Harry Bowling was [...] left school at fourteen to supplement the family income as an office boy in a riverside provisions' merchant. He was called up for National Service in the 1950s. Before becoming a writer, he was variously employed as a lorry driver, milkman, meat cutter, carpenter and decorator, and community worker. He lived with his wife and family, dividing his time between Lancashire and Deptford. We at Headline are sorry to say that THE WHISPERING YEARS was Harry Bowling's last novel, as he very sadly died in February 1999. We worked with him for over ten years, ever since the publication of his first novel, CONNER STREET'S WAR, and we miss him enormously, as do his many, many fans around the world.

Also by Harry Bowling

When The Pedlar Called
As Time Goes By
The Chinese Lantern
The Glory and The Shame
Down Milldyke Way
One More for Saddler Street
That Summer in Eagle Street
Waggoner's Way
The Farrans of Fellmonger Street
Pedlar's Row

The Tanner Trilogy
Backstreet Child
The Girl from Cotton Lane
Gaslight in Page Street

Paragon Place
Ironmonger's Daughter
Conner Street's War

The Whispering Years

Tuppence to Tooley Street

Harry Bowling

headline

THE WHISPERING YEARS
first published in Great Britain in 1999
by HEADLINE BOOK PUBLISHING

TUPPENCE TO TOOLEY STREET
first published in Great Britain in 1989
by HEADLINE BOOK PUBLISHING

First published in this omnibus edition in 2004
by HEADLINE BOOK PUBLISHING

A HEADLINE paperback

10 9 8 7 6 5 4 3 2 1

ISBN 0 7553 2250 9

Printed and bound in Great Britain by
Clays Ltd, St Ives plc

Papers and cover board used by Headline are natural, recyclable
products made from wood grown in sustainable forests. The
manufacturing processes conform to the environmental
regulations of the country of origin.

HEADLINE BOOK PUBLISHING
A division of Hodder Headline
338 Euston Road
LONDON NW1 3BH

www.headline.co.uk
www.hodderheadline.com

The Whispering
Years

To my granddaughter Poppy with love

Prologue

November 1952

The heavy night rain had eased, but the morning air was wet with saturating mist already polluted by the sulphurous smoke from coke fires, lit against the cold of that inhospitable Saturday morning in riverside Bermondsey.

It should have been a day for huddling by the fire and brewing more tea, for staying in off the streets, but it was, after all, Saturday, when the markets beckoned and food queues had to be faced, and for Sue Parry there was a visit that had to be made, unavoidable after the letter that had filled her with trepidation and unease.

As she threw the covers back and slid her feet down on to the small rope mat by her bed she sighed sadly. A few short months ago she would have been woken with a cup of tea, and in the front room the fire would have been drawing up nicely. Her mother would be buttering the toast and Aunt Sara would be sitting by the fire, her dressing gown pulled tightly round her thin frame, her grey hair looking tortured by the metal curlers which did little if anything to enhance her appearance. Now though, on that cold Saturday morning, Sue Parry was alone.

Back in August Aunt Sara had left to find other

accommodation after a bitter row, and then before the month was out Lucy Parry had suddenly been struck down with pneumonia and died two days later in the Rotherhithe infirmary. Sue was still trying to come to terms with the loss of her mother and the stark changes in her life, her days and nights filled with soul-searching and restlessness. She was getting married early in February and her mother would not be there, nor would Aunt Sara, and neither would Charlie Foden. Not now. Uncle Charlie she had called him, the man who was to have escorted her down the aisle, but now it was unthinkable and he would have to know the reason why.

The first-floor flat in Rye Buildings had been the family home for less than two years, ever since Cooper Street was emptied under a slum clearance order, and as the young woman reached for her dressing robe she thought about the forced move and how it had affected her mother. She had seemed to fade a little every day, and Aunt Sara too had become more and more morose and unreachable.

As she walked out of the bedroom Sue brushed her fingers over the framed photo of Alan. He was smiling up at her, looking smart in the navy-blue dress uniform of the Royal Signals. Alan Woodley, the rock she clung to, the one stable part of her life, the man she had loved and who had loved her since forever, it seemed. He had seen the letter and understood. 'Better to get it sorted once and for all,' he had agreed, 'otherwise the unanswered questions'll come back to haunt you, to haunt us both.'

There was just time for two cups of strong sweet tea and some toast in front of an unlit fire before setting off, and as the young woman turned into the Old Kent Road the rain started to fall heavily once more. She hurried through the dreary drizzle, tightly wrapped in a heavy black coat, the collar turned up to a chiffon scarf tied loosely round her neck. Her blond, shoulder-length hair was partly concealed under a matching black beret, and she stepped carefully across the puddles in her wedge-heeled shoes and dark stockings. The small handbag she had tucked under her arm contained the letter, and one other, addressed to her mother and postmarked Bristol 1943.

There was no real need to use the derelict Cooper Street as a short cut to Charlie Foden's flat in Lynton Road but she found her feet taking her in that direction, and as she turned the corner Sue sighed deeply. Two years and still the houses remained, boarded up and ghostly, sounds of children long gone, the presence of women chatting on door-steps just a memory, but the old Victorian gas lamp still there halfway along the turning. Two wasted years while the Council and the town planners argued and still there seemed to be no solution in sight. The street remained abandoned to its past.

Charlie Foden looked surprised as he answered the knock. 'Well, if it ain't young Susan. Come in, gel.'

The young woman walked into the small parlour and took off her rain-sodden beret. 'I needed ter talk ter yer, Charlie,' she said.

The older man helped her off with her coat and hung it behind the door. 'I'm sorry I've not been round ter see yer since yer mum's funeral,' he said guiltily. 'Yer know 'ow it is, all good intentions, but I ain't bin too good lately. Nuffing bad – I just bin a bit off colour.'

Sue sat down by the fire and ran a hand over her hair. 'About the weddin', Charlie,' she began hesitantly.

'It's all right, gel, I'll be there, never fear,' he said, smiling. 'Now, can I get yer a nice cuppa?'

Sue shook her head as she slid her handbag down by her feet. 'No fanks, Charlie.'

He eased himself into the chair opposite her. He was a stocky man in his mid-sixties, with a full head of hair, white now but still inclined to wave, and a broad face with wide-spaced hazel eyes. He clasped his gnarled hands together and leaned forward slightly. 'What is it, Sue?' he asked, seeing the troubled look on her pretty face.

For a moment or two the young woman stared down at her hands, then she took up her handbag before fixing him with her pale blue eyes. 'Charlie, there's only one way ter say this,' she told him with a sigh. 'I can't let yer give me away at the weddin'.'

Charlie looked surprised and a little wounded. 'It's your choice, gel, but it'd be nice ter know what I've done ter make yer change yer mind. It must be somefing. You always called me Uncle Charlie, remember?'

Sue gave him a pale smile. 'The day before the funeral I was goin' frew Mum's fings an' I came across a bundle o' letters. They were tucked away in the back of 'er dressin'-table drawer, tied up wiv pink ribbon. Every one of 'em was postmarked Bristol, an' all from you. I've read 'em all, Charlie, but even before I did I knew the truth.'

'What did yer know, gel?' he asked quietly.

'That you an' my mum were – were lovers.'

For a few seconds Charlie's eyes fixed on hers. 'I don't deny it, an' I wouldn't try to,' he replied.

Sue lowered her head, and when she raised her eyes again to meet his they were misted. 'I was wiv Mum when she passed away, an' she called out your name. Not my dad's name, but yours. They were 'er dyin' words. I was shocked, naturally, but I thought the two of you 'ad got tergevver after me dad was killed, which would 'ave bin

4

understandable. You was always good to us an' I know Mum leaned on you many times when fings were bad.'

'But the letters you found told you ovverwise,' Charlie prompted her.

She nodded her head slowly. 'You an' me mum were cheatin' on Dad. It was goin' on before the war started.'

'That's true, an' ter be John Blunt I don't regret it,' he said plainly. 'I don't expect you to understand, not from your position, but the fact is it wasn't some lustful, grubby affair. Me an' yer mum both fought against it 'appenin', but the mutual attraction was too strong, an' that's the gist of it.'

Sue opened her handbag and took out the more recent letter. 'I've thought of nuffing else since I 'eard your name on Mum's lips,' she said quietly. 'I was goin' ter say somefing at the funeral, but I just couldn't. It wasn't the right place. There was plenty o' time ter dwell on it afterwards, though. Too much time, but I did try to understand. After all, I couldn't change anyfing. My mum 'ad obviously loved you so I felt it was best ter bury the past an' get on wiv me own life. I still intended fer you ter give me away, but this week I got a letter from Aunt Sara, and as I read it all the old doubts an' questions came floodin' back.'

'Doubts? Questions? I don't understand yer, gel,' Charlie said with a frown.

'You'd better read this letter,' she answered, holding it out to him.

Dear Sue,

I hope you and Alan are keeping fit and well. As for me, I am not in the best of health. It's my heart, so the doctor tells me.

I bumped into Mrs Roach last week and she told me

that you and Alan were tying the knot in February. It's good news and I wish you all the very best on the day. I will not be at the church but I'll be thinking about you both. Try not to feel too badly towards me. I was guilty of harsh words on the day I left, but your poor mum did not spare me either, God rest her soul.

Do me one favour, Sue. Get someone else to give you away. Charlie Foden doing the honours would be an insult to both your mother and your father's memory. Charlie Foden is a bad man, and I should know. He was behind the beating your father got from the Coleys. He coveted your mother from the start, and nothing he ever did to help was done out of kindness. Even I was not safe from his lecherous intentions, as he made quite clear to me on numerous occasions. He despised your father, played on his weaknesses and almost got him killed. It was a bone of contention between me and your mum, but she saw no harm in him, not even when it was brutally obvious, staring her in the face.

I could say more but I don't want to upset you too much, now that your future happiness lies ahead of you. Suffice it to say that Charlie Foden will have to live with his sins the way we all have to, and one day he will be called to answer for them. I hope he will be able to face Wally Coates in the hereafter.

Think kindly of me if you can. I was very close to your mother despite what you might think.

My love to you and Alan, and may God go with you.

Aunt Sara.

Charlie's face had grown dark with anger as he read the spidery handwriting and when he had finished he handed the letter back with a shaking hand. 'The woman certainly showed her true colours,' he growled. 'Do you believe all that rubbish?'

'I don't know what ter believe any more, an' I'm all confused,' Sue sighed. 'Who was this Wally Coates? I've heard the name mentioned once or twice but it was always whispered. What did Aunt Sara mean by it?'

Charlie allowed himself a brief smile. 'I'll tell yer somefing, Sue. Yer muvver used ter look on the time we were tergevver as the whisperin' years, an' that just about summed it up.' He stood up slowly and reached up to the mantelshelf for his pipe and tobacco pouch. 'I understand why yer feel the way yer do,' he said quietly, 'an' I'll 'ave ter go along wiv yer wishes, but I would like ter fink that you'll keep an open mind on that woman's rantin' fer the time bein'. There's always two sides to a story an' yer've not 'eard mine yet.'

'I'm listenin', Charlie,' she said spiritedly. 'I've not planned ter go anywhere else this mornin'.'

'In that case I'll make us a cuppa, an' then you'll be able to 'ear it,' he answered.

Outside the rain beat down on the cobblestones and rattled the windowpanes. It bounded up from the pavements, ran gurgling down the swollen drains and cascaded from a broken gutter across the street. Charlie Foden sucked on his pipe as he glanced through the net curtains, then he turned and made himself comfortable in the chair facing the young woman. 'It 'ad been much like terday when I first walked inter Cooper Street,' he began. 'The winter of '35 it was. I was soaked ter the skin an' it was still rainin', an' gettin' dark . . .'

Chapter One

November 1935

For two days and nights the yellow choking fog had blanketed the mean Bermondsey streets, but on Friday morning heavy rain cleared the air and continued falling all day. Now, in the chill evening, water was coursing down the drains and the cobblestones were clean and glistening. With some relief the tired man dragged himself into the warmth of Joe's fish and chip shop in the Old Kent Road, the clothes on his back wet through and his saturated trousers sticking uncomfortably to his legs.

Two younger men were in front of him at the counter, hungrily eyeing the food as Joe the Italian scooped up a portion of chips from the stainless steel fryer into a small piece of greaseproof paper and then flipped a piece of haddock on top. 'Tenpence 'a'penny. You wanna wally?'

'Nah, that'll do,' the taller of the two answered with a momentary glance at the large jar of dill gherkins standing on one side of the counter.

Joe dropped the bundle of food on to a pile of newspaper sheets and finished the wrapping. 'You wanna fish an' chips?' he asked the second man.

'Nah, we're sharin' this,' he laughed as they left the counter.

Italian Joe stirred the vat of chips and scooped a large wire sieveful from the boiling fat before looking up enquiringly at Charlie Foden. 'It's a bad night,' he remarked.

The sodden customer nodded as he pushed his cap back from his forehead. 'Same again,' he said, reaching into his coat pocket for the coppers.

While Joe was wrapping his order Charlie glanced over at the two young men. They were standing by a table and the taller one was sprinkling salt and vinegar on to the chips. ''Ere, you 'alve the fish. Yer 'ands are cleaner than mine,' he said.

With the fish and chips carefully shared out the young men ambled out into the rain and Charlie turned to pick up his bundle. 'D'you know Cooper Street?' he asked.

Joe scratched his wiry grey hair. 'It'sa behinda Croft Street. You knowa Croft Street?'

Charlie shook his head. 'Nah.'

'Yer walka that way,' the Italian told him, jerking his thumb to the right. 'Yer see-a da big-a clothes shop. Turna da left. That'sa Croft Street. Cooper Street's da nexta street yer come to. Righta da bottom.'

Charlie thanked him, liberally sousing and salting his food before stepping out into the wet night. A deep doorway some way along the road gave him shelter while he wolfed down the fish and chips before, licking his lips, he set off again, hoping that the room had not already been taken.

At number 8 Cooper Street Lucy Parry was busy gathering up the used crockery. She was an attractive woman in her mid-thirties with fair hair and deep blue eyes set in an oval face. She wore an apron tied tightly round her waist which accentuated the curve of her hips, and as she piled up the used plates she was frowning. 'What did they

10

actually say, then?' she asked.

George Parry looked up at her from the armchair by the fire and shrugged his shoulders. 'The manager just said that they'd 'ave ter look at the situation carefully, bearin' in mind the drop in sales.'

'What else do they expect?' Lucy said. 'Three million on the dole an' no sign of any relief. That's what it said on the wireless yesterday.'

George sighed and sagged back in his chair. He was a slightly built man just a year older than Lucy, with thinning dark hair and grey eyes which tended to widen when he spoke. He worked in the gift department of William Knight's tobacco company in Shoreditch and he had known for some time that the firm was intending to suspend its gift coupon scheme. 'It'll mean the sack fer the 'ole twenty-five of us,' he said. 'That's the long an' short of it.'

'Won't they transfer some of yer?' Lucy asked.

'Where to?' he retorted. 'There's no vacancies anywhere else in the firm. Some o' them'll be gettin' their notices as well, I shouldn't wonder.'

Lucy took up the plates. 'Well, it's not werf worryin' too much about it just yet. Fings might look up. They say one door shuts an' anuvver one opens.'

George Parry grimaced at her show of spirit. There were no doors opening in Bermondsey at the moment, he thought. All the local factories were on short time or going that way, and on the very rare occasion when a job was advertised the firm was swamped with applicants who seemed quite capable of murder to land the position.

'Daddy, I'm tired.'

George reached down and picked his four-year-old daughter up in his arms. 'It's all right, darlin'. Mummy'll see ter yer soon.'

Lucy gave her husband an irritated look. 'Can't you put the child ter bed fer once? Yer know what I've got ter do ternight. There's all those clothes need darnin' an' ironin', an' I gotta sort that copper out. It's all clogged up.'

'All right, all right, don't go on about it,' he replied sharply, giving Lucy a hard look. 'Come on, sweet pea, Daddy's takin' yer up ter bed.'

Susan rested her blond curls on her father's shoulder as he carried her out of the room and Lucy sat down at the table with a sigh. George was not normally snappy, but she knew why he was in this mood. He was worried over his job, and also not too happy about her decision to take in a lodger. He knew that the few extra shillings would come in handy but he had been angry at her for not discussing it with him first. What was the use, she asked herself? She knew what his reaction would have been. He would have ended up by saying that she should do as she saw fit. George was not the most inventive or demonstrative of men and it was always left to her to make the decisions and take the initiative. He was a good man, it was true, and she knew he loved her and Susan above all else, but at times he could be infuriating with his indecisiveness.

'She was asleep soon as 'er 'ead touched the piller,' George said as he came back into the parlour.

'Sara's late,' Lucy remarked as she looked up at the chimer on the mantelshelf.

George followed her glance. 'Yeah, she's normally in by now.'

Lucy stifled a smile. 'I expect she's got 'erself tied up wiv some new-fangled idea at the fellowship. Last time it was patchwork quilts. Spare us anuvver quilt, please.'

George forced a smile and then his face became serious again. 'I know she can be tryin' at times, but yer gotta take fings inter consideration,' he said. 'She's not 'ad the best o' luck over the years, an' she's not too well at the moment.'

Lucy looked at him quizzically. 'I'm sure Sara's well. She just likes ter put fings on a bit. She should get out an' about a bit more instead o' sittin' in that chair from mornin' till night. The church fellowship's the only place she goes to. And it would be nice ter see 'er take a little more pride in 'erself.'

'What d'yer mean? She keeps 'erself clean an' tidy,' George said quickly.

'I'm not disputin' that,' Lucy replied. 'What I'm sayin' is she could do somefing about that 'air of 'ers. I've offered ter perm it for 'er. She could dress a bit younger, too. She looks like an old woman in those long frocks an' skimpy cardigans she wears. Christ, George, she's only forty, not sixty.'

'You should 'ave anuvver word wiv 'er,' George suggested.

'I'm fed up wiv talkin' to 'er,' Lucy said, frowning. 'She's your sister, you should do it. She'd take it more kindly comin' from you.'

George leaned forward in his armchair. 'Yer don't regret us takin' 'er in, do yer?' he asked.

'Course I don't,' Lucy lied. 'I'm used to 'er ways by now. 'Ow long's it bin, four years?'

'Goin' on four,' George corrected her. 'It'll be four years next March when me mum died. Sara came to us at the end o' March. What else could we 'ave done but take 'er in? There's no way she would 'ave stayed in that old 'ouse alone, bearin' in mind 'ow nervous she is.'

Lucy nodded and reached for her sewing box. Sara's stay was only supposed to be short-term, she thought, until she could find something suitable. After nearly four years she treated the house as her own and there was no way she was even considering leaving.

The sound of a key in the lock heralded Sara's arrival and she came into the parlour with a dripping umbrella which she placed in the hearth. 'What a terrible night,' she said in greeting. 'It's absolutely pourin' down.'

'Never mind, it's got rid of the fog,' Lucy said tartly.

Sara made herself comfortable in her favourite chair by the fire. 'Mrs Phelps ain't none too good,' she remarked. 'She wasn't at the club ternight. That nice Reverend Beeney was, though. I made 'im a cup o' tea an' 'e told me 'ow nice it was. 'E liked those rock cakes I took along, too. It's nice ter be appreciated.'

Pity you don't try making the tea here some time, yer scatty mare, Lucy thought.

'I fink I'm goin' down wiv somefing,' Sara announced. 'I've got this sharp pain keeps catchin' me in me left side. I'm sure it's me kidneys.'

'There's only one that side,' Lucy pointed out. 'It could be stones, or those rock cakes yer made. You didn't eat any yerself, did yer, Sara?'

'There's nuffing wrong wiv my rock cakes,' Sara replied indignantly.

'No, nothing a sledgehammer wouldn't put right,' Lucy muttered under her breath.

'I fink I'll take me cocoa up ter bed wiv me,' Sara said. 'This side's playin' me up somefing awful. If yer wouldn't mind, Lucy.'

The younger woman put her darning down on the table and went to boil the milk, and as soon as she was out of the room Sara leant towards her brother. 'You should 'ave put yer foot down when she got the idea ter take in a lodger,' she growled. 'Yer can't be too careful these days. There was

14

a woman murdered in 'er bed a few weeks ago over in
Brixton an' it turned out it was the lodger what killed 'er.'

'Where did yer 'ear that?' George said, smiling.

'It was in the Sunday paper,' Sara replied. 'An' you
shouldn't laugh about it neivver. When yer take people in
yer don't know anyfing about 'em. They could be wanted
by the police, or escaped prisoners.'

The sharp knock made Sara jump and she frowned as
George got up to answer it. 'Who could it be at this hour?'
she wondered.

'We'll soon find out,' he said. 'It could be one o' those
escaped convicts after a room fer the night.'

'Don't mock,' Sara implored him, her eyes wide and
frightened.

George Parry opened the front door to a bedraggled
figure standing in the rain. 'Yeah?'

'The name's Charlie Foden, I've come about the room. Is
it still goin'?'

George nodded. 'Yeah. Come in out the rain. I'll fetch the
missus.'

Lucy was standing in the scullery mixing the cocoa in a
large beaker and she heard what was said. 'There we are,
luv. I've put two sugars in. All right?'

Sara glanced along the dark passageway as she nodded.
'I'll go straight up. Yer don't want me in there when yer
talkin' business,' she said in a low voice. 'You just be
careful. It's a bit late at night fer anyone ter come askin'
after a room.'

'Sara, fer goodness' sake,' Lucy sighed.

'You can make light of it, but I'm very wary o' those
sort,' Sara muttered as she climbed the stairs to her back
bedroom.

George offered his armchair to Charlie but the visitor

declined. 'I'd better not, I'm wet frew,' he said. 'It'll make yer seat all wet.'

''Ere, take a dinin' chair, then,' George told him.

Lucy came into the parlour, smiling, and Charlie stood up quickly. 'I'm Charlie Foden an' I've called about the room.'

'I'm Lucy Parry an' this is me 'usband George.'

Charlie reached out and shook hands with him. 'Nice ter meet yer.'

'The room's still vacant, but first fings first,' Lucy said cheerfully. 'You look like you could do wiv a cuppa.'

'I'd be more than grateful,' Charlie said, smiling.

'I'll do it,' George offered, wanting to let Lucy sort things out herself.

'I should begin by tellin' yer that I am in work,' Charlie said as George left the room.

'That's good,' Lucy replied. 'The room's on the bend o' the stairs an' it's quite small but cosy. There's a fire in there an' the bed's nice an' comfortable. There's a wardrobe fer yer clothes as well. The rent's as on the advertisement, twelve an' six a week wiv breakfast or fifteen shillin's if yer want the evenin' meal. Did yer see the notice yerself?'

'Yeah, in the paper shop in the Old Kent Road.'

Lucy appraised him and liked what she saw. There was a calm expression on his open face as he sat holding his saturated cap in his large hands. He was obviously a manual worker, she decided. His wet greying hair was thick and inclined to curl about his ears and his shoulders were wide, giving him a powerful appearance. 'Are you from round 'ere?' she asked.

'Walworth Road, but I've bin lodgin' in Lucas Street, off of Abbey Street,' he explained. 'The places 'ave bin condemned an' we've all 'ad ter get out. At the moment I'm stayin' at the workin' men's 'ostel in Tooley Street but it's not ideal.'

'I'm sure it's not.'

'I'm a docker.'

'I understand fings ain't too rosy in the docks neivver,' Lucy remarked.

'I get one or two days' work as a rule,' he replied. 'The rest o' the week most of us 'ave ter bomp on at the labour exchange. It's not good but we're better off than many.'

George came in with the tea and Charlie drank his down gratefully. When he had finished, Lucy led the way up to the small bedroom and lit the gas mantle. 'As you can see, it's quite 'omely.'

'It's very nice an' I'd be glad ter take it, wiv the evenin' meal,' he told her.

She glanced at his sodden garments. 'Right, then. First fing is ter get yer somefing ter put on while I dry those clothes out. You're bigger than my George but there's a large dressin' robe be'ind the door that'll fit, an' I'm sure I can find some long johns an' a vest you can squeeze into. Just leave yer wet stuff outside the door. Me an' George usually 'ave a bite o' supper before we go ter bed, cheese or a brawn sandwich wiv a cuppa. Can I get yer one?'

'That'll be smashin',' Charlie said, smiling gratefully. 'An' by the way, I do appreciate yer takin' a chance wiv me.'

'Why? Yer not some escaped convict, are yer?' Lucy said, grinning.

He looked embarrassed. 'No, I'm 'armless, I assure yer.'

As Lucy was leaving the room she stopped and turned back to him. 'By the way,' she said quickly. 'Me 'usband's sister's stayin' wiv us fer the time bein'. She's a spinster an' gets a bit ratty at times, but take no notice of 'er. I thought

I'd better put yer on yer guard.'

Charlie smiled at the expression on her face. 'Fanks fer warnin' me,' he said.

George was poking the fire when Lucy came into the room. 'I noticed 'e 'ad no luggage wiv 'im,' he remarked.

'Yeah, I noticed too.'

'Don't yer fink it's a bit strange?'

'Not really. It doesn't mean anyfing.'

'Doesn't it?'

'George, what yer gettin' at?'

'Someone on the run wouldn't let 'imself be bowed down wiv luggage.'

'Nor would someone who stormed out of the 'ouse after a row,' Lucy countered.

George put down the poker and eased himself back into his chair. 'I dunno, there's somefing about the bloke I can't put me finger on an' it's bovverin' me.'

Lucy looked at him closely. 'You don't fink 'e's a criminal on the run, do yer?'

'No, but there's somefing . . .'

It was cosy and warm in the room on the bend of the stairs and Charlie Foden felt at ease as he reached for his pipe and tobacco pouch on the chair by the bed. The makings had stayed dry in the oilskin wrapping and once he had got the pipe glowing he picked up the tatty old wallet from the chair and opened it. There were two sepia photos inside the flaps. One looked stern and military, a picture of himself as a young fusilier taken just before he went to France in 1916, and smiling up at him from the other was a beautiful young woman with classical features and hair that hung in long ringlets over her shoulders. Charlie closed the wallet with a deep sigh and placed it back on the chair. Outside the rain was easing and he could hear the clanging sounds of metal on metal and screeching wheels from the nearby freight yards. He drew on his pipe and blew the smoke upwards to the cracked ceiling as he took stock of his situation. He was forty-eight and had taken his share of kicks, suffered loss, and made mistakes which had cost him dearly, but there had to come a time when life finally turned in an upward direction, when a man could again enjoy some of the good things in the world, live contentedly and walk tall once more. That might be some way off as yet, he thought, but it had to start somewhere. Why not here, now?

The tap on the door startled him and he wrapped the dressing robe around him as he got up from the bed.

'There's some bread an' cheese an' I 'ope yer like strong tea,' Lucy said cheerily.

'It's the only way ter make it,' he said, smiling.

The rain had finally stopped and a lone star shone down from among the driven clouds. Yes, it had to start somewhere, Charlie told himself with conviction as he sipped his tea.

Chapter Two

Charlie Foden stepped out of number 8 Cooper Street and stood for a moment or two looking up and down the small turning. The rain had given way to a bright Saturday morning and already he could feel the pleasant warmth of the winter sun on his face. His coat and trousers were badly creased but at least they were dry, he thought. His boots felt damp, though. The sooner he picked up his suitcase from the hostel the better.

As he stood at the front door taking his bearings, Mrs Goodwright from number 7 opposite nudged her next-door neighbour, Mrs Black. 'Who's that?' she asked.

Ada Black peered through her glasses, then took them off to get a better view. 'Must be the Parrys' lodger,' she replied.

Emmie Goodwright huffed. 'Didn't take 'er long ter get fixed up, did it?' she remarked. 'She only put the ad in the shop a few days ago ter my knowledge.'

Ada folded her arms over her ample bosom and nodded. 'There's a lot movin' inter the area lately,' she said. 'It's the factories, I expect. There's always the odd job goin' in one o' them. Pearce Duff's took a couple on last week, so Mrs Reefer told me. 'Er ole man got a start there. Two years 'e's bin out o' collar.'

21

'My ole feller's bin out o' work more than that,' Emmie replied stiffly. 'It knocks the stuffin' out of a man after so long. I know by 'im. So moody 'e is. I'm frightened ter talk to 'im at times. Bites me bloody 'ead off.'

'Your Bert's all right, Emm,' her neighbour remarked. 'It's nuffing a few weeks' work wouldn't put right.'

'That's what I was just sayin'.'

'Yeah, well, we know 'ow it affects 'em bein' on the dole.'

Emmie Goodwright sensed that Ada was beginning to drift off on one of her mental rambles and felt that enough was enough. 'Well, I can't stand 'ere chattin' all day. I gotta get me shoppin' done,' she said quickly.

The two watched Charlie Foden set off along the street and Emmie brushed her hands down her clean apron. ''Ow long d'yer reckon 'e'll last there?' she asked.

'What d'yer mean?' Ada replied with a frown.

'Sara Parry, that's what I mean.'

'Oh, I see. Well, it depends whevver the bloke lets 'er get to 'im or not,' Ada said. 'We all know what a miserable cow she is. If she gives 'im too much grief 'e might decide ter piss off.'

'Couldn't blame 'im, could yer?'

'Not really.'

'Oh, well.'

'I'll pop in later,' Ada told her friend.

Charlie bought a pair of socks at Cheap Jack's stall in the Tower Bridge Road market and then called into a shoe shop nearby. Wearing his new brown brogues he made his way to the hostel in Tooley Street and was surprised at the activity going on outside. Men were milling around the entrance and the warden was trying to keep order. 'Now look 'ere, it's no good you all tryin' ter get in at once,' he growled. 'Mr Coley'll see you all in good time. Now just line up an' be patient.'

Fred Wilson spotted Charlie and pulled a face. 'They're all goin' mad 'ere this mornin',' he said, shaking his head. 'Coley's recruitin' again.'

'Who's Coley?' Charlie asked.

'Yer tellin' me yer never 'eard o' the Coley bruvvers?' Fred said disbelievingly. 'I thought everybody knew those nasty bastards.'

'Well, I've never 'eard of 'em,' Charlie told him. 'Let's pop in Ted's café an' you can put me in the picture.'

Fred Wilson was at a loose end that Saturday morning and was quite happy to oblige. The two men sat clutching huge mugs of tea inside the steamy café and when Fred had painstakingly rolled a cigarette he jerked his thumb over his shoulder. 'Those poor bastards don't know what they're lettin' themselves in for,' he began. 'Every now an' then the Coleys get a subber, an' they—'

''Ang on a minute,' Charlie interrupted. 'What's a sub-ber?'

Fred smiled. 'Sorry. I fergot you ain't familiar wiv the buildin' game. One o' the big buildin' firms get a large contract an' they subcontract some o' the jobs. That way they don't 'ave to employ too many new workers an' people like Coley can take on casuals fer next ter nuffink. The big firms don't lose by it – they get their cut an' everyone's 'appy, 'cept the poor bleeders Coley takes on.'

'That bad, is 'e?' Charlie said, sipping his tea.

Fred Wilson shook his bald head slowly. 'Worse. I worked fer the buggers once. Never again.'

'What work is it they do?' Charlie asked.

'Pipe layin', mainly,' Fred explained. 'This contract's fer

sewage pipes by all accounts, an' that can be a killer. Yer gotta go down furvver fer sewage pipe layin' an' yer diggin' clay. 'Ave you ever dug out clay?'

'No, but I can imagine.'

'Yer can't, Chas, not till yer've actually done it. A lot don't last the day, an' if yer do yer so tired an' full of aches yer just fall inter bed exhausted. Yer gotta remember too that Coley needs so much done every day an' 'e's on yer back all the time, 'im an' 'is bruvver. They're 'ard men an' they'll get their quota by 'ook or by crook, even if it means thumpin' a few 'eads.' Charlie looked unimpressed and Fred leaned forward on the marble table. 'I've seen Frank Coley drag a poor sod out the trench an' give 'im a right-'ander before tellin' 'im ter piss off. That feller 'ad worked most of the week an' was dead beat. Coley didn't pay 'im any wages an' the poor bleeder was in no position to argue. Take it from me, Frank Coley's a real bad 'un, but there's a lot'll tell yer that 'is younger bruvver Ben's even worse.'

''Ow do they get away wiv it?' Charlie asked, frowning. 'Workers 'ave rights. What about the union?'

Fred snorted. 'Union? What union? The Coleys won't entertain any union an' they get away wiv it. They recruit casual labour from places like the 'ostels an' dole queues an' they rule by fear, an' any talk by the men o' gettin' themselves organised is likely ter get 'em sorted out good an' proper. They've got a few gangers runnin' the jobs who are as 'ard as them, so you can see it ain't no good complainin'. You eivver sign on an' do the work wiv yer mouth shut or yer give 'em a wide berf. Once was enough fer me, I can tell yer.'

Charlie drained his mug. 'Well, it's bin nice talkin' ter yer, Fred. I'm off ter pick up me suitcase. I got meself a nice little lodgin's.'

'I'm sorry ter see yer go,' Fred replied, 'but yer better out of it. There's gonna be a lot o' sad, sorry faces in the 'ostel next week.'

Charlie picked up his case from the office and saw the welter of people in the dining hall at the end of the corridor. Wanting to get the smell of the place out of his nostrils he strode briskly off into the morning sunshine.

Sara Parry sat by the fire holding a saucer under her chin while she sipped a cup of tea. Drinking tea was a refined art as far as George's older sister was concerned. The brew had to be weak and milky, with a half-teaspoon of sugar, and not too hot. Given a suitable concoction Sara would spend quite some time sipping at her cup while she expounded her opinion on whatever the current topic of conversation happened to be. It usually conflicted with Lucy's opinion, but the younger woman thought it better to ignore her silly ways than to create an atmosphere in which Sara would sulk, often for days.

''E's collectin' 'is fings at the 'ostel,' Lucy told her.

''Ostel?' Sara said with feeling. 'Is that where 'e's bin stayin'? I 'ope 'e don't bring any bugs or fleas in 'ere.'

'Workin' men's 'ostels are usually clean, not like the flop-'ouses,' Lucy answered.

'Well, I'm still worried,' Sara went on. 'It's always the way when yer take people in. We don't know anyfing about 'im. I really don't know why yer decided ter take a lodger. After all, yer not much in after the food's taken inter consideration. That sort usually eat yer out of 'ouse an' 'ome, if yer let 'em.'

Lucy bit on her tongue as her temper rose. Sara had little room to talk. She paid very little towards her keep and had been cosseted from the day she arrived. 'I fink you'll find 'e's a decent bloke, Sara,' she said. ''E seems very friendly an' 'e is workin'.'

'Well, we'll just 'ave ter wait an' see, won't we?' the older woman replied haughtily. 'I must say I'm gonna feel uncomfortable wiv 'im sittin' round the table wiv us.'

Lucy forced a smile. 'Who knows, 'e might even brighten the place up fer a change. It's not bin very cheerful lately, yer gotta admit.'

'Well, it's understandable,' Sara said sharply. 'George is naturally worried about 'is job an' 'e's the breadwinner. Some women go out office cleanin', but you can't, can yer? Not till Susan starts school.'

Lucy was tempted to suggest that Sara herself might feel a lot better if she dragged her arse out of that chair and found an office-cleaning job. She could just see her, off to work beneath a pig-filled sky. 'If George loses 'is job I'll 'ave ter go out ter work,' she said. 'George can look after Sue, an' you can pitch in, can't yer?'

Sara looked horrified. 'I wouldn't be much 'elp, not wiv my chest,' she replied with a pained expression. 'An' you can't expect George ter do all the fings you 'ave ter do.'

Lucy watched her sister-in-law slide the bottom of her cup across the edge of the saucer yet again and wanted to scream. 'D'yer want anuvver cup?' she said out of desperation.

'Presently,' Sara said. 'By the way, I'll need ter go ter the wool shop in the Old Kent Road later, once the streets 'ave aired. It's fer the church fellowship.'

'I'm sure the streets are aired by now, Sara,' Lucy said, a note of irritation stealing into her voice. 'Leave it too late an' it'll start turnin' cold.'

Sara placed the cup and saucer down on the table and held a hand to her back. 'I'm sure there's somefing wrong wiv my kidneys,' she groaned. 'Lucy, 'ave you gotta go out any more?'

'No, why?'

'You wouldn't like ter collect the wool for me, would yer? I don't fink I could make it ter the shop the way my back is this mornin'.'

'Yeah, I'll collect it, if yer tell me what it is.'

For the first time that morning Sara raised a smile. 'George should be in soon. I'll put the kettle on, shall I?'

Lucy would normally tell her that she would do it, and that was exactly what Sara expected to hear. 'All right, if yer don't mind,' she replied instead. 'I'll just slip upstairs an' sweep the lodger's room out before 'e gets back.'

Sara looked a little hesitant as she lit a match and reached for the gas tap. Lucy knew how she hated lighting gases, especially when there was air in the pipes. As the jet belched Sara shut the tap off quickly and stood back, and at that moment George walked into the house carrying Sue in his arms. 'You all right, Sara?' he asked as he put the child down and looked into the scullery.

'Yer'll 'ave ter get these pipes blown,' she declared with irritation. 'Yer know I get frightened lightin' the gas.'

'Where's Lucy?' George asked.

'Where's Mummy?' the child demanded, tugging at Sara's dress.

'She's upstairs,' Sara told her. 'Don't pull me dress like that, Susan. It's naughty.'

George looked at his sister enquiringly.

'She's tidyin' the lodger's room up,' Sara puffed. 'I dunno why, it was done yesterday. She fusses too much.'

George lit the gas and put the kettle over the flame. 'Go an' sit yerself down, Sara,' he said, smiling. 'I'll make the tea. Come on, Sue, let me take yer coat off. Look, there's

27

yer dolly. Now sit down at the table an' I'll find the dolly's clothes.'

When George put the biscuit tin of dolls' clothes down on the table Sue flipped open the lid and it dropped with a clatter on to the stone floor.

'Do be careful, child,' Sara scolded her. 'I've got a bad 'eadache as it is.'

The sharp tone of her voice brought tears to Sue's eyes and she jumped down from the table and ran out into the passage as her mother was coming down the stairs.

'What's the matter, luv?' Lucy asked with concern as the child buried her head in her skirt.

'Aunt Sara shouted at me,' she mumbled in a tiny voice.

'Whatever for?' Lucy said, directing her words at Sara.

'She banged that tin down on the floor an' I told 'er ter be careful,' Sara complained. 'I've got a splittin' 'eadache.'

'If you went out an' got some air in the mornin's instead of sittin' on yer arse all day yer wouldn't get those 'eadaches,' Lucy growled.

'I'm not well enough ter go gallivantin' about in this weavver,' Sara retorted indignantly.

'This weavver? It's a nice mild day, it'd do yer good.'

'Not the way I feel.'

Lucy gave her a stony look and took herself off to the parlour. The woman's getting worse, she thought, scowling. It's about time I had a word with George. Throwing childish tantrums and constant petty bitching are one thing, but upsetting the child like that for the slightest reason is another matter entirely. It's a pity she can't find a man to take her off our hands. George is feeling it too, but being her brother he suffers her in silence. Well, I won't, not for much longer. 'Is that tea ready yet, Sara?' she called out loudly.

'George is doin' it,' Sara replied as she walked into the parlour and sat down in her armchair with a heavy sigh. 'Is there any aspirin?'

Lucy reached for her handbag. ''Ere's two,' she said, imagining shoving the whole packet down her sister-in-law's throat.

'Can yer get me some water?' Sara asked in a small voice.

A few minutes later Charlie Foden knocked at the front door. 'I've got me case,' he announced, grinning at Lucy. 'Bought a pair o' shoes, too. Feelin' a bit more civilised now.'

Lucy smiled back as he stepped into the passageway. 'When yer've put yer case in the room I'd like yer ter meet our Sara,' she said, rolling her eyes in warning. 'An' you 'aven't met Sue yet.'

'Sue?'

'My daughter. She's four years old.'

Charlie nodded. 'Give me a minute,' he replied as he hurried up the stairs.

Susan came scurrying into the passage and followed him up to his room. 'Are you our lodger?' she asked, standing in the doorway.

'Well, as a matter o' fact I am,' he answered, kneeling down in front of her. 'An' who might you be?'

'I'm Susan an' I'm four.'

'An' do you live 'ere?'

'Yes. Wiv my mummy an' daddy.'

'An' Aunt Sara?'

'Yes, but she makes me cry sometimes. She's very grumpy.'

'Oh, an' why's that?'

'She shouts at me.'

'I wouldn't shout at you.'

'What's in that case?' Susan asked.

'All my clothes an' fings.'

'What fings?'

'All sorts o' fings.'

''Ave you got any dollies?'

'No. I'm too old ter play wiv dollies any more,' he chuckled.

Lucy had come up the stairs and was standing behind her daughter enjoying the chatter.

'I've got a dolly an' I've got lots o' dollies' clothes. Would yer like ter see 'em?'

Lucy bent down and scooped the child up. 'Now leave Mr Foden alone,' she said fondly. ''E's got some unpackin' ter do.'

'It's all right. I was really makin' some 'eadway there,' Charlie remarked with a smile and a wink in Sue's direction.

'I don't fink yer'll do as well wiv our Sara,' Lucy told him drily. 'She's got one of 'er bad 'eadaches. P'raps yer'd better come down an' say 'ello, though.'

Charlie followed his landlady down the stairs and entered the parlour behind her.

'Sara, I'd like yer ter meet our lodger, Mr Foden.'

'Charlie'll do, if yer've no objections,' he said pleasantly as he took a step towards her armchair.

Sara allowed him to take her limp hand. 'Pleased ter meet yer, Mr Foden, I'm sure,' she said without enthusiasm. 'Will yer be stayin' fer long?'

'I can't say,' he replied with a shrug. 'Maybe as long as you'll all 'ave me.'

Lucy gave him a smile and suddenly caught her sister-in-law's look of distaste. If Sara had her way Charlie Foden's stay would be very brief indeed, she realised.

Chapter Three

Lucy had made a meat pie for the Saturday evening meal and served it with boiled potatoes and mint peas. George sat at the head of the table with his daughter to his left, who seemed quite pleased to have Charlie on the other side of her. Lucy faced the lodger across tureens and was gratified to hear him say that the pie smelled delicious. Sara sat lackadaisically at the opposite end, and glanced at the cutlery before she began to eat. It was a habit that always irked Lucy, and she gave George a quick glance, but her husband was already tucking into the meal.

Sue seemed to manage quite comfortably with her knife and fork and she occasionally gave Charlie a coy look. His collusive wink made her smile and Lucy knew that one friendship at least was being forged. 'That's a good gel. Eat it all up now an' yer'll be as big as Mr Foden,' she said, smiling.

'Call me Charlie.'

'Can I call yer Charlie too, Charlie?'

'Yeah, course yer can.'

When everyone had finished the meal Lucy got up and gathered the plates. 'There's stewed apples an' custard fer afters,' she told them.

The tea was brewing under a cosy out in the scullery, and

while Lucy served up their portions George carried the laden tea tray into the parlour. Outside the temperature had dropped and a river mist was creeping into the backstreets, but in the Parrys' parlour the fire was glowing and the licking flames reflected in the blue china cups intrigued the little girl, who sat at the table with her chin cupped in her hands as she drifted towards a wonderland of fairies and wizards, magic wands and shooting stars.

'She looks tired,' George observed.

Lucy nodded. 'There we are. Now eat it all up,' she said, putting the small portion in front of Susan.

When the plates were scraped clean and hunger was satisfied, the Parrys and their lodger leaned back in their chairs and began to get a little better acquainted.

'You work in the docks, then, Charlie?' George said.

'Yeah, I'm a plain docker. I work on the quay; the stevedores work the barges an' ships' 'olds,' Charlie explained. 'Mind you, there's very little work there at the moment, same as everywhere else. I'm lucky ter get two days' work a week. Usually it's only one day.'

'Yeah, it's bad all round,' George replied with a sigh. 'I'm sweatin' over my job foldin' up very shortly. I work fer a tobacco firm over the water, in the gift-wrappin' department, an' now the company are talkin' about stoppin' the gift coupons. If they do that it'll mean the dole queue fer all of us.'

Lucy wanted to steer the conversation away from unemployment and misery and she was pleased when Charlie quickly changed the subject. 'I noticed that photo on the mantelshelf,' he said. 'You was in the Navy.'

George's face brightened somewhat. 'Yeah. I went in the boys' service when I was sixteen an' I did twelve years' full service,' he replied. 'I came out ter get married, but I'm still on the reserve. They pay us a few bob every year an' it comes in very 'andy. I was an artificer.'

'You could be pulled back in if there was a national emergency?' Charlie queried.

George nodded a little self-importantly. 'Yeah. Knowin' all about marine engines means that I'd be straight in.'

'I read that the Germans are mobilisin' under that man 'Itler an' we're startin' ter build up our Navy,' Sara cut in.

Charlie glanced down the table. 'Yeah, that's right. There's bin quite a bit about it on the wireless lately. At least it'll put some more jobs people's way.'

Sara looked pleased with herself and wanted to impress a little more with her knowledge of current affairs. 'Of course, it doesn't 'elp when the Italians march into a poor, 'armless country like Ethiopia. Fascist bullyin', just like Franco in Spain.'

Lucy hid a smile. Sara was going to wind herself up if she wasn't careful and start one of her nasty headaches. 'More tea, anybody?' she asked, reaching for the teapot.

Sara passed her cup and saucer over. 'If it's not too stewed,' she said fastidiously.

Lucy got up and took the teapot into the scullery to add some hot water, and Sue turned and tapped Charlie on the arm. 'I've got a tin box fer my dollies' clothes,' she announced.

'That's nice,' Charlie replied.

'Would yer like ter see 'em now?'

'Sue, let Charlie be,' George told her crossly. ''E doesn't wanna see dollies' clothes.'

Charlie saw the child's face drop abruptly and felt for her. 'Of course I would,' he enthused.

Sue jumped down from her chair and hurried out of the room as George grinned, raising his eyes to the ceiling.

'She spends hours dressin' an' undressin' that doll of 'ers,' he said.

'She's a little smasher,' Charlie remarked.

The child was soon back clutching the biscuit tin and she lifted the lid carefully, stealing a quick glance at Sara. 'Look, this is dolly's,' she said, holding up a tiny woollen vest.

'What a lovely jumper,' Charlie replied.

'That's not a jumper, it's a vest,' Sue corrected him quickly.

'Oh, I see. An' what's this?' Charlie asked, picking up a cardigan from the box. 'I know, it's a woolly coat.'

'No it's not, it's a cardigan,' she told him with a look of long-suffering superiority. 'Anyone knows that.'

'So do I now,' Charlie said, chuckling.

'Come on, leave Charlie alone, Sue. It's time fer your beddy-byes,' George reminded her.

'Night, Charlie.'

'Night night, luv. Sleep tight.'

Lucy placed the fresh tea down on the table and took Sue by the hand. 'I'll see to 'er. Pour the tea, Sara.'

George reached up to the mantelshelf for his cigarette makings. 'Care fer a roll-up?' he asked.

Charlie nodded. 'I smoke a pipe, but I'm confinin' it ter me room,' he said. 'The tobacco I use is a bit strong. I would like a roll-up, though.'

George pulled some tobacco strands and a strip of rice paper from the cigarette tin and passed the container over. 'We've bin lucky as a family so far,' he said, looking serious. 'Most o' the poor sods in the turnin' are out o' collar an' findin' it 'ard ter put a meal on the table. The Naylors' two boys were sittin' on the doorstep eatin' bread an' marge fer their tea yesterday an' they ain't got a decent

34

pair o' shoes between 'em. Then there's the Whittles. Bill Whittle's bin out o' work fer almost three years now. 'Is wife's an invalid an' they've got five kids. They're existin' on the UAB money, such as it is. It's the same story at almost every 'ouse yer knock on in this turnin', an' it's the same everywhere else. Where's it all gonna end?'

Charlie had rolled his cigarette and was sliding it thoughtfully between his fingers. 'I dunno,' he replied with a sigh.

'It'll end when we're in our boxes,' Sara declared as she handed over the tea. 'It's the fate o' workin' people. Yer can get so far an' then somefing 'appens ter put yer back. There's too many people chasin' too few jobs, an' wiv mass unemployment there's always ovver fings that come wiv it, such as epidemics an' disorder. It'll take anuvver war ter sort fings out, I'm sorry ter say.'

Charlie lit his cigarette and blew a cloud of smoke towards the ceiling. Maybe Sara was being melodramatic, he thought, but there was something in what she said. The influenza epidemic of 1918 had cost him dearly, as it had many thousands of others, and its virulent spread was linked to poor housing and living standards. Since then the old hovels had been pulled down and sewage now flowed through pipes instead of the gutters, but many people today were existing just above starvation level, and there was no easy way up.

'Are you married, Mr Foden?' Sara asked.

'Yeah, but we've lived apart fer quite a few years now,' he told her.

'I'm sorry. I shouldn't 'ave asked,' Sara replied with unaccustomed humility. 'I was just curious, the way you 'ad wiv Sue. I imagined you'd 'ad children of yer own.'

'It's OK, it doesn't upset me ter talk about it,' Charlie

reassured her. 'It was a long time ago when we split up, an' ter be honest I fink we'd both realised early on that the 'ole fing was a mistake from the start. But there you are. None of us are perfect.'

George was surprised at his sister's rare show of interest, but felt encouraged by it. She could be trying at times, and was quite capable of driving a lodger away with her tantrums and attitudes. 'Sara keeps very busy at the church fellowship,' he said. 'She's always involvin' 'erself in some-fing or ovver. What's the latest business, Sara?'

'Mr Foden doesn't want ter know about such fings,' Sara said quickly.

'On the contrary, I'd be very interested,' Charlie replied with a smile.

'It's patchwork quiltin',' she informed him. 'We're makin' quilts fer those in need, an' there's a big demand as you'd imagine.'

'That's very commendable,' Charlie remarked.

Sara looked suddenly embarrassed. She stood up and gathered together the dessert dishes. 'I'd better make a start on the washin' up while Lucy's gettin' Sue settled,' she said.

George looked across at Charlie as soon as Sara had left the room. 'Me sister gets a bit morbid at times but she's very feelin',' he explained quietly. 'She spent a lot o' time lookin' after our mum, till the day the ole lady died as a matter o' fact, an' then she found she couldn't live in the empty 'ouse. Me an' Lucy told 'er she could stay wiv us fer a while an' she's bin 'ere ever since. We don't mind really, even though she's got 'er funny ways.'

''Aven't we all?' Charlie replied with a smile.

'Sara never 'ad a steady boyfriend,' George went on. 'Our mum was very critical o' the few lads who did come callin' earlier on. She seems to 'ave accepted the way fings are an' she's 'appy in 'er own way.'

Charlie took another drag on his cigarette and stared down for a few moments at the dying glow. How easy for George to make that assessment, he thought, and how wrong it probably was. Sara didn't strike him as a happy woman, though he had to admit that he hardly knew her. Who was it said everyone was an island unto themselves?

Lucy came back in and slumped down in the armchair. 'She's off ter sleep,' she announced. 'She got me readin' to 'er.' She smiled as she glanced at Charlie. 'She wanted ter know if you was gonna stay wiv us fer a while, 'cos she finks you're a nice man.'

Charlie grinned. 'Kids an' dogs, I never fail. It's adults I 'ave trouble wiv.'

'Sara's started the washin' up,' George told her.

Lucy gave him a hard look. 'All right. I'll take over in a minute or two,' she replied irritably. 'After all, it won't 'urt 'er ter do it once in a while.'

Charlie stood up. 'Well, I'll leave yer in peace,' he said. 'I've a couple o' letters ter write.'

'Look, you're welcome ter stay down 'ere as long as yer like,' Lucy said quickly. 'That's right, ain't it, George?'

'Yeah, course it is,' George agreed. 'We want yer ter treat this 'ouse as yer own. As far as we're concerned you can come an' go as yer please.'

'I appreciate that an' I'll bear it in mind.' Charlie smiled. 'I do 'ave a letter or two ter get off, though. By the way, the meal was excellent.'

'What d'yer fink of 'im?' Lucy asked as soon as she heard the bedroom door close.

'I fink 'e's a nice bloke,' George replied. ''E's certainly made strides wiv young Sue.'

'I've never 'eard Sara get so involved in the conversation neivver.'

''Ow old d'yer fink 'e is?' George asked.

'I dunno, about forty-five, forty-six. The grey 'air makes 'im look older.'

'Sara asked 'im if 'e was married an' 'e said 'e was, but they'd bin livin' apart fer years.'

'I guessed 'e was married,' Lucy said. George reached for his tobacco tin and she stood up. 'Well, I'd better see what our Sara's gettin' up to,' she sighed.

Along the narrow backstreet at number 20, Minnie Venners was preparing to make her own personal protest, if there was anyone out there who would take note or heed. People could not be expected to put up with things the way they were for ever, she told herself. Something would have to give. Perhaps soon the powers that be would scrutinise the whys and wherefores that had caused Minnie Venners to do away with herself. It shouldn't be too difficult for them to arrive at an answer. Her neighbours knew the score. They would tell of a woman whose husband was out of work for four years, during which time he changed from a lively Jack-the-lad into a man frightened of his own shadow, willing to take any nonsense from scum who weren't fit to lick his boots. They would tell of a woman widowed prematurely, losing her husband to a sudden heart attack. One or two of her closest friends would talk of a woman living on a pittance who had exhausted her supply of items for the pawnshop. They knew the score. Anyway, there was no sense in dwelling on it all. The decision had been made and that was that. First the gas. A tanner's worth would do nicely. Must put that down on the note as a PS, she thought. 'It was my last tanner.' It would add a bit of light relief to the proceedings.

Right then, where's that cushion, she wondered? The one with the hole in it. I should change by rights. This dress is a bit tatty. But the other one isn't much better. God, what am I worrying myself like this for? Talking of God, I hope he understands. I think it's the Catholics who say that suicide is a mortal sin which closes the door to heaven. Well, that's up to them, but I think that the good Lord'll understand. Albert will be there waiting, I'm sure. He'll be there to see me through.

The sharp knock on the front door made Minnie start and she screwed her face up in agitation. Who could it be at this hour? I won't answer it and they'll think I've gone to bed, she said to herself.

The knock was repeated, louder this time, and Minnie cursed as she hurriedly put the note in the dresser drawer and strode along the passage. Whoever it was had seen the parlour light and knew she was still up.

''Ello, gel. Sorry ter knock this late but it couldn't wait.'

Minnie stared at her best friend Elsie Farr. 'What couldn't wait?'

'Me Jenny's gone inter labour an' it's due any minute. Yer gotta come quick.'

'Me? Why me?'

''Cos Jenny wants yer there.'

'What about the midwife?'

'Jack's gone for 'er, but she might not get 'ere in time. The baby wasn't expected till next week, as yer know. Come on, Minnie, quick as yer can.'

Minnie grabbed her coat and key from the peg and hurried out of the house, slamming the door behind her.

'Jenny knows yer used ter do the birthin' round 'ere, an' I fink she prefers you ter that 'orse-faced ole cow of a midwife,' Elsie went on as they hurried along the street.

'It's bin a long time since I 'elped a baby inter the world,' Minnie told her breathlessly.

A cold, lonely moon looked down on the Bermondsey backstreet as the first wail filled the stuffy bedroom.

'It's a boy an' it's got everyfing it should 'ave,' Minnie said, smiling at the hot face of the young mother.

Elsie boiled another kettle and made some tea while Minnie removed the bloodstained rubber sheet from the bed and tidied the room, and later, once Jenny had been settled with the newborn baby in her arms, the two older women sat facing each other across the table.

'I'm so glad you was still awake when I called ternight, Minnie,' Elsie remarked.

'A few minutes later an' I wouldn't 'ave bin.'

'I bet that midwife'll stink o' booze when she does get 'ere.'

'It's a lovely little mite.'

'They all are, ain't they?' Elsie grinned happily. 'Seein' 'em pullin' them funny faces makes yer ferget all yer trials an' tribulations. 'Ere, I almost fergot ter tell yer, what wiv all the excitement.'

'Tell me what?'

'Mrs Bolton's put 'er notice in. She's movin' down ter Kent ter be near 'er daughter, so I've spoke fer you, if yer still interested.'

'Interested? Elsie, I'm down ter me last tanner. Of course I'm interested.'

'I'll give yer a knock in the mornin' then, shall I?'

'I'll be ready. An' fanks, Elsie.'

'No, I should be fankin' you.'

'As it 'appens the fanks is due ter your Jenny,' Minnie replied, and seeing Elsie's puzzled frown she smiled. 'I'll tell yer why termorrer, but now I wanna take one more peek at the baby. I fink I'll give the little 'un me tanner ter start off its money box, an' a smackin' big kiss ter go wiv it.'

Chapter Four

The church bells of St Mark's rang out on a cold, gloomy November Sunday and as always Emmie Goodwright and her best friend Ada Black listened to them at Ada's front door. 'I always fink it's a lovely sound to 'ear on Sunday mornin's, them bells,' Emmie remarked.

Ada nodded as she leaned against the doorpost. 'Yeah. It makes yer feel sort o' charitable, like they're sayin' ferget yer worries an' troubles an' come ter church.'

Emmie could not always follow her friend's line of thinking and she frowned. 'Charitable? I'd like ter be in a position ter be charitable, Ada, but when you ain't got two pennies ter rub tergevver yer can't fink about charity.'

'Nah, yer don't get me meanin'. I'm talkin' about inside, bein' charitable in the way yer deal wiv ovvers.'

'Oh, I see.'

Ada doubted it but went on anyway. 'When I 'ear them church bells I wish I was a regular churchgoer, often as not. I fink about gettin' meself all spruced up an' goin' ter the mornin' service, an' singin' those lively hymns like "Onward Christian Soldiers" an' . . . an' . . .'

' "Jesus wants me fer a sunbeam",' Emmie offered.

'That's a Sunday school hymn fer kids,' Ada snorted. 'No, seriously though, Emm, I really do get the urge ter try it one Sunday. Why don't me an' you go?'

'What, now? This mornin'?'

'Nah, soon. Next week maybe.'

'I dunno about that,' Emmie said, stroking her chin. 'I ain't bin inside a church since ole Mabel Stubble passed away.'

'Blimey, Emm, that was donkey's years ago. I remember that turn-out. Wasn't that when Mrs Branch from Lynton Road conked out durin' the service?'

'Nah, yer gettin' mixed up. Mrs Branch conked out at Mrs Turnbell's funeral, 'er who fell under the dray in the Ole Kent Road. Anyway, it was years ago, an' I'd feel ashamed goin' back inside there after so long.'

'Yeah, I s'pose so,' Ada conceded. 'As long as we try ter live a decent life an' don't go upsettin' anybody we're as good as all those who go ter church regular.'

The bells ceased to chime and a few minutes later the ice cream man pedalled his tricycle into the street and rang his own bell loudly. Children came running and formed a circle round the curious vehicle.

'Now line up prop'ly. I can't serve yer all at once,' the vendor growled.

Emmie shook her head slowly. 'Yer know, it amazes me,' she said thoughtfully. 'Those kids are wearin' cardboard in their shoes an' most o' their farvvers are out o' collar, but they still seem ter find the pennies.'

'I'm glad I ain't got little ones ter fend for,' Ada remarked.

'Me too,' Emmie agreed. 'It must be a nightmare fer people wiv young families, the way fings are.'

'Mind you, though, the pubs are still full on Sunday mornin's, an' that's after five years o' chronic unemployment,' Ada pointed out.

'Yeah, but it's a different fing nowadays,' Emmie said, scratching the tip of her nose. 'My Bert was only sayin' the ovver week 'ow the blokes sit wiv the one pint where before it'd be gone like soapsuds down a drain'ole. 'E said there's none o' that "Wanna drink?" soon as someone walks in. Everyone buys their own now.'

Elsie Farr came hurrying along the turning. 'Mornin', ladies,' she said breezily. 'Our Jenny 'ad a little boy! Late last night it was born. Minnie Venners delivered it. We couldn't get the bloody midwife till it was all over. I'm gonna report 'er ter me doctor when I see 'im. I 'ate ter fink what might 'ave 'appened if Minnie 'adn't 'a' bin up, 'cos it was late.'

'She's a very nice woman,' Ada remarked. 'She used ter do a lot o' birthin' at one time, till those new-fangled midwives come on the scene.'

'Sorry I can't stop,' Elsie told them. 'I gotta get the *News of the World* before they sell out. There's a bit in there about that dirty ole git from Borough Road who's up fer bigamy. Apparently 'e's got four wives on the go. Would yer believe it?'

''Ow do they get away wiv it, that's what I'd like ter know,' Ada tutted.

'They do in the Arab countries,' Emmie cut in. 'Those sheiks 'ave a tentful.'

'Yeah, but they're only concubines.'

'Concubines, porcupines, it still ain't right. One woman should be enough, even fer the likes o' them.'

'It's the sun what does it,' Ada said knowingly. 'Makes 'em fruity.'

'If that's the case I'll get my ole feller ter sit in the sun when it comes out next,' Elsie chuckled as she hurried off.

Charlie Foden finished putting a polish on his best black boots out in the backyard and looked up to see George watching him from the doorway.

'I wondered if yer'd care fer a pint,' he suggested.

'I was gonna ask you the same,' Charlie told him.

'The Mason's Arms in Lynton Road's about the best pub round 'ere,' George said.

'Right then, let's go.'

The two men stepped out of the house into the overcast morning and walked along to the intersection with Lynton Road. As they turned left past the bootmender's on the corner Charlie noticed that the shop on the other corner was boarded up. George saw him looking at it. 'That was a florist's up until a few weeks ago,' he said. 'Before that it was an oil shop, an' if I remember rightly it was a green-grocer's fer a spell. Nobody seemed able ter make it pay.'

The Victorian houses with their steps leading up to the front doors stretched away into the distance, and across the road a head-high red brick wall hid the railway track and freight yards.

'Nice places,' Charlie remarked. 'Bit noisy though, I should fink.'

George nodded. 'It used ter be worse at one time. We could 'ear the racket from our 'ouse. It went on right frew the night.'

They reached the pub and George led the way into the public bar. 'Wotcher, Mick,' he greeted the tubby landlord. Mick mumbled a reply and glanced quickly at Charlie. 'This is my new lodger, Charlie Foden,' George informed him.

'Mick Johnson,' the landlord said, holding out his hand. 'Are you from round 'ere?'

'Walworth, until recently,' Charlie replied.

George put a ten-shilling note down on the counter. 'I'll 'ave a pint o' bitter,' he said, and turned to Charlie.

'The same fer me, please.'

While the landlord poured the drinks Charlie took a quick look round. There were only a couple of elderly men propping up the counter on either side of him, and it struck him how few people there were in the place. A piano stood idle under a large figured window and in the far corner two young men were playing darts. The wrought-iron tables in the bar were mostly occupied by old men smoking pipes and one or two elderly women, all with blank, sad faces as they guarded their half-empty glasses. It was a sign of the times, the new lodger reflected. A far cry from the days when the ships came continually and the Tooley Street pubs were packed to overflowing.

'Wanna pint, Bill?'

'Nah, I'll get these.'

'Fancy a chaser?'

'Yeah, why not?'

'Give 'im a large 'un.'

Now the men stood quietly as they were called off, the few lucky dockers working the day and then going home sober. The rest made their way to sign on at the labour exchange, 'bomping on' as they termed it, and they all waited patiently for the ships to call again, the quays to ring out with expletives and the tall cranes to swing to and fro with their awkward sets, hauled up from the holds and expertly landed on the wet quays and waiting transport. Once there had been constant queues of traffic on the Tower Bridge approach as the centre span was raised repeatedly on the changing tides, but now the tide could change without a single lift.

The two men stayed at the counter after their drinks were

served and when George had taken his first sip he pulled out his tobacco tin. 'This place used ter be packed out every Sunday lunchtime,' he remarked.

'Yeah, I was just finkin' about 'ow it is at the docks an' wharves nowadays,' Charlie replied. 'It's bin five years now an' no sign of any change fer the better.'

George brought the makings up to his mouth and licked the rice paper. 'I ain't told our Lucy, but it's cut an' dried at the factory,' he said quietly. 'We're all gonna be put off in two weeks' time. I know I should 'ave told 'er, but the time never seems right.'

'I'm very sorry to 'ear that,' Charlie replied sympathetically. ''Ave yer got any plans?'

George shook his head slowly. 'I've bin frew all the papers an' tried factories over the water but it's always the same answer. P'raps I'll get a part-time job be'ind the bar. 'Ow about it, Mick?'

The landlord was serving a nearby customer and he snorted. 'I've just 'ad ter lay our evenin' barmaid off,' he said. 'The pub trade's the worst I've known it in twenty years. What's even worse, they're closin' the road off soon. They're diggin' it up fer new sewer pipes. That'll be 'alf me daily trade gone fer a burton. A lot o' the local firms' carmen call in 'ere at lunchtime. They won't be able ter get down 'ere now, will they?'

The old man who had just been served looked across the counter at Mick. 'Who's got the contract, any idea?' he asked.

'I dunno,' Mick answered. 'Does it matter?'

'Yeah it does, if yer lookin' fer a job diggin',' the customer replied quickly. 'If it's a main contract job the firm'll bring their own labour, but if it's subbed out there'll be some work fer the locals.'

'The Coleys 'ave bin recruitin' in Tooley Street,' Charlie informed him.

The old man looked disgusted. He held out his gnarled hands, palms upwards, and slowly turned them over. 'I used ter be in the game, an' these ole mitts o' mine 'ave bin wrapped round more shovels than I care ter remember,' he said in a measured voice. 'I've worked fer some decent firms in me time 'an I've also worked fer some right real bastards, but from what I've 'eard the Coley bruvvers take some beatin'. There's a couple o' young shavers who come in 'ere now an' then an' they was tellin' me they got a start wiv the Coleys down in Rovverhive. They said it was like bein' on a chain gang. Two weeks was all they could stick of it, an' then they 'ad a bloody 'ard job gettin' their wages.'

''Ow do they get away wiv it?' Charlie asked, already knowing the answer from talking to Fred at the hostel.

'Fer a start they're non-union,' the old man replied. 'Then there's a couple o' gangers in charge an' by all accounts they're nuffing more than animals. They'd fight King Kong if the money was right. They work the men flat out an' constantly bribe 'em wiv the promise of a big bonus at the end o' the contract. Course it's all pie in the sky an' yer don't find out till it's too late.'

George looked suddenly depressed. 'I'm game fer most fings but I couldn't work in a trench, diggin' away all day. It'd kill me.'

'Nah it wouldn't,' the old man said. 'Yer get used to it, an' if yer not too tall yer back'll stand up to it. Yer shoulders an' yer legs get stronger too. It's the tall blokes who suffer most wiv their backs, 'specially when yer get down ter the clay.'

George and Charlie began to feel more and more miserable as the old man elaborated on the hardships of trench digging, and as soon as they could they took their fresh drinks over to a far table. Only a few more customers came into the bar, but one of them caused a few heads to turn. The man was big, six foot three in his socks, with broad shoulders and lean hips. His neck was bull-like and he walked over to the counter with a confident swagger. Small dark eyes stared out of a wide flat face and his jawline was square, knotted with hard muscle. The landlord said something to him as he ordered a beer and he smiled, showing a set of large white teeth.

The old man Charlie had talked to at the bar got up and walked unsteadily to the toilet, and when he came back he stopped to lean over the table. 'Did yer notice that big geezer who just come in?' he asked. 'That's Sharkey Lockwood, the Coleys' right-'and man. 'E used ter wrestle at the Bermon'sey baths under the moniker o' The Vikin'. 'E's got an easier job now though, overseein' the poor sods who make the mistake o' signin' on wiv the bloody slave-drivers, an' considerin' 'e ain't bin in 'ere fer some time I'd say it's a pound to a pinch o' shit the Coleys 'ave got the contract. Sharkey's come in 'ere 'specially ter put the word out. Next week they'll be queuein' up outside, poor bleeders.'

George and Charlie finished their drinks and left the Mason's Arms to walk the short distance home. When they entered the house the smell of roast potatoes and beef cooking filled the passageway and George reached down for Sue as she came towards him. Charlie smiled at the little girl and hung his coat up on a hook by the front door. Even Sara was ready with a weak smile, and as Charlie walked into the scullery to wash his hands Lucy looked up from slicing the meat. 'What did yer fink o' the Mason's Arms?' she asked with a smile.

'It was pretty quiet,' Charlie replied.

'We go in there occasionally on a Saturday night,' she told him, 'but I prefer the Star in the Old Kent Road. It's much livelier.'

Charlie's eyes inadvertently strayed down to the tight-fitting blouse Lucy was wearing and he looked up quickly, but not quickly enough, and the young woman did not mistake what she had seen for a brief second in his frank hazel eyes.

Along the small turning there were houses where the money had not stretched to a joint of beef. The Marchants had mutton stew, and Ada and Joe Black sat down to corned beef and cabbage. Emmie and Bert Goodwright enjoyed a lamb chop apiece, while at number 16 Mrs Belton discovered that the chunk of corned beef she had kept for the Sunday meal was mouldy right through and she and her two boys had bread and jam instead. Sid Belton was not concerned. He was sitting in the Dun Cow, slowly slipping into a state of sublime intoxication which let him forget that regular meals on the table required money in his wife's purse. Annie Belton never forgot and she was feeling angry and bitter, as she often did these days, but Sid wore a stupid grin on his face as he pushed his empty glass across the counter and handed the barman the last of his dole money.

Chapter Five

November was ending the way it had begun, with yellow fogs and clammy mist, and on the last Friday of the month George Parry climbed down from the number 42 bus and walked the rest of the way home with his employment cards in his coat pocket. It was stupid of him not to have let Lucy know what had been going on at the factory during the past week, he realised now. He could have cushioned the blow, but he had been praying for the impossible, that the firm would have a last-minute change of heart and hold on to their workers. That sort of thing only happened in fairy stories. This was stark reality, and the truth of the matter was that from Monday morning he would be joining the rest of the human jetsam at the labour exchange.

Inside the house it was warm and cosy, and Charlie eased his position in his armchair as Lucy came into the parlour to lay the table. 'Can I do anyfing?' he asked.

She gave him a quick smile. 'No, it's all right, fanks. Everyfing's under control.'

Charlie watched as his landlady arranged the knives and forks around the table and brushed the spotless tablecloth with the palm of her hand. 'Are you OK?' he enquired in a quiet voice.

'Yeah, of course,' Lucy replied quickly. 'Does it look as

though there's somefing wrong?'

'You just look a bit worried, that's all,' he said in embarrassment.

Lucy laid a large spoon in front of Sue's place and folded her arms over her clean apron as she turned towards him. 'I'm sorry if I jumped,' she said. 'Yeah, I am a bit worried. When George gets 'ome from work 'e's gonna tell me that 'e's got 'is cards.'

'P'raps not,' Charlie said supportively. ''E was only sayin' last night that nuffing definite 'ad bin decided as yet.'

Lucy smiled wryly. 'You ferget I'm married ter the man. I can read 'im like a book. I know 'e's only bin tryin' ter protect me, but I wish 'e 'adn't. Whatever 'appens we face it tergevver.'

Charlie looked up at the determined young woman and noticed how the tightly fitting apron accentuated her figure. Her fair hair looked nice too, the way she had of gathering it up carelessly and tying it at the back of her neck. He liked to see her uncovered small flat ears and the high forehead, the soft blue eyes and the movements of her expressive mouth. She was chewing on her lip nervously and Charlie stood up and glanced through the net curtains into the street. 'Do yer fink I should slip round ter the surgery an' escort Sara back?' he suggested. 'The fog's thickenin'.'

'No, she wouldn't fank yer for it,' Lucy told him. 'You know 'ow independent she is. Ter be honest I don't know why she bovvered ter go out on a night like this. She only wanted some more of 'er backache pills an' she's still got a few days' supply left.' Charlie pulled a face and rolled his dark eyes, which brought a smile to Lucy's face. 'You 'ave to admit she is tryin' at times.'

The front door opened and shut and George walked into the parlour, hardly casting the lodger a glance as he reached out to give Lucy a peck on her cheek. 'It's bin a bad day,' he said hesitantly.

'I know the worst, George,' she replied, 'so don't try to ease it out.'

He reached into his coat and pulled out the green and buff-coloured employment cards. 'I was 'opin' against 'ope, but—'

Lucy cut across him. 'Look, it's not your fault. We both knew it was comin'.'

'I'm very sorry, George,' Charlie added.

Lucy took control. 'Right then, you sit down an' I'll make us some tea, then I'll 'ave ter fetch our Sue. She's playin' next door wiv Gracie.'

'Where's Sara?' George asked as he slipped out of his coat.

'Gone ter the doctor's fer more backache pills,' Lucy told him, momentarily glancing towards Charlie.

At number 10 the two young children played happily together, untroubled by all that was happening around them, but for Roy and Mary Chubb it was a difficult day. Mary was still tormented by the fact that her husband had gone along to Lynton Road that morning. 'But yer've never done that sort o' work before,' she pointed out once again.

'I've done some buildin' labourin' in the past an' it's much about the same,' Roy replied. 'Anyway, I'm fit an' strong, an' if Danny Albury can do it so can I.'

'Yeah, but Danny Albury's used ter the work,' Mary reminded him. ''E was on the council road gangs fer a few years ter my knowledge.'

'Anyway, it's done now,' Roy said firmly. 'I start work on Monday in Lynton Road an' if I get on all right there's an option ter get a start at the next job in Southwark Park Road.'

When her husband had told her of his intentions that morning Mary had felt sick inside. Only the previous week Lucy Parry had been talking to her about the Coleys' impending recruitment in Lynton Road, and she had hoped that her husband wouldn't get any ideas about signing on. He was fit and strong, it was true, but he was a carpenter by trade, not a ditch digger, and there would be some building site jobs coming up soon, if he could just be a little more patient. After all, there were still a few shillings left in the jug, and with his dole money, a pittance though it was, they wouldn't exactly starve just yet. 'I'm just worried about yer,' she told him. 'I've 'eard so many stories about those slave-drivers.'

'An' who from?' Roy replied quickly. 'Lucy next door, an' where did she get 'em from? Yer can't afford ter take too much notice o' people. Remember it'll be December in a few days' time an' before yer know it Christmas'll be 'ere. The money's gonna come in very 'andy, an' if I 'ave ter sweat fer it, so be it. I tell yer this, Mary, I'd sooner sweat fer a few bob than 'ave ter stand in those dole queues waitin' fer an 'and-out. It's soul-destroyin'. We're like the walkin' dead shufflin' along in line till we get ter the counter. It feels like beggin', an' me wiv a trade.'

Mary got up and put her arm round his shoulders as he slumped back in the armchair. 'I understand, luv,' she said softly, 'an' I know 'ow yer feel. I just wanna keep yer in one piece.'

Roy chuckled. 'Don't you worry about me,' he told her. 'I can use a shovel as well as the next man.'

Mary leaned over and kissed him gently on the forehead. 'I know yer can,' she replied.

★ ★ ★

At number 2 Sammy Strickland leaned back in the armchair and puffed on his cigarette. 'I was surprised 'ow many was there,' he remarked to Peggy, his long-suffering wife. 'I got there early like yer told me an' I thought ter meself, Sammy, yer got a chance 'ere, son. 'Alf the men in front o' me must 'a' bin in their late fifties an' most of 'em didn't look all that strong.'

'You're in yer late fifties,' Peggy reminded him.

'Yeah, but I got a bit o' meat on me. At least I looked the part,' he replied. 'Anyway, this geezer comes out o' the shed an' walks along the line starin' at us all, so I give 'im a wink, just ter let 'im know I was keen.'

'Yeah, I bet yer did,' Peggy said disbelievingly.

Sammy ignored the sarcasm. 'Then the geezer goes up ter the first man in line an' asks 'im a few questions, an' suddenly 'e jerks 'is thumb an' ses, "Yer no use ter me, piss off." The next few in line get told ter go an' wait in the shed an' then 'e comes up ter me. "What's yer name?" 'e said. "Sammy Strickland, sir," I told 'im smart like. "Ever done any diggin' before?" 'e asked me. "Plenty," I told 'im. "Who for?" "St Mary's," I said. "Are you takin' the piss?" 'e growled. "No, I done a spell o' grave diggin'," I explained. Wiv that 'e jerks 'is thumb an' tells me ter get lost.'

'Ignorant git,' Peggy exclaimed. 'An' what did yer say to 'im? I 'ope yer did say somefing to 'im.'

'Do me a favour, gel,' Sammy puffed. 'The geezer was built like a brick shit'ouse. 'E even 'ad muscles on 'is muscles. I just left the line an' done me little trick.'

'What yer talkin' about, Sammy?'

'I slipped in the shed when 'is back was turned an' just waited.'

'Well, go on.'

Sammy flicked his cigarette stub into the hearth. 'It seemed like ages till the bloke come in, an' when 'e did 'e took all our names an' addresses. 'E told us ter be by the shed at seven firty sharp on Monday mornin' an' we'd be given wellin'ton boots an' a boiler suit each. 'E also said there was a certain amount o' work that 'ad ter be done every day, an' if we didn't reach our quota we wouldn't get our full pay fer that day.'

'An' what is the full pay?' Peggy asked impatiently.

'Fifteen bob a day.'

'So do yer start on Monday or not?' Peggy asked with irritation mounting in her voice.

''Ang on a minute, I'm comin' ter that,' Sammy told her with a frown. 'When the geezer finished takin' our names 'e told us we could go, an' as I walked out o' the shed 'e grabbed me by the scruff o' the neck an' pulled me back inside. "I thought I told yer ter piss off," he said. "I didn't 'ear yer," I told 'im. "Well yer do now, so scram," 'e shouted.'

'So yer didn't get the job after all,' Peggy said, puffing loudly.

'Nah. 'E said it was me 'ands.'

'What d'yer mean, yer 'ands?'

'The geezer took a gander at 'em an' said they 'adn't done an 'ard day's work fer years.'

'Well 'e was bloody well right,' Peggy growled.

Sammy reached down for the morning paper and sighed as he searched for the comic strip page. There wasn't much to laugh at these days, he thought, but that page did make him smile.

'So what's yer plans now, Sammy?' Peggy asked him after a while.

'I thought I might go an' see Ben Toland later on.'

'What for?'

'Ter see if 'e can fix me up wiv a couple o' days' work.'

'Paintin', yer mean?'

'What else?'

''E might not 'ave anyfing fer 'imself.'

'Buller Morris was tellin' me Ben's got the contract ter paint the Trocette cinema,' Sammy informed her.

'Well, what yer waitin' for?'

'Ben'll be in the Mason's by now an' I'm skint.'

Peggy sighed heavily as she fished into her purse. ''Ere, take it, an' fer Gawd's sake try an' get yerself fixed up. That's me last 'alf-crown.'

Lucy called next door and Mary Chubb led her into the parlour. 'Sue, 'ere's Mummy. Now you an' Gracie gavver up those toys, there's good children.'

Lucy sat down and smiled bravely at her best friend. 'Well, it's 'appened at last,' she said with a sigh.

'George's job?'

'Yeah. 'E came in wiv 'is cards this evenin'.'

'I'm sorry, luv.'

Lucy shrugged her shoulders. 'We knew it was comin' but you always 'ope that there's a change of 'eart at the last minute. I know George was finkin' the same as me. Still, it's 'appened, an' we've just gotta get on wiv it like everyone else round 'ere.'

Mary pulled on her dark hair as she stood watching the children reluctantly putting the toys into a cardboard box. 'Look, they're all right fer a bit longer. Roy's gone out fer a pint. Let's me an' you 'ave a nice cuppa.'

Gracie immediately tipped the box of toys on to the floor and giggled at Sue.

'Now keep the noise down, you two,' Lucy warned them.

Mary was soon back with the laden tea tray. 'My Roy's found a job,' she said with little enthusiasm.

'Good fer 'im. Where?' Lucy asked.

Mary pulled a face. ''E starts wiv the Coleys on Monday.'

'Oh no,' Lucy said quickly. 'They're bloody slave-drivers. Remember George was tellin' me they work their men really 'ard.'

Mary nodded. 'What could I do, though? Roy's just about at breakin' point. The way 'e is 'e'll take anyfing.'

'Yeah, I can understand,' Lucy replied. 'There's Christmas just round the corner, an' 'ow d'yer tell kids there ain't no Farvver Christmas this year?'

'There won't be fer a lot o' kids, I'm afraid,' Mary said sadly.

Lucy watched her friend as she poured the tea. She had put on weight round the hips and her face too looked more full. Her dark eyes still sparkled and her skin was comparatively smooth and unlined. 'Mary, I dunno 'ow yer do it,' she said suddenly.

'Do what?'

'Keep yerself lookin' 'alf yer age.'

'Go on wiv yer.'

'No, I mean it. Yer do.'

'Well, it's not the good life nor the money, that's fer sure,' Mary said, grinning.

Lucy took her tea and leaned back in the armchair. ''Ow 'as all this affected you an' Roy?' she asked.

'What, 'im bein' out o' work fer so long, yer mean?'

Lucy nodded. ''Ow d'yer cope wiv it?'

'Well, at first it wasn't too bad,' Mary recalled. 'We 'ad a few bob saved up an' Roy expected ter get a start before long, but when it dragged on inter weeks an' then months an' the money we'd saved 'ad all gone we both got really shirty wiv each ovver. It got to a stage where I wouldn't let 'im near me an' then when I did want 'im 'e'd turn 'is back on me. It was as though we were punishin' each ovver fer what was 'appenin' to us, as though it was our fault. One night we came close ter blows an' suddenly we hugged each ovver an' cried on each ovver's shoulders. That night we emptied our grief, an' sat till the early mornin' talkin' everyfing over. We're closer now than ever, Lucy, though we still 'ave our little differences. I got on at Roy this evenin' about 'im takin' that job wiv the Coleys, but it's different now. We draw the line an' refuse ter step over it. It's what you'll 'ave ter do, luv. It'll get 'ard, believe me, an' when yer fink nuffing else can 'appen it will.'

Lucy looked sad. 'I wish I could 'ave 'elped yer more,' she said.

'You 'ave 'elped us, as much as yer could,' Mary replied. 'I've not forgotten the bits an' pieces you give us, but yer won't be in a position ter do it now, not any more. Yer'll be makin' friends wiv the pawnbroker, like most o' the people in this street. Where it was beef it'll be mutton stew, an' yer'll learn ter scrape an' scheme.'

Lucy's eyes filled with tears. 'I've bin wrong, Mary,' she said quietly. 'I've shut me eyes an' ears ter the rest o' the people in this street. George was workin' an' we 'ave decent meals. I've even taken in a lodger. I'm doin' all right, fank you very much. I didn't notice the neighbours wiv brown paper bundles under their arms, an' if I did I ignored it. That would never be me. Oh, no. I'd never resort ter takin' a pair o' best sheets over ter the pawnbroker's. I'd never 'ave ter put cardboard in me shoes or wear a patched-up dress. I've even got a winter coat.'

Mary put her empty teacup down. 'Now you listen ter me,' she told her. 'We all do the best we can fer our loved ones. We all try ter be that little bit better, 'cos it's in our nature. But there comes a time when circumstances stop yer. Poverty don't pick its victims at random, it sweeps over all of us one way or anuvver. One man loses 'is job an' it puts anuvver man out o' collar. Sooner or later we're all swimmin' fer our lives, our 'eads just above water, an' that's when yer sit down an' take stock, just like me an' Roy did. Yer decide ter fight it, swim fer it or go under. There's no middle ground, only the shore.'

'We'll be all right,' Lucy said. 'I'll see to it. George is inclined ter be a bit weak when decisions 'ave ter be taken, an' sometimes 'e lets fings get on top of 'im, but I'll be 'is crutch. I won't let 'im go under.'

'Good fer you, luv,' Mary said, smiling. 'Fancy anuvver cuppa?'

Lucy nodded. 'So what d'yer fink of our new lodger, then?' she asked casually.

''E looks very respectable,' Mary replied. 'Quite attractive, too. I spoke to 'im yesterday, just passed the time o' day, an' 'e introduced 'imself. 'E told me 'e's very 'appy wiv everyfing an' the food was excellent, which made me smile. Your lodger's a very shrewd man. 'E knew that livin' next door I'd most likely tell yer what 'e'd said.'

'Yeah, 'e's very nice,' Lucy remarked. ''E 'as a way wiv Sara an' I'm sure she fancies 'im. She asked me ter perm 'er 'air for 'er last week.'

'Well well, what d'yer know?' Mary said with a cheeky grin. 'An' what about you? Do you fancy 'im?'

'Mary!' Lucy said indignantly. 'I'm an 'appily married woman.'

'Which don't necessarily mean that yer can't fancy

someone else,' Mary pointed out. 'You can look at the goods wivout buyin'.'

Lucy smiled dismissively, but deep inside she remembered how Charlie had occasionally given himself away with a lingering gaze or a surreptitious glance. The effect on her was increasingly exciting. She could not deny that she liked it whenever his eyes strayed, but refused to read anything into it. She was happily married and that was that. 'I don't see 'im that way,' she replied. 'Besides, 'e must be ten years older than me.'

'Which doesn't mean a fing,' Mary persisted. 'An older man can bring 'is own charm an' experience.'

Lucy felt that the conversation was getting a little dangerous and she might say something she could regret if pressed any more by her forthright friend. 'I expect you're right, but I like ter play it safe,' she said.

'Don't we all,' Mary replied, grinning.

Two tired young children slept soundly that night, but George Parry twisted and turned until the first streaks of dawn rose in the winter sky and he fell into fitful sleep.

Chapter Six

Monday morning dawned cold and dreary, and as Roy Chubb left the house he was feeling a little nervous. Stories were rife about the way the Coleys handled their workers, but he thought that if he could get through the first day without any mishaps then he had a chance. Mary had fixed him up with a packet of brawn sandwiches and had bought him a pair of thick angler's socks at the market to go over his own when he wore the wellington boots.

As he turned into Lynton Road he saw the men gathering up ahead. A wooden barrier had been placed across the turning and an arch-shaped shed of tarpaulin had been set up on the pavement. Next to it was the small wooden hut which the Coleys operated from. Roy could see Danny Albury from number 5 and a few other faces that were familiar.

'Right then, you lot, come an' get yer gear,' Sharkey Lockwood called out as he stepped from the shed.

For a few minutes there was chaos as men tried to sort out their boot sizes and grab boiler suits which would come somewhere near to fitting them.

'Oi, you. You can see they're too big,' Sharkey's voice rang out. 'The size is marked inside the top o' the boots. Surely yer know yer own size. An' what d'yer fink you're doin'? Put the poxy boiler suit on, don't try it up ter yer like some big nancy-boy. Oi, you. If yer fixed up get outside an' make room fer the ovvers. Come on, 'urry up, we start work in five minutes.'

Roy Chubb scrambled into his working gear and joined the rest of the men beside a marked area in the middle of the street, and after a few minutes Sharkey ambled over and took one of the men by the arm. 'Now, me an' 'im are gonna start off by loosenin' a few o' the cobblestones an' I want yer ter pick 'em up an' stack 'em all over there near the kerb,' he told them. 'Once we've got the first few out the rest'll lift easy.'

Willing hands soon cleared the prised-up stones and Roy found himself at work with a pickaxe. It took no time at all to remove all the cobbles inside the chalked area and when they were finished Sharkey called the men round him. 'Now, there's ten of yer an' I want yer ter work in pairs,' he explained. 'One'll use the pickaxe an' the ovver the shovel. Spell each ovver wiv the tools an' it'll be easier. Space yerselves out; I don't want anyone reportin' ter me wiv a pickaxe in 'is 'ead. Now as yer dig down move forward, like yer cuttin' steps.'

''Ow far down's the pipes?' one young man asked. 'We don't wanna pierce 'em, do we?'

'What's yer name, son?' Sharkey asked him.

'Watson. Gerry Watson,' he replied.

'Well, Mr Watson, it was good of yer ter point that out, but yer gotta realise that you an' the ovvers are employed ter dig, not fink. I'll do the finkin' round 'ere. If yer must know, the pipes are over six feet down, so yer won't reach 'em just yet awhile. What I want from you is a nice straight trench an' no conversation. Just keep yer lip buttoned over that big mouth o' yours an' me an' you'll get on like an 'ouse on fire. Right then, get on wiv it.'

Once Sharkey had gone into the hut the young man looked up at Roy and gave him a sheepish grin. 'I'd 'ave put one on 'is chops, 'cept I need the work,' he remarked.

Roy returned the grin. Already he felt the heat building up inside his uncomfortable boiler suit as he brought the pickaxe down on the exposed hardcore. The secret was to pace himself, he thought. It was going to be a long day and his back was already beginning to feel the strain.

'Oi. Silly git,' Sharkey yelled. 'Why are yer chuckin' out on that side when everyone else is chuckin' out the ovver side?'

'Sorry, I wasn't finkin'.'

'Yer don't 'ave ter fink. Just copy the ovvers, or is that too much to ask?'

By ten o'clock the digging crew were at waist level in the trench and Sharkey took the boiling kettle from the coke brazier and turned back into the hut.

A heavily built man with a balding head and a flat wide face looked up from a blueprint spread out in front of him. ''Ow's it goin'?' he asked.

'Well, I've 'ad better crews, but they seem ter be gettin' stuck into it,' Sharkey told him.

Ben Coley smiled, displaying a gold tooth. ''Ow many yer keepin'?'

'Eight, same as last time. I got me eye on two.'

Coley leaned his arm on the sloping work surface while he waited for Sharkey to make the coffee. The system they used worked well. At first the men would set to work trying to show willing, but then as the toil wore on the obvious signs would be there. For some it became torture trying to lift a clay-filled shovel clear of the hole, and for others the wear and tear on the hands made it impossible to carry on.

'Oi, you, it ain't break time yet,' Sharkey called out from the hut.

'Just takin' a minute's breavver,' the man replied.

'Yer take a break when I tell yer, not before,' the ganger shouted at him. 'Piss off an' get changed.'

'But I'm only—'

'Are yer deaf as well as idle? Get changed an' quick about it.'

Gerry Watson mumbled something which Roy did not catch, and then he tried to look industrious as he saw Sharkey approaching.

'You seem to 'ave quite a bit o' trouble keepin' that trap shut,' the ganger growled. 'Would you like ter join 'im?'

Gerry looked up at the sorry figure making his way to the shed and shook his head vigorously. 'I'm dumb from now on,' he said, pushing his shovel into the soil with gusto.

At ten thirty Ben Coley stepped out of the hut and blew a whistle, and the digging crew scrambled out of the trench to a well-earned ten-minute break. At the kerbside there was a large metal container filled with steaming tea and an array of chipped enamel mugs. Roy grabbed one and, having observed the man ahead of him, followed suit by dipping his into the tea.

'I don't fink I'm gonna last the day, let alone the week,' someone said nearby.

'Wait till we get down ter the clay,' Gerry groaned.

Roy studied his blistered hands and felt that he too would be very lucky to last the week. 'We'll just 'ave ter grit our teeth an' carry on,' he said with bravado.

A man sitting nearby leaned forward to catch Roy and Gerry's attention. 'I take it yer've met Ben Coley,' he said, and they answered with a shake of their heads. 'That was 'im wiv the whistle. Long as Frank stays away we'll be all right. 'E's the bastard. Sharkey's like a pussy cat next to 'im.'

The whistle sounded all too soon and the work got under way once more. Clods of clay were thrown up to the side of the trench and the men grew more and more fatigued as the morning wore on. Suddenly a shout rang out and Roy could see two men grappling at the front of the line. All work stopped as the two combatants fell in a heap, and when one man tried to separate them a cry went up. 'Leave 'em alone. Let 'em fight it out.'

Sharkey came running over and dropped down into the hole, tearing the two apart and holding them at arm's length. 'What's goin' on?' he growled.

'That stupid git nearly done me wiv the pickaxe,' one of the fighters said.

'It was nowhere near yer, yer bloody cry-baby.'

'Who you callin' a cry-baby?'

'What's goin' on 'ere?'

The men turned to see the huge figure of Frank Coley standing legs apart at the edge of the trench. He was inches taller than Ben and at least two stone heavier. His thick grey hair was swept back over his ears and his grey eyes glinted as he stared down coldly at the scene below. 'Fetch 'em both up 'ere,' he demanded.

Once they had scrambled out of the trench Sharkey prodded the men towards the workmen's shed.

'Who started it?' Frank asked as he sat down on the trestle table and rested his foot on a bench stool.

''E did,' the two said in unison.

'Do yer like fightin'?' Frank asked them. 'Well, do yer?'

'We just got a bit—'

'I asked you a question an' I expect a sensible answer. Do you like fightin'?'

The men shook their heads. Coley stood up and suddenly brought the back of his hand across the face of the taller one, drawing blood from a split lip. 'Would yer like ter fight me?'

The man shook his head as he licked his damaged lip.

'What about you? Would you like ter fight me?'

The other one stepped back a pace, fearing the same treatment. 'No, sir.'

Frank Coley grabbed him by his overalls and pulled him close. 'I don't allow fightin' on my jobs,' he said quietly. 'If anyone gets involved in fightin' they get put off right away, is that understood?'

The man nodded and was suddenly caught with a back-hander.

'I said is that understood?'

Staggering back, the man mumbled a reply and turned to run from the shed, only to see Sharkey barring his way.

'Sit down, the pair of yer,' Coley snarled. 'You were on fifteen bob a day, right? A mornin's work makes it seven an' a tanner. We gotta knock off two bob fer the 'ire o' yer gear an' then there's a shillin' tea money ter do down. I make that four an' a tanner we owe yer.' The two men nodded, wanting to get away from what had to be a dangerous maniac. 'Yer'll 'ave ter call back fer yer money termorrer afternoon.'

As the two chastened workers hurried off in different directions Frank Coley stepped from the shed. 'Right, lads, stop what yer doin' an' listen ter me,' he ordered. Seven tired faces stared up at him as he stood above them. 'You lost one worker this mornin' fer takin' an unofficial break an' yer lost anuvver two fer fightin'. So there's just seven of yer left. We'll replace the ovvers termorrer, but in the meantime there's work ter do. I want them pipes cleared o' soil an' ready fer takin' out termorrer. Any complaints?'

The silence gratified Coley and he looked around at the blank expressions. 'Now I want yer ter listen carefully ter what I'm gonna say,' he went on. 'We pay fair wages an' we expect a fair day's graft. But it seems that recently some of yer 'ave taken umbrage fer certain reasons known only ter yerselves. Complaints 'ave bin submitted at the employment exchange an' wiv the buildin' unions. We don't entertain unions an' we don't like you geezers spoutin' yer mouths off in the wrong direction, like wiv the local rags an' public busybodies. If yer do, be sure we'll get ter find out an' woe betide anyone we catch. We're talkin' about survival 'ere, yours as well as ours. We stay in business an' you don't starve. Do yer job an' yer'll be took on fer our ovver contracts in the area. Mess us about an' yer'll regret it, be sure. Right then, back ter work.'

Harold Wicks considered that he had been treated very unfairly. After all, it wasn't a crime to take a couple of minutes' rest. And to crown it all he had been sent packing without any wages – not that he'd earned that much. They could have paid him for the morning's work, though, but the gits seemed to do just what they liked. Well it wasn't fair and a man had his rights. He'd make an official complaint at the labour exchange and see what they could do. Maybe it'd shake the Coleys up a bit if the union got involved as well. They should know what was going on at these non-union jobs.

Harold Wicks managed to scrape up enough coppers for a half-pint at the Mason's Arms that evening, and recognising one of the diggers from the site who was sitting alone he wandered over. ''Ere, Joe, did yer know I got chucked off the job wivout a penny?'

'No I didn't.'

'The way I see it I should 'ave bin paid fer the hour an' 'alf I worked,' Harold complained.

'I should go back termorrer an' ask fer it,' Joe Lambert advised him, knowing full well that the man wouldn't dare.

'I'm not gonna waste me time wiv those 'orrible bastards,' Harold sneered. 'I'm gonna make an official complaint at the labour exchange about the way I bin treated. I'm gonna see the union people as well.'

'I don't s'pose they'd be able to 'elp much, what wiv the Coleys bein' non-union,' Joe remarked.

'We'll see,' Harold said confidently.

Joe Lambert was a friendly soul who liked nothing more than a pint of beer and a cosy chat in a friendly pub, and after Harold Wicks had left he got into conversation with two men who were already discussing the digging works outside.

'I've done a bit o' diggin' in me time,' one was saying.

'Can't say as I 'ave,' his companion replied. 'That sort o' graft's too 'ard fer me, what wiv me dodgy back.'

'They're doin' the sewer pipes by all accounts,' the other man said. 'It's bloody 'ard work, especially when yer get down ter the clay. I done a spell wiv that firm once. Only lasted a week. They're poxy slave-drivers.'

Joe Lambert decided it was time to make his contribution. 'I started on there this mornin',' he put in. 'They certainly want their pound o' flesh. They chucked one bloke off the site fer takin' a breavver an' they ain't paid 'im a sausage. As a matter o' fact I was just talkin' ter the bloke. 'E reckons 'e's gonna report 'em. Fat lot o' good that'll do.'

'In my opinion I fink 'e'll be better off keepin' 'is trap shut,' the first man remarked. 'If the Coleys get ter find out the bloke's bin makin' complaints about the firm they'll tune 'im up, that's fer sure.'

Amongst the few customers at the Mason's Arms that night was a gentleman by the name of Lennie Chivers, and most people who knew him were convinced that Lennie would sell his mother into slavery, if the price was right. Lennie came cheaply, and he knew where the Coleys' ganger did his drinking. For the cost of a pint he gave Sharkey Lockwood a full account of what he had overheard.

Harold Wicks never did put his complaint in at the labour exchange. Smouldering rags poked through his letterbox and then a verbal warning from a third party about the consequences of poking his nose into Coley affairs was enough to convince him that a few shillings' compensation was not good enough danger money.

Chapter Seven

Lucy Parry and her best friend Mary Chubb sat chatting together in Mary's scullery on Monday evening. With the door pulled to they were safe in thinking they would not be overheard, and while Roy was snoring in the parlour they spoke openly of their worries.

'When I saw those 'ands I nearly cried,' Mary was saying. 'The blisters 'ad busted an' there was all congealed blood round 'em. I made 'im soak 'em in salt water an' then I smarmed 'em wiv Vaseline. Gawd knows 'ow they'll be by termorrer.'

'Well, if 'is 'ands ain't any better 'e won't be able ter work,' Lucy told her. 'Yer gotta be careful they don't go septic.'

'You try tellin' 'im,' Mary groaned. ''E's so bloody obstinate at times.'

'I can understand it,' Lucy said, sighing. 'It's the manly fing. I'm tough, I can cope.'

'Yeah, but Roy's a carpenter not a bloody ditch-digger. 'E ain't used ter usin' a shovel all day.'

'Well, 'e 'ad the guts ter try it,' Lucy remarked. 'A lot wouldn't. 'E's only finkin' o' you an' little Gracie.'

'Yeah, I know that, but 'is 'ealth's gotta come first. I don't want 'im gettin' blood poisonin'.'

'Just see 'ow 'is 'ands are in the mornin',' Lucy advised. 'If they're no better tell 'im about Tom Creasey.'

'Tom Creasey?'

'You remember ole Tom, the feller in Lynton Road who 'ad to 'ave 'is leg off an' died o' blood poisonin'.'

'I thought it was an 'eart attack killed 'im.'

'It was, but I don't s'pose Roy'd know that.'

Mary forced a grin. 'What about you? You must be worried sick about George.'

Lucy nodded. ''E 'ad ter sign on this mornin'. 'E joined a long line o' people an' when 'e finally got ter the counter the bloke told 'im 'e was in the wrong queue. You 'ave ter give 'em all yer details when yer first sign on as unemployed.'

'Yeah, that's right. I know from what Roy told me. Apparently they 'ave a special queue fer tradesmen.'

Lucy smiled briefly. 'I know I shouldn't laugh, Mary, but George was tellin' me that when 'e finally got ter the counter this mornin' an' the clerk asked 'im what 'e'd done fer a livin' 'e told 'im 'e was a gift wrapper. 'E said when the clerk chuckled an' made some stupid remark 'e wanted the floor to open up. That's my George fer yer.'

Mary got up from the table and filled the kettle at the chipped stone sink. 'I was finkin', Lucy. Me an' you might be able ter do a bit of office cleanin'.'

'An' what about the kids?'

Mary smiled as she lit the gas under the kettle. 'We could both look fer a job, an' then if we get lucky we can take turns.'

'I'm not wiv yer,' Lucy said, frowning.

Mary sat down again and folded her arms over her ample bosom. 'Look, let's say one of us is lucky enough ter find somefing. The first week I'll go an' you can mind the kids, then the second week I'll 'ave the kids while you do the work. That way we can both earn a few bob. All right, it won't be much, but it'll be better than nuffing.'

'Assumin' we do find somefing, 'ow we gonna get away wiv it?' Lucy asked.

'No one's ter know,' Mary replied, smiling.

'What about the forelady, or the supervisor?'

'We don't go fer those sort o' jobs,' Mary told her. 'We only go after key jobs. You know the sort I mean, like small offices where yer let yerself in.'

Lucy nodded slowly. 'It might work, an' as yer say it'll mean a few bob fer both of us.'

Mary smiled. 'Even if we are found out we could say that you, or me, was standin' in frew illness. They wouldn't care, long as the place was gettin' cleaned.'

'Mary, you're a gem,' her friend said, grinning.

'It comes out o' desperation.'

'Yeah, an' I'll be gettin' as shrewd as you before long,' Lucy said pointedly.

'There's anuvver fing I got in mind,' Mary went on.

'An' I know you'll tell me.'

Mary stood up as the kettle began to sing and reached for the tea caddy. 'I 'eard that yer can get old tram sheets at the depot in New Cross.'

'Tram sheets? What's them?'

'They call 'em destination rolls,' Mary explained as she spooned tea into the china pot. 'You've seen the tram conductor windin' 'em round. They're made o' linen an' Mrs Venners got one fer free at the depot the ovver day. She showed me. What yer do is soak them in salt water an' then peel off the black paint round the edges, cut 'em up an' fold 'em ter make 'em look like bedsheets.'

'Mary, are yer feelin' all right?'

'Fer uncle's benefit. Uncle, the pawnbroker.'

'Yer mean yer pawn 'em?'

'That's what Mrs Venners did,' Mary informed her. 'She cut the roll an' folded it flat an' then tied it up in a bundle. She tore the corner o' the brown paper parcel just enough ter make the pawnbroker fink she was pawnin' a pair o' good linen sheets. The best fing is, she's managed ter get four bundles out o' one roll. Mind you, she's gotta go ter four different pawnshops.'

'An' 'ope that one of 'em doesn't decide to open the parcel,' Lucy reminded her.

Mary shrugged. 'Well, in that case it'll just be a question o' blaggin' it out. What can they do? They can only chuck yer out o' the shop.'

'I s'pose it's all about survivin',' Lucy said, sighing.

The kettle boiled over and Mary grabbed the handle with an ironing pad. 'When we're desperate we revert ter desperate measures,' she declared.

'George might be lucky,' Lucy said with little enthusiasm. ''E may get somefing soon. I don't want 'im 'avin' ter stand in the dole queues day after day, week after week. It'll crucify 'im.'

Mary took two teacups and saucers down from the dresser and then gave the tea a stir. 'Look, luv, I don't wanna depress yer,' she said in a quiet voice, 'but yer gotta face up ter George possibly bein' out o' work fer some time. There's just nuffink doin' anywhere. There's no work in the factories, not while they're on short time, an' in Roy's case every buildin' site 'e's tried 'as bin fixed up wiv carpenters. People don't realise just 'ow bad it is out there, till their own ole man gets put off.'

'You're right,' Lucy replied. 'I've tended ter shut me eyes an' ears ter what's goin' on, but I'm beginnin' ter come ter terms wiv it.'

'Of course yer will,' Mary said with conviction. 'Me an' you are survivors, we're all survivors. We can cope, an' when fings do buck up we'll still be around ter pick up the pieces.'

Rain started to fall, drumming down on the tin bath hanging in the Chubbs' backyard. A distant roll of thunder crashed and Roy Chubb stirred in his chair. Sharkey Lockwood was coming towards him wielding a large shovel, his face contorted and a wild look in his dark eyes. Sharp pain ran up Roy's arm as he tried to fend off the madman and he woke up with a start, realising that he was clenching his fists hard.

'Are you all right, Roy?' Mary asked in concern as she came hurrying into the parlour. 'We 'eard yer shout out.'

'Yeah. I was dreamin',' he replied, wincing as he slowly opened his clenched hands. He looked up at Lucy and gave her a brief smile. ''Ow's George, luv?'

Lucy returned his smile. 'Bearin' up. 'E signed on this mornin'.'

Mary bent down over Roy. 'I fink I'll do those 'ands again before yer go ter bed,' she said.

Lucy touched her friend gently on the arm. 'I'd better get goin', luv. See yer termorrer.'

As she walked back into the house Lucy saw Charlie coming down the stairs clutching a soiled handkerchief.

'It's OK. Young Sue's just woke up cryin',' he said reassuringly. 'She's 'ad a bit of a nosebleed.'

'Where's George?' Lucy asked as she made for the stairs.

''E 'ad ter go out.'

'Go out? Where?'

Charlie shrugged his shoulders. ''E never said.'

Lucy hurried up the stairs and saw that her daughter was settled and breathing easily. Charlie had followed her back up and stood in the bedroom doorway behind her. 'I wet this and pressed it on the bridge of 'er nose,' he said. 'It seemed ter do the trick. I was a bit worried in case she was frightened of me but she was fine. She called me Charlie.'

'I'm very grateful. She does get the occasional nosebleed an' that's all I do, put a wet cloth on her nose.'

They went back down into the parlour and Lucy looked at the chimer in the centre of the mantelshelf. 'Sara's late again,' she remarked. 'Flirtin' wiv that new vicar, I expect. I'm worried about George, though. It wasn't fair of 'im expectin' you ter play nursemaid. Where could 'e 'ave gone, I wonder?'

''E might 'ave gone fer a drink,' Charlie suggested. ''E most likely needed it after terday. Those dole queues take some gettin' used to.'

'I can imagine,' Lucy said. 'Fancy a cuppa?'

'That'll be nice.'

The rain became heavier and thunder sounded loudly as Lucy stood in the scullery waiting for the kettle to boil. She saw flashes of lightning through the net curtains and counted the seconds till the thunder rolled.

'I make that almost over'ead,' Charlie said as he walked through.

Lucy turned quickly. 'Yeah, two seconds, two miles away.'

Charlie averted his eyes for a few moments then fixed her with a steady gaze. 'Look, I know it's none o' my business but George did ask me if I'd 'old the fort fer a few minutes till you got back. 'E also checked that Sue was sleepin' soundly before 'e left.'

'I'm not angry, just surprised,' Lucy replied with a frown. 'It's so unlike 'im ter go out durin' the week, an' on a night like this too.'

'I might be wrong, but I've a feelin' 'e just wanted ter sit quietly wiv a pint. Just ter get 'imself sorted out, come ter terms wiv what's 'appened.'

'You know, you're very perceptive, considerin',' Lucy said, and immediately wished she hadn't made the remark.

'Considerin' what?' Charlie asked with a smile.

'Now I'm gettin' embarrassed,' she said, turning her back on him while she spooned tea leaves into the china pot. 'What I meant was, p'raps people livin' alone don't often get in the 'abit o' noticin' what ovver people are goin' frew.'

'Ah, but I'm not alone,' Charlie replied. 'There's you an' George, an' young Sue, not fergettin' Sara, o' course. An' then fer all you know I might be 'avin' a passionate affair wiv some lady who lives nearby.'

'In that case it'd 'ave ter be durin' the day,' Lucy said, turning towards him and smiling. 'You're 'ere almost every night.'

Charlie sat down at the table. 'Well, I s'pose that's true. No, there's no one in my life an' there 'asn't been fer some time now.'

'Is there any chance you an' yer wife'll ever get back tergevver again?' Lucy asked.

'No chance at all,' he told her. 'The whole fing was a sham from the very beginnin'. I s'pose we were both tryin' ter make up fer the past . . . past loves, past 'appiness. We were just substitutes fer each ovver. Can you understand what I mean?'

Lucy nodded slowly. 'Yeah, I believe I do. I take it there was someone once, someone who was very special to yer.'

Charlie did not answer. Instead he took out a folded black leather wallet from his back pocket and opened it. 'She was seventeen when this photograph was taken,' he said quietly as he handed it to her.

Lucy studied the sepia print of a young girl with deeply waved flaxen hair and a winsome smile. 'She's very beautiful,' she remarked.

'I first met 'er when she was eighteen,' Charlie said, his expression growing serious. 'I was in my late twenties at the time an' in the army. I'd bin wounded in France an' I was recuperatin' at a military 'ospital. She was a trainee nurse. She came from a very wealthy family.'

'What was 'er name?' Lucy enquired.

'Charlotte. Charlotte Farrington.'

Lucy looked down at the photograph once more then handed it back to Charlie. 'I'm sorry. I feel as though I've bin pryin',' she said respectfully.

'No, it's nice of yer ter be interested,' he replied. 'We were very much in love. It seemed to 'appen so quickly, an' then it was all taken away.'

'She died?'

'In the 1918 flu epidemic.'

'I'm so sorry,' Lucy said with genuine feeling.

Charlie's face relaxed slightly. 'It's a long time ago,' he said thoughtfully. 'Though sometimes it doesn't seem like it. Seventeen years. I was a long time comin' ter terms wiv Charlotte's death, an' then just when I felt I was startin' ter live again I met Claire. She'd lost 'er first love on the Somme in '16 an' we found ourselves bein' drawn ter-gevver, by our mutual loss really. Claire was a beautiful woman who reminded me of Charlotte an' she often said I favoured 'er first love in looks an' build. We were both hostages ter the past an' it couldn't work.'

Lucy looked at his dark eyes and sensed the pain and frustration he had struggled with. 'Do you see yerself ever marryin' again?' she asked hesitantly.

He shook his head. 'Claire's a staunch Catholic. She

would never agree to a divorce.'

Lucy got up suddenly, the tea almost forgotten. 'I'm sorry. I bet yer fink I'm a nosy bitch.'

'No, not at all,' Charlie replied quickly. 'I was ready enough ter talk about it. Sometimes it's good fer a man to unburden 'imself.'

'That applies ter women too,' Lucy said, 'though we tend ter use our own sex as a floggin' post.'

They sat in the quiet scullery sipping their tea, and occasionally Lucy glanced up at the battered alarm clock on the dresser. 'What could 'ave 'appened ter Sara?' she wondered.

The answer was soon forthcoming when George's sister let herself into the house wearing a secretive smile. 'I'm sorry I'm late, Lucy. You weren't worried, were you? Yer knew where I was.'

'Yeah, but yer could 'ave met wiv an accident on the way 'ome.'

'I've bin voted on ter the committee,' she said smugly. She raised her voice. 'Did you 'ear, George?'

'George is out,' Lucy told her.

'Out? Out where?'

'I wish I knew.'

'Didn't you ask 'im where 'e was goin' when 'e went?'

'I was next door talkin' ter Mary.'

'I do 'ope 'e's all right,' Sara said nervously.

Then something banged against the front door and Sara put her hand up to her mouth. Lucy stood up but Charlie took her by the arm. 'Yer'd better let me go,' he warned her. 'It could be a drunk.'

When he opened the door Charlie found George leaning sideways, his outstretched arm supporting him against the doorpost. 'I'm 'fraid I'm . . . I'm . . .'

'Come on, pal, let's get yer out o' the rain,' Charlie said kindly.

George leaned heavily on him as he walked along the passage to the warm scullery, where he collapsed into a chair at the table. 'I went fer a drink,' he slurred.

Lucy forced a smile. 'I can see that,' she replied.

'I needed time ter fink. I . . . I knew it was . . . was . . . but yer see . . .'

'Look, I'd sooner wait till termorrer fer the post-mortem,' she told him crossly. 'Now let's get yer upstairs an' you can get those wet clothes off yer before yer catch yer death.'

George tried to stand but slumped down again in the chair. Charlie bent down and took his weight. 'Come on, pal, let's do as she said, shall we?'

George nodded and allowed himself to be helped out of the scullery and up the stairs.

'Fanks, Charlie. I can manage all right now,' Lucy said, giving him a grateful smile.

For a while Charlie sat on the edge of his bed, deep in thought as he puffed on his pipe. The rain had stopped and the quietness was undisturbed but for an occasional clatter from the freight yards. He could not deny it, the faint stirring in his loins and the quickening of his heartbeat as he thought about her. She was a very attractive woman and she was getting under his skin in a dangerous way. What of her, he wondered? Had he stirred her feelings too? Despite himself, he could not help hoping so.

Chapter Eight

Coley's ditch diggers managed to stay together as a unit during a bitterly cold last week in November. Harold Wicks was replaced by a giant of a man who handled a shovel like a dinner fork, but there were no replacements for the two sacked for fighting and the work force was now down to eight. Gerry Watson realised that he had inadvertently upset Sharkey Lockwood on the first day and he made sure that he never slacked nor spoke a word while the ganger was anywhere around. Joe Lambert, the digger accosted by Harold Wicks, was another worker who seemed quite at home using a shovel, but Roy Chubb and Danny Albury were suffering.

'I can't understand why me 'ands are so bad,' Roy groaned to Danny during their midday break. 'I'm a bloody carpenter by trade an' I'm used ter workin' wiv 'em.'

Danny shook his head. 'It's those shovels an' picks we gotta use. They're all old an' rough, an' then yer gotta take inter consideration yer've bin out o' collar fer some time. Yer 'ands soon get soft. I soak mine in salt water every night. It 'elps 'arden 'em up a bit.'

Gerry Watson still looked in pretty good shape and after washing down the last of his cheese sandwich with cold tea he took out his tobacco tin. 'Well, there's anuvver week's work fer us, if we can stick it,' he remarked. 'It's December next week an' the dosh'll certainly come in very 'andy.'

'Are yer married, Gerry?' Danny Albury asked.

The young man nodded. 'Yeah, an' I got two God ferbids, one of each. Me gel's four an' me little sproggo's just two.'

Danny jerked his thumb in the direction of the marked-out area further along the long turning. 'That'll give us a week at least,' he reckoned. 'Maybe even two. It's longer than this trench.'

'Don't you believe it,' Gerry said dismissively. 'Sharkey'll be on our backs the minute we start work there, you mark my words. 'E'll still want it finished by the weekend.'

As the crew left the hut to go back to work Joe Lambert sidled up to Roy and the others. 'See that big ugly git over there? Wally Coates? Watch what yer say in front of 'im,' he hissed. ''E's one o' the Coleys' men.'

The week dragged on and rain fell on Friday, making it harder to get the clay out from around the damaged pipes. When the job was finally finished an exhausted team of diggers expected to be paid early and sent home, but Sharkey had other ideas. 'Yer bein' paid till five so yer might as well get those cobbles up ready fer Monday,' he told them.

As the bedraggled men prised up the flintstones Sammy Strickland strolled past. He knew how close he had come to getting a job with the Coley brothers and he still had the occasional nightmare. His wife Peggy had been on to him to 'put himself about', as she termed it, since he would never find anything until he did, but Sammy wasn't all that worried. He had his unemployment money and Peggy had a regular job at the baker's shop in the Old Kent Road. They wouldn't starve, and if the worst came to the worst he could always get a few days' work helping on the stalls at the market, like in the past. Right now, though, he was quite happy to stand in the drizzling rain and watch other men toil.

'Bloody weavver's bad, ain't it?' he said out of genuine sympathy to the nearest worker.

'Poxy.'

'Don't they give yer no oilskins when it's pissin' down?'

'Nah.'

'Bloody disgustin'.'

'Yeah, it is.'

'You lot should go an' see the ganger. I would if it was me gettin' soaked ter the balls.'

Unknown to Sammy the man in question was eyeing him from the hut. 'Who's that geezer chattin' ter the men?' he asked.

Frank Coley strolled over to the doorway. 'Gawd knows,' he said. 'Go out an' send 'im on 'is way, Sharkey. 'E's 'oldin' up the works.'

As the big man stepped out of the hut he was immediately spotted by Gerry Watson. 'Yer better piss off, mate,' he said out of the corner of his mouth. 'Our ganger's in a bad mood.'

'People like that don't scare me,' Sammy told him with feigned grit. 'The bigger they are the 'arder they fall, that's my motto.'

'I 'ope you ain't disturbin' my boys,' Sharkey growled at him.

'Nah, just watchin',' Sammy replied.

'Yer'd better be on yer way,' he was advised. 'There's nuffink ter see round 'ere.'

'I can watch, can't I?' Sammy said with spirit. 'It's a free country.'

'The rest o' the country might be, but not this bit,' Sharkey declared. 'I rule this bit an' I'm sayin' yer should piss off an' leave my men alone.'

'I ain't touched 'em,' Sammy replied.

'Now look, I'm a very reasonable man when yer get down to it,' Sharkey told him, 'but I don't take kindly to any little git like you givin' me lip so piss off while yer in front.'

Sammy saw the menace in the ganger's eyes and decided to take heed. 'You should fit 'em out wiv oilskins in weavver like this,' he remarked, sauntering off as calmly as he could.

Charlie Foden found time hanging heavy on him lately. There had only been one day's work at the docks in the past few weeks and he had spent his time keeping warm in the reading room of the local library, which prompted Lucy to chide him. 'Look, yer don't 'ave ter spend all yer time there,' she emphasised when he told her. 'This place is yours ter come an' go in, an' there's always a fire 'ere an' an armchair ter sit in.'

'Yeah, I know, Lucy, but yer don't want me under yer feet all day long.'

'Yer won't be under my feet,' she assured him. 'I'll be busy around the place, an' I might get a cleanin' job soon.'

'That'll be good.'

'Me an' Mary next door are gonna try an' get one between us,' she went on. 'It won't be much comin' in but at least it'll keep the wolves away from the door.'

'An' yer'll share the kids?'

''Ow did yer guess?'

'It didn't want much workin' out,' he said, smiling.

'I wish my George would crack 'is face wiv a smile now an' then,' she said sadly. 'I know 'e must be very worried but I've tried dozens o' times ter tell 'im that bein' out o' work's no crime. Trouble is 'e ain't come ter terms wiv it yet. Like the ovver night. I've never seen 'im drunk since our weddin' day, an' it came as a bit of a shock.'

'I fink it done 'im good ter let off a bit o' steam,' Charlie remarked.

Lucy merely nodded, recalling that night when George came home soaked to the skin and hardly able to walk, let alone talk. He had gone out with the intention of having a solitary pint while he thought things out, but unfortunately he had let himself get dragged into the company of a group of factory workers who had been paid off that evening. The beer was flowing and he drank more than he should have. There were other jobs available, the newly unemployed workers believed, so why not take heart? It was just a matter of time.

Late in the evening he left the friendly company and staggered home alone, stopping to rest awhile on a park bench in St Mark's churchyard, as far as he could remember. He had probably not given a thought to the rain, nor to the fact that he had spent over ten shillings on a round of drinks. Lucy was supposed to understand.

She had tried, aware of how he must be feeling inside. He had always been able to provide for her and Sue and now he had lost the means. It was a question of pride and self-esteem, and she had got his wet clothes off and eased him into bed without a word of complaint, but she failed to understand how he could have been so careless as to lose his final pay packet. Surely he hadn't spent it all. It wasn't among his wet clothes and she could only guess that it had dropped out of his pocket either in the pub or when he sat in the church garden on his way home.

It had been hard the following week. The rent could not

be found and the tallyman had to be persuaded to forgo his weekly payment. Mary Chubb had been a lifesaver, though, lending Lucy a pound out of the meagre savings she had been putting away for Christmas. George himself was distraught at having been so careless, but he had made matters worse by constantly carping about his run of bad luck. There was a bad atmosphere about the house for a few days and Sara had not helped with her miserable mood. The new vicar at St Mark's was apparently involved in a torrid affair with a pretty deaconess and it had come as a terrible shock to George's sister, who had felt that she herself was making headway in cultivating the cleric's affections.

Secretive to obsessiveness, Sara kept her feelings bottled up and told no one what was going on, but Lucy guessed that her sister-in-law's frame of mind had something to do with the church. It had to be; there was little else in her life which would have triggered off such sullenness.

'Don't serve me up anyfing,' Sara said. 'Me stomach's playin' me up.'

'Shall I get yer some tomato soup an' a slice o' bread?' Lucy offered.

'I just told yer me stomach was bad,' Sara puffed. 'Tomato soup'll only make me sick.'

'What about a couple o' slices o' bread an' marge?'

'I keep tellin' yer I don't want anyfing,' Sara growled.

'Well sod the lot o' yer then,' Lucy said with emphasis. 'I'm just about fed up wiv it.'

'That's right, take it out on everybody,' Sara replied in a raised voice. 'I 'ope yer don't leave 'im out.'

Lucy sighed. 'What yer talkin' about?'

'You know what I'm talkin' about.'

'If I did I wouldn't 'ave to ask yer, now would I?'

Charlie had just come in from the street and heard the

sharp exchange. 'Evenin', folks,' he said, smiling sheep-ishly as he walked into the parlour. 'It looks like the fog's comin' in again.'

Sara stood up quickly, and without answering him she hurried out of the room with a haughty expression on her face.

'Take no notice,' Lucy told him. 'She's just bein' 'er usual charmin' self, bloody silly cow.'

Charlie stood for a moment, feeling in the way. 'Where's George?' he asked.

''E's gone after an advert in the *South London Press*,' she replied. 'It's fer a school caretaker.'

'Fingers crossed,' Charlie said, giving her a wide smile.

'What about you? What you bin doin' all day?'

He shrugged his wide shoulders and sat down facing her. 'There was no work this mornin', so I went ter the library an' then I killed time at the dockers' club. Played a few games o' darts, an' one ole chap insisted on a game o' shove-'a'penny. It turned into a marathon, actually.'

Lucy looked into his soft eyes and felt sorry for him. Charlie must be feeling the strains and stresses of being on short time just like everyone else, she thought, but he never showed it. His smile was never far away and she admired the inner strength of the man. He had so much self-control and seemed to ooze confidence. That wife of his must have been mad to let him go, she reflected, immediately cursing herself as she felt the hot flush rush into her cheeks. She was at it again, allowing herself to become far too inquisi-tive and intrigued. It was a dangerous game to play, even within the confines of her own mind. She was a married woman with a child and he was an older man carrying the baggage of a failed relationship. The barrier had to stay in place and he, like her, had to be aware of it.

''Ave you always bin a docker?' she asked as casually as she could.

He nodded. 'Me farvver worked in the docks an' I followed 'im in, but I've got no son ter pass me ticket on to, which makes me wonder if I should look around fer somefing else. After all, there's no work there ter speak of an' the future prospects don't seem all that good.'

As Lucy leaned forward to prod the fire with a brass-handled poker Charlie noticed how the heat from the coals flushed her face, and his eyes lingered on the black velvet strip at the nape of her neck where her fair hair was gathered together carelessly. She was a lovely woman, and in another time, another place, her portrait might well have graced the walls of an ancestral home. She would be in the company of giggling young women, of course, but her large blue eyes would constantly glance over in his direction. He would be in the dress uniform of the Light Horse, trying to seem relaxed on the eve of his regiment's departure for the Crimea. Her eyelashes fluttered as he boldly walked over and bowed stiffly. She stepped forward, her heart beating a little faster, and rested her hand on his proffered arm, allowing him to lead her on to the marble floor. The string quintet were warming to the occasion and he took her in his arms, tripping gaily among the couples to the delight of some and the envy of others.

'They make a fine couple, don't you think, Wheatcroft?'

'A marriage, surely, once the regiment gets back, Manvers.'

'Rather a premature assumption, I fear, Wheatcroft old chap. We'll be staring down the barrels of the Russian cannon to be sure.'

'Good lord, they've waltzed straight out on to the balcony,' Fairclough remarked.

'I'd cross her name off that dance card if I were you, Herbert old fruit,' his fellow officer suggested.

Charlie smiled to himself. The novel he was reading had taken him far away from the poverty and deprivation of thirties Bermondsey to a time of gallantry and honour, but now the beautiful Lucy Parry and he were back in the real world and the drama was left to run its full course on the tattered pages.

'I'm sorry the dinner's gonna be a bit late ternight,' Lucy said. 'I'll serve it up as soon as George gets in. 'E shouldn't be long now.'

'It's OK, Lucy, there's no rush on my part.'

She gave him a smile. 'You looked miles away just then.'

'If you only knew,' he said, smiling back at her.

They heard the front door and George walked in looking downcast. 'No luck,' he announced. 'It went yesterday.'

Sue ran into the room with her picture book and went over to her father. 'Daddy, will you read me my book?' she asked.

'In a while, luvvy,' he said as he took off his coat and hung it behind the door.

Sue was impatient and came over to Charlie. 'Can you read me my book, Charlie?' she asked him.

He lifted her on to his lap and opened the pages. 'Well, well,' he said in a shocked voice. 'There's no crunchy giant in this book.'

'Who's the crunchy giant, Charlie?'

'Well, 'e's really a nice crunchy giant an' 'e looks after the nice children.'

'Not the naughty ones?'

'No, not the naughty ones.'

'Will 'e look after me?'

'Yes. If you get lost in the forest the nice crunchy giant

will be there ter show you the way 'ome.'

'Is there a bad crunchy giant?'

'Yes, but the nice crunchy giant doesn't allow 'im in the forest.'

'I like the nice crunchy giant,' Sue said in a tiny voice as she nestled her head against Charlie's chest.

He glanced up at Lucy with a bemused look on his face, and she smiled at him. 'Crunchy giant indeed.'

Sara joined the others at the table after a little coaxing from Lucy, and Charlie, feeling that somehow he might have been partly responsible for her upset earlier, was particularly attentive. 'More gravy, Sara?' he asked. ''Ow's the 'eadache?'

Lucy glanced at George with a brief collusive smile on her face and he looked across at Sara. His sister seemed to be enjoying the attention, judging by the way she rallied. 'I'm sorry the job 'ad gone, George,' she told him. 'Never mind, better luck next time.'

He put a brave face on and gave her a smile. 'Yer lookin' better, Sara.'

'I feel better this evenin',' she replied, glancing quickly at Charlie.

Lucy caught the look and the intonation of her sister-in-law's voice and then checked herself. No, surely not. She wouldn't be trying to let Charlie know she was available. It was ridiculous even to consider such a thing. He was not her sort. He was rough, tough, the sort of man Sara would normally steer clear of.

For a few moments Lucy felt extremely irritated but then she pulled herself together. Who was she to be so judgmental, and why should the idea irk her so? She was being stupid. Opposites did attract, and why should it not work for Charlie and Sara?

'Do you read much, Charlie?' Sara asked.

'Quite a bit,' he replied. 'Do you?'

'Yes, I do. I like period romances.'

'I like the old classics.'

Lucy got up to gather the dirty crockery. Much as she disliked herself for thinking it, she preferred Sara when she was having one of her tantrums or sick headaches. That she could tolerate, but this was something again.

Chapter Nine

Another week of hard toil, another pay packet to weaken the spectre of Christmas without the basic trappings, and for Gerry Watson it was one more stepping-stone towards the shore. His children would now be able to open a few presents on Christmas morning, and the money might even stretch to a bottle of port. Another week's work and the outstanding bills could be paid, which would ease the pressure and allow Amy to begin with a clean slate at the butcher's and the grocer's.

Ben and Frank Coley were feeling pleased with the team's progress, and once the next trench was excavated and the pipes replaced they would be able to get on with the last phase on the main sewer at the far end of Lynton Road.

'We'll 'ave ter go eight feet down before we reach the brickwork,' Ben reminded his brother as they stood together in the saloon bar of the Mason's Arms. 'It'll need ter be a shutterin' job, an' we can't afford any balls-ups. It 'as ter be ready fer the brickies right after Christmas. The twenty-seventh, as a matter o' fact.'

''Ave we got any carpenters on our books?' Frank asked.

'That geezer Chubb told me 'e was a carpenter by trade,' Ben said, taking a swig from his glass of whisky.

Officially the pub did not open till five thirty, but Mick

97

Johnson made an exception in the Coleys' case. Their workers were to be paid out in the public bar and they would feel duty bound to buy at least one drink before going home. Keeping in with Ben and Frank was no bad thing, the landlord considered, though his wife Freda did not feel as enthusiastic as he.

'They're a couple o' no-good bastards, if yer want my opinion,' she said plainly, 'an' that ganger they've got is as bad as them. 'E's an 'orrible git. 'E treats the poor blokes like slaves.'

'Yeah, but yer gotta remember the Coleys are on a tight schedule,' Mick explained. 'They're subbers, an' if they fall be'ind they don't get any more contracts. Besides, most o' those workers need a kick up the arse now an' again.'

'Don't talk stupid,' Freda replied angrily. 'They're men who've bin out o' work an' desperate enough ter take any job they can get.'

'Well at least they get decent wages,' Mick said defensively.

'Don't make me laugh,' Freda snorted contemptuously. 'Would you like ter work in a waterlogged trench shovelling clay fer fifteen bob a day, an' then find out at the end o' the week yer've bin charged two bob fer overall cleanin' an' anuvver shillin' fer the tea?'

'Who told yer that?' Mick asked quickly.

'Sammy Strickland.'

'Yer can't believe what 'e ses.'

'Well I do,' Freda said firmly. 'Anyway, why should 'e lie?'

Mick shrugged his shoulders as he threw the bolts back and opened for business.

As the men filed into the public bar and lined up by the

far table Ben and Frank Coley came round from the saloon. 'There's anuvver week's work available on the pipes, if yer up to it,' Ben announced with a dark smile. 'Then, if all goes well, we've got work for yer right up till the end o' December on the main sewers at the end o' the turnin'. So it's up ter you.'

Sharkey Lockwood came into the pub carrying a blue money bag in his huge fist. 'Right then, let's get you lot o' lazy gits sorted out,' he said, sitting down at the table.

Gerry nodded as he was handed his pay packet and immediately opened it to take out some silver coins. One pint then straight home, he told himself.

Danny Albury and Joe Lambert paired off for a game of shove-'a'penny while Roy Chubb stood with Gerry at the counter. 'That main sewer job'll be a bloody 'ard graft,' he remarked.

Gerry nodded. 'I've done a bit o' main sewer work,' he said. 'Yer gotta go down deep ter reach the roof o' the tunnel, an' the trench 'as ter be shuttered.'

'Yeah. I've done a bit o' shutterin' work,' Roy told him.

'I'd let Coley know,' Gerry suggested. 'If yer get the job it'll be a sight better than 'umpin' bloody great shovel-loads o' clay all day long.'

'I dunno,' Roy replied, stroking his chin.

'I do. Tell 'em,' Gerry pressed him. 'It'll mean a few extra shillin's in yer pay packet.'

Roy drained his glass. 'I'll bear it in mind,' he said as he made ready to leave.

At that moment Ben Coley ambled over. 'Do I remember you tellin' me you're a carpenter by trade?' he asked.

Roy nodded. 'That's right.'

'Ever done any shutterin' work?'

'We've just bin talkin' about that,' Gerry told him.

Coley gave him a cold stare and then turned back to Roy. 'Well 'ave yer or not?'

'Yeah, I 'ave,' Roy replied.

Coley put a pound note down on the counter. 'Get these two a drink, an' the same again fer me,' he ordered Mick. 'Listen, Chubb, that main sewer job's gonna require shutterin'. We'll pay yer an extra shillin' a day ter take care of it, OK?'

Roy nodded. 'Yeah, I'll do it,' he said, trying not to look too enthusiastic.

Ben Coley picked up his change and left the counter with a parting shot at Gerry. 'Keep yer trap shut an' yer might be around ter see 'ow it's done,' he said with a cruel grin.

Lucy and Mary took their children along with them to the tram depot at New Cross on Friday afternoon.

'I 'ope we're gonna be able ter carry the bloody fing,' Mary remarked.

'We'll manage. We'll take turns,' Lucy replied with gusto. 'We could even get two if they're not too 'eavy.'

'Can yer tell us where the foreman is?' Mary asked a uniformed tram driver.

'You ain't come fer a job, 'ave yer?' the bewhiskered man queried with a wide grin. 'We ain't 'ad a woman tram driver 'ere since the strike.'

'Nah. We've come ter see the foreman on private business,' Lucy told him.

'Yer'll be wantin' the supervisor,' the driver replied. 'See that office over there? If 'e's not in there 'e'll be in the workshop. Trouble is yer never can find ole Winkle when yer need 'im.'

Lucy and Mary crossed the wide terminus, holding on to

Sue and Gracie who were giggling together about the driver's whiskers.

Mary looked into the office. 'Mr Winkle?'

There was a loud guffaw from two of the occupants and a growl from the other. 'I'm Mr Winkless, the supervisor,' he said. 'What can I do for yer?'

''Ave yer got any old destination sheets ter give away?' Mary asked.

'Nah, I'm afraid we don't, not any more.'

'We know a woman who was given one two weeks ago,' she pointed out.

'Yeah, but that was then. We're not allowed ter give 'em away any more.'

'Why's that, then?'

'Don't ask me, luv. It's just company policy.'

'What d'yer do wiv 'em then?' Lucy asked quickly.

'I dunno. It's not my department.'

'But you're the supervisor.'

'Look, I ain't responsible fer everyfing that goes on in this depot,' the man said irritably. 'I s'pose the sheets get sent back ter where they come from.'

'Well, fanks fer yer co-operation,' Mary said sarcastically.

As they tramped across the covered concourse the driver with the whiskers stood watching them. 'Did yer see ole Winkle?' he asked, chuckling.

'Yeah, an' we didn't get much of a response from 'im,' Lucy said sharply. 'I reckon 'e took offence at us callin' 'im Winkle.'

''Ave yer come fer ole sheets?' the driver asked.

'As a matter o' fact we 'ave,' Mary told him.

'Some'ow I thought you 'ad.'

'That was observant of yer.'

The driver looked around quickly then leaned a little closer to them. 'I gotta tell yer it got a bit out of 'and, the number o' people callin' in fer those sheets, an' the guv'nor 'ad ter put a stop to it,' he explained. 'I could see 'is point. There's trams comin' in an' out of 'ere all day long an' yer can't 'ave members o' the public turnin' it into a market-place. I tell yer what yer can do, though. If yer go down the alleyway at the side o' the depot an' go round the back yer'll see the workshop. If there's any sheets about they'll be stacked up by the workshop dustbins. An' fer Chrissake keep 'old o' them kids. It's no place fer them, nor you fer that matter.'

Ten minutes later two happy women and their children stepped on to a number 38 tram. 'Can we put these under the stairs?' Mary asked the conductor.

He gave her a grin. 'I thought they stopped givin' those fings away,' he remarked.

'So they 'ave, but Mr Winkle took pity on us,' Mary replied with a straight face.

Come storm, hail, or fireballs from heaven, it would be safe to assume that Mrs Black and her next-door neighbour Mrs Goodwright would be out in it, if only to keep in touch with what was going on in the street. Even on that Friday evening with the fog thickening, the two hardy souls stood chatting with their coat collars turned up and their hands thrust deep into their pockets. Visibility was down to a few yards, but they persisted with their sentry duty and were suitably rewarded.

'What's Mary Chubb got there?' Emmie Goodwright asked.

'I dunno, but Lucy Parry's got one as well,' Ada Black commented.

''Ere, Bert,' Emmie called into the passage. 'Come out 'ere a minute.'

Bert did as he was bid. 'What's up?'

'What's those fings them two've got under their arms?'

''Ow the bloody 'ell am I s'posed ter know?' Bert growled.

Emmie watched the two women go into Lucy's house. 'I'd love ter know what they were,' she said.

'Yeah, so would I,' Ada replied.

'Why don't yer come inside out of it,' Bert grumbled. 'Yer lettin' all the fog in.'

Emmie reluctantly gave up the watch, but promised herself she'd get to the bottom of the mystery before long.

Sammy Strickland had had a hard week. Three times he had been close to getting a job and it was becoming frightening. On each occasion he had left his long-suffering wife Peggy sitting with her fingers crossed, and on each occasion she had been both deflated and angry when he came back with that by now familiar hang-dog look on his angular face. It was unbelievable, she sighed to herself. Most of the men in the street and in the immediate area were unable to find one position to go after, let alone three. Sammy seemed to pick chances out of a hat, but for some reason he was never successful. The digging job was a prime example, but there were other jobs he might have landed, with a little decorum and a sprinkling of luck.

'What was it this time?' she asked.

'I was too old.'

'Too old?' she queried. 'Ter be a nightwatchman?'

'Yeah. It bloody well upset me, I can tell yer.'

'An' that ovver job yer went for, they said you was too young.'

'Yeah. That was a nightwatchman's job too,' he replied, making himself comfortable by the fire.

'An' the ovver job? More bloody excuses.'

Sammy shrugged his shoulders. 'It ain't my fault, luv,' he said, putting on his bad-luck face. 'It seems I'm never gonna get a start. It's makin' me ill.'

The only thing that would make Sammy ill was if someone actually gave him a job, she thought. 'So yer too old, too young an' . . .'

'An' too bloody nice, that's my trouble,' he groaned.

'You could 'ave looked a bit more mean an' nasty when yer walked in the place,' Peggy told him.

'I did,' Sammy replied. 'I put on me worst face ever. As a matter o' fact I looked at me reflection in a shop winder before I went in an' frightened meself. Anyway, I never fooled 'em. Still, when yer come ter fink of it, yer wouldn't like me bein' a debt collector, now would yer? Not you. You're the kindest person ever. You're the first to 'elp anyone out an' yer don't brag about it, that's what really pleases me. Some people never stop goin' on about what they do, but not you.'

Peggy could not help but enjoy such silver-tongued flattery, and she leaned back in her chair. 'I've never bin one ter blow me own trumpet,' she remarked.

'That's what I bin sayin',' Sammy agreed. 'An' yer'd be upset if yer knew I was chasin' people up fer money who didn't 'ave a pot ter piss in.'

Peggy had to agree. 'Never mind, luv, somefing'll turn up,' she said consolingly. 'Now, what d'yer want fer supper? I got a slice o' brawn left in the cupboard . . .'

Chapter Ten

The folk of Cooper Street could not say with certainty just how long the bootmender's shop had been there on the corner of the turning. Ada Black said that as far as she could recall it was there when she moved into the street, and she'd lived there for twenty-five years. Emmie Goodwright was a little more specific. 'Nah, it was later than that,' she declared. 'It opened up the year o' the armistice.'

'Are yer sure?'

'Yeah, 'cos I moved in 'ere in '15 an' it was a tripe an' onion shop then.'

'Nah. The tripe an' onion shop was round the corner in Lynton Road.'

'I don't fink so.'

'Well I do,' Ada said firmly. 'I remember goin' round there on Friday nights fer me farvver's supper. They used ter sell 'alf sheep's 'eads an' skate's eyeballs. Me ole dad loved skate's eyeballs.'

Peggy Strickland was drawn into the controversy while she was on her way to the market. ''Ere, Peg, when did that bootmender's open?' Ada asked her.

'About nine o'clock, same as usual,' she replied.

'Nah, I mean when did ole Staples start 'is business up?'

'Gawd only knows,' Peggy said, stroking her chin. 'My

Sammy'll know. There ain't much 'e don't know about round 'ere.'

The speculation had arisen after Ada saw the notice that Jimmy Staples had pinned up in his shop window.

'I can't believe it,' Emmie said when Ada told her.

'Neivver can I,' Ada replied. 'Fings must be bad fer ole Staples ter call it a day.'

'I bet 'e's made 'is pile, the time 'e's bin 'ere,' Emmie remarked. 'I expect 'im an' Marfa'll end up in some nice little cottage in the country.'

Her prediction was way off the mark, and if the truth were known Jimmy and Martha Staples were trying to close down as quickly as possible without fuss and bother, not wanting to attract too much attention.

'They're sendin' a van ter take the stitcher,' Martha reported.

Jimmy nodded. 'They'll take the sheets o' leavver as well, I expect.'

'What about the rest o' the stuff?'

'There's nuffink werf floggin', 'cept me knives,' Jimmy told her, 'an' I'm keepin' them. I can still repair our own shoes if I got me knives an' the last.'

Martha was assailed by a deep sadness as she handed him a mug of tea. Jimmy was a craftsman and his repairs had always stood up to the crucial tests, the games of street football and a week's toil on the cobblestoned dock quays, but now people in the area were finding it impossible to scrimp together enough money for boot and shoe repairs and using cardboard and folded newspaper instead to line their worn-out soles. The sales of leather goods had trickled almost to a halt, and the belts and handbags which Jimmy Staples sold as a sideline had all been returned to the makers at a distinct loss.

'Where's it all gonna end?' Martha sighed.

'Gawd only knows,' Jimmy said heavily as he threw the bolts on the shop door for the last time.

The Staples' one-time customers Ada and Emmie were basically kind people, and though they were under the erroneous impression that the bootmender and his wife were retiring to the country in comfortable circumstances they still felt that a little going-away present would be nice. Nothing much, maybe a set of the jugs or glasses which could be bought cheaply enough at any of the Sunday markets.

'It's too late,' Minnie Venners told her friends the following morning when they sounded her out. 'They've gone.'

'Already?'

'They must 'ave left last night,' Minnie explained.

'They could 'ave waited till we 'ad a chance ter say goodbye,' Ada said stiffly.

'Well good riddance then, that's what I say,' Emmie growled.

In truth the Staples would dearly have loved to say their goodbyes before leaving the business Jimmy had run for over thirty years, but try as they might they had found it impossible to satisfy all their creditors. They left Bermondsey for good, moving into a small flat in Walworth, and the following Monday Jimmy started work as a factory clogmaker with an old-established company near London Bridge.

'I'd say it was a bloody disgrace if you was to ask me,' Sammy Strickland remarked to Peggy when he returned home with the evening paper.

'What is?'

''Avin' ter go right up ter the Old Kent Road ter get a

newspaper an' fags,' he replied as he took off his wet coat. 'Did yer know it's pissin' down out there?'

'Yeah, I can see,' Peggy said as she skimmed a film of fat off the mutton stew.

'There's only two shops in this street an' they're both boarded up,' Sammy went on. 'Surely someone can see the sense in openin' up one of 'em as a tobacconist, or a grocer's shop.'

'It's understandable, the way fings are. There's no money about.'

'Banks lend money ter start businesses up,' Sammy pointed out.

'Tell me somefing I don't know.'

'I could get a loan,' Sammy suggested confidently as he kicked off his sodden boots.

'Who'd be stupid enough ter lend you money, pray?'

'Any bank manager wiv 'alf a brain in 'is 'ead.'

'Don't talk tripe.'

Sammy assumed a superior air as he warmed his hands over the open fire. 'I'm talkin' sense, an' you'd agree wiv me if yer'd just shut yer gob long enough to 'ear me out.'

'Go on then, Mr Clever, I'm all ears,' Peggy said sarcastically.

'Yeah, I can see,' Sammy remarked with a grin. 'No, let's be serious fer a minute. I got a policy on me life an' it was took out more than forty years ago.'

'This is the first time I've 'eard of it,' Peggy replied, frowning.

'I'd fergot all about it till this mornin', ter tell yer the truth,' Sammy confessed.

'An' what made yer fink about it this mornin'?'

'It was when I was gettin' the paper,' he explained. 'While I was waitin' ter get served I 'eard this geezer tellin' the bloke be'ind the counter that shopkeepers could get a business loan if they 'ad some sort o' security. I got ter finkin' about those two boarded-up shops in the turnin' so I 'ad a few words wiv the papershop bloke. 'E told me the geezer 'e was talkin' to worked next door at the insurance agency. 'E said 'e advises people who wanna start up in business. As I was walkin' back 'ome it struck me that I've got security wiv that old insurance policy. It must be werf a fortune, considerin' 'ow old it is. I remember when me dad retired from the slaughter'ouse. 'E said it was a little somefing if I ever fell on 'ard times.'

'So yer got the idea o' usin' it as security against a loan,' Peggy reiterated. 'Would yer mind just tellin' me an' puttin' me out o' me misery. Fer what?'

'To open up one o' those shops.'

'Yeah, I'm already wiv yer there, but what as?'

'An oil shop.'

'An oil shop?'

'An' why not?' Sammy said indignantly. 'Just fink about it. No matter 'ow poor people are, they still try ter keep their 'ouses clean an' warm. I could sell the usual fings, such as whitenin' fer steps, dusters, mops an' bug tapers. Then there's paraffin o' course, turps an' nails an' tin tacks. There's no end to it. I could sell canes, there's certainly a need fer canes round this area. A lot of oil shops sell mugs an' enamel teapots an' kettles. Just fink of it, Peg. The shop would never be empty, what wiv one fing an' anuvver.'

Peggy was becoming impressed. 'An' you'd serve in the shop all day, every day?'

'Too bloody true,' he told her with enthusiasm. 'I'd be as 'appy as a pig in shit.'

'Well in that case, me little porker, you should go an' take that policy up ter the insurance agency an' see 'ow much you can raise on it,' Peggy concluded.

The second phase of the Coley workings had been completed on time, and now less than two weeks before Christmas the main sewer excavation was about to start. On the evening of Friday the thirteenth Ben Coley and his brother Frank were making final preparations with Sharkey Lockwood in the saloon bar of the Mason's Arms. 'We'll need ter take on a few more men,' Frank recommended.

Ben nodded. 'Yeah, five or six should do it. Maitland's 'ave confirmed that they want the brickies ter make a start on Friday the twenty-seventh.'

'We'd better make it six then,' Frank said. 'There's no margin for error on this job, not if we're out ter get the big one.'

Sharkey had caught his warning glance and knew just what was expected of him. All the diggers had been retained for the main sewer job and Roy Chubb had been assigned the job of shoring up the workings, but it was going to be a tricky operation. The thick clay level had to be removed from around the crumbling brick tunnel in two phases, considering the depth of the workings, and with only six extra hands involved it would be far from easy. 'Couldn't we stretch it to eight or nine?' he suggested.

Frank Coley leaned across the table. 'Up till now we've taken these jobs fer peanuts, just ter get our foot in the door, an' we've made it pay by keepin' the labour costs to a minimum,' he said pointedly. 'Maitland's know the score. This is a government contract they've got, an' if they can complete on time they stand ter get the big one, the job o' renovatin' the 'ole sewer system in Bermon'sey an' Rovverhive. Tests an' inspections 'ave shown that it's crumblin' everywhere, an' winnin' the contract would earn them a fortune. So yer see, we're puttin' ourselves in a good bargainin' position. I've bin assured by the Maitland people that they'll give us all the work we can 'andle if we complete this job on time, an' at an improved contract price, so if we get an' 'undred per cent from every man on the team we'll be fine.'

Sharkey nodded compliantly, hiding his anger. He knew that the men would work till they were exhausted, and the hundred or so feet of old sewer tunnelling would be uncovered on time. If not he would be held responsible, rather than Frank Coley and his six extra hands. It made no sense. They could afford to break even on this contract, considering the work which would come their way if they did – and at an improved rate. It was sheer bloody-mindedness, he fumed.

On that Friday morning Charlie Foden drew the last of his savings out from the post office, a grand total of two pounds ten shillings, and bought a small Christmas tree at the East Lane market. The trader tied it up and Charlie walked home to Cooper Street with it tucked under his arm. The remaining money wouldn't go very far, he thought, but it would certainly help the family through a very hard time.

'You shouldn't 'ave,' Lucy reproved him mildly, grateful for his kindness.

Charlie smiled awkwardly. His gesture had been prompted the previous evening when Sue clambered on to her father's lap and asked him to read her a story. George had chosen a seasonal tale, and as he turned a page the child spotted the coloured picture. 'Where's that?' she asked.

'Fairyland,' George replied.

'I'd like ter live in Fairyland.'

'An' the children all looked out of the window an' saw

that the snow was fallin' 'eavily,' George read on.

'Why is there a tree in that 'ouse?' Sue asked him.

''Cos it's Christmas. It's a Christmas tree.'

'Why can't we 'ave a Christmas tree in our 'ouse?'

'Because in Fairyland they can go an' pick a tree from the forest but where we live people 'ave ter buy them,' George told her with a kiss on her forehead.

'Can we buy a tree fer Christmas?'

'Not this Christmas, darlin'. Maybe next Christmas.'

'My friend Gracie's got a Christmas tree in 'er 'ouse,' Sue said in a sleepy voice. 'Gracie said 'er daddy bought it ter put the presents under. Will we 'ave presents?'

'If you're a very good gel,' her father replied softly.

Charlie caught the look of desperation on George's face as he glanced at Lucy and he was filled with anger. He got up, took his pipe from his pocket and walked out to the backyard for a smoke. It was little enough to ask for, he thought. The right of a man to provide for his wife and children by earning a fair wage. His pride in a profession, a trade or simple muscle power which put bread on the table, clothes on the family's backs and shoes on their feet. Yes, and a few little extras, such as a Christmas tree with one or two presents laid out beneath it.

'Are you all right, Charlie?' Lucy asked as she looked out of the scullery door. 'It's cold out 'ere.'

He tapped his pipe against the heel of his boot and looked up. ''As Sue gone ter bed?' he asked.

Lucy nodded. 'She was dead tired.'

'Is George OK?'

'Yeah, I fink so. 'E's settlin' 'er.'

Charlie stood up from the rickety old chair. 'While you was gettin' the tea ready George told me 'e'd 'eard that the Coleys were recruitin' again,' he said in a serious voice. 'It was Danny Albury who told 'im. Don't let 'im go after the job, Lucy, or at least try an' talk 'im out of it.'

''E's not mentioned anyfing ter me,' she replied. 'Obviously I'd try ter stop 'im, but 'e's gettin' really worried now. 'E'll take anyfing ter get a few bob fer Christmas.'

'Fings'll turn out all right,' Charlie said quietly.

'You're a big 'elp,' Lucy replied.

Charlie felt his face colour slightly. 'I'm sorry,' he said, misunderstanding her.

'No, I mean it, Charlie,' she emphasised with a warm smile. 'Whenever I get ter feelin' low or a bit down in the mouth, you're there wiv a few kind words.'

'It's nice ter be appreciated,' he said, returning her smile.

Lucy reached out and touched his arm. 'It was a good day when you came ter stay,' she said with feeling.

For a moment time stood still as he looked steadily into her blue eyes. He made no attempt to hide his feelings, concentrated calmly in his molten gaze. Her physical presence was working on him like magnetism and he felt himself slowly being drawn into its field of power, where the invisible, ineluctable forces of life would bring them together, just as night followed day, as the sun climbed in the morning sky. Was she mocking him now, her eyes laughing, her mouth trembling at the corners to hold a smile at bay, or was she merely amused by the intensity of his large dark eyes? Whatever the truth, it made him feel warm inside as the momentary spell passed and he followed her back into the house.

Chapter Eleven

George came down the stairs and smiled briefly at Lucy.
'She's gone off ter sleep but she seems a bit 'ot ter me. I
'ope she ain't goin' down wiv anyfing.'

'I'll go up an' take a look in a while,' Lucy told him.
'Look, there's a few bob in the jar. Why don't you an'
Charlie go out fer a pint?'

He shook his head firmly. 'I wonder you could even
suggest it. We're gonna need every penny, especially
after . . .'

'Look, there's no good 'arpin' on it,' she said bluntly.

'But I feel terrible about it,' he went on. 'I just don't
know 'ow it 'appened.'

'Take the money an' 'ave a pint,' Lucy said with a note of
impatience in her voice. 'There's anuvver week not touched
yet. Yer might be lucky at the labour exchange next time.
Some blokes are. Mrs Farr's son-in-law got a start last
week.'

George nodded reluctantly and took the jam jar down
from the dresser. 'I'll take the 'alf-crown,' he told her.
'That's if Charlie fancies goin' out.'

'Yer'd better ask 'im. 'E's sittin' in the parlour.' George
seemed hesitant and Lucy gave him a firm look. 'Well go on
then,' she sighed.

Charlie needed no persuasion and he grabbed his coat from the back of the door. The two men walked through the misty evening streets, past the boarded-up shops, and when they reached the Mason's Arms in Lynton Road they found the public bar unusually full. Ben and Frank Coley were sitting alongside Sharkey behind two tables which had been hastily pulled together, facing a line of men.

'What's goin' on?' Charlie asked the landlord as he waited to be served.

'They're takin' on a few extra workers,' Mick Johnson told him. 'It's fer the main sewer job startin' next week at the far end o' the turnin'.'

''Ow many are they lookin' for?' George asked.

'Six, as I understand.'

Freda Johnson came over and leaned on the counter. 'They paid the diggers off soon as we opened this evenin',' she said, 'but they made those poor gits wait around till just now.'

'It's nuffink ter do wiv us,' Mick reminded her.

'It looks bad, though.'

'What d'yer mean?'

'What I say,' Freda retorted sharply. 'It makes it look like we've encouraged those two ugly gits ter keep the men waitin' so they'd spend a few bob in 'ere.'

'Well they didn't, did they?' Mick growled back at her.

'Of course not. What did you expect?'

Charlie saw that there were at least a dozen men in line and the one at the front seemed to be arguing with the older Coley. 'Sixty or not I can still pull me weight,' he said indignantly.

'Sorry, try anuvver time,' Frank Coley told him.

The man mumbled something as he walked away and the

men at the end of the line looked a little more hopeful as they shuffled forward.

Charlie turned to say something to George Parry and saw the pensive look on his face. 'You ain't finkin' what I fink you're finkin', are yer?' he asked.

'What 'ave I got ter lose?' George replied. 'I can stick it till Christmas.'

''Ave you ever done any ditch diggin'?' Charlie asked him. 'Yer'll be chuckin' clods o' wet clay up out o' the trench an' by the end o' the day yer 'ands'll look like raw meat. It's a killer of a job.'

''Ave you ever done any ditch diggin'?' George countered.

Charlie shook his head. 'No I 'aven't, but I know those that 'ave. I saw the state they got in.'

George suddenly put down his glass of beer. 'Like I just said, what 'ave I got ter lose?' He walked off to join the line.

Charlie shook his head sadly as he leaned on the counter. There was nothing he could say or do, short of physically restraining the man. George would have to learn the hard way.

The line moved forward and more men were turned away. Four had been accepted and the last six in line realised that the odds had shortened to three to one.

'What experience 'ave you 'ad?' Ben asked the man at the head of the line.

'I've worked fer Langhams, Mowlems an' Williams, general labourin',' the man replied.

'What was yer last job?'

The man stifled a cough. 'It was wiv Williams. On the new quay they've built at the Surrey Docks.'

'Williams subbed out that contract,' Ben informed him. 'Slaters done the job.'

'Yeah, I know, but I—'

'Sorry. Next one.'

Charlie had been watching the exchange and he felt sorry for the man as he shuffled off. Sharkey Lockwood was grinning evilly as he mumbled something to Frank Coley and the two laughed loudly.

'I rue the day Mick allowed that pile o' shite inter this pub,' Freda said close to Charlie's ear.

'That ganger seems a charmin' sort, I must say,' he replied.

''E's nuffink but a big bully,' the landlady remarked with distaste. 'It only wants someone ter stand up to 'im an' 'e'd run a mile.'

Charlie felt she was probably being a little naive but he nodded nevertheless. 'I don't doubt it.'

The man in front of George was taken on and Frank Coley closed the large notebook at his elbow. 'Right then, that's sorted,' he said.

George leaned his hands on the table. 'Can't yer make room fer one more?' he asked.

'What d'yer fink this is, a workmen's charity or some-fink?' Coley growled.

'I can work as 'ard as the next man,' George persisted.

'I ain't disputin' that,' Coley replied. 'The books are full an' that's the end of it.'

'Can't yer put me down as a standby?' George asked him.

'Standby fer what?'

'In case any o' the ovvers don't turn up.'

'If yer wanna be a standby feel free,' Lockwood cut in. 'Be at the workin's at seven thirty sharp an' if someone don't turn up you can ask ter take their place. Mind you, yer won't be alone, so don't expect ter get a start.'

'Wouldn't it be better ter put a few standbys down in the book?' George asked.

Frank Coley's face darkened. 'Don't you start tellin' us 'ow ter run our business,' he grated. 'Now piss off out of it.'

George hesitated as he searched for a reply and he suddenly felt Charlie's hand on his shoulder.

'There was no need fer that,' Charlie remarked, his wide eyes fixed on Frank Coley. 'What my pal said made sense, ter me at least.'

The older Coley returned the stare. He prided himself on being a good judge of men and he felt sure that this character's confidence was not just a front. After all, it wasn't every day of the week that he and his team would be confronted in such a way. 'Look, it might make sense ter you, pal, but it's not the way we do fings, OK?'

'It's your prerogative,' Charlie said quietly, 'but it don't cost much ter let a man retain a bit o' dignity.'

'Oh, I see,' Frank Coley replied with a smirk. 'Would you prefer us ter say, "Sorry, sir, try again next week"?'

'Well, it would sound a bit better than tellin' a bloke ter piss off after waitin' in line,' Charlie said calmly.

Sharkey Lockwood leaned forward over the table. 'Are you 'is keeper?' he asked, nodding his head towards George.

'I don't believe I was talkin' ter you,' Charlie said dismissively.

'Well I'm talkin' ter you,' Sharkey stormed.

'Save that big mouth o' yours fer the diggin's,' Charlie told him, menace in his widening eyes.

Frank Coley laid his hand on Sharkey's arm and then got up out of his chair, motioning Charlie towards the counter. 'Look, I'm sorry if yer pal's upset by the way I spoke,' he said in a civil tone of voice, 'but it don't always sink in when we turn 'em down. Some of 'em can get stroppy, yer know.'

'Yeah, I can understand that,' Charlie acknowledged, 'but it don't take no longer ter be polite to 'em.'

Coley did not reply immediately, beckoning instead to Mick Johnson. 'Give us a drink, will yer, Mick, an' one fer this feller an' 'is pal.' Then he turned to face Charlie. 'I didn't get yer name, by the way.'

Once the introductions had been made Frank Coley invited them over to a spare table in the far corner of the bar. 'Let's sit awhile,' he suggested.

They made themselves comfortable and the contractor took a large gulp from his whisky and soda. 'An' what d'you do fer a livin'?' he asked.

'I'm in the docks,' Charlie replied.

'I understand it's a bit iffy at the moment,' Coley remarked.

'That just about sums it up,' Charlie agreed.

George took a quick swig from his pint. 'It's only one day a week, ain't it, Charlie?' he said.

'You'd do better workin' fer me,' Coley let fall with a smile.

'No fanks,' Charlie replied quickly. 'I wouldn't be much good on a shovel. Now give me a crane-set ter load on to a lorry or a cargo o' wine ter store an' there'd be no 'oldin' me.'

'I don't mean diggin',' Frank said. 'I was finkin' more along the lines o' ganger. That's if yer've considered surrenderin' yer docker's ticket.'

'Well, I've got no sons or nephews ter pass it on to,' Charlie told him. 'At the moment the job's a waste o' time an' I 'ave bin tempted ter chuck it in.'

Frank Coley put down his drink and straightened up.

'Look, I'm gonna put me cards on the table,' he said finally. 'I was impressed by the way yer took yer pal's part, an' no less by the way you 'andled my ganger. Yer didn't let 'im ride roughshod over yer, though I should say in passin' that 'e won't ferget it. I fink you'd make a decent ganger yerself, an' I need anuvver one fer the workin's after Christmas. There's a big contract in the offin', providin' we don't mess up on the job we start next week. We'll be workin' on two sites at once. You'd control one an' Sharkey the over.'

''Old on a second,' Charlie urged him. 'I don't know the first fing about ditch diggin'.'

'What d'yer need ter know? It's somefing yer'd pick up wiv no trouble. Bein' a ganger ain't about wieldin' a shovel, it's all about 'andlin' men. I'm considered ter be a good judge of a bloke an' I'd say wivout fear o' contradiction that you'd be able to 'andle the men every bit as good as Sharkey. Better, in fact. A good ganger gets the best out of 'is crew an' that's what I need, the best effort I can get. It's crucial if we're ter make a go o' this new contract.'

'If I agreed, when would yer expect me ter start?' Charlie asked.

'Next week,' Coley replied. 'Yer'd spend the week wiv Sharkey ter find yer feet an' then yer'd be on yer own. We've gotta clear over seventy feet o' main sewer so that the bricklayers can set ter work repairin' it, an' if we can manage it on time we'll get the length o' River Lane ter sort out by the end o' January. I'll pay yer six quid a week an' a decent rise when we win the new contract. What d'yer say?'

Charlie looked steadily at Frank Coley and saw the hardness in the man's deep-set eyes. There was no charity being offered here, only an opportunist deal that served Coley's purpose. From what he had said the firm stood to make a lot of money, providing they could hit their targets. 'I'll accept your offer on two conditions,' he answered in a measured tone.

'I don't usually settle fer conditions,' Coley told him, 'but go on.'

'Firstly I can't start till Tuesday. I need ter get a leave of absence from the Dock Labour Board. Secondly, yer give my pal George a start on Monday.'

Coley's eyes narrowed and his jaw muscles tightened. 'That's out,' he replied sharply. 'I've got me quota an' there's no changin' it now.'

Charlie smiled. 'Considerin' what's openin' up for yer, one extra man's wages pales to insignificance, in my opinion. Anyway, it's bin nice talkin' ter yer, Frank. Sorry it didn't work out.'

Coley drained his glass and pulled a face as the fiery spirit burned his throat. 'You'd throw a good opportunity away fer that reason?'

'Yeah I would.'

'Fer a pal?'

'George ain't exactly a pal. I lodge wiv the family.'

Coley shook his head slowly and his face relaxed. 'I gotta say George should consider you as a pal, an' fink 'imself lucky. All right, it's agreed.'

Charlie finished his own drink. 'You'll get a fair day's work out o' both of us, you can be sure,' he replied.

Lucy glanced up at the clock again and it did not go unnoticed by Sara, who was busy casting off stitches around the neck of a cardigan she was knitting. 'They're late,' she remarked. 'I do 'ope Charlie's not plyin' 'im wiv drinks. George never could drink that much.'

'Charlie's got no money ter waste,' Lucy said quickly. 'I

expect they're just 'avin' a good chat.'

A few minutes later the two men came in and the women were bemused by their humorous expressions. 'What's bin goin' on?' Lucy asked.

'Yer'd better ask Charlie,' George explained with a sly grin.

'Maybe you should explain,' Charlie retorted. 'You started it off.'

'An' you ended it,' George said, grinning.

Lucy raised her voice. 'Will one of yer please tell us what's bin 'appenin'.'

Charlie followed George's lead by sitting down at the table. 'Well, it was like this . . .'

Sammy Strickland had lost no time in making preparations to become a trader and to that end he got the name of the insurance man from the paper shop before calling into the insurance agency next door. 'I'd like ter see Mr Beecham, please,' he requested.

'What is it related to?' the receptionist asked.

'Business.'

'Business?'

'Yeah. My business,' Sammy emphasised, getting a little irked by the young woman's attitude.

'Just one moment, I'll see if 'e's available.'

Twenty minutes later a fidgety Sammy was shown into a large office.

'Sorry for keeping you, Mr Strickland,' Beecham said. 'Now what can I do for you?'

'Yer might as well call me Sammy, considerin' we're gonna be associates,' the prospective trader said, smiling broadly.

'We are?'

'Yes sir.'

'Can you be a little more specific?'

''Ow much more specific do I need ter be?' Sammy said triumphantly as he took out the policy from his coat pocket. 'Cast yer meat pies on this.'

Beecham studied the document for a few moments before looking up at his visitor. 'Am I right in supposing that you're thinking of submitting this policy as security against a loan?'

'Right on the button, pal.'

Beecham winced noticeably at the unwonted familiarity and studied the policy again. 'It was issued in 1880, fifty-five years ago,' he remarked.

'Yeah. Me farvver gave it ter me before 'e snuffed it,' Sammy told him. ''E said it'd come in 'andy one day.'

'Can you remember what year that was?' Beecham asked.

'What, when 'e give us the policy, or when 'e snuffed it?'

'When he gave you the policy and when he died.'

'Now let me see.' Sammy pulled on his bottom lip. 'I remember it 'cos it was me twenty-first birfday.'

'When your father died?'

'No, when 'e gave me the policy. It was a birfday present, so me dad said.'

'And how old are you now, Mr Strickland?'

'Fifty-five.'

'That would be thirty-four years ago.'

'Yeah, that sounds about right,' Sammy said, frowning with confusion.

'Now what year was it when your father died?' the insurance man enquired.

'Er, 1914.'

'Twenty-one years ago.'

'Look, I'm gettin' all confused wiv these dates,' Sammy complained.

'I'm sorry, Mr Strickland, but I'm trying to ascertain who's been responsible for the premiums.'

'The payments, yer mean?'

'Exactly.'

'Well, it wasn't nuffink ter do wiv me,' Sammy said quickly. 'I just took it ter be a present like me ole man said. I mean ter say, yer not expected ter pay fer yer own presents, now are yer?'

'Well, if your father kept up the payments until he died all well and good. It would be worth something,' the agent explained. 'But I have a nasty feeling that the premiums were not paid, which makes the policy not even worth the paper it's printed on.'

'Oh my good Gawd!' Sammy gasped. 'That connivin' ole bastard. That's why 'e gave it ter me, 'cos 'e couldn't afford ter pay it.'

'Look, I think it might be better if I keep this policy for the time being,' the agent said. 'I'll write you out a receipt for it. Give me a week and I should have some news, one way or the other. Just book another appointment for this time next week. The receptionist will arrange it.'

Sammy left the office feeling deflated, and when he got home he slumped in the armchair. 'When yer down, yer down,' he groaned. 'I've bin sittin' on that policy fer thirty-four years an' not a penny's bin paid on it all that time.'

'So it can't be used as security?' Peggy queried.

'The insurance man told me that if me farvver paid the premiums till 'e died then it would be werf a few bob,' Sammy explained, 'though it still wouldn't be enough ter stand as security against a business loan. But me an' you

125

know very well that my ole farvver was as tight as a nun's arse. Me poor ole muvver struggled till the day she died. There was never any extras fer 'er, Gawd rest 'er soul. Nah, that stingy ole bastard gave the policy ter me so 'e wouldn't be responsible fer it. I can just imagine 'im finkin', let 'im pay fer it, 'e's the one who'll benefit.'

'I wish the ole git 'ad reminded us ter keep up wiv the payments,' Peggy remarked.

''Ere, steady on. That's my dad yer talkin' about,' Sammy said with a big smile.

Chapter Twelve

Charlie Foden hadn't envisaged much trouble getting a leave of absence and he was right. 'As long as yer keep yer dues paid,' the union official reminded him. 'One less standin' on the line every mornin' gives anuvver poor bleeder a chance of a scratch.'

Charlie left the office in Tooley Street and immediately bumped into Fred Wilson, his friend from the men's hostel.

''Ow the bloody 'ell are yer, Charlie?' Fred asked. 'I ain't seen yer around.'

Charlie told him what had happened since their last meeting and Fred pulled a face. 'Yer gotta be orf yer 'ead workin' fer those no-good bastards,' he growled. 'After all I told yer. Some people never learn.'

Charlie put his arm round Fred's bony shoulders. 'Come on, pal, let's walk up ter the café,' he said, grinning.

The older man was quick with advice as they sat sipping huge mugs of sweet tea. 'Yer gotta let the men see yer no pushover,' he stressed. 'But yer gotta be fair wiv 'em too. They'll sum it all up. Sometimes, when yer back's fair breakin' an' yer arms are done in, a five-minute break comes as a godsend. Sometimes yer gotta be 'ard too, Charlie. Yer might spot a bloke who should never 'ave got the job in the first place. Yer better finishin' 'em up before they end up killin' themselves, or somebody else.'

'It's a shutterin' job, main sewers.'

Fred pulled a face. 'Sewer work can be dangerous, Chas, so watch out,' he warned. 'Make sure the feller doin' the shutterin' knows 'is onions, an' keep the timbers checked fer slippage. I've seen men buried under tons o' clay, 'ad ter dig 'em out, so don't take any chances. If I know the Coleys they'll go the cheapest way, an' that means no steel clamps, only timbers. It just means yer gotta be extra careful.'

Charlie smiled gratefully. 'Yer've bin a big 'elp, Fred,' he told him. 'I'm goin' in green.'

'You'll be OK. Just remember what I said,' Fred urged him. 'One fing more before yer shoot off, watch that ganger Sharkey Lockwood. I know quite a bit about 'im. 'E'd shop 'is own muvver for a few bob. 'E's a bully an' 'e'll pick on anyone 'e knows won't stand up to 'im. As a matter o' fact 'e used ter wrestle at the baths but 'e wasn't all that good. Before that 'e fancied 'imself as a boxer but I can tell yer now, 'e's got a glass chin. That's why 'e turned ter wrestlin'.'

Charlie smiled. 'That's somefing I'll keep in mind, Fred,' he said.

'I 'ope yer do, ole sport,' Fred replied.

That morning the main sewer diggings were being scratched over, with the top layer of soft soil soon removed. George Parry was expecting a very hard day, and after talking to Roy Chubb next door he had rubbed Vaseline into his hands, bandaged up the palms and then put on a pair of woollen gloves with the fingers cut away. He felt as prepared as he would ever be and prayed he would be able to last the first day out, remembering that Roy had said the first day was the killer.

Sharkey smiled at the sight of George wearing his mittens as he struggled into his boiler suit. 'I see we're lookin' after our 'ands, then,' he remarked sarcastically. 'Playin' the pianner ternight, are we?'

George bit back a suitable reply and merely smiled, but Sharkey was not finished. 'I want yer ter pair up wiv Wally Coates,' he said. ''E'll show yer the ropes.'

While they were coming out of the shed Roy Chubb managed to pass on Joe Lambert's warning that Coates was a stool-pigeon for the Coleys, and George resolved to be careful as he set to work. He was dwarfed beside the giant Wally, who handled a pickaxe like a child with a toy. 'Mind yerself,' were the only words he uttered all morning, along with a few mumbled orders for George to remove the soil he had loosened.

The new recruit worked as steadily as he could, knowing that he had to pace himself or be exhausted by lunchtime. He was pleased that his hands felt reasonably comfortable beneath their protection and he ignored the face-pulling of Coates, who seemed to find the mittens amusing.

''Ow yer doin'?' Roy asked as they scrambled out of the trench for the morning tea break.

'Apart from me back I'm fine,' George replied.

'Yer'll get used to it,' Roy said supportively. 'Swing the shovel from the shoulders – it'll ease yer back off.'

All too soon the men were back in the trench and by lunchtime they had made good progress.

''Ow's it goin'?' Ben Coley asked when Sharkey walked into the hut.

'No problems,' Sharkey replied as he picked up the mug of coffee Ben had made.

'Who yer gonna get rid of?' Ben enquired.

Sharkey shook his head. 'I know Frank wanted a space

made fer that Parry geezer, but I ain't 'ad reason ter kick any o' the ovvers out, not yet anyway. They've all got their 'eads down.'

'Well, yer better get it sorted before Frank gets 'ere. 'E's due at two o'clock,' Ben reminded him.

'If it was left ter me I'd out Parry,' Sharkey growled. 'The man's 'andlin' the shovel like some ole pouf. I can see Wally slowly gettin' the needle wiv 'im.'

'Parry stays,' Ben said firmly. 'An' tell that big gorilla ter keep off 'is back.'

Sharkey ambled out to the diggings and looked along the line of workers, all busy and now down to their waists in the trench. He spotted Gerry Watson, and with a sly grin he walked over to stand directly above him in the small gap between the workings and the growing pile of thrown soil. The young man swung a laden shovel and the earth landed on the ganger's feet. 'Sorry, boss. Didn't know yer was standin' there,' he said quickly.

'I'm big enough ter be seen,' Sharkey scowled.

'Yeah, but—'

'Don't start arguin',' the ganger sneered. 'That's the trouble wiv you, yer don't know when ter button that big trap o' yours.'

Gerry did not understand the reason for Sharkey's antagonism but he was aware that he had got off on the wrong foot from the start and knew that it was only a matter of time before things came to a head. This seemed like the moment, and with a show of pluck he drove the blade of the shovel into the loose soil and stood upright, his head tilted back to meet Sharkey's stare. 'I fink yer must 'ave got out the wrong side o' the bed this mornin',' he said. 'There's bin no damage done.'

The men near Gerry gritted their teeth and carried on

working, knowing that he had overstepped the mark.

Sharkey leaned forward over the young man. 'I 'ad you marked down fer a loud-mouthed git an' I wasn't wrong. You're paid ter work, not keep spoutin' yer bloody mouth off.'

Gerry knew that it was useless arguing with the big ganger. Any further remarks on his part could cost him physically, as well as in his pocket. He shrugged his shoulders and made to scramble out of the trench.

'Where d'yer fink you're goin'?' Sharkey growled.

'Yer want me out of 'ere, don't yer?'

'I'll tell yer when I want yer out o' there.'

Gerry reached for his shovel once more. 'I'll get back ter work, then.'

'Don't you ever listen?' Sharkey snarled hatefully. 'I'll tell yer when yer work, I'll tell yer when yer take a break, an' in your case I'll tell yer when yer can take a piss.'

Gerry clenched his hands into two tight fists, dearly wanting to jump out and attack the man, but he knew that he would stand no chance. Better to keep cool and make a dignified exit, he decided. He quickly clambered out the other side of the trench and unbuttoned his boiler suit, glaring at Sharkey across the divide. 'OK, you win,' he said calmly.

'Put yer gear in the shed an' piss off, an' be quick about it,' the ganger shouted.

Gerry Watson rubbed his sore hands together and turned his back on the workings. There would be very few presents for the kids this Christmas, he thought regretfully as he made his way home, but at least Amy had managed to get them a toy each from the market last Saturday.

On Monday morning Lucy went next door with Sue and sat chatting with Mary while the children played together.

'I've 'ad those sheets in soak fer a few days,' Mary told her. 'I've stuck a load o' salt in the water ter 'elp loosen the paint.'

'When we gonna start peelin' 'em?' Lucy asked.

'We could make a start ternight, if yer can manage it,' Mary replied.

'I'll be in soon as I can,' Lucy said. 'George'll get Sue off ter bed. 'E's better at it than me, anyway.'

''E might not be, not ternight,' Mary warned her. 'The first night my Roy got 'ome from the diggin's 'e just flopped in the armchair an' couldn't move. I 'ad ter give 'im 'is tea on a tray.'

'Yeah, I've not stopped finkin' about 'ow George is gettin' on,' Lucy said, sighing. 'Don't get me wrong, 'e's strong enough, but ditch diggin' ain't the same as wrappin' parcels, is it?'

'Don't worry, Roy'll keep an eye on 'im, I'm sure.'

'Charlie's startin' there tomorrow.'

'Yeah, so yer said.'

Mary had always considered herself to be fairly perceptive, and recently she had noticed a slight change in Lucy's voice whenever she mentioned Charlie. It was hardly tangible, but there was a new enthusiasm there. She talked about him as if she was discussing a member of the family, Mary thought, but then a lodger who ate with them and shared their home would grow to seem like one of the family. 'The kids are all right fer a minute,' she said. 'Let's show yer those sheets.'

The two women went out into the tiny yard which was almost filled by the old tin bath and Mary lifted up the edge of one of the sheets. For a few moments she picked at the thick rubbery black paint and only succeeded in stripping off a small sliver. 'It's still not soaked enough,' she sighed.

'Did yer tell Mrs Venners we got the sheets?'

'Yeah. She said ter let 'em soak in salt water fer a few days, an' that's what I done.'

'Did she say 'ow long it took 'er ter strip the paint off?'

'Well, she did say it wasn't easy.'

''Ow long did it take 'er, Mary?' her friend coaxed her.

'She reckoned about a couple o' weeks.'

'Just ter get the paint off round the bloody edges?' Lucy said disbelievingly.

'As a matter o' fact, she ended up strippin' the 'ole lot off,' Mary told her reluctantly. 'Apparently she took one o' the bundles up ter that pawnbroker's in New Cross and 'e opened the parcel. Gave 'er a right mouthful, so she said. Anyway, once all the paint's off the linen'll iron up lovely. At least we'll 'ave a couple o' pairs o' new sheets.'

Lucy looked reluctant but she shrugged her shoulders. 'If we're ever gonna get them done we need ter start now,' she said.

'Well, come on then.'

'Shall we 'ave a cuppa first?'

'A good idea.'

While Mary was in the scullery making the tea Lucy sat by the fire, watching the two children playing in a corner with Gracie's cardboard box of toys. Sue was intrigued by a rag doll she had just found amongst them and Gracie was trying hard to put a vest on one of her small china babies. The toy's face was scratched and one eye and an arm were missing but Gracie spoke to it gently, transported to a world of make-believe where its kind caught cold, cavorted wide-eyed and talked back. The dolls were ancient, damaged and falling to pieces and Lucy smiled sadly. There would be very few replacements or additions to the cardboard box this Christmas, she thought. There was a small Christmas tree standing in her parlour, though, decorated with paper chains and a few sprigs of holly.

'There we are,' Mary said cheerfully as she came into the room and set down a laden tea tray.

The children came over to the table and Mary gave them each a cup of milky tea with a chocolate biscuit. 'Now don't spill it,' she warned.

Outside the temperature was dropping and snow clouds were gathering, and as Lucy sat back in the armchair and sipped her tea she suddenly chuckled.

'What's tickled you?' Mary asked.

'I was just finkin'. 'Alf an hour out there in the yard pickin' at those sheets an' our fingers'll be droppin' off.'

'Yeah, we do time fings right, don't we,' Mary grinned.

'I reckon they'd be better laid out in the sun ter soften. Anyway, we won't get much time ter spend on 'em if we get that key job, will we?'

'Yeah. Ada Black was s'posed ter call this mornin' if she 'eard anyfing,' Mary reminded her.

The two children finished their tea and walked out of the parlour each carrying a doll, prompting Mary to ask them where they were going.

'We're takin' our dollies fer a walk,' Gracie told her.

'Ask a silly question,' Mary said to Lucy with a shake of her head.

Gracie led the way into the scullery and peeked through the net curtains at the filled bathtub. 'Shall we bath the dollies?' she suggested.

Sue's face lit up at the prospect and she hunched her shoulders excitedly as Gracie put a finger to her mouth and gently lifted the door latch. Undeterred by the cold the two girls set about dipping the dolls into the icy water. Sue's doll became entangled in the sheeting and as she pulled on it the arm came off in her hand. Gracie reached further into the bath trying to pluck it up and only succeeded in soaking her dress.

'I'll get it,' Sue told her as she moved round the tub.

Gracie pulled the sheeting aside to help and Sue was immediately drenched. Suddenly the whole thing ceased to be an adventure, and with the two dolls back on dry land two very wet and by now very cold children hurried into the warmth of the house.

'Oh my good Gawd!' Mary gasped. 'Just look at yer both. Yer'll catch yer death o' cold. Get them clothes off.'

'You've bin very naughty,' Lucy said sharply.

It was not long before the two children were warm and dry, wrapped in bath towels in front of the fire.

'That's the trouble wiv leavin' it there full o' water,' Mary said, sighing.

'Yeah, well, it's only natural that kids would wanna play wiv the water,' Lucy replied supportively.

'I really dunno what we should do about it,' Mary said, stroking her chin.

'Nah. It's awkward, really.'

'I s'pose we could let Mrs Venners 'ave the sheets.'

'Yeah, I s'pose so,' Lucy replied, trying not to sound too enthusiastic.

'We won't 'ave much time, anyway.'

'Not really.'

'Is that settled, then?'

Lucy nodded casually, but she felt relieved inside. 'I don't fink I'd 'ave bin able ter bluff it out at the pawn-broker's,' she remarked.

Mary chuckled. 'Nah, me neivver.'

'Yer still OK about that key job, though, ain't yer?'

'Course I am,' Mary replied quickly as she reached for the teapot.

Lucy sipped her fresh tea and then looked up at Mary. 'I was just finkin',' she said. 'As far as I understand it, those key jobs are fer little offices where yer let yerself in an' out before they come ter work in the mornin's.'

'So?'

'Well, why can't the work be done in the evenin' instead?'

'There's no reason as far as I can see.'

'We could do a job each in the evenin's, providin' the fellers don't mind lookin' after the kids fer an hour or two.'

Mary nodded. 'If that scatty mare Ada does come over we could go after the job an' see if it'd work out doin' it that way. If it does we could look fer anuvver one.'

Lucy put down her teacup, hoping that Mary was not going to have any second thoughts about the original money-making idea. 'Want me ter give yer an 'and takin' them sheets out of the bath?' she offered.

'Would yer?' Mary replied gratefully. 'I'm gonna be glad ter see the back o' the bloody fings, ter tell yer the trufe.'

Chapter Thirteen

George Parry came home that evening from his first day at the diggings looking exhausted and hollow-eyed, and when Sue came running up to him as she always did he found it painful bending to lift her up into his arms.

Lucy let the child hug him for a few moments then took her from him. 'Daddy's very tired, so you be a good little gel an' let 'im 'ave a rest,' she told her.

As George washed his hands in the soapy water Lucy had made ready for him he winced painfully.

''Ow did it go, luv?' Lucy asked as she stood over the gas stove stirring the gravy.

He gave her a hard look. The cake of Sunlight soap was stinging his raw hands, his back was aching badly, and what with the sniggering he had had to endure from his work partner throughout the day, he had just about had enough. 'It's a job,' he answered flatly.

'Yer must be dead tired,' Lucy said kindly. 'You go in an' get warm by the fire an' I'll get yer a nice cuppa.'

Normally George would have been grateful for the thought, but tonight he felt irritable and utterly jaded and he walked out of the scullery without another word.

'Come an' sit 'ere by the fire, luv,' Sara told him as she got out of her armchair. 'You must be dead tired.'

George gave her a weak smile and flopped down heavily.

'Look at yer poor 'ands,' Sara said, tutting. 'They look raw.'

He glanced down at them for a second or two and nodded. 'They'll 'arden up after a few days.'

Lucy came into the parlour with a mug of tea. 'There you are,' she said. 'Yer'll feel better after this.'

George sipped the tea, becoming aware of Sara staring into the mantelshelf mirror as she pulled on her mousy hair. In his current frame of mind he felt like telling the silly bitch to sit down, but he gritted his teeth instead and stared down at the glowing coals.

'George?'

'Yeah?'

'I've bin tempted ter get Lucy ter do me a perm,' she announced.

George looked up at her. 'Yer 'air's all right as it is,' he told her without enthusiasm.

'It's not. Just look at it.'

George was not going to let himself get dragged into a conversation about hairstyles and he shrugged his shoulders. 'Please yerself,' he replied abruptly.

'I will,' Sara said with spirit.

George gave his sister a quick glance. What was the matter with her, he wondered? It must be something to do with that church committee. 'Are yer goin' out ternight?' he asked.

Sara nodded. 'I've got a church outin' meetin',' she said importantly.

'Will the vicar be goin'?'

'No,' Sara replied quickly. 'Why d'yer ask?'

'No reason, 'cept you said 'e was a nice bloke who took an interest in all the church functions.'

'Well I've 'ad good reason ter change me mind,' Sara told him coldly. ''E's left the Church – well, our church, that is. 'E ran off last week wiv one o' the deaconesses from St Jude's.'

'I'm sorry,' George replied, trying not to smile at the expression on his sister's face.

'There's nuffink ter be sorry about,' Sara said offhandedly. 'It's no skin off my nose, but I 'ave ter say it does reflect on the good name of the church.'

'Yeah, I s'pose so,' George sighed as he eased his aching back in the armchair.

Sara finally finished twiddling with her hair and sat down facing him. 'You look dead beat,' she remarked.

'Tea'll be in five minutes,' Lucy announced, putting her head round the door.

'Where's Charlie?' George asked.

'Up in 'is room,' Sara replied as she fingered her hair once more. Charlie would like her hair shortened, she felt sure. He was a man of few words, no doubt stemming from being alone so much. But he was responsive when drawn out and his opinions made good sense. He was a man she could suffer, given the chance, and she wanted to believe that he felt the same. She must get Lucy to fix her hair, and maybe she could wear the dress that her sister-in-law said made her look shapely. At the time Lucy only said that to turn her off the dress, but things had changed. She wanted to look shapely, wanted to be seen, and noticed. She wanted Charlie to notice her, make her feel a real woman, not a predictable fixture in her brother's home.

When the evening meal was over George sat chatting to Charlie while Sara helped Lucy with the washing up.

'It got to a stage when I wanted ter crown 'im wiv the

shovel,' George growled. 'Apparently 'e's a Coley man. All the news goes back via 'im.'

'I know it's difficult, but yer gotta shut yer mind ter the piss-takin',' Charlie advised him. 'When that new contract starts, if it starts, there'll be better wages fer a kick-off. OK, it's not the sort o' job any of us would normally do, but fings are tight. There's millions out o' collar an' anybody wiv a job ter go to must consider themselves lucky.'

'Well I don't feel lucky,' George grumbled. 'At this moment I feel like I'm gonna break in 'alf.'

'Give it a few days an' yer'll feel a little more human,' Charlie said, smiling.

'Yeah, at least it's not fer ever.'

Sara came back into the parlour and gave Charlie a weak smile. 'I'm due at the church at eight o'clock,' she told him. 'I'm worried about the fog. It seems ter be comin' down thick.'

'Do you 'ave ter go out ternight?' George asked her.

'I do really,' she replied. 'It's a very important meetin'. Decisions 'ave ter be taken ternight. We can't just leave it.'

'Would yer like me ter walk along wiv yer ter the church?' Charlie suggested.

Sara shook her head. 'I couldn't expect yer ter go out on a night like this, just fer me.'

Charlie smiled indulgently. Sara certainly knew how to twist her words. 'Gimme a shout when yer ready,' he told her.

At ten minutes to eight Charlie offered Sara his arm as they stepped out of the house on to the damp, greasy pavement. It was something she had not experienced since her youth. John Balcombe, it was. She was eighteen and he two years older. They were getting close, to the extent of walking out arm in arm, but her mother felt that she was too young to form a lasting attachment with any boy, however honourable his intentions. John Balcombe tried to overcome her mother's resentment and Sara's own problems of divided loyalty, but one evening the young man's anger exploded and he walked away, leaving the old lady smiling with satisfaction. She had known all the time that he wasn't the one for her vulnerable daughter, and nor were any of the other young men who dared to throw their hats into the ring.

'It's nice of yer ter see me ter the church,' Sara said now.

'It's OK,' he replied with a mischievous smile. 'After all, it can be a bit scary on a foggy night. The old imagination can play tricks, like seein' some dark character steppin' out o' the fog in front of yer brandishin' a carvin' knife.'

'Don't, Charlie. Yer scarin' me,' Sara said in a childish tone of voice as she took the opportunity to grip his arm more tightly.

They crossed the main road and walked through the church gardens to the huge oaken door, where Charlie took his leave.

'Enjoy the meetin',' he said.

'Fanks, Charlie.'

'Look, if yer've got any idea when yer gonna be finished I could call back for yer,' he suggested.

Sara shook her head. 'It's all right. One o' the men lives in Lynton Road an' 'e'll walk back wiv me. Fanks anyway, though.'

Charlie made his way back to Cooper Street deep in thought. For the past few days Sara had been extra pleasant to him. He had put her initial reserve down to natural mistrust, and the difference now had begun to concern him. He could recognise the signs and felt that she was making a play for him in her own individual way. The sly glances, the hanging on his words, little tokens that warned him to be careful. In retrospect it had been foolish of him to walk Sara to the church, but he knew that had he not offered George would have, and tonight he was in no fit state to leave his chair.

In the house, Lucy sat down by the fire and kicked off her shoes. 'Sara seems ter like Charlie, don't yer fink?' she said.

George nodded. 'I 'ope she don't go readin' anyfing into 'im takin' 'er ter the meetin',' he replied. 'Charlie's a loner, an' there was no ulterior motive, I'm sure.'

'No, of course not,' Lucy agreed. 'Though yer gotta understand Sara's position. She's on 'er own, same as Charlie, an' she must feel it at times. An' let's face it, Charlie's an attractive man, an' 'e keeps 'imself respectable.'

'What about you?' George asked suddenly. 'Do you find 'im attractive?'

'I've never took that much notice, really,' she lied.

George looked at her closely. ''Ave I changed lately?' he asked.

'What d'yer mean, changed?'

'What I said, changed.'

'D'yer mean since yer've bin out o' work?'

'Yeah.'

'No, I don't fink so,' Lucy replied, ''cept fer bein' a bit edgy at times, which is quite natural, what wiv the worry o' providin' fer the family an' everyfing.'

George shifted uncomfortably in his chair. 'Yer don't fink I've bin neglectin' yer lately, do yer?'

'Nah, of course not.'

'It 'as bin a few weeks now since we . . . you know.'

'George, I've bin too worried an' tired lately ter fink o' that,' Lucy said quickly.

He nodded towards the small Christmas tree standing in a

china pot by the window. 'It's little fings that get to a man when 'e's on the floor. Yer feel like a failure fer not bein' able ter provide, an' then somefing like that 'appens.'

'Like the lodger bringin' 'ome a Christmas tree?' Lucy said with irritation. 'Fer God's sake, George, it was only a little gift, fer Sue mainly. You remember when she was sittin' on yer lap an' you was readin' to 'er. You 'ad ter tell 'er we wouldn't be 'avin' a tree this year an' it must 'ave got to 'im. 'E's a kind man, luv.'

'Yeah, an' I appreciate 'is thought, but—'

'Look, I've 'eard enough, so don't keep goin' on, George,' she said in exasperation. 'Yer feelin' sorry fer yerself an' it's showin'.'

'No I'm not,' he retorted.

'Look, let's stop right now, before we get into an argument,' Lucy suggested. 'I'm gonna make a pot o' tea.'

George rested his head back against the armchair and closed his eyes in an effort to think clearly. Lucy had always been rather demanding in bed and their love life up until recently had been very good, he thought. But it had cooled now and noticeably so. Neither of them had seemed very keen to initiate anything and it had reflected in their day-to-day lives. Gone were the little endearments, the sweet nothings, the looks that passed between them after a night of love, and in their place was an edginess, a reluctance to sit together chatting in the evenings, and now they had a way of turning their backs on each other when they climbed into bed.

Any further thoughts were quickly quashed when Sue came bounding into the parlour. 'Daddy read me a story,' she demanded.

George opened his eyes and straightened himself in the armchair before taking his daughter on to his lap. 'Right now, let's see,' he said with a large yawn.

She leaned back against him, her face turned up to his as he opened the nursery rhyme book and began with the misfortune of Humpty Dumpty.

'This one next,' the child urged, her hands on the pages.

'Don't be in such a rush,' George told her more forcefully than he intended, and it made her pull a face. 'Right then. Jack an' Jill . . .'

Sue took the book from him and closed it as she slid from his lap. The nursery rhyme she wanted to hear next was on another page. With the book under her arm she made for the door and turned briefly, giving him a look which was like a spear through his heart. He was failing them all: Lucy, Sue, and even Sara, whom he found difficult to talk to lately. The worry and degradation of being made redundant had got to him, and that day in the trench he had felt like an imbecile beside the giant Wally Coates and his silent sneering. He detested the man, the job and the exploitation of it all, but there was nothing he could do about it, except try to leave his frustrations and anger at the diggings.

Lucy stirred the tea slowly, her thoughts centred around Charlie and the effect he had had on her since his arrival. He was hardly out of her mind and it troubled her. Making his bed, even just being in his room, conjured up romantic fantasies, and she knew that if she was not careful things could very soon get out of hand. All Charlie needed was a little encouragement and he would respond, she felt sure. His eyes lingering covetously on her was proof enough, as were his efforts to please.

He had shown her without one word that he desired her and it made it all the more exciting.

Late that evening Ada Black knocked at Mary Chubb's front door. 'I know it's a poxy night ter be out but I 'ad ter come 'an see yer, gel,' she began as she was shown into the cosy parlour. 'There's a key job goin' at Dolan's in Tooley Street an' I only found out this evenin'. It's a small office next door ter the post office. I found out from the man in the tobacco shop opposite when I 'anded my key in. 'E 'olds the keys fer a lot o' the jobs along there. Apparently the last cleaner wasn't suitable an' they gave 'er the push. Don't ask me why, I never enquired. Anyway it's yours, if yer want it.'

'Want it? Course I want it,' Mary replied with a grin. 'Who do I 'ave ter see about gettin' took on?'

Ada sat down by the fire and puffed as she loosened the top button of her thick coat. 'Go round ter Dolan's at ten o'clock termorrer mornin'. The bloke'll be expectin' yer.'

'I'm very grateful, Ada,' Mary said. 'Can I get yer a cuppa?'

'Yeah, why not? Where's Roy, by the way?'

''E's upstairs tryin' ter settle Gracie,' Mary told her. 'I expect 'e's fast asleep 'imself by now. 'E was absolutely bushed when 'e got in ternight.'

'George next door started work there terday, didn't 'e?' Ada queried.

'Yeah. I saw 'im comin' down the street this evenin'. 'E looked all in as well.'

'I don't doubt it,' Ada remarked with a downturned mouth. 'Those Coley bruvvers are bloody slave-drivers. You earn yer corn workin' fer that pair of ugly bastards.'

'Yeah. I can tell by the state o' Roy when 'e gets in at night. Right then, let's get that kettle on.'

Ada stretched her legs out in front of the fire as Mary came back into the parlour. 'Once yer get yerself sorted out at Dolan's yer might be able ter wangle it like I do,' she said.

'Wangle it?'

'Yeah, go in ter please yerself, like me. Sometimes I do the cleanin' in the evenin's an' sometimes in the mornin's. It makes no difference ter them, as long as the offices are clean an' shipshape before they get in.'

'That sounds a good idea.'

The two sat sipping their tea by the roaring fire and suddenly Mary's face broke into a grin. ''Ere, yer don't know if Mrs Venners fancies any more tram sheets, do yer?' she asked.

'I'm sure she would,' Ada told her. 'She can pick those sheets faster than anyone in the turnin'. I saw a pair o' bedsheets she made out o' one of 'em. Really nice they were. She 'emmed all the edges an' embroidered a little pattern in the corners.'

'Well, I've got two an' she's welcome to 'em,' Mary said. 'Ter be honest I'll be glad ter see the back of 'em.'

'Couldn't yer get on wiv 'em?'

Mary laughed. 'Me an' Lucy Parry 'ad a go but we found it was takin' too long. We would 'ave still bin pickin' away next Christmas.'

Chapter Fourteen

Charlie Foden felt apprehensive as he walked along to the Lynton Road diggings with George Parry. 'I'm wonderin' if I've done the right fing,' he said. 'Anyway, it's too late ter turn back now.'

'Not really,' George replied. 'I feel like doin' just that right now.'

'Yer'll be OK when yer get used to it,' Charlie said supportively. 'Yer'll be glad yer stuck it out when yer draw yer pay on Friday.'

George nodded. 'I can stand the shovellin' an' the diggin', an' I'll get used ter those poxy overalls an' rubber boots we 'ave ter wear, but I'm gonna blow apart if that ugly big git Coates winds me up again terday.'

Charlie looked at him with concern. There was a distinct note of desperation in George's voice and he was reminded of what Fred Wilson had told him. They were all going to be working in shuttered trenches and accidents were very prone to happen. If George lost his head in that situation it could spell disaster.

'So yer decided ter give it a try,' Sharkey said as the two men arrived at the site.

'That's what we arranged,' Charlie replied with a calm smile.

George went into the men's changing shed and Sharkey nodded his head towards the hut. 'Ben Coley wants a word wiv yer before yer start,' he said.

Charlie stepped into the confined space of the hut and saw the big man crouched over an unrolled blueprint. 'Yer want ter see me, Mr Coley?'

Ben stretched out his hand. 'Welcome ter Coley Bruvvers. I don't stand on ceremony 'ere. I'm Ben an' I'll call yer Charlie. Yer know what I expect: a good day's work from the men. Watch the slacker an' the trouble-maker, keep a tight rein on 'em all an' don't stand no back-chat. It's one fing I won't abide. Sharkey's word is law ter them, an' so will yours be. Anyway, I've gotta go an' see the main contractors soon so I'll leave you in Sharkey's capable 'ands. Anyfing yer wanna know, just ask 'im an' 'e'll be only too glad to oblige.'

The December day was cold, a raw coldness that seemed to eat into the bones, and the sky above was patched with slate-grey snow clouds as the men filed out of the long tarpaulin shed wearing their ill-fitting, mud-caked overalls and cumbersome wellington boots. Soon they would be glad of them, once they were slithering and slipping in the slimy clay, but for now the diggers' faces were pinched with discomfort and awkwardness.

Sharkey walked up to the trench as the men clambered in. 'There's a bit of a way ter go yet so get to it,' he bawled out.

Charlie stood at his elbow, watching for any reaction, but all he saw were the blank expressions and bowed backs as the working day began. ''Ow far down 'ave they gotta go?' he asked Sharkey after a while.

'They'll strike the brick at about six feet,' he replied. 'Then it's a matter o' clearin' the soil an' clay round the outside o' the tunnel.'

'What about the shutterin'?'

'What about it?'

'When d'yer start proppin' up the sides?'

Sharkey swung his boot at a large pebble which skidded back into the trench. 'Soon as they reach the brick,' he answered as though he thought Charlie should have known.

'I can't see any wood lyin' around.'

'It's bein' delivered this mornin',' Sharkey replied as he turned on his heel and walked back towards the hut.

Charlie had purposely worn his heavy hip-length sea coat that he used on the quayside and he pulled its large collar up around his ears as he strolled along the length of the trench. George and Wally Coates were digging at the far end and as he approached he saw that the big man was wielding the shovel. Huge clods of earth were being thrown on to a rapidly rising mound at the side of the trench and Charlie quickly got the impression that Coates was working in competition with the rest. Occasionally he would look along the line and then put his head down again, grunting under the weight of the clay.

George looked up as Charlie stood over him and nodded briefly before taking another swing with his pickaxe at a section of hard soil.

Coates rammed the shovel into the earth and reached out his hand. ''Ere, give us that poxy pickaxe,' he growled.

George stepped back a pace while the big man set about loosening the hard clog, and after a while Coates stood upright. 'That's ready ter shovel out now,' he declared, 'so get to it.'

'I was usin' the pickaxe, remember,' George said calmly, reassured by Charlie's presence.

'Yer was, yer mean,' Coates replied. 'Get it shifted.'

George did as he was bid, but Coates was not satisfied.

'Come on, or the ovvers'll beat us to it,' he growled.

'So what?' George said scornfully.

Wally Coates threw down the pickaxe at George's feet and grabbed him by the front of his overalls. 'I'm not gonna be seconded by that lot,' he snarled. 'There's not a decent digger amongst 'em.'

Charlie felt a sudden anger at being ignored. 'Oi, you,' he shouted at Coates. 'Take yer 'ands off 'im an' get back ter work. This ain't a competition.'

To his surprise the big man acquiesced and picked up the shovel. George smiled up at Charlie and retrieved the pickaxe. 'Don't worry, we'll be first,' he said to Coates as he set to work once more.

Charlie walked back into the hut to roll a cigarette and saw that Sharkey Lockwood was missing. It figured, he thought. He was being left to supervise without any firm knowledge of how things should be done, and he had half expected a trick like this. Sharkey was undoubtedly hoping that something would go wrong and it was a sure bet that he had sloped over to the Mason's Arms to sit in the warmth, waiting.

'We're down ter brick,' Coates shouted out.

Charlie came hurrying out of the hut and saw the big man freeing his boots from a pile of earth which had become dislodged from one side of the trench. 'Roy, come up 'ere,' he called out.

The carpenter fought his way along the slimy bed of clay and saw the concave wall of the trench. 'I'd better get started,' he said. 'That side looks very weak.'

'We've got no wood yet,' Charlie told him. 'It should be 'ere soon, though. Anyway, yer know where yer gotta start now.'

It was early afternoon when a lorry finally drew up, and

the driver jumped down and went over to Sharkey, who had only just arrived back at the diggings with a smell of whisky on his breath. 'I've got on all we could find,' he said. 'Some of it ain't all that clever.'

'It'll do,' the ganger replied. 'Just back yer lorry over 'ere an' me an' Charlie'll 'elp yer unload it.'

'What's 'e mean, some of it ain't all that clever?' Charlie queried.

'Some of it's old wood,' Sharkey explained. 'It'll make no difference though, as long as it's wedged properly. By the way, yer'd better get inter some overalls. Some o' the wood's oily. There's a pair in that cupboard'll fit yer.'

Charlie slipped into the overalls and was glad he had. The wood was slimy, full of oil and grease, and there were lengths which were badly split. 'We'd better put these worst ones ter one side,' he suggested.

'Nah, put it all tergevver. It'll do,' Sharkey replied. 'We ain't after doin' a pretty job – it's only shutterin', fer Gawd's sake.'

Charlie picked up a plank of wood which had a large wide split running almost from end to end. 'This piece is useless, fer shutterin' or anyfing else,' he insisted.

'Let the carpenter sort it out,' Sharkey said with finality.

Sleet started to fall later in the afternoon and by five o'clock it had turned to snow as the men clambered out of the diggings for the day. Roy Chubb had managed to shore up a long section but he looked concerned as he came up to Charlie. 'I don't like it,' he said anxiously.

'What d'yer mean?' Charlie asked.

Sharkey interrupted them. 'Get yer overalls off,' he growled. 'I wanna lock up.'

While the three men were walking the short distance home George turned to Charlie. 'You certainly shut Wally

151

Coates up,' he said, grinning. 'I never got a bad word out of 'im after that. Mind you, 'e never spoke a word of any sort fer the rest o' the day.'

Charlie gave him a wry smile. 'Don't let it fool yer,' he replied. ''E won't ferget, so be on yer toes.'

Roy remained quiet until they were nearly home. 'A lot o' that wood I used was rotten right frew,' he said then. 'It might be an idea ter see if they can get some new timbers. I really need four by fours.'

'Tell me, Roy, 'ave you ever done any shutterin' work before this job?' Charlie asked.

'Yeah. Most carpenters workin' on buildin' sites get a fair amount o' shutterin' jobs. It's all part an' parcel o' the work. Why d'yer ask?'

Charlie turned to face him outside the house. 'I need ter be sure you know what yer talkin' about when I go an' see Coley termorrer,' he answered. 'If the request's comin' from someone who knows the business 'e'll be less likely ter refuse.'

Roy pulled on his front door string and pushed the door open. 'I tell yer this,' he said. 'While it's snowin' it'll be all right, but if there's a thaw an' the snow turns ter slush then we've got a problem. The walls are gonna be runnin' an' those rotten timbers might not 'old.'

'I'll see what I can do,' Charlie told him. 'In the meantime yer'll just 'ave ter use the best of what yer got.'

Roy smiled cynically. 'That's the trouble,' he said. 'All the poxy wood's the same.'

Will Jackson was in his late thirties, happily married with two young children. His wife Paula worked part time at the bagwash factory in Long Lane, but Will had never had a steady job for as long as he could remember. He earned a living as a handyman, gardener and stall helper, and by doing other jobs which sometimes he preferred not to talk about. Will was willing, and nothing was too small or too large for him to tackle, given the chance.

The Reverend Clarke acquired Will's services on a frequent basis, helping to tend the church gardens, and the market men used him to fetch from their sheds when their stocks were running low. Mrs Black paid him to unblock her guttering and he seemed to be unplugging the drain in Mrs Venners' backyard on a regular basis. In fact on most days of the year Will found himself gainfully employed, until the depression began to bite. Now the market men hardly ever ran short of stock, and Mrs Venners managed to unblock the drain herself with a long stick. Mrs Black had not experienced any more trouble with her guttering, and if she did it would be a question of getting her husband to sort it out. As for the Reverend Clarke, he still got the handyman to do a little gardening, but on a very limited basis.

Will Jackson knew that he could hardly join the dole queues. He had no employment cards to present and no employer to blame for being out of work, so he decided he had to make some adjustments. He chopped firewood and tied it up in little bundles which he sold at front doors, and to supplement the meagre income he ran errands, fetching coke from the gasworks and people's clean washing from the bagwash factory in an old bassinet, and all the while he struggled to get by.

Always on hand with a cheery disposition, Will had endeared himself to local people, in particular those in Cooper Street where he lived himself. They felt mean not giving him the odd jobs as before, but money was very tight and they hoped he would understand.

Once in a while one of the neighbours did offer Will a bit

of work, and on Tuesday morning Mary Chubb was glad to see Will coming into the turning with the morning paper under his arm. 'It's a raw mornin',' she remarked.

Will nodded. ''Ow's the firewood?'

'I'll need two bundles termorrer,' she told him. 'By the way, I got a job needs doin' but I'm a bit wary of askin'.'

'I'm not likely ter bite yer 'ead off,' he replied with a smile, 'so tell me what yer want done.'

'I've got two big tram sheets out in my backyard,' Mary explained. 'They was soakin' in a bathtub but I've managed ter get 'em out. They're 'angin' over me line an' I gotta get rid of 'em – they're makin' the place feel like a bloody shit-tip. Mrs Venners picks the paint off 'em an' she told me she'd be glad of 'em. I'd take 'em to 'er meself but they're too 'eavy while they're still wet. I could wait till they're dry, I s'pose, but I'm scared our Gracie'll pull 'em over on top of 'er.'

'So yer want me ter deliver 'em for yer?'

'If yer'd be so kind.'

Will nodded. 'Give us a tanner an' consider it done,' he told her.

Mary gave him a shilling and Will was happy, though he had a bit of a struggle as the two weighty sheets were still soaked through. Mrs Venners was happy too, having them delivered to her backyard, and she took the opportunity to broach the subject of her old wringer. 'I gotta get rid of it,' she explained. 'It won't wring out. Just look at the rollers – they're all split. As a matter o' fact I've bin waitin' fer the totter ter call round the street but I ain't seen bugger all of 'im.'

Will stroked his chin and suddenly smiled to himself. 'Leave it wiv me,' he told her.

On Tuesday night Will Jackson broke into the premises

which was formerly the bootmender's and was glad to see that he had remembered correctly. There in the backyard was a rusting wringer with its rollers intact. He had first seen it on the evening he delivered some cardboard boxes Martha Staples had asked him to get for her, and that was when he had learned in confidence that she and her husband were moving out of the street within the next few days with only as much as they could carry in large suitcases and boxes, which meant leaving the wringer behind. Mrs Staples had told him it was a shame really. Only a few weeks previous she had got the rollers replaced.

It did not take long for the street handyman to remove the two heavy rollers, but as he stepped out into the street with one under each arm his heart missed a beat. Directly opposite, lit up by the streetlamp, was Ron Sloan the beat bobby, talking to Sammy Strickland.

'No, yer can't go rootin' in trenches fer bloody firewood,' the constable told him sternly.

'But it's not proppin' up anyfing,' Sammy tried to explain.

'What d'yer mean, not proppin' up anyfing?'

'It's just lyin' there amongst the dirt where the wall collapsed.'

'I'd better take a look meself,' Ron Sloan declared.

Just then Will Jackson hurried past, holding his breath. 'Evenin', constable.'

'Evenin', Will. 'Ere, where yer goin' wiv them?'

'I'm takin' 'em 'ome,' the handyman told him.

'Where d'yer get 'em?'

'Mrs Staples left 'em in 'er backyard for me.'

''Ow did yer get in?'

'Over the back wall.'

'That's breakin' an' enterin'.'

155

'I never broke anyfing,' Will said defensively.

Sammy Strickland was grinning widely. 'I was there when Mrs Staples told Will 'e could 'ave the rollers. Honest ter God I was.'

Ron Sloan chewed on his chinstrap for a few moments. 'I'll see yer termorrer about them,' he said. 'Right, Sammy, show me where this wood is.'

The not-to-be shopkeeper led the way to the diggings feeling angry with himself. He should have gone back there later and got the wood. He could have collected enough to keep the house warm right through the winter. Instead, he had to open his big mouth. 'Look, there's loads of it. Someone must 'ave just frew it in there,' he said, pointing into the hole.

'That's not bin thrown in,' the constable told him. 'That's collapsed shutterin', an' I'm tellin' yer now ter keep out o' that trench. It looks ter me like some more's likely ter go at any time.'

Sammy nodded, knowing full well what had really happened. After dark he had made his way to the diggings and with the aid of a length of wood he had prised the main prop loose and levered on the side wood till the wall collapsed. As well as cocking a snook at the insufferable Coleys, it had almost provided enough free fuel for him to open a stall, which he could have built out of more of the wood. Him and his big mouth!

Will Jackson breathed a sigh of relief as he stepped into his house, promising to buy Sammy a pint next time he bumped into him. Now he had to negotiate a price for the renovation of Mrs Venners' old wringer.

The deal was done on Minnie Venners' doorstep half an hour later. 'I'll fix new rollers on it, clean off all the rust an' oil the cogs,' Will promised her. 'Oh, an' I'll also give it a coat o' brown gloss paint.'

'An' 'ow much is that little lot gonna set me back?' Minnie asked him.

'Call it a dollar,' Will told her.

Minnie shook her head. 'I can't afford a dollar.'

'Call it three an' a tanner, then.'

'Nah. I just ain't got it,' Minnie said.

'All right, seein' it's you. 'Alf a crown. 'Ow's that sound?'

'That sounds better,' Minnie told him.

Will smiled. 'Right then. I'll make a start termorrer.'

Constable Ron Sloan walked along Lynton Road listening to the noises from the freight yard. It had been a long spell, which thankfully was due to end at midnight, and all he had had to deal with throughout the shift was a devious character carrying a pair of wooden rollers on the King's highway, and another by the name of Sammy Strickland, who would no doubt stay warm even if hell froze over.

Chapter Fifteen

On the cold December morning that Charlie started work as a ganger, Mary Chubb made her way to Tooley Street and was interviewed for the cleaning job at James Dolan, Dairy Products Ltd.

'I'm Mr Cuthbert, office manager. Do sit down, Mrs . . . er . . .'

'Mrs Chubb,' Mary told him.

'Yes, of course.' Cuthbert took off his glasses and smiled out of a flat pallid face. 'The job entails the cleaning and polishing of all the offices, and the toilets, of which there are three. You will collect the key from the tobacconist opposite. He opens up at seven o'clock in the morning and if you pick the key up as soon as he opens it'll give you two hours to get the work done. By the way, you will also be expected to keep the insides of the windows clean. We'd expect them to be done once a week. The office opens up sharp on nine, but I'm a natural early riser and I often get into work before the morning rush. Obviously I don't mind you finishing off after I've arrived, but in any case I would like you to be finished by nine o'clock latest when we open for trading.'

Mary smiled in acknowledgement. 'I understand.'

Cuthbert pushed his desk chair back and got up. 'You'll

be on trial, of course,' he said. 'We'll review the situation after two weeks. Is that all right with you?'

'Yes, that'll be fine,' Mary answered as she stood up.

Cuthbert seemed to linger at the door with a sickly smile playing around his lips and his eyes glancing over her body in a way that made her shiver. 'I'm sure we can work things out to our mutual satisfaction, Mrs Chubb,' he told her. 'And I want you to know that I'm always here should you need anything. Good luck.'

Mary walked to the tram stop with an image of the manager's pallid face in her mind and she began to wonder. Key jobs in cleaning were hard to come by and most women were glad to hold on to them. What had caused the last incumbent to give up this one? It could have been any of several reasons, but Mary had a feeling she was soon going to discover the right one.

Feelings were running high at the diggings on Wednesday morning, with Sharkey Lockwood bawling out the men as they struggled to clear the timbers from the trench. 'Come on, get 'em all out an' stack 'em by the side,' he shouted. 'No, not like that. Dig the poxy wood out, don't try an' tug it free. Oi, you, don't stand there gawkin'. Go an' fetch two more shovels.'

Charlie had changed into overalls and he grabbed one of the shovels the worker brought up and jumped down into the trench. Sharkey took the other one and together they prised the remaining timbers free.

'If I find out who's responsible fer this I'll crucify 'em,' he growled to Charlie.

'Someone wiv a grudge, that's fer sure,' Charlie replied.

'This delay is gonna put the Coleys in a right poxy mood,' Sharkey said, standing up to take a breather while the team removed the last of the wood.

Charlie glanced at the wall of earth where the shuttering had been and noticed two deep score marks. 'That's where it was levered off,' he pointed out.

Sharkey nodded. 'I knew it was no accident,' he scowled. 'The rest o' the wall's too firm an' dry. Shutterin' just don't fall down fer no reason.'

Roy Chubb was examining the timbers. ''Ere, there's 'alf the plankin' missin',' he remarked.

'Ben Coley'll go mad when I tell 'im we've gotta get some more,' Sharkey groaned.

'Well there's no ovver choice, is there?' Charlie said.

'We'll need a poxy nightwatchman now,' the ganger said as he stabbed the blade of his shovel into the clay bed. 'Right then, Chubb, yer'll 'ave ter do what yer can wiv what's left till see the boss.'

Roy shook his head as he grabbed up a length of timber. 'This is gonna be like tryin' ter make a piece o' furniture out o' matches,' he said with a derisory laugh.

Ben Coley's face grew black when he saw what had happened. 'I'm not gonna buy new bloody timbers, that's fer sure,' he growled. 'Get that yard man to 'ave a good sort-out. Surely there's enough wood lyin' round the yard.'

'What about a nightwatchman?' Sharkey asked him.

'I s'pose we'll 'ave ter take one on now,' Coley replied. 'I'll get on ter the labour exchange soon as I get a minute.'

The digging got under way once more and Roy Chubb worked hard to shore up the sides where Wally Coates had first uncovered the brickwork of the crumbling main sewers. Sharkey had left the site to organise the yard man into finding fresh timbers and Charlie breathed a little easier. 'C'mon, lads, get yer backs into it,' he called out as he walked along above the excavation. 'Level that earth out beside the brickwork an' yer can take a ten-minute breavver.'

The men wondered if they were hearing things. Ten-minute breaks outside the specified times were unheard of, but it was a small treat to look forward to nevertheless and they worked with a will to uncover more of the dilapidated sewer, which had been damaged in no small way by a combination of natural earth movement and the constant vibration from the nearby freight yards.

At eleven thirty, in the absence of both Sharkey and Ben Coley, Charlie called a break, and as the men sat resting on the edge of the workings the novice ganger ambled up to Wally Coates. 'I don't expect ten minutes' pause is gonna put us be'ind in any way,' he remarked. 'In fact it'll give you lads more incentive ter push on even faster. Don't you agree, Wally?'

The big man nodded. 'It's a welcome break,' he answered, an unconvincing note in his voice.

'If the boss man does find out then we know who's told 'im, don't we,' Charlie said with an edge to his words.

Wally Coates understood that he was being warned in no uncertain manner and he bit back on a smart reply. He had been lined up as a future ganger, but now it seemed his chance of promotion was further off than ever with the arrival of this cocky man who acted as though he had always been in the business. He felt his time would come soon, though, and when it did a few scores would be settled.

Sammy Strickland reached the front of the dole queue on Wednesday morning and made his usual dramatic plea for a job. 'I know fings are very tight but I'm desperate,' he said.

'If you'll just move to the next window I'll send someone along to see you,' the clerk told him.

Sammy was suddenly consumed with panic. This was very unusual. It looked like they were actually taking notice of him for once and it could be tricky.

'Ah, Mr Strickland,' the dole officer said as he appeared at the window. 'If you'll come along to the end I'll let you into the office.'

Sammy was shown into a comfortable seat facing the officer who sat upright at his desk. 'Is there anyfing wrong?' he asked fearfully.

'Wrong? Of course not. Why do you ask?'

'Well, as you know, I've bin comin' 'ere on an' off fer years now an' never got a start,' Sammy explained. 'So I said ter meself, Sammy I said, this can't be an offer of a job, it's gotta be somefing else.'

'Well I can assure you, Mr Strickland, there's nothing wrong,' the officer replied. 'Everyone who signs on here has a work record, and when we get employers phoning in with job offers we try to match them with suitable candidates. Now I remember clearly that you once called in with a request for a nightwatchman's job.'

'Twice,' Sammy corrected him.

The official continued regardless. 'I see here too that you are a trained shepherd. Rather a rare occupation in London, wouldn't you say?'

'Yeah, but it's true, strike me dead if it's not,' Sammy said, superstitiously crossing his fingers. 'When I was a young shaver I 'elped ter look after the royal cattle in Regent's Park. They wandered around on the grass an' they were my responsibility. If they 'ad too many little 'uns I 'ad ter cut their nuts off too.'

'Amazing,' the official remarked. 'Now to get back to the present. The nightwatchman's job. It's at the Coley Brothers' workings in Lynton Road. They require a man who is reliable and conscientious, and able to safely guard the workings through the night.'

'That's right up my street,' Sammy replied with a breezy grin. 'The workin's would be safe as 'ouses while I was on the job.'

'Well I'll make you out a green card and you can present it to Mr Coley,' the official said, smiling amicably.

The threat of being landed with a job had initially put the fear into Sammy, but he had bucked up immediately when he learned who it was with. He had about as much chance of getting the job with that rag-taggle outfit as becoming a shepherd once more. 'I'm very much obliged, sir,' Sammy said dutifully. 'I'll go there straight away.'

'Oh, you must,' the officer told him. 'We have more than forty applicants on our books who are unemployed night-watchmen, and if it doesn't work out with you and Mr Coley we can always offer it to someone else.'

Sammy thanked the official profusely and set off with a satisfied grin on his face. Looking for work was becoming a hazardous profession, he realised. One day he was going to come unstuck, and he would have to be very careful in future.

Mary and Lucy were discussing the latest developments over their usual cup of tea and Mary was at pains to tell her best friend that their little scheme might prove to be a bit trickier than they thought.

'Ter be honest 'e seemed a dirty ole git, the way 'e leered at me,' she said. 'You know the sort, all eyes that undress yer. Actually 'e wasn't all that old, but it was 'is face. 'E looked sort o' dead from the neck up.'

Lucy giggled. 'You do 'ave a way o' describin' people.'

Mary smiled back. 'The fing I didn't like was when 'e

told me 'e got in ter work early in the mornin's. I wouldn't wanna be cleanin' there while 'e was standin' over me, lecherous ole git.'

'So what d'yer reckon?' Lucy asked.

'I'll start termorrer as arranged an' see 'ow it goes,' Mary replied. 'Once I get ter know the tobacco shop bloke I might be able ter get the key off 'im in the evenin's. I'll bring Gracie in before I go, if that's all right.'

'Yeah, course, but it means draggin' 'er out o' bed early,' Lucy said.

'She's always awake early anyway.'

'If she's still tired you can put 'er in wiv our Sue.'

'Yeah, course I can.'

'Well that's settled then.'

'Yep.'

'Good luck wiv the letch.'

'Don't worry. I'll end up clonkin' 'im if 'e gets unnecessary.'

Sammy Strickland made his way to Lynton Road and paused near the diggings to catch his breath. This wasn't something a man could just rush into, he thought. Better to amble up and exchange a few pleasantries with the chaps before presenting himself to the management. Besides, him standing there over the hole might jog the loud-mouthed ganger's memory and the rest would be easy. 'Good afternoon, boys,' he said. 'Workin' 'ard, I see.'

The toil was torture for the back, arms and shoulders and generally exhausting, and no one in the trench had enough spare energy to feel pleasantly disposed towards the onlooker.

'I should piss off if I was you,' Danny Albury managed. 'Before Sharkey gets back.'

'As a matter o' fact I've come fer a job,' Sammy announced.

Danny's partner Joe Lambert quickly looked him up and down. 'There's no vacancies fer diggers,' he told him.

'I ain't come ter dig. I'm the new watchman – if I'm lucky, that is,' Sammy answered.

Just then Ben Coley put his head out of the hut. ''Ere, is that the bloke who was 'ere before? The bloke you saw off?'

Sharkey followed Ben's gaze. 'Yeah, that looks like the same geezer. I wonder if 'e's come ter gloat.'

'Go an' fetch 'im over,' Ben growled.

Sharkey strode up to him. 'Oi you, ain't you the silly git I sent packin' last week?'

'Nah, yer made a mistake,' Sammy said pluckily. 'I've come ter see the guv'nor an' I was just passin' the time o' day wiv yer lads.'

'Get in there,' Sharkey scowled, motioning towards the hut and following him inside.

When Sammy saw the look on Ben Coley's face he swallowed hard. This was going to be difficult, he decided. 'Er . . . er, Mr James sent me round,' he stammered.

'An' who might Mr James be?' Ben Coley asked him with a burning stare.

''E's the manager o' the labour exchange in Walworth Road.'

'Yer mean 'e sent you about the watchman's job?'

Sammy smiled bravely. 'Right first time.'

'An' I s'pose you fink you're very smart,' Ben snarled.

'What d'yer mean?'

'Last night someone tore all the shutterin' down in the trench an' now you appear askin' fer the nightwatchman's job. Very convenient.'

''Ang on a minute, yer got me all wrong,' Sammy told him. 'Last night I come past the trench on me way 'ome from the pub an' I saw that all the sides were down. I wasn't ter know if there was someone trapped under there or not, so I did the best fing I could do, I went an' fetched Ron Sloan.'

'Who the bloody 'ell's Ron Sloan?'

''E's the beat bobby. Nice copper, actually, one o' the best.'

'An' what did 'e 'ave ter say?'

''E knew all about it. 'E'd already chased away some kids who were messin' about wiv the wood.'

'So it was kids?'

'Yeah.'

Ben Coley's dark eyes narrowed. 'If I thought you were lyin' ter me I'd—'

'I wouldn't lie ter yer, honest I wouldn't,' Sammy said quickly. 'If yer don't believe me speak ter Ron Sloan. 'E'll be along presently.'

Ben leaned back on his stool and glanced at Sharkey. 'What d'yer reckon?'

Sharkey leaned towards Sammy menacingly. 'If you was employed as our nightwatchman an' those kids came back what would yer do?'

'I gotta be straight wiv yer,' Sammy gulped. 'I'd run an' fetch the copper.'

'An' meanwhile the kids create merry 'ell in the trench.'

'I'd tell 'em ter piss orf first,' Sammy said weakly.

'An' what if they took no notice?'

'Then I'd go after 'em wiv this,' the little man said with spirit, triumphantly pulling a wicked-looking scimitar out from underneath his coat. 'I'd chase 'em off wiv this an' I'd be swingin' it round in the air like this ter frighten the crap out of 'em.'

Ben Coley and Sharkey both staggered backwards as Sammy demonstrated. 'Take it easy, yer dopey git,' Ben shouted, 'or yer'll do us all an injury.'

Sammy carefully replaced the short sword inside his belt and took a deep breath. 'I 'ad to apply fer this job or I'd 'ave lost me dole money,' he explained, 'but ter tell yer the trufe I wouldn't be much good ter yer as a nightwatchman.'

'Why's that?' Ben asked.

'I can't stay awake after ten o'clock at night. Always bin in bed early, ever since I was a kid. I'm frightened o' the dark, yer see. I can't 'elp it, it's just one o' those fings.'

''Ere, give us that bloody form,' Ben growled. He scribbled 'NOT SUITABLE' in capitals in the appropriate box and handed it back. 'Take this back an' tell Mr What's-'is-name ter send someone 'alf sensible next time. Now piss orf.'

Sammy waited until he was out of sight before doing a little jump and clicking his heels together the way Buddy Ebsen did on the films. Peggy wasn't going to believe this, he thought, smiling victoriously.

Chapter Sixteen

The last few days leading up to Christmas were bitterly cold, but the threatening snow held off and the Coley workmen were able to make good progress. They kept their heads down, not wanting to present the management with any reason to put them off, and both Sharkey and Charlie Foden found that they had little to do except prowl the workings and occasionally move the men about to keep the level of digging even. Roy Chubb was grateful for the few new timbers delivered but they were nowhere near enough and he prayed that the cold weather would continue. Any rise in the temperature could well cause movement in the soil around the trench as it softened, and heavy rain would put severe strain on the shuttering.

Charlie suggested getting some steel adjusting clamps to reinforce the shored-up walls but Ben Coley shook his head adamantly. 'They're not all that good an' a lot o' contractors prefer wood,' he replied. 'You just leave us ter decide. If we needed steel clamps we'd 'ave got some.'

Roy Chubb was dismissive of Coley's attitude as he walked home with George and Charlie. 'They used metal clamps on every site I ever worked on,' he said. ''E's just makin' excuses.'

George had been strangely quiet and Charlie guessed that

Wally Coates was giving him a hard time. He had seen the tension on George's face and Wally's disdain for his partner as he patrolled the line. It was a strained coupling but in one sense it brought out the grim determination of the smaller man to pull his weight, despite the difference in their build and strength. Splitting them up would be the easy option, Charlie knew, but then Coates could be expected to antagonise his new partner and the progress of the diggings might well suffer as a consequence.

As the three men walked into the street the evening before Christmas Eve Charlie casually asked George if everything was all right, guessing what he might say.

'I want shot o' that no-good git on the next job,' George blurted out. 'I don't fink I could stand much more of 'im.'

'What's 'e bin saying?' Charlie asked.

'It's what 'e's not bin sayin',' George replied with a scowl. 'I'm gettin' the dumb treatment. All right, I know yer can't split us up on this dig, but I want a new partner on the next one. If I don't I'll end up clobberin' 'im wiv me shovel, so 'elp me I will.'

'Leave it ter me,' Charlie told him. 'If we get the job in Dock'ead that Ben Coley was talkin' about there's gonna be some changes made. It'll be a big job o' work, an' wiv a bit of luck it'll last through the year. There's literally miles of defective sewers in Bermondsey, so Coley was sayin'.'

George was not impressed. He was hoping to be long gone from ditch digging before the next year was out.

Lucy had an amused expression on her face as her husband and Charlie stepped into the house. 'Remember ter say 'ow much yer like Sara's 'air,' she whispered at the door. 'I finally got round ter doin' it this afternoon.'

George played along as he walked into the parlour.

'What've yer bin doin' wiv yerself, Sara? You look different,' he commented.

She patted the tight curls with her fingers. 'Well then, what does it look like?'

'Very nice,' George told her.

'Yes it does,' Charlie echoed. 'It makes yer look younger.'

'Not too young?'

'No, it's just right,' he assured her.

'I 'ad ter get it done,' Sara told them. 'I was gettin' depressed wiv it the way it was.'

Sounds of childish merriment rang out from upstairs and Lucy went into the passageway. 'Now don't get too excited you two or there'll be an accident,' she called out.

George looked irritated as he sat down heavily by the fire. 'I fink Mary's got it easy, palmin' Gracie off on you all the time,' he said.

'She's no trouble,' Lucy responded quickly. 'An' she don't palm the gel off on me all the time. She looks after our Sue quite a lot.'

'All that screamin' an' shoutin',' George said. 'She'll be too excited ter get ter sleep early an' then she'll be in an' out of our bedroom all night.'

Lucy caught Charlie's eye but the lodger averted his gaze quickly, bending down to loosen the laces in his boots.

'It's Christmas, George, the kids are gonna be excited. It's only natural,' she told him.

'They do get more excited when they're tergevver, though,' Sara cut in.

'Well of course they do. So did you when you was their age,' Lucy replied sharply.

George could see an argument brewing and he looked up at Lucy. 'Is tea gonna be long?' he asked. 'I promised

Danny Albury I'd go fer a game o' darts ternight at the Dun Cow.'

'It'll be ten minutes,' Lucy said, going out to check on the meat pie finishing off in the oven.

A loud bump sounded overhead and Sara touched her temple with the tips of her fingers. 'Mary Chubb's gone out ternight, that's why Lucy's bin mindin' Gracie,' she told her brother.

'I see,' George mumbled as he picked up the evening paper.

'Somefing about a job.'

'Oh yeah?'

'There's bin a bit o' whisperin' goin' on between Lucy an' 'er next door,' Sara went on. 'I 'eard 'em talkin' in the scullery about this cleanin' job.'

George felt in no mood to listen to his sister's bitching and he looked up at her with a frown. 'Mary Chubb's got a cleanin' job, that's all it is,' he said testily. 'Nuffing wrong in that.'

'I'm not sayin' there is,' Sara replied quickly. 'Long as Lucy don't get no ideas about me lookin' after Sue while she goes out ter work. I couldn't be up an' down those stairs, not the way I am.'

'Lucy wouldn't dream of leavin' Sue ter do a cleanin' job,' George assured her.

'I would 'ope not,' Sara replied, keen to have the last word on the subject.

Charlie glanced over at George and saw that he had buried his head in the paper. Sara was staring moodily into the fire and suddenly he wanted to shout aloud, bang the table, stamp his feet, anything to break the charged atmosphere. He rolled his sleeves up and walked out to the scullery.

Lucy was bending over the oven and she straightened up quickly to let him pass her. 'There's some 'ot water in the kettle,' she told him.

Charlie filled the small enamel bowl in the sink and reached for the cake of Sunlight soap. 'It's gone a bit quiet in there,' he remarked with a grin.

Lucy smiled back and then quickly took the soap from him. 'Don't use that, it's only fer washin' clothes,' she said. ''Ere, use this.' She picked up a new bar of Lifebuoy from the dresser.

Charlie took the packet, the tips of his fingers closing over hers. 'You really look after me, don't yer?' he smiled.

'An' why not?' Lucy replied, withdrawing her hand slowly. 'You're part o' the family.'

Charlie soaped his hands and forearms. 'I'm a payin' lodger, Lucy, which brings me ter the question o' payment. I've bin givin' it a bit o' thought an' I reckon wiv all the food you supply an' the washin' you do fer me, fifteen shillin's don't seem enough. I'd like yer to accept a pound a week.'

'Well now,' Lucy said with a saucy grin spreading across her face. 'That's a one-off. A lodger who feels 'e's not payin' enough.'

'I'm serious, Lucy. I'd like ter make it up to a quid.'

She picked up a clean cloth and pulled the meat pie from the oven, puffing with the sudden heat in her face, and she ran the back of her hand across her hot forehead. 'If you really insist,' she conceded. 'I'm quite 'appy wiv the arrangement as it stands, ter tell yer the trufe. Your comin' 'ere ter stay 'as bin like a breath o' fresh air.'

'It's also allowed me ter get ter know a very nice lady,' he replied.

'Yes, Sara's very sweet under that front she puts on,' Lucy joked.

Charlie grinned at her sly humour, then his face grew serious. 'I 'ave ter say yer do make me feel like part o' the family. In fact I find meself finkin' about you quite a lot durin' the day, an' sometimes when I'm in my room late at night.'

Lucy stared at the meat pie as she prodded it with a fork, an unreadable expression on her face.

'It's gettin' so I'm finkin' about you all the time,' he said in a low voice.

She turned towards him, her face flushed, her full breasts firm under the flowered apron she wore. 'I fink about you too, Charlie, an' I 'ave ter remind meself I'm a married woman.'

He glanced down at his feet momentarily, then when he raised his eyes again to meet hers the look in them was unmistakable. 'I can't 'elp the way I feel, Lucy,' he said. 'God knows I've tried. I know it's wrong. You're a married woman wiv a good carin' 'usband an' a crackin' little daughter, an' what's more I'm a guest in your 'ome. It makes it all the 'arder. Maybe I should consider movin' somewhere else.'

Lucy shook her head quickly. 'Don't, Charlie, don't even fink that way. I'd be miserable an' lonely if you left us. I've come ter lean on yer, see yer as a tower o' strength, an' it means so much ter me. It can never be more than that, but I can dream. We both can. Let fings stay the way they are. Let's not spoil it all.'

'Yeah, you're right,' he sighed. 'I was stupid to even mention the way I feel.'

'No yer not,' she said with a tremor in her voice. 'I've seen the way you look at me, the way you watch me, an' it's

174

excitin'. I feel a warmth inside, an' I can take comfort from what yer've told me.'

They heard the telltale squeak as George got out of his armchair and Charlie grabbed the towel while Lucy turned to cut the pie into sections.

'I didn't suggest it before, Charlie, 'cos yer said yer was gettin' an early night,' George said as he walked into the scullery, 'but if yer change yer mind yer welcome ter join us at the Dun Cow.'

'That's good of yer, mate, but I really do feel tired,' Charlie told him. 'I don't seem to 'ave your energy.'

The younger man felt pleased with the compliment. He had started at the diggings wondering if he would last the day but sheer cussedness and determination had made him stick it out. Now his hands were calloused and hard, his back was strong and his arms were more muscular than they had ever been. He had learned from the other more experienced diggers to shut off his mind and work at a steady pace and he survived. Now he felt able to hold his own with any of them, including the detestable Wally Coates, which made the situation between them all the more fraught with danger. George knew that one day it might well blow up into a violent confrontation and he suspected that Coates was feeling the same way. He tried to put it from his mind and hoped that the pairings would be changed when the new contract started after Christmas. 'Last day termorrer, then,' he said as he snapped off a small piece of pie crust.

'Yeah. It should be a bit easier,' Charlie replied. 'We've got the best part o' the brickwork uncovered. Who knows, we might get away a bit earlier.'

'I don't want no shop talk in my 'ouse,' Lucy declared with mock severity as she playfully tapped Charlie's arm.

'George, 'ave you washed yer 'ands?'

He winced as she waved him towards the sink. ''Urry up.
I'm dishin' the food up now.'

Light snow started to fall later that evening as George
left the house and Lucy propped the coconut mat up
above the bottom of the scullery door against the draught.
Sara had intended to go out to the fellowship but when
George remarked that it was snowing as he went out she
shivered and moved nearer the fire. Now she was reclining in her armchair, her face red with the heat as she
dozed fitfully.

'What a picture,' Lucy said, grinning at Charlie.

Both knew that Sara was very devious. She could feign
sleep and listen to other people's conversation, and for that
reason they were a little careful what they said.

'Tell me, Charlie, are you intendin' ter stay wiv the
Coleys next year?' Lucy asked as she sat down facing him
at the table.

He shrugged his shoulders. 'I dunno. It all depends 'ow it
goes. If they get the big contract fings should start to
improve, conditions an' paywise. If not there'll be a few
disgruntled diggers on their books.'

''Ow's George copin'?'

''E's doin' fine, considerin'.'

'Wally Coates?'

''E told yer about 'im then?'

'Yeah, 'e did.'

'Unfortunately there's always one on every site,' Charlie
sighed, 'an' ter make matters worse the man's a grass.
Everyone's gotta be very careful what they say an' do
around 'im.'

'Keep yer eye on George, Charlie,' she said with concern.
'I know 'e's not a man ter make trouble but everyone's got a

breakin' point, an' from what 'e told me last night 'e's very near it.'

'Yeah, I know,' Charlie replied quietly. 'Don't worry. Coates won't attempt anyfing while I'm around, but George must keep calm an' refuse ter rise ter the bait. I know it's 'ard but it's the only way.'

'I wish 'e could get somefing else, but there's no work anywhere, it seems.'

'I wouldn't worry yerself too much,' Charlie told her kindly. 'Any work experience is valuable, an' at least George is lookin' very fit. 'E'll find somefing better in the new year, I'm sure.'

Lucy smiled impishly as she reached across the table and touched his arm, at the same time nodding towards the sleeping Sara. 'Well, I fink it's time I made a cup o' tea fer you an' me,' she said rather loudly.

Sara started to move in her chair and suddenly groaned as she straightened her neck. 'Deary me, I must 'ave dropped off,' she said.

Lucy narrowed her eyes. 'I don't s'pose yer fancy a cuppa yet, Sara?'

'I'd love one as a matter o' fact,' she replied. 'I feel parched.'

'I just wondered,' Lucy said, winking at Charlie as she got up from the table.

Next door the Chubbs were already sipping their tea by the fire and Mary was explaining her campaign plan to Roy. 'We decided ter wait till after Christmas,' she told him. 'It'll give me a chance ter get ter know the paper man a bit better. As a matter o' fact I fink 'e'll be OK, but yer never know. Best ter play it careful.' She paused to take another sip.

'Well, go on,' Roy urged her.

'So far the office manager's bin comin' in every mornin' about 'alf eight,' she said, 'just as I'm finishin' off the toilets. The first week after Christmas I'm gonna get in a bit earlier so I can get away before 'e arrives, an' if I don't get any comebacks Lucy's gonna do the followin' week. The ole goat won't be none the wiser.'

'Unless 'e comes in earlier still, just ter catch yer out.'

'Why should 'e do that?'

''E might guess yer doin' the job in the evenin's.'

'Why should 'e?'

'The shop bloke might tell 'im.'

'Nah, we'll prime 'im up. It'll be no skin off 'is nose. Anyway, I'll give it a try, an' if it works out me an' Lucy are gonna look out fer anuvver key job nearby an' we can do the two tergevver. It'll be better if there's two of us, especially round the Tooley Street area when it's dark.'

'Well I 'ope it works out fer yer,' Roy said, yawning wearily.

'It will, as long as yer don't mind lookin' after Gracie fer a couple of hours in the evenin',' Mary reminded him.

'I told yer I don't mind, but what about George?' he asked.

'Lucy seems ter fink 'e won't mind eivver,' she answered. 'The money'll certainly come in 'andy.'

Roy eased back in his chair. 'I just 'ad a thought. S'posin' yer can't get the key any earlier in the mornin's, what then?'

'The paper shop opens up at 'alf six fer the delivery boys,' Mary told him.

'Well, fingers crossed then.'

'I won't be really 'appy though till you get a better job,' she remarked with concern. 'I worry over yer workin' in that trench.'

'There's no need ter worry,' he replied dismissively. 'It'll do till I can get somefink decent. I'm always on the look-out.'

'Yeah, I know you are.'

'At least I'm pretty well left alone doin' the shutterin', an' it's better than usin' a pick an' shovel all day,' he told her.

Mary shook her head sadly. 'I try ter keep cheerful, but it's 'ard, especially when fings seem like they're never gonna improve. I tell meself that fings can't get any worse, an' then they do. I wouldn't mind if we could put a few shillin's by.'

'But you 'ave,' Roy reminded her.

'Yeah, an' then I've 'ad ter dig into it.'

'That's what it was for, an emergency.'

'I know, Roy, but wouldn't it be nice ter get a few bob saved wivout 'avin' ter touch it? We could take a week somewhere like Margate, or Brighton. Gracie could go in the sea paddlin' an' we could walk along the promenade.'

'Fish an' chips at a seafront café,' Roy added.

'Lookin' out of our digs an' watchin' the sun go down over the water,' Mary fantasised.

'Me takin' you in me arms an' tellin' yer 'ow much I love yer,' Roy said in a deep voice for effect. 'We'd go ter bed an' I'd pull yer close . . .'

'Yeah?'

'I'd kiss yer neck an' yer ears, then I'd gently . . .'

'Yeah, go on,' Mary urged him.

'I can't. Gracie's just walked in the room.'

Mary giggled and went to him, her arms encircling his neck as she kissed his cheek. 'Do you feel tired?' she asked.

Roy shook his head. 'Not really.'

'Let's go ter bed anyway,' she said, gently chewing his ear.

Maurice Oakfield folded the tatty, holed blanket and made it into a cushion of sorts to sit on in his sentry box, as he called it. The brazier was glowing nicely and Maurice felt at peace with the world as he set about boiling water for his midnight tea. The beat bobby would be along soon and he usually spent some time sharing the brew and chatting about this and that, which helped pass the long night away.

The deep trench stretched out from the sentry box to the end of the turning and Maurice made his usual patrol along its length at regular intervals, for the Coley nightwatchman was a creature of habit.

Up in the night sky the clouds were gathering and the falling sleet was changing to large white flakes. It was a pity, he thought to himself. Earlier it had seemed as though it would be a good night to study the heavens, which Maurice, being an enthusiastic amateur astronomer, did on a regular basis. He'd seen a glimpse of Orion that evening, with reddish Betelgeuse and bright Rigel in the hunter's leg, but any further stargazing was impossible now with the weather closing in. It mattered not, Maurice decided. If he could somehow shield the nightlight he carried in his pocket he might be able to read another chapter of *Nicholas Nickleby*. Charles Dickens was one of his favourite authors and the pupils he had once taught were left in no doubt as to which of the classics they should concern themselves with.

Maurice leaned back and reminisced while the water was getting hot over the brazier. 'Come out here, Smythe, and bring me your notebook. Be quiet, Gates. And you too, Kelly. This is supposed to be an English lesson and it's degenerating into bedlam.'

Mr Chips would have been proud of him, he thought, or at least his creator James Hilton would have. His pupils had been proud of him too, he knew. Smythe came to visit the school just before he left for France and so did Gates. Kelly too paid a visit and was encouraged to speak to the class about the rigours and dangers of serving their country at sea. They were all long gone now, but he still heard their high-pitched voices in the playground and saw them file past in their uniforms of khaki and navy blue, as if in spectral tribute to their favourite master. The sound and fury of that terrible time was history now, but on his lonely vigils the former teacher often wondered how many of those young lives had been enfolded for ever into the quietness of the night.

The water was coming to the boil and Maurice prepared to make the tea. It was a far cry from the insipid tea and scones in the master's room at college, but it mattered not, he decided. A sentry is a sentry, whether in the palaces of Rome, on the ramparts in Elsinore, or in a backstreet in Bermondsey.

The snow was falling fast now and already the cobbles were disappearing under a carpet of white. Behind the wall that ran along the turning the sounds of freight being assembled split the stillness of the night and Maurice heard the steady footsteps of the approaching beat bobby. Life as a nightwatchman was not all that bad, he reflected. It had its compensations: the occasional genial conversation; time for uninterrupted reverie, stargazing and reading; time to refresh the mind, sharpen the wits and revisit the classics, though his enjoyment of things cerebral was undeniably poorer without the hungry minds of a young class to feed.

The water was boiling but first Maurice consulted his pocketwatch. It was one thirty. The tea would have to wait, he decided. After all, he was a creature of habit, and it was time to patrol.

Chapter Seventeen

Charlie Foden walked the length of the trench at one o'clock on Christmas Eve, looking down at the uncovered Victorian brickwork that reminded him of a long reptile. Here and there the workmen were leaning against the crumbling tunnel waiting for orders and beginning to feel the cold penetrating them, now that the hard slog was over. One or two glanced up at him hopefully as he passed by but Charlie knew the decision to pull them out of the workings was up to Sharkey. He walked back to the hut where the ganger was drinking coffee and pulled up a stool. 'I don't see the sense in keepin' the men in the trench,' he remarked. 'The job's finished an' they'd be better off sittin' in the shed.'

'Ben Coley makes the decisions an' 'e ain't 'ere,' Sharkey answered.

'When's 'e due in?'

'I dunno. I ain't 'is keeper.'

Charlie fixed the ganger with his eyes. 'I'm gonna get the men out,' he said firmly.

'They stay there till Coley gets in,' Sharkey replied with a note of menace in his voice.

Charlie got up slowly and faced him. 'Surely 'e won't mind. There's nuffink for 'em ter do.'

'That's up ter Ben,' Sharkey said.

Charlie was suddenly filled with anger at the ganger's intransigence. 'I'm gonna pull the men out an' I'll take full responsibility,' he declared.

'I wouldn't if I were you,' Sharkey growled, his eyes flaring.

'Yer not gonna try an' stop me, are yer?'

'You're walkin' a thin line, Charlie. Don't overstep it.'

'Let me tell yer somefink,' Charlie said, leaning on the bench top. 'I fink you agree wiv me that those men should be out o' that trench but yer too worried what the Coleys might say. You wouldn't want them ter fink yer've gone weak all of a sudden. I've got you taped, Sharkey. Under that 'ard exterior you're just the same as me.'

'Piss off,' the ganger growled as he turned away.

Charlie stepped out of the hut into the bitter cold air. 'Right, men, out yer get,' he called down the line.

The enthusiastic scramble made him smile to himself and he jerked his thumb towards the shed. 'Yer can't get changed yet 'cos there might be some more tidyin' up ter do, so get in there an' keep the noise down.'

As he walked back to the hut he saw Ben and Frank Coley coming along the street. Both looked pleased with themselves and they nodded to Charlie.

'Are we finished?' Ben asked him.

'All done an' levelled off,' Charlie answered. 'I've pulled the men out o' the trench in case yer wanna check the brickwork. Yer can't do it wiv 'em all loungin' against it.'

Frank nodded. 'I'll take a look, then I wanna talk ter the men,' he announced.

There was an air of expectancy when Frank Coley led the way into the long tarpaulin shed. 'Right, men,' he began.

'I'm pleased ter tell yer that from next Monday we'll be startin' diggin' at River Lane in Dock'ead. It's a main sewer contract an' part o' the 'ole sewage renovation scheme fer Bermondsey. It'll mean regular work fer at least a year an' you lot'll be retained. Anuvver fing. We're gonna operate a bonus scheme. If the target's reached each week there'll be an extra fifteen shillin's in yer pay packet, but if we fall be'ind I'll assume there's some slackin', an' that means two men'll get the push an' be replaced from names on the waitin' list. Fair enough?'

The men nodded, voicing their agreement, and as the noise level rose Frank Coley held up his hand. 'We're pleased wiv the effort you've put in, so we're lettin' yer go early. Yer can get changed now an' collect yer wages in the Mason's Arms before yer push off 'ome. Merry Christmas, men.'

Charlie felt a sadness welling inside him as he looked round at the men's happy faces. The few shillings in their pay packets were hardly recompense enough for the hard, back-breaking week's toil, and the small perk of an early day was little enough appreciation for their efforts, which had enabled the Coleys to secure the lucrative main contract. A bonus in the men's pay this week would have been a far better gesture, but Frank and Ben Coley were shrewd, cold-hearted businessmen who were using the hard times to their advantage. While there were ten men waiting for one vacancy they could afford to operate with a rod of iron. The present workforce had been primed to suit and they worked like zombies, knowing full well that any misdemeanour, however slight, would mean a swift return to the dole queues.

Charlie turned and followed the Coleys out of the shed. 'I'd like a word, Frank,' he said.

Coley gave him an enquiring look. 'In the office,' he replied.

Ben turned to his brother. 'Me an' Sharkey'll start the payin' out. I'll see yer in the pub later.'

Frank led the way into the hut and sat down on the high stool. 'What is it?'

'I understand the new job's gonna start in two separate sections,' Charlie said.

'Yeah, that's right,' Coley replied. 'Ten men per section. The new men we're takin' on 'ave all worked fer us before so there'll be no novices ter worry about. You an' Sharkey'll each 'ave ten workers in yer team an' 'e'll get the new men.'

Charlie nodded. 'The reason I wanted ter see yer is, I've got a problem wiv Wally Coates. Nuffink I can't 'andle, but I want yer ter know that if it comes to it I won't 'ave no 'esitation in doin' what Sharkey does when someone don't shape up.'

'Who's Wally's partner?' Frank asked.

'George Parry.'

Frank Coley smiled. 'Still lookin' out fer that pal o' yours, I see.'

'George Parry's bin no trouble,' Charlie assured him. 'In fact 'e's turned out ter be one o' the best diggers on site, which I 'ave ter say 'as surprised me. Nevertheless 'e's got Wally Coates on 'is back all the time. The two don't get on an' Coates is upset that 'e can't wind Parry up.'

'So what am I s'posed ter do about it?' Frank asked testily.

'Let Sharkey 'ave Coates on 'is team.'

Frank shook his head. ''E stays wiv you. If I take 'im out it'll seem like you're callin' the tune. Anyway, Sharkey's gonna 'ave the new men ter deal wiv, so I don't wanna saddle 'im wiv someone like Coates. I will 'ave a word wiv the man, though.'

Charlie nodded. He knew it was useless to pursue the matter any further, but at least he had tried.

Bill and May Whittle were facing their trials and tribulations with a resolve that drew favourable comments from their neighbours, themselves struggling to get by this Christmas. Mrs Venners, the Whittles' next-door neighbour, was saddened by the fact that May Whittle was not getting any better, and she noted that the blue tinge in her face had become more prominent this last few weeks. May was finding it a great strain caring for her husband and five sons, all still at school, and the onus fell on Bill to take on more of the responsibilities of running the home and family. Things had not been made any easier early in November when Bill was thrown out of work. He took comfort in being around during the day to do more in the home, but he was desperately afraid that he would not be able to pay the bills or provide decent food for his growing boys.

''E's such a nice man too,' Minnie Venners remarked to Elsie Farr's daughter as she held the new baby in her arms.

'So are the boys,' Jenny replied. 'They're very polite, good-natured little kids.'

'It must be a terrible worry fer poor ole Bill,' Minnie said. 'I'd like ter be able ter take 'em a bag o' shoppin' but we're all in the same boat as them really. I s'pose I could spare a cup o' sugar an' maybe a few spoons o' tea, but yer can't go knockin' at their door wiv little bits an' pieces like that, can yer?'

Jenny nodded. 'I've got a tin o' corned beef they could

'ave an' p'raps a few biscuits, but like yer say yer can't give 'em odds an' sods like that. It'd be like we were feedin' sparrers.'

Minnie suddenly brightened up. 'Yeah, that's right,' she said, 'but if we 'ad a whip-round in the street for 'em an' people put in what they could afford in the way o' food it'd mount up.'

'That's a good idea,' Jenny told her. ''Ere, you can start wiv this corned beef.'

'Got a carrier bag, Jenny?'

'Yeah, 'ere's one.'

'Right, let's get started.'

Ada Black donated a cup of sugar and a knob of cheese while her friend Emmie, not wanting to be outdone, gave a tin of condensed milk and a few Oxo cubes as well as a pat of margarine wrapped in grease-proof paper.

Mrs Naylor felt bad about not being able to add to the food collection but she had a new scarf and gloves which her sister had knitted for her. They were a shocking pink and they made her shudder every time she looked at them. 'What was the silly mare finkin' of?' she had ranted. 'I wouldn't be seen dead in these.'

The lurid scarf and gloves went into the hamper along with a pair of lisle stockings and Mrs Naylor felt quite relieved.

The cups of sugar donated gradually mounted up and by the time Mrs Venners reached the end of the street the carrier bag felt quite heavy. Homemade jam, tins of beans, a packet of salt and a few less practical items were accepted with profuse thanks and a tear or two by the ailing May Whittle, but she was at a loss for words when Will Jackson turned up with half a dozen bundles of firewood, and the promise to replace her cracked parlour window free of charge.

At number 16 Annie Belton threw another piece of wood on to the flames and sat back in her armchair to await the arrival of her husband Sid. There was time yet, she thought. He wouldn't dream of coming home until the Dun Cow turned out. Not that it mattered, though. He would be too drunk to assess the situation clearly and when he had fully recovered his senses the shock of what she had to show him would send him straight back to the pub.

'Why don't yer chuck 'im out, Muvver?' Annie's elder son Reggie said, scowling. 'The drunken ole bastard ain't never bin any good ter none of us.'

'Don't you talk like that about yer farvver,' Annie said sharply. 'Whatever 'e is 'e's still yer dad.'

'Reggie's right,' Mick Belton cut in. 'If it wasn't fer you goin' out cleanin' an' doin' that part-time job at the baker's we'd bloody well starve.'

'You two boys 'ave gotta remember that yer farvver wasn't always like 'e is now,' Annie told them. 'Once upon a time 'e was a smart man.'

'Yeah, once upon a time,' Reggie said mockingly. ''E's a bloody disgrace now.'

''E ain't werf a carrot now, Muvver,' Mick growled.

'Now don't you two start sayin' anyfing when 'e gets in,' Annie warned them fearfully. 'I don't want any trouble.'

'Last night 'e was in a bad mood when 'e got 'ome an' you took all the abuse wivout sayin' a word,' Reggie reminded her. 'At one point I thought 'e was gonna give yer a right-'ander. I tell yer now, Muvver, if 'e as much as lifts an 'and ter yer when 'e gets in I'm gonna do 'im good an' proper.'

'Yeah, an' I'll kick six buckets o' shit out of 'im too,' Mick added.

'Don't you worry, 'e wouldn't touch me,' Annie said, smiling at their concern. ''E never 'as done an' I don't s'pose 'e'd start now.'

''E might just, when yer show 'im that,' Mick remarked, nodding towards the brown envelope propped up on the mantelshelf.

'No 'e won't.'

'Just let 'im try, that's all,' Reggie said with venom.

Lucy Parry relaxed in the armchair by the roaring fire and George sat opposite her, cuddling Sue whose eyes were drooping with sleep. Sara sat facing the fire next to Lucy and she hummed in time to the carols coming over the wireless. The table had been moved back to provide more room and Charlie was sitting at George's elbow in an easy chair with the evening paper resting on his lap.

'The pubs'll be packed ternight,' Lucy remarked.

'I'd sooner be by this fire,' George answered as he moved Sue into a more comfortable position.

'I used ter go dancin' on Christmas Eve,' Sara told them.

'Who wiv?' George asked, intrigued.

'Wiv a young man I knew.'

'I didn't know you could dance.'

'Well yer do now.'

'Talkin' of dancin', do you dance, Charlie?' Lucy asked.

'I did frequent the dance 'alls when I was a young buck,' he replied, 'but I wasn't all that clever at it.'

Sara seemed amused by something she had recalled. 'Shall we all 'ave anuvver glass o' port?' she suggested.

'It's yours ter decide,' Lucy reminded her.

Sara smiled. 'I was really surprised when they called

out my number at the fellowship. It was the main prize: a bottle o' port, a bottle o' sherry an' a large Christmas puddin'.'

'Good fer you, Sara,' Lucy said as she held out her glass.

'More port, Charlie?' Sara asked, smiling sweetly at him.

'I'd be delighted to join you,' he replied, assuming a refined accent as he too held out his glass.

Lucy gave him a humorous smile. 'This is very cosy,' she remarked, and as Sara handed her back the replenished glass she raised a toast. 'May the good spirit of Christmas bless us all.'

'I'll drink ter that,' Charlie said.

'Yeah, 'ere's ter peace an' goodwill,' George added.

'I'm tired,' Sue said in a croaky voice.

'I'll take you up in a few minutes,' George told her.

'I wanna be asleep before Farvver Christmas comes,' the child said anxiously.

'You will, my love,' Lucy replied in a cooing voice.

Sara sighed deeply. 'There'll be many round 'ere who won't be gettin' a visit this year,' she remarked.

George got up with Sue holding tightly to his neck. 'I'll get 'er in bed,' he said.

Lucy stood up and planted a kiss on the child's forehead. 'Sleep well, darlin',' she whispered.

The fire was burning low and Lucy refuelled it with a large knob of coal. Outside an icy wind was blowing from the north, hiding the stars from view behind thick dark cloud. At the diggings in nearby Lynton Road Maurice Oakfield struggled with the nightlight in his sentry box and gave up as the wind increased. Constable Ron Sloan walked slowly along Cooper Street, chewing on his chinstrap and looking forward to a cup of hot sweet tea with Maurice, and at number 16 the Belton boys waited with their anxious mother for the homecoming of the prodigal father.

Lucy Parry poked at the large knob of coal that was starting to flare and listened to the wind rattling the windowframes. 'It'll snow in the night, I'm sure,' Sara remarked.

Suddenly a muffled noise sounded outside.

'What was that?' Sara said with a horrified look on her thin face.

'I dunno. It sounded like someone screamin',' Lucy replied.

'Don't open the door,' Sara warned her fearfully.

Lucy ignored her and hurried out to the passage, followed by Charlie. 'Better let me take a look,' he told her.

As he opened the door they saw him, a drunken figure reeling in the middle of the road. Blood was coming from his nose and he was struggling to stay on his feet.

'It's Mr Belton,' Lucy said in a shocked voice.

'An' don't come back, you drunken ole bastard,' a young voice yelled out.

Lucy and Charlie looked along the turning to see Annie Belton being comforted by her two sons.

''E punched our muvver,' Reggie called out.

'So we give 'im what for,' Mick added.

Sid Belton staggered towards the pavement. 'It's all 'er fault,' he slurred. 'We've bin given notice ter quit.'

'Piss off an' don't come back,' Reggie Belton shouted after him.

Charlie ushered Lucy back into the house and closed the front door just as George came down the stairs. 'I saw it from the bedroom,' he said. 'Looks like they've given their ole man a right pastin'.'

Lucy sighed sadly. 'Christmas, the season of goodwill to all men, unless yer name's Sid Belton. Mind you, 'e 'ad it comin' to 'im. C'mon, let's finish off Sara's port.'

Chapter Eighteen

For most of the folk in Cooper Street the festive holiday had seemed little more than a normal weekend, and the prospect of a happy new year seemed especially remote for the Belton family. Annie was beside herself, wondering what she could do, if anything, about the official brown envelope sitting on her mantelshelf. For the Parrys and the Chubbs it had been a restful time. The small presents passed around had been accepted gratefully, everyone knowing just how hard it had been to raise the money for the luxuries.

'Go careful, both of yer,' Lucy called out as her husband and Charlie set off for the diggings in Dockhead through a carpet of fresh snow.

Roy answered their knock and caught them up halfway along the turning. 'It's a nice day ter go back ter work,' he remarked sarcastically.

'Summer's a long way off,' Charlie said, hunching his shoulders against the chill wind.

George remained quiet as they walked out of the street. Never very talkative in the mornings, he was feeling less inclined to say anything on this particular day. Having to work alongside Wally Coates again made him feel on edge, and he worried about what was in store at the new

195

workings. Things couldn't go on the way they had been for much longer.

The men walked quickly past the Lynton Road workings and turned right over the wide bridge that spanned the railway, crossing Southwark Park Road and finally coming out into Dockhead, the riverside district of tall warehouses, wharves and old tenement buildings. Smells of hops, spices and pepper greeted them and the sour tang of river mud rose in their nostrils as the receding tide laid it bare.

Frank and Ben Coley were already at the site talking in earnest with their ganger, and when the three men from Cooper Street arrived Frank beckoned to Charlie. 'I was just puttin' Sharkey in the picture,' he said. 'The soil round this area is very unsettled. The Electricity Board 'ad two cave-ins when they were layin' new power cables last summer an' they said there's water runnin' underground from the Thames. It'll mean we've gotta keep our eye on the shutterin'. I'm orderin' new plankin' fer a start an' I want every inch propped up securely. We're gonna be runnin' on a tight schedule an' there'll be no room fer delays. One o' Sharkey's new men is used ter shutterin' an' 'e's bin primed already. Make sure your man knows the score too. Get your team down the lane ter the ovver marked-out area, Charlie, an' you, Sharkey, you get movin' on this stretch. Right then, let's get ter work.'

River Lane ran parallel with the river, narrow in places but widening out to take traffic along a roughly cobbled surface. The lane afforded access to wharves and warehouses at its widest part, and where it narrowed into little more than an alley it served as a shortcut to the foot of Tower Bridge.

While the excavations were taking place River Lane would be closed at the narrow end and made accessible to light transport only, and Charlie thought about this as he led his men along towards the barrier. Of the two trenches to be dug, his would pose more problems in that it would have to be cut narrow, with less room to manoeuvre, while Sharkey's trench could be wider.

'At least we won't 'ave any lorries an' 'orse an' carts passin' back an' forwards while we're in the trench,' Roy remarked.

Charlie nodded, realising the added dangers passing traffic would pose on that unstable ground. 'Right, lads, let's make a start,' he said, then looked directly at Coates. 'An' remember we're not in a contest ter see if we can outdo Sharkey's team. Remember as well, we'll be workin' in a narrow trench, so be extra careful. Space out safely an' let's make sure we earn that bonus.'

At six thirty that morning Mary Chubb called into the paper shop in Tooley Street to collect the Dolan's key. Jack Crompton opened up at that time every day to sort out the morning newspapers he had started to sell a few months ago. He had a team of paper boys who delivered to the tenement blocks and flats in nearby backstreets and he felt that the extra profit coming in from the deliveries was worth the early rise.

'Mornin', gel,' he said cheerfully as Mary walked into his shop.

'Mornin', Jack. It's a cold 'un.'

'There we are.'

Mary took the key. 'Er, Jack. Would you mind if I collected the key in the evenin' from termorrer?' she asked gingerly.

He shook his head. 'I'd like to, gel, but ole Cuthbert's put the block on it. I did it fer the last cleaner till she got found out, an' Cuthbert told me the key can only be given out in the mornin's now.'

'What difference can it make to 'im?' Mary said. ''E's still gettin' the work done whichever way.'

'I shut at six thirty every night,' Jack explained, 'which means yer wouldn't be able ter give me the key back till the next mornin', an' Cuthbert don't like the idea of 'is cleaner 'avin' the key in 'er possession all night, not after the business in Long Lane.'

'What was that?' Mary asked.

Jack Crompton added several newspapers to a pile and put them all into a wide canvas bag. 'This woman used ter do cleanin' at an office in Long Lane,' he explained. 'One night while she was workin' 'er 'usband an' 'is mate were pickin' the lock of the safe in a director's office. They managed to open it an' they cleaned out over two thousand quid by all accounts. Of course she pleaded ignorant an' said 'er ole man must 'ave copied the key wivout 'er knowledge an' gone in the office after she'd left that evenin'. Trouble was, there was one o' them new-fangled time-locks on the safe an' the police knew exactly when the lock was picked. They stop goin' when the safe's opened, apparently, an' the time put 'er in the office while it was all 'appenin'.'

Mary smiled. 'If I was out ter rob the firm I could get the key copied anyway,' she pointed out.

'An' if there was no sign o' forced entry you'd be the prime suspect,' Jack reminded her. 'They'd wear yer down, gel, till yer confessed.'

'I s'pose yer right,' Mary replied. 'Never mind, it was werf a try.'

He smiled back at her. 'I'm sorry. If it was left ter me I'd let yer 'ave the key in the evenin's, but it's our Kate, yer see.

She frets over the least little fing an' after that ovver business she'd worry 'erself sick if I let yer 'ave it.'

'I understand,' Mary said.

That morning Ernest Cuthbert arrived at twenty minutes past seven. 'Nice holiday, Mrs Chubb?' he enquired.

'Nice, but very quiet.'

'I thought I'd get in early this morning,' he said as he took off his grey mackintosh and trilby. 'I've got a backlog of work to catch up on. Nothing like an early start to get the blood flowing.'

Mary looked at his pallid face and thought it was going to take more than an early start to get his blood flowing. 'I expect you're right,' she replied.

'I stay pretty fit, you know,' he went on. 'Long walks and early to bed, that's the secret.'

Mary was standing with a duster in one hand and a handbrush in the other. 'I'm just about to—'

'Are you concerned about fitness, Mrs Chubb?'

'No, I can't say I am.'

'Actually it was my wife who introduced me to body fitness,' he said. 'She's a naturist, you see. We both practise it whenever we can. Not in this weather, of course – well, not outside. In the home, though. We find it very restful walking around with no clothes on.'

Mary struggled to keep a straight face. 'What about in the summer?'

'We go to a naturist club in Sussex,' Cuthbert revealed.

His eyes strayed over her body and Mary guessed what he was thinking. 'Well, I'd better finish off,' she said quickly.

'Have you ever thought about joining a naturist club?' he asked in a low voice.

'Good God no,' she replied, shocked at the question.

'I could give you the address of my club,' he continued regardless. 'I think that once you've tried it you'll be itching to take your clothes off at every opportunity.'

Mary nodded briefly and hurried out of the office with a hasty excuse. Cuthbert seemed to be working himself up into a lather, she thought, and she would have to be careful not to encourage him in any way. She wondered about the last cleaner. Had he got to her with his views on nudism, or could it have been—

'Mrs Chubb,' he called out. 'Have you a minute to spare?'

When Mary walked back into the office Cuthbert was standing by his desk holding a magazine. 'Here we are,' he said, 'you can have this. It'll let you know a little more about naturism.'

Mary took the magazine and mumbled her thanks as she went back to her chores. Wait till I tell Lucy, she thought to herself.

Maurice Oakfield had been transferred to the new workings now that the main contractors were renovating the brick-work in Lynton Road, and being of an enquiring mind he was keen to inspect the site. Very close to the river, he thought. There'd be night mists sweeping in. Cold too, though the warehouses and wharves would help shield some of the wind. Might be a good place to put the sentry box, here by the gap between the two diggings. Must have a word with Mr Coley.

Satisfied, he made his way to the nearest pub and ordered a ginger ale. 'Thought I might introduce myself,' he said to the landlord. 'I'm the nightwatchman at the River Lane sewer job.'

'Sooner you than me, mate,' the landlord replied. 'I'd be

a bit nervous o' that place at night.'

'Oh, an' why's that?'

'Well, it's steeped in 'istory round 'ere as yer might expect, an' there's always stories.'

'You're perfectly right,' Maurice agreed. 'I'd imagine there are a few ghosts walking the lanes by the river on cold dark nights.'

'An' it doesn't worry yer?'

'Not in the slightest,' Maurice answered positively. 'Ghosts can't harm you.'

'Well I wouldn't like ter be chained to one,' the landlord said with a shudder.

Maurice finished his ginger ale and felt that his finances might stretch to another. 'Fill my glass, stout yeoman,' he said cheerfully.

An elderly man walked into the quiet pub just as Maurice took up his refill and the landlord nodded to him. 'Mornin', Godfrey,' he said.

'Mornin', Stan,' the old man replied. 'I see they're startin' work at the River Lane.'

'Yeah, an' this is the nightwatchman who'll be on the site.'

The old man chuckled. 'Glad it ain't me. Sittin' there all night wouldn't be my cup o' tea. 'Ow d'yer pass the time sittin' in that little box?'

Maurice smiled indulgently. 'I read by the light of my nightlight if the wind's not too high, and then there are the stars to watch, if the sky remains clear. I take a regular stroll – well, it's a patrol really, just to make sure all's well – brew tea over the brazier and think about all sorts of things. It's quite pleasant on a friendly night, but I have to be honest, it's not much fun when the rain beats down and dowses the fire, or when an icy wind chills the bones.'

'What about the spirits?' the old man asked.

'Spirits? You mean ghosts?'

'Spirits, ghosts, phantoms, they're all the same,' Godfrey replied. 'River Lane was notorious at one time fer sightin's. People used ter come in this pub quakin', 's that right, Stan?'

'That was before my time,' the landlord answered. 'People don't use River Lane so much now.'

'Well I can assure yer that the spirits used ter congregate there at certain times,' the old man went on. 'Used ter be a prison back in the Elizabethan days. It was mainly used fer naval prisoners: deserters, mutineers an' the like. The ole chronicles tell of the prisoners bein' starved an' tortured an' then they chucked the bodies in the river on the tide. Yeah, they say there's a regular assembly o' spirits at certain times down in River Lane. I don't mean ter frighten yer, but a man who's gonna do nightwatchin' in a place like that should be forewarned.'

'And for that I thank you, sir,' Maurice said elegantly. 'I will be on my guard.'

'Course, yer probably won't see anyfing unusual,' Godfrey continued, 'but it's the ground bein' disturbed. That won't 'elp. Last time they were workin' in River Lane the trench caved in an' two blokes were buried under a load o' soil. They were lucky ter be dug out alive.'

Maurice bade them goodbye and went home to his lodgings to get some sleep before his night on duty, and Godfrey Thomas took his place at the counter. 'I 'ope I didn't put the fear up 'im,' he said, chuckling.

'I don't fink yer did,' the landlord replied. ''E seemed a very cool customer.'

''E won't be if those ghosts start roamin',' the old man replied sagely.

★ ★ ★

At the diggings the work was getting under way and Roy Chubb was busy preparing the best of the planking for the job of propping up the slimy, muddy soil. 'We're gonna 'ave trouble if we're not careful,' he remarked to Charlie when the ganger walked up to him. 'The soil's like paste, even wiv this bitter weavver. If it gets milder it's gonna turn inter sludge an' then we'll know all about it.'

'I'm gonna go an' see Coley about that new plankin' 'e's promised us,' Charlie told him. 'I don't want Sharkey claimin' it all fer 'is team.'

Just then there was a shout from the far end of the trench and Charlie could see Danny Albury holding up his hand.

'It's Joe Lambert,' Danny said as Charlie came running. 'There's somefing wrong wiv 'im.'

The trench was barely knee-deep along its length and the distressed digger was hauled out and lowered on to the mounting pile of rubble to recover.

'It's me chest,' Joe rasped. 'I was shovellin' out an' suddenly this pain caught me. Christ! I thought I was gonna die fer a minute.'

Charlie saw how the colour had drained from the man's face. 'Get in the shed,' he told him, 'an' if the pain don't ease up soon yer'll 'ave ter go ter the 'ospital.'

'What d'yer fink it is?' Danny asked.

''E could 'ave pulled a muscle in 'is chest,' Charlie suggested. ''As 'e bin coughin'?'

'Yeah, 'e 'as,' Danny replied. 'It was a sort o' raspin' cough.'

Charlie walked over to the shed. 'Can yer manage ter get 'ome under yer own steam, Joe?' he asked.

'Yeah, course I can,' the digger answered.

'Right then, on yer way,' Charlie urged him. 'That could

be a dose o' pleurisy yer got.'

'I've never bin troubled wiv anyfing like that before,' Joe declared.

'Anyway, yer better get it seen to right away,' Charlie said as he helped him on to his feet.

Sharkey's trench was not free of incident either on that first morning, and it served to upset the local clergy.

'Well I'll be stuffed,' Ginger Gordon exclaimed as he uncovered a skull, complete with teeth. 'I wonder 'ow old this is?'

'Donkey's years I expect,' his partner replied. 'We could be diggin' over a plague pit fer all we know. They say there was a burial place round 'ere in the dark ages.'

'Better leave it fer Sharkey ter see,' Ginger said as he placed it carefully on the edge of the trench.

Lofty Williams the carpenter picked up a piece of splintered planking and hammered it into the soil before setting the skull on top of it. 'There we are,' he said. 'That 'ead's gonna jump down an' bite the ear off anyone who starts slackin'.'

The men set to work once more and the skull was forgotten until Father O'Riorden chanced to walk through River Lane. 'Holy Mary Mother of God!' he roared. 'Is this how you heathens treat our departed? Get it down, this instant!'

'Where can we put it?' Ginger asked him.

'Certainly not back in the soil,' the reverend father raved. 'Get something to put it in, and should you dig up any more human remains put them with it. They will all have been desecrated by you gaggle of pagans and need the holy blessing of reconsecration. Holy Mother! What next?'

'Silly ole git,' Ginger muttered as the irate father stormed off to seek out the Coleys. 'It was only a bit of a skeleton.'

'I can see you ain't a Catholic,' Lofty Williams remarked.

'No I ain't,' Ginger replied. 'Are you?'

Lofty shook his head slowly. 'We ain't 'eard the last o' this, not by a long chalk,' he said.

'Why's that?' Ginger enquired.

'That was Father O'Riorden,' Lofty told him. ''E's all fire an' brimstone.'

'Yeah, maybe, but 'e's still a silly ole git,' Ginger said as he buried his pickaxe in the cold damp soil.

Chapter Nineteen

Though they drank toasts to the new year, 1936 began in much the same vein for the Coley diggers. The bitter weather continued and the unremitting, thankless toil seemed never-ending. As soon as the trenches were cleared for the bricklayers to start work a new section was to be opened up in nearby Morgan Street, and then once the contractors had finished renovating the two lengths of uncovered sewer in River Lane and the surface was made good the remaining fifty-yard length linking the two was to be dug up, on which score the two gangers were summoned to the hut.

'I want you two ter take a look at this blueprint,' Frank Coley said as he unrolled the large drawing on the bench-top. 'The reason we left a gap between the two trenches was the unstable soil conditions, marked 'ere in colour. One long trench would 'ave weakened the ground ter such an extent that there might well 'ave bin a large cave-in. Now you know we've got an arrangement wiv the contractors fer them ter fill in an' resurface the road wiv their mechanical equipment, but in this case there's a problem usin' the 'eavy machinery in the lane due ter the unstable soil conditions, so they've asked us ter do the job by 'and an' then they'll use a light road roller ter make good the surface.'

Coley paused to look at each of the gangers in turn. 'Now as yer know, the idea was ter tackle the Morgan Street section next week while they were brickin' up 'ere, but there's bin a change o' plan. We reckon the freezin' weavver'll prevent any natural slippage, so we're gonna press on wiv excavatin' the middle section which'll leave the 'ole lot ready fer the brickies next week. We've got the okay from the contractors, providin' the full length o' the trench is made safe fer their men ter work in. That means it's gotta be securely shuttered.'

'We'll need more new timbers,' Charlie told him. 'Some o' that wood we've got now is rotten.'

Coley nodded impatiently. 'We'll take care o' that. Now, I'm givin' you two o' Sharkey's team, Charlie, an' I want yer ter get that middle section dug out by the weekend. All right, I know it's cuttin' it fine, but that's the way it goes.' He turned to the other ganger. 'Sharkey, you can start right away in Morgan Street, then next week we can go back ter normal, everyone workin' in Morgan Street till we're called back ter fill in 'ere. It'll save us a few days by doin' it this way an' it'll make sure we don't 'ave the contractors breavvin' down our necks.'

Charlie was not happy about it. 'It's a tall order, expectin' the section ter be finished in two days, even wiv two extra men.'

'Tell 'em we're uppin' the bonus to a quid,' Coley replied. 'That'll fire 'em up.'

'What about Joe Lambert's replacement?' Charlie asked.

'You'll 'ave 'im termorrer for sure,' Coley answered.

Lucy and Mary were holding a council of war. 'Trouble is, I can't get the key till 'alf six,' Mary explained, 'an' the lecherous ole goat's bin comin' in at 'alf eight every mornin'.'

'It makes yer wonder about the last woman,' Lucy remarked. 'Did 'e try it on wiv 'er?'

Mary shrugged her shoulders. 'I wouldn't be at all surprised. When I saw Ada Black down the market she asked me 'ow I was gettin' on there, but I didn't say anyfing to 'er about 'im. Yer know what a mouth an' trousers she can be at times.'

Lucy sipped her tea. 'P'raps it'll be better if you carry on fer a bit longer,' she suggested, 'unless the ole goat gets too much to 'andle. Once 'e accepts yer won't play 'is little game 'e might start comin' in later.'

'I was 'opin' we could work the oracle there,' Mary said, pulling a face. 'I explained it ter Roy an' 'e could see what I was gettin' at. I told 'im that if we could manage ter do the job in the evenin's we could look out fer anuvver key job nearby an' do the two tergevver, as it wouldn't be very nice goin' up ter the likes o' Tooley Street at night an' those dingy offices'd be creepy places fer a woman ter work on 'er own. Anyway 'e said 'e wouldn't mind lookin' after Gracie while I was gone.'

Lucy stared into the fire for a few moments. 'I gotta tell yer, my George ain't too keen on me goin' out cleanin' at night. Course I 'ad ter go an' put me foot in it by sayin' it was really about 'im not bein' too keen on 'avin' ter look after Sue. 'E got really shirty. 'E's so irritable lately. 'E tends ter jump at the least little fing.'

'An' 'ow are you an' Charlie?' Mary asked with a sly grin.

'I don't know what yer mean,' Lucy answered with a wide smile.

Mary leaned back in her chair. 'I fink yer do,' she said.

Lucy waved her hand dismissively. ''Ere, let's 'ave anuvver look at that magazine the bloke gave yer.'

Mary giggled as she took it out from behind the cushion and reopened it. 'Just take a look at that feller,' she said. 'Don't it make yer feel sick?'

Lucy pulled a face. 'If I looked like 'er I'd wanna 'ide in a dark cupboard, not strip off fer everyone ter gawk at me.'

Mary flicked through the pages. 'Oh my good Gawd,' she exclaimed. 'She must be all o' twenty stone.'

Lucy pulled a face as she looked over her friend's shoulder. 'Get 'im,' she remarked. 'Look at the way 'e's eyein' that woman up. Dirty ole git.'

Mary quickly flipped through the remaining pages and then shut the magazine. 'D'yer fink we're bein' 'orrible?' she said. 'Those people must take it seriously.'

'Point is, does that Cuthbert bloke take it seriously, or is 'e just an ole letch?'

'I dunno,' Mary said, reaching for the teapot. 'By the way 'e talks about it I s'pose 'e does, but it's the way 'e 'as o' lookin' at me what makes me fink different.'

Lucy handed over her empty cup. 'Like I said, maybe you should carry on by yerself fer the time bein'.'

'Coward,' Mary teased with a disarming smile.

Stan Mapson, the landlord of the Bell, was chatting to two of his regulars at the counter while Godfrey Thomas sat nearby listening to the conversation.

'Yeah, they've started diggin' up Morgan Street,' the landlord was saying. 'As a matter o' fact we 'ad the night-watchman in 'ere earlier. Strange bloke if you ask me. 'E seemed educated an' pretty well turned out. Not yer usual nightwatchman. What d'you reckon, Godfrey?'

''E's right,' the old man replied. 'I 'ad 'im down as a teacher ter tell yer the trufe.'

'Yer could be right,' Stan Mapson remarked. 'There's

fousands o' people out o' collar who are glad ter do anyfing fer a few bob.'

The taller of the two customers nodded. 'I wouldn't be fussy. I ain't worked fer over two years now.'

'I'm the same as Bill,' his friend agreed. 'I'd even do a bit o' that diggin' if it wasn't fer me back. It wouldn't stand up to it, more's the pity.'

Bill Walters grinned. 'That's your excuse an' yer stickin' to it, ain't yer, Tom?'

Godfrey sidled up to the counter. 'Me an' Stan was sayin' 'ow the place 'as got a bad name, but the bloke didn't seem at all put out. I don't fink 'e believed us.'

'What d'yer mean, got a bad name?' Tom Smith asked.

'You know, ghosts walkin' in the dead o' night an' that,' the old man explained.

'Is that a fact?' Bill queried.

'Yeah. Apparently there used ter be a prison in Morgan Street many years ago,' Godfrey recounted, 'an' when one o' the poor bastards in there snuffed it they'd chuck 'im in the river, by all accounts, an' let 'im drift out ter sea on the tide. The gaol was fer navy men, yer see, an' I s'pose they saw it as a fittin' end.'

'Well from what yer've told me I wouldn't care ter be a nightwatchman on that job,' Bill remarked.

'Me neivver,' Tom added.

Stan Mapson grinned broadly. 'I can just imagine the watchman's reaction if one of us crept in the turnin' in the dead o' night clangin' a few stones in a tin can or somefink. I bet 'e'd be off like a shot.'

'Especially if we was wrapped up in an ole sheet an' groanin' like we was in agony,' Bill said, grinning back.

Time hung heavy for Bill Walters and Tom Smith, and in the warm public bar of the Bell there was time enough to dwell on the subject of ghosts walking abroad and unhappy spirits wailing. The time eventually came for serious negotiation with Stan Mapson about the possibility of adding another pint to their slates, and with a favourable result the two men were able to spend another hour by the fire.

''Ere, I was just finkin',' Tom said after a lengthy silence. 'What if me an' you 'ad a bit of a laugh wiv that nightwatchman?'

Bill chuckled. 'Yeah, I'm game fer it.'

'We could find somefink ter put over us an' we could clang somefink ter make it more scary,' Tom went on.

The two sat plotting eagerly until even they felt that it was time to let someone else share the fire, and as they walked to the public library in the bitter weather the plot was fully hatched.

Charlie got his replacement on Thursday morning, a morose, heavily built man in his forties who introduced himself as Norman Gill and had little else to say, but he gave the impression of being able to cope with the heavy toil. In addition there were the two men from Sharkey's team who seemed happy at the change as they joined the rest in the shed, and Charlie took the opportunity to spell out the situation before they started work.

'We've only got terday an' termorrer ter get this job finished, so we've gotta put our backs into it,' he began. 'Now, the ovver two sections are well shuttered an' I don't want 'em weakened when we link up wiv 'em. Wally, I'm changin' yer partner. You can take Norman 'ere as George's replacement. I don't fink Joe Lambert'll be comin' back just yet awhile so George, you can work alongside Danny Albury.'

'Why not give the new man ter Danny?' Wally complained. 'Why should I 'ave 'im?'

'Because I said so,' Charlie growled at him, then he looked over at Norman Gill. 'It's all right. Wally likes a moan now an' then, it's nuffink personal. That right, Wally?'

The giant mumbled something under his breath and the two from Sharkey's team glanced quickly at each other and smiled.

'That's put 'im in 'is place,' Fergus remarked.

'Too bloody true,' Derek replied.

The work started with a vengeance. Wally Coates was eager to show the new man that he was under the wing of the best digger on site, while Fergus and Derek worked well as a pair, and with George happy to be away from the contemptible Coates it was a determined team that bent their backs, all eager to finish on time and earn the added bonus.

During the early part of the day Roy Chubb helped out on a shovel and Charlie joined him, preferring it to standing around on a bitterly cold morning. Wally Coates swung his pickaxe into the soil and levered it loose, matched all the way by Norman Gill, who quickly removed it with little effort.

'They make a good pair,' Charlie remarked to Roy as they took a breather.

'Yeah. I'm glad yer gave George a change. It was gettin' 'im down, an' ter be honest I thought once or twice 'e was gonna steam inter the big ugly git.'

Fergus took a quick breather and motioned towards Charlie. 'That's somefing yer never see wiv Sharkey.'

'Nah, yer right,' Derek replied. 'That miserable sod wouldn't dream o' gettin' 'is 'ands soiled.'

Charlie concentrated his efforts on getting the diggers to work as hard as they could with encouraging comments and a ten-minute spell of rest for each pair in turn, and by the end of the morning they had made excellent progress.

Wally Coates and Norman Gill sat together on a pile of rubble while they took their break. 'No disrespect ter you, but I don't go a lot on the ganger piss-ballin' me about,' Wally remarked. 'Yer get used ter workin' wiv one bloke.'

'Yeah, I know what yer mean,' Norman replied. 'Soon as we started work I could tell that yer bin in this game a long while. You can always tell.'

Wally raised a rare smile. 'I bin doin' it since I was in me twenties,' he said. ''Alf o' these blokes are chancers. There's not one decent digger amongst the lot of 'em.'

Norman was not disposed to a prolonged chat and he took out his pipe and tapped it against the heel of his boot. 'Yeah, I can see that,' he agreed.

Wally fell silent and Norman puffed thankfully away on his briar until their break time was up, and late that afternoon after working flat out the duo scraped the last of the soil away to expose the roof of the sewer tunnel. The rest of the team were not far behind, and when Roy Chubb began to fix the shuttering Charlie breathed a huge sigh of relief. His method was paying off, he decided. The ten-minute break during the day had been a wise move and finishing the job by tomorrow evening now looked a lot more likely.

That evening Maurice arrived on the dot to begin his nightly vigil, and soon he had his brazier burning merrily with pieces of scrap wood and old newspapers he had brought with him. A few coals and then some dampened coke provided by the company finally had the brazier white hot and Maurice leaned back against the wooden sentry box to enjoy the warmth on a bitterly cold night.

As the midnight hour drew near something clandestine was happening at the far end of River Lane. 'Does this look all right?' Bill asked.

'Yeah, course it does,' Tom replied as he glanced at the tattered old bedsheet his friend was wearing round his flour-whitened face and over his shoulders. 'What about me?'

'It's enough ter frighten King Kong,' Bill told him as he put a handful of pebbles into a tin can. 'Right, let's go.'

Maurice was getting ready to make his periodical patrol when he heard a clanking noise and then the sound of wailing. He got up quickly and moved to his right, peering down the curve of the lane to see two shrouded figures coming along in his direction. Maurice swiftly crossed to the left of the narrow turning and hurried into a darkened warehouse doorway. His heart was beating fast and he fought to control his breathing. This was idiotic, he reasoned. Ghosts and spirits could not physically harm anyone, other than causing a heart attack by their very presence.

The two ghostly figures drew nearer and Maurice could clearly see them now and hear the metallic clanking which seemed to be coming from under their shrouds. He held his breath as they passed the doorway, making for the sentry box, and suddenly his face creased into a smile. The ghost to the rear was not floating, it was walking on two feet. The shroud had slipped slightly and a pair of dirty hobnailed boots were clearly visible.

Years ago at Whiteacres High School the sixth-form pupils had staged a ghostly gathering in the nearby woods, but their intention to march on the school dormitories to frighten the younger pupils had been scotched by the form masters, who joined in the spirit of the prank and turned the tables. Now would be a good time to re-enact the counter-plot, he thought.

Bill and Tom had reached the sentry box, their wailing echoing in the narrow lane, and they exchanged grins when they realised that the nightwatchman had run away.

'What's that?' Bill exclaimed as he heard the scraping sound.

'I dunno,' Tom said in a low voice.

The scuffing noise got louder and suddenly a wailing filled the lane.

'I'm gettin' out of 'ere,' Bill said fearfully.

'Wait fer me,' Tom screamed out, struggling desperately to disentangle himself from his tattered shroud.

From his concealed position next to a pile of earth Maurice watched the men dash terror-stricken from the lane, and when he re-emerged with a smile on his face he saw the two tin cans lying by the sentry box. 'Oh well, time for my patrol,' he thought to himself with some satisfaction as he picked them up.

Throughout the rest of the night the ex-teacher kept the fire banked up, did his patrols and managed a chapter of *The Hound of the Baskervilles* with the aid of his nightlight, untroubled by spirits, or jokers with brains addled by them.

Chapter Twenty

On Friday morning the diggers at the River Lane site set to work with a determination to finish on time and earn their bonus, and Roy Chubb passed down the fifty-yard stretch fixing pieces of planking against the sides as the soil was removed from around the tunnel. Wally Coates and his new partner were soon out in front of the others as the clay level was reached, and Charlie felt a little concerned as he went over to where Roy was cutting a length of timber on a makeshift saw bench. 'Make sure yer keep an eye on those two,' he warned. 'The way they're goin' they could cause us a problem if those walls ain't propped securely. They're two feet lower than the rest an' we can't ignore it. I should tell 'em to ease up a bit an' let the ovvers catch up, but it wouldn't go down well wiv Coates. The bloody idiot sees this as some sort o' contest an' it seems the new bloke's just as bad.'

Roy picked up a long length of thick timber and laid it down on the saw bench. 'Look at this,' he said. 'It's split in places an' there's a load o' wood rot in it. I thought we was gettin' some decent timbers.'

'I'll 'ave annuver word wiv the Coleys soon as one or ovver of 'em shows up,' Charlie told him. 'They seem to 'ave left us ter get on wiv it.'

217

'Anyway, it looks like we'll be done on time,' Roy remarked.

'I'll get Coates an' Gill out fer a ten-minute spell while you get some shutterin' up at their end,' Charlie said, sticking his hands deep into the pockets of his reefer jacket. He walked down the line beside the ever-growing piles of earth and clay.

Coates clambered out of the workings with a satisfied smile on his face and Gill followed him. 'Look at that lot,' he sneered. 'Didn't I tell yer?' He cupped his hand to his mouth. 'Oi, Parry, what's the 'old-up?'

George swung the pickaxe hard and levered it against the stubborn clay before looking up. 'Get knotted,' he growled back.

Danny Albury gripped him by the forearm. 'Don't take any notice. 'E's tryin' ter wind you up.'

George took another forceful swing with the pickaxe. 'I'm not standin' fer much more of it, whatever yer say, Danny,' he replied. 'I took enough piss-takin' while me an' 'im were workin' tergevver an' I ain't takin' it now.'

Danny threw a loosened lump of clay out of the trench and stabbed the blade of his shovel back into the protesting soil. 'Look, George, I'm a bit older than you an' I've got a lot more experience in this game,' he said as he pressed his foot down on the edge of the shovel. 'I've come across the likes o' Wally Coates on plenty o' diggin' sites in the past. They're bad news. Coates ain't got no family ter consider, an' as long as 'e earns enough ter pay 'is keep at the workin' men's 'ostel an' keep 'imself in beer 'e don't give a toss. 'E gets pleasure out o' goadin' 'is workmates an' you 'appen ter be the one 'e's pickin' on at the moment. What you 'ave ter remember is, yer kept up wiv 'im when you two were teamed up an' it annoyed 'im, so now yer workin' wiv someone who's 'alf sensible you should ignore 'im.'

George took up his pickaxe once more. 'I'm more than 'appy ter be workin' wiv yer, Danny,' he remarked. 'We make a good team.'

'Oi, Parry! Is that pickaxe too 'eavy for yer?' Coates shouted.

'It's not too 'eavy ter bury in that fick 'ead o' yours,' George responded.

'Feelin' tough are we?' Coates growled as he scrambled on to his feet.

'Oi, you! Where the 'ell d'yer fink you're goin'?' Charlie yelled as he hurried along the line. 'Yer break's over. Get back in that trench the pair o' yer.'

'Don't worry, it'll keep,' Coates called out to George as he went back to work.

Maurice Oakfield was feeling pleased with himself as he strolled along to the Bell with a small brown paper parcel under his arm. 'Mornin', mine host,' he said breezily as he walked into the public bar.

'Well if it's not Mr Nightwatchman,' Stan Mapson replied. ''Ow's it goin'?'

'Mustn't complain,' Maurice declared, wanting to delay the presentation till the right moment.

The landlord had not been privy to the outcome of the River Lane spookery. In fact he had seen nothing of the two perpetrators, who were feeling too embarrassed to go into the Bell that morning. 'What'll it be?' he asked.

'A ginger wine if you will,' Maurice told him, looking round the bar as he placed his parcel down on the counter.

Just then the elderly Godfrey Thomas walked in, and when he saw Maurice he looked surprised. 'I didn't expect you ter be 'ere,' he remarked.

'Oh, and why's that?' Maurice enquired.

'I understand there was some strange goin's-on in River Lane last night.'

'You could say that,' the watchman said, smiling. 'It seems the place is prone to visitations. As a matter of fact I did see an apparition last night, but I'd be interested to learn how you know about it.'

Godfrey looked uncomfortable. 'Someone was tellin' me this mornin'. They said the local bobby was s'posed to 'ave seen somefing ghostly movin' about in the lane.'

'I could have done with that policeman's assistance last night,' Maurice told him. 'It was nearing midnight when I banked up the fire, and suddenly I heard a wailing and a clanging noise. I looked down the length of the trench and then I saw it.'

'Saw what?' the publican asked impatiently.

'It's hard to describe,' Maurice continued, milking the moment. 'I could see two white shrouded figures coming towards me. Strangely enough, they appeared to be floating along. It was really frightening, I can tell you.'

'So what did yer do, run?' Godfrey asked.

'Good Lord no,' Maurice said positively. 'That would have been the wrong thing to do. No, in these sorts of situations it's better to stay put, and let the spirits, ghosts, or whatever see that you mean them no harm. And let's face it, how do you harm a ghost?'

'What, then?' the publican asked.

'Well, I slipped into a doorway and watched points,' Maurice went on. 'The two spirits came right past me, and do you know what?'

'No.'

'I noticed that the ghost bringing up the rear was actually wearing boots. Remarkable, don't you think?'

'Yer mean they wasn't ghosts?' Godfrey queried.

'Just a couple of young men out for a bit of fun,' Maurice answered.

'Ah, but they could 'ave bin real ghosts wearin' ordinary boots just ter fool yer,' the landlord ventured.

Maurice unwrapped the parcel and held up the tin cans. 'These are what they used for the clanking noise,' he replied. 'Anyway, I thought it was time to do a spot of wailing myself, and when I did the two young men ran from the lane like bats out of hell.'

Stan Mapson shook his head slowly. 'I wanna shake yer 'and, pal,' he laughed. 'I really admire the way you 'andled that situation. What yer drinkin'? It's on the 'ouse.'

'In that case I'll have a whisky in the ginger wine, if you please,' Maurice told him.

Lucy sat by the fire helping Sue to identify the large coloured letters of the alphabet, and as the child responded in a sing-song voice Sara nodded to her sister-in-law. 'She's pretty good.'

'She'll be startin' school this year, won't yer, luv?' Lucy said encouragingly.

'Time certainly flies,' Sara sighed. 'Last year seemed ter flash by, which suited most. It was a year we'd all want ter put be'ind us.'

Lucy had long since fathomed her sister-in-law. She was never very talkative except when it suited her, and it was obvious now she would be seeking a favour. 'You asked me if I'd tong yer 'air terday. D'yer still want me ter do it?'

'I'd be very much obliged,' Sara replied.

Lucy smiled to herself. Of course it was Friday, and Sara usually made an effort to smarten herself up at weekends. Once her hair was done she would be certain to put on her fawn dress with the dark brown figured pattern over the bodice, and she'd use a light powder and a spot of rouge on her pale cheeks as a finishing touch before taking her place by the fire around the time the men got home. It had become painfully obvious that she was out to create a favourable impression on Charlie Foden, who had become rather embarrassed by it all, as had George, judging by his uncharitable comments the previous evening. 'The silly woman should get out more, an' I don't mean ter the church. She's involved wiv that fellowship business enough as it is, an' I'm sure it's not doin' 'er any good.'

'I know it's embarrassin' fer Charlie the way she carries on at times,' Lucy replied, 'but yer gotta feel a bit sorry for 'er. Let's face it, we know she fancies 'im but she just doesn't know 'ow ter go about it.'

'Maybe it's just as well,' George remarked. 'She'd only get a kick-back. If there's anyone 'ere Charlie fancies it certainly ain't our Sara.'

'An' what's that s'posed ter mean?'

'Come off it,' George replied curtly. 'Anyone can see 'e fancies you. I've seen the way 'e stares at yer at certain times.'

'Now you're bein' stupid,' Lucy told him. 'I've never bin aware of 'im starin' at me.'

'Yer would say that, wouldn't yer?' George retorted. ''E only wants 'alf a chance an' 'e'd be there.'

'That's ridiculous,' Lucy said with feeling. 'I'd never give 'im the chance an' I'm sure 'e'd never take advantage. As a matter o' fact I see 'im as a member o' the family now, an' if you was honest yer'd say the same.'

George leaned back in his chair. 'Don't get me wrong. I like Charlie, but I wouldn't trust 'im where you was concerned.'

Lucy realised that she should be angered by her husband's comments but instead a raw, fearful excitement had risen in her belly. Charlie did fancy her, and he had said as much. Only the agreement they had made kept him from making his move, but his eyes mirrored his true feelings and she relished his every glance.

Sue had had enough of the alphabet book and she slid down from her mother's lap. 'Can I go an' play wiv Gracie?' she asked.

'No you can't,' Lucy told her. 'I've gotta start the tea soon, and in any case you're due fer an early night ternight, madam.'

'Will you 'ave time fer me 'air?' Sara asked.

Lucy nodded and stood up. 'Move away from that fire an' I'll get the tongs,' she said.

Sue climbed into Sara's vacant chair and watched while her mother set to work, testing the heated tongs by closing them over a piece of brown paper before using them on Sara's lank mousy hair.

'I've bin finkin',' Sara said after a while. 'Would Charlie feel it was a cheek if I invited 'im ter the fellowship next week?'

Lucy had to stifle a giggle. 'No, I shouldn't fink so,' she answered, 'but ter be honest, Sara, I don't fink 'e'd care ter go. It's not somefink Charlie'd take to.'

'I dunno,' Sara said. 'There's a few men at the meetin', widowers who go there fer company.'

'Charlie's not a widower,' Lucy said quickly, 'an' when 'e needs company 'e goes up the pub wiv George or down ter the dockers' club.'

'Do yer fink 'e likes me?' Sara asked.

Lucy was surprised at her sudden frankness. 'I'm sure 'e does, but I don't fink 'e's lookin' fer female company.'

''Ow d'yer know?'

'Charlie's lived on 'is own fer some time now,' Lucy pointed out, 'an' like most men 'is age, 'e's come to accept that way o' life.'

''E's not that old,' Sara replied quickly. ''E's only in 'is mid-forties. A man's s'posed ter be in 'is prime at that age, an' besides, 'e don't come over ter me as bein' celibate by choice. I fink 'e just needs a little bit of encouragement an' 'e'd be all fired up.'

'Sara!' Lucy said in mock horror. 'You've got a naughty mind.'

Sara smiled smugly. 'I'm just makin' an observation.'

The younger woman knew that her sister-in-law had hit on the truth, but Charlie had no designs on Sara, and unless she was made to realise the fact there was only heartbreak and unhappiness ahead for her. 'There we are, all done,' she said. 'Just let me give it a quick brush out, then I'll 'ave ter be gettin' on wiv the tea.'

Danny Albury had decided to stay for a drink at the Mason's Arms but the other three diggers from Cooper Street walked home together through the gathering mist, and Charlie felt pleased with the way the day had gone. There had been no hold-ups, and even Frank Coley had raised a brief smile when he arrived to find that the work had been completed on time. George Parry was happy to be free at last from working alongside Wally Coates, but Roy Chubb was very thoughtful. He had been hard put to it shoring up the sides of the trench to his own satisfaction and he had fussed over the job, aware that he was working with sub-standard wood. Next week there would have to be some answers forthcoming, he told himself. Why hadn't Coley done what he promised and supplied new timbers?

Any cave-in would doubtless be blamed on shoddy workmanship rather than the lack of proper materials, and it was vital that the request for more new timbers should be recorded and witnessed.

Across the small street Ada Black stood at her front door with her coat collar turned up against the chill as she chatted to her best friend Emmie. 'It's gonna be a foggy night by the look of it,' she remarked.

'Yeah, it looks like it,' Emmie replied. 'I've told our Bert ter bank the fire up. I won't be movin' far from it ternight, that's fer sure.'

Elsie Farr came hurrying into the turning with the evening paper. 'It's gonna be a foggy one ternight,' she said as she came up to her neighbours.

'I was just sayin' that to Emmie,' Ada replied. 'By the way, 'ow's the baby?'

''E's gettin' on lovely,' Elsie told her. 'Our Jenny's lookin' forward ter gettin' back ter work an' I'm lookin' forward ter mindin' 'im.'

'It's a shame she's gotta leave the little mite while 'e's so young,' Ada remarked, 'but if needs be.'

'She's got no option,' Elsie said a little sharply. ''Er Len's out o' work again.'

''Ere, 'ave you 'eard 'ow Sammy Strickland got on terday?' Emmie asked.

Elsie shook her head. 'Peggy told me this mornin' 'e was goin' after a job at the tannery, but I ain't seen anyfing of 'er since.'

'I dunno where 'e finds 'em,' Emmie went on. ''E's always goin' after jobs but 'e never ever gets one. I wish 'e'd let our Bert know. I'm gettin' sick an' tired of 'im under me feet all day. 'E's gettin' sick of it all too. It ain't right fer a man ter be mopin' about all day.'

'Well, I'd better get indoors an' start on the tea,' Ada said reluctantly, not wanting to leave the other women chatting together in case she missed any juicy gossip.

'Yeah, I gotta go,' Elsie told them.

Emmie Goodwright nodded. 'I s'pose I'd better be off too,' she said.

None of them was feeling confident enough to take the initiative, and it wasn't until Bert Goodwright came to the door to see what was keeping Emmie that the conference broke up.

Chapter Twenty-One

During the early hours of Saturday morning strong winds came in from the west, sweeping away the thick night fog and ushering in dark, threatening clouds. By dawn heavy rain was falling, with thunder rumbling in the distance, and as the Cooper Street womenfolk got ready to make their usual trip to the markets the storm broke in earnest. Torrential rain lashed the little houses, bouncing up from the pavements and cobblestones and running down into the gurgling drains.

At number 8 George and Charlie were both enjoying a lie-in and Sara had woken up with one of her headaches, which prompted her to go right back to sleep again, but downstairs it was less quiet. Sue and Gracie knelt together on a chair in the scullery watching the deluge and listening to the clanging sound as the rain pounded the tin bath hanging on the yard wall. Behind the children Lucy and Mary sat at the scullery table listening to their chattering.

'I get in that every Friday. Well, I fink it's when it's Friday,' Sue was going on.

'D'you remember when we got all wet?' Gracie said, giggling.

'Yeah, when we was barfin' our dollies.'

'My dolly's not very well, but I'm gonna give 'er some

227

medicine an' she'll soon get better.'

'Shall I get my dolly's clothes?' Sue suggested.

Her little friend did not seem too enthusiastic and they continued to stare out at the driving rain. 'My daddy said we gotta 'ave rain ter make fings grow,' Sue remarked, 'but I don't like it. We can't go out ter play when it's rainin'.'

'We could play 'ospitals,' Gracie said, scratching her head. 'You could be the nurse an' I'll be the mummy.'

It was Sue's turn to show reluctance. 'Nah, we always play 'ospitals. I wanna go out an' play in the yard.'

'Well you can't,' Lucy told her. 'It's absolutely fallin' down.'

'When will it stop?'

''Ow do I know?'

'This afternoon,' Mary cut in. 'So you two 'ad better find somefing ter do in the meantime.'

'Let's go upstairs an' look at my books,' Sue said.

Gracie slid off the chair and went over to Mary. 'Mum, can I go an' get my books?'

'I'll get 'em later,' Mary said quickly. 'Now you two go upstairs an' play.'

'An' don't make too much noise. Aunt Sara's in bed. She's not very well,' Lucy added, with a meaningful glance at Mary.

The children wandered from the scullery and Lucy got up to put the kettle on. 'I've bin givin' it some thought about that job,' she said. 'Yer've got used ter the money now, an' I'm a bit worried in case it don't work out. You'd be the loser.'

'Well I say let's take a chance,' Mary answered. 'This last two days ole Cuthbert 'asn't bin comin' in early an' I've bin finishin' at twenty ter nine. Me wages are left on the desk in 'is office so I can't see 'ow it won't work out. If 'e does 'appen ter come in early an' catch yer out just say I'm not well an' I asked yer ter fill in fer me. Anyway, you could do wiv the few bob same as me.'

Lucy shook her head. 'Nah, it was an 'are-brained scheme, Mary. I'll wait till there's anuvver key job goin' up that way an' then we can do like we said, knock the two jobs out tergevver.'

'Are yer sure? Really sure, I mean?' Mary asked, looking a little concerned.

'Yeah, really.'

Her friend watched while Lucy took the boiling kettle off the gas and filled the china teapot. 'Is George all right?' she asked.

'Sort of.'

'That's no answer.'

Lucy shrugged her shoulders. 'Ter be honest, Mary, 'e's not bin the same man since 'e lost 'is job, but who is? Takin' that job diggin' wasn't a very good idea as far as I'm concerned, but you know George. 'Is pride wouldn't let 'im stand in those dole queues day after day, week after week. All right, I know fousands an' fousands are compelled ter do it, but it was drivin' 'im scatty. D'you know, 'e's 'ardly bin near me since 'e was put off, an' on the rare occasion it does 'appen it's over before I get goin'. I'm sure it's become a sort o' duty to 'im. Keep 'er 'appy an' let's get some sleep. Trouble is, it don't keep me 'appy, an' I can't seem ter talk to 'im about it wivout endin' up 'avin' a barney.'

'I'd say 'e's takin' a chance, especially wiv anuvver man in the 'ouse,' Mary replied. 'What if yer turned ter Charlie fer comfort?'

Lucy shook her head quickly. 'I couldn't, much as I like the feller.'

'Yeah, yer say that, but yer never know,' Mary persisted. 'It could just be that one time when yer desperate fer arms round yer an' some lovin', an' George ain't there, but Charlie is. It 'appens.'

Lucy smiled indulgently. As well as being very observant Mary was never one to pull her punches, but her comments were welcome. She had always been there for Lucy and a good shoulder to cry on. Nothing Mary could say in good faith would be taken the wrong way and the woman knew it. 'Ter be honest it wouldn't be that 'ard fer it to 'appen,' she said quietly. 'Charlie ain't all that good at 'idin' 'is feelin's. I see the way 'e looks at me sometimes an' there's no mistakin' it. If I give 'im 'alf a chance 'e wouldn't need promptin'.'

'George is a fool,' Mary replied plainly. 'You an' 'im 'ave gotta get fings worked out or I can see big problems.'

Lucy sighed as she poured the tea. 'I'm all mixed up,' she confessed. 'On the one 'and I want George ter notice I'm there an' make the occasional fuss o' me, an' on the ovver 'and I don't want 'im near me. Does that make any sense ter you?'

Mary smiled. 'Yeah it does. I reckon you fancy Charlie strong enough ter go wiv 'im an' yer want a strong enough excuse. Bein' neglected as a red-blooded woman gives yer that excuse.'

Lucy added sugar to the tea and passed a cup over to Mary. 'I tell yer somefink,' she said. 'Yesterday there was a letter came fer George, from the Royal Naval Reserve. They wanna know if 'e'd like to apply fer a promotion course ter petty officer. 'E was really bucked up about it an' although 'e wouldn't commit 'imself I'm certain 'e's gonna say yes. It'll mean 'im goin' ter Portsmouth fer a few weekends, an' when 'e showed me the letter I was pleased fer 'im, but I was also excited about the weekends at Portsmouth. D'yer know what I'm sayin'?'

'It's not 'ard ter guess,' Mary answered. 'It'd leave you an' Charlie alone in the 'ouse. Apart from Sara, of course, but she goes out occasionally.'

'Exactly, an' I was filled wiv guilt,' Lucy told her. 'Then I got ter finkin'. S'posin' I do let Charlie know I'm available an' me an' 'im do get at it while George is away, what 'arm could it do? It wouldn't be somefink wiv weddin' bells at the end of it. It'd just be a mad fling. 'E's bin on 'is own fer a long while an' I'm not exactly the contented wife. It could be very good fer both of us, an' it might even 'elp ter get me an' George closer.'

'A lot o' people say that a bit on the side sometimes 'elps ter strengthen a marriage,' Mary replied, 'an' I s'pose they always will, but it could be disastrous if fings don't go the way you want 'em to. What you an' Charlie get up to while George is away is your business, but as far as I can see, it 'as ter be spelt out from the start. No commitment from eivver of yer. Make sure it don't get serious ter the extent that yer can't stay away from each ovver. In ovver words enjoy it fer what it is an' carry on bein' the dutiful wife, if you can bear it.'

Lucy sipped her tea, thinking about what Mary had just said. She was right, of course. Her marriage was solid, built on firm ground, and George was a good husband, despite his recent lack of feeling. She would rather die than let it flounder. 'I can bear it,' she said, smiling.

Since he had been confronted by Ron Sloan the beat bobby, Will Jackson had been very careful to keep his distance, for the time being at least. On that wet Saturday morning, however, he was keen to enlist the services of Sammy

Strickland in a moving job, and he hadn't given the police-man a second thought. 'I can't do it on me own, Sammy, an' I thought you might like the chance to earn a few coppers,' he said as the two stood inside his front door.

'I'm always ready to earn a few shekels, but I gotta be careful o' me back,' Sammy told him. 'That's why I gotta know just what this job entails. I can't go movin' pianners, wringers an' those sort o' fings.'

'I dunno exactly what Mrs Bright wants movin' but she ain't got no pianner, that's fer sure.'

''Ow d'yer know if yer don't know exactly what she 'as got?'

''Cos she said it'll all go on a barrer.'

'Well, that's different.'

'So yer gonna give us some 'elp?'

'If the price is right.'

'I'm chargin' 'er firty bob an' 'alf a crown fer the barrer, 'cos that's what Tommy Dougan's chargin' me fer the loan of it,' Will explained. 'So we earn fifteen bob each.'

'Sounds reasonable.'

'I should say it is. It's only from Lynton Road ter Macklin Street, which is just round the corner. We could be done in 'alf an hour.'

'Right then, I'm wiv yer.'

'I told the ole gel I'd be there by twelve,' Will said, 'so if we get our skates on we could start now an' be finished by then.'

'Where's the barrer?' Sammy asked.

'In Tommy Dougan's yard.'

'Where's that?'

'In Briar Street.'

'That's a bit of a way.'

'It ain't far.'

'Far enough.'

'Now look, are you wiv me or not?' Will asked crossly.

'Yeah, course I am.'

'Well you go an' fetch the barrer while I go round ter see Mrs Bright.'

'Why me?'

''Cos it'll save time,' Will told him. 'By the time you get the barrer round ter Lynton Road I'll 'ave all 'er bits an' pieces packed away in the cardboard boxes she's scrounged. Now when yer go inter Briar Street from the Old Kent Road yer'll see a red door on yer right about 'alfway down the turnin'. That's Dougan's yard door. Just go in an' give 'im the 'alf-crown an' tell 'im Will Jackson sent yer. All right?'

'An' where's the woman live?'

'Number 10 Dennis 'Ouse, Lynton Road.'

'Right, I'm on me way.'

The street's handyman hurried through the driving rain to the block of council buildings in Lynton Road and when he arrived out of breath Mrs Bright had a cup of tea waiting. 'Them stairs 'ave bin killin' me,' she groaned. 'I really can't tell yer 'ow 'appy I am ter be movin' back into a little 'ouse. These buildin's are murder. You 'ardly ever see yer neighbour, an' when yer do yer can't stand gassin' at the front door like yer can when yer live in an 'ouse.'

''Ow come yer moved 'ere in the first place?' Will asked.

'I 'ad no option,' the woman told him. 'The place I lived in was condemned an' they stuck me in 'ere. Only fer a few months till we find an 'ouse, they said. Two bloody years ago that was an' I've kicked up merry 'ell ever since. Anyway, they finally found me a place in Macklin Street, fank Gawd.'

'Right then,' Will said, rubbing his hands together. 'Is this the lot?'

'Yeah, except the big stuff.'

'Big stuff? What big stuff?'

'The joanner an' me wringer.'

'Bloody 'ell, I didn't know yer wanted fings like that moved,' Will said, looking round the room. 'When I came round last time yer said it'll all go on a barrer.'

'Well it will, though not all at once, I grant yer.'

'I wish yer'd said that at the time,' Will puffed. 'Movin' pianners an' wringers is dearer than ordinary stuff.'

'Well I 'ave ter say I thought you was very reasonable wiv yer prices,' Mrs Bright said sweetly.

'It'll cost an extra 'alf a quid.'

'That's all right.'

'Anyway, where's the pianner?'

'Wiv the wringer.'

'An' where's the wringer?'

'In the pram sheds down the alley,' Mrs Bright told him. 'The council let me use two o' the sheds ter store 'em or I'd never 'ave agreed ter come 'ere in the first place.'

Will Jackson set about packing up Mrs Bright's bits and pieces and soon Sammy Strickland arrived looking hot and bothered. 'That bloody barrer's 'ard work empty,' he growled. 'The wheels need a good oilin'.'

Will knew that if he moved the small cartons first he would never get Sammy to come back for the wringer and piano. 'There's bin a change o' plan,' he said hesitantly.

Sammy looked suspicious. 'Go on then, tell me.'

Before he had finished explaining the helper shook his head sternly. 'Sorry, Will, but I just can't do it, not wiv my back.'

'It's only round the corner.'

'I don't care if it's next door.'

'I'll do the 'umpin'.'

'I don't care what yer do, I ain't movin' no pianner.'

Will scratched his head in consternation. 'Not fer an extra 'alf a quid?'

Sammy stroked his chin. 'All right then, but if me back goes I'll 'ave ter leave it ter you.'

The two manhandled the piano from the pram shed and pushed it along the alley to the pavement, and then Will tipped the barrow on its end. 'We'll lean the joanner backwards an' then we'll be able ter pull the barrer back upright wiv it on it,' he said.

The job was not as hard as Sammy had feared and they were soon pushing the laden barrow along Lynton Road. Getting the instrument off the barrow in Macklin Street was no harder, but it took some considerable negotiation getting it into the house, and some tutting from Mrs Bright before they settled it in the parlour.

'Look at the bloody scratches on it,' she complained.

'They was there before we started,' Will replied irritably.

'Yer better bring the cardboard boxes next,' she told them. 'I got all me fings in the boxes an' I can't make a cuppa till they get 'ere.'

The barrow wheel was squeaking badly by the time the two removers got back to Lynton Road, and after they had finished loading up the six heavy cartons Sammy sat down on the kerbside to catch his breath. 'That wheel's gonna seize up before we've finished, mark my words,' he said.

Will was eager to get the job done and he leaned his weight against the shafts. 'C'mon, Sammy, give us a push,' he urged him.

As they reached Mrs Bright's house the wheel locked solid. 'There we are, what did I tell yer?' Sammy said self-righteously.

Will Jackson was not going to be beaten. 'We'll let it cool

a bit while we fetch the wringer,' he decided.

'Yer mean we're gonna push it round 'ere?' Sammy said, a look of horror on his pale face.

'Yeah, unless you got any better ideas.'

Mrs Bright came out of the house frowning. 'Yer fergot ter pack me teapot,' she told Will.

'Oh, no. I remember now. I left it on the drainin' board.'

'Fetch it wiv the wringer,' she ordered, 'an' don't ferget ter make sure yer shut the front door tight when yer leave.'

The two were feeling decidedly jaded by the time they had manoeuvred the rusting wringer into the street, and to make matters worse the rain had started to fall once more.

''Ang on while I go an' get that poxy teapot,' Will said testily.

Sammy leaned his weight against the wringer and it started to move. Encouraged, he continued, knowing that Will would not be far behind.

''Ello, 'ello,' a voice called out over his shoulder and Sammy turned quickly to see PC Ron Sloan strolling up to him. 'An' where yer goin' wiv that?'

'I'm 'elpin' me mate,' Sammy told him.

'It wouldn't be the 'andyman by any chance, would it?' the constable queried.

Sammy nodded. 'Yeah, Will Jackson.'

Just then the man himself came out of the block entrance carrying the teapot. 'Oh my Gawd!' he exclaimed.

'Stoppin' fer a tea break are we, Will?'

'Nah, we're movin' someone.'

Ron Sloan sucked on his chinstrap and rocked back and forth on his heels as he glared at the handyman. 'Why is it every time I bump inter you lately there seems ter be a wringer involved? You ain't collectin' 'em, are yer?'

'Nah, we're movin' it fer Mrs Bright,' Sammy cut in. 'It's

236

only round the corner so we thought we'd push it instead o' puttin' it on the barrer.'

'So yer've got a barrer?'

'Yeah, but the wheel's seized up, so we left it in Macklin Street where Mrs Bright's movin' to.'

Ron Sloan looked suspicious. 'Let's take a look at this barrer,' he said.

The two removers accompanied him into Macklin Street and stood watching while the policeman walked round the old contraption. 'It ses "Tom Dougan" on the side,' he observed. 'Did you get this from Tom Dougan's yard?'

Sammy nodded. 'Yeah, I did.'

'Well I'm afraid yer in trouble, me ole beauty,' the policeman said in a grave voice. 'Tom Dougan called in at the station ter say someone walked off wiv 'is barrer.'

'That can't be right,' Will interjected. 'I sent Sammy ter get the bloody fing. I'd already made the arrangement wiv Tom Dougan ter loan it an' 'e said it'd be 'alf a crown. Sammy paid 'im, didn't yer, Sammy?'

The older man looked decidedly uncomfortable. 'Well, as a matter o' fact I didn't actually give 'im the money.'

'Why not?' the constable asked.

'Well it was like this, yer see. When I got there Tom Dougan was walkin' off up the street wiv this ovver geezer an' I saw the barrer standin' in the kerb outside the shed, so I thought 'e'd put it out ready. I decided ter take it an' pay when I fetched it back.'

'Well you'd better bring that wringer round an' then get the barrer back ter Dougan quick as yer can,' the policeman told them. 'I'll be poppin' in ter see Tom later an' it better be back there, or else.'

The two men struggled to push the wringer into Macklin Street and finally set it in place in Mrs Bright's backyard.

'I 'ope you intended ter pay Dougan when yer took the barrer back,' Will remarked. 'Or was yer 'opin' you could put it back wivout bein' noticed an' pocket the 'alf-crown?'

'As if I'd pull a dirty trick like that,' Sammy said with a haughty look.

'I'm sorry I can't offer yer a cuppa,' Mrs Bright said as she settled her bill. 'I ain't got the cups unpacked yet.'

Sammy leaned on the barrow. 'The wheel don't seem so stiff now,' he remarked. 'I fink I can manage it OK.'

'You won't 'ave to,' Will told him sternly. 'I'm comin' wiv yer, just in case.'

Chapter Twenty-Two

It had rained on and off all through the weekend and on Monday morning a drizzle was still falling. The temperature had risen too and Roy Chubb was feeling worried as he joined his two workmates and walked briskly out of Cooper Street. 'I'd like ter take a look at the River Lane site,' he said. 'It's on our way ter Morgan Street.'

Charlie nodded. 'You ain't worried about that shorin', are yer?' he asked. 'It looked a good safe job ter me.'

'Yeah, but there's been so much rain over the weekend it could 'ave moved,' Roy told him.

George Parry had his hands tucked into his coat pockets and his head held down against the rain, and as usual he had little to say. His thoughts were elsewhere on that particular morning and he had already made up his mind to go for the naval promotion course. Had he been able to predict what lay ahead that day he would have turned back home there and then.

The three made the slight detour into River Lane and Roy breathed a sigh of relief when he looked down into the muddy trench. 'Well, nuffing seems to 'ave shifted since we left it on Friday evening,' he remarked.

'I told yer it was a good job,' Charlie said, grinning. 'Just make sure yer do a good job in Morgan Street.'

'We ain't sure what the subsoil's like there,' Roy pointed out. 'Morgan Street runs directly down ter the river, remember.'

'What's the drill?' George asked unexpectedly. 'Is it gonna be one long trench, or are we doin' it in sections like River Lane?'

'One long section,' Charlie told him.

'Well I 'ope I can get the opposite end ter Wally Coates an' that ovver idiot 'e's workin' wiv,' George growled.

'I'll see what I can do,' Charlie answered.

Although Danny Albury lived in Cooper Street he always made his own way to work, and was already changed by the time his partner arrived. 'Stay clear o' Coates terday, George,' he warned. ''E's in a right ole mood.'

'That's nuffink unusual,' George replied.

'I ain't seen 'im as bad as this, though,' Danny said. 'Apparently somebody's nicked 'is pocket watch.'

'When was this?'

'Last night in the lodgin' 'ouse by all accounts.'

'I didn't know 'e could tell the time,' George remarked with a grin.

Wally Coates was sitting by the entrance of the shed, and as George and Danny walked past him he gave them both a hard stare.

'Shall I ask if anyone's got the time?' George joked.

Danny pulled a face. 'I wouldn't if I were you,' he muttered.

The two changed quickly into their overalls and wellington boots, and George pulled a woollen scarf out of his overall pocket and wrapped it loosely round his neck.

'Knit that yerself did yer?' Coates asked in a mocking voice.

'Yeah, plain an' purl,' George answered. 'You should try

it sometime. It's quite easy really, but then again maybe not. Yer need at least 'alf a brain ter learn knittin'.'

Wally Coates stood up quickly, his eyes wide with anger, huge hands rolled into tight fists. 'You've bin askin' fer this, Parry,' he snarled as he moved forward.

George quickly put the long heavy table between him and the hulking digger. 'Calm down, Coates, or yer'll be doin' the walk,' he told him.

'If I do the walk it'll be over your mangled body,' the big man growled.

Roy Chubb was standing outside the shed talking to the other carpenter Lofty Williams when Coates made his lunge at George and he jumped back in, grabbing the giant round his middle. 'All right, calm down,' he said quickly.

Coates threw him off as though he were a child, and using the bench seat to clamber up on to the table he dived at the smaller man with a roar.

''Old tight, Sharkey's comin',' someone called out.

George had gone down under the bully's weight and he fought like a wildcat to get free, suddenly feeling as if his head would burst as Coates grabbed him round the throat.

'What's goin' on 'ere?' Sharkey called out as he hurried into the long shed.

'Get 'im off George!' Danny implored the ganger.

Sharkey stood back a pace and turned away from the flailing arms and legs. 'Right, you lot, let's get ter work,' he shouted. 'C'mon, not in a minute, now!'

'Stop 'im, fer Gawd's sake!' Danny screamed at Sharkey.

Alerted by Roy, Charlie rushed into the shed, leaned over and grabbed Coates's hair at the back, yanking hard until the man's head was arched enough for him to slip his other hand round his neck. 'It's over, big man, now let's get ter work,' he said breathlessly as he shoved Coates away, then he turned his attention to George. 'You too, George, there's work ter do, at the opposite end.'

Sharkey stood next to Charlie, watching the men take their digging tools from a pile and set to work on the trench. 'Coates ain't no slouch,' he remarked. 'I wonder why 'e didn't turn on you?'

'I should 'ave thought that was obvious,' Charlie replied. ''E gets a few privileges as the Coleys' eyes an' ears, but even they wouldn't sanction 'im settin' about a ganger an' 'e knows it.'

'Yeah, I can see that, but that's if the man's finkin' straight, which I don't fink 'e was.'

'Well let's assume 'e prefers ter mark time,' Charlie said with a sardonic smile. ''E'll get round ter sortin' me out, if 'e can, I've no doubt.'

'I expect yer wonderin' why I didn't pull 'em apart,' Sharkey said as he slid his hands into his jacket pockets.

'It did cross me mind.'

'I was quite 'appy ter pick up the pieces,' Sharkey explained. 'I've got no time fer eivver of 'em, but if I tried ter sack 'em I'd be overruled by Frank Coley, so why should I risk gettin' 'urt?'

Charlie looked along the line. ''Ow d'yer wanna work this one?' he asked.

'It's a twenty-man workforce an' we're talkin' about an eighty yard stretch,' Sharkey replied. 'Let's share it. We'll walk the line tergevver an' then spell each ovver.'

'Sounds OK,' Charlie said. 'One fing, though. If we do well terday we'll be startin' ter shore up the sides termorrer an' we'll need more decent timbers, not that woodworm-ridden rubbish we've bin usin'.'

'What d'yer expect me ter do?' Sharkey asked.

'Back me up when I see the Coleys.'

'Yeah, OK.'

As the mounds of shifted earth started to grow at the side of the workings heavy rain and driving winds made working conditions very difficult, and before long sludge ran back into the trench and the men gritted their teeth and grunted with exertion as they heaved out shovelfuls of mud that seemed to weigh a ton.

Mary Chubb hurried along Tooley Street and went into the papershop a few minutes after Jack Crompton had opened up.

'You're sharp this mornin',' he remarked.

'Yeah. I got someone comin' ter see me later an' I wanna get done early,' Mary told him.

'Don't owe 'em any money, do yer?'

'I shouldn't fink so,' she replied, smiling.

As she crossed the wide thoroughfare and stepped out of the gloomy winter's morning into an equally gloomy set of offices Mary felt flat. She knew she should have been glad to get a key job, which was considered far better than working for a cleaning company. She knew also that Gracie was being well cared for in her absence and Lucy had refused to accept any money for the chore, but she could not shake off the depression. She and Lucy had planned to share the job but since her friend had changed her mind the initial enthusiasm had vanished. Maybe another key job would come up soon, she hoped, and then they could share the jobs as planned.

Lorries and horse carts were arriving to load and unload at the Tooley Street wharves and warehouses, and purposeful footsteps sounded outside as the early workers turned up to begin another day. In the Dolan offices Mary worked with a will, and after cleaning the toilets she glanced up at the clock in Cuthbert's office. It was eight thirty and she set about her final chore, polishing Cuthbert's large desk.

Suddenly he was there, standing by the open door, still holding his briefcase and rolled umbrella, his watery grey eyes staring out of a pale face. 'Good morning, Mrs Chubb,' he said in his reedy voice.

Mary was taken aback. 'You scared me,' she gulped. 'I never 'eard yer come in.'

'I'm very sorry,' he replied as he slipped his umbrella into the stand and struggled out of his light mackintosh. 'I seem to have missed you in the mornings. As a matter of fact the trains have been a little erratic this past week or so, but I'm pleased to say that the Southern Railway appear to have overcome their problems and I hope to see more of you now.'

Mary smiled and set to work polishing the desktop. Not if I can help it you won't, she thought. 'There we are, I'm just about finished,' she told him.

He looked disappointed. 'Wouldn't you like to stay for a coffee?' he asked. 'I have the facilities to make some.'

'No, really,' she said, smiling. 'I need ter get back 'ome. I 'ave somebody lookin' after my daughter an' I don't like ter take liberties.'

'I'm sure they wouldn't mind if you were a few minutes late,' Cuthbert pressed.

'No, really.'

He walked over and eased himself into his large padded desk chair. 'Tell me, Mrs Chubb, would you have any objection to me addressing you by your Christian name?'

'It's Mary,' she said.

'That could be the oldest Christian name of all,' he said with a stab at humour. 'Tell me, Mary, did you have a chance to view the magazine I gave to you?'

'Well I . . . I sort of . . .'

'It's quite all right,' he assured her. 'I understand your reluctance to admit to perusing a rather forward periodical, a publication that some people would find rather objectionable.'

'I didn't find anyfing bad in it,' Mary replied. Cuthbert's eyes were moving again and she felt uncomfortable. 'Well, I'd better be off,' she said quickly.

'Mary, can I ask you something?'

'Yes?'

'After studying that magazine does the thought of communing with nature excite you? Can you imagine the sense of freedom when a naked body is offered to the elements, the wind cooling the hot brow, stinging rain chastising the flesh, and the warm spring sunshine gently caressing and stimulating the sensuous regions? It's something to live for, believe me.'

'I must admit I didn't look at it like that,' Mary replied, trying not to laugh aloud at the way his voice sounded as he delivered his flowery speech.

Cuthbert raised a finger as a gesture for her to wait and he reached down into a bottom drawer and brought out a key. 'This is not just an ordinary key,' he said with conviction. 'This key represents freedom and exquisite pleasure. On any given day, at any time, I can climb the stairs to the top floor and use this key to let myself out on to a flat section of the roof. The design of the building makes that part completely private. It is there that I take off all my clothes and experience a freedom of expression, and the exquisite sensation of the elements assailing my nude body. Can you understand? Could you envisage joining me there at some time? If you can, and do so, you will feel as I do, experience pleasures heretofore denied you. Think on it,

Mary, and reread the magazine with a more enlightened outlook. You may surprise yourself.'

Mary nodded as she moved backwards from the room. 'Good day, Mr Cuthbert,' she faltered.

Jack Crompton gave her a cheery nod as she walked into his shop and handed him back the key. 'See yer termorrer,' he said.

'I doubt it very much,' she answered.

Chapter Twenty-Three

The morning rain had never let up and by lunchtime when the bedraggled workmen climbed out of the deepening trench they were feeling decidedly miserable. They had cut down at an angle to hold the sides in place but already sludge was oozing into the workings.

'I can't start shorin' it up yet,' Roy said to Charlie as the two stood watching the men slouch into the shed.

Charlie was determined that there would not be a repeat of the morning's rumpus and he was pleased to see that George and his partner Danny Albury had moved down to the far end of the shed, away from Wally Coates and Norman Gill who always sat by the entrance. 'It's like a bloody powder keg,' he sighed. 'It only wants one word out o' place, one bad look, an' it could all be off.'

'I don't fink George is gonna provoke 'im again,' Roy answered, 'but as far as Coates is concerned I dunno.'

He turned his back on the shed and walked over to where the timbers were stacked. 'There's not much good stuff 'ere,' he said as Charlie joined him. 'See fer yerself, most of it's sodden.'

'As I said, I'll 'ave a word wiv Ben Coley soon as 'e gets back,' Charlie told him.

Roy was not impressed. 'It's like talkin' ter that bloody

shovel. We're gonna need more plankin', good or bad, ter shore up over eighty yards o' trench.'

It was late afternoon before Ben Coley made an appearance and he nodded impatiently when Charlie mentioned the need for some more timber. 'Leave it ter me,' he grumbled. 'I'll get some out 'ere first fing termorrer.'

Charlie walked along the line and noticed that George and Danny had stationed themselves far enough away from Wally Coates and his partner to avoid any backchat, but had he heard their conversation he would have been concerned.

'I ain't finished wiv 'im yet,' George growled. 'Next time 'e 'as a go at me I'm gonna crown 'im, mark my words.'

'It ain't werf it,' Danny replied. 'Just ignore 'im.'

The muddy state of the trench slowed the work, and by five o'clock when the men scrambled out of the workings the tunnel roof had still not been uncovered.

In Cooper Street the rain trickled off Ada Black's umbrella as she stood at her front door chatting to Emmie. 'I was talkin' ter Paula Jackson at the market this mornin',' she announced. 'Apparently 'er Will was complainin' about Sammy Strickland.'

'Oh?'

'Yeah. It seems Will got Sammy ter give 'im a bit of 'elp wiv this movin' job 'e 'ad an' 'e sent 'im ter fetch this barrer from Tom Dougan,' Ada explained. 'It'd all bin arranged, yer see. Anyway, the dopey git saw a barrer outside Dougan's shed an' 'e just took it wivout askin' first. As it 'appened the barrer was due to 'ave the wheel sorted out an' by the time they'd finished it was ruined. Somefink ter do wiv it seizin' up an' causin' the axle ter twist.'

'Well it would do,' Emmie said, without understanding what Ada was talking about.

'The outcome was, Dougan told the pair of 'em ter bugger off an' not expect ter borrer any more barrers,' Ada went on. 'Paula told me 'er Will was gutted. 'E always gets barrers from Tom Dougan.'

'I dunno 'ow Peggy Strickland stands that bloke of 'ers,' Emmie remarked, 'an' I dunno why Will Jackson asked 'im ter lend an 'and. 'E'd 'ave bin better askin' Charlie Pease.'

'Well I reckon she's got the patience of a saint meself,' Ada replied. 'She was tellin' me that Sammy went fer anuvver job in the week. It was at the tannery in Long Lane apparently. She said 'e come back grinnin' all over 'is face an' she thought 'e'd finally clicked, but then 'e showed 'er what the bloke 'ad put on 'is green card. It was somefing about 'im bein' allergic ter leavver dyes. O' course Peggy went on at 'im about not wantin' ter get a job an' comin' in grinnin' like a Cheshire cat, an' Sammy told 'er 'e was only grinnin' 'cos 'e was still alive. Can you imagine? The story was, they was takin' 'im round the tannery an' showin' 'im the pits where they soak the skins when the silly git chucked a dummy, an' it was only the quick finkin' of the foreman what stopped 'im tumblin' 'eadfirst inter the chemicals. The foreman told 'im later that one mouthful o' that stuff in the pit would 'ave killed 'im stone dead.'

'Not Sammy,' Emmie chuckled. ''E'd 'ave just sprouted a pair of 'orns.'

''Ere, I saw Sara Parry walkin' up the street yesterday,' Ada said. 'I thought she looked quite nice fer a change. She'd obviously 'ad 'er 'air done an' she was wearin' a decent coat.'

'She was probably off ter the fellowship,' Emmie replied. 'P'raps she's got a bloke there.'

'I doubt it,' Ada remarked. 'She's a typical spinster. Flat shoes, long clothes, old-fashioned 'airstyle an' a silly 'at.

Yer don't attract the blokes lookin' like that, do yer?'

On the contrary, a certain Randolph Cadman had thrown his cap into the ring in pursuit of Sara Parry's favours, only to realise that no one else had bothered, which the enlightened suitor, who introduced himself with the suffix Civil Service, retired, found very encouraging.

Currently he was a member of St Mark's fellowship, recruited for the choir and recently voted on to the committee alongside Sara, which pleased him even more. It pleased Sara too, who felt that he was a very good tenor as well as a very knowledgeable and thoroughly nice man. Now perhaps the committee could get back to normal functioning after the trauma of the young reverend's recent elopement.

Randolph Cadman hoped so too, for his own reasons.

When darkness fell the rain finally ceased, and as Maurice Oakfield settled down at the new site in Morgan Street he felt the damp air seeping in from the river. It was the sort of night that chilled the bones, and he paid particular attention to making sure his fire burned bright. He was also very keen to catch a glimpse of a few constellations that night, such as Pegasus to the west, Leo in the east and maybe even Cygnus, but for the moment very few stars showed through the banks of cloud that still crowded the dark sky.

Morgan Street was yet another commercial byway in the Dockhead area, much the same as River Lane. Alongside the grimy warehouses fed from the nearby Thames were a couple of allied manufacturing concerns, a harness maker serving the many horse transport firms in Bermondsey, and a rope-yard, whose high-quality ropes and cables spanned a thousand of the barges and freighters using the Pool of London and the local wharves. The end of the turning farthest from the river led into Tooley Street with its large tenement blocks, built by trusts to replace the workers' slums of the late nineteenth century. Gloomy and badly lit, Morgan Street was a place the local people neither cared nor needed to use, and after dark only reckless lovers sought its solitude.

Maurice was quite prepared for a lonely vigil. He had not made the acquaintance yet of the local bobby, but he was content to pass the night away reading and viewing the changing night sky, weather permitting. What Maurice was not prepared for was the old man who shuffled along the turning after midnight and stopped to admire the glow of the brazier. 'It's a cold damp night for sure,' he said through his long scraggy beard.

Maurice smiled. 'Come closer, sir, and feel the warmth,' he replied, saddened to see the rags that passed for clothing on the man's bony frame.

'It's very decent of you,' the stranger said in a cultured voice. 'I was on my way to Barstow's.'

'Barstow's?'

'It's a derelict warehouse on the river's edge,' the old man explained. 'It's a place a man can get his head down and there are sacks galore to wrap up in. I've had many a cosy night at Barstow's, even at the height of winter.'

Maurice lifted his iron teapot from a grid which he had fixed to the side of the brazier. 'Would you care for some tea?' he asked.

'That's very civilised of you, sir,' the old man replied.

Maurice filled his own mug and the one he had kept for Ron Sloan when he paid him a visit. 'Sugar?'

'Two, if you please.'

Maurice passed the tea over and pulled up the makeshift saw bench which Roy Chubb used. 'There we are, sit yourself down for a few minutes,' he said.

The stranger did as he was bid, and as he gratefully sipped his tea Maurice studied him. His hands were smooth, with long thin fingers that might once have elicited music from keys or strings, but his frame was narrow and bowed, as though deprived of regular nourishment and creaking under his own private burden. The collar of his long brown tattered overcoat was pulled up round his ears and he wore a grease-stained trilby cock-eyed on his head. His feet were shod in down-at-heel boots tied up with string, and most noticeable of all was the drooping blue wild flower that was pinned to the front of his coat.

'I'm William Darcy, a man of the open road,' he said, smiling through his beard.

'Maurice Oakfield, nightwatchman for Coley Brothers, civil engineers,' Maurice replied. The two shook hands and he was surprised at the visitor's strong grip. 'This is what you might call a temporary job,' he added. 'I hope to go back to my vocation very soon. I'm a teacher.'

'That's very good,' the old man said. 'I hope you do. Anything less would be a waste.'

'More tea?' Maurice asked.

'You're most kind,' William said, holding out his empty mug.

The two sat in silence for a while, then the old man said something which made Maurice frown. 'Are the nights quiet?'

'Very much so,' Maurice replied. 'Few people need to venture here at night.'

'No, I was referring to the noises. I hear them while I'm waiting for sleep to come at the warehouse.'

'What sort of noises?'

'Dull booming,' William told him. 'Like a distant drum.

A whistling noise, like wind gusting through trees, and a deep, almost inaudible groan that rises and falls at certain times.'

Maurice forced a smile. 'I'm afraid this is my first night in this area, so I wouldn't know of any undue noises.'

'Yes, I'm aware of that,' the tramp replied. 'I walk through this turning every night. Be circumspect, but take heart. You're not in any danger. I believe the sounds are from another time, when Morgan Street was a riverside meadow crowned with a gallows and gibbet, and people came with their children to witness the executions while they drank beer and ate their bread and cheese. I've been able to study the history of this place and it's no wonder the sounds remain. It has a violent past, you can be sure.'

Maurice looked skyward for a few moments, catching a glimpse of a bright star he imagined to be Sirius before the moving cloud hid it from view, then he fixed his eyes on the old man. 'Do you think the digging in this street would have upset the balance of things?'

'It would have disturbed things, undreamt-of things that we know little about,' William answered in a quiet voice.

Maurice felt a shiver run down his back and he rolled his shoulders. 'I'll be careful not to add to the noise,' he said with a smile. 'I'm paid to guard this site, and that's what I intend to do, come hell or high water.'

'And I will outstay my welcome if I'm not careful,' the old man replied, 'so I'll say goodnight to you, and fear not. Remember, the darkest part of the night is just before the dawn.'

Maurice watched him leave. 'Goodnight, William,' he called out.

The tramp answered with a wave of his bony arm, and then he was gone, swallowed up in the dark night.

Maurice banked up the fire, made his regular rounds and sat reading with the aid of his nightlight. Occasionally the night sky opened out between the clouds, like a window into eternity, and he was able to pinpoint the stars and constellations he was familiar with. It stayed quiet, apart from the earthly sounds of a fussing tugboat's whistle, the late tram rattling through nearby Tooley Street, and the crackle of the burning log on the brazier.

When the men arrived at the diggings Maurice took his leave, and on impulse he decided to take a look at Barstow's warehouse. He found nothing but a large open space next to the Shad Thames wharves. 'Was this where Barstow's warehouse stood, constable?' he asked the passing policeman.

'Yes, sir. It was pulled down back in the twenties, I believe.'

Maurice was not ready for his bed, so he made his way to the local library. 'Have you any local newspapers from the twenties in your archives?' he enquired.

'Come this way,' the librarian replied.

Maurice was led down to a basement room, complete with a very large polished table and shelves full of heavy binders along the four walls. He spent more than two hours searching the old papers and then he found what he was looking for in a June 1924 edition of the *South London Press*.

'Bermondsey Says Goodbye'
The people of Bermondsey lined the streets today for the funeral of William Darcy, the well-known local character who called himself a man of the open road. William tramped the streets and slept rough, and he was never seen without a wilted flower pinned to his

coat. He always had a kind word and a cheerful smile for everyone he encountered.

He was said to have been educated at Eton and then went on to serve as a First Lieutenant with the Royal Fusiliers in France during the Great War. Disenchanted by his war experiences, William Darcy gave up a promising career in banking and chose to live his life walking the streets and relying on the goodwill of the people of Bermondsey for sustenance.

He seemed an uncomplicated man, but his death will remain a mystery. What made him end his life by jumping into the River Thames?

Maurice Oakfield hardly noticed the people passing by as he walked home lost in thought. Had he dreamed it all? What other possible explanation was there? One thing was for sure, though. His self-imposed period of rehabilitation was now over, and he would apply to be reinstated at the college as soon as possible.

Chapter Twenty-Four

When the diggers started work on the dull Tuesday morning early in January they did not imagine that the day was going to be any different from the rest, and as they set about clearing the earth around the buried sewer tunnel there was the usual friendly banter between them, with the exception of Wally Coates and his partner. They were left to their own devices and totally ignored during the short breaks which had now become the norm. Any attempt at good-natured persiflage would incur a frosty reply at the least, and more likely a stream of abuse from the giant of a man who seemed devoid of humour and tended to treat everyone with utter contempt.

As expected, Coates and Gill were making fast progress, and as they dug deeper around the tunnel that afternoon Roy Chubb began the shoring-up process beside them. Lofty Williams, the other carpenter, began his task at the other end of the trench and as Charlie made his way along the ridge he felt pleased that everything was going as planned. By this evening the twenty-man team would be almost finished. One more day would see the job out, and then the men would learn from Frank Coley that the main sewer excavation was to get underway, along the whole of the eastern side of Tooley Street down as far as Jamaica Road.

At four o'clock the rain started again and soon it was lashing down. Sludge from the piles of earth at the side of the trench ran back into the diggings and the trench walls became soggy and unstable. Charlie worked under Roy's guidance helping to fix the shuttering and Sharkey joined Lofty Williams at the opposite end.

'I don't see any sense in tryin' ter go deeper ternight,' Charlie told his fellow ganger. 'What d'you reckon?'

Sharkey nodded. 'We'd better get the men out of our way while we finish off. They can sit in the shed till it's time ter knock off.'

The diggers needed no coaxing and they scrambled out of the trench by way of the raised platforms used to make the removal of soil easier, but Danny Albury hesitated, bending down with his hand pressed to the side of his stomach.

'What's wrong?' George asked him with concern.

'It's OK. I get the cramp now an' then an' it's just caught me,' he said through clenched teeth.

'It ain't an 'ernia, is it?' George asked.

Danny shook his head, gingerly straightening himself up. 'Nah, it's just the cramp. It ain't troubled me fer some time.'

'Give us yer pickaxe,' George said.

Danny passed it to him and George threw it out of the trench, then as he picked up his shovel he saw Wally Coates coming towards him.

'I fink me an' you 'ave got some unfinished business ter see to,' the big man growled.

'Give it a break, Wally,' Danny cut in. 'What 'appened yesterday is all over an' done wiv.'

'You keep out o' this,' Coates snarled. 'This is between Parry an' me.'

"As someone bin windin' you up?' Danny asked him.

'Leave it, Danny,' George said quickly, turning to face Coates. 'I'm surprised you ain't got yer dummy wiv yer. Is 'e fed up wiv you pullin' 'is strings?'

Coates's eyes widened and he suddenly lunged forward but Danny stepped in front of him. 'Look, I ain't aimin' ter get the bullet fer scrappin', an' nor should you,' he growled. 'Why don't yer piss off out the trench an' let us do the same.'

'Get outta me way, you little rat,' the giant roared.

'Make me.'

Coates grabbed at him and slammed him roughly against the side of the trench, drawing back his fist to hit him, and George quickly swung the shovel with all his force. It smashed into the side of Coates's head and he staggered backwards a pace then fell heavily against a shoring prop, dislodging it as he collapsed into the bottom of the trench. Suddenly soil and sludge was pouring into the diggings and in seconds Wally Coates was completely buried under earth and fallen timbers. Danny had been lucky and he managed to struggle out of the morass as his partner frantically scooped the muddy earth from around his waist and legs.

Charlie had seen what happened as he stood by the side of the workings and he shouted out for the others to help the buried man before jumping into the trench himself and trying desperately to free him before he suffocated.

'What's 'appened?' Sharkey yelled down.

'Wally Coates is under that lot,' Charlie shouted back at him. ''E's gonna need an ambulance, an' a doctor as well.'

'I'll use the phone box in Tooley Street then I'll chase up

the doctor.' Sharkey turned on his heel and dashed along the turning.

There was no shortage of volunteers to get the big man out. Charlie scraped the sludge away with his bare hands as the other rescuers dug frantically, and the ambulance bell was sounding as they reached him. Sharkey had managed to summon a doctor from his practice in Tooley Street and willing hands helped him down into the trench.

'Get this prop off 'is 'ead,' one of the rescuers shouted as the doctor bent down over the still figure.

A stretcher was lowered and within minutes Wally Coates was being rushed to Guy's Hospital.

During the rescue operation George and Danny had stood to one side, and now as Charlie came towards them they could see the worried look on his face.

'Is 'e dead?' George asked fearfully.

Charlie nodded his head slowly. 'It looks that way.'

George dropped down on to the wet earth. ''E was comin' for me an' 'e was gonna 'ammer Danny,' he groaned. 'Jesus God, what 'ave I done?'

'Now you listen ter me,' Charlie hissed. 'When anybody asks yer what 'appened this is what yer say. Coates was 'avin' a dig at yer about you bein' slow but you an' Danny ignored 'im, then as 'e started ter climb out the trench 'e suddenly slipped an' fell backwards, dislodgin' the prop as 'e fell. Just remember, that's what 'appened an' there was nuffink you could do ter prevent it.'

'What about the mark on 'is 'ead from the shovel?' George said in panic.

'It must 'ave bin caused by the 'eavy prop that was layin' across 'is face when we got to 'im,' Charlie answered. 'Clean the mud off that shovel right away an' there'll be nuffink ter show.'

Frank and Ben Coley looked anxious as they came out of the hut after speaking briefly with Charlie.

'Send the men 'ome, Sharkey,' Frank told him, 'but make sure Parry an' Albury stay in the shed. I wanna see 'em. You two come inside right away.'

When they crowded into the hut Ben Coley pulled two stools out from under the bench and motioned Sharkey and Charlie to sit beside him. Frank pulled his chair over to the closed door and sat with his back resting against it. 'The doctor told me that Wally Coates is dead,' he began. 'It'll mean an inquest. Now I know you saw what 'appened, Charlie, but I want George Parry an' Danny Albury ter tell me their version. You told me they saw it 'appen.'

'Yeah, that's right, an' they're both shocked rigid,' Charlie answered.

'This could balls everyfing up,' Coley growled. 'I was duty bound ter report the accident ter the police an' they'll be sendin' someone round later. In the meantime there's questions need answerin'. What was Coates doin' up that end o' the trench? What caused 'im ter slip? After all, 'e knows 'is way round a trench. Was the shorin' secure? The answers we get are gonna be crucial. If it points ter malpractice or skylarkin' then the individuals concerned can be dealt wiv an' no blame'd be attached ter the management, but if the accident was caused by bad workmanship, insecure shorin' or weakened timbers then we're gonna be 'eld responsible, an' I don't need ter spell it out. We'd lose the contract an' any furvver work fer Maitland's.'

'Some o' those timbers that come away 'ad split in 'alf,' Charlie told him.

Frank Coley looked worried. 'Is there any new plankin' lyin' around 'ere?' he asked.

Ben Coley shook his head. 'The delivery's due termor-rer.'

Frank glared at him. 'You'd better get it delivered right away, before the police arrive,' he said quickly.

Ben grabbed his coat. 'I'll take care of it.'

Frank turned to Charlie. 'Will yer go an' fetch George Parry?'

Charlie was soon back with the ashen-faced workman, having quietly reminded him to stick to his story, and Frank Coley waved him towards Ben's empty stool.

'Look, I know this must 'ave bin a terrible shock, but we 'ave ter know just what 'appened,' he impressed on him. 'Take yer time an' tell us exactly what yer saw.'

George drew a deep breath and explained as calmly as he could how he and Danny were being taunted, and how when they did not respond Wally Coates turned to leave and slipped backwards as he tried to get out of the trench, dislodging the main cross prop as he fell.

'You never pushed 'im, or caused 'im ter slip?' Frank asked, staring hard at him.

'Certainly not.'

'Why should Wally Coates 'ave it in fer yer?'

'I dunno. I never slacked or left the bulk o' the work to 'im when we were teamed up,' George said with spirit, 'but fer some reason best known to 'imself 'e was always gettin' on ter me.'

'All right, you can go. I'll speak ter yer again termorrer,' Frank told him. 'Let's 'ave Danny Albury in.'

Danny's version of the incident matched that of his partner and Frank Coley gave him a dark look. 'Now listen ter me,' he said. 'If Parry caused the accident in any way an' you don't come clean you'll be just as guilty as 'im, so yer better fink about it.'

The little digger stood up to his full height and looked Coley square in the eye. 'I know it's common knowledge that Parry an' Coates never got on, but when the big man come along the trench an' started goadin' 'im an' me we took no notice. 'E called us a few choice names an' went ter get out o' the trench. That's when 'e slipped. Like I already told yer, it was a pure accident.'

'Tell me,' Coley continued. 'Did Coates go off fer 'is lunch break or did 'e stay in the shed?'

''E stayed in the shed an' ate 'is grub like the rest of us,' Danny answered.

'Right, you can get off 'ome,' Coley told him. 'I expect the police are gonna be askin' you an' Parry some more questions termorrer.'

After the digger had left Frank Coley turned to Charlie. 'I got a feelin' those two were lyin',' he remarked pointedly.

Charlie turned on him angrily. 'I've already told yer I saw Coates slip. If they're lyin' so am I, an' I assure yer I'm not a liar.'

Coley raised his hand in a conciliatory gesture. 'I'm not callin' you a liar,' he said quickly. 'I'm suggestin' yer might 'ave missed somefink, bin distracted fer a moment.'

Charlie shook his head slowly. 'I was standin' right above Parry an' Albury when Wally Coates fell. They were nowhere near 'im.'

Frank Coley nodded. 'OK. Sharkey, you'd better wait around till Ben gets back wiv those timbers. You too, Charlie. The police'll need a statement from somebody who saw what 'appened.'

It was after eight o'clock when Charlie walked into the house and Lucy met him in the scullery with a look of concern in her eyes. 'You must be worn out,' she said. 'George told me what 'appened. It's just terrible.'

As Charlie rolled up his shirtsleeves Lucy filled the bowl with hot water. 'I've kept yer meal in the oven. I 'ope it ain't too baked up,' she remarked.

'I 'ad ter stay be'ind ter give the police a statement,' he replied as he dipped his hands into the bowl.

'I'll take this in fer yer,' Lucy said as she took the plate from the oven.

'Don't bovver. I'll eat out 'ere,' he told her. 'It'll save you layin' the parlour table again.'

Lucy moved behind him as he sat down, placing her hand lightly on his shoulder as she reached across him to get a knife and fork from the dresser drawer. 'George came in lookin' as white as a ghost,' she said. ''E's left 'alf 'is tea. Mary popped in an' said Roy came in lookin' all shook up even though 'e never saw what 'appened.'

'It's natural,' Charlie replied. 'I've seen it on the quayside. A man gets killed or badly 'urt an' it brings it all 'ome ter yer. It could 'ave bin you.'

'What's gonna 'appen now?' Lucy asked.

'There'll be a post-mortem,' Charlie explained, 'an' then there'll be an inquest, so the police said.'

Lucy placed her hand on his shoulder once more and he felt the slight pressure of her fingers. 'Get on wiv yer tea. We can talk later,' she said.

The hour was late and the fire burned low when Charlie sat facing Lucy in the parlour. 'I was glad when Sara decided ter go ter bed,' Lucy remarked. 'I'm sure she made George feel worse the way she was goin' on about it before you came in. She wants ter know the ins an' outs of a nag's arse.'

Charlie had had no chance to talk with George alone that

evening before the troubled man went off to bed, but he had seen the fear in his eyes when he told him how he had been questioned by the police and asked to give a statement about all he had seen. He hoped George would continue to keep the truth from Lucy, but he was less than optimistic. He knew that it was playing on George's mind and before very long he would confess to her. He would have to speak to him as soon as possible and try to make him see that it wouldn't help anyone to dwell on what had really happened. Better to let it rest where it was, however hard. ''E'll be all right in a few days,' he said reassuringly, 'once the initial shock wears off.'

'Well at least 'e's got this weekend at the naval reserve,' Lucy replied. 'It'll 'elp take 'is mind off it.'

Charlie stared into the fire for a few moments, then his eyes met hers. 'Are you all right?' he asked quietly.

'Why d'you ask? Do I look tired or somefing?'

'No. You look very nice, as a matter o' fact, but I can see the worried look in yer eyes,' he said with a brief smile.

'I am worried about George,' she answered. 'When 'e told me about the man bein' buried alive I went all cold. I suddenly realised just 'ow dangerous that job can be. It could 'ave bin George, or you.'

'I'd try not ter worry too much,' he said softly. 'These sorts of accidents aren't very common where all the necessary precautions are taken. Roy put that shorin' up an' 'e did a good job. It wasn't 'is fault it collapsed. The man who was killed was a big feller. I'd say 'e weighed all of eighteen, nineteen stone.'

Lucy felt her cheeks grow hot and raw excitement course through her body as she watched him speaking. At that very moment she wanted him to take her in his arms, hold her tightly and kiss her breathless, but she fought the need, as she had to, averting her eyes and breathing in deeply in an effort to calm herself. This was crazy. Every time she allowed her emotions to run rampant would only strengthen her desire for him, but she wanted him to know just how she felt, wanted him to need her every bit as much as she desired him. Yes, it was crazy, but deep down inside she knew that there would come a time when their mutual feelings would inevitably overwhelm them both. 'Are you 'appy 'ere, Charlie?' she asked suddenly.

The question took him by surprise. 'I've felt at 'ome in this 'ouse from the very first night I arrived,' he answered.

'You wouldn't leave us, would you?' she said. 'I couldn't imagine one day wivout you bein' 'ere.'

'I won't leave you, Lucy,' he told her softly. 'I wouldn't want ter go frew a day wivout seein' yer, talkin' to yer, watchin' the way you move about, the way you 'ave of dealin' wiv fings.'

'Like our Sara?' she said, smiling, trying to bring some sanity into their dangerous game.

'Yeah, like Sara fer instance.'

Lucy looked up at the clock on the mantelshelf. 'I'd better get off ter bed,' she said almost reluctantly. 'George might be lyin' awake.'

'Yeah, me too,' he replied. 'Lucy?'

'Yeah?'

'I'd like very much ter kiss you goodnight,' he said huskily, rising from his chair.

She took his outstretched hands in hers as she got up and allowed him to pull her to him. His kiss on her trembling lips was soft and warm and very brief as he held her close, and when she moved back, still held in his strong arms, she knew that there was no going back. His kiss had told her all she wanted to know and she shivered with pleasure. 'Goodnight, Charlie,' she said quietly.

'Goodnight, Lucy.'

Chapter Twenty-Five

All work had stopped at the Morgan Street diggings, and when the men reported for work on Wednesday morning they were told to wait in the shed. Charlie pulled George Parry and Danny Albury to one side and warned them that the police would want to speak to them first. Then he looked around at the anxious faces of the men. 'Now listen ter me,' he began. 'We're all sorry this tragedy 'appened, even though none of us liked the man, so least said the better about any confrontations wiv 'im. I'm referrin' ter the little set-to in 'ere the ovver mornin'. It could be seen by the police as a reason fer a revenge attack, so I don't want any of yer ter mention what 'appened. Is that understood? As far as you lot are concerned you've never witnessed any confrontations.'

The men chatted amongst themselves, but Danny and George both sat quietly while they waited to be interviewed by the police.

Charlie stepped outside and immediately saw the police car drive into the turning. He looked back into the shed and motioned for George and Danny to join him. 'They've just arrived,' he told them. 'Just try ter stay calm when they ask yer what 'appened. Remember, apart from you two I was the only one who saw the accident.'

'Yeah, but it wasn't an accident,' George mumbled.

'You'd better pull yerself tergevver, George,' Charlie retorted angrily. 'Yer didn't mean ter kill the man.'

''E's right, mate,' Danny said, putting his arm round George's bowed shoulders. 'You was only lookin' out fer me. If we just stick ter the same story we'll be OK.'

'Right, I've gotta see Frank Coley,' Charlie announced. 'Now just remember what yer gotta say, 'cos if yer don't get it right I'm gonna be dragged right into it as well.'

Frank Coley's face was dark with anger as he faced his two gangers in the work hut. 'I've just 'ad words wiv Pat Lawrence from the contractors,' he told them. ''E threatened ter tear up the contract if we don't get this business sorted out quickly.'

'There's only 'alf a day's work left on the site,' Sharkey cut in. 'Can't we get it finished?'

'Nah, we 'ave ter wait till the coroner's man inspects the cave-in spot,' Frank replied. 'At least we've bin able ter replace some o' those old timbers, so they can't put the accident down ter bad wood. As fer the shorin', they'll see that the rest of it's safe an' solid, so there's no reason fer 'em ter say it was bad workmanship.'

'As we've already said, we gotta make sure they 'ave no reason ter suggest it was management negligence,' Ben Coley reminded them, 'an' ter be honest I'm a bit worried about this goadin' business concernin' Coates.'

'What d'yer mean?' Charlie asked quickly.

'Granted yer split Coates an' Parry up when yer found out about it,' Ben went on, 'but why was Coates allowed ter come along almost the 'ole length o' the trench ter sort Parry out after bein' told like the rest ter get out?'

Sharkey and Charlie exchanged quick glances. 'I was standin' above the middle o' the trench when I saw Coates comin' along an' I asked if 'e was deaf or somefing,' Charlie told him. ''E just ignored me, an' the accident 'appened too quick fer me to do anyfing ter stop it. That was what 'appened an' that's in me statement.'

'There'll be an inquest, an' let's 'ope the coroner ends up satisfied,' Frank said with emphasis. 'If 'e ain't then we're effectively out o' business. That much was spelled out by Pat Lawrence.'

The policemen stepped out of their car and the coroner's man in civilian clothing introduced himself to the Coley brothers. 'If you'll show me where the accident happened,' he requested.

While the official began his inspection the uniformed sergeant took both men's statements in the hut and then went to the workmen's shed to speak with the rest of the diggers.

'I'll be sending a photographer along some time today,' the coroner's man told the Coleys, 'and once he's finished there'll be no reason to hold you up any further.'

'You two might as well get off 'ome,' Frank said to his gangers. 'I want you in bright an' breezy termorrer, so we can 'ave that trench ready to 'and over by lunchtime at the latest. We've gotta keep the contractors sweet now.'

Charlie joined George and Danny outside the shed and as they set off home he noticed how relieved the two looked.

'The sergeant was a real nice bloke,' Danny remarked. ''E didn't rush us or anyfing, an' 'e said that we did the right fing not lettin' Coates wind us up.'

''E asked me about all the goadin',' George added. 'I just told 'im that me an' Coates didn't get on an' when I asked yer fer a change o' partner yer got me one. There was one fing, though. The copper wanted ter know if I'd ever lost me temper when me an' Coates worked tergevver an' I told 'im it never bovvered me that much. I said I put it down ter the man's ignorance. I also told 'im that none o' the men got on wiv 'im an' we all tended ter stay away from 'im as much as we could.'

'Yer did well, both of yer,' Charlie said with a smile. 'Now yer gotta put it ter the back o' yer minds. Nuffink good's gonna come if yer dwell too much on it.'

'I blame meself fer what 'appened,' Danny frowned. 'I got Coates's back up an' George did what 'e did ter save me gettin' a pastin'.'

'An' you stood up ter the bully ter save George gettin' a pastin', so it's neivver one nor the ovver,' Charlie told him forcefully. 'Do like I say an' put it where it belongs, an' don't start losin' any sleep over it. After all, nuffink can be changed. It's 'appened an' that's that.'

The tragic incident was very soon on everyone's lips in Cooper Street and Peggy Strickland was prompted to tell Ada and Emmie that it came as no surprise to her. 'If you'd seen my Sammy that day 'e went fer the nightwatchman's job,' she said with a sour look. ''E came 'ome really upset. Coley told 'im 'e wasn't suitable an' Sammy 'ad a right ole go at 'im. After all, it don't take much sense ter look after a bleedin' 'ole in the road, does it? I mean ter say, it ain't goin' anywhere. Then there was the time Sammy took a stroll when they was diggin' up River Lane an' 'e stopped ter chat wiv the blokes, like yer would. Coley sent this great big bloke out the office after 'im an' 'e threatened 'im.'

'Who, Sammy did?' Emmie asked.

'Nah, the bloke threatened Sammy.'

'Sounds a right nasty firm ter work for,' Ada remarked.

'They certainly want their pound o' flesh,' Peggy said disgustedly.

'Lucy Parry's lodger works fer the Coleys as well,' Ada told her.

'So I 'eard,' she answered. ''E's a ganger, by all accounts.'

Emmie nodded. 'Mary Chubb's ole man works there too.'

'Mind you, there's not much ovver work fer 'em ter do, is there?' Ada went on. 'My ole man would 'ave gone there fer a job if 'e was a few years younger, but they don't take anyone on who's over fifty.'

'My Sammy's over fifty,' Peggy said.

'Yeah, but 'e was applyin' fer a nightwatchman's job, not as a ditch digger,' Emmie reminded her.

Ada slid her hands deeper into the sleeves of her coat. 'While I fink of it,' she said. 'Did you know that Sara Parry's gone an' got 'erself a bloke?'

'Never.'

''S true. Quite a presentable bloke too.'

'Where'd yer 'ear this?'

Ada quite liked being able to pass on snippets of information and she took her time in replying. 'Well as it 'appens,' she began with suitably conspiratorial glances, 'I was standin' by Tommy Atwood's fruit stall when Mrs Penfold came up an' said 'ello. I 'adn't seen 'er fer Gawd knows 'ow long, so I asks 'ow she was an' she was tellin' me about 'er nervous breakdown. She put it down ter the worry she's 'ad wiv 'er ole man. Anyway, the doctor told 'er she should get out a bit more so she joined the muvvers' union at St Mark's. Then she got to 'ear about this fellowship they've got there an' she went along one evenin'. Apparently they do all sorts o' fings there, like sewin' an' embroidery, an' they make fings fer Christmas bazaars.'

'Go on,' Emmie said impatiently.

Ada looked up and down the turning. 'Mrs Penfold got chattin' ter Sara Parry an' they struck up a friendship, like yer do, an' after a few meetin's Sara confided in Mrs Penfold that she quite liked this bloke who'd recently joined the fellowship.'

'I thought it was only women who went ter the fellowship?' Emmie queried. 'Surely men wouldn't be interested in sewin' an' embroidery?'

'Nah, they 'ave discussion groups,' Ada told her, 'an' they do oil paintin' an' fings like that, accordin' ter Mrs Penfold.'

'Did she say what the bloke looked like?' Emmie wanted to know.

'Mrs Penfold reckons 'e's quite smart,' Ada went on. 'She said 'e's fifty or thereabouts, a bit podgy an' a bit shorter than Sara but 'e talks nice an' 'e seems ter like 'er.'

'Well I 'ope 'e can put up wiv 'er moody ways,' Emmie remarked uncharitably. 'That woman never seems two minutes alike. One day she'll be all friendly an' anuvver time she'll walk right past yer.'

'Yeah, she's done it ter me,' Ada replied, 'but I don't fink she means ter be off'and. She's just a bundle o' nerves.'

Emmie nodded. 'It could be the makin' of 'er, I s'pose.'

With the Morgan Street diggings made ready for the bricklayers and the River Lane site filled in there was no more work available and the men were paid off.

'Well, it's back ter the bloody dole queue,' Danny sighed.

''Ow long d'yer fink it'll be before the next job starts?' one of the diggers asked.

'Gawd knows,' his partner replied. 'Nuffink's gonna 'appen till this inquest takes place.'

274

'I 'eard the contractors are blamin' the Coleys fer the cave-in,' another chipped in.

''Ow we gonna know when we can come back ter work?' the first man asked.

'By word o' mouth, the way it always goes.'

'Mind you, I'd like ter be in a position where I could tell the Coleys ter stick the poxy job right up their arse,' Danny remarked, 'but the way fings are at the moment I don't fink there'll be much chance o' that.'

The men left the site with their few hard-earned shillings in their pockets and the nagging worry that it might be some time before they could earn any more.

On Thursday night at the fellowship Sara helped to serve the tea and biscuits, and then with a feigned look of surprise found that she was sitting next to Randolph Cadman. 'I never saw you there,' she said sweetly.

'I'm honoured,' he replied with a smile. 'This is a very nice cup of tea, but then that's not surprising with you making it.'

Sara smiled coyly. Randolph could be so charming, she thought, and it made it much easier for her to converse with him. How different from Charlie Foden, who never seemed to respond to her when she tried getting to know him better. Maybe it was just as well. He was a rough diamond with little finesse, and much as she would have liked him to take notice of her there would always be that between them. Perhaps if she'd had Lucy's cheek and brashness she would have made better progress, but that sort of demeanour was alien to her. Besides, she had had very little experience where men were concerned, and she was not the sort of person who could flaunt herself. It would have been necessary with Charlie to make him realise that she was interested in him, but it wasn't with Randolph. She could be herself and not have to put on an act for his benefit.

'How's the choir comin' along?' she asked him.

'Very well, Sara,' he replied. 'I'm rather rusty but a few practice sessions will soon bring back the volume. It all stems from the diaphragm, you know. Down here,' he said, tapping his midriff.

Sara smiled. 'Would you care fer some more biscuits?' she asked.

Randolph shook his head. 'I'm afraid I'm off my food at the moment,' he told her.

'Oh dear. Nuffink serious, I 'ope?'

'No, it's nothing really, but when certain pressures build up they do tend to affect me that way. I suppose I'm a born worrier.'

'You say certain pressures,' Sara probed. 'Are they ter do wiv your work?'

He nodded. 'I work in the City, you see. Actually I'm employed by a City broker and you'll appreciate what a bad time we're having. Shares everywhere have fallen to a disastrous low and some, or I should say most, of our clients have lost considerable sums of money. It will improve, of course, but not in the short term. Trying to safeguard their investments in such a financial climate has become a terrible responsibility and a very hard burden to endure.'

'It must be awful for yer.'

He sighed deeply. 'The worst thing of all is knowing that there is a solution, and not being able to be part of it.'

Sara found that the conversation was beginning to go over her head but she persevered. 'Isn't it possible?' she asked.

He smiled indulgently. 'There is one essential condition,' he told her. 'A few of my colleagues have decided to break away from the company and go into the stocks and shares business on their own. They want me to join them, but it comes down to an old chestnut. Ready cash. With collateral we could buy certain shares at a ridiculously low figure and sell them for a large profit. It's a foolproof scheme with these particular shares because we have inside information that a bid is going to be made very soon by an old-established company, which would send them climbing to a record level. The fact of the matter is that we have to buy the shares before the knowledge becomes public. That's the problem.'

'It sounds very excitin'. I only wish I was in a position to 'elp yer,' Sara said sincerely.

'You're very kind,' Randolph replied, 'but even if you were in a position to help financially I couldn't possibly expect you to take the gamble on my word alone. Good lord, I could be a confidence trickster for all you know.'

'Never,' Sara said with a passion which surprised her. 'I'm a good judge of a person an' I know you'd never trick anyone.'

Randolph felt the time was ripe and he reached out and gently squeezed her hands in his. 'What a lovely thing to say,' he said softly.

Sara felt her cheeks getting hot. This was very intimate, and it sent all the right messages through her body. Here was a man she could feel perfectly at home with, a man who treated her as though she were Dresden china. 'It's a pity, really,' she said. 'I do 'ave one or two valuable possessions in the way o' jewellery, but they couldn't be put up as security, could they?'

He stroked his chin for a moment or two. 'That would

depend on the value,' he replied. 'The newly formed company could get a substantial bank loan, providing we have the necessary collateral. Rings, bracelets, necklaces and paid-up insurance policies and endowments are acceptable.'

Sara held out her hand palm down and he saw the large ruby flash in the uncertain light. 'That's a remarkable ring,' he said, nodding. 'It must be very valuable.'

'I've got a five-stone diamond ring at 'ome that was left ter me by my poor muvver, God rest 'er soul,' she told him. 'There's bin times when I've bin tempted ter pawn 'em, but I couldn't bring meself ter do it, desperate as I was.'

Randolph's eyes lingered on the ruby ring for a few seconds, then he looked up at her and smiled. 'Do you know,' he said, 'I don't think I've ever met such a nice, trusting person before, but rest assured, I wouldn't even consider accepting personal items of jewellery from my friends as security, and especially not from you. It wouldn't be right. It would be asking too much from someone who's only known me for a very short time.'

'It seems as if I've known yer for ages,' Sara replied, flushing slightly.

'I too feel as though you and I are old friends,' he declared. 'Sara, I want you to know that I came to this fellowship out of loneliness, and I know that meeting you was meant to be. It was fate. You and I are two kindred souls and I want to get to know you much better. Come to Brighton with me this weekend.'

Sara looked shocked. 'I couldn't. It wouldn't be right,' she said quickly.

Randolph laughed aloud. 'Good lord, you don't think my intentions are anything but honourable, do you? We'll have single rooms at a little seafront guesthouse I know, and the sea air will do wonders for you, even in winter.'

'I don't know. It's all so sudden,' Sara said hesitantly.

'Say you will and make me a very happy man,' he entreated her with a disarming smile.

'All right, I will.'

Chapter Twenty-Six

Frank Coley's face was a dark mask as he prodded the tabletop with his forefinger. 'Charlie Foden was lyin' as far as I'm concerned,' he growled. 'I'd bet any money George Parry was the cause o' Wally Coates's death, 'im an' that idiot Danny Albury.'

Ben Coley quickly looked round the saloon bar of the Mason's Arms to make sure his irate brother was not being overheard. 'I go along wiv that,' he said. 'Coates never slipped. 'E was clubbed.'

Sharkey sat moodily contemplating his pint. He knew the Coleys well and suspected that something nasty was brewing in Frank Coley's head.

'There's no way we're gonna find out, though,' Ben added. 'They'll stick ter their story an' leave us sweatin'.'

'Yeah, an' we could effectively be put out o' business,' Frank replied. 'That coroner's man was payin' a lot of attention ter the timbers by the cave-in an' I 'ad this feelin' 'e suspected they'd bin changed.'

'Nah, I don't fink so,' Ben said dismissively.

'I didn't like the way 'e walked the length o' the trench to inspect the rest o' the shutterin',' Frank went on. 'There was a lot of old wood used. It's gonna feel like a long time before that inquest gets under way. If the outcome's down ter misadventure an' we get criticised fer bad workmanship we can say goodbye ter the rest o' the contract. Maitland's won't look at us, not wiv that government-sponsored deal they've got.'

'Well there's no sense in worryin' about it now,' Ben answered. 'There's nuffink we can do ter change fings.'

'That's a matter of opinion,' Frank said, smiling evilly.

Ben looked at him and grinned. 'What's in that schemin' brain of yours?' he asked.

'It'd be a different fing entirely if eivver Albury or Parry owned up ter bein' the cause o' Coates's death,' Frank remarked. 'It'd put us in the clear, wouldn't it?'

Sharkey sat up straight in his seat as the brothers looked at him. 'Now wait a minute,' he said quickly. 'I ain't gonna go beltin' it out of 'em. I don't fancy goin' down fer GBH.'

'I wouldn't want you ter get involved, Sharkey,' Frank told him with a grin, 'but wiv your influence an' know-ledge, I'm sure you could get a couple o' reliable lads ter give Parry an' Albury a good goin'-over. I don't fink they'd 'ave too much trouble knockin' the truth out of eivver of 'em. Just tell 'em ter make sure they don't go over the top. We don't want any killin's on our 'ands, after all. We've gotta be kept out of it. See what yer can do, will yer?'

Sharkey nodded. 'I'd better be makin' some enquiries, then,' he said, getting up from his chair. 'What's the figure?'

'They get a tenner each now an' anuvver tenner when the job's done,' Frank replied. 'But make sure they're reliable. They can say they're friends o' Wally Coates, but under no circumstances do I want our names mentioned.'

Sharkey left the Mason's Arms with mixed feelings. He knew a few of his old pals down on their luck who would jump at the chance of earning twenty pounds for a short job of work, but there was also a sense of misgiving nagging at his insides. If the Coleys were put in a corner they'd act like rats and go for the throat – his throat if it suited them.

The troubled ganger made his way to Dockhead and walked into the Crown public house, ordering a pint of bitter and a large whisky chaser as he looked around for familiar faces. The germ of an idea was growing in his mind and he had to think it through thoroughly. Any slip and he would end up like a slice of meat between two rounds of bread.

On Thursday morning George Parry and Danny Albury joined the long winding dole queue at the labour exchange in Mollings Street off the Old Kent Road. They had decided enough was enough as far as working for the Coleys was concerned, and they would wait on the chance of getting offered some other work, however remote.

The queue seemed to go on for ever and it was over an hour before the two were anywhere near the front entrance. Men stood with shoulders slumped, blank looks on their gaunt faces and hands stuffed deep in their coat pockets against the chill day.

'I dunno if we've done the right fing,' George said despondently. 'What chance 'ave we got wiv this lot in front of us.'

'Well, at least we'll be able ter register fer unemployment money,' Danny told him.

'Yeah, I s'pose yer right,' George agreed.

''Ere, look at that geezer,' Danny said quickly.

George glanced down the line and saw a tall thin man walk up carrying a screwed-up newspaper in his hands and say something to one of the men.

'Go on, piss off,' the man scowled. 'Don't come that one wiv me. D'yer fink I'm stupid or somefink?'

'I'm not lyin' ter yer, pal,' the newcomer told him. ''E said 'e'd mind me place while I went fer some chips.'

'Who did?'

'The bloke who was standin' next ter yer.'

'Yer never said anyfing ter me,' the man in front spoke up.

'Nah, not you, the ovver bloke what was 'ere.'

'No one's moved away since I was 'ere,' the first man said sharply.

'Well I assure yer I'm not tellin' porkies,' the newcomer replied.

'Look, piss off while yer still able,' the first man growled.

Suddenly the line was broken as men started pushing and shoving, then fighting erupted, and the chancer found himself on the ground with blood dripping down his chin on to his chips. Around him there seemed to be a general fracas. Men who one minute before had been standing peaceably in line were now like a pack of rampant animals as hits were thrown at random and blows received were given back with interest.

Two elderly women who were passing by suddenly spotted one man throw a cowardly punch to the back of someone's neck and they waded in with relish, raining blows on his head.

'Stop it! Stop it, d'you hear!' a loud voice yelled out, and slowly the fighting began to calm down. 'This behaviour is disgraceful. I'm inclined to close this exchange down for the day.'

'Give us a chance, guv,' one of the men called out through bruised lips. 'It was some dodgy 'Erbert who started it all. We've queued up 'ere fer hours all peaceful like.'

'Very well then,' the official replied, 'but if there's any repeat of this disgusting behaviour I'll make sure you don't get seen to today.'

Danny shook his head. 'I've never seen grown men act like this before,' he remarked. 'It's like they were waitin' fer the chance ter steam in.'

George raised his eyebrows and shrugged. 'It's bottled-up anger,' he answered. 'There's gotta be anuvver way o' dealin' wiv this, surely. 'Avin' ter stand fer hours on end in a dole queue is soul-destroyin'. It makes yer feel useless. Well, it does me.'

'It does that to all of us,' Danny said quietly.

The man who had started the rumpus came walking down the line still clutching soggy chips in a grubby piece of newspaper. 'I'm pushin' orf 'ome,' he told a man standing in front of Danny. 'They're all bloody mad 'ere.'

'Well go on then, piss orf, don't tell me,' the man retorted.

'Fancy a chip?'

'No I don't want one o' yer poxy chips.'

'No need ter be nasty about it.'

'Piss orf.'

'All right, I'm goin'.'

George looked at Danny and smiled. 'That's 'ow we'll end up if we 'ave much more o' this,' he muttered.

The man in front turned round and nodded towards the departing chancer. 'That's Manny Corrigan,' he told them. 'Daft as a brush 'e is. Last week 'e came 'ere wiv an ole tom on 'is arm. Pissed out o' their brains the pair of 'em. Gawd knows where 'e gets 'is money from.'

'I saw 'im singin' in the streets round the Elephant an'

Castle,' another man remarked. ''E sells oddments out of a suitcase down East Lane as well.'

Danny glanced at his friend. 'P'raps we should try that,' he said, grinning.

They eventually filed through the door into the relative warmth, and after another lengthy delay they finally reached the counter and signed on as unemployed.

Mary and Lucy were having their regular get-together and Gracie stood obediently by the armchair while her mother pinned two pieces of linen together round her middle. 'There'll be enough 'ere fer you ter make one as well,' Mary told her neighbour. 'Minnie Venners said she'd given me enough fer two dresses. I thought it was nice of 'er. I told 'er she shouldn't feel obligated. Those tram sheets would 'ave still bin in the bathtub if I 'adn't given 'em to 'er.'

'Too bloody true,' Lucy replied.

Mary brushed the creases out of the material and looked up at her friend. 'I showed Roy that magazine,' she said. ''E was really shocked. Until then I'm sure 'e thought I was exaggeratin' about that lecherous ole git.'

'Anyway, you're well out of it,' Lucy told her. 'You just fink what might 'ave 'appened on that roof wiv 'im.'

'It don't bear finkin' about,' Mary said, shivering.

Gracie started fidgeting and Mary held her by the shoulders. 'Just a tiny bit more an' you can go an' play wiv Sue,' she coaxed.

'What yer gonna do when yer've sewed it up?' Lucy asked her.

'I'm gonna dye it green an' put some fancy lace round the collar an' sleeves, an' at the bottom,' Mary said, smiling confidently.

Lucy waited till the child had gone to find her friend, then she leaned forward in the armchair. 'Sara's started courtin',' she said quietly.

Mary looked surprised. 'That's one fer the book. Who is it? D'yer know 'im?'

Lucy shrugged her shoulders. 'She came 'ome last night full of it. It's bin goin' on fer a few weeks by all accounts, an' this feller wants 'er ter go ter Brighton wiv 'im this weekend.'

'Bloody 'ell, 'e ain't wasted any time.'

'Sara was quick ter point out that it was all above board. They're gonna 'ave separate rooms.'

'Is this someone from the church?'

'Yeah, the fellowship.'

'Did she tell yer what 'e's like?'

'She said 'e's good-lookin' an' very charmin', an' 'e sings in the choir.'

'An' 'ow old is 'e?'

'About Charlie's age.'

'Good fer 'er,' Mary remarked. ''Ere, d'yer reckon 'e'll creep in 'er room in the middle o' the night an' take 'er by surprise?'

'Not by surprise, if I know Sara. She'll be expectin' 'im.'

'P'raps it'll be the makin' of 'er,' Mary chuckled.

'I was gettin' worried about 'er, ter be honest,' Lucy confided. 'She started playin' up ter Charlie fer a while but she was makin' it look so obvious it was embarrassin' 'im. Poor Sara, she didn't 'ave a clue 'ow ter go about it.'

'Which is just as well, I should fink,' Mary replied. 'Especially if Charlie wasn't interested.' She gathered up the offcuts of linen and caught Lucy's eye. 'George's off an' all this weekend, yer said.'

'Yeah. It's gonna seem strange.'

287

Mary gave her a sly grin. 'I don't s'pose Charlie's goin' anywhere, is 'e?'

Lucy averted her eyes. 'I dunno really.'

Mary sat back in her chair and picked some strands of cotton from her flowered apron. ''Ow long 'ave we known each ovver, Lucy?' she asked suddenly.

'Ages. Ever since I moved inter the street.'

'Well, as an old friend I feel I can say this. Whatever you an' Charlie get up to, don't let it ruin yer marriage.'

'We're not gonna get up to anyfing,' Lucy said quickly.

'Don't try ter kid a kidder,' Mary told her with a cheeky grin. 'You're crazy about the bloke. I see the look in yer eyes every time yer mention 'is name. It's OK, yer don't 'ave ter fight it. Just remember ter keep it on a sensible level.'

Lucy knew that it was useless to pretend any longer. Mary knew the truth but she was right about another thing too. Nothing was more important than her marriage, and if any lapse did occur it would have to remain just that, a fleeting pleasure. Something to be enjoyed in passing, like a moment out of time. 'You're sayin' all this about me an' Charlie,' she smiled, 'but I don't really know if Charlie's interested in me.'

'Now I know yer gotta be jokin',' Mary snorted. 'Anyone wiv 'alf a brain can see it. Sara can, an' so can George, an' I bet yer George only tolerates 'im as a lodger 'cos 'e finks you're not interested yourself.'

'Well, I 'aven't given 'im any reason ter fink ovverwise.'

'Don't. An' be careful,' Mary warned her. 'George might seem preoccupied wiv all that's 'appened lately, but 'e ain't stupid.'

Lucy sighed sadly. 'Do you know, Mary, I fink if me an' Charlie cuddled in front of 'im 'e wouldn't notice? We seem to 'ave become like strangers to each ovver. I can't remember the last time 'e showed any interest in me. The times I've wanted ter reach out fer 'im in bed but 'e's bin snorin' 'is 'ead off.'

'It 'appens in the best o' marriages at times,' Mary said reassuringly, 'an' the times we're livin' frew at the moment ain't exactly conducive ter bein' 'appy in bed. We take our burdens up those stairs wiv us at night instead o' leavin' 'em be'ind. I reckon everyone must lie in bed wonderin' where the next penny's comin' from, an' 'ow they're gonna pay the bills. I'm no different from you in that respect. You an' George are gonna come frew it. Just make sure yer don't pull the rug from under the pair of yer.'

'Mary, you're a gem,' Lucy told her warmly. 'But yer do go on at times. Over an hour I've bin sittin' 'ere an' not one cup o' tea's passed me lips. Shall I put the kettle on?'

Mary got up. 'Leave it ter me,' she said with a crooked smile. 'Just sit back an' get yer rest while yer can.'

Although the diggers had been paid off Sharkey and Charlie had been told to report for work the following morning, and Frank Coley was feeling confident as he spoke to them. 'All bein' well we'll be gettin' back ter normal soon an' we'll need ter let the men know,' he said. Then he turned to Ben. ''Ave we got all their addresses?'

His brother nodded. 'Most of 'em are 'ere, in the note-book. There's also the name of a pub against some of 'em so we could contact 'em quickly when the work gets underway again.'

Frank took the notebook from Ben and flipped through the pages. There were blanks beside Danny and George's names and he looked up at Charlie. 'What about your two pals?' he asked. 'Do they still use the Mason's?'

Charlie nodded. 'Occasionally.'

Sharkey made a mental note. He would be expected to pass on the information to the two ruffians he had recruited, who were ready and waiting to earn their wages.

Frank Coley reached for his coat. 'Yer'd better come wiv me, Ben,' he said. 'We've got some talkin' ter do.' Then he looked back at the gangers. 'Mind the fort, will yer? We'll be back soon as we can.'

Once they were alone Sharkey pulled out a stool from under the bench and sat down heavily. 'Yer know they won't rest until they nail Parry an' Albury,' he remarked tentatively.

'Yeah, I know, but they won't,' Charlie replied. 'It wasn't 'ow it 'appened an' they can't prove ovverwise.'

Sharkey clasped his large hands together on his lap and leaned back against the bench. 'Ter be honest I don't care if Parry did clobber Coates,' he went on. 'The man was a troublemaker, an' 'e wouldn't 'ave bin tolerated in ovver firms. 'E suited the Coleys, though. They could trust 'im ter keep 'em informed.'

'Yeah, then they got you ter do the business for 'em,' Charlie replied coldly.

'It's what I'm paid for, an' if I showed any weakness it'd be taken advantage of by the men,' Sharkey said, shrugging his shoulders. 'You know I'm right. Fortunately fer you, though, you 'aven't needed ter get rid of anyone yet.'

'If it crops up I 'ope I do it in a more civilised way than you,' Charlie answered.

Sharkey narrowed his eyes and smiled mirthlessly. 'We all 'ave our methods.'

Charlie gave him a hard look as he stood up. 'I'm goin' outside for some fresh air,' he said offhandedly.

'Wait a minute,' Sharkey urged him. 'There's somefing

yer need ter know, but first, I want your word you'll keep what I tell yer strictly between us two.'

'Can yer trust my word?'

'I believe I can.'

Charlie sat down once more. 'Go on then, Sharkey.'

'The Coleys told me that the inquest's set fer next Friday, an' they asked me ter line up a couple of 'eavy geezers ter sort Parry an' Albury out before'and. The idea's ter knock the trufe out of 'em, then make sure they admit as much at the inquest.'

Charlie looked shocked. 'They've told the trufe already,' he said quickly. 'An' s'posin' they do agree ter change their story ter save a beatin', what's ter stop 'em stickin' ter the trufe at the inquest? They could even tell the coroner they've bin threatened. 'E'd be obliged ter bring in the police.'

Sharkey smiled scornfully. 'You don't know these geezers. They're not gonna stand arguin' the toss first. They'll just say they're Wally Coates's pals an' steam in. Once Parry an' Albury 'ave bin well seen to they'll be told what ter say at the inquest, an' if they don't do as they're told they can expect more o' the same. An' I gotta tell yer it won't stop at that. They'll be made aware that their families'll be included next time. That's 'ow this sort work.'

'You've got some right nice friends,' Charlie said sarcastically.

'They're no friends o' mine,' Sharkey replied quickly. 'I was just asked ter recruit someone who could do a good job. What you gotta understand is, the Coleys could go under if the inquest verdict goes boss-eyed. They're desperate, an' they'll do what they 'ave ter do.'

'Which means that Parry an' Albury are gonna be obliged ter go into 'idin' till the inquest.'

'That's about the strength of it.'

'If they do get waylaid an' forced ter change their story it'll fly in the face of what I'll be sayin', or 'ave the Coleys lined me up too?' Charlie asked with a searching stare.

'No, they'll just sort Parry an' Albury out. It'll be their word against yours, an' the coroner's gonna realise that you've got good reason ter lie,' Sharkey reminded him. 'You were the ganger in charge. As far as 'e's concerned you couldn't be 'eld responsible fer a man slippin' over an' causin' 'is own death, but yer could be if there was a confrontation an' you failed ter nip it in the bud.'

'Parry an' Albury were tellin' the trufe,' Charlie said firmly.

'You try tellin' the Coleys as much,' Sharkey growled. 'Like I said, I ain't bovvered eivver way about what 'appened, but I ain't intendin' ter be the patsy if it all goes wrong. They'll stick me in the frame if they 'ave to.'

''Ow they gonna play it?' Charlie asked.

'They know where Parry an' Albury live an' they'll pick their time.'

'When will it 'appen?'

'Soon as possible,' Sharkey said, 'bearin' in mind the inquest is only a week away.'

Charlie felt relieved that George would be out of the area that weekend, but he was worried about Danny Albury. The man was too brave for his own good at times. Standing up to Wally Coates had taken some nerve and he would do the same with the heavies, which would only make matters worse. 'Why don't you give those scum bruvvers the elbow an' go back ter wrestlin'?' he remarked.

'I might even do that,' Sharkey replied with a brief smile.

Charlie stood up to leave. 'I don't s'pose you're worried about what I might fink of yer,' he said quietly, 'but I want

yer ter know I appreciate you takin' a chance in tellin' me.
I'll tell yer somefing else too. I'm glad we never needed ter
come on 'ead to 'ead.'

'Yeah. It could 'ave bin a right ole set-to,' the ex-wrestler
replied. 'Let's go get a drink. They won't be back yet.'

Chapter Twenty-Seven

On Friday evening Charlie Foden held a council of war at the Mason's Arms. Sharing a table with him at the far end of the public bar were George Parry, Danny Albury and Roy Chubb.

'Are you sure she's all right?' Charlie asked Danny.

'Look, you can take my word fer it,' the dapper man replied. 'Freda Johnson's as good as gold. I know fer a fact she's bawled Mick out plenty o' times fer gettin' too cosy wiv the Coleys. She told me 'e's servin' in the saloon ternight so 'e won't even know we're 'ere. Not that it matters. We're allowed ter come in fer a drink, surely ter Gawd.'

Charlie nodded. 'Now this is straight from the 'orse's mouth, so listen carefully an' don't make light of it,' he began, staring at Danny and George in turn. 'You two 'ave 'ad yer cards marked. The Coleys 'ave got a couple o' bruisers ter sort you out. The idea is to 'ammer the truth out o' the pair of yer, an' make yer confess that you caused Wally Coates's death.'

Both looked shocked. 'They can't do that,' Danny said quickly.

'S'posin' we went ter the police an' said we've bin threatened?' George added.

Charlie shook his head. 'Let me try ter put yer in the picture,' he went on. 'In the first place the Coleys 'ave got someone ter recruit the two geezers, an' as far as they know it's prob'ly one o' Coates's mates who's puttin' 'em up to it. The Coleys' 'ands are clean. What's more, the person who warned me 'as got my word I won't drop 'im in it, so if yer go ter the police they won't be able ter do anyfing. They'd need proof.'

'What's this all about?' George asked.

'The inquest is set fer next Friday,' Charlie explained, 'an' if they can get a confession out of eivver one of yer before then, they can use it as evidence that the management weren't ter blame fer Coates's death. That leaves 'em in a position ter talk terms wiv the main contractors fer the rest o' the trenchin' contract.'

Danny Albury seemed puzzled. ''Ow do they know who we are?'

'They've bin given both yer addresses an' they know the pubs you use,' Charlie told him. 'They only need ter make a few enquiries anyway. They could say they're ole friends or somefing, an' someone could point you out.'

'If they threaten us we could promise ter say anyfing an' do the opposite at the inquest,' Danny said.

'They won't threaten yer, they'll come at yer,' Charlie stressed, 'an' by the time they'd finished wiv the two of yer you'd say anyfing an' stick wiv it. If yer didn't, they'd come back at yer families as well as you. That's the dangerous sort they are, believe me.'

'What can we do about it?' George asked.

'Well in your case you'll be away fer the weekend,' Charlie reminded him, 'an' we can sort somefing out when yer get back on Sunday night. As fer you, Danny, yer gotta stay off the street. Make sure yer know who's at the door if there's a knock, an' if yer don't then don't answer.'

'I usually go out fer a pint on Saturday nights,' Danny groaned.

Roy Chubb had been silent so far, but now he smiled. 'I like a drink on Saturday nights too,' he said. 'I'll come an' collect yer.'

'Not on yer own yer won't,' Charlie said bluntly. 'Yer'd need ter be mob-'anded.'

'You know Benny an' Fatty Wallace, an' Les Green?' Roy asked, looking at Danny. 'We'll call round tergevver. We all use the Swan on Saturday nights.'

'I don't go out on Sundays,' Danny said, 'but what about when me an' George go down the labour exchange on Monday mornin'?'

'We'll work somefing out later,' Charlie answered. 'In the meantime be extra careful. I'll be 'avin' a discreet word wiv Ron Sloan soon as I can. I'll put 'im in the picture an' 'e'll be able ter keep a look-out fer any strange faces lurkin' about in the vicinity.'

'I'll warn a few o' the lads ter be on the look-out as well,' Danny added.

Charlie drained his glass. 'I might be wrong, but I got an idea they won't try anyfing this weekend,' he said thoughtfully. 'They'll wait till early next week.'

The group left the pub together and walked briskly into Cooper Street. 'Remember what's bin said, Danny, an' take care,' Charlie told him as they reached the little man's front door.

Sammy Strickland left his house on Friday evening and strode off towards the Dun Cow in the Old Kent Road. That week he had earned a wage helping out with some house painting, and when he had laid out the money on the scullery table Peggy felt quite faint. 'I dunno what ter say,' she gasped.

'There's nuffink to say,' he replied. 'I done it fer you. I was just about sick an' tired o' seein' you struggle, an' when ole Fuller offered me the work I jumped at it. Actually there might be some more o' the same comin' up but I'll wait till next week ter see 'im. I ain't gonna go wastin' money lookin' fer 'im at the Dun Cow.'

'Is this every penny yer've earned?' Peggy asked.

'Every penny, love.'

'Well you take a coupla bob back an' go an' get yerself a drink. You've earned it,' Peggy told him with a smile.

Sammy was not aware of the large man who had watched him come out of the turning and had now fallen into step a few yards behind him. Nor did he see the other bulky figure who came up and joined the first man. Sammy's mind was on that pint of frothing beer, and as he stepped into the public bar he licked his lips in anticipation.

'It looks like it's gonna be a nasty old night,' the stranger remarked casually to Sammy as he and his colleague stood next to him at the counter.

'Yeah, it does,' Sammy replied as he gratefully pulled the brimming glass towards himself.

The man ordered two pints of bitter and turned to face Sammy. 'I take it you're a local round these parts, pal,' he said amiably.

'All of firty years,' Sammy told him with a smile.

'You'd most likely know Danny Albury an' George Parry, then.'

'Know 'em? I live in the same street as them.'

The big man smiled. 'Me an' my mate Frank 'ere used

ter work wiv 'em, yer see, an' we was 'opin' we'd bump into 'em in 'ere. They told us once they used the Dun Cow.'

'Not very often,' Sammy replied. 'They use the Mason's Arms or the Star on the corner o' Kingsley Street.'

'Fanks, pal,' the big man said. 'We'll pop in there later. It'd be nice ter see 'em again.'

Sammy drank his beer with relish and decided that one more pint was in order, and as he reached into his trouser pocket Will Jackson walked in.

'Wotcher, Sammy, 'ow yer doin'?' he asked.

'Not so bad. What about you?'

'Fings are a bit quiet lately, which is ter be expected,' Will replied, taking out a handful of copper from his pocket.

'Leave it ter me,' Sammy told him. 'I 'ad a good week by way of a change.'

The two carried their pints over to a vacant table and Will took out his tobacco tin, a serious look on his wide face. 'I just come from Alice Albury's,' he said. 'I'd put a new pane o' glass in 'er scullery winder an' as I was clearin' up the mess Danny walked in. 'E looked worried out of 'is life an' 'im an' Alice went inter the parlour. I could 'ear Danny talkin' quickly but I wasn't earwiggin'. Anyway, they called me in a few minutes later an' Danny told me 'e's 'ad 'is card marked. 'Im an' Alice are in a right ole state. Worried out o' their lives they are.'

'What's it all about?' Sammy enquired.

Will Jackson sipped his pint. 'Apparently there's a couple o' nasty geezers after givin' 'im an' George Parry a goin'-over.'

'George Parry as well?'

'Yeah. It's over that accident at the diggin's in Morgan Street, so Danny told me. These two geezers are out ter make 'im an' George change their story of 'ow it 'appened.'

'What for?'

'I dunno. Danny was sayin' it's so that the Coleys don't take the blame,' Will replied. 'It was all a bit over me 'ead, but I can tell yer Danny looked really worried. So did Alice. I bin asked ter watch points an' let 'em know if anyone strange comes askin' questions.'

Sammy's face had slowly lost its colour as Will was talking and he now looked as white as a freshly laundered bedsheet. 'Don't look round, just keep yer eyes fixed on me,' he hissed.

'What's the matter?'

'I'll tell yer what's the matter,' Sammy gulped. 'I just bin approached by two big geezers at the counter askin' about Danny an' George.'

'Oh my good Gawd!' Will gasped. 'What did yer tell 'em?'

'They said they was ole workmates an' they wanted ter meet up wiv 'em again, so I told 'em they usually go in the Star or the Mason's Arms.'

'Yer never.'

'I did.'

'Bloody 'ell.'

'What we gonna do, Will?'

'What you gonna do, yer mean,' Will said sharply.

'I'll 'ave ter go an' warn 'em ter keep away from those pubs,' Sammy decided.

'Yer'd better tell 'em what those two geezers look like as well, so they'll 'ave 'alf a chance o' dodgin' 'em,' Will advised him.

Sammy studied his glass of beer for a few moments and then a smile started to play around the corner of his mouth. 'I've got an idea,' he said.

'It better be a good one,' Will growled.

'Look, you finish yer pint an' then walk out the pub,' Sammy told him. 'I'll see yer in the Samson in about ten minutes.'

As soon as Will Jackson had left Sammy sidled up to the counter and stood next to the two bruisers. 'Did yer see me talkin' ter that bloke just now?' he asked them. ''E lives in the turnin'. 'E told me they've just took Danny Albury ter the Rovverhive Infirmary in an ambulance. Suspected appendicitis by all accounts.'

'That's bad news,' the man nearest to him answered.

'Anyway, yer'll be able ter visit 'im in there,' Sammy went on. 'Maybe take a few grapes in. I'm sure Danny'll appreciate it. Well, must be off. I'm 'avin' a drink wiv me bruvver-in-law later when 'e comes off duty. 'E's the local beat bobby. Nice feller. A bit 'ard wiv the Jack-the-lads at times, but 'is 'eart's in the right place.'

As Sammy left the Dun Cow the bigger of the two thugs drained his glass. 'C'mon,' he said quickly.

'Where we goin'?' the other asked.

'I can smell somefing fishy 'ere,' the first man replied. 'We're gonna pay a trip ter the Rovverhive Infirmary an' find out if a Mr Albury was admitted this evenin'.'

When Will Jackson left the Dun Cow and made his way along to the Samson he almost bumped into the local bobby. 'What, no wringers?' the policeman remarked, looking down at the smaller man with a sarcastic smile. 'You must be slippin', Will.'

'I'm strickly kosher these days,' he replied. 'I gotta fink o' Paula an' the two kids.'

'Nice to 'ear yer say it,' Ron Sloan said, rocking back on his heels.

Will Jackson looked up at the policeman with an earnest expression on his face. 'Does your beat go as far as the Old Kent Road?' he enquired.

'Just about. Why d'yer ask?'

'As far as the Dun Cow?'

Ron Sloan shook his head. 'What's this all about, Will?'

The handyman cast a quick glance along the street. 'I just bin 'avin' a drink in there wiv Sammy Strickland an' 'e pointed out these two ugly great geezers who are after sortin' out Danny Albury an' George Parry.'

'What for?'

'Yer'd need ter talk ter Sammy about the whys an' wherefores,' Will answered. 'All I know is those two geezers are out ter make George an' Danny change their statements at the inquest on that bloke who got killed in Morgan Street.'

'If that's the case they're duty bound ter report it ter the police,' Ron said emphatically. 'What's more, if you can identify these two men you should go wiv 'em too.'

'It ain't as simple as that.'

'No, it never is,' the policeman growled.

'If you could see Danny Albury or George Parry they'd be able ter put yer in the picture,' Will suggested.

'I might just do that,' the policeman told him. 'Now can yer give me a description o' these two villains?'

Will shook his head. 'I only got a quick flash of 'em, but Sammy was talkin' to 'em before I arrived at the pub an' 'e'd remember what they looked like.'

Ron Sloan nodded. 'Is Sammy likely ter be in before the pubs turn out ternight?' he asked.

'Yeah. I'm on me way ter see 'im at the Samson now,' Will replied, 'but Peggy wouldn't allow 'im ter stay out that late.'

302

PC Sloan knocked at the Alburys' front door and saw the curtains move in the parlour before his knock was answered. Later he called at the Parrys' house and faced Lucy's wrath. 'My George would never 'arm a fly,' she insisted. 'An' who in their right mind's gonna admit ter somefing that never 'appened, especially when it could get 'em inter trouble, even get 'em sent ter prison?'

'People do some strange fings when they're frightened, Mrs Parry,' the policeman remarked, then turned his attention to Charlie. 'You say you were warned about what's bin planned on the premise that yer'll keep yer contact's name secret. Well let me tell you somefing. If this ever gets ter court you'll be summoned as a witness an' you'll be on oath. You might well find yerself in contempt, which, as I'm sure yer know, could land you in prison.'

'Yeah, I realise that,' Charlie replied quietly.

Ron Sloan got up to leave. 'I'm obliged ter put what's bin said in my report, so if I were you I'd get round the station first fing termorrer an' see the Super.'

Lucy showed the policeman out and then walked back into the parlour with a dark look on her pretty face. 'I've got a nasty feelin' I'm bein' kept in the dark,' she complained.

George leaned back in his chair. 'There's no way they can make me lie about what 'appened in that trench,' he said firmly. 'Wally Coates slipped an' fell back on the shorin' prop. 'E was a big man an' 'is weight dislodged it. That's what me an' Danny saw, that's what we put in our statements an' that's what the coroner'll be told. It's the trufe.'

Charlie hated lying to Lucy, but it was for the best, he thought. 'Yer can't go wrong wiv the trufe.'

'I wonder if we should do as Ron Sloan suggested?' George said.

'If we do I gotta keep my contact's name out of it,' Charlie told him, 'come what may.'

'I'm sure they'll understand,' George replied.

Lucy got up and collected the tray of used crockery from the table. 'I was 'opin' Sara wouldn't walk in while that copper was 'ere,' she remarked. 'Those sewin' evenin's don't run all that late as a rule.'

That particular sewing evening had in fact finished early, due to the heating boiler having broken down, and as the women filed out of the church Sara was thrilled to see Randolph standing in the porch. 'I thought I'd look in to see if you'd like me to walk you home,' he said, smiling. 'It's a nasty night.'

'That's very nice of yer.'

'I managed to see Mr Saward this morning,' he told her. 'Things are looking good.'

'You mean you'll be able ter get the business started?'

'Well, it all depends on my being able to raise the necessary funds,' Randolph said as they walked along Lynton Road. 'I'm hopeful, and if it works out the company could be in full flow by the summer. We'd be financially established and in a position to challenge the big fish. Believe me, Sara, the prospects are almost frightening in their intensity.'

'I'm so thrilled fer you, Randolph,' Sara said sweetly. 'I want you ter remember what I said. You're more than welcome ter use my jewellery as security. I've got every confidence in you.'

'I must admit it would solve a problem or two, but I stop short of asking you. It's just too much to expect.'

'Don't be so silly,' Sara told him in her childish voice. 'If all else fails yer must ask me, do you promise?'

'I promise.'

They had reached the corner of Cooper Street. 'Goodnight, Sara,' he said, taking her hand in his and giving it a little squeeze.

'Goodnight, Randolph.'

He quickly kissed her cheek and walked away, leaving her with a satisfied smile on her pale face which was suddenly wiped away as she saw PC Ron Sloan leave the house.

'Whatever's 'appened?' she gasped as she hurried into the parlour.

'It's all right, calm down, Sara,' George told her. 'Ron Sloan was only tellin' us that the inquest's fixed fer next Friday.'

'But you already knew that.'

'Yeah, but the copper never knew I knew,' George said, smiling.

'I was worried out o' me life when I saw 'im come out the 'ouse,' Sara went on. 'There's always somefing comes up ter spoil a nice evenin'.'

'So you 'ad a nice evenin'?' Lucy said.

'I did, and when I came out o' the church there was Randolph waitin' to escort me 'ome.'

'That must 'ave bin nice,' Lucy replied, trying to look serious.

'I 'ope yer'll be careful this weekend,' George remarked.

'George, Sara's not a child, she's a mature woman,' Lucy said quickly, giving Charlie a brief glance. 'She's goin' ter Brighton, not Timbuctoo.'

'Yeah, but she 'ardly knows this Randolph feller,' he replied. 'Yer read so many bad stories in the papers an' I'm just warnin' 'er ter be careful.'

'Randolph's a real gentleman an' I'm goin' ter be well looked after this weekend,' Sara said indignantly.

Yeah I bet you will, Lucy thought, and she smiled amiably at her sister-in-law. 'You just 'ave a nice time,' she said.

Chapter Twenty-Eight

Police Constable Ron Sloan had been the beat bobby around the Cooper Street area for a number of years and he was known to everyone. Many a young buck had been turned aside from the road to incarceration by a judicious clip round the ear at a most impressionable age, and many a usually law-abiding citizen had been let off when apprehended in suspicious circumstances by the discerning bobby, who knew only too well that desperate men took to desperate measures. Ron Sloan was no soft touch, however, as many a local publican would testify after seeing him break up a fight or calm down an enraged customer.

The constable took his job seriously enough to have turned down the chance of becoming a sergeant, which would have effectively taken him from his beat, and he was at his best in difficult situations.

'Yer'd better 'ave a word wiv the Super,' the station sergeant told him after reading his report.

Ron Sloan was able to convince his superior that it could all be sorted out satisfactorily if he was allowed to deal with it informally, and to that end he was given permission to change to early shift beginning on Saturday morning.

'Any chance of a cuppa, Sammy?' he asked the very surprised chancer who answered the rat-tat in his nightshirt.

'Bloody 'ell, don't you ever sleep?' Sammy growled as he showed Ron in.

'Sammy, I wanna use your parlour fer a while this mornin'. Is that all right?'

''Ere, you ain't bringin' a dodgy woman in 'ere, are yer?' Sammy asked, wide-eyed.

'Don't be silly. I've got a nice little woman at 'ome,' Ron Sloan told him. 'I'm after watchin' points.'

'Is it ter do wiv what I told yer last night?'

The policeman nodded. 'I got a gut feelin' they'll be turnin' their attention towards George Parry an' they may even call on 'im. I 'ope they do, then you can make a formal identification.'

''Ere, I ain't goin' ter court ter pick 'em out, so you can get that right out o' yer 'ead,' Sammy said with passion.

'They won't be goin' ter court if they don't do anyfing,' the PC told him. 'That's what I'm after, sortin' this before it gets nasty.'

'Right, I'm wiv yer,' Sammy said, grinning. 'Now you do what you 'ave ter do while I make the tea. Peggy's 'avin' a lie-in this mornin'.'

Ron nodded. 'I'll 'ave a quick cuppa, then I'm gonna pop over ter see the Parrys before George leaves.'

Bonny Watson and Snatcher Bayliss sat by the window in a steamy café off Lynton Road and slurped tea from large mugs.

'I don't like it. I don't like it one little bit,' Snatcher was saying. 'It's as though we're bein' watched.'

'Look, d'you still wanna earn that score, or 'ave yer gone bottly all of a sudden?' Bonny asked.

'Course I wanna earn it, an' I ain't gone bottly,' he replied. 'It's just that we've bin took on, an' I'm askin' meself fer why? Danny Albury wasn't admitted ter the 'ospital last night. Why should that ole boy tell us ovver-wise?'

''E could 'ave got the 'ospitals mixed up.'

'Cobblers. 'E sussed what we were up to an' wanted ter put us off the scent.'

Bonny grinned. 'If I was asked fer someone's where-abouts I'd be cagey, 'specially if the blokes looked like we do.'

'What's the matter wiv us?' Snatcher said indignantly.

'Well, we're not exactly yer average person's idea of good ole pals, are we?'

'Nah, I s'pose not,' Snatcher conceded, rubbing at his cauliflower ear.

'Now come on, drink up. We're gonna join the street corner mob,' Bonny told him.

'Street corner mob?' Snatcher frowned.

'Yeah. There's always blokes standin' round on street corners on Saturdays. We're gonna make a few discreet enquiries. Well, I am. You just keep stumm.'

Bonny was right, and as they strolled casually up to the three men lounging on the corner of Cooper Street by the boarded-up cobbler's shop they were given suspicious looks.

'Me an' my pal just got moved on from the corner o' Mason Grove,' Bonny growled. 'I dunno what the bloody copper thought we was after. We was only watchin' the draymen puttin' the beer in the pub. Can't stand round anywhere these days.'

'Our bobby don't mind us 'angin' around on this street corner,' Mike Stiles told him. 'Long's we don't start shy-'ikin' people.'

''E must be a decent copper, that's all I can say,' Bonny

replied. 'That bastard Priestly ain't 'appy unless 'e's 'avin' a go at somebody.'

Women were passing to and fro carrying shopping bags and the rag-and-bone man came trundling his barrow into the turning as the young men lounged against the shop hoarding. Bonny took the opportunity of checking the door numbers and pinpointed George Parry's house.

'Where d'you come from?' Dennis Grainger asked.

'Down the Blue,' Bonny told him.

'D'you know the Ashley bruvvers?' Ted Wicks enquired.

'Yeah. They're a bit 'ard,' Bonny remarked.

'Yer don't mess wiv them,' Snatcher cut in.

Ted Wicks looked at Snatcher's mutilated ear and decided that the Ashleys must really be a hard crowd if someone looking like him was wary of them. 'You look like you can take care o' yerselves,' he ventured.

'We do our scrappin' in the ring,' Bonny informed him. 'We do a bit o' wrestlin'.'

The three loungers were full of questions but Bonny suddenly cut them dead, nudging his friend as he spotted three men coming out of number 8. 'C'mon, Snatch, we've got some business ter take care of,' he said quietly.

As agreed, Charlie Foden and Roy Chubb escorted George towards the bus stop in the Old Kent Road, and as they disappeared out of the turning the curtains at number 2 moved very slightly. 'I bloody well knew it,' Ron Sloan growled. 'Quick, Sammy, take a gander.'

'Yeah, that's 'em,' the chancer replied. 'Yer couldn't mistake those two. They look like they've done fifteen rounds wiv Pedlar Palmer.'

Ron Sloan waited until the two wrestlers left the turning, then he slipped out of the house and trailed in their wake at a reasonable distance. As planned the three friends walked along Croft Street, ignoring Bell Alley, a quiet shortcut which would take them into the Old Kent Road directly opposite the bus stop. Bonny and Snatcher kept back a little and stood looking in a shop window as the three joined the bus queue.

'What now?' Snatcher asked.

'I don't bloody well know,' Bonny scowled.

A number 21 bus pulled up at the stop and the lurkers noticed that only one of the three men boarded the bus.

'This is a waste o' time,' Snatcher groaned.

'No it ain't,' Bonny said sharply. 'That was Parry who got on that bus. I know 'im by sight now. The ovver two are 'is minders.'

Snatcher was not convinced. It could be a ploy to mislead them, he thought. The man could get off at the next stop and wait for his escort to arrive. 'What we gonna do, foller the ovver two?' he asked as the minders set off back to Cooper Street.

'Nah. We'll 'ang around on the corner an' see if the ovver geezer makes a show.'

'Yer mean this Albury bloke?'

'Who else,' Bonny said with contempt.

Snatcher ignored it. Bonny considered himself to be the brains of the partnership but there were times when Snatcher had to question it, though silently. This little job of work was going wrong before it got underway and the twenty pounds he would receive for his trouble was going to be well earned, Snatcher knew that much. As they turned back from the bus stop they were immediately confronted by Ron Sloan, who had stepped out of the alley.

'Don't I know you two?' he asked, hooking his thumbs in his polished belt.

'I don't fink so,' Bonny replied quickly.

'Someone pointed you out ter me an' told me you've bin askin' 'im questions.'

'We ain't bin askin' questions, 'ave we, Snatch?'

'Nah, course not.'

'Well, I must 'ave bin mistaken then,' the constable said with a sly smile. 'But just so you an' me know where we stand, let me put yer in the picture. My name is Ron Sloan an' I'm the beat bobby fer Cooper Street an' the surroundin' manor. Everyone knows me an' I know everyone back, which makes it nice an' cosy. When I'm off duty I've got eyes an' ears lookin' out fer fings, know what I mean? Then when I come on duty I can get on wiv keepin' the peace, fer my people's benefit, if yer get my drift. Well, do yer?' he asked in a slightly raised voice, and the two men nodded dutifully. 'Now it's come ter my attention that you two are after sortin' out a couple o' my people, an' it grieves me, so let me make it all nice an' clear. If I see eivver o' you 'angin' around the neighbour'ood again I'm gonna come down on yer so 'ard yer'll fink a bloody great wall's fell on yer, an' before yer've got over the shock I'll 'ave yer down that station an' charge the pair o' yer wiv everyfing I can make stick – loiterin' wiv intent, threatenin' conduct, conspiracy ter commit a felony, conspiracy ter pervert the course o' justice, abusive language, resistin' arrest, treason an' mutiny on the 'igh seas. Want me ter go on?'

The two villains merely shook their heads in shock and the constable tapped his breast pocket. 'Yer'll notice that I ain't got me little book out an' wrote yer names down,' he reminded them. 'I don't need to. I never, ever ferget a face. That'll do fer me. Now on yer way, an' if yer know what's good for yer remember everyfing I've said. By the way, you can 'ave my name an' number. 143, Constable R. Sloan.'

'Big-'eaded git,' Bonny growled as the two slouched off.

'That's it as far as I'm concerned,' Snatcher declared. 'Sharkey can keep 'is poxy score.'

'I'm gonna 'ave words wiv 'im,' Bonny replied. 'It's as if everyone round 'ere knew what we was up to an' was waitin' fer us ter make our move.'

'Come on, then, let's see if we can find 'im,' Snatcher said. 'I reckon 'e'll be in the Crown by the time we get there.'

Sara Parry felt her heart flutter a little as she took her seat in the morning train to Brighton. Randolph was sitting close and she could feel his shoulder touching hers. It made her feel quite young again and she sighed.

'Are you all right, my dear?' he asked.

'I'm feelin' very well,' she replied, smiling at him.

Randolph leaned his head back against the white linen square. 'First class is the only way to travel,' he remarked. 'It gives one a feeling of importance. Not in a pompous sense, you understand, more by way of being catered for, as opposed to all that confounded finger-snapping and doffing of caps in the presence of the mine owner or the works manager. Sitting here in this carriage we could be a double act on the music halls, a lord and his lady, or even runaway lovers being pursued by the lady's wicked stepfather who has designs on her.'

'Oh, Randolph, you make it all sound so romantic.'

'It's my aim to please, to make you feel gay.'

'You do, you do.'

At the Redhill stop another passenger entered the compartment and sat in the seat facing them. He was elderly and wearing the collar of holy office. 'A miserable day,' he said politely.

'Yes it is,' Randolph replied.

'Going to Brighton?'

'Yes. Are you?'

'No, I'm getting off at Haywards Heath. Visiting an old friend.'

'That's nice,' Sara said with a smile.

'Are you taking the baths?' the cleric asked.

'No, just the air and the rest,' Randolph told him.

'Good place for that, is Brighton,' the cleric went on. 'I served in London for many years, in Hoxton and Shoreditch to name but two parishes. Now in my autumn years I'm serving the parishioners at Plough-Deeping, little more than a hamlet near Redhill. Still plenty of work to do there, though. There are souls to be saved everywhere.' He drew out a wallet from inside his coat, opened it up and took out a crumpled photograph. 'There it is, Plough-Deeping. Rather quaint, wouldn't you say?'

Randolph looked at the photograph and passed it to Sara. 'I see they have a village pump,' he remarked.

'Yes, all the water for the village is drawn from that pump,' the cleric replied. 'There are plans to lay water pipes but it's still some way off, I'm afraid. Question of funds, you understand. I did ask the Redhill council to help finance the project and I got a rather tart reply. They suggested I should contact my own governor for help.' He raised his eyes towards the ceiling of the compartment.

Sara tutted and Randolph shook his head. 'Disgusting,' he declared.

At Haywards Heath the cleric stood up and held out his outstretched hand over Sara's head, then Randolph's. 'May the good Lord go with you,' he said reverently.

They watched as he climbed down from the carriage and disappeared into the crowd. It was then, as the train pulled out of the station, that Randolph noticed the small card lying at his feet. The vicar must have dropped it, he thought as he leaned down to pick it up while Sara was still looking out of the window.

Bernard Goggings
Entertainer extraordinaire. West End
trained. Theatre and music hall. Home
and holiday bookings accepted at short
notice. Children's party specialist.
Puppets, magic and party games.
Your satisfaction guaranteed.
Contact Bernard on ROD 1769.

'What a nice man,' Sara remarked.

'Very talented too, I should say,' Randolph replied with a smile.

'I could sense the piousness o' the man,' Sara said. ''E seemed very open an' honest.'

'I agree,' Randolph answered, secretly pocketing the card.

Bernard Goggings had walked along the platform and then re-entered the train further down just as the porter waved his green flag. That couple were too wrapped up in themselves to be of assistance, he thought. Better to concentrate on the elderly ladies. Water pipes for Plough-Deeping would be an expensive project and every penny helped. Of course the rare five-pound note instead of the customary one-pound bills would contribute handsomely to the endeavour, or rather the well-being of Bernard Goggings on his working trips to the south coast.

In the privacy of their compartment Randolph took Sara's hand in his. 'I do hope you enjoy the brief respite from London, dear,' he said quietly.

'I'm sure I will,' Sara told him. 'I 'ope you do too.'

'I'm sure I will,' he said, crossing his fingers by his side.

'Randolph?'

'Yes?'

'What was that place the vicar mentioned?'

'Plough-Deeping.'

'I bet I'd 'ave a job tryin' ter find it on the map,' she remarked.

'I'm sure you would,' he said, hiding a smile.

Chapter Twenty-Nine

When Charlie arrived back at the house Lucy met him with an anxious look on her face. 'I've bin so worried,' she said. 'I was imaginin' all sorts o' fings.'

Charlie squeezed her arm gently as he stepped into the dark passageway. 'There was no need to,' he told her. 'They wouldn't try anyfing wiv three of us. Anyway, George got the bus an' 'e seemed quite cheerful.'

'Yeah, I expect 'e was,' Lucy said grudgingly. ''E's out of it, but Danny Albury's not, an' nor are we.'

Charlie followed her into the parlour and sat down in the armchair by the warm fire. 'Where's Sue?' he asked.

Lucy eased herself into the armchair facing him. 'She's playin' next door. I'm gonna collect 'er in a few minutes.' She sat forward in the chair. 'I'll put the kettle on.'

Charlie leaned forward and placed his hands over hers. 'Look, there's no need ter get all agitated 'cos we're on our own,' he said with a smile. 'Sit fer a while. Talk ter me.'

Lucy smiled back at him. 'Do you realise this is the first time you an' I 'ave bin alone in the 'ouse?'

'The thought did occur ter me,' he replied.

Lucy slowly withdrew her hands from beneath his. 'I thought George might 'ave made some comment about it before 'e left but 'e was more concerned about not missin' 'is train,' she said, raising her eyes expressively.

''E was worried about leavin' yer in case those blokes called,' Charlie replied, 'but I assured 'im I wouldn't leave you on yer own fer a minute while 'e was away.'

'That should 'ave made 'im fink,' Lucy said with a brief smile. 'Just put yerself in 'is place. Would you be all that 'appy ter leave yer wife alone in the 'ouse wiv the lodger?'

'Well, that all depends on the lodger,' Charlie answered. 'I mean, 'e could be a lecherous ole goat, or a bookworm, or 'e could be genuinely attracted ter the lady o' the 'ouse.'

'Where d'yer put yerself amongst that lot?' she asked.

'Don't you know yet?' he replied quietly.

She nodded. 'I've known fer some time, an' I knew fer sure the night you kissed me.'

'I'd bin wantin' ter do that fer a long time,' Charlie confessed. 'I just looked at yer an' wanted desperately ter feel yer against me, take yer in me arms an' kiss yer, an' I tried ter resist it, but I couldn't. When I asked yer I truly expected yer ter say no, but yer never did. Yer let me kiss yer, an' 'old yer close fer a few seconds, an' it was wonderful.'

'It was fer me too,' Lucy said quietly. 'That night I went up ter bed still feelin' yer lips on mine an' I sat on the edge o' the bed fer ages, just finkin'. I needed time ter calm down, an' as I sat there I became more an' more irritated by George's snorin'. I became angry, Charlie. I started ter blame 'im fer what I'd done, an' then I hated meself fer bein' so selfish. I can't 'elp it, though. George doesn't seem ter know I exist lately. I sometimes fink if I confessed ter lettin' you kiss me 'e'd merely nod an' bury 'is 'ead in the paper.'

'It'd be easy fer me ter come on ter yer if that was the case,' Charlie said, 'but we both know it's not like that.

George loves yer, but it's bin 'ard fer 'im lately.'

'It's bin 'ard fer ovver men too,' she replied. 'Do they all ignore their wives as well?' She looked fixedly at him and he shrugged his shoulders. 'You're a good man, Charlie, an' I respect yer fer sayin' what yer did, but I need love an' attention just like any ovver red-blooded woman. Sometimes I feel my life is merely tickin' away like a clock, an' each day I'm gettin' a little bit older. I feel I'm missin' out on so much.'

Charlie looked down at his feet for a few moments and then his dark eyes came up to meet hers. 'If somefing 'appened between us, 'ere an' now, would yer stop feelin' like you were missin' out, or would you end up 'urtin' more inside? There'd be no future in it fer eivver of us. We're both married an' you wouldn't leave George, nor would I be able ter get a divorce.'

Lucy reached out and rested her hand on his. 'What are yer tryin' ter tell me, Charlie?' she asked quietly. 'Are yer excusin' yerself fer not makin' any more passes at me?'

'No, Lucy, I'm tryin' ter be honest an' up front,' he replied in a husky tone that made her feel sick with excitement. 'I'm lettin' you know that I understand what the situation is. I'm not a young man any more, and you're a wife an' muvver. We can't make each ovver promises, we can't make plans tergevver. Stolen hours, that's all we can 'ave, an' all we can ever 'ope for. I wish it could be so much more but it can't, an' I'd 'ave ter live wiv that an' make it enough fer me, but it might not be fer you.'

'I could live wiv that, Charlie,' she said in a voice she hardly recognised. 'I know I can't expect the world or turn back the clock, but I'd enjoy every second we 'ad tergevver an' live fer the next encounter.'

'Wiv you an' me livin' under the same roof?'

'It'd 'ave ter be that way. It's the only way. Every day I'd see yer, an' I'd take comfort in 'earin' your voice, watchin' yer smile an' shiverin' wiv pleasure every time yer looked at me in that certain way.'

Charlie rose slowly from his chair and reached out to her. She came to him and their bodies melted together as he found her eager lips. Time seemed to stand still as she held on to the kiss, her sweetness arousing him, stroking and rubbing her lips against his to excite him still further. Then, his strong hands clasping her to him, she moved her head back to look deep into his burning eyes. 'You know I want yer, Charlie,' she gasped.

He smiled in the way she had come to adore. 'I've never needed anyone more than I need you right this minute,' he told her. 'I feel like a youngster, achin' fer the chance ter love yer fully an' completely.'

'Don't, Charlie,' she breathed. 'I'm shakin' all over.'

He moved back half a pace, still holding her by the shoulders. 'You are beautiful, an' just lookin' at yer takes me breath away.'

She rose up on tiptoe and kissed him quickly on the lips. 'Let me calm down a bit, Charlie,' she said. 'Sit down while I make the tea, an' then I've gotta fetch Sue from next door.'

The wintry sun peeped fitfully from gathering clouds and a chill wind came off the sea as Randolph and Sara walked along the Brighton promenade. She held his arm lightly and occasionally he glanced at her as they made for the Cadogan Hotel.

'I'm still not sure I should be doing this,' he told her.

'Don't be so silly,' she chided him. 'It's only an appraisal, after all's said an' done.'

'Yes, but it's the principle of the thing.'

'Principle my eye,' Sara said with a passion that surprised her. 'If the jeweller gives us a good evaluation then you can feel more confident in yer future negotiations. You've explained it all an' I'm 'appy ter be in a position to 'elp yer. Let's just see what 'e 'as ter say first.'

The doorman in his olive-green uniform gave them a polite nod as they stepped into the warmth of the Victorian hotel, and Sara was immediately taken by its splendour. The ornate ceiling seemed as high as a cathedral's and huge gilt and crystal chandeliers hung down along its length. The black and white marble floor and oak furniture were complemented by rose-flowered tapestry and covers, while on a discreet dais to one side of the large reception area a pianist tinkled away on a beautifully polished Steinway. Ahead, a wide flight of stairs led up to a balcony which encircled the lower area like a halo, and it was there that Samuel Horowitz was waiting, his bulky frame reclining in a plush lounger.

'Ah, Randolph. How good to see you again,' he declared, getting up and smiling to show his small, tobacco-stained teeth.

They shook hands and then Randolph encouraged Sara forward with his hand on her back. 'This is the young lady I was telling you about, Samuel,' he said.

Sara held out her gloved hand and the Russian Jew took it gently in his much larger one, debonairly inclining his head. 'A pleasure I'm sure,' he told her.

Randolph looked around the balcony. 'Can you do the appraisal here?' he asked.

'I think we should go over by the window,' the jeweller replied. 'It's the lighting, you see. A jewel is like a living thing – it reacts to natural light.'

Sara found herself sitting at a wrought-iron table by a

large window and she watched intrigued as the jeweller polished the ruby ring with a piece of blue velvet. He then took out a jeweller's eye-glass and studied the ring for a few moments. 'Yes, it's undoubtedly Burmese,' he remarked. 'Mined in the Mandalay area. It's identifiable by its depth of colour. Rubies from Ceylon are more pink and the Siamese type are darker in colour. This particular ruby is exquisitely cut and quite valuable. The mounting was most probably done in South Africa. I would hazard a guess at three-quarter carat. Yes, this is a very valuable ring. Is it insured?'

Sara shook her head. 'It was left ter me by my muvver,' she told him. 'My farvver gave it to 'er when 'e returned from the Boer War.'

'Well, I can assure you this ring would gladly be accepted as security for a considerable sum,' Horowitz said, looking at Randolph. 'If sold it would fetch over two hundred pounds, I should say.'

Sara had been waiting for this moment and she quickly delved into her handbag. 'What about this one?'

Randolph looked taken aback. 'Sara, no,' he said quickly.

She brushed away his objections. 'I was keepin' this as a surprise.'

Horowitz studied the diamond ring carefully, grunting once or twice. 'Yes, once again it is very good quality. The diamonds are South African white, brilliant cut and very well matched, and the setting is very ornate. Early Victorian I would say. Very good workmanship indeed.'

Randolph shook his head slowly. 'Sara, you shouldn't.'

'An' why not, pray? These two tergevver would allow yer ter go fer a large loan.'

The two men exchanged satisfied smiles and Horowitz stood up to go. 'I look forward to seeing you at the next session, Randolph,' he said, extending his hand.

'What session did 'e mean?' Sara asked as soon as they were alone.

'Oh, it's nothing of importance,' Randolph told her. 'We belong to the same club. It's a City thing, merely boring men talking about boring subjects over insipid coffee. C'mon, my dear, let's you and I go back to our rooms and we'll see about arranging a meal.'

Sara felt happy and quite light-headed as they walked back along the promenade in the failing light. What an adventure this was.

Sue hurried into the house and stood poised in the parlour doorway with a picture book tucked under her arm. 'Uncle Charlie, will you read fer me?' she asked.

'Of course, my little love,' he said, grinning.

'Not the first one 'cos it makes me 'ave bad dreams,' the child told him as she clambered up on to his lap. 'Read me that one.'

'But I always read yer that one,' Charlie complained with a pouting bottom lip.

'This one then,' Sue replied, flipping the pages over quickly.

'Could I tell yer the story about the nice crunchy giant?' he asked.

'If yer like, but it won't make me 'ave bad dreams, will it?' the tot queried with a serious look on her pretty face.

'Now sit still on Uncle Charlie's lap,' Lucy told her. 'I'll 'ave yer tea ready very soon, an' then it's an early night fer you, missy.'

Charlie gave Lucy a reassuring smile and leaned back comfortably in his armchair, letting Sue nestle against his chest.

'Once upon a time there was a crunchy giant who was very nice really,' he began. ''E lived all alone in the forest but 'e was becomin' very lonely. All 'is friends 'ad left an' there was no one 'e could talk to or play wiv, so the crunchy giant decided ter leave the forest an' go an' live wiv a nice family who would take care of 'im. 'E walked all day an' was becomin' very tired an' 'ungry when 'e arrived at Coopertown. It 'ad rained all day an' the giant was not only 'ungry an' tired, 'e was wet all the way frew to 'is skin.'

'Was that like when me an' Gracie got wet washin' our dollies in 'er mummy's barf?' Sue enquired.

'Yes,' Charlie replied, his eyes straying to Lucy, who had seated herself at the table. 'Anyway, the crunchy giant knocked at one o' the 'ouses which looked very warm an' cosy, an' 'e said, "Is there any room 'ere fer a lonely giant who loves children?" an' the man sent a lady out ter see the giant, an' when 'e saw 'er 'e gave a very big sigh. She was the most beautiful lady 'e 'ad ever seen. "Come in out o' the rain," the lady said, an' the crunchy giant stepped inter the warm parlour. 'E was given a lovely meal, 'is clothes were dried an' 'e went ter bed in a cosy bedroom that 'ad a nice fire, an' before 'e went ter sleep the crunchy giant said 'is prayers. 'E fanked Jesus fer givin' 'im a lovely 'ouse to live in an' a lovely lady who could care fer 'im, an' fer makin' sure that 'e would never need ter feel lonely again. I don't know if the giant lived 'appily ever after, 'cos there was a page missin' in the story book about the crunchy giant, but I would fink 'e did live 'appily ever after, an' when I find that page I'll find out fer sure.'

Lucy came over and took the sleepy child up into her arms. 'I won't be long,' she told him in a soft voice. 'Put the kettle on, Charlie.'

Chapter Thirty

The cold, damp night had closed in and the thickening fog glowed eerily in the light of the Victorian streetlamps that lined the Bermondsey backstreets. It was a night for sitting round a warm fire, listening to soft music on the wireless and letting the cares of the day fall away as eyelids grew heavy and heads drooped.

There would be no Saturday night reverie for Margaret Lindsey, however, and her lonely footsteps echoed along Lynton Road as she walked quickly by the large patch of light issuing from the Mason's Arms. This must be it, she told herself as she reached the boarded-up corner shops. She saw the street sign and went down the small turning, glancing up at the door numbers until she came to number 8. It was going to take some explaining, but it had to be done while there was still time.

Lucy's face grew frightened as she heard the heavy knock and Charlie got up quickly. 'Stay 'ere,' he told her firmly.

'Be careful, Charlie. It's late fer people ter come knockin'.'

When he opened the front door Charlie was surprised to see the middle-aged woman standing on the doorstep with a worried look on her pale face.

'I'm very sorry ter trouble yer, but does Sara Parry live 'ere?' she asked hesitantly.

Charlie nodded. 'Is there anyfing wrong? 'As anyfing 'appened to 'er?'

The woman shook her head. 'No, but it's important I speak ter someone close to 'er.'

'Yer'd better come in out o' the fog,' Charlie told her.

Lucy had come out to the passage and she led the way back into the parlour. 'I'm Lucy Parry, Sara's sister-in-law,' she said. 'Won't yer take a seat, 'ere by the fire?'

'I'm Margaret Lindsey. It's OK, I'll sit at the table if yer don't mind. I don't wanna get too warm.'

'Is Sara all right?' Lucy asked with a puzzled frown.

'I 'aven't seen 'er, but I'm sure she is,' the visitor replied. 'I understand she's gone ter Brighton fer the weekend.'

'Yeah, that's right.'

'An' the man she's wiv is Randolph Cadman?'

'Yeah.'

Margaret smiled wryly. 'In actual fact 'is real name's John Lindsey an' 'e 'appens ter be my 'usband.'

'Oh my God!' Lucy exclaimed. 'Poor Sara. She's besotted by 'im. She finks 'e's wonderful.'

Margaret nodded slowly. 'Yes, I can understand that,' she replied. 'John 'as that effect on women. A proper charmer at times, but 'e can be nasty an' cruel. I've seen that side of 'im as well durin' the past few years.'

''Ow did yer find out our Sara was seein' 'im?' Lucy asked.

Charlie had been hovering by the door, and he coughed to get Lucy's attention. 'Shall I put the kettle on?' he said.

'Would yer, Charlie?' she replied with a smile.

The visitor rested her hands on her large handbag and sighed deeply. 'I fink I'd better start from the beginning. I married John Lindsey seven years ago an' two years after we were married I discovered that 'e was involved wiv anovver woman. I don't know 'ow long it'd bin goin' on, 'e wouldn't tell me, but I found out later that 'e'd talked 'er inter partin' wiv a large sum o' money as well as valuable jewellery an' bonds. Apparently 'e'd conned this woman inter believin' that 'e was involved in startin' up a company in the City an' stood ter make large sums of money by buyin' an' sellin' short term. A year later 'e was at it again, an' when I found out I left 'im. Soon after that 'e was arrested an' sent ter prison fer three years fer embezzlement. When 'e finally came out we got back tergevver again. 'E promised me faithfully 'e was a changed man, an' I believed 'im. Fings seemed ter be goin' very well fer us, until . . .'

Lucy watched as the woman delved into her handbag and pulled out an envelope. 'This letter addressed ter me arrived last week,' she went on. 'I'll spare yer the details but it said that John was busy wormin' 'is way into a lonely woman's affections at the fellowship of St Mark's Church in Bermondsey, and 'e was operatin' under the name o' Randolph Cadman. The writer o' the letter said that she 'erself 'ad bin taken in by 'is charm while she was there, but when 'e suggested that she might like ter get involved in makin' a lot o' money by puttin' up 'er jewellery as security she got suspicious. She got a man friend ter make enquiries before partin' wiv any of 'er valuables an' 'e was able ter find out about the embezzlement charge, an' 'e also got 'old of a photo o' John taken at the time 'e was sent ter prison. The woman went on ter say that she left the fellowship as soon as she discovered the truth, but recently she bumped inter one of 'er friends who was still there an' found out that Randolph Cadman was becomin' very friendly wiv a Sara Parry, anovver o' the lonely women who seem ter frequent the meetin's.'

'Didn't yer know yer 'usband was a member o' the fellowship?' Lucy asked.

Margaret shook her head. 'I thought John was playin' in a darts team at our local pub on Wednesday nights. That was what 'e told me 'e was doin'.'

Charlie came into the parlour with a laden tray and Lucy filled the cups with strong hot tea. 'Did yer approach 'im about it?' she asked.

The visitor nodded. 'We 'ad a big row an' I walked out. That was the day after I got the letter an' I 'aven't seen 'im since, nor do I want to.'

''Ow did the woman get your address?'

'It was easy, though it grieves me ter say it,' Margaret replied. 'She knew where I lived. She'd bin in my 'ouse wiv John while I was workin'. While we were rowin' 'e actually told me as much, bold as brass. Anyway the woman said in the letter that she felt it was 'er duty ter prevent some ovver poor woman from bein' duped as she nearly was, an' the best way ter nip it in the bud was by lettin' Cadman's wife know what was goin' on. She was right. I can't stand by an' see someone bein' conned out o' their valuables by that snake of a man. I 'ad ter let 'er know what was goin' on. I 'ad ter find out where Sara lived, so I decided ter pay a visit ter the church. I spoke ter the vicar an' told 'im everyfing. I'm sure 'e thought I was makin' it all up at first, but I managed ter convince 'im that it was true an' I asked fer Sara Parry's address so I could warn 'er.'

Lucy handed the woman a cup of tea. 'I'm very grateful to yer fer the warnin',' she said, 'but 'ow did yer find out about 'em goin' ter Brighton fer the weekend?'

Margaret sipped her tea. 'As a matter o' fact the vicar

didn't 'ave Sara's address, but luckily there were two members o' the fellowship in the church at the time. They were doin' some flower arrangin' or somefing, an' they produced a notebook wiv all the members' addresses in. One o' the women knew that Sara was plannin' ter spend this weekend in Brighton wiv a friend. She said Sara 'ad bin unusually bubbly when she told 'er, an' seein' the attention Randolph Cadman, as 'e calls 'imself, was payin' 'er it wasn't 'ard ter guess who the mysterious friend was.'

Lucy shook her head slowly. 'I can't believe it of Sara,' she sighed. 'Usually she's so suspicious o' strangers, especially men.'

Margaret smiled coldly. 'My 'usband's a charmer, as I've already said, an' it seems that lonely women are easily taken in by 'im. A lot came out at 'is trial, an' if you'd 'ave bin there you'd understand better.'

'Our Sara's not a wealthy woman,' Lucy said, frowning. 'She 'as a couple o' nice rings that were left to 'er, one she 'ardly ever wears. She keeps it in a drawer by 'er bed.'

'Are they valuable, would yer know?'

'They could well be, but I've never asked 'er. The ruby ring she wears all the time. It's a large stone.'

'Would yer know if she's got any insurance on 'er life, or an endowment?' Margaret asked.

'Only a small life policy. Just enough ter bury 'er.'

'No bonds?'

'No, I'm pretty certain she 'asn't got anyfing like that stashed away.'

Margaret finished her tea and put the empty cup down on the table. 'I 'ope I'm wrong, but I'd bet Sara's bin encouraged ter get 'er rings valued.'

Lucy stood up. 'I won't be a moment,' she said, hurrying out of the room. Less than a minute later she was back. 'The diamond ring's not in the drawer,' she announced. 'She must 'ave took it wiv 'er.'

'It figures,' Margaret replied. 'You must try ter warn 'er as soon as she gets 'ome. I just 'ope it's not too late.'

Sara Parry sat on the edge of her bed in the small guesthouse near the seafront and smiled happily. She and Randolph had had a fish supper at a nearby restaurant and they had gone back to their rooms so that he could make one or two urgent business calls. Poor Randolph, she thought, he never seemed to stop working. He was wonderful. All her life she had wanted to be loved and cherished by the man of her dreams, but it had never transpired, until now. As a young woman she had cared for her ailing mother and stayed loyal to her while the rest of her siblings were making a life for themselves. She had tried to form one or two friendships but her mother was terrified of being abandoned and had usually managed to put a stop to it, one way or another. She was dead now, and there was no hardness in her daughter's heart towards her memory, only sadness and frustration at being totally unprepared and too lacking in confidence to forge a friendship and romance with a man. Her attempts to make Charlie Foden aware of her had been pathetic, she knew only too well, and they hadn't been helped by the obvious attraction between him and Lucy. The casual glances they shared and their ready smiles were quite obvious to her and she hoped George hadn't noticed anything. He was her brother and she loved him, and it had hurt her to think that Charlie Foden was trying to make up to Lucy under his very nose. George was quiet and not very demonstrative whereas Lucy was inclined to flightiness at times, and Sara realised that she would have to keep an eye on the potentially dangerous situation.

As she sat ruminating Sara studied her fingertips and vowed to let her nails grow. She would have to do something about her hair, too. She wanted to look her best for Randolph, wanted to please him, and she suddenly experienced a little shiver. He had always been the perfect gentleman, had assured her that his intentions were honourable, and she had to trust him. He would be knocking soon to take her down to the bar for a nightcap and she did not want to disappoint him by declining. Alcohol went to her head very quickly and she could not remember the last time she had set foot in a public house, but a small sherry in pleasant surroundings would do her no harm, and it might even help her to sleep.

Lucy came into the parlour and giggled as she saw Charlie hunched in the steaming tin bath in front of the fire. 'This is the largest towel I've got an' I've warmed it over the gas,' she told him.

Charlie strove to hide his embarrassment by pretending to hunt for the soap. 'Fanks, Lucy. I won't be long,' he replied.

She made no attempt to leave the room. 'Would yer like me ter scrub yer back?'

He smiled sheepishly. 'If yer want.'

Lucy came over and hoisted her long dressing gown above her knees before bending down beside the tub. ''Ave yer got the soap?'

Charlie was roused by her show of shapely thigh and he quickly handed her the bar of Lifebuoy. 'It must be nice to 'ave a place wiv a built-in bath,' he remarked.

'Those new council buildin's 'ave got bathrooms,' she replied as she dipped the soap in the water beside his leg.

Charlie leaned further forward to hide his nakedness and Lucy smiled. 'It's the first time I've seen yer wivout yer shirt on,' she said saucily. 'I always imagined yer to 'ave an 'airy chest.'

Charlie felt the soap gliding over his back and he chuckled. 'I 'ope yer not disappointed.'

She shook her head as she squeezed water from the flannel over his lathered shoulders. 'I wouldn't mind if yer was bald all over, Charlie,' she told him.

He looked at her and liked the way she had pulled her hair up on top of her head and fixed it with a black velvet band. He could see her small flat ears and her slim neck and he shook his head slowly. 'Lucy, you're a very attractive woman,' he said with quiet sincerity.

She giggled again as she rinsed his back with the flannel. 'It's a good job you never saw me in the bath, or yer might 'ave changed yer mind.'

'As a matter o' fact I was tempted ter see if yer wanted me ter scrub your back, but I thought it might give yer the wrong impression.'

'No, I'd 'ave liked that, Charlie.'

He splashed water into his face and rubbed his fingers through his thick greying hair. 'I'd better get out,' he said, taking the towel from her.

She stood up but made no attempt to leave the room. 'OK, go on then.'

His look of surprise brought another giggle from her and she turned and walked to the door. 'I'll put the kettle on,' she told him with a saucy wink.

Charlie dried quickly and slipped on a heavy dressing gown, knotting the belt tightly. The bath had to be emptied and the fire was burning low.

Outside the temperature had dropped and the fog had

disappeared. In its place a thin film of frost covered the cobblestones and pavements and shrouded the roofs of the small houses, tiny crystals of ice glistening in the wan light of a crescent moon. Inside the house Sue slept peacefully in her warm bed and downstairs Lucy and Charlie sat facing each other by the glowing fire, sipping tea and trying to look innocent and unaffected, but Lucy felt excitement growing steadily in her belly. Charlie knew that the gods had conspired that evening to provide the opportunity, and he had read the signs. He knew he must not fail. It had been a long time, and he had resigned himself to leading a celibate life, until that fateful night when he knocked on the door soaked to the skin. Seeing Lucy for the first time had jolted him from his complacency and over the past two months he had come to desire her with an intensity which made it harder than ever to disguise.

She put her empty cup down on the table and stretched leisurely. The time for pretence was over. Tonight she was going to seduce him if she had to. She stood over him, almost tormented by the thrilling inside her. 'Charlie.'

'Yeah?'

'That night you asked me fer a kiss. Did yer fink about it afterwards? I mean, did it make yer feel good?'

He stood up slowly. 'I went ter sleep still feelin' yer lips on mine,' he said huskily.

'It's my turn now, Charlie,' she replied. 'Kiss me.'

He reached out and pulled her gently to him. He could feel her firm, rounded breasts against his chest and her thighs touching his. He smelt the scent of her body and the aroma of her freshly washed hair, and he closed his eyes as he found her eager lips. It was a kiss that transformed them. Her mouth was open hungrily and her tongue tantalised his as she threw her arms round his neck. All her passion, all her repressed feelings seemed to be released in one wild moment and she pressed her need against him, rubbing her sex against his stiff manhood. There was no going back now, no memory of guilt or betrayal, only the desperate need to be fulfilled in an explosion of love.

He stepped back a pace and swept her up in his strong arms, and as he climbed the flight of stairs she let her head rest against his chest. His room was lit by a solitary gas lamp and warmed with a small fire, and the curtains had been pulled against the cold night. She sighed with pleasure, closing her eyes as he eased her down on to his bed and lay beside her, gently moving her dressing gown away from her heaving breasts. Her nipples were hard and she shivered as his lips savoured them. More, she thought, more, and reaching up to him she slid his dressing gown off his broad shoulders and arms and cupped his head in her hands, urging him down towards her smooth flat belly. There was no time to be coy and she arched herself as he explored lower and lower. He tasted her sweetness, felt her swollen cherry, caressed it vigorously with his tongue. In an intensity of forbidden delight she moaned, throwing her head back as she felt an ecstasy rising through her body. Charlie's sensitive probing and licking had found her most intimate spots and suddenly she could hold out no longer. She gave a deep groan and clenched her fists tightly as her love juice flowed.

Charlie gently stroked her belly, waiting for her throes of passion to subside, then he rose up and slid his arm under her waist, easing her over on top of him. Her legs locked against his flanks and she lowered herself down for him to enter her with a groan of unadulterated pleasure, riding him like a stallion, driven into delicious abandonment as he raised himself up on his elbows and clasped her hips, moving with her sensuously. She could feel her passion overwhelming her once more and knew that he was struggling to contain himself too. 'Charlie!' she cried. 'Oh, Charlie!'

Chapter Thirty-One

Sara Parry wiped her eyes and looked with disgust at her puffed image in the bathroom mirror. 'Whatever did 'e see in you in the first place?' she muttered to herself tearfully. 'You're nuffing but a stupid, frustrated old maid an' yer can't seem ter do anyfing about it.'

Sara went back into the bedroom and sat down despondently on the edge of the bed. It had all started so well, too. He had escorted her down to the bar on Saturday evening and she had enjoyed the convivial chat, fortified with two glasses of sherry, one more than she intended, and she had felt quite daring. When they finally returned to their rooms she had taken Randolph's arm at the door and kissed him on the lips, making some silly remark about nice girls wouldn't do that sort of thing, and naturally enough he had taken it as a come-on. Unfortunately, she had been unprepared for what happened next.

His knock was soft and his eyes reflected a gentleness as he came into her room a few minutes later. He sat holding her hand as he confessed to wanting to make love to her, but she had laughed him off. Mistake number one, she sighed.

His eyes seemed to burn with desire and he pressed her down on to the bed to kiss her protesting lips. He was not to know, how could he know, that she had never experienced the love of a man in her whole life and was still as pure as the driven snow. He should have been gentle, arousing her slowly with patience and panache, and he would have done so, she felt sure, had she confessed to him her ignorance of carnal matters. Her silent protestations only served to make him feel that she was toying with him and he became angry. For one terrifying moment she was convinced he was going to rape her, but he brought himself under control and turned away, sitting with his back to her. 'Do you find me repulsive?' he asked suddenly.

'Of course not,' she replied tearfully. 'You took me by surprise. I wasn't prepared.'

He sighed deeply, not knowing quite what she meant. 'You and I have got on so well, Sara, I really thought you wanted our relationship to progress. You must forgive me.'

At that moment, she now realised, she could have made it all right, but still she could not bring herself to explain to him her lack of experience. 'We'll both feel better after a good night's sleep,' she told him weakly.

Back in his room Randolph Cadman, alias John Lindsey, poured himself a stiff drink. The stupid woman was playing games with him, he fumed. Who the hell did she think she was? Certainly no raving beauty. He would have to employ a different tactic if he was to make the weekend a success after all, financially speaking.

On Sunday morning Randolph was all charm as he escorted Sara along the quiet seafront. Gulls dipped and dived, driven ashore by the choppy conditions in the Channel, and the sky was full of rain-laden cloud. Ahead they could see the pier half shrouded in mist, and apart from an old man exercising his dog they had the promenade to themselves.

They took lunch at a little pub tucked away in a narrow

cobbled street and spent the afternoon sitting in the comfortable lounge at the guesthouse reading the Sunday papers.
Randolph went out at five o'clock, saying he had to get a
printed valuation from Horowitz, and Sara was left to her
own devices. She had at first decided to take a short nap, but
resisted the urge when she noticed the couple sitting nearby
being served with coffee. She folded her newspaper and
attracted the attention of the elderly waiter. A few minutes
later she was served with China tea and she took out a
ten-shilling note from her handbag.

'Wouldn't you like me to put it on your bill, Mrs
Devenish?' the man enquired.

'No, I'd sooner pay, thank you.'

The waiter was soon back with a few coins in a small
silver salver and Sara deliberately left a shilling as a tip.

'That's very kind of you, Mrs Devenish,' the man said,
smiling.

'I fink yer've got me mixed up wiv someone else,' Sara
told him.

The waiter looked perplexed. 'I saw you at breakfast with
Mr Devenish and I assumed . . . I'm terribly sorry.'

'The name of the man you saw me wiv is Randolph
Cadman.'

The waiter was quite obviously embarrassed. 'I'm sorry.
My eyes aren't what they used to be. I'm afraid I mistook
Mr Cadman for Mr Devenish who was here a few weeks
ago.'

Sara smiled and thought no more about it. Her mind was
too full of how she would handle the coming evening.
Maybe Randolph would not try anything on again, and in
that case it wouldn't matter too much if she cried off from a
night at the bar or at a pub by saying she had a bad
headache. If, however, he made his intentions clear, she

would have to make him understand that she needed encouragement and guidance in the art of love-making.

As she sipped her tea on the soft cushioned divan Sara began to romanticise, and she decided to place last night's little episode in the bin of experience gained. If anyone could steal her heart and make her a fulfilled woman it was Randolph.

On Sunday morning PC Ron Sloan knocked at number 8 with the news that he had frightened the two ruffians off. He looked pleased with himself as he sipped his tea in the parlour, flanked by Lucy in her dressing gown and Charlie with his shirt buttoned carelessly. 'I 'ope I didn't call too early,' he said, trying not to smile as he stared at Charlie's crooked collar.

Lucy shook her head and pulled her dressing gown closer around her shapely figure. 'I was up, an' so was Charlie,' she told him.

'Sara's still in the land o' nod, I take it,' he remarked with a grin.

'No, as a matter o' fact she's gone ter Brighton fer the weekend,' Lucy replied.

Ron Sloan raised his eyebrows slightly. 'Good fer 'er. An' when's George due back 'ome?'

'Ternight,' Lucy answered. 'I'm dyin' ter find out 'ow 'e got on.'

The constable looked enquiringly from one to the other for a moment and then eased back in the armchair. 'I got 'em dead ter rights watchin' you an' George an' Roy Chubb at the bus stop,' he said, addressing Charlie. 'I don't fink they'll bovver ter show their faces round 'ere again, unless the ante's upped an' they fink it's werf it fer the extra money, so yer still gotta be careful. Keep yer eye out an' let me know if yer see any dodgy characters lurkin' about. By the way, yer might 'ave a word wiv the geezer who warned yer in the first place. 'E might know the score.'

Charlie nodded. 'Yeah, I will, soon as possible.'

The policeman took another sip of his tea. ''Ow's Sara takin' all this?' he asked suddenly. 'Or are yer keepin' it from 'er?'

'She doesn't know anyfing about it,' Lucy told him. 'It's better she don't know, the way she is. In any case, she doesn't answer the door if I'm shoppin' an' she's 'ere on 'er own.'

Ron Sloan nodded. 'Well, I'd better pop over an' 'ave a word wiv Danny Albury.'

As soon as the constable had left Charlie took Lucy by the arm. 'C'mon, darlin',' he said, 'before that bed gets cold.'

She took his hand and followed him up the stairs and into his room.

'I love you, Lucy Parry,' he said, pulling her to him.

'I love you too, Charlie,' she sighed.

Charlie undressed again quickly and Lucy took off her dressing gown before they slipped under the covers. He sought her lips and she turned and snuggled up close, feeling his strong body pressing against her. 'Charlie?'

'Yeah?'

'Do yer believe me when I say I love yer?'

'Of course I do.'

'But is it possible ter love two men at the same time?'

'I fink so, though I can't say as I've never loved two blokes at once.'

Lucy kissed his neck and ran her fingers through his matted hair. 'Do you realise we've only known each ovver fer less than three months?'

Charlie brushed a strand of hair from her face. 'It seems I've known yer fer ever.'

'Charlie?'

'Yeah?'

'Charlie, yer not just treatin' this as a bit o' fun, are yer?'

He propped himself up on one elbow and looked down into her troubled eyes. 'It is fun, 'owever intense it is,' he said softly. 'Neivver of us are available, marriage-wise I mean. I'm mad about yer an' I want us to enjoy the pleasures we're sharin', not feel guilty about it.'

'I try not to, Charlie. But some'ow I can't 'elp feelin' a little scared.'

He kissed her quickly on her open lips and laid his head on the pillow beside her, slipping his arm across her and cuddling her to him. 'Look, George'll be 'ome this evenin', an' Sara termorrer,' he said quietly, an' we'll 'ave very little chance ter be alone tergevver. I'll look at yer an' I'll want yer desperately. You'll look at me an' remember this week-end, an' we'll need all the patience we possess ter see us frew. We'll 'ave ter grab our chances when we can, an' in between we'll carry on in the way we always 'ave. You'll be the dutiful wife an' mum, an' I'll be the respectable lodger. The secret we share'll see us frew the lonely times an' the desire'll be tenfold when we do get the chance ter make love.'

'I can wait, Charlie,' she answered with a deep sigh, 'as long as you're there, as long as I can see yer an' 'ear yer voice.'

'An' I'll watch yer movin' about the 'ouse, I'll savour the sway of yer body an' the way yer smile an' pout at times, an' I'll save all me lovin' fer that special time we'll share.'

Lucy rolled on top of him and moved her hips sensuously against his, bringing him to a full erection, and she licked her tongue around her dry lips as she felt him enter her. His slow erotic rhythm sent shivers of pleasure coursing along her spine and she could feel his hot breath on her face as the loving became intense. She drew her knees up, raised herself and arched her body backwards to take all the pleasure she could as his hands cupped her full breasts, and he gasped to feel her eager thrusting. He fought to hold back his explosion till she was ready and then as she groaned and shuddered he jerked involuntarily and felt his love flow free.

They were lying close, wrapped up in each other's arms, when they heard a movement on the stairs. The door creaked open and Sue looked in. 'Mummy, I couldn't find yer. I'm firsty.'

'All right, darlin',' Lucy said. 'Go back ter yer room an' I'll get yer a drink.'

Charlie had lain perfectly still beneath the bedclothes and when the child went out again he jumped out of bed and grabbed his trousers. 'I 'ope she didn't see me,' he said with a worried look.

Lucy was more calm. 'She's still 'alf asleep. She won't remember any o' this.'

Charlie looked at the clock on the chair by his bed. 'Christ, it's turned eleven.'

Lucy grinned as she slipped on her dressing gown. 'Don't time fly when yer enjoyin' yerself?'

'It's a good job Sue didn't come in a few minutes earlier,' he said, smiling sheepishly.

'I didn't expect 'er ter wake up too early, after the time she went ter bed last night,' Lucy remarked. 'It must 'ave bin all of ten o'clock.'

Charlie took a clean pair of socks from the tallboy drawer. 'I need ter see Sharkey Lockwood at lunchtime,' he said, grunting as he bent over to put them on.

'You be careful, Charlie,' she told him. 'You mind they don't take it out on you.'

He grinned lopsidedly. 'No chance.'

'Mummy.'

'All right, darlin', just comin',' Lucy called back.

Ada Black and Emmie Goodwright braved the cold Sunday morning to have their usual confabulation and Ada looked a little irritated. 'I dunno what's goin' on in this street lately,' she remarked. 'I saw Ron Sloan come out o' the Stricklands' early yesterday mornin' an' then 'e knocked on the Parrys' front door.'

'Did 'e go in?' Emmie asked her.

'Yeah. 'E was in there fer a good 'alf hour.'

'I wonder what that was all about?'

'Gawd knows.'

'It makes yer fink,' Emmie said, shaking her head slowly.

'Did yer know George Parry's away this weekend?'

'No. Where's 'e gone?'

''E's doin' a weekend at the naval barracks in Chatham by all accounts,' Ada said. ''E's still in the reserve, yer see, an' Mary Chubb was tellin' me 'e's doin' some trainin' fer promotion. She said if 'e passes 'e'll be a petty officer.'

'That's nice.'

Ada looked quickly up and down the turning before leaning closer to her friend. 'Lucy an' Charlie Foden are on their own this weekend. Sara's gone ter Brighton wiv that chap she's met.'

'The one at the fellowship?'

'Yeah.'

'I bet George is all on edge, leavin' them two in the 'ouse on their own.'

'It's only natural, ain't it?'

Emmie slid her hands further into her coat sleeves. 'I don't fink there's anyfing goin' on between 'em, or George would 'ave known. Even if 'e just suspected somefing 'e wouldn't go an' leave 'em tergevver, surely ter Gawd?'

'Yer never know, do yer?'

'Nah, yer right.'

'Mrs Albury told me the inquest's this Friday.'

'It'll be in all the papers, I should fink.'

'Well, I'd better get in an' start the dinner.'

'Yeah, me too. What yer got?'

'Lean ribs.'

'I got some sausage-meat. My ole man likes that wiv some taters an' gravy.'

Frost still clung to the cobblestones as Charlie made his way along to the Crown in Dockhead, where with a bit of luck he hoped to find Sharkey. A chill wind met him on the corner of Lynton Road and he pulled the collar of his coat up round his ears, but inside he was glowing.

Chapter Thirty-Two

Sharkey Lockwood sat slumped on a bar stool in the saloon as Charlie pushed open the door and walked in. He looked enquiringly along the polished counter at the newcomer and forced a brief smile. 'I expect yer've come ter tell me the game's up wiv those two prats,' he said.

Charlie laid a half-crown on the counter and jerked his head towards Sharkey's glass. 'Same again?'

The bigger man nodded. 'Yeah, why not?'

Charlie leaned sideways on the counter facing the ganger. 'Yeah, they are a couple o' prats,' he remarked with slightly narrowed eyes. 'All they achieved was ter get everyone in the street watchin' out fer 'em, an' the local copper marked their cards too.'

Sharkey smiled cynically. 'You only get what yer pay for an' the Coleys weren't prepared ter dig deep inter their pockets,' he replied. 'Physically they were more than capable, but they ain't got a brain between 'em.'

Charlie took a sip of his beer. 'You was aware o' that when yer picked 'em, wasn't yer?'

Sharkey looked noncommittally at his co-ganger. 'I 'ad my reasons.'

Charlie nodded his head slowly. 'Parry an' Albury are gonna stick ter their story at the inquest on Friday,' he said

347

matter-of-factly, 'an' in the meantime they'll be escorted everywhere they go. They won't even use the bog unless there's someone standin' guard.'

'That's nice,' Sharkey said sarcastically.

'The thought occurs ter me,' Charlie went on. 'You're gonna be obliged ter face the Coleys, an' I can't see them bein' too 'appy about the way fings 'ave turned out.'

'That's my problem,' Sharkey replied. 'I've talked wiv those two idiots I recruited an' they're sure someone's bin doin' some talkin'.'

Charlie smiled. 'They could be right.'

Sharkey drained his glass and pulled the fresh one towards him. 'I'm goin' back ter wrestlin' again,' he announced. 'As far as I can see the Coleys are on their way out an' I'm not 'angin' around fer the end. It won't be very nice, that's fer sure.'

'I'll come an' see yer first bout,' Charlie told him with a grin. 'I 'ope it'll be werf the entrance fee.' He drained his glass and held out his hand. 'Well, I'll see yer at the inquest, pal,' he said warmly.

'Take care, pal,' the big man replied.

Sara Parry joined Randolph for a late evening meal at the guesthouse on Sunday evening and she was very surprised by what her escort had to say.

'There it is in black and white,' he told her, passing the slip of paper across the spotless tablecloth. 'The ruby's a large stone of high quality and the setting is perfect. It'll serve to raise a very considerable sum if we can use it along with the diamond ring as security. Of course it would have to be deposited at the bank, and you have to be certain in your own mind that the decision is a sensible one. If you have any doubts I want you to tell me now, right this minute.'

'I trust you, Randolph,' Sara replied. 'I'd trust you wiv my life.'

He smiled gratefully. 'If there was any chance, however remote, of you losing your valuable assets I would cancel the whole project, but I know that very soon we'll be up and running. Neither of us will ever need to look back.'

Sara returned his smile, suddenly feeling elated. 'Randolph,' she almost whispered. 'You won't leave me alone tonight, will you? Promise.'

He reached across the table and closed his hand over hers. 'I promise,' he replied.

Sara lowered her head, feeling quite emotional. It would be all right tonight, she swore to herself. It had to be. This chance would never present itself again and she must grab at it with both hands.

Thomas Walburton was now approaching sixty-seven, and he had been in the hotel business since leaving school. At first he had worked as a bell-boy at some of the best hotels on the south coast, going on to become porter and receptionist during the heady days of yore, when music hall stars and politicians of note came there to relax and pursue their own private pastimes. Thomas had a pleasant personality and a smart appearance, which earmarked him for a job waiting on tables at the very exclusive Ambassador Hotel in Brighton. He learned fast and enjoyed many years attending upon some of the most famous and most notorious in the land. His mind was sharp and he prided himself on never forgetting a face.

Mrs Charlotte Blake had managed the Westland guest-house for the past five years and she had been saddened to see the rapid deterioration in her neighbour after his retirement from the hotel business at the age of sixty-five.

She spoke to her employer in glowing terms of Thomas Walburton's capabilities and was able to get him a part-time job there as a waiter. Thomas now had a new lease of life and was eternally grateful to Charlotte for her kindness.

They often shared their breaks and chatted amiably over cups of tea in the staff room behind the reception desk, and on this particular Sunday evening Thomas was feeling somewhat upset.

'I must be getting past it,' he sighed. 'I felt awful when I was corrected by Mrs Devenish . . . I mean Miss Parry.'

'I shouldn't place too much importance on it, Thomas,' Charlotte told him. 'None of us are perfect.'

'But I was so sure,' he went on. 'In fact I'd have bet everything I had on being right. It's very upsetting.'

Charlotte could see that her old friend was indeed quite distressed and she had an idea. 'Thomas, will you do me a favour?' she asked. 'I can't leave the reception area, but could you fetch me the guest book from my office? You'll find it on the shelf by my desk.'

While he was off on the errand Charlotte quickly scanned through the guest signatures in the reception book and found the signature of Harold Devenish beneath that of Benjamin Rosamin. She then compared it with Randolph Cadman's and smiled smugly.

'Here it is,' Thomas said as he marched back into the staff room.

Charlotte opened the book and scanned the pages of photographs, signatures of notables on letter headings, and messages from appreciative guests. 'I thought I was right,' she said, grinning widely.

Thomas looked bemused. 'What's that?' he queried.

Charlotte stabbed her forefinger at a photograph.

350

'Remember when the Rosamins got wed?' she asked him. 'This is a group photo. It was taken in the dining room. Look in the background at the other guests. Do you recognise anyone in particular?'

Thomas took out his glasses and sniffed loudly as he put them on. For a while he studied the photograph and then a large smile creased his face. 'I was right,' he said triumphantly. 'There he is, Mr Harold Devenish, alias Mr Randolph Cadman. What's going on, Charlotte?'

She shook her head slowly, a serious look appearing on her wide, open face. 'I don't know, but I don't like it,' she replied thoughtfully.

Thomas stroked his chin. 'I've seen them at work over the years, believe me,' he remarked. 'Con men, preying on gullible, lonely women, and if you were to ask me I'd say that Miss Parry falls into that category.'

'Really it's none of our business,' Charlotte reminded him. 'There's not a lot we can do.'

Thomas shook his head. 'I'd hate for us to stand aside while that poor woman gets fleeced for every penny she owns. We could show her the photograph.'

'I don't know,' Charlotte said hesitantly.

Thomas was adamant. 'You must let me approach the poor lady,' he urged her. 'You know I'd do it very discreetly.'

She thought for a few moments. 'Do it, Thomas.'

Sara waited. It was getting late and she had had time alone to compose herself. There had been the opportunity too for a hard think, and she now knew the way ahead.

'Darling, are you sure?' he asked quietly as she welcomed him into her room.

'You've no need to ask, Randolph,' she replied. 'Last

night I was all at sixes an' sevens. I was overcome an' I made it seem so wrong. Will you forgive me? Please.'

He took her in his arms and kissed her gently on her trembling lips before leading her by the hand towards her bed.

'Please be gentle wiv me, Randolph,' she gulped nervously.

He hid his distaste as he took her by the shoulders and eased her down on to the counterpane. The silly woman must be all of fifty, he thought, and she was acting like a young virgin. 'I'll love you most gently, and you'll be fulfilled as a woman, even beyond your wildest dreams,' he told her grandiloquently.

She lay down under his prompting and felt him lowering his body on to her, and she shivered in expectation. He rubbed up and down like a terrier for a few moments then lifted himself off to slide her nightdress up from her milky white thighs. His hands were warm and sweaty and she closed her eyes and felt her face grow hot as he explored her most secret parts. He used his fingers in a practised way designed to relax her taut muscles and then he exposed himself to her. She gasped at his size and feared she would never be able to accommodate him, but there was no going back now and she let him close in on top of her. Suddenly he was going inside her and she felt the stretching and the sharp pain as her maidenhead was torn. She gasped at his ferocious movement and her fingernails drew blood from his back as she slid her legs further apart. He was dripping with perspiration in the short time he needed to climax and then with a deep shudder that she felt inside her he ejaculated.

Sara was teetering on the edge of an unknown abyss when he exploded and she clung to him, wrapping her legs round his waist as she used his still hard member to bring herself to completion. He pulled away from her quickly as though suddenly shamed, and she lay back and looked up at him. Gone was the confident look, the warm light in his eyes. Instead she saw a naked expression of disgust. It was hard to bear, but his mute regard, crucifying as it was, told her all she needed to know.

On Monday, a damp, dreary January morning, Charlie Foden took his leave of the Coleys, telling the brothers that he was going back to his job in the docks. They took the news with little more than sullen looks, but Frank Coley had a parting shot. 'I just 'ope the inquest turns up the right verdict, fer all our sakes,' he said meaningfully.

'There's no need ter fuss over us,' George remarked when Charlie arrived back at the house and told him he would accompany him to sign on. 'They wouldn't try anyfing at the labour exchange, not wiv everyone millin' about.'

'Yer most likely right, but it's better ter be on the safe side,' Charlie replied. 'Anyway, it's only till Friday. Once the inquest's over it'll be too late fer 'em.'

Lucy watched as the two men walked across the street to knock at the Albury house and her heart fluttered as she thought of that weekend of love. Her memory of those wonderful hours was tempered by a sickly feeling of guilt, the endlessly nagging awareness that she had been unfaithful to George, but she dared not dwell on it. She knew she would end up putting all the blame on her devoted husband, using his lack of passion, his surly ways of late, to justify what had happened, and it wouldn't be fair. She was about to go back indoors when she spotted Sara coming along the turning.

'You look frozen,' she said by way of greeting as her sister-in-law reached the house. ''Ow did it go?'

Sara shrugged her shoulders as she stepped inside. 'No better than I expected,' she replied.

Lucy took her coat from her and went into the scullery to put the kettle over the gas, and by the time she went back into the parlour Sara was sitting in her usual place and warming her hands as though nothing had happened. Lucy felt suddenly angry but she fought to control herself as she sat down facing her. 'Look, I dunno 'ow ter tell yer this, but yer gotta know sooner or later.'

'Tell me what?' Sara said quickly.

'Saturday night there was a woman called,' Lucy explained. 'She told us she was Randolph Cadman's wife. In fact Cadman's not 'is real name. It's John Lindsey. The woman 'eard from a friend who goes ter the fellowship that you an' 'er 'usband were gettin' very close an' she was worried yer'd get taken on like all the ovvers.'

'Taken on?'

'Yeah, get relieved of yer valuables.'

Sara raised a smile. 'Randolph wants me ter put up me rings as security against a big bank loan,' she said. ''E told me there's no risk attached an' in a few months I'll make a large profit as a share'older.'

Lucy stared at her sister-in-law with anger boiling up inside her. 'Ain't you bin listenin' to anyfing I've said?' she exclaimed. 'Randolph Cadman's a con artist. 'E's out ter fleece yer fer every penny 'e can get.'

Sara's smile grew. ''E won't fleece me.'

'Yer've still got yer rings?'

'Too bloody true.'

'We thought the worst,' Lucy told her.

'I was lucky. I was warned off,' Sara answered. 'The rings are safe in me 'andbag an' Mr Randolph Cadman'll be waitin' in the tearooms at London Bridge Station fer me this afternoon. I'm s'posed to 'and 'em over to 'im there. Actually 'e wanted me ter pass 'em over last night but I told 'im I wanted ter do it right by puttin' 'em in their boxes first.'

'Sara, you amaze me,' Lucy said with new-found respect.

Sara smiled again briefly, then her face changed. 'I've never trusted men, an' ter be honest I've never felt relaxed in their company,' she said quietly. 'This episode makes me realise once an' fer all that I could never ever take up wiv a man, sad as it sounds. I missed the boat years ago, when I was too young ter worry about their intentions. Now I 'ave ter be content wiv livin' the life I live an' enjoyin' ovver pleasures. What little I 'ave got out o' this affair, if you could call it that, will be enough fer me. We all 'ave our memories, Lucy.'

The younger woman wanted to throw her arms around her and comfort her with soft words, until Sara spoiled it all by saying, 'One man can breed trouble, but two men under the same roof spells disaster, so be told.'

Lucy went into the scullery to make the tea feeling uneasy. Sara's words had troubled her, but it was what she hadn't said that really frightened the young woman.

Chapter Thirty-Three

The women of Cooper Street were out early on Friday morning, wrapped up against the cold as they stood at their front doors waiting and talking together in low voices. For some the verdict would mean little if anything, but for others it would be the final chapter in the Coley saga which had been the major talking point around meal tables and by the fireside on the long dark wintry nights.

George Parry was uneasy as he put a quick polish on his best boots. His stomach was knotting with a sickly feeling and his wife Lucy picked up on it that morning.

'You can't go out wivout 'avin' any breakfast,' she told him. 'I 'ad it all wiv Sara this mornin'. I'll do yer some toast – it'll settle yer.'

George looked at her with a puzzled frown. 'Did Sara say where she was goin'?' he asked.

Lucy shook her head. 'I asked 'er an' she just said it was unfinished business. I've never known 'er ter go out so early. Now what about some toast?'

He nodded compliantly. Lucy was right. 'Just one slice,' he sighed.

Charlie Foden had been up for hours, it seemed. He had fetched the morning paper and was now seated at the scullery table flipping through the pages, a mug of tea by his hand. How could he stay so calm and collected? George thought with irritation as he cast a critical glance at him. He had as much to lose as anyone, more maybe. He had been the ganger in charge on that terrible day and it would be noted by the coroner.

'Mornin', folks,' Mary Chubb said cheerily as she walked into the scullery. 'Lucy, can Roy come in an' wait? 'E's bin ready fer hours an' 'e's gettin' under me feet.'

'Of course. There's no need to ask,' Lucy chided her.

Mary smiled. 'Roy said 'e feels like 'e's goin' to a funeral.'

'I'll be glad when it's all over meself,' George sighed.

Lucy gave Charlie a quick glance and smiled to herself. He was reading something in the paper that appeared to interest him and was oblivious of what was going on around him.

'Mornin', Charlie,' Mary said pointedly after getting no initial response from him.

'Sorry, luv, I was jus' readin' this bit about the docks,' he replied. ''Ow's Roy?'

'You might well ask,' Mary answered with a sigh. ''E's like a cat on 'ot bricks.'

George was standing by the yard door looking a little anxious. 'Shouldn't we make a move?' he suggested.

Charlie folded the paper and stood up. 'Yeah, we might as well. We'll give Roy a knock,' he said to Mary as he reached for his coat.

Danny Albury sat waiting. 'What's the time, Alice?' he called out.

'It's ten past nine, five minutes on from the last time you asked me,' she said sarcastically as she popped her head into the parlour.

'I'll 'ave ter get this bloody clock fixed,' he told her as he rocked the chimer standing on the mantelshelf.

'That's 'ow the bloody clock got broke in the first place,' Alice scolded him. 'Yer s'posed ter wind the poxy fing, not shake the works out of it.'

'I'd better get goin',' he declared. 'I fink I'll go an' give George an' Charlie a knock.'

Alice waited while he put his coat on and then gave him a quick peck on the cheek. 'Good luck, luv,' she said. 'Yer'll be all right.'

The Coley brothers were at the courthouse early and they took their seats at the back of the large room. Frank looked along the row and nudged his brother. 'I guessed they'd be 'ere,' he remarked.

Ben followed his brother's gaze and saw the two Maitland men sitting impassively in the far corner. 'I thought they'd send their messenger boys,' he growled.

The room started to fill up, and when Charlie and Roy walked in closely followed by Danny and George an usher led them to the front row.

Not too far from the Bermondsey courthouse, in the tearooms opposite London Bridge Station, another drama was about to unfold.

'You should have insisted it didn't matter about the boxes,' Horowitz remarked irritably. 'You could have got the rings last Sunday and we'd have been long gone. Instead, we've lost a full week. This is just a sheer waste of time.'

'You don't understand,' Cadman replied quickly. 'She was a difficult woman to handle, believe me. I had to treat her with kid gloves. She's been too long without a man and it was far from easy getting her interested in the first place. She'll be along as promised.'

'What time's your train?' Horowitz asked.

'Eleven thirty from Paddington,' Cadman told him.

The fence nodded. 'We'll meet up at the Royal Hotel in Exeter tomorrow afternoon, providing I can dispose of the rings by this evening.'

Cadman sipped his coffee. 'It'll certainly be a change plying our trade in the west country,' he remarked.

'Yes, I'm looking forward to it,' Horowitz replied. 'It's getting a bit hot here in south London.'

Sara had surprised herself with her ingenuity. On Monday afternoon she had gone to the tearooms with a note one hour before she was due to turn up. She described the two men to the manageress and asked her if she would be so kind as to hand them the message when they arrived around four o'clock.

Cadman had cursed at the delay, but her being incapacitated with a very heavy cold could not have been foreseen, he had to admit, and he hoped, as the note said, that she would shake off the chill in a few days if she stayed indoors and would definitely be there to hand over the jewellery at eleven o'clock on Friday morning.

The respite gave Sara all the time she needed. A visit to the fellowship and a frank discussion with all the members was followed by an extraordinary meeting to plan the way ahead, which Margaret Lindsey attended with another victim of her husband's deception she had managed to encourage along. Then there was one thing left to do.

Sara looked pale and nervous as she entered the tearooms on Friday morning and Cadman was very attentive, greeting her with a kiss on the cheek and helping her into a chair. 'I hope you feel better, Sara,' he said. 'I take it you've got the rings?'

She nodded, reaching into her handbag. ''Ere they are,' she told him.

Suddenly the tearooms seemed to be full with milling people and Margaret Lindsey looked down on her cheating husband with contempt. 'It's all over,' she declared quietly. 'You're finished.'

'I believe you 'ave somefing o' mine,' her companion said to him scornfully.

Cadman looked aghast at the women and Horowitz got up from his chair. 'I think I'd better leave you to it,' he said with a nervous smile.

A detective barred his way. 'I don't think you're going anywhere just now, Stymie,' he said firmly.

'What is this, Randolph?' the fence appealed to him.

'I think you'd better accompany us to the station and get this sorted out,' the policeman suggested.

Sara was still grasping the two rings and she smiled with satisfaction as she dropped them into her handbag. 'You won't be needin' these where you're goin',' she said with venom.

The coroner looked over his thick-rimmed glasses as George Parry took the stand. 'Your statement here mentions that the deceased was constantly goading you,' he said in a hoarse voice. 'Can you be a little more precise?'

George clasped the rail in front of him. 'We worked as a team fer a few weeks an' durin' that time Wally Coates kept on about me bein' too weak ter do the job properly.'

'How did you respond?'

'I ignored 'im.'

'You never argued with him?'

'No, I never did.'

'Did you ask to be put with another worker?'

'Yes.'

'And were you?'

'Charlie – I mean Mr Foden – put me wiv Danny Albury.'

'And did you get on with Mr Albury?'

'Yes, very well.'

'I want you to describe in your own words the events which led up to the death of Mr Coates,' the coroner said.

'Mr Foden ordered us inter the shed, an' as me an' Danny were gettin' ready ter leave the trench Wally Coates came towards us. 'E started goin' off about us bein' a liability ter the rest o' the workers but we ignored 'im.'

'Go on, Mr Parry.'

'''E turned an' spat down by our feet an' started ter climb out o' the trench,' George explained. 'Suddenly 'e slipped on the mud an' fell backwards on to a cross pole that was supportin' the walls. It collapsed under 'im, an' before we could do anyfing about it the walls on both sides caved in. 'E was buried completely.'

'Mr Parry, are you sure you never touched the deceased at any time while he was there with you?'

'Yes, I'm certain.'

'What did you do to help?'

George hesitated for a few moments. 'Mr Albury was partly covered by the cave-in an' once I was sure 'e could get out OK I joined in wiv the ovver men tryin' ter free Mr Coates.'

'That'll be all, Mr Parry.'

Danny Albury was next on to the stand and he was asked the same questions, which he answered in a loud voice. As he was about to step down the coroner held up his hand. 'Just one more question, Mr Albury,' he said. 'Was your ganger, Mr Foden, aware of what had happened?'

'Yes. 'E was organisin' the rescue,' Danny told him.

'Thank you. That'll be all.'

Roy Chubb was the next worker to be called and he stood with his shoulders thrown back like a sentinel while the coroner scanned the sheaf of papers in front of him.

'Mr Chubb, you were employed by Coley Brothers as a shuttering carpenter.'

Roy looked a little hesitant. 'No, I was employed as a digger, but they knew I was a carpenter by trade so they gave me the job o' shutterin'.'

'As a carpenter would you be expected to perform the shuttering operation?'

'At most buildin' firms, if it was needed,' Roy told him.

'Now I want you to think about my next question and answer truthfully,' the coroner said in a consequential voice. 'In your opinion, was the wood you were using sub-standard?'

'Some of it.'

There was a low murmur around the room and the coroner held up his hand for silence. 'Was the wood holding up the walls where the deceased was buried sub-standard in your opinion?'

'No.'

'Oh?'

'I'd complained about the condition of it an' the ganger ordered some new planks,' Roy explained.

'But the rest contained some sub-standard timbers, you say.'

'Yes.'

The coroner turned a page and looked over his glasses. 'Mr Chubb, are you familiar with the adjustable metal props which are used by some building firms in similar conditions?'

'Yes.'

'Do you prefer them?'

'It depends.'

'Will you elucidate for us?'

Roy took a deep breath. 'Wooden wedgin' props are 'ammered inter place while the metal sort 'ave arms that are extended by a screw thread. Too much pressure can cause the timbers ter split, an' sometimes cold weavver causes the metal ter shrink while they're in place just enough ter loosen the grip. It's a matter o' choice, an' the conditions on the job at the time.'

'Would you have preferred to use the metal type on the diggings in Morgan Street?'

'No, I was 'appy wiv the wood props.'

'That'll be all, Mr Chubb, and thank you for your clear and concise explanation,' the coroner said with a brief smile.

Frank Coley leaned towards Ben. 'That wasn't too bad,' he hissed into his ear.

'Will Charles Foden take the stand.'

The mumble of voices was stilled once more by the coroner raising his hand. 'Mr Foden, you were employed as a ganger by Coley Brothers, is that correct?'

'Yes.'

'And were you in charge of the men in the trench when the fatal accident occurred?'

'Yes I was. I was sharin' the responsibilities wiv Mr Lockwood.'

'And it was you who gave the order for the men to leave the trench?'

'Yes.'

'Did you see the deceased walking along the trench at that time?'

'Yes, an' I asked 'im if 'e was deaf,' Charlie replied.

'Mr Coates took no notice of your instruction?'

'I fink 'e was goin' to, but 'e wanted to 'ave a few words wiv Mr Parry an' Mr Albury first.'

'Go on, Mr Foden.'

'A few words were said by Wally Coates an' then 'e turned 'is back on Parry and Albury an' started ter climb out o' the trench. I saw 'im slip an' fall back on the cross-prop. 'E was a big man, about sixteen, seventeen stone, an' the prop was dislodged.'

'It didn't snap?'

'No, it got dislodged.'

'Mr Foden, I understand that Mr Parry came to you with a request to be paired with another partner during the diggings. Did he say why?'

''E was bein' got at by Mr Coates.'

'Got at?'

'Mr Coates treated Mr Parry wiv contempt,' Charlie explained. 'Anyone who worked wiv Coates would 'ave bin liable ter the same bullyin'. The man was a loner an' very unsociable.'

'In your opinion.'

'In the opinion of all the ovver workers,' Charlie said plainly.

'As a ganger shouldn't you be responsible for stopping this bullying and harassing?' the coroner asked.

'I did as much as I could,' Charlie replied. 'I warned Coates on a number of occasions, but apart from standin' beside 'im all day I couldn't totally stop 'im.'

'Not even by threatening him with dismissal?'

'It wouldn't 'ave worked. Coates was a company man.'

'A company man?'

'Yeah. 'E was a long-time employee who could only be

dismissed by the guv'nors themselves,' Charlie told him.

'One last question, Mr Foden. Are you satisfied, in your own mind, that you did enough to get better quality timbers supplied for the shuttering?'

'Every time I asked the company fer stronger timbers they sent a few new planks, but it was never gonna be enough.'

'Thank you, Mr Foden,' the coroner said, taking off his glasses to stroke his brow.

The policeman attached to the coroner's court then made his appearance on the stand and his statement was devastating. 'I inspected the timbers which the rescuers said had been thrown to one side during their attempts to free the deceased and I found them to be mainly dry. In my opinion they would have been sodden if they had supported wet and muddy walls for a few days. I mentioned this fact to Mr Frank Coley but he was noncommittal.'

'Are you saying that the original timbers had been replaced?'

'It's a distinct possibility in my opinion,' the officer replied.

The last witness to go on to the stand was Frank Coley and he stood upright and expressionless as the first question was put to him. 'Mr Coley, did you authorise the timbers to be changed at the scene of the accident?'

'Certainly not.'

'Did you comply with your ganger's requests to supply new timbers for the shuttering?'

'Only one request was made an' I ordered new timbers myself straight away.'

'Enough for all the shuttering?'

'Yes.'

'Then can you explain why a section of the trench was

supported with sub-standard timbers?'

Coley took a deep breath. 'I employ gangers ter take care o' the operation an' it's usual fer them ter make sure the shutterin' work carried out is safe. If the timbers are not up ter scratch then the carpenter informs the ganger who sees me. As I said, only once was I asked ter replace bad timbers an' I did so, immediately.'

The coroner glanced up at the clock. 'We'll break off for lunch now and reconvene at two o'clock,' he announced.

The two Maitland observers telephoned an initial report and Sir Isaac Maitland nodded his head as his works director offered his advice.

Charlie and George went out with Roy and Danny to slake their thirst at a nearby pub, and very little was said as they sat around a table with their pints in front of them. It had been a draining couple of hours, and Danny summed it up for them all as he leaned forward in his chair and rubbed the back of his neck with a gnarled hand. 'I feel like I've done a day's work in the trench,' he groaned.

At two o'clock the coroner began his deliberations. 'It is clear from the evidence I've heard this morning that the deceased brought the accident upon himself by his insistence on going to an unfamiliar part of the trench to berate Mr Parry and Mr Albury. His bulk was a contributing factor in the dislodgment of the supporting prop which he fell on top of, and with no involvement or interference from Mr Parry and Mr Albury which might well have precipitated a misadventure I can only bring in one verdict. Accidental death.'

He held up his hand as the murmuring grew louder. 'I wish to add a rider, however,' he went on. 'Although it would be impossible to declare whether or not stronger supervision could have prevented the tragedy in this particular case, it poses the question. I would also say that until legislation comes into force to compel contractors to obtain safety certificates from building inspectors, the building industry should seriously consider implementing a voluntary scheme.'

The coroner's words of wisdom were heard and digested by the two company observers and they hurried back to the Maitland offices at Waterloo.

'Shall I inform them, sir?' the works director asked.

'No, get Pat Lawrence to do it,' Sir Isaac Maitland replied. 'After all, he has been in regular contact with the Coleys, and I'm sure he'll let them down gently.'

Hard on the heels of the Maitland observers were the local newspaper reporters, and the tenor of their dispatches would serve to supply the people of Cooper Street and the surrounding area with much food for thought, and rumour.

Chapter Thirty-Four

The Maitland executive waited a few days before delivering the communiqué to their sub-contractors, just long enough for the local newspapers to report on the Morgan Street inquest. It made their decision seem all the more appropriate in the circumstances, and in taking the decision they had the old-established company would appear to be retaining their impeccable record in the building industry.

Frank and Ben Coley were expecting the worst. The coroner's rider had been picked up on by the press, and in particular by the *Weekly Journal* which included it in their editor's comments, and the brothers fumed as they read it. It seemed that too many accidents were taking place in the building trade and the implementation of proper safeguards was long overdue. The editor was scathing about lack of proper supervision, untrained personnel and the cost-cutting methods of sub-contractors which must be stamped out. It was all very commendable, the Maitland executive agreed, and they promised in a statement to the *Journal* that in future they would thoroughly vet any further sub-contractors they used.

'We've bin done over,' Frank growled to Ben as they sat in the saloon bar of the Mason's Arms. 'It'll be back ter scratchin' fer a livin' now, an' I put it down ter that parcel o' shite we took on.'

'You took on,' Ben reminded him as he twirled his glass of whisky.

'I took on, you took on, what does it matter?' Frank scowled. 'We could 'ave avoided this if that idiot Sharkey 'ad picked a couple o' geezers wiv a bit o' sense.'

'I dunno so much,' Ben disagreed. 'The writin' was on the wall. We should 'ave watched points more, instead o' leavin' those two gangers ter sort everyfing out.'

'Yeah, but I still say Parry an' Albury caused Coates ter slip an' Foden saw what went on,' Frank insisted. 'Wiv a bit o' persuadin' they'd 'ave told the truth at the inquest an' the verdict would most likely 'ave bin one o' misadventure, which we could 'ave used to our advantage. The onus then would 'ave bin on skylarkin' instead o' bad workmanship, 'cos that's what that poxy paper's alludin' to.'

Ben shook his head slowly. 'You won't face it, Frank,' he said plainly. 'Whatever the verdict Maitland's would've wanted out. It's all bad publicity an' they've got too much ter lose wiv their main sewer contract.'

Frank drained his glass and his eyes narrowed as he stared at his brother. 'I've realised we should 'ave paid fer a couple o' professionals ter sort Parry an' Albury out an' next time I won't penny-pinch.'

'What d'yer mean, next time?' Ben asked with a frown.

'I ain't finished wiv them, nor Foden, not by a long chalk,' Frank answered.

The women of Cooper Street had read the local newspapers and Ada mentioned the *Journal*'s editorial comment to Emmie as they stood at their usual spot by Emmie's front door. 'Charlie Foden was the ganger an' 'e was partly ter blame fer the accident,' she told her. 'It said in the paper that the supervision left a lot ter be desired.'

Emmie nodded. 'It must be pretty awful 'avin' that on yer conscience.'

'Too true,' Ada agreed. 'It said in the papers that the bloke who got killed was at logger'eads wiv George Parry an' Danny Albury. Yer'd fink the firm would 'ave bin able ter sort it out before it got out of 'and.'

'They should 'ave sacked the bloke, or all of 'em, come ter that,' Emmie said firmly.

'Well, it's too late now,' Ada concluded in a voice that told Emmie that that particular topic of conversation had been exhausted.

There was an angry mood in the Parry household and Lucy was adamant as she faced Charlie across the parlour table at teatime. 'I fink that reporter wants shootin',' she fumed.

'It was the editor,' Charlie corrected her.

'I don't care who it was,' Lucy told him, 'they shouldn't try ter put the blame on you an' that ovver ganger, what's-'is-name.'

'Sharkey Lockwood.'

'The way that editor went on anybody'd fink you killed the poor sod yerself. It was a pure accident, fer Chrissake.'

'It's all down ter sellin' papers,' George cut in. 'They never consider people's feelin's.'

Sara refrained from comment as she worked away on a piece of embroidery, her thoughts focussed on that Sunday night when Randolph Cadman came to her room at the guesthouse.

Lucy looked at Charlie and saw the pain in his face. He was trying to make light of the whole thing but he hadn't fooled her. How she would have liked to go to his bed once more and hold him in her arms, let him love her and take away his anguish. It would have been nice just to sit on his lap by the fire and run her fingers through his thick hair. He liked that and said it relaxed him. Anything, just to tell him how much she wanted him, but it was nigh on impossible. George was going to the naval centre again next weekend but Sara would be housebound, she was willing to bet.

It was as though Charlie had read her mind. He looked over at her with a desire that Lucy had come to recognise only too well and it made her shiver. Was he feeling as frustrated as she was?

George stood up and stretched, tired of watching Sara working away at the piece of cloth. 'I'm gonna go fer a stroll,' he announced.

'At this time o' night?' Lucy queried.

'It's only 'alf nine,' he told her. 'I need some air.'

'Why don't yer go fer a pint?' she suggested.

In reply he patted his pocket and smiled. 'I'm boracic.'

Lucy stood and reached up to the mantelshelf for her purse. 'Take this,' she said, handing him a half-crown. 'It's all right, I've got enough ter last till yer dole money.'

George took the coin with a brief smile. 'Don't worry, I won't be out o' collar fer very long,' he assured her. 'I'm gonna do the rounds termorrer.'

'Look, I'm not worried, George,' she replied quickly. 'I know you're doin' yer best ter get work, but yer can't get any if it's not there ter be 'ad.'

He looked serious-faced as he went out and Sara looked up momentarily. 'Where's George gone?' she asked.

''E's gone ter get pissed,' Lucy said unkindly.

'I beg yer pardon?'

''E's gone ter stretch 'is legs,' Lucy told her impatiently.

Sara poked at the fire and pointed to the coal scuttle.

'You wouldn't like ter fill it, would yer, Charlie?' she asked him.

'Yeah, sure,' he replied, getting up quickly.

Lucy was trying to control her irritation towards Sara but finding it increasingly difficult. Most nights she would have gone to bed earlier than this but tonight it seemed she was intent on staying up late. Was it because George was out of the house? 'Would you like a cuppa, Sara?' she asked.

'I'd love one.'

'I'll put the kettle on, then.'

Charlie came back into the scullery clutching the coal scuttle and saw Lucy standing by the gas stove. 'Sara must be feelin' the cold,' he said, smiling.

'Put that down an' 'old me,' she whispered.

He looked at his messy hands but Lucy came to him. 'I want a kiss,' she sighed.

He held her, careful not to let his hands touch her dress, and she reached up to him, her lips hungrily closing over his. 'I love yer an' I want yer, Charlie,' she said huskily.

'I love you too,' he told her, his eyes straying to the door, half expecting Sara to walk in on them.

'When, Charlie? When are yer gonna love me?'

'I need to, I want to, but it's so difficult.'

They heard the chair squeak in the parlour and Charlie quickly picked up the scuttle.

'I fink I'll kill Sara,' Lucy said, grinning. 'I'll poison 'er.'

Charlie turned back in the doorway. 'Do it quick,' he muttered.

It was getting late when Sara decided that her eyes were not up to any more sewing and she eased herself out of her armchair. 'I fink I'll take a drink up ter bed wiv me,' she announced.

Lucy gave Charlie a quick glance then got up. 'All right, Sara. I'll do it.'

'No, it's all right, I'll make it,' Sara insisted. 'The last one wasn't sweet enough. I can't stand cocoa wivout enough sugar.'

'Please yerself,' Lucy replied.

They heard her footsteps on the stairs a few minutes later and Lucy saw that it was ten thirty by the clock. She glanced at Charlie. 'George'll be in soon,' she said.

Charlie reached his hand across the parlour table and laid it on hers. 'Yeah. There'll be times, darlin',' he replied in a low voice.

She sighed deeply. 'That first time we made love. I felt guilty then, but I don't now, Charlie. I can't wait fer us ter get tergevver again. Say you feel it too.'

'I do,' he answered. 'We agreed we'd 'ave ter be patient, but sometimes I get desperate. I feel I wanna carry yer off, like a desert sheik. I dream about sweepin' you up on ter my white stallion an' gallopin' off inter the moonlight.'

'Yeah, go on,' she told him with her chin propped on her hands.

'Well, I'd take yer ter my tent at the oasis an' we'd be alone beneath the stars. I'd lay yer down on exotic silks an' I'd make love to yer all night. We'd love as never before an' when we'd finally become exhausted you'd sleep the sleep o' love there in my arms.'

Lucy sighed, realising that her cheeks had grown hot. 'Charlie, you amaze me,' she said.

'When I'm wiv you I amaze meself,' he said quietly.

'What are we gonna do, darlin'?' she asked with anxiety in her voice.

'The way I see it, we've got no choice but ter wait till the opportunity arises,' he answered. 'We've got somefing special, Lucy, a magic that won't disappear just because we can't make love whenever we feel like it. In fact I try ter use it ter my advantage. I watch yer, watch the way yer move, catch the look in yer eyes an' the love inside me grows. I pray fer the chance ter make love ter yer, Lucy, an' I wait.'

'But you're so calm an' collected,' Lucy said. 'You can 'andle it. I'm findin' it almost impossible.'

'I didn't say it was easy, but we've gotta play it the only way we can. There's no ovver way. We take each day as it comes,' an' let the love flourish inside us.'

'I wish I could put inter words what I feel, Charlie,' she said, her eyes filling. 'I 'aven't got your way wiv words, but you must know.'

'I know,' he replied softly.

They heard the front door open and Charlie quickly grabbed up the newspaper while Lucy slipped into the armchair and closed her eyes.

George looked pleased with himself as he walked into the room. 'I was at the Mason's,' he said. 'I 'eard that the Coleys were in there earlier. Apparently they've lost the Maitland contract. Freda told me. She was well pleased. She can't stand those Coleys.'

Lucy stretched and yawned. 'I didn't know it was so late,' she said, yawning again. 'Did you 'ave a nice drink, George?'

'Yeah. I played a few games o' darts wiv Danny.'

'Can I get yer some supper?'

'No I fink I'll get ter bed. I'm feelin' bushed.'

Charlie folded the paper and rubbed his hands over his eyes. 'Yeah, it must be catchin',' he said, smiling.

'You should come out wiv me next time,' George told him. 'Anyfing's better than watchin' Sara sewin'.'

'Or fetchin' the coal,' Charlie joked.

Lucy was the last to go upstairs to bed, after sliding the bolts and raking the ash from the fire. George was already slipping off to sleep and she lay next to him, listening to his irregular breathing. She reached out and touched his arm gently. 'G'night, George.'

He grunted something unintelligible and turned on to his side. Lucy sighed deeply and stared up at the cracked ceiling, partly illuminated by the glow from the streetlamp. How easy it would be to wait until George was snoring his head off then creep into Charlie's room, but she would have to run the gauntlet. Sara was unpredictable and she was a light sleeper. No, she mustn't even think about it. Our time will come soon, Charlie, she thought to herself as she turned over and buried her head in the cool pillow.

Chapter Thirty-Five

The poorly dressed menfolk standing in the winter dole queues shivered against the winds from the east and prayed for the snow which hadn't come. The temperature would rise a few degrees, and there would be some casual snow-clearing work available at the council yard.

Charlie had managed to talk his way back into work at the docks but there was little trade and only one day's labour a week most of the time. As for George Parry and Danny Albury, they stood in line at the labour exchange and dreamed of a job offer, anything that would bring a few shillings into the home.

The winter days wore on and the cold weather persisted till the end of February, when a fitful sun began to show its face a little more often. During that time the relentless ritual continued and Charlie joined his friends in the queue most days, now feeling a little less conspicuous as he walked through the turning. At first the tongues were wagging constantly and the sudden silence as he passed by his women neighbours told him what the topic of conversation was. He began to feel like a murderer and wanted to scream out his innocence to the whole street, but his good sense prevailed. Better to ride it out and let the women tire of it all, he decided. They would soon have something else to gossip about.

Throughout the depressing days of forced idleness Charlie found his salvation in the few stolen moments he spent with Lucy. George was now going to the naval barracks every weekend until he took his exams in March, and it was left to Sara to determine whether or not they could be alone.

'I might go ter the church ternight,' Sara declared, 'but then again I might not. It all depends on 'ow I feel, an' the weavver.'

Lucy gritted her teeth and drew a deep breath before using a little guile. 'I wouldn't,' she said. 'Yer know 'ow you suffer wiv yer back.'

As far as Sara was concerned it was all right for her to announce a backache or a chill coming on but she objected to anyone else pre-empting her health bulletins. 'There's nuffing wrong wiv my back at the moment,' she scoffed.

'You could stay in an' listen ter band music wiv me an' Charlie,' Lucy went on with her fingers crossed behind her back. 'We love that brass band music.'

Sara always felt that brass band music brought on her headaches and she gave Lucy a hard look. 'I don't fancy listenin' ter that noise all evenin',' she said firmly.

'If yer do go out try ter get back a bit early,' Lucy told her. 'I worry if yer out too late.'

'I can look after meself, thank you very much,' Sara retorted. 'Us on the committee 'ave ter wait till last – there's always someone wiv a problem.'

'Well, just see 'ow yer feel later,' Lucy conceded.

Charlie tried to appear disinterested behind the evening paper. He thought that Lucy was playing a very tricky game, but he felt reassured when he saw the look of defiance on Sara's face. She would go out tonight in a blizzard just to be awkward, he felt sure.

As the days grew longer and the winds changed to the west it became obvious that there would be no snow-clearing this year. A warm summer would certainly create a few jobs, though. The breweries often took on casuals during good weather, and the many bottle-washing firms operating under the Bermondsey arches took on extra female workers.

'Mary's goin' ter get 'er name down at Bentley's,' Lucy told George one evening. 'I fink I'll go wiv 'er. Susan an' Gracie'll be startin' school at Easter.'

George shook his head. 'Mary can do what she likes but I don't want you bottle washin',' he said firmly.

'Why ever not?' Lucy replied sharply. 'The pay ain't bad an' it's an eight-hour day.'

George looked angrily at her. ''Ave you ever seen those bottle washers?' he asked. 'They 'ave ter wear clogs an' great big rubber aprons an' caps, they've got their 'ands in water all day an' the bloody place reeks of ammonia. I know 'cos Danny's wife used ter do that work an' she told me all about it. All those bottle washers are the same.'

Lucy ignored George's objections and went with Mary anyway. Sara continued to hold the lovers to ransom, and Charlie marvelled at Lucy's new-found deviousness.

'Sara?'

'Yeah?'

'I was finkin'.'

'What about?'

'Well, you're on the committee an' you must 'ave some input.'

'So?'

'Well, the church is always lookin' out fer ways to 'elp

the poor. Couldn't you organise a sewin' circle?'

'We 'ad one,' Sara told her.

'Yeah, but that was mainly fer baby clothes an' fings. I was finkin' more o' gloves an' scarves.'

'Who for?'

'Those poor gits on the dole queues, an' that'd include George an' Charlie.'

Sara stroked her chin for a few moments. 'I s'pose I could suggest it,' she replied. 'The trouble is gettin' the wool. It costs money, yer know.'

'Yeah, but the church ain't short of a few bob, an' I'm sure they'd go along wiv the scheme if someone like you was pushin' it. All right, I know the winter's nearly over, but they could get a good supply o' gloves an' scarves ready fer next winter.'

Sara looked smug as she considered the idea. 'Well, I 'ave got some clout on the committee,' she said. 'I'll bring it up next week.'

Lucy dreamed of her sister-in-law spending her weekends at the fellowship and she noticed that Charlie had his fingers crossed too.

During the spring a new face joined the Cooper Street men on the dole queue. 'Mornin', lads,' he said cheerily as he slipped in behind them. 'Tod Franklin's the name, anyfink's me game.'

'What's Tod stand for?' Danny asked.

'Nuffink. I was christened Tod,' the newcomer replied.

Danny did the introductions and patted Charlie on the back. ''E was our ganger,' he said proudly.

Charlie studied the newcomer and felt that his face was familiar. He was short and dapper, with a dark complexion and a full head of grey wavy hair. 'D'you ever get in the

Mason's Arms?' Charlie asked.

'Occasionally, but I use the Crown at Dock'ead most times, when the funds allow,' Tod replied.

Danny got into a lengthy conversation with him and George joined in from time to time. Charlie listened, feeling a little puzzled. He had noticed the man standing to one side of the queue as they arrived and knew he had joined them purposely. He was to learn the reason why before too long, but for the moment the chatter was light-hearted and trivial.

With the signing on completed Charlie led the way out of the exchange and stood in the afternoon sunlight debating whether or not to go to the library for an hour or so. Roy had decided to do the rounds of the local builders and he wandered off with his hands in his pockets. Tod Franklin came out and sidled up to Charlie and the others. 'Do you lads fancy a cuppa at Sadie's café?' he asked. 'I got the price.'

Danny nodded. 'I ain't got anyfing better ter do.'

George accepted too and Tod looked at Charlie. 'What about you, big man?'

Guessing that Tod Franklin had a reason for his offer he nodded. 'Yeah, why not?'

They walked round the corner to the steamy café and found a table while Tod ordered the tea, and it was not long before the short man came to the point. 'Tell me, gents,' he began, pushing his mug to one side and resting his arms on the table. 'Do you ever get desperate when yer standin' in that dole queue? I mean desperate enough ter take a chance ter get some money? I know I bloody do.'

'Yer mean like thievin',' Danny said.

'Exactly.'

'Well that depends,' George cut in. 'Yer don't rob yer

own, do yer, an' in any case they'd most likely 'elp yer look fer fings werf nickin'.'

'Nah, I was finkin' o' somefing else,' Tod told them.

Charlie frowned. 'Are yer talkin' about ware'ouse breakin'?'

Tod smiled. 'What if I told you gents there was a nice bit o' money ter be earned wiv little trouble an' no danger involved?'

'Are yer tellin' us the gear's just sittin' there waitin' ter be nicked?' Danny said incredulously.

'It's not there yet, but it will be very shortly,' Tod replied, 'an' I'm lookin' fer a team o' lads I reckon I can trust to 'elp me nick it.'

'You reckon you can trust us?' Charlie asked.

'I'm a good judge o' character,' Tod went on. 'I get the feelin' you can be trusted ter keep yer gobs shut, even if yer don't fancy the little caper.'

Charlie gave him a hard stare. 'I'm still a little puzzled why yer should pick us out fer this caper as yer call it,' he said. 'You could 'ave approached anyone in the queue.'

'That's true,' Tod replied, 'but most of 'em are on their own or in twos. I could see you three were pals an' I can't use anyfing less than a three-man crew. We'll need one more as well unless any o' yous can 'andle hydraulic cranes.'

'I work in the docks,' Charlie told him. 'I can work cranes.'

'Look, 'ear me out an' then go away an' fink about it,' Tod suggested. 'There's no rush. If yer decide ter go in wiv us phone this number. It's me bruvver's – 'e runs a news-agent's.' He handed Charlie a slip of paper with the phone number printed on it. 'If yer don't fancy it, don't bovver ter get in touch. I'll understand. If I ain't 'eard from yer by this time next week I'll start lookin' fer anuvver team. OK, lads, now listen in . . .'

Lucy looked worried as she sat in Mary's parlour on that bright morning, watching her friend pouring the tea with a sly smile on her face.

'I could tell when I brought Susan back the ovver evenin',' Mary told her. 'The atmosphere was electric.'

'Me an' Charlie are just good friends,' Lucy said dismissively.

'Well you could fool me,' Mary replied.

'I know Charlie fancies me, but I got George an' Susan ter consider,' Lucy reminded her.

''Ow long 'ave we known each ovver?' Mary asked.

'Donkey's years.'

'An' are we best friends?'

'Course we are.'

'Well why don't yer come clean?' Mary laughed. 'You an' Charlie are lovers, ain't yer?'

Lucy slumped down in her chair. 'Is it that obvious?'

'Ter me it is,' Mary replied, handing her the tea.

'I didn't want it to 'appen but it did, an' now we can't keep our 'ands off each ovver, when we get the chance,' Lucy said, sighing. 'Don't get me wrong, I still love George, an' yer might find that 'ard ter believe but it's true, as God's my judge it's true. I couldn't even fink o' leavin' 'im, even though our love life's practically dried up, but when Charlie touches me I'm on fire. I can't resist 'im.'

Mary made herself comfortable in an armchair facing her friend. 'We all try ter squeeze the best out of our lives,' she said quietly. 'You get from Charlie what yer can't from George, but you gotta be sure in yer mind about fings. Is it just about 'avin' it off, or could it get like the love you 'ave fer George? If it's goin' that way then I'd say yer've got problems. One day there'll be a choice ter make an' it won't be easy. I fink 'avin' the 'ots fer someone wanes wiv time an' if there's nuffink deeper then it's not too difficult ter finish.'

'You sound like you've bin there,' Lucy remarked with a smile.

Mary shook her head as she smiled back. 'No, I'm only talkin' as I see it,' she replied. 'There's bin times when me an' Roy 'ave turned our backs on each ovver an' we both got irritable, but the love was still there an' it grew, I'm convinced it did. We don't indulge nearly so often as what we did a few years ago, but nevertheless we cuddle an' kiss, an' try ter please each ovver in all sorts o' ways. That's love, ter my way o' finkin', Lucy. I imagine it's what you've got wiv George, in fact I'm sure it is, but yer've found someone who can give you all that George can't or won't, an' yer need ter see it fer what it's werf. Get what yer can out of it but don't burn yer bridges, luv. George'll be there for yer when you an' Charlie are just a memory.'

Lucy shuddered. 'That's somefing I can't come ter terms wiv,' she said. 'If Charlie left me now I'd die, I know I would.'

'Now, yeah, but let it run a course, an' come an' say that ter me then.'

Lucy finished her tea and put the empty cup down on the table. 'I could never keep anyfing from you, could I?' she said quietly.

'That's what friends are for, luv,' Mary told yer. 'Yer secret's safe wiv me, but now I know the score I can be there for yer when fings get bad, an' they will, believe me. Live fer terday, take all yer want from the affair, but remember life still goes on in its 'umdrum way an' generally it's comfortable an' stable. We need that too.'

Lucy stood up to go and suddenly she put out her arms and they embraced. Mary patted her back as though comforting a frightened child. 'Be 'appy, luv,' she said quietly.

Chapter Thirty-Six

The three friends from Cooper Street had agreed that they should take a couple of days to think about Tod Franklin's plan and that it would have to be a unanimous decision to go ahead. George also suggested that Roy Chubb should be made aware of the possible escapade but when he was approached he immediately shook his head. 'I don't need any time ter fink about it,' he said firmly. 'Count me out. I've got a chance of a start wiv a buildin' firm in Deptford very shortly an' that'll do fer me.'

Danny made his home available for the next get-together, knowing his wife would be visiting her sister that day. 'Besides, it's better than meetin' in some café or pub,' he remarked. 'Yer never know who might be earwiggin'.'

'Well, lads, we've all 'ad time ter fink. 'Ow d'yer feel about it?' Charlie asked as Danny brought in the tea.

'I'm game,' Danny said without hesitation. 'I've given it a lot o' thought. I've never done anyfing like this before, but all my life I've never 'ad two 'a'pennies ter rub tergevver, an' I've come ter the conclusion it don't pay ter be honest these days.'

'What about you, George?' Charlie asked.

'Yeah, count me in,' he replied. 'I dunno 'ow long I can go on linin' up at that labour exchange, an' fer a pittance.

It's drivin' me mad. All right, we're takin' a chance, but I fink from what Tod Franklin's told us it's good odds.'

Both Danny and George looked at Charlie, knowing that the go-ahead rested upon his decision.

'Like you lads I spent a lot o' time finkin' about this, an' I was impressed by Franklin's know-'ow,' he told them. ''E's obviously took a lot o' time plannin' fings out, an' the fact that 'e's worked at the firm makes a big difference. So the answer's yes. I'm wiv you.'

Danny grinned broadly as he poured the tea. ''Ere, get that down yer,' he said cheerily. 'I fink fings are finally gonna look up.'

'I'll drink ter that, even if it's only tea,' George said, grinning.

The number 82 bus trundled through Rotherhithe Tunnel and pulled up in Commercial Road, where the three conspirators alighted and made their way through drizzling rain to the nearby Grapes public house. It was fairly busy in the public bar and Tod was waiting for them. 'We'll move inter the saloon,' he said. 'It's quieter in there.'

Having led them to a vacant table in a corner of the bar and got in a round of drinks, he sat quietly rolling a cigarette with a ghost of a smile on his lips, seeming totally calm as he looked from one to another. 'Right, lads, the caper's on fer Friday,' he said, licking the cigarette paper. 'The two drums o' tobacco were delivered yesterday an' my pal tells me that they'll be started on next Monday. So yer see we've gotta act fast. Now, I've got some sketches wiv me an' I'll explain just what everyone 'as ter do. If we digest this properly an' stick ter the letter, everyfing'll go off like a dream. Oh, an' one more fing before we go over it all. The buyer's agreed ter the price I quoted 'im. An' so 'e should. We're talkin' about two drums, each containin' over three 'undredweight o' compressed pipe tobacco of the finest quality.'

The three leaned forward over the table as Tod laid out his first sketch. 'Now this is the point of entry,' he began . . .

Mary Chubb thought that her husband seemed very preoccupied at teatime and she put it down to his worrying over money. He had told her that there might be a job coming up for him very soon but she had heard it all before and preferred not to build her hopes up too much.

Roy sat staring into the empty grate for a long time after he had finished his tea with the evening newspaper lying forgotten at his feet, and Mary could stand it no longer. 'Look, there's somefing troublin' you, Roy,' she said as she seated herself in the armchair opposite him.

'Nah, I'm just a bit tired.'

'Don't try an' fob me off,' she told him sharply. 'I know you well enough. There's somefing on yer mind.'

He looked at her and saw that there was no use attempting to keep it from her so he leaned forward in his chair and clasped his hands together. 'George, Charlie an' Danny Albury are takin' a gamble,' he said.

'What d'yer mean, takin' a gamble?' she asked with a frown.

'They're gonna do a job.'

'What sort o' job?'

'They're plannin' on breakin' into a ware'ouse,' he told her. 'They're after nickin' some drums o' tobacco.'

'Bloody 'ell!' Mary exclaimed. 'Does Lucy know?'

'No she doesn't an' you mustn't tell 'er. George don't wanna worry 'er.'

'Where did they get this idea from?' she asked, looking shocked.

'A geezer in the dole queue. 'E's planned it all.'

'I would 'ave thought they 'ad a bit more sense,' Mary remarked with an exasperated sigh.

'They asked me ter go in wiv 'em but I turned it down.'

'I should bloody well fink so,' she replied with passion. 'All right, I know fings are bad an' there's no money about, but stealin' ain't the answer. S'posin' they get caught. Imagine what it'd do ter Lucy an' their Sue. It don't bear finkin' about.'

'Now look, I want yer ter promise me yer won't let on ter Lucy,' Roy said firmly.

'I won't say anyfing,' she sighed. 'I just 'ope it goes off OK.'

Roy picked up the paper but he couldn't concentrate on it. Had he done the right thing in turning down the chance of earning a decent few quid, he wondered? Would they think him a coward?

Mary got up and went to him, gently kneading his shoulders. 'I've bin finkin',' she said. 'I'm proud you 'ad the guts ter say no, even if it made yer look bad in their eyes. You could 'ave jumped at the chance of the money, but no money in the world'd make up fer you bein' locked away fer years. Me an' Gracie need you 'ere wiv us frew these bad times. We can cope if we're tergevver, but I couldn't if you wasn't there wiv us, an' just fink what it'd do ter Gracie.'

Roy felt distinctly better. Mary was right in what she said, he realised. It made no difference what his friends might think of him. Mary and their daughter came first.

Charlie and George had it planned, and Lucy was told that there was to be a darts final at the Star on Friday evening and drinks were to be served free to the team.

'If we win we may be back a bit late so I wouldn't wait up,' George remarked.

Lucy stole a glance at Charlie and he gave her a sly wink. 'Keep yer fingers crossed fer us,' he said with a smile.

Danny was ready and the three men made their way to the bus stop in Jamaica Road. Charlie carried the key which Tod had supplied and he tapped his coat pocket to reassure himself. Nothing must go wrong tonight, he told himself. Come tomorrow they would all be well breeched.

The rain had ceased and the night was clear with a pale crescent moon shining down from a velvet sky. The river mud was bubbling at low tide and its odour lingered in the air along the narrow riverside lane in Wapping as the three neared Conroy's wharfage. They saw Tod waiting in a doorway and he smiled at them. 'The copper's bin frew an' 'e won't be back fer two hours,' he reported. 'I'll be 'ere at exactly nine o'clock. I'll pull up as planned below that crane an' you be ready ter let the drums down. One at a time fer safety. Like I said, I don't want 'em sent down tergevver. I've seen 'em slip out o' slings before when they come down doubled up. OK then, lads, let's get goin'.'

They watched him hurry off to fetch the lorry and George and Danny followed Charlie into the alley that led down to a flight of stone steps known by the locals as Lover's Walk. Charlie took out the key and removed the rusted padlock that secured the reinforced sliding door at the side of the warehouse. He reached through the iron grille of the lift to depress the locking lever, slid the grille to one side and stepped into the lift, repeating the procedure with the other grille which led into the large storage area. Tod had explained that although the lift was robust enough to take the two drums it would be difficult to manhandle them out from the alley and on to the lorry, whereas the crane would drop them into place with no effort.

George joined Charlie in the storage area while Danny slid the door back into place and replaced the padlock. He then made his way to the front of the building and Charlie let him in through the emergency fire door which could only be opened from the inside. The three men hurried up the dusty stone stairs to the third floor where the drums had been stored and Danny's eyes lit up as he spotted them. ''Ow we doin' fer time?' he asked.

Charlie took his pocket watch out of his coat pocket. 'Eight forty-five,' he told him. 'We'd better get started.'

Slowly and methodically the two large drums were manoeuvred across the wooden floor towards the front crane door and Charlie slid the bolt, ready to kick the door open and drop the flap into place when Tod drove up.

'Right, let's get this crane workin',' he said quickly.

George and Danny watched as he switched on the power to fill the water tank and in a few minutes the pressure had built up. Charlie tugged sharply on the operating cord and as the crane rope grew taut he gave a sigh of satisfaction. 'Right, it's ready,' he told them. 'Get the slings. Careful now. That's right, roll it over the rope an' take up the slack. Right, loop it an 'old it up while I 'ook it ter the crane.'

Tod Franklin looked at his watch as he reached the transport yard and saw that it was ten minutes to nine. 'They're cuttin' it short,' he growled to himself.

The swish of tyres and the blazing headlights startled him and he stepped to one side as the car drove quickly into the yard. 'Are they on the premises?' the inspector asked.

Tod nodded. 'They were about ter go in when I left 'em,' he replied.

The police inspector gathered his men around him and glanced quickly from one to another. 'Now you all know your positions and I want you to be as quiet as possible,' he began. 'The object of the exercise is to wait until the goods are visible in the loophole and then we go in. All the exits will be manned and Johnson and Skeets will go up with me to make the arrests. Holland, your back-up team will follow us up the stairs in case we need assistance but for God's sake stay well clear of the loophole. Remember we'll be three floors up and I don't want any of you falling from there, understood?' The police operatives nodded and mumbled their replies and the inspector turned to Tod Franklin. 'Right then, get aboard and take it easy. Just act as you've planned.'

Tod started up the five-ton, drop-side Leyland and drove slowly from the yard. It had been a lengthy bit of work for him and he was looking forward to going up to Manchester for a few weeks' rest as soon as it was all over.

Danny leaned on the attached drum. 'What time d'yer make it, Charlie?' he asked.

Charlie glanced at his watch once more. 'It's two minutes ter nine.'

The waiting seemed interminable but now the three men heard the sound of the lorry approaching and it was time to move. Charlie kicked open the crane door and dropped the flap, and as Danny and George leant their weight to the drum he pulled on the crane rope. It took up the slack and he kicked the suspended drum outwards as the lorry drew up below. Suddenly the lane was lit up like a theatre as the police cars turned on their headlights. Charlie could see men running into position and he swore. 'We've bin tumbled!' he shouted. 'Quick! The stairs!'

As they ran up to the top floor they heard the metallic voice of the police loud-hailer. 'Come down quietly and give yourselves up. There's nowhere to go.'

George led the way as they hurried on to the flat roof and Charlie brought up the rear. The adjacent warehouse roof looked tantalisingly near yet it was too far away to reach and Danny leaned over the edge. 'We'd never make it if we tried ter jump,' he gasped.

Charlie hurried across towards Danny and suddenly he felt the floor give way beneath him, and he was falling . . .

Chapter Thirty-Seven

November 1952

Sue leaned back in the armchair and blew long and hard through her pursed lips. 'I tell yer, Charlie, if it 'ad bin anyone ovver than you who told me about those days, about me dad an' all that ovver stuff, I'd never 'ave believed 'em,' she said. 'I find it 'ard ter believe anyway.'

Charlie leaned forward in his seat. 'Yer know I wouldn't lie ter yer, luv,' he replied. 'Sara got it all wrong, but ter be fair she didn't know anyfing. It was all kept from 'er.'

'I fink she must 'ave realised that you an' me mum were lovers,' Susan said quietly, 'though she never actually said it in 'er letter.'

Charlie nodded. 'You know, I really 'ave a soft spot fer Sara, despite 'er vindictiveness, an' 'er troublemakin'.'

Sue smiled at him. 'As she got older she got more 'ateful towards men but she wouldn't 'ave a bad word said against me dad, so that left you.'

'Poor Sara,' Charlie sighed. 'I even feel a bit sorry fer 'er,'

The young woman suddenly realised that the rain had stopped and the sun was breaking through. 'I was only five when you got caught in that ware'ouse,' she remarked.

'When you went away I cried buckets. Me mum an' dad told me you 'ad ter go a long way away ter work but I wanted yer there, ter read me those picture books an' tell me those stories about the crunchy giant.'

'You remember those stories,' he said, smiling.

Sue nodded. 'Yeah, I remember, but there's still so many questions I wanna ask yer.'

'Then ask me,' he told her.

She gazed at his calm face for a moment or two. 'When me dad killed Wally Coates did it affect 'im badly? I knew 'im ter be a gentle, kind man. I can't imagine 'im doin' such a terrible fing.'

Charlie took her hands in his and looked into her pale blue eyes. 'Those times changed people, there's no two ways about it,' he answered. 'Imagine yer dad slavin' in that trench hour after hour, day after day fer a pittance, wiv his 'ands raw as meat an' 'is back ready ter break, an' all the time 'e was plagued by Wally Coates who wouldn't leave 'im alone. Yer dad put up wiv the bullyin' an' the bad-mouthin', 'cos, like yer say, 'e was a kind and gentle person an' 'e couldn't find it in 'is 'eart ter retaliate. P'raps if 'e 'ad Wally Coates would 'ave left 'im alone. Anyway, it was only when Coates grabbed 'old o' Danny Albury that 'e picked up the shovel an' swiped 'im. Yer dad never actually killed 'im, 'e was suffocated by the earth on top of 'im, but we 'ad ter keep on at yer dad fer some time tryin' ter make 'im see it as it really was or 'e would 'ave gone out of 'is mind. 'E was adamant too that yer mum mustn't know, but now I think it would 'ave bin better if she 'ad known. It would 'ave surely drawn them closer.'

'I might sound naive an' stupid, but I can't imagine me dad gettin' involved in that break-in neivver,' Sue told him.

'But then yer've explained 'ow desperate fings were an' 'ow tight the money was.'

'Those dole queues, an' constantly 'avin' ter say no when yer wife an' kids wanted somefing, turned a lot o' men's minds,' Charlie said. 'People got desperate an' the possibility of makin' fings easier by takin' a few chances was 'ard to ignore. Yer dad didn't need ter be persuaded, Sue. 'E jumped at the chance, the same as me an' Danny Albury. On reflection we should 'ave bin a bit more patient, sussed the bloke out before we agreed ter go in wiv 'im, but 'e sounded plausible enough an', like I say, we never 'ad a brass farthin' between us at the time.'

'You said me dad an' Danny got away that night,' Sue reminded him. 'Tell me exactly what 'appened.'

'When I went frew the rotted wooden trapdoor I fell feet first an' broke me ankle on landin',' Charlie told her. 'I was soon caught, but from what I could 'ear I knew they 'adn't caught yer dad or Danny. It was only when I was sentenced that I found out what 'appened. Before I was sent down yer mum was allowed a few minutes wiv me an' yer dad 'ad told 'er everyfing. It turned out that 'e'd found a long ladder on the roof an' 'im an' Danny stretched it between the two ware'ouses an' crawled across the gap. They did the same on the next roof an' managed ter shimmy down a drainpipe on ter the top of one o' those box cranes yer see at some wharves. They used the crane's wall ladder ter reach the quay an' waded frew the mud ter some nearby steps. Yer mum said yer dad come in covered from 'ead ter foot in mud an' shakin' like a leaf. I 'ave ter say they were dead lucky. It took the police a few minutes ter break in the ware'ouse, an' by that time yer dad an' Danny were long gone.'

'An' you got three years,' Sue added.

He smiled sheepishly. 'Unfortunately I got a stern judge an' 'e set out ter make an example o' me. Trouble was there'd bin a lot o' pilferin' goin' on in the docks at the time.'

'It couldn't 'ave 'elped you not lettin' on who was wiv yer.'

Charlie nodded. 'I told the police I'd bin recruited by a couple o' strangers who'd bin told I was a docker an' knew about cranes. I'm sure they didn't believe me an' I don't fink the judge did eivver.'

'Did Mum come an' visit yer while you was away?' Sue asked.

'Once or twice wiv yer dad, but then I got transferred ter Durham prison an' it was too far ter come, an' they couldn't afford the fare anyway.'

'Was it bad, Charlie?'

'Yeah, it was bad enough.'

'I'll never ferget the day you came 'ome,' the young woman said. 'I was eight years old an' I remember showin' yer me gas mask.'

'Yeah, an' you was upset 'cos they never gave yer a Mickey Mouse gas mask,' Charlie grinned.

Sue studied her fingernails for a few moments. 'Did you an' Mum pick up on the affair?'

'Fer a few weeks,' he answered, 'but then war was declared. Yer dad was called up straight away an' Sara took it on 'erself ter be yer mum's unwanted chaperone. She 'ardly left the 'ouse. It went on that way till the Blitz started. Then . . .' His voice faltered.

'Go on, Charlie,' she urged him. 'I wanna know everyfing.'

He lowered his gaze for a few moments, then his eyes came up to meet hers. 'The Surrey docks were still burnin' from the day raid an' the bombers were back,' he recalled.

'Sara was at the local street shelter an' me an' yer mum were alone. It was the last time we made love. Two weeks later I was transferred ter Bristol ter work in the docks there an' I only got ter see yer mum every so often at weekends, if I could get away. Yer dad was on convoy duty in the Atlantic an' Roy Chubb was in the air force.'

'But you sent those love letters from Bristol,' Sue pointed out. 'The last one was in 1943.'

'That's right, but they were only expressin' the way I felt an' 'ow I wished fings could be back the way they were,' he explained. 'Fer a long time I'd sensed that yer mum was bein' drawn back closer ter yer dad. I truly fink she expected 'im ter be killed an' she was missin' 'im bad. I remember comin' 'ome fer a weekend. It was the summer of '41 an' yer mum an' Sara were sittin' at the front door in the warm sunshine when I walked inter the turnin'. I 'adn't even 'ad time ter say 'ello before the telegram boy drew up on 'is bike an' 'anded yer mum the dreaded buff envelope that told 'er yer dad 'ad bin lost at sea. I tried me best ter comfort 'er but Sara took charge an' I left after a while. I knew then that the affair between us was over. I didn't doubt that we'd stay good friends, but that was all it would ever be from that day on.'

'Did me mum ever write back ter yer?'

Charlie smiled and shook his head. 'Yer mum told me more than once she was the world's worst letter writer,' he replied, and then his face became serious. 'There was one letter, though. It came a few weeks after yer dad was killed. I want yer ter read it, Sue. It might 'elp you understand a bit better.'

Sue watched while he got up and went over to the dresser. He opened a drawer and took the letter out from under a pile of papers. She saw that his hand was shaking as he handed it to her and the sad look on his face made her heart melt.

Dear Charlie,

I know you'll be surprised to get this letter after me telling you how bad I am at writing, but I just had to let you know the way I feel about things. Yes, Charlie, I really love you and I always will, and it was strong enough to overcome my deep sense of guilt. But things are different now. George is no longer with me and I only have the memory of him. I no longer have the chance to make things up to him for the respect I lost. I found the courage to cheat on him during his life-time, if courage is the right word, but I find I can't cheat on him now that he's dead. I know that you'll find this hard to understand and I'm not sure I fully understand myself, but please try to see it as I see it. You know I loved George and while he lived I was able to use his failings as a reason for the deceit. His death killed something in me and I can't find fault with him any more, and it tears me apart. Loving you is the best thing that ever happened to me and I'll take the love I have for you to my grave. Think well of me, Charlie, and keep warm memories in your heart, as I will surely do of you. Let's stay friends and let's meet without guilt or strangeness. Continue to smile for me as you always do and I'll be happy to remember the whisper-ing years.

May God bless you, Charlie.

My love for ever,

Lucy.

Tears dropped on to the letter and Sue closed her eyes as she handed it back to him. Charlie put it away in the drawer and came over to sit facing her.

'We were good friends, Sue,' he said quietly, 'an' as the years slipped by the friendship blossomed. We could meet as your mum said, wivout guilt or strangeness. She did love yer dad, you can be sure, and she loved me too in 'er own way. I can live wiv that, an' I 'ope that letter 'elps you understand an' forgive both of us. I loved George as a bruvver.' Charlie stood up and gathered the used teacups. 'I'll make us anuvver cuppa an' then I want yer to meet someone. It's all right – she only lives along the landin'.'

The red November sun was molten in a clear sky and the pavements were drying out as Charlie led the way along the stone balcony. He knocked on the last door but one and gave Sue a reassuring smile as they waited.

'Well, if it ain't young Sue Parry,' Alice Albury said as she opened the door. 'Come in, come in. Yer'll 'ave ter take me place as yer find it. I can't get about the way I used to, not any more. It's me legs, yer see. I'm plagued wiv arfritis. Sit 'ere, luv. Charlie, pull up that armchair.'

'Sue's engaged ter be married,' Charlie told her. 'She's gettin' married early next year.'

'Tell me somefink I don't know,' Alice snorted. 'Alan Woodley's a fine young man. Credit to 'is family. I've known the Woodleys fer years.'

'Me an' Sue's bin 'avin' a chat about the ole days in Cooper Street,' Charlie remarked. 'Remember that time I broke me ankle?'

Alice shook her head slowly and tutted. 'You was a naughty boy, Charlie, an' if I didn't know you better I'd 'ave sworn you led my Danny on.'

'You know I wouldn't 'ave done that, luv.'

Alice smiled. 'We was just grateful yer didn't let on about who was wiv yer. Danny an' George would 'ave gone away too. Oops! 'Ave I put me foot in it?' she said quickly.

Charlie smiled. 'She knows all about it,' he assured her.

'Charlie was a good friend ter my Danny as well as yer farvver,' Alice went on. 'Did 'e tell yer about Wally Coates?'

Susan nodded. 'I fink 'e's told me just about everyfing,' she replied with a smile.

'Your farvver was protectin' Danny in that trench an' it was Charlie who got it all sorted out,' the old lady said. 'My Danny, Gawd rest 'is soul, thought the world o' Charlie.'

Charlie looked up at the mantelshelf and pointed to the framed photograph. 'That was taken durin' the Blitz,' he remarked.

'Get it down, Charlie,' Alice told him.

He did as she asked and handed it to her.

'Don't yer fink Danny looked 'andsome in 'is ARP uniform?' she said, and then her face grew sad. 'That was taken a few days before Webber Buildin's copped it. Danny was 'elpin' ter get the poor bleeders out an' a main wall fell on 'im. 'E didn't 'ave a chance. They gave 'im a lovely write-up in the local papers. I was pleased about that.'

'Your Danny was an 'ero, Alice,' Charlie told her quietly.

'Yeah, 'e wasn't scared of anybody,' Alice said proudly. She looked at Susan. 'I remember the time your dad got drunk. It was just after Charlie got sent down, an' everyone knew that the Coleys were be'ind it. Anyway, yer dad was goin' off in the pub about it an' those awful gits got to 'ear. They waited on 'im as 'e came out an' steamed into 'im. They would 'ave killed 'im if it wasn't fer Danny an' ole Ron Sloan the beat copper. Danny waded in wiv 'is fists an' Ron Sloan 'appened ter turn the corner just in time. 'E cracked Ben Coley over the crust wiv 'is truncheon an' my Danny knocked Frank Coley out cold wiv a milk bottle. Lucky fer your dad, it was. A few minutes later an' I don't know what would've 'appened. Those Coleys didn't mess about.'

Sue turned to Charlie. 'Didn't you ever try ter get yer own back on 'em?' she asked.

'I thought about nuffing else while I was locked up,' he told her. 'As soon as I got out I made enquiries, but that was as far as it went. Life itself 'ad taken care o' Frank Coley. 'E'd suffered a stroke an' was paralysed down one side, an' Ben 'ad gone missin'. Nobody seemed ter know where 'e was, but I found out later that 'e was contractin' up in Liverpool. 'E did come back ter London, but it was a bad move. 'E was killed when a flyin' bomb landed on a buildin' site in Dock'ead.'

'You spoke about Sharkey Lockwood,' Sue reminded him. 'What 'appened to 'im?'

''E's still about,' Charlie replied. ''Aven't you ever seen that bloke wiv the scales in East Lane on Sundays?'

'The guess-yer-weight man?'

'That's 'im,' Charlie said, smiling. 'It's a bit of a comedown fer Sharkey, but 'e always liked an easy, uncomplicated life.'

Alice eased her position in her armchair and looked at Charlie. 'I'm goin' again this year as usual, even if I 'ave ter be pushed in a wheelchair,' she said firmly. 'Will you be there?'

'I will,' Charlie told her, 'even if I 'ave ter push yer all the way.' He looked across at Sue. 'Alice visits Danny's grave every November on the anniversary of 'is death. So do I.'

Susan suddenly felt drained and she looked at Charlie

appealingly. 'I really must get me shoppin' before every-where closes,' she said.

The November day was giving way to a chilly evening as Sue Parry saw him coming towards her. She put down her laden shopping bag and hugged him.

'I was gettin' worried,' he said.

'So was I,' she replied. 'I 'aven't seen yer fer hours.'

'Did yer get it all sorted out?' he asked as he picked up her shopping.

'Almost,' she told him. 'There's one more visit I need ter make soon an' I want yer there wiv me.'

'Don't tell me, let me guess,' he replied. 'Aunt Sara.'

'Right first time,' she said, feeling with pleasure his arm tighten round her waist.

Epilogue

They were there in St Mark's churchyard, the people of Cooper Street, and they waited patiently in the mild February sunshine.

'I do love a weddin',' Ada Black remarked.

'So do I,' Emmie replied. ''Specially when it's one o' yer ole neighbour's kids.'

'Wouldn't Lucy be proud if she was 'ere terday?' Ada said.

'She is,' Emmie told her. 'She'll be lookin' down on 'er an' young Alan, an' she'll be pleased. 'E's a lovely boy.'

Ada nodded. 'Yeah, they're a good match.'

'I just 'ope they 'ave it a bit easier than we did,' Emmie said.

The Stricklands were standing next to them and Sammy felt the need to say his piece. 'They will, luv,' he said positively. 'There's plenty o' work now an' there's new 'ouses an' buildin's goin' up all round. Kids o' terday 'ave got a chance, where we 'ad ter scratch around fer a pittance.'

Peggy Strickland hid a smile, wondering how Sammy would have fared as a young man in today's world. Someone would have managed to shove a job down his throat, despite his hatful of excuses to make himself unemployable. 'Yeah, it was 'ard fer us in those days,' she said mildly.

There was a murmur of excitement as someone spotted the car and Ada checked that she had her confetti in her handbag.

'Bloody 'ell! See who's just walked in the gates,' Emmie exclaimed.

Ada turned to see Ron Sloan accompanied by his wife, still upright at seventy and still looking every inch the beat bobby.

'I always felt reassured when I saw 'im walk in our turnin',' Emmie told her. 'It's different terday. They're all ridin' round in cars.'

Will Jackson and his wife Paula were standing nearby and Will's mind went back to the day he was apprehended with a pair of wringer rollers. 'Nice ter see yer, Ron. An' you, luv,' he said.

'Nice ter be 'ere,' the ex-policeman replied.

'I bet yer miss the ole turnin',' Will remarked.

Ron nodded with a smile. 'Yeah, I do. The backstreets are all slowly disappearin' now.'

'Ain't much call fer wringers these days eivver,' Will said with a grin.

The bridal car drove into the churchyard and the chauffeur alighted smartly to open the rear door. Charlie stepped out and helped Susan climb out as she nervously hoisted up her long white wedding dress.

Gracie Chubb was chief bridesmaid and she gave her best friend a supportive smile as her mother helped her adjust the folds of her gown. The bystanders entered the church while the photographer took a few snaps of Susan and her escort by the car, and every head inside the church turned as the opening bars of the wedding march boomed out. Charlie felt the young woman's warm hand on his arm and he threw back his shoulders as he led her down the aisle, casting his eyes briefly to the pews on both sides. He couldn't see her, but he heard the soft murmurings and the whispered words of appreciation as he and the beautiful bride in her flowing white dress walked slowly towards the altar.

Beams of early spring sunlight shone through the stained glass window above the altar and fell in pale spangles of colour on the two young people to be wed, and Charlie was happy.

She came late and eased herself quietly into a back-row pew. She was pale and thin, the gossamer veil of her new hat covering her face. She listened to the words being said and the vows being taken and stood with the rest to sing the cheerful hymn, suddenly aware that there was no hymnal on the rack in front of her.

''Ere, luv, share mine,' Mrs Venners said to her.

The congregation stood to watch the bride and groom walk down the aisle as man and wife and Sara shed a tear.

They were gathering outside for the photo call and Charlie eventually walked across to her. 'Will yer join me in a drink at the reception?' he asked.

'I don't fink so,' she replied. 'I just wanted ter see Susan get wed.'

'But she needs you ter be there,' Charlie said quietly. 'We're all she's got, me an' you. Besides, I gotta do a speech an' I'd feel much less nervous if you was there, Sara.'

She looked at him for a few seconds and then something like a tremor passed across her face. 'Can you fergive a wicked ole lady?' she asked him as she looked down at the ground.

'There's nuffink ter fergive,' he told her with a smile.

Sara pressed her frail hand on top of his, and shed another tear.

Tuppence to
Tooley Street

To the memory of my parents,
Annie and Henry Bowling.

With special thanks to Edie Burgess for her help,
advice, and her special knowledge – what a gal!

Chapter One

Dunkirk

A blood red sun was dipping down behind a clump of trees and evening shadows lengthened across the flat French countryside as the two soldiers journeyed towards the coast. Private Danny Sutton felt deathly tired under the weight of his pack. He glanced at Albert Sweetland, the young soldier from the Royal Norfolks, as he trudged along with a cold determination, his thumbs hooked through his pack-straps. Danny gritted his teeth and cursed to himself as he tried to keep up.

The road the two soldiers travelled was busy. Laden trucks drove past carrying battle-weary troops. Civilians rode past on bicycles with large bundles slung across the handlebars, and occasionally a horse-cart went by carrying French women and their young children perched on top of their salvaged belongings. Up ahead, the tar-black pall of smoke from the burning oil installations at Dunkirk was rising high in the already darkening sky. The guns had ceased and it was strangely quiet. A faint bird-song sounded from a hedgerow and Albert held up his head.

"That's a jay. First I've heard this year," he said.

"Is it? I wouldn't know a jay from a cock robin," Danny replied irritably. "I can reco'nise a sparrer though," he said as an afterthought. "Plenty o' sparrers in London. Quite a few chickens as well. They keep 'em in their backyards where I come from."

1

Albert grunted and hoisted his pack higher onto his sore shoulders.

The two soldiers lapsed into silence. The mention of chickens had conjured up visions of food which niggled at their empty bellies. Danny tried to forget that he hadn't eaten all day. Christ! What a mess, he thought. Two starving infantrymen without a rifle and a round of ammunition between us. He puffed and hoisted his backpack higher onto his shoulders. They had to reach the coast as quickly as possible. The bloody remnants of the British Expeditionary Force were being squeezed into a pocket around the port of Dunkirk. Danny and Albert had seen their units decimated, and now the German Panzers were closing in behind them.

A breeze had sprung up and Danny shivered. The stocky figure of Albert plodding on steadfastly in front made the young cockney feel a grudging admiration. The country boy was not the most talkative soldier he had met but he seemed able to go on marching for ever. They could smell the stench from rotting carcasses of farm animals and it mingled with the acrid smell of the burning oil dumps as darkness settled over the French fields. It was May 29th, and only a few days away from Danny's twenty-first birthday. He was feeling pessimistic about his chances of being around to celebrate the occasion. If he didn't find a place to rest pretty soon he felt sure he would fall asleep on the march and sink beneath the muddy ditchwater. He tried to focus his mind on home. He attempted to picture his family in Dawson Street, and Kathy from the next turning, but all he saw were the faces of his comrades as they faced the onslaught of the German troops.

An old woman shuffled slowly along the road, her frail body bent forward in the shafts of the creaking cart which rattled and jumped over the uneven surface, the contents swaying and bobbing around; a shrouded figure sat slumped in the back. When the woman reached the two

2

soldiers she stopped and put down the shafts. She looked at them with baleful, sunken eyes and her lips moved silently. They could see she was very old: her face was skeletal and her hollow cheeks puffed out with her exertions; her dark clothes hung in tatters and her skirt touched the cobbles. Slowly she turned her head as they passed, her eyes narrowed, and she mumbled something, then her body bent as she picked up the shafts and set the cart into motion once more. The shrouded figure on the bundles rocked back and forth and Danny caught sight of the face. His flesh crawled and he gripped Albert's arm. "Gawd Almighty! Look at it!"

Albert stared at the grey, bloated face of death and he turned his head away. "It's been dead for at least a week," he muttered, unable to decide whether the corpse was male or female.

"It's tied on," Danny whispered.

They could now smell the stench and Danny retched into the hedgerow. He felt Albert's hand on his shoulder and he straightened up. He had looked upon death before, but this was different. "Let's go," he said, shuddering.

They trudged on for a few paces then both reluctantly looked back down the lane. The stretch was deserted. There was no sign of the cart.

The light had faded and Albert quickened his pace. Danny tried to keep up with him, and after what seemed an eternity the two young soldiers reached the edge of Dunkirk. For a while they trudged wearily along the bomb-damaged streets, then Danny leaned against a wall. "It's no good, Albert. I'm done in," he said breathlessly. "We gotta find a place ter kip fer the night."

Albert pointed to a row of shattered shops further along the road. "What about there? The roof looks solid at least."

They walked over and entered a small shop. Inside a group of soldiers from the Middlesex Regiment sat propped against the walls. One of the soldiers nodded at

3

them and then pointed to the back of the shop. "There's a tap out back," he said.

The two went outside into a small courtyard and washed the dust from their dry throats before filling their water bottles. Danny raised his pale blue eyes to the dark sky. A few tiny stars twinkled through the smoky clouds, and he thought of his home in Bermondsey. His folk might be looking at those same stars right that minute. He thought of Kathy and vowed to put things right with her if he ever got out alive . . .

He knew he had done wrong by taking her for granted. She had always been there when he needed her. It had always been him and Kathy ever since they were youngsters. She had been content just to be with him and he had to mess everything up. The other girls never meant anything to him; he could hardly picture their faces now. But there was the image of Kathy, strong and clear in his mind, as it had been throughout the long months away, filling him with a sense of calm. Only now it was too late. His sister had told him in her last letter that Kathy was seeing someone else.

Albert had gone back inside and now Danny bathed his feet and used the last of the boracic powder on his raw heels. He rummaged through his pack and found another pair of socks and a field dressing. Once he had bound up his feet and put on the clean socks he felt a little better. The desire for food was giving way to tiredness and he went back into the dusty interior and slumped down beside Albert. The young soldier who had first spoken to them leaned over and nudged Danny. "Ain't yer 'ad any food terday?" he asked.

Danny shook his head. "Me stomach finks me froat's bin cut, mate."

The soldier grinned. "Don't worry. Oggy Murphy's out on the scrounge. 'E'll find somefink."

Time passed and Danny felt his head drooping. Albert was already snoring, his head resting against the

4

crumbling plaster. Suddenly there was a commotion. Danny looked up and saw a huge soldier standing in the shop doorway. He walked in to ragged cheers from his comrades. He was bareheaded and his shaven skull shone in the light of the candle. His features were large and his fleshy lips were parted in a wide grin. "Oggy's got the goods," he said in a bellowing voice.

He placed a sack down on the floor and immediately one of the soldiers grabbed at it. Oggy cuffed the young man smartly around the head. "Wait, me beauty. There's bottles in there!" he growled.

Everyone was now wide awake. Oggy laid down a bundle beside the sack and grinned at the group. "Wait fer it," he said as he reached into the sack.

Soon Oggy had spread out the contraband on the dusty floor. There were six bottles of red wine and two sticks of bread. Oggy then opened the bundle and produced three tins of corned beef and a chunk of mouldy-looking cheese. Last of all he felt into his uniform pocket and took out a packet of Craven A cigarettes.

"Cor! Where d'yer get that lot, Oggy?" the young soldier said admiringly, rubbing his head.

The ugly giant of a man touched the side of his nose with the tip of his finger. "Never you mind, sonny. Oggy could get court-martialled fer nickin' officers' grub an' comforts."

The food was shared out as fairly as possible and everyone in the room ate in silence. The wine tasted like vinegar but it helped the food down their dry throats. When the meal was finished some of the troops lit cigarettes, and Oggy pulled out a wooden pipe and packed it to the brim with tobacco which he took from a greasy pouch.

The loosely hanging shutters rattled in the wind and gunfire sounded in the distance. After a while the soldiers began to fall asleep. Albert was snoring again, his head tilted forward onto his chest. Danny tried to think about home but tiredness prevented him from

5

focusing clearly. His head drooped and he fell into a fitful sleep.

Danny was awakened by the noise of the Middlesex troops mustering outside the shop. Albert was in a dead sleep and he jerked violently as the young cockney shook him by the shoulder. "C'mon, Albert. It's time ter go," he said, yawning widely.

In the grim light the two trudged slowly down towards the harbour. The scene that met them caused the two comrades to look at each other in disbelief. Thousands of troops were milling around, and long ragged lines of exhausted soldiers were wading out into the water in an attempt to board the small craft that were coming inshore. One large transport ship was moored at the jetty, and the long line of troops was four deep as the loading went on. The queue stretched back to the sea road and military police struggled to keep order.

"It looks 'opeless," Danny said, puffing hard. "We'll never get aboard that ship."

Albert pointed to the beach. "Let's catch a rest in them dunes. The tide's coming in. There'll be more boats soon."

The two had only just made the dunes when the air attack started. Planes dived out of the sky and bombs fell, exploding in the water around the transport ship. The long line of waiting troops dived for cover as more planes swooped low and machine-gunned the defenceless men. Screams of the wounded and dying rose above the roar of the aircraft and the noise of the gunfire from the ship. Bullets whipped up the sand and soldiers were caught as they tried to clamber aboard the overturning craft. The bodies of the dead floated back to shore.

Danny lay beside Albert in the dunes as the aircraft made repeated runs over the churning water; they pressed their faces into the sand and waited, hardly daring to move a muscle. As the carnage went on, thick, black smoke filled the sky and the lifting sun became red. When at last the planes roared off out to sea, the two young soldiers picked themselves up and dusted the sand from their uniforms. They could see the transport still intact by the jetty. Already the lines were forming up once again and more men began to wade out towards the few boats that were still afloat. Stretcher bearers moved along the beach and soaked, grey-faced men moved into the shelter of the dunes. A small group of bedraggled troops came by and one called out to Danny and Albert. "We're trying La Panne. It's hopeless here."

Danny looked at his pal. "Where's that, Alb?"

Albert pointed along the sea road. "It's a couple o' miles on. What d'yer reckon?" he asked, looking at Danny.

The young cockney slumped down into the sand. The thought of another two miles walking on his raw and blistered feet made him feel sick. He looked around. At that moment he felt ready to give up. "Let's wait till the tide comes right in, Alb. There'll be more boats then," he said unconvincingly.

Albert was feeling too exhausted to argue and he slumped down beside Danny.

The sun rose overhead and the planes came back. The intermittent strafing went on until the sun began to fall towards the west, and then there was a lull. Danny mustered his last reserves of energy and stood up. "C'mon then, Albert," he groaned. "Let's try that uvver place while it's quiet."

They left the dunes and walked wearily along towards La Panne. The road was busy, and they reached their destination only to see the dunes crowded with exhausted soldiers. As they walked along the sands a voice called out to them, "No luck at the jetty then?"

The two looked over and saw Oggy's men sheltering in a hollow. They went and sat down beside the shivering Middlesex lads. One of the soldiers nodded towards the sea. "We all got dumped in the drink, jus' when we reckoned

7

we'd made it. We 'ad ter tow Oggy back. 'E can't swim.''

Oggy looked embarrassed. ''All right, all right. Don't tell everybody. Yer won't get a medal fer it,'' he growled.

The soldier grinned and turned to Danny. ''The boat we got on was a small fishin' boat. The feller told us they're sendin' a lot more soon. That's what we're waitin' for.''

''What 'appened ter the bloke?'' Danny asked.

The soldier's face suddenly became sad. ''Poor sod didn't make it. 'E got a bullet in 'is back. 'E only come ter 'elp us,'' he said, looking down into the sand.

A breeze began to blow, chilling the soldiers as they waited on the sands. The strafing had ceased completely and an eerie quietness settled over the dunes. Danny suddenly turned to Albert. ''What did yer do in civvy street, Alb?'' he asked.

''I was a clerk in a firm that sold farm machinery. What about you?''

Danny eased his position in the sand. ''I was a bookie's runner. Me ole man wanted me ter go in the docks wiv 'im, but I wasn't 'avin' none o' that. 'E's bin in the docks all 'is life. All 'e's got ter show fer it is 'ands like dinner plates an' bronchitis frew workin' out in all weavvers.''

''You going back to being a bookie's runner?'' Albert asked.

Danny grinned. ''When I get out o' this mess I'm gonna get rich. Don't ask me 'ow, but I'm gonna make a pile. I might even do a bit o' buyin' an' sellin' like those Yiddisher boys over the Mile End Road.''

It was late afternoon when a flotilla of small craft appeared on the horizon. As the boats drew near to the shore the aircraft returned without warning and strafed their attack. Men were stranded in the water and those waiting on the sands ran back into the scant shelter of the dunes. One young soldier from the Middlesex saw an upturned boat floating near the water's edge and he ran towards it. Machine-gun fire cut him down and his body floated face up in the water. Oggy's men jumped up and raced down towards the shore. Danny and Albert were following behind when the country lad fell face down in the sand. Danny could see the growing red patch on the back of his uniform blouse.

"C'mon, Alb! Get up!" he screamed, bending down and dragging his pal into a sitting position.

Albert groaned as Danny tried to lift him.

"Can yer stand, Albert?"

Albert coughed and flecks of blood appeared on his lips. The young cockney looked at the white face of his comrade. "They've got the boat upright, me ole son," he said. "C'mon, you can make it."

Albert coughed again. "It's no good. Help me to the dunes. I'll be okay," he gasped.

Oggy was in the boat and pulling his pals in with him. He shouted for the two to get a move on, but Danny realised that Albert was not going to make it and he waved the boat away.

Planes were still strafing the beach as Danny half carried and half dragged Albert back to the meagre shelter of the dunes. When he had propped his pal up against a sand mound he searched through Albert's discarded pack and found a field dressing which he pushed beneath the country lad's battledress to stem the bleeding. Albert opened his eyes and groaned. Danny gave him a sip of water from his field bottle and Albert leaned his head against the sand.

"You go on. I'll be okay," he mumbled.

"Shut up, yer silly bleeder," Danny said gently. "They ain't takin' stretcher cases on the boats. Soon as one comes in I'll carry yer out. Leave it ter me."

As he looked along the sands Danny could see stretcher bearers running along to pick up the wounded. He could see Oggy's boat riding out a few yards offshore. The men had oars in the water and the big soldier was standing up in

9

the prow waving frantically. "C'mon! We're waiting fer yer!" he bellowed out.

The young cockney stood up and tore off his battledress. "All right, Albert," he said. "We're gonna make that boat. Did yer 'ear me?"

Albert's face was grey and he tried to speak. Danny bent over him and held his face in his hands. "Listen, Alb. Yer'll 'ave ter grit yer teef, me ole mate."

Albert screamed with pain as Danny hoisted him to his feet and dropped him onto his shoulder. Danny's feet sank in the soft sand as he moved slowly down towards the water's edge. His breath came in short gasps and sweat was running into his eyes. His legs buckled under him and he fell. "Okay, Albert. One more try. We can do it!" he said panting.

Albert was past caring. His eyes had glazed and his mouth hung open.

"Get up, yer stupid bastard, can't yer?" Danny screamed at him. "I'm not leavin' yer ter die on a Froggy beach! Wake up! Wake up!" he shouted, shaking the lifeless body roughly.

A firm hand gripped his shoulder. Danny looked up through clouded eyes and saw a medic standing over him. "Go for the boat, son. We'll take care of your pal."

Tracer cut across the sky as Danny stumbled into the cold water and swam for the boat. Oggy reached out a huge hand and hoisted the breathless cockney aboard. Danny dropped onto the planking shaking and Oggy patted the young man's back.

"Yer did yer best, son. Yer couldn't 'ave done more," he said quietly.

Danny pulled himself up and looked back to the shore, to Albert's lifeless body. Oggy's men were pulling on their oars and the boat began to move slowly away, fighting against the tide. The big ships were getting larger against the evening sky and the overcrowded lifeboat was headed for the nearest of them. Low-flying planes were roaring over the shallow waters, raking the helpless boats with machine-gun fire; men screamed as they were hit and went over the side. Danny saw the plane coming towards the boat.

He felt no pain as he fell into the cold sea. He could not move his limbs and he waited for the sea to swallow him. The last thing he remembered was the ugly face of Oggy Murphy beside him in the water.

Chapter Two

On the night of the 30th of May 1940 a military vehicle emblazoned with a large red cross left the quayside at Dover and drove the few miles inland to the red-brick Cavendish Home for the Elderly. The hospital stood in spacious grounds where flower beds were set amid chestnuts and willows. The walls of the buildings were covered with vines and a wide gravel drive led up to the entrance from the gates. Until the German army had swept across Europe, the place had been a serene refuge for the elderly and convalescent. Now it had been converted into a military hospital, filled with feverish activity as the casualties from France were brought in from the boats.

The vehicle pulled up at the entrance and medical orderlies quickly took off the stretchered wounded. A pretty dark-haired nurse helped wheel one of the casualties into the operating theatre, and two hours later she was on hand to take the unconscious soldier into a high-ceilinged ward. Throughout the night the young man lay comatose. Sounds of the night outside and sounds in the ward could not invade his sleep, but as the early morning rays of sunlight stole across the high white ceiling and lit up the white walls, the young soldier opened his eyes.

Danny Sutton's drugged mind stirred and he saw a whiteness everywhere. He began to wonder whether he was dead. His pain-wracked body sent signals to his befuddled brain and he knew he was still alive. There was no pain in heaven, and he knew he was not in the other place, for it was too white and bright. A wave of sickness overcame him and a soft body pressed against his head as

13

he was attended to. He could smell soap and he felt soft, cool hands on his forehead. Danny breathed out deeply and sank back into a heavy sleep.

For two days and nights the young soldier drifted between sleep and consciousness. He was transported far away in his fitful dreams. He was back on the beach at Dunkirk and his screams were ignored. He was back home, and he searched for his family. He heard iron-rimmed wheels on cobblestones and he saw Kathy, but she walked past him. He could see his family gathered around the kitchen table. His father wiped his large hand across his straggly moustache as he read the letter. His glasses were set on the end of his nose and the sleeves of his collarless shirt were rolled up high. His grey-haired mother dabbed at her eyes with a tiny handkerchief and tears rolled down her thin, lined face. Danny could see his three sisters: Maggie, the eldest, sat beside her husband Joe; Lucy held the hand of Ben, her fiancé; and Connie, the youngest, who was a year older than Danny, sat beside her mother and sobbed loudly. Maggie's two young children were playing in a corner. In his dream Danny was sitting at the table but his family ignored him. He felt himself being drawn away from the room and he struggled, trying to bang on the table. He opened his eyes with a start and the pretty nurse patted his forehead.

"You've been dreaming," she said in a soft, lilting voice.

As the days passed slowly Danny grew stronger. He began to wait impatiently for the pretty dark-haired nurse to come on duty, and when she changed the soiled dressings around his chest he could smell the fragrance of her hair. He had been told that a shell splinter had pierced his lung and another fragment had been removed from his thigh. The wounds were healing slowly, but after one week he was able to be wheeled into the sweet-smelling gardens of the hospital.

One afternoon Danny was sitting in the warm sunshine.

The fresh smell of new-mown grass hung in the air, and early butterflies fluttered amid the spring flowers. The retreat seemed far away from this peaceful scene. Danny saw the nurse walking towards him and noticed how her hips swayed slightly. She wore a cape around her shoulders which flapped as she walked, and when she reached him she stood with her arms folded. Danny saw the pretty flush of her cheeks and noticed how her dark hair was swept up around her tiny ears. He had heard about patients falling for their nurses and he could quite understand it, if all nurses looked like her. She reminded him somehow of the girl back home — the one he had lost — and his eyes fixed on hers.

She smiled at him. "I'm going back on duty soon, soldier boy. I'm supposed to take you back, or you'll miss your tea," she said in her sing-song voice.

"Danny's the name," he grinned. "What's yours?"

"I know it's Danny, but we're not supposed to get fresh with our patients," she grinned back.

The young cockney started to propel his wheelchair, but the nurse stopped him, as a sharp pain shot between his ribs.

"And what do you think you're doing, Danny Sutton?"

"I was jus' goin' ter push me chair over ter the seat," he said. "You could sit down an' talk ter me fer five minutes."

"Just five minutes," she said in mock seriousness as she walked around the wheelchair and pushed her patient over to the wooden bench.

The sun was slipping down in the afternoon sky and already a pink tinge lit up the western horizon. It was cooler now as a very slight evening breeze rose. It rustled a loose strand of the girl's hair and she patted it down as she talked.

"Why do you insist on knowing my name?" she asked.

Danny grimaced. "I can't keep on callin' yer 'nurse'. It sounds too . . . I dunno."

"Let me tell you, Danny. If Sister heard you calling me anything but nurse I'd be in trouble."

15

"I wouldn't get yer inter trouble. I'd only use yer name when we was alone — like now," he persisted.

"Listen, soldier boy, we're not likely to be alone. And anyway, you'll be off in a few more days."

Danny looked into her dark eyes. His hand went up to his chest and he grinned. "I'm goin' ter 'ang this out as long as possible. I'd really like ter get ter know yer better, honest I would."

The nurse flushed slightly and glanced into Danny's pale blue eyes. His vivacity attracted her and she warmed to his serious look. She noticed the way his fair hair tended to curl above his ears, and the way he had of grinning suddenly. She liked the humorous twitch of his mouth and the way his eyes seemed to widen when he spoke. "They'll be sending you to the other hospital in a few more days," she said smiling.

"What uvver 'ospital?" he asked.

"Why, the convalescent hospital up in Hertfordshire. It's supposed to be very nice there."

"Cobblers! I like it 'ere fine," he said quickly.

The young nurse's eyes opened wide in surprise. "Danny Sutton! Don't use that word! I don't like it."

Danny touched her arm and she stiffened noticeably. "I'm sorry," he said. "It's jus' that, well, I'd like you an' me ter get ter know each uvver better. 'Ow the 'ell am I gonna find out more about yer up in bleedin' wherever it is?"

"Okay," she replied in resignation. "My name is Alison Jones. I'm twenty-two, and I come from Cardiff. Is that enough to be going on with? Now come on, I've got to get you back for tea. By the way, if you mention my name in front of Sister or the doctors, I'll never speak to you again. Is that understood?"

Danny grinned and raised his hands in mock fear. "Understood, Alison."

When he got back to the ward, Danny learned that only the more seriously wounded were to get visitors. The others would have to wait until they reached the convalescent hospital. He was not unduly worried; he did not want his parents to see him until he became more mobile. He thought about the letter he had scribbled, telling his family that he had only a few scratches. He knew that they wouldn't believe him. His mother would cry into her handkerchief, while his father would polish his glasses and read the letter again. He pictured the scene back in Dawson Street, Bermondsey. The neighbours would call round to commiserate, and that would only start his mother crying again. He thought of Kathy, the girl from the next street, and wondered if she would get around to dropping him a line.

Casualties had been crowded into the old vine-covered buildings, and as soon as the less severely wounded were able to travel they were transferred to other hospitals around the country. Danny found himself waiting with a dozen or so soldiers at the hospital gates for the coach to arrive. It was only three days since he had persuaded Alison to tell him her name. He had managed to snatch a few minutes alone with her once or twice and she had told him a little about herself. She came from a mining family; her father had been killed in a pit accident when she was a child, and her mother had been left to bring up a large brood with little help. Alison told him about the hardships during the miners strike, and how the illnesses often caused by coal-mining affected the families in the Welsh Valleys. She said she would have liked to study medicine but it had been impossible, and nursing had been the only alternative. She told him that nothing else mattered to her. Danny responded by telling her about his home in dockland and how his family had suffered during the strikes for better working conditions. Her wide dark eyes had become sad when he told her the stories he had heard from his mother, of his father coming home bloodied on more than one occasion after clashes with the police at the dock

17

gates. Alison's frank sympathy had surprised him. She said that there had been many dark stories when the army had been called in to threaten the striking miners in the coalfields. Danny had become captivated by her pretty looks and lilting voice as she chatted away to him. He wanted very much to see her again when he got his medical discharge, although Wales seemed a very long way from his home in the grimy, rundown area of London's dockland. He felt that Alison liked him, and he wondered whether she would agree to meet him again. She had seemed happy and relaxed in his company, but when he had attempted to find out about her life outside the hospital she had been quick to change the subject. He wondered whether or not there was someone else in her life, and he became anxious. His feelings for Alison had grown during those all too brief interludes, and he realised that he was now beginning to think of the Welsh nurse rather more than of Kathy back home.

The coach pulled up at the gates and the waiting patients were hustled into their seats. Danny looked around urgently as his name was called and an orderly helped him to climb aboard. There was no sign of Alison. He sat down despondently and stared out of the window as the coach driver climbed aboard and started up the engine. Suddenly he saw Alison. She waved at the driver and he opened the door for her. She came along the aisle, her face flushed, and when she reached Danny she quickly gave him some letters which she had in her hand. "Good luck, soldier boy," she said lightly.

Danny looked up into her dark eyes and she bent her head and kissed him lightly on his cheek. He could find nothing to say but he gave her a huge grin as she stepped off the coach.

The driver pulled into the Three Counties Hospital near Hitchen after a tiring journey and the casualties found themselves billeted in prefabricated wards; the hospital

18

had been built in 1938 to accommodate the possible civilian casualties in the event of war. Danny settled quickly into the routine and he was cheered by the fact that he could now get around with the aid of a stick. After a week at the hospital his parents visited him. Alice Sutton fussed over him and said how thin he was looking on the hospital food; Frank Sutton sat uncomfortably on a small garden seat and tried to have a word with Danny when his wife ran out of things to say. Danny felt uncomfortable with them and was glad when it was time for them to go. He felt guilty for his lack of patience as he watched his parents walk arm in arm through the hospital gates. They seemed to have aged; his father was still robust, but his thinning hair had gone completely grey. His mother was lined and frail, and she looked diminutive beside his father. Danny couldn't understand why it had been so difficult meeting his parents, and he felt sad as he turned and limped back into the ward.

After the weekend visits the hospital settled down to its usual routine. Danny spent most of his time in the hospital grounds. His wounds had largely healed and he could now walk without the aid of a stick. He realised that his twenty-first birthday had passed and he had hardly even remembered it. The days passed slowly until he was finally pronounced fit enough to travel home. The documentation was completed and he had his medical discharge book, a travel warrant, some back pay and a bundle of dressings. As he was piling his belongings into a suitcase Danny saw a figure hobbling towards him. "Well I'll be blowed. Look who it is," the soldier said, grinning widely. "Remember me?"

Danny recognised the soldier as one of Oggy's crowd. " 'Course I remember," Danny said loudly with a huge smile. They shook hands, and the slight young man sat on the edge of Danny's bed and ran his fingers through his wiry hair. His face became serious. "I saw yer mate cop it. I didn't fink you was gonna make it ter the boat."

Danny shook his head. "I can't remember much after you lot pulled me aboard."

The soldier eased his plastered leg. "Me, you an' Oggy was the only ones ter make it."

Danny gasped. "I felt sure Oggy drowned. 'E couldn't swim, could 'e?"

The wiry-haired lad laughed aloud. "If you ever bump inter that ugly gypsy yer'll 'ave ter buy 'im a pint. 'E saved your life. We was 'oldin' on ter that upturned boat fer dear life. Oggy 'ad yer roun' the neck. We was in the water fer ages before we was picked up. Me an' you ended up in different 'ospitals."

"Where did Oggy go?" Danny asked.

"Back to our depot, I s'pose. 'E never 'ad a scratch on 'im. I tell yer mate, 'e saved both of us that night. I was ready ter give up, but 'e kept on shoutin' fer me ter 'old on. What a great feller, that Oggy Murphy."

" 'E sure is," Danny said quietly with a smile. " 'E can get pissed at my expense any time."

"Me too," the soldier said, nodding his head. "They give out medals fer less than what Oggy did."

Danny finished his packing and clipped the case shut. The two shook hands and the young cockney walked out into the bright sunshine to wait for the coach that would take him to the station. He felt a sudden dismay. The lifeboat had been packed with soldiers and only three of them had survived. The day seemed to have grown cold, and he was glad when the coach finally arrived at the hospital gates.

War-time King's Cross was full of life. There were uniforms everywhere, servicemen moved about the station with kitbags slung over their shoulders, and sandbagged entrances and exits were flanked by large war posters. Military policemen stood in pairs, biting on their chinstraps and eyeing the itinerant servicemen with a cold severity. Danny stared hard at one pair as he walked past them, but they ignored him. He saw placards outside a kiosk tempting the travelling public to read more about the capitulation of France, and he was struck by the serious expression on everyone's face. The news was bad. He had managed to catch some of the radio bulletins while he was at the hospital, although the matron had forbidden the nurses to let the patients listen. Danny had heard about Italy declaring war on Britain, and it made him think of those Italians who lived around the docks. Some had shops, like the Arpinos and the Lucianis. He had played with Tony Arpino as a kid; together the two of them had got into their first scrape with the police. Danny remembered how Tony, who was a year younger than him, had run home crying after a cuff around the ear from the street bobby, and his enraged father had taken the belt to him for bringing disgrace upon the good name of Arpino. Danny himself had scooted off home with two large cooking apples still stuffed down his trousers, his head ringing from the whack. Danny wondered what would happen to the Italian families. The news broadcasts had said that the Italian nationals were being rounded up and interned and he did not expect to see Tony Arpino or Melissa Luciani around dockland. The whole thing seemed ridiculous to him — Tony was as cockney as anyone in Dawson Street.

Danny walked through the station exit lost in thought and the scene that met him at the busy junction brought him to a halt. Everywhere there were signs of war. Neatly stacked sandbags fronted office buildings and public institutions; there was a public shelter near where he stood; outside, a poster demanded retribution, and another implored everyone to 'Dig For Victory'. Trams and buses all wore a canvas-like material on their windows, and every building had the criss-cross pattern of brown paper strips over its larger panes of glass. The traffic noise on that Friday afternoon in June 1940 made Danny feel light-headed. He wanted to get away from the stir and disquiet of King's Cross and back home to his own familiar surroundings. First though, he needed a cup of tea. There was a stall only a few yards away outside the station; he gripped his almost empty suitcase and went up to the counter. The only other customers were two taxi drivers who were talking loudly together. The stall-owner looked at Danny cross-eyed and he ordered a mug of tea. As the tea was being poured into a cracked mug one of the taxi drivers nudged his mate and then looked up at the stall-owner. " 'Urry up with that pie, Sid," he said.

Sid peered over his beaked nose at the leering cabbie. "Can't yer wait five minutes?" he moaned in a nasal tone. "Bloody pie ain't warm yet."

Danny put down a threepenny bit and picked up his mug from the soaking wet counter. As he sipped the hot tea he watched the cabbies. The vociferous one returned his stare. "Joinin' up, son?" he asked with a smirk on his face, his eyes glancing down to the suitcase at Danny's feet.

The young cockney looked hard at the cabbie. Danny sensed an unpleasant seriousness and aggression in the cabbie and he was not prepared to be insulted. He took the mug away from his lips and his eyes hardened. "No. I work the 'alls," he said quietly.

"You on stage then?"

"That's right."

The cabbie looked down again at Danny's suitcase. "You a magician or somefink?" he smirked, looking at his silent friend for support.

Danny's eyes glinted. "Matter o' fact I'm a ventriloquist," he said. "Trouble is, I've 'ad me dummy nicked. You wouldn't like ter earn a few bob, would yer?"

The stall-owner turned and roared with laughter as he banged the hot pie down on the counter. "Got yer there, didn't 'e?" he rasped.

The cabbie's round face flushed and he looked away from Danny's challenging stare. "Poke yer pie," he sneered as he turned on his heel and walked away from the

22

stall. Danny exchanged a smile with the other cabbie as he moved off to catch up with his friend.

Sid looked at the young cockney. "Are yer joinin' up, son?" he asked quietly.

Danny put the mug down on the counter. "No, I'm goin' back 'ome. I was at Dunkirk."

Sid's crossed eyes lit up. " 'Ere, son, you 'ave this pie on me. Best pies in norf London, straight."

Danny took the hot pie and fished into his trouser pocket for some change. "I can pay. I've got money," he said.

"Nope, I insist yer take it. Me an' my ole Dutch cried when we 'eard about it on the wireless. Must 'ave bin terrible out there."

Danny nodded and bit into the steaming pie. A few customers came up to the stall and Sid became very busy serving tea and shovelling fresh pies into the metal box on top of the tea urn. Danny thanked him and picked up his suitcase. As he walked away Sid turned to his customers and said knowingly, " 'E was at Dunkirk. 'E only looks a kid."

Danny walked along the busy thoroughfare until he came to King's Cross Road. A few yards down he saw a bus stop where a queue was beginning to form in the early evening coolness. Danny had been waiting about ten minutes when a number 63 bus came into sight. The queue shuffled forward anxiously as the bus squeaked to a halt. The conductor leant out from the platform and counted the passengers on. "No pushin'. There's anuvver one behind," he shouted authoritatively. He pressed the bell as Danny stepped on the platform. "Put yer case under the stairs, son. Full up inside. Yer'll 'ave ter go on top."

Danny climbed to the upper deck and found the last remaining seat beside a dapper-looking man in his sixties. He had a well-trimmed goatee beard and wore a pair of gold-rimmed spectacles. The bus jerked away from the stop, accelerating quickly as it moved down the King's

Cross Road. Danny saw the long queue outside the working men's hostel waiting for their chance of a bed, and the second-hand book market traders packing away for the day. Farringdon Road was heavy with lorries, taxis and horse-drawn carts, and to his left Danny caught a glimpse of the now deserted Smithfield Meat Market. The bus passed under Holborn Viaduct and reached Fleet Street before it stopped. The hustle and bustle of the City had always fascinated Danny, but it now seemed there was a strangeness in the way people hurried by. Everyone seemed to have a serious expression, and nearly everyone was carrying a newspaper under his arm. There were no smiles, and no one was standing still. As the bus got under way again and started over Blackfriars Bridge Danny saw the exodus from the City as crowds flowed along the pavements overlooking the river.

The little gentleman next to Danny chuckled and tapped the window. "Look how calm that River Thames is down there beneath all those frantic people," he said.

Danny smiled cautiously. The bus had reached the centre of the bridge, and down below the grey water sparkled in the evening sunlight. Barges were moored up for the night, crane arms were secured against the closed and bolted warehouse loop-holes, and the ebbing tide lapped lazily against the mud-streaked stanchions.

"That is the greatest river in the world, young man," the man continued. "There are longer rivers and wider rivers, but where else is there one with such character? It's our heritage," he said with conviction, his small eyes glaring at Danny through his spectacles.

"You're right there, pop. It wants some beatin'," Danny grinned.

The old man nodded his head. "I know I'm right. And yet those crowds we just passed, they seem to walk over that river without even noticing it."

"Well, I s'pose they see it every day. They mus' get fed up wiv the sight of it," Danny said.

24

" 'When a man is tired of London he's tired of life'," the man said, his eyes twinkling. "I worked in the Royal Mint for more than twenty-five years, young man. Do you know where that is? Well let me tell you, I walked over Tower Bridge twice each day for all that time. I never once got fed up with the sight of Old Father Thames. It *is* London. Without that river this city would be nothing. London would dry up like a desert. It's your heritage, young chap."

The bus stopped at the Elephant and Castle junction and the old gentleman bid Danny farewell. Danny eased up against the window and the vacant place was taken by a large lady who puffed noisily as she sat down. He stared out of the window, excitement building up inside him as he recognised the familiar sights of South London. At the Bricklayers Arms he got off the bus and walked towards the river. The evening was cool and clear, and starlings were chattering noisily in the leafy plane trees. The quiet thoroughfare had taken on a cloak of war. Windows were criss-crossed with brown paper strips and sandbags were piled against factory entrances. He saw the shelter signs, the war posters, and the arrow that pointed to the first-aid post. He noticed the splashes of white paint on the kerb stones, and around the boles of the large trees. He glimpsed the iron stretchers strapped to the roof of a passing car, and up ahead the huge imposing mass of Tower Bridge.

He could now smell the Thames and the docks, the spices and fruit, and the pungent smell of vinegar as he walked past a quiet factory. At Tooley Street he turned left and saw the familiar wharves and warehouses to his right. Small streets led off opposite the large buildings and it did not take him long to reach Clink Lane. The next turning was his street.

The slanting hitching post was still leaning towards the wall and the little houses on both sides of Dawson Street still looked as he had remembered them. The railway arch

25

at the end of the turning had been given a coat of paint, and Granny Bell's front step gleamed as white as ever. Danny saw the Brightman children swinging around a lamppost on a piece of fraying rope, and ginger-haired Billy, the Birkitts' youngest, sitting in the gutter slowly counting a pack of cigarette cards. Billy Birkitt stared at Danny with a fixed grin. Danny smiled back, but he did not know that young Billy was only displaying the gap where his two front teeth had been. He spotted Crazy Bella who was standing arms akimbo in her doorway. She gave him a stare and then went in.

Nothing seemed to have altered in the months he had been away. His own front door was closed; it still had the same cracked knocker-pad and the withered weatherboard. Number 26 Dawson Street was like every other house in that tumble-down turning: the windows were clean, the front step was whitened, and the street door sorely needed a lick of paint. Danny stood outside his house for a few seconds before he knocked. Apart from Crazy Bella and the children no one had seen him. He raised the knocker and banged it against the plate. His mother opened the door and stood staring at him.

" 'Ello, Mum,'' Danny said. ''Well ain't yer gonna let me in?''

Chapter Three

Alice Sutton looked up at the mantelpiece and noticed that the clock had stopped. She got up and put on her glasses before opening the glass door of the chimer and moving the minute hand around to the half-hour. Still the clock did not start ticking. She fished out a key from beneath the ornate stand and wound up the twin springs. A sharp tilt woke up the pendulum, and the clock started again. Alice could have sworn that she had wound the thing that very morning. It was supposed to be a seven-day timepiece, at least it had been when it was given to her and Frank as a wedding present more than thirty years ago. It's getting old, like the two of us, Alice thought.

"Good job Dad didn't see yer do that, Ma," Connie laughed. "Yer know 'ow 'e fusses over that clock."

Alice grinned and sat down amidst her three daughters. Tonight she felt happy and contented. For the first time since last October, when Danny had gone off to France, the family were all together — all except the two grand-children, who should be in the land of nod by now, she thought. Tomorrow she would be spoiling the kids. Tonight it was the turn of her grown-up children to be fussed over, and she got up again to gather up the tea things.

"Stay put, Mum. I'll make us a fresh pot," Maggie volunteered.

Connie got up and followed Maggie out into the scullery. The back door was ajar and voices could be heard coming from the small yard, where the men of the family were gathered for a quiet drink.

Alone in the parlour with Lucy, Alice turned to look at her daughter, eyes filled with concern. Lucy had seemed rather quiet at tea time, she thought. It was a pity, because everything had gone off so well. The large rabbit stew had been ample and the plum duff with treacle was scraped clean from everyone's plate. The little wooden table looked nice with its linen tablecloth and best dinner plates. She had squeezed seven places around the table, and Connie had helped out by eating her dinner sitting in the armchair. Even Frank looked well scrubbed and sober, although he had stopped off on his way home from work for a couple of pints, as was his usual custom on Friday nights. Alice had noticed that Danny struggled to finish his meal, but she would soon get him used to her big meals again and get some meat on his bones.

Lucy was staring down at the empty grate and Alice leaned back in her chair and folded her arms. "Well, out with it, girl. What's troublin' yer?"

"Oh it's nothing, Mum. Really it's not."

Alice pulled a face. "If there is somefink worryin' yer, I wanna know."

Lucy sighed and looked into her mother's lined face. "It's Ben. The tribunal is on Monday and I'm worried about the outcome. We've talked about this before, Mum. Ben said it's no good us thinking of getting married until this thing is sorted out. Ben might have to go to prison, or be sent on war-work somewhere. It's so worrying."

Alice stared at her daughter. Lucy was in many ways different from the rest. She had been very bright at her lessons and had attended the central school. She had even learned to speak in a way that was different from the others. Lucy sounded her aitches, which had, at first, caused problems with the others until Alice put her foot firmly down. "If she's gettin' a good education it's nat'ral fer 'er ter speak proper. She'll get a good job one day, an' I don't wanna 'ear any more mickey-takin' from any of yer. Is that understood?"

Everyone in the Sutton family paid attention to their mother when she spoke up, and the mickey-taking ceased. Now, as the latest of Lucy's problems emerged, the matriarch was ready with a sympathetic ear and good advice.

"Listen, my girl, you've chosen yer partner. One day, God willin', yer'll 'ave 'is children, but in the meantime yer gotta face up ter fings. There's a war on, people are dyin', an' a lot more will go before there's a peace. Your Ben 'as decided 'e ain't gonna kill anybody, even the bloody Germans. All right, 'e's got 'is point o' view, same as all of us. Trouble is, there's a lot in the papers an' on the wireless about those anti-war people, like Mosley an' 'is crowd o' Blackshirts. Then there's the Communists, an' all those uvver bloody aliens. People tend ter lump 'em all tergevver. It reminds me o' that ole Irish chap me an' yer farver saw up on Tower Hill once. 'E was speakin' to a crowd, an' 'e said, 'Those who are not fer us, are agin us'. That's what yer up against, me girl. That's what Ben is up against. 'E's gonna find it 'ard an' it's gonna get 'arder. People in the pubs an' on the street are gonna shun 'im. They're gonna call 'im a coward an' all the uvver names they can lay their tongues to. It won't be easy, but yer gotta be prepared fer it. If 'e's really the feller yer want, then stan' by 'im. Oh, an' anuvver fing. Yer gonna get some nasty letters, mark my words. They did it in the last war. People used ter send white fevvers frew the post. Anyway, if yer prepared, it won't be so bad. Just you remember, whatever 'appens round 'ere, Ben's always welcome in this 'ouse. Neighbours can turn funny if they like, but this family stays tergevver. We've always bin a close-knit family, an' that's the way it's gonna stay."

Lucy's brown eyes filled with tears and she hugged her mother.

Out in the backyard of 26 Dawson Street, four men sat in the darkness. The night was cool, and stars were shining down from a clear sky. The black-out regulations were being enforced rigidly, but the back door was kept ajar, letting just enough light out to illuminate the crumbling stone floor and the crate of ale. Danny sat in a broken-down armchair, his father squatted on an upturned bucket, and Ben and Maggie's husband Joe shared a bench made up of a plank of wood stretched over empty tubs. Ben was the only one who wasn't drinking. Danny sipped his glass of beer and found that he wasn't enjoying it. The meal had seemed huge and the events of the evening had tired him. The greetings from his sisters had been tearful and he had felt embarrassed. Joe and Ben had pumped his hand, and his father had hugged him tightly until his chest hurt. Their questions too had been fast and furious. Danny wanted to forget his recent experiences, but the questions opened new wounds and made him feel shaky. He shivered although the night was warm.

Joe Copeland was talking. "The ships 'ave bin turnin' round quicker than ever lately. We've bin doin' late shifts fer the past fortnight."

"Careful, Joe," Frank piped in. "Yer can get an 'eavy fine fer careless talk."

The men laughed and Frank shifted his weight on the pail. "You can laugh, but I bet that poor ole feller in the paper ain't laughin' after yesterday."

"What was that, then?" Danny asked.

'Well, 'e was goin' on about all these taxes, an' some ole biddy reported 'im. Next fing yer know 'e's summonsed. The ole beak give 'im six weeks. I tell yer, yer gotta be careful what yer say these days."

"Yeah, it's what they call emergency powers," Joe said, pouring himself another drink. "I 'eard a funny one last week. There's this ole geezer who's got a car. 'E's a manager of a big business. Well 'e just so 'appens ter leave 'is motor car outside the Town 'All while 'e gets some permits renewed. Anyway, up comes a bluebottle an' checks 'is car. 'E finds it ain't immobilised, or so 'e finks, 'an 'e only goes an' lets all the tyres down. Not bein' satisfied wiv that, 'e goes an' sticks a summons on the car. 'Course when the bloke comes an' sees the copper doin' 'is party piece, 'e nearly 'as a fit. What the copper didn't know was that the car *was* immobilised. Instead of takin' the rotor arm out, the driver took the wire off the coil or somefink. Anyway, it was just as good. This geezer's fumin'. 'E runs back in the Town 'All an' phones up the 'ead one at the local police station. Accordin' ter the feller what told me, this bloke an' the 'ead copper were ole drinkin' mates. The outcome was, there's a copper pumpin' up the tyres wiv a foot pump, while the 'ead one an' this geezer are 'avin' a right ole piss up in the boozer next door.''

The laughter made Maggie put her head round the door. ''What's goin' on out 'ere? Filfy jokes, I expect,'' she said.

'No, I was jus' tellin' 'em about that car-owner who 'ad 'is tyres let down.''

Maggie grinned. ''Don't laugh at 'is silly tales. Yer only encouragin' 'im. I fink 'e makes them stories up, honest I do.''

The men were still laughing as Maggie took the tea into the parlour.

Dawson Street was dark, with the two lampposts out of service for the duration of the war. The black-out curtains were effective, and the distant stars offered scant relief from the darkness. The two corner shops at the Tooley Street end of the turning, the oil shop and the tatty little sweet shop, were shuttered and deathly quiet, and the only sign of life came from The Globe public house which stood on the corner of Clink Lane. Inside the pub a piano was knocking out one of the old favourites. The door of the jug-side opened and closed, and a woman came out. She walked quickly, a shawl draped around her hunched shoulders. She turned into Dawson Street and hurried to number 23. The woman was mumbling to herself as she

31

fumbled the key into the lock and pushed open the door. As she let herself in the gas jet in the passage went out. Without taking her shawl off, she reached up and dropped a sixpence into the meter slot and turned the handle. The coin dropped and she chuckled.

Back in The Globe Annie Barnes was worried. Annie lived in Dawson Street, and she knew Crazy Bella very well. Bella never ventured out at night, least of all to change coppers up for a sixpence. If Bella's gas ran out she would sooner light candles. And something else worried Annie Barnes. Two weeks ago Bella had had one of her turns. She had stood in the middle of the street and threatened to blow the whole turning up sooner than let the Germans get it. Fortunately, old Doctor Kelly was on his rounds and he had managed to get Bella indoors and settled very quickly. No one had paid much attention to Bella's threats except Annie. Her husband used to work for the gas board, and he had said how easy it was for a gas leak to prove disastrous. Annie got even more worried when Bill told her about the explosion in Prentis Street some time ago, where a whole row of terraced houses had been demolished by a gas leak.

Annie Barnes quickly finished off her Guinness, buttoned up her coat and hurried out to see her friend Alice Sutton. Alice would know what to do. In any case, she wasn't going to knock on Bella's front door on her own. Bella scared the living daylights out of Annie Barnes. As she passed number 23, Annie shivered and crossed the street. At the Suttons' front door Annie stopped and looked over her shoulder before rat-tatting loudly.

The women of the Sutton family were sitting together in the parlour, drinking tea and talking about the possibility of getting Maggie's two children evacuated. There had been an air raid warning on the Monday of that week, although it had been a false alarm. The all clear had sounded hours later, and the only effect it had was to make people jumpy the next day from their loss of sleep. It had made Maggie realise however that the children would be much safer away from London. She had talked it over with Joe, but he was unhappy with the idea of sending them away. Already there were bad stories about the reception some of the evacuees had encountered and many families had got their children home after the initial panic at the outbreak of war. Maggie struggled with her conscience and she was listening to what her mother had to say about it.

"It strikes me," Alice began, "that no matter what decisions you make, it's in the 'ands o' the Almighty. I always say, what will be, will be. There's nuffink anybody can do about it. I mean yer could send the kids away, an' you an' Joe could get killed, Gawd ferbid. You'd 'ave a couple of orphans on yer 'ands."

"Don't talk like that, Mum. You're givin' me the creeps," Maggie said.

"Well it's no good tryin' ter dodge the issue," Alice went on. "None of us know what's gonna 'appen. There's those bloody leaflets they put frew the door last week. Did I show yer? Anyway, it's about what ter do if there's an invasion. Cor, it turns yer cold jus' ter fink about it."

Connie was sitting on the floor, her hands clasped around her knees. She looked up at her sister, her blue eyes open wide. "I know, why don't you go wiv the kids? You 'aven't got a job or anyfing ter worry about."

Maggie looked at her disapprovingly. "Don't be silly. 'Ow could I go an' leave Joe? I mean, there's 'is food, an' yer know 'ow useless 'e is in the 'ome. I bet if I was away the place would go rotten. 'E can't even boil an egg."

"Well 'e'd bloody well 'ave ter cope. Lots o' men 'ave done it," Connie retorted. "The Arrowsmiths 'ave all gone away. Freddy Arrowsmith manages."

Maggie laughed aloud. " 'E's got a fancy woman, everybody knows that. She does 'is washin' an' ironin', an' she cooks fer 'im. Who knows, I might go away, an' 'fore yer know it, Joe's found 'imself a fancy woman?"

It was Connie's turn to laugh. "Don't be silly, Maggie. Joe's not that sort."

"Don't yer be so sure," said Maggie. "All men are the same. They want their bread buttered on both sides. Mind you, I'm not sayin' Joe would stray. It's jus' that I'm not gonna give 'im the chance."

The loud rat-tat made the women jump. "Who the 'ell can that be?" Alice said quickly, getting up and leaving the room.

There was a murmur of voices and then Alice called out, "Frank! I want yer."

The family hurried out into the passage. "It's all right everybody. It's Missus Barnes. She's worried about Bella. You wait 'ere. Me an' yer dad are goin' over there."

Frank put on his coat and followed Alice out into the street. The turning was deserted and dark. The two of them accompanied Mrs Barnes across the cobbles and knocked loudly on number 23. There was no answer. Frank bent down and peered through the letter box. Suddenly he straightened and pushed Alice aside.

"Stand back!" he shouted as he threw his weight against the front door. It gave easily and Frank stumbled into the dark passage. The smell of gas was strong. He put his hand up to his mouth and ran through into the scullery. Crazy Bella was lying on her back with her head on a pillow inside the open gas oven; she looked up at Frank, her staring eyes glowing cat-like in the darkness. Frank reached for the gas taps and discovered that they were not turned on. He left Bella lying there and staggered back into the passage. The gas jet on the wall was hissing and unlit. He turned it off quickly and ran back into the tiny scullery and opened up the window. Half carrying and half dragging Bella he succeeded in getting her out onto the pavement.

"Keep yer eye on the silly ole cow," he said. "I'm goin' ter see if I can get Doctor Kelly."

* * *

The chimer on the Suttons' mantel showed five minutes to midnight. Ben and Lucy were saying goodnight at the front door; Maggie and Joe had already left; and Connie had gone to bed. Danny sat in the parlour with his parents, his eyes heavy with tiredness. His father was noisily sipping his tea.

"What I can't understand is why she didn't turn the gas stove on. Seems a silly way ter do yerself in, if yer ask me," Danny said.

"Doctor Kelly reckons that ole Bella 'ad no intention of doin' 'erself in," Alice said, passing a mug of tea to her son. "I'm inclined to agree wiv 'im. Doctor Kelly reckons she was doin' it all fer somebody ter take notice. An' we did, didn't we?"

Frank put his empty mug down on the table. "Yer right there, Alice," he said.

" 'Ave they took 'er away?" Danny asked.

"No, Doctor Kelly give 'er a sedative. 'E said 'e's comin' ter see 'er termorrer. I was talkin' to 'im afterwards," Alice went on. "What 'e reckons 'appened was that she went purposely ter get that sixpence. She was tryin' to attract attention. They all know she don't venture out at night. Somebody in the pub was bound ter take notice, an' sure enough, somebody did."

"What about the gas?" Danny queried.

"Well, what we fink 'appened," interrupted Frank, "was that she put the tanner in the meter after the gas 'ad run out. She was so concerned about settin' it all up, she forgot about the passage gas jet. Jus' fink of it. She sticks 'er 'ead in the gas oven an' nearly gets gassed wiv' the passage jet. Silly ole cow."

"Don't be like that, Frank luv," Alice said. "She's ter be pitied. She ain't got a soul in the world, 'cept us folk in the street. If it wasn't fer you, she'd be laid out on a slab right now."

Frank got up and stretched. "It's Annie Barnes she should be grateful to. Anyway, I still fink she's a silly ole cow," he grinned, winking at Danny. "Well I'm off ter bed. Nice ter 'ave yer 'ome, son. C'mon, Alice. It's bin a long day. Let's get some shut-eye."

Danny climbed the stairs to his room and lay down in the darkness. He was exhausted after his first night back home and was grateful his family hadn't pressed him too much when he declined to go to the pub. He smiled as he recalled the look of disappointment on his father's face and how he had brightened up when it was suggested that he fetch a few quarts of ale from the 'off sales'. Danny stared up at the cracked ceiling, which was illuminated by the pale moonlight, and cupped his hands behind his head. His thoughts turned to Kathy Thompson and the night they had parted. Kathy had been moody all evening and when they returned from the Trocette Cinema they had stood in her doorway. He remembered trying to kiss her but she pushed him away.

"You seem ter fink you can grab 'old o' me an' kiss it all better. Well I'm tellin' yer now, Danny. Yer'd better make yer mind up who you are s'posed ter be takin' out. I ain't playin' second fiddle ter that trollop Janie Arnold."

"What yer talkin' about?" he shouted, his eyes narrowing.

"You know very well," she replied. "You was seen in The Crown wiv 'er. You was all over the silly cow, so I was told."

Danny grabbed Kathy's arms. "Who told yer that?"

"Never mind who told me. But I'm tellin' yer this — eivver yer stop playin' around, or me an' you are finished. I can't believe yer doin' this ter me again, Danny. All the time I've known yer, yer never change. Yer've always bin the same. I'm sick o' tellin' yer, an' sick of 'earin' what's goin' on be'ind me back."

"Well if yer believe uvver people before me p'raps it's better if —"

There was a loud clattering at the end of the turning and as Danny looked up Kathy stiffened and stepped into the open doorway. Charlie Thompson had turned the corner blind drunk and he had staggered into a pile of rubbish. He swore loudly and kicked out at some empty tin cans he had knocked over. Danny knew that Kathy was terrified of her father. She had told him how he often threatened to throw her out of the house, and how he knocked her mother about viciously when he came home drunk. Kathy had backed into the passageway. "I've gotta go," she said. "Farver'll kill me if 'e finds me out 'ere while 'e's in that state."

"Wait a minute, Kathy," Danny said.

Charlie Thompson did not appear to have seen them. He reeled across the pavement and leant against the wall. Danny watched in disgust as he bent over and was loudly sick.

"Kathy, wait."

"I can't, Danny," she sobbed, as she closed the door on him.

The young cockney stood still for a few moments then walked away in confusion. Charlie Thompson was still leaning against the wall with his head hanging down.

It was the last time Danny saw Kathy before he went off to war.

Chapter Four

Danny woke up in panic, his whole body soaked in sweat. He could still hear the Company Sergeant screaming out for everyone to watch their flank. He sat bolt upright in his bed and grasped the iron bedrail with both hands, his breath coming in short pants. Gradually, his pounding heart began to slow down and he was able to recover his breath. He swung his legs over the side of the bed and rested his head in his hands. A beam of morning sunlight lit up the tattered carpet by the side of his bed and felt warm on his bare feet.

Danny wiped the cold sweat from his face and neck with the sheet and looked around the small room. It hadn't altered since he was a lad. The old wardrobe in the corner was the one he used to hide in, and the marble-topped washstand with its cracked china bowl and water jug was the same one he used to hide his secret possessions in. The door was always sticking, and it needed to be tapped in a certain place to free it. Danny leaned forward and pulled on the lift-up handle. The door would not budge. From down below came the grinding noise of the wringer being turned and the sound of the wireless set next door blaring out a popular tune.

Danny look at the alarm clock which stood on a chair beside the bed — it showed 10.30 a.m. His right leg felt stiff and the puffy scar on his ribs itched. The noise of the wringer ceased and he could hear Connie singing in the yard. Danny got up slowly and peered through the window. His sister was pegging out the washing, her fair hair covered with a headscarf and her feet encased in a pair of

39

carpet slippers; an apron was tied tightly around her trim figure and knotted at the back. Danny stared down into the yard for a few seconds before getting dressed. He felt tired and shaky as he opened the bedroom door and walked out onto the landing between the two flights of stairs.

The kettle was boiling over as Danny entered the scullery. Connie rushed in from the yard and turned off the gas tap. " 'Ello, bruv. We wouldn't wake yer. Mum's gone shoppin' an' Dad's gone fer the paper." Connie poured the boiling water into the teapot. "Did yer sleep well?"

"Like a log," Danny lied.

"Want some brekkie? We've got bacon an' eggs, or eggs an' bacon?"

"Go on, finish what yer doin'," Danny answered. "I'll get meself somefink."

Connie grinned. "Get in the front room, bruv. I'll call yer when it's ready. Mum said we've gotta make a fuss o' yer fer a couple o' days, then yer can fend fer yerself, okay?"

Danny smiled as he went to the sink and splashed cold water over his face. Connie handed him the towel and watched closely as he dried his face. "You look pale. D'yer feel all right?"

Danny threw the towel over the back of the chair. "Tell yer the trufe, I was fast asleep an' I 'eard this screamin'. I thought yer got yer fingers caught in the mangle. Then I realised it was only you singin'."

Connie laughed, her white teeth flashing. "Don't be lippy," she said, tossing her pretty head in the air. "Now get in the uvver room out o' me way while I do yer breakfast."

The Globe was full of the usual Saturday morning crowd. The public bar buzzed with conversation as dockers and stevedores from the backstreets piled in for their 'constitutional'. Becky Elliot, the buxom barmaid, and the 'Missus', Harriet Kirkland, busied themselves behind the bar, while in the more sedate saloon Eddie the guv'nor leant on the counter listening to Biff Bowden, the proud owner of Shady Lady. Eddie was a slight man in his mid-fifties, with a clipped moustache and heavily tattooed arms. His sandy hair was well brushed and kept in place with brilliantine. He was a straight-backed character who prided himself on the cleanliness of his pub, a fetish that had stayed with him since his time as a drill sergeant in the Queen's. Biff was a regular to the pub, a robust character in his late forties with a hearty laugh. His moonface remained impassive when he was sober, but when inebriated Biff's features became excessively animated, contorting his face into outlandish expressions.

Biff remained poker-faced as he raved about the exploits of Shady Lady.

"I tell yer, Eddie, that dog clocked the fastest time it's ever done on Monday. It'll walk its next race, you mark my words."

"Well if I'm gonna stick a few bob on it I'll want it ter run, not walk," Eddie said pointedly, winking at the group who stood to one side of the counter.

The owner of Shady Lady was not easily put off. Biff was knowledgeable about nearly every money-making scheme that had been devised in the area — he had been the creator of most of them. Biff could spin a good tale and get backing for his ventures — and he was versatile. He had been known to sell patent medicines in the street markets, and he had once peddled a hair restorer which was guaranteed to produce a mop of curly hair. He also marketed a certain 'tonic' that was supposed to have wondrous powers, especially where there was a flagging sexual desire. Biff Bowden always produced evidence to support his claims: in Petticoat Lane he had a hulking bystander who swore he was once at death's door and the medicine had saved him; in the lesser markets a curly-haired

41

individual testified that he was once bald; another said he had rekindled the burning passions of youth, and that at sixty-plus he was still adding to his brood. At one market in North London, a woman had rushed up to Biff Bowden's fellow conspirator and said that if he was still producing children, they were certainly not hers, and she had chased her startled spouse from the market. Biff had quietened the alarm by saying that the tonic must have made the man over-sexed, and he was sold out in no time at all.

If Biff had a weakness, it was his inability to pick a winner. Most of his hard-earned money was lost at the dog tracks. It had seemed to him that the obvious answer was to get a dog of his own. Unfortunately Shady Lady was lazy — a diet of Guinness and sausages did not appear to be successful — and on two occasions at least the dog didn't even bother to leave the trap. But Biff would not give up, and he engaged the services of a trainer who was finally able to get the greyhound at least to run around the track. Eddie Kirkland told his pals that in his opinion Shady Lady was on a new diet, which probably included Biff's special tonic.

It was around noon when Danny walked sheepishly into the public bar and sidled up to the counter. The Globe was his local and he was prepared for some sort of reception. Becky Elliot took him completely by surprise however by grabbing his face in both hands and planting a kiss on his lips.

"If it ain't me ole Danny boy come ter see me," she laughed.

Danny wiped the scented lipstick from his mouth as well-wishers slapped him on the back and asked how he was.

Becky called the guv'nor into the public bar. "C'mon an' see who's just walked in, Eddie." The guv'nor shook hands warmly and told Becky to give Danny a pint on the house. Harriet Kirkland came over and put her hand on Danny's. "Nice ter see yer back, luv. Are yer okay?"

Danny nodded, his attention divided by people who

wanted to buy him drinks and others firing questions at him.

"Leave the boy alone," Becky said, prodding one of the customers in the ribs with her finger. "Let 'im drink 'is beer in peace, can't yer?"

When the excitement died down Danny took his drink and sat down to talk with 'Bonky' Williams and Johnny Ross. The two of them had been friends of Danny's from school days. They were all about the same age and Bonky lived two doors away from Danny. He had got his name when, as a youngster, he lost his eye in an accident. The glass eye that he wore was often removed and laid down in front of unsuspecting victims in The Globe. Eddie Kirkland had threatened to bar him from the pub on more than one occasion, but Bonky spent well, and any altercation was quickly overcome by the lad buying drinks for the offended party. Johnny Ross was slight and dark-skinned. He limped noticeably owing to a tubercular ankle which had developed when he was very young. Johnny Ross had been involved in a few shady activities, and he was known to the police. He lived in Bermondsey Lane and worked as a labourer in the local vinegar factory.

The Globe was packed and getting noisy and Becky's raucous laughter could be heard above the din. Bonky was getting drunk and his good eye roved around the bar. Johnny nudged him. " 'Ere. Don't you start yer tricks. We don't wanna get chucked out of 'ere."

Bonky grinned. "It's okay, I'm jus' lookin'."

Johnny turned his attention to Danny. "What yer gonna do now yer 'ome, me ole son?"

"I dunno," Danny replied. "I've gotta sign on the Labour Exchange an' get me cards on Monday."

"Take my tip, Danny, don't let 'em palm yer orf wiv any ole job. Tell 'em yer a nerve-case, an' yer gotta get somefink quiet. Tell 'em yer can't stand noisy jobs."

"See if they've got a vacancy fer a shepherd, that's a quiet job!" Bonky piped in.

"You be careful, Danny boy, if yer get too lippy they'll suspend yer. Yer gotta be as crafty as they are," Johnny warned him. "You take 'is case. Go on, Bonky, tell 'im about you gettin' suspended."

Bonky drained his glass and put a ten shilling note down on the table. " 'Ere, get a round in, Johnny. We gotta cheer our ole mate up. 'E don't look 'is ole natural self." He grinned and turned to Danny. "Yer look sort o' different. You okay, son?"

Danny put his glass down and leaned back in his chair. "I feel pissed. Mus' be outta practice. Tell us about yer gettin' suspended, then."

Bonky laughed. "Bloody scream it was. This geezer sends me fer a job at a glass factory down near Dock'ead. I goes inter the office an' there's a real darlin' sittin' down at the desk. 'Course I get me Woodbines out an' asks 'er fer a light. 'We don't allow smoking in here,' she says in a posh voice. Well straight away I've copped the needle. I'm sittin' there dyin' fer a fag, when the phone goes. 'Mr Jones will see you now,' she says in this snotty voice. So in I goes all meek an' mild. I've got me clean scarf on an' I've 'ad a nice shave. I even took me 'at orf. Well, I takes one look at this geezer an' straight away I don't reckon 'im. 'E's got shifty eyes an' 'e's wearin' a collar two sizes too big. Now, I'm standin' in front of 'im an' 'e ain't asked me ter sit down or anyfing. 'E asks me if I can count. 'Yeah, 'course I can, mate,' I tells 'im. 'My name is Mr Jones,' 'e ses, all posh like. When 'e tells me what I'm s'pose ter do I done me piece."

"What did 'e want yer ter do then?" Danny asked, trying not to laugh.

"What did 'e want me ter do?" repeated Bonky. " 'E wanted me fer a glass inspector! D'you know what a glass inspector does?"

"Well 'e inspects glass, I s'pose," Danny said, his eyes widening.

"I'll tell yer what a glass inspector does," Bonky went

on. " 'E sits in front of a machine all day long, an 'e looks at all the bottles goin' along the belt. They give yer an 'ammer, and when a bottle goes past that's got a flaw in it yer gotta smash it. Nine hours a day sittin' on this stool, waitin' ter smash bottles. I ask yer, 'ow could anybody stay sensible doin' a job like that? If I'd took that job, me uvver eye would 'ave gorn in a couple o' weeks.''

Danny burst into laughter. "Did yer tell 'im ter poke the job?"

Bonky looked indignant. "Gimme credit fer a bit o' sense, Danny boy. I 'ad ter play me cards right, didn't I? If 'e puts 'Refusal' on me green card I'm in bovver at the labour office. I 'ad ter get 'im finkin' I'm stupid, see. I got me chance when this office gel walks in the office wiv some papers. This geezer gives 'er a right lecherous look like the dirty ole git 'e is, an' I takes me eye out, wipes it on me scarf, puts it back an' I lets me tongue 'ang out as I watches 'er walk out the office. Yer should 'ave seen 'is face. 'E must 'ave fought 'e was about ter take on a pervert. 'E looked jus' like ole Bert Adams did when I stuck me eye on the table one night when 'e was pissed. Anyway, 'e scribbles 'Not Suitable' on me green card an' 'e ushers me outta the office like I've got galloping cock-rot, which suits me fine, 'cos I don't fancy gettin' suspended.''

Danny looked at Bonky with a puzzled expression. "I fought Johnny said yer got suspended.''

"No, it wasn't that time. This was anuvver time.''

Danny breathed a sigh of relief as Johnny came back with the filled glasses, and when Bonky Williams went off to the toilet Danny shook his head at Johnny. "Bonky's gettin' worse. 'E jus' gave me a real ear-'ole bashin'.''

Johnny laughed. "If yer ask me, I reckon Bonky's goin' orf 'is 'ead. Twice last week 'e took 'is eye out. And once in front o' Mrs Brown from the Council. She went potty. I fought Eddie was gonna ban 'im fer sure.''

The hour hand moved around towards two o'clock and Danny was feeling the effects of the drink. Bonky had got

45

himself involved in a conversation at the bar counter. A couple of latecomers whom Danny recognised as friends of his father walked over and shook hands, but Danny politely refused their offers of drinks; it was time to leave while he was still able. He finished his beer and made to get up.

Johnny looked up at the clock. "You goin' already? It's only two o'clock."

Danny nodded. "Yeah, it's a long time since I've 'ad a good drink and I'm feelin' a bit pissy."

"What about ternight? Fancy comin' out fer a pint? We're 'avin' a drink wiv Tony the bookie, up The Crown. 'E's 'avin' a bit of a knees-up at 'is place afterwards. There should be a few birds there, Danny boy. Tony always 'as good parties — if 'e's 'ad a good day then the booze is flowin'."

"Okay," Danny replied, "if I get a couple of hours sleep this afternoon I might feel all right. I'll see yer at The Crown about 'alf-eight."

It was warm and sunny as Danny left The Globe. Tooley Street was quiet and deserted on that Saturday afternoon, with the wharves and warehouses closed for the weekend. In the 'Pool' — as the adjacent stretch of the Thames between London Bridge and Tower Bridge was known — small ships pulled against their anchors on the high tide, and out in the mainstream laden barges tethered in groups lay low in the water. The high sun lit up the silent quayside and the tall, still cranes, and it shone down on the white stonework of the Tower of London. A few strollers peered down from the grimy old London Bridge, but Tower Bridge was empty, except for the lonely City of London policeman who stood impassively, hands clasped behind his back, gazing downriver. The scene was peaceful and quiet, although the more discerning onlooker would not have been fooled; there were signs of war preparations. Fore and aft of the moored ships the tell-tale shapes of mounted guns beneath their tarpaulin covers could be seen. One of the ships wore the scars of battle where cannon shells had pierced the metal plating high in the bow. For the present the ships rested at anchor, but the usual feverish activity would begin on Monday morning, and on the evening tide the Tower Bridge would raise its cantilevers in salute as the craft sailed out of the Pool to join the Atlantic convoys.

Dawson Street was noisy. A group of children were playing tin-can copper and a baby wailed in its bassinet. Aproned figures stood chatting in doorways, and outside number 14, old Charlie Perkins sat in his wicker chair, holding a clay pipe steady with a forefinger crooked over the brown-stained stem. His face was expressionless and he seemed oblivious to the noise of the children. To the street's inhabitants, the sight of Charlie sitting outside his front door was as familiar as the street lampposts and the railway arch at the end of the turning.

Danny walked unsteadily down the street and veered around Charlie Perkins's outstretched legs. The railway arch seemed to be floating before his gaze and he blinked a couple of times. At his front door he swayed and peered closer at the number. He pulled hard on the knotted door string and almost fell headlong into the passage. Lucy came out from the parlour, her face showing her disgust at his condition.

"You're drunk," she muttered darkly.

Danny put his finger up to his lips and grinned lop-sidedly. He opened his mouth to say something, but changed his mind. Slowly and deliberately he climbed the creaking stairs and staggered into his bedroom.

It was after six o'clock when Connie carried a mug of tea up to his room and found him lying face down on the bed. She put the tea down on the chair and sat on the edge of his bed. The gentle pressure of her hand on his shoulder aroused Danny from the depths of sleep, and in his semi-conscious state he thought the hand on his shoulder was pushing him under the water and Danny called out in terror.

Connie ruffled his hair, "Danny! Danny, it's me, Connie. I've got yer tea. C'mon, it's turned six."

The bed springs squealed as Danny turned over and looked up at the concerned expression on Connie's face. His head was pounding and his mouth felt parched. He attempted a grin and Connie grinned back. "Don't tell me, you've bin in The Globe, an' everybody bought yer a drink."

Danny reached for his tea with a shaky hand and swallowed a mouthful before replying. "I met Bonky an' Johnny Ross," he said.

"That's strange," Connie mocked, "what are those two doin' in The Globe?"

Danny sat up against the bedrail and sipped his tea. "Bonky Williams ain't changed," he said. " 'E's still messin' around wiv that glass eye of 'is."

Connie shuddered. "I can't stand them two. Johnny Ross is the worst. Dirty git wanted ter take me out last week. 'E said there was a party goin' on somewhere."

Danny looked serious. "You keep away from Johnny Ross. I don't want you ter get 'urt."

"Don't you worry about me, bruv," Connie laughed. "I'm goin' steady."

"Oh, an' who's the lucky feller then?"

Connie looked down at the floor, her cheeks flushing slightly. " 'Is name's Jimmy Ellis, an' 'e's in the Navy."

Danny showed mock horror. "Not Jimmy Ellis?"

"You know 'im?" Connie asked.

"Know 'im? Course I know 'im, they call 'im 'ugly Ellis'."

Connie looked angry. " 'E's not ugly. Jim's good lookin', an' 'e's very nice."

Danny put his hand on her arm. "I'm only pullin' yer leg. I've never met the bloke, but if yer say 'e's good lookin' I'll take yer word fer it."

Connie stood up. "You comin' down fer yer tea? There's fish an' chips keepin' 'ot in the oven. I can't stay 'ere chattin', I've got a date ternight.'' She made for the door then turned. "By the way, bruv, 'ave you bumped inter Kathy Thompson yet?''

"Not yet," Danny answered, swinging his legs over onto the floor. "Why d'yer ask?''

"No reason, 'cept I know yer used ter go out wiv 'er.''

"That was a long while ago," Danny replied.

Connie went to say something, then changed her mind and walked out of the room.

Danny went down to the scullery and washed in the stone sink. The cold water revived him and the pounding in his head eased slightly. When he went into the parlour Lucy looked up from her armchair. "Hello, how's your head?''

Danny put his hand up to his forehead. "Thick," he whispered.

Lucy got up. "You'd better sit in the chair. I'll fetch your tea, it's in the oven.''

Danny sat at the table with his head resting on his hands. When Lucy came back with his meal Danny sat up straight in his chair. "Where is everybody?" he asked.

"Mum and Dad have gone over to see Dad's cousin in Guy's. She's very ill. And Connie's upstairs getting ready to go out.''

"You in ternight?" Danny asked as Lucy sat down facing him.

"Ben's coming round later. We're going up West to see a concert." Lucy answered, her forefinger drawing imaginary circles on the tablecloth.

Danny speared some chips on his fork and started eating. After a while he put down his knife and fork. "You worried about Ben?" he asked. "The tribunal I mean.''

Lucy folded her plump arms and leant on the table. "Naturally I'm worried . You see, Ben's very sensitive, he couldn't hurt a fly. Apart from running the youth club, he's a regular church-goer. His parents were the same. He feels that killing is wrong, and he won't change his

49

thinking. Ben won't put a uniform on. All right, I know you don't agree with his point of view, and I know you don't like him very much, but I hope to get married to him one day."

Danny scratched his head and looked into his sister's dark eyes. "Listen, Lucy, it's not that I don't like Ben, but 'e's different from me. I can't take 'im up The Globe fer a pint, 'cos 'e don't drink. I can't 'ave a conversation wiv 'im, 'cos we don't speak the same language. We're worlds apart. I know Ben's not gonna change, an' nor am I. Yer gotta see that. One fing's fer sure though, if you an' Ben wanna get married, you'll get no trouble from me. Ben's okay, and while we're on the subject I'll tell yer somefink else too. 'E ain't no different from the rest of us in one respect. Killin' people *is* wrong. The 'ole bloody war's wrong. The way Ben sees it is that if everybody 'eld the same views as 'im there'd be nobody ter fight the war. Trouble is, life ain't like that. Nuffink's gonna change. There'll always be some bloody maniac ready ter start a war, an' there's no shortage o' people ter do the dirty work. Maybe Ben's got the right idea, I dunno. Good luck to 'im anyway. 'E'll be all right at the tribunal."

Lucy smoothed the tablecloth and leaned back in her chair. "I've never heard you talk like this before, Danny. Everything was one big joke to you. You've got all serious."

Danny pushed his plate away and picked up his teacup. "I tell yer, sis, what I've seen of the war 'as made me fink. I lost a few good mates, an' I've seen what the war does ter people, but d'yer know what shook me most of all? I was trampin' along wiv our company, we were goin' up ter relieve anuvver regiment. Casualties were bein' brought back an' we got off the road ter make room fer 'em. Right where we stopped was a stone memorial. There was plenty o' names on that stone, I can tell yer. It was from the 1914 war. And there we was doin' it all again twenty-six years later. I got ter finkin', 'ow many more stones they gonna

50

put up when this lot's over? I tell yer, Lucy, I wanted ter run as far as I could, away from what I was seein'. Maybe Ben 'as got the right idea — I only wish most o' the Germans agreed wiv 'im.''

Lucy stood up and playfully ruffled his fair hair. "You know what Dad would say if he was here?"

Danny laughed. "Put the kettle on," he mimicked.

On the stroke of seven there was a knock on the front door and Danny went to answer it. A young sailor was standing on the doorstep. "I'm Jimmy. Is Connie there, please?" he said with an eager expression on his face.

Danny looked out of his bleary eyes at the slim young man who was a few inches shorter than his six feet. "I guessed who yer was. Connie's bin tellin' me all about yer bad 'abits.''

Jimmy was abashed. "Oh!" he breathed, still looking wide-eyed at Danny.

Danny's face relaxed. "C'mon in, I was only jokin'.''

The young sailor stepped into the passage and removed his cap to reveal a mop of wavy blond hair. His baby face turned towards the stairs as Connie came hurrying down and took hold of his hand. "This is my 'orrible bruv, Danny," she said, looking at him affectionately. " 'E's bin out celebratin', Jimmy, so 'e can't see yer very well."

The two shook hands and Danny motioned to the parlour. "D'yer wanna cup o' tea?"

Connie put her hand on her brother's arm. "Look, bruv, Jimmy's only got a few days' leave an' I'm claimin' all 'is spare time. Besides, I'm not gonna sit an' listen ter you two men talkin' about the war. C'mon, Jimmy, or we'll miss the big picture."

Danny stood by the front door and watched as his sister walked up the turning holding on to Jimmy's arm, chatting and laughing. The young cockney smiled to himself. Connie was his favourite, and he hoped that nothing would ever happen to mar her happiness.

Chapter Five

The sun had left the room and slipped down behind the lop-sided chimney pots. Danny looked into the old faded mirror over the washstand and adjusted the knot of his tie. The clock showed twenty to nine. He patted down his hair with both hands and looked down at his polished shoes. His best grey suit felt tighter than it had when he left the hospital. He undid the buttons of the jacket and peered into the mirror once more. The fading light gave the room a sombre look and Danny felt a desire for company. He opened the door and heard his father's voice talking to his mother. He hurried down the stairs and put his head around the parlour door. Frank looked up from his paper and Alice stopped sewing.

"You're not goin' out again, Danny?" she asked, looking quite amazed.

"Leave the boy alone, Alice. 'E's turned twenty-one yer know," Frank chided her.

"I know," his wife retorted, "but I'd 'ave thought 'e'd 'ad enough fer one day, 'spesh'ly in 'is condition."

Danny grinned. "Hush, Ma, people'll fink I'm pregnant or somefink."

Frank chuckled. " 'E'll know when 'e's 'ad enough, Alice. 'E'll fall over!"

Danny made to leave, then turned. "By the way, 'ow was yer cousin, Dad?"

"Very weak," Frank replied. "Mind you, she's turned ninety, yer can't expect much."

Danny dropped his gaze with a nod. "Well I'm off

folks," he said quickly. "Don't wait up, I might be goin' to a party."

Frank leaned back in his armchair. "All right fer money?"

Danny nodded. "I'm okay, fanks. I didn't get a chance ter spend much terday."

"So I 'eard," Frank said, looking over his glasses at Alice.

The evening was still warm, with heavy storm clouds rolling in. It was still light enough to see the pavement in the blacked-out streets as Danny made his way to The Crown in Dockhead. His leg felt more comfortable now, and he had padded his chest with a few turns of bandage and a cotton wool dressing. At the outset he walked briskly but he became breathless as he crossed the Tower Bridge Road and he slowed his pace. It was fairly quiet as he continued on to Dockhead. A few couples strolled arm in arm along Tooley Street, and a number 68 tram rattled noisily past. Danny walked by a surface shelter with its sandbagged entrance, and it reminded him of Dunkirk. Farther on he saw the large grey spire of St James's Church showing up against the angry sky. His thoughts turned briefly to Alison. I should have written to her, he thought.

The Crown stood back from the main road. No light shone out, but sounds of merrymaking reached Danny's ears while he was still some distance away. He reached the saloon, pushed open the door and went in. The room was filled with tobacco smoke, and there was a strong smell of perfume.

Johnny Ross called out to him. "Over 'ere. I fought yer wasn't comin'. Yer late."

Danny grinned. "I got a few hours' kip. I'm okay, as long as yer don't lean on me."

Johnny pointed over to a tall, wavy-haired individual who was talking to a young woman. "That's Tony. Looks like 'e's pulled a bird."

54

A barmaid came over and set some drinks down on the counter in front of Johnny, who pointed in Danny's direction. "An' a mild an' bitter fer me mate, luv."

The barmaid gave Johnny a sweet smile as she reached for a glass and proceeded to pull on the pump handle. Johnny's eyes looked down at the barmaid's low-cut V-necked dress and her eyes flickered at him.

"Pour yerself one," Johnny said, winking at her suggestively.

Danny had been casting his eyes around the bar and suddenly he saw Kathy. His immediate reaction was to look away, but he found himself staring at her. She looked even prettier than the picture of her he had carried in his mind during all those months in France. He felt a surge of jealousy when he realised Kathy was not alone. She was talking to a well-dressed, thick-set man whose hair was combed smartly back from his forehead. Danny estimated the man to be in his mid-thirties. As he watched the couple Danny noticed that Kathy seemed to be disagreeing with her companion, she kept shaking her head and he was getting more agitated.

Johnny observed Danny's interest. " 'Ere, cop yer drink, Danny boy, an' take yer covetin' eyes off 'er," he said. "That bloke spells trouble fer the likes of us."

"Who is 'e?" Danny asked, still looking in Kathy's direction.

"That's Jack Mason. 'E used ter run the Elephant and Castle mob a few years ago. 'E done porridge fer GBH. 'E still runs wiv the mobs, so I'm told. That sort o' geezer don't go out of 'is way ter 'elp ole ladies across the road."

Danny sipped his beer and paid little attention as Johnny Ross attempted to bring him up to date with the news in dockland. Kathy had seen him now. Her eyes caught his and held his gaze for an instant, then she deliberately moved around slightly so that she was out of Danny's line of vision. Her stocky companion was still in view however, and Danny could see him nodding his head vigorously. More people crowded into the bar and soon he could not see either of them. It was getting stuffy in the saloon bar and presently Johnny nudged his pal. "Let's move inter the uvver bar, there's more room in there," he said.

The small room that separated the saloon from the public bar was mainly used for darts. A few regulars sat around against the wall, and customers came through to use the toilets. Danny bought more drinks and leaned against the counter.

Johnny jerked his thumb in the direction of the clock. "We're goin' roun' Tony's soon's the pub closes. We'll take a crate wiv us, jus' ter show we're willin'. By the way, Elsie said she's comin' round later."

"Who's Elsie?" Danny asked.

"Elsie's that darlin' be'ind the bar. 'Er ole man's doin' bird, an' Elsie's lonely."

Danny shook his head and grinned. "You'll be lonely if 'er ole man finds out."

Johnny shrugged his shoulders. "Elsie's ole man's doin' a long stretch. From what she tells me, 'e was always playin' around 'imself."

"That makes no difference," Danny persisted. " 'E mus' get visits. Somebody's only gotta grass yer up an' 'e can soon get one of 'is mates ter sort yer out. It wouldn't be the first time it's 'appened."

"Don't worry, Danny boy, Johnny Ross can look after 'imself. 'E don't scare me."

Danny Sutton raised his glass. " 'Ere's to yer, Johnny. I 'ope yer stay 'ealfy."

Johnny clinked his glass against Danny's. "Nice ter see yer 'ome in one piece. Now yer gotta start earnin' some shekels. First of all though, yer gotta get fixed up wiv a bird. Yer don't wanna start mopin' about, do yer?"

Danny grinned and looked back into the crowded bar. Johnny puffed hard. " 'Ere, 'old up! You ain't finkin' o'

56

takin' up wiv that Kathy again, are yer? I'd leave well alone. She's got a villain on tow, an' as it 'appens them two are comin' ter the party. We don't want claret all over Tony's carpet, 'e would get the needle.''

"Don't yer worry, Johnny. I'm finished wiv fightin', an' I've got me discharge book ter prove it.''

It was almost closing time when Kathy walked into the small bar. Her cotton dress hugged her figure and Danny noticed how her large brown eyes seemed to sparkle as she gave him a smile. " 'Ow are yer, Danny? Connie told me you was 'ome.''

"I'm fine, an' you?''

"I'm okay.''

Danny shuffled uncomfortably. "Johnny tells me yer might be goin' ter Tony's party.''

"Yes, I'm just off ter powder me nose," Kathy laughed.

"I'll see yer there then. We can 'ave a chat," Danny said, catching Johnny's dark look.

Kathy began to look uncomfortable. "Matter o' fact I'm wiv somebody," she said.

"That's okay," Danny said with a shrug of his shoulders. "We can still say 'ello, can't we?''

"Course we can," Kathy said as she walked off to the ladies' room.

The loud voice of the barman calling time spurred Johnny into action. "C'mon, me ole son. Give us an 'and wiv the crate.''

Danny reached into his pocket and Johnny stopped him. "There's nuffink ter pay. The guv'nor owes me. I done 'im a favour last week. 'E's gettin' off lightly.''

The crate containing a dozen bottles of light ale was passed over the counter, and they each took hold of a handle. "C'mon, Danny, let's get roun' there, it's only in the next turnin'," Johnny said, winking at Elsie as he walked to the door.

Outside the night was dark, with a waxing moon peering out from heavy cloud. Johnny limped along on his bad ankle and Danny too found himself limping.

Johnny started giggling. "You know what, if the birds could see us two now, we'd 'ave as much chance of pullin' 'em as Biff Bowden's dog's got of winnin' the Grey'ound Derby."

"I wouldn't worry," Danny laughed, "yer don't 'ave ter do it standin' up."

"Don't you be so sure," Johnny countered. "Elsie likes it standin' up!"

Three stone steps led up to Tony Allen's house in Dock Street. The front door was ajar. It looked impressive with its varnished surface and brass knocker. Once inside the two men put the crate down in the hallway, and Danny looked around. "Christ! It makes a change ter see an 'ouse wiv electric light," he said, standing on one leg and flexing the other.

Tony had already heard them and he came out into the hallway and nodded to Johnny. "Is this Danny?" he said, holding out his hand. "Johnny told me about yer bein' at Dunkirk. Must 'ave bin 'ell. You just enjoy yerself, son. 'Elp yerselves ter drinks."

"Let's go an' chat up the birds, Danny, before Elsie gets 'ere," Johnny grinned.

In the large room there was a piano at one end, and there were gilt-framed pictures of mountains and lakes around the walls. Easy chairs were spread about the room. The red carpet was thick underfoot, and heavy velvet curtains kept the light in. A Japanese fire screen hid the hearth, and up on the high mantelshelf there were iron statues of rearing horses. The centrepiece was of gilt, and it caught Danny's eye — nude figures were draped in various poses around the clock-face, and the whole piece was mounted on a marble plinth. Johnny noticed that his pal was staring at the ornament. "Yer don't get somefink like that on Cheap Jack's stall, do yer?"

"All this mus' be werf a fortune," Danny remarked, his eyes moving around the room.

"Yeah, Tony's got a lot o' contacts apart from 'is bookie's business," Johnny informed him. "In fact, 'e's gonna put a bit o' business my way later. I'll tell yer about it termorrer — we can't talk 'ere."

The room was getting full and the piano player began to tinkle away on the keyboard. People started singing and the drinks flowed. Elsie flounced in looking hot and bothered in her fur stole. She came over to Johnny and kissed him on the mouth. Soon after, Kathy came into the room escorted by Jack Mason. The two looked serious-faced, though Kathy relaxed slightly when Tony Allen went up to them. Danny sat in one corner of the room, his drink held in his hand. Johnny was joking with Elsie and occasionally he slid his hand over her behind as Elsie snuggled up to him. And when the piano player started playing a waltz she dragged Johnny into the centre of the room and almost smothered him in her ample bosom as she danced around dreamily. Danny watched the pair gyrating, and then his eyes turned to Kathy again. She was over in the far corner of the room, looking stern as she sat cross-legged in an armchair. Her escort seemed to be ignoring her as he talked animatedly with Tony and two other men. Danny tried to catch her eyes but she appeared to be avoiding his stare. A few more couples got up to dance and someone pulled Kathy into the centre of the large room. She waltzed around, looking bored with the whole procedure, while her partner acted as if he were taking part in a dancing contest. A middle-aged lady asked Danny if he would care to dance, but with a brief smile he told her that he had a stiff leg, and immediately he regretted having said it. The lady showed concern and started to explain her own medical history, but then someone grabbed her and whisked her off into the dancing group. Danny got up and refilled his glass. As he walked back to his chair Kathy and her partner danced near to him. Kathy's eyes met his, and she raised hers to the ceiling in anguish as her feet were stamped on yet again.

Danny sipped his drink and looked around; everyone seemed to be with someone. Two girls who had walked into the party unescorted were now chatting happily with a group of young men. Danny began to wish he had stopped at home. The piano player broke off to get a drink and Kathy resumed her place in the armchair. Jack Mason looked around briefly and then carried on talking with Tony Allen.

Another ten minutes and they can stuff this party, Danny thought as he finished his drink.

"What's wrong wiv yer leg then, luv?" somebody asked him.

Danny looked around to see a large lady leaning over his shoulder. Her face was flushed and he could smell strong perfume and see the sweat lines running down her heavily powdered face. She was grinning, with her thick-painted lips parted to show large teeth.

"Somebody put a bullet frew it," Danny said sharply.

"Good Gawd! You a soldier?" she asked.

"I was till I got this," Danny replied.

"Why, you don't look old enough ter be a soldier, does 'e Muriel?"

"No," Muriel said, without taking her eyes off the bald-headed suitor by her side.

The big lady tut-tutted and lost interest in Danny's wounded leg. She returned to Muriel's crowd, to Danny's relief.

Over in the far corner Kathy was shaking her head at Jack Mason and she looked distressed. Jack gesticulated with a wave of his arm and turned his back on her and Kathy suddenly got up and made for the door. Danny watched as she took her coat down from the clothes-rack, said something to the woman who had been serving the drinks, then quickly left. Danny stood up and with a quick glance in Jack Mason's direction he put his glass down on the sideboard and walked casually towards the door. Danny walked out into the hallway and let himself out into the street. It was too dark to see far but he could hear Kathy's footsteps up ahead. Quickening his pace he got closer. Kathy's high-heeled shoes clicked faster on the pavement and Danny called out, "Kathy! It's me! Danny!"

Kathy continued walking. "Leave me alone, Danny! I'm goin' 'ome!" she called out.

"Wait, Kathy! I can't walk fast! I wanna talk wiv yer!"

The footsteps halted and when Danny reached her he was panting. He saw the tears falling down her cheeks and her eyes shining in the darkness.

"Let me walk yer 'ome at least," he pleaded.

Kathy dabbed at her eyes with a small handkerchief and smiled through her tears. "It looks like you need somebody ter see *you* 'ome," she said.

Danny put his hands into his trouser pockets and fell in beside her. "I'll be okay in a minute. It was stuffy in that party, I wasn't enjoyin' it one little bit."

"Nor was I," Kathy said.

"I could see that. Is Jack Mason your steady bloke?"

"Do you mind if we don't talk about Jack Mason?" Kathy said sharply.

"All right, let's talk about me then," Danny grinned. "Let's see, I'm a war 'ero, an' I'm off ter see the King next week ter get me Victoria Cross! King George'll say: ' 'Ow did yer manage ter be so brave?' an' I'll say: 'It was nuffink, Your Majesty, we're all the same in Bermon'sey'."

Kathy laughed aloud and took his arm. "Was it really bad in Dunkirk? I'm sorry, it must 'ave bin terrible. What I meant was, was it bad fer you? Gettin' 'urt like yer did."

Danny pulled up his coat collar against the cool breeze and shrugged his shoulders. "Tell yer the trufe, Kathy, I was out cold when I got pulled out o' the water. I don't remember anyfing till I woke up in the 'ospital. I found

61

out later that some feller 'eld on ter me, even though 'e couldn't swim a stroke 'imself. 'E supported the pair of us by clingin' on to an upturned boat. If anybody deserves a medal 'e does, I wouldn't be 'ere if it wasn't fer 'im.''

The two reached the end of Dock Street and turned into Dockhead. Although the night was dark, the half-hidden moon seemed to bathe the streets in a faint light. They approached Shad Thames, a narrow turning where wharves and warehouses loomed high and sombre. Danny chuckled, and Kathy pulled on his arm. ''What's wrong?''

''Jus' somefing I thought of,'' Danny said, still chuckling.

''C'mon then, let us in on the joke.''

''All right,'' Danny said, leaning his head in her direction, ''when the lads used ter pull the birds — sorry, girls — they used ter say to 'em, ' 'Ow would yer like ter see Butler's new crane?' They'd tell 'em all about 'ow big an' tall it was, an' they'd take 'em down ter Butler's Wharf in Shad Thames.''

''I see,'' Kathy grinned, shaking her head in mock disgust. ''All those dark alleyways an' dark doorways, I see. An' I s'pose you took quite a few girls down there?''

''Not many,'' Danny smiled.

''Were they disappointed they never got to see the new crane?''

''You'll 'ave ter ask them,'' Danny said with a shrug of his shoulders.

Kathy was quiet for a second or two, then she pulled on his arm again. ''I s'pose you was finkin' about askin' me ter come down an' see the crane?''

Danny put on his innocent look. ''No. But it is a short-cut that way.''

The two veered off and walked down the deserted Shad Thames. High wharves towered above them as they walked the cobbled lane. Various smells hung in the night air — the aroma of spices and the eye-watering tang of pepper mingled with other more obscure odours. Shad

Thames was full of pungent, exotic wares, and the loneliness of the place made them shiver. Kathy clung tightly onto Danny and he could feel her body pressing onto his arm. He looked at her and in the half-light could just make out her dark hair, pale complexion, and her full lips, and he shivered.

Half-way along the lane Danny stopped, took his hands from his pockets and turned to face Kathy. Without saying a word he moved in close to her and clasped her shoulders. She did not resist as he pulled her to him and kissed her on the lips. Her mouth opened beneath his as the kiss became more urgent. For some time they stayed locked in an embrace, then when they moved apart Danny took her hand and led her the few paces into a doorway.

The night was silent and they could hear their own heartbeats. Kathy put both arms around his neck and Danny could feel her slim body against his chest, and her thighs touching his. His hands sought her, opening her coat, and moved gently over her soft, smooth breasts. He bent to kiss her neck, and Kathy shuddered, her head held back as his lips moved over her throat. She could no longer think clearly, there was only the urge to meet his caresses and feel his passion. She needed him to love her more than anything in the world.

Together they drew back into the deepest shadows of the doorway, and their breathing became a rhythmic panting.

"Love me, Danny! Please!" she whispered harshly in his ear.

For a while neither of them spoke. Then finally Kathy moved away from his embrace. She buttoned up her coat and took his arm. "I've wanted you to do that ever since that Saturday night before you went away, Danny," she said.

The young man looked at the girl who stood with him in the dark recess and his face relaxed into a smile. "You don't know 'ow many times I thought about that night since I left," he said quietly.

They started walking again, their footsteps echoing along the silent and deserted lane. They were silent as they turned from Shad Thames into a side road and continued on past the huge brewery. The smell of hops hung in the air, and as they came out once again into Tooley Street rain started to fall. Each was thinking about the suddenness and the fantasy of the experience they had shared only a few minutes ago. Danny could not get the picture of Jack Mason out of his head, it hung like a dark cloud over him, and he was tortured by a feeling of possessiveness. Yet he knew that Kathy was not about to become his; he could sense her inner conflict as she walked beside him to the corner of Clink Lane. She held his arm tightly, but at the same time she had become distant and rigid.

Kathy stopped a few doors away from her own house. "We'd better say goodnight 'ere. I don't want ter let me dad know I've bin out this late."

Danny looked skywards and felt the rain beginning to fall on his face. "What about us, Kathy? Can I see yer again?"

The young girl sighed deeply and put her hands up onto Danny's coat lapels. "It's no good, I'm goin' steady wiv Jack Mason. Let's leave ternight fer memories. It's somefink I'm never gonna ferget, really, Danny. It was special ternight."

Danny's face darkened. "You frightened of 'im?"

"Who, Jack? 'Course not. All right, me an' 'im 'ad a bust up, but I don't wanna worry yer wiv me troubles. It's not your concern anyway."

"That's just it," Danny replied, taking her by the shoulders and squeezing her tightly. "It is my concern. Only a little while ago we made love. It was great, we're good tergevver. We can make a go of it again."

Kathy resisted his attempts to pull her close to him. "Listen, you've bin frew a terrible time. You're gonna

64

find yer feet again soon, an' when yer do you'll see this as . . . just an experience. Let's jus' remember ternight. We'll still see each uvver about, an' when we meet in the pub or in the street, we'll look at each uvver an' there'll be somefing special there. Let's leave it at that, Danny. Any uvver way an' it's gonna be trouble an' 'eartbreak fer both of us.''

Danny tried to pull her towards him but Kathy pushed him away. "No, Danny. Look, I've gotta get in, my dad's givin' me a bad time as it is.''

Danny relaxed his grip and Kathy kissed him suddenly on the lips and turned away. He watched her trim figure disappear into the darkness.

Chapter Six

Sunday the 30th of June 1940 dawned clear and dry after the night rain. The sun rose early, and outside the Globe the winkle stall was set up ready for trade. The paper shop in Tooley Street sold out of the *News of the World* early, and all the local church bells remained silent. People gathered outside their tumbledown houses in the backstreets to discuss the progress of the war, while across the English Channel the German High Command were drawing up plans to invade.

The Sutton household was awake early as usual. Frank polished his Sunday best shoes in the yard, and Maggie brought her two children around to see Danny. Both Terry and Reggie tore up the stairs and bounded onto Danny's bed, demanding to see his 'soldier's gun'. Alice was already peeling the potatoes in the scullery sink, and Lucy was on her way round to meet Ben and then on to the Methodist church in Tower Bridge Road for morning service. The Sabbath in Dawson Street was a day when the doorsteps gleamed white, lace curtains looked freshly starched and, weather allowing, old Charlie Perkins put his wicker chair outside number 14 and prepared himself for another day's hard thinking. Crazy Bella appeared and reappeared at her front door, and the kids were their normal noisy selves — even noisier when the toffee-apple man cycled into the street. In a way it was just like any peace-time Sunday, except that during the previous week everyone in the turning had had a leaflet tucked into their letterboxes, and the street folk now had time to talk about it.

Mr and Mrs Brightman stood at their front door and listened to Granny Bell's furious outburst. "I tell yer, Flo, if I'd 'ave caught the cow-son I'd 'ave given 'im what for. Fancy comin' round 'ere wiv that leaflet an' fright'nin' the bleedin' life out of us all. All this talk about us bein' invaded — scaremongerin', that's all it is. Them bastards 'ave gotta get 'ere first. D'yer fink our boys are gonna stan' back an' let 'em come 'ere? Course they ain't. Anyway, can yer imagine them Germans walkin' down this street an' catchin' a dekko of ole Bella? She'd scare the daylights out of 'em. They'd soon piss orf."

Mrs Brightman wasn't so flippant about the leaflet. "Well I dunno, Granny. Me an' Maurice 'ave bin talkin' about evacuatin' the kids, ain't we, luv?"

Maurice Brightman nodded, and by the time he had thought of a response, Granny Bell was off again.

" 'Vacuation my foot! What d'yer wanna send yer poor little mites away for? Strikes me you people wanna get rid of yer kids. Nobody sent their kids away in the last war, and we 'ad the Zepp'lins ter contend wiv then. They was 'orrible fings, like great sausages floatin' in the sky."

Flo Brightman slipped her hands under her apron and pulled a face. "Yer gotta understan', Gran, it wasn't the same in the last war. Fings are different now. I mean, look 'ow they bombed them towns in Spain. We saw it on the news at the Tower Kinema, didn't we Maurice?"

Maurice nodded and opened his mouth to speak but Granny Bell started in again. "I ain't bin ter the pictures fer years, not since my ole man died, Gawd rest 'is soul. I read it in the papers though. I can't make 'ead nor tail of it. Them Spanishers are fightin' each uvver, ain't they?"

Maurice had read all about the Spanish Civil War and he was about to enlighten Granny, but she wasn't finished. "I still say yer should keep yer children round yer. Anyfing could 'appen to 'em in the country. I remember ole Sadie Murgatroyd tellin' me years ago about those gypsies who stole a little boy from 'is 'ouse. Know what they done to 'im?''

Mr and Mrs Brightman shook their heads.

''They broke the poor little sod's legs, so 'e'd be double-jointed. They was gonna put 'im in a circus as an acrobat or somefink, accordin' ter Sadie Murgatroyd.''

The Brightmans left Granny Bell sweeping her front doorstep and went into their house to worry some more.

It was opening-time when Maggie's husband Joe called round for Frank, and the two of them took a leisurely stroll up to The Globe. Danny had promised to pop in later, but first he wanted to see his pal Tony Arpino. Connie had told him that the Arpinos had not been interned because they had taken out British citizenship long ago, but the Lucianis had not been so fortunate. Connie had said how upset Tony was about being parted from Melissa. It was commonly known locally that one day the two Italian families would be united through the marriage of Tony and Melissa.

As Danny walked towards Bermondsey Lane, where the Arpinos had their grocery shop, he was deep in thought. Last night still seemed unreal, it had all been so sudden. He desperately wanted to see Kathy again, but she'd seemed so sure about staying with Jack Mason. Maybe she was right, maybe he should leave things the way they were. Then he remembered he hadn't written to Alison and he decided to do so today for sure. If Kathy wouldn't see him then maybe Alison would. But it could be difficult. The Channel ports were out of bounds to normal travellers — it was in the morning papers — so he would have to find out when she could get leave, and maybe meet her somewhere. She might even come to London.

The Arpinos' shop was open when Danny arrived. Lou Arpino was piling tins of peas onto a shelf, and when he saw Danny Sutton step through the doorway he raised his hands above his head and knocked half a dozen tins onto the floor.

"Hey, Danny! How's a ma boy?" he called out, his olive face breaking into a wide smile.

"I'm okay, Lou. 'Ow's the family?"

Lou's dark eyes shone as he leaned over the counter and grasped Danny's hand. "Hey, Mamma! Tony! Come a see what's a come in da shop."

The buxom figure of Sofia Arpino appeared in the doorway at the back of the shop. Her raven hair was tied up in plaits which covered her ears, and she had a white crocheted shawl draped loosely around her wide shoulders. When she saw Danny she came around from behind the counter and took his head in both hands and planted a kiss on his forehead. "Danny Sutton! It's good you come back. Didn't I say Danny will be okay, Lou?"

Lou Arpino put his arm around her shoulders. "We see da papers an' we 'ear da news. Mamma cried, didn't you Mamma? She prays for your safety. It's a good to see you."

Danny grinned, "It's good ter see you two again. Where's Tony?"

Lou Arpino leaned his head around the door and called out to Tony. Sofia's face became serious. "You heard about the Lucianis? Tony is very upset, he's not seen Melissa since they come to take them away. It's a very sad."

Tony appeared in the doorway and his eyes lit up. He came over and threw his arms around the young cockney. "It's great ter see yer, Danny boy. We all knew you'd be okay. Your Connie told us yer got wounded —'ow d'yer feel now?"

"I'm all right, Tony. 'Ere, I'm sorry about Melissa an' 'er family. Are yer gonna get ter see 'er?"

Tony's face darkened. "I don't know where they've all gone. They're puttin' 'em all over the country. Melissa said she'd write, soon as she could. I've jus' gotta wait, nuffink else I can do."

Danny looked at Lou Arpino. "Can yer spare 'im fer 'alf an hour?"

Lou nodded and Danny put his arm around Tony's

shoulders. "C'mon, let's get a drink, an' I'll tell yer all about those French girls."

The two walked out of the shop and Sofia dabbed at her eyes. Lou watched them as they sauntered up the street, and then he went back to his shelf-filling. Sunday customers came and went, and some passed by the shop, preferring to take their custom to the English shop owner further up the street. The war had already touched the Arpino family, just as it had the Lucianis.

In The Globe that Sunday midday the landlord felt uneasy. Eddie Kirkland had been in the business a long time and he had a nose for trouble. He had seen his share of bar brawls and right now he could smell one brewing.

At first he had paid no attention to the strange crowd of dockers in one corner of the public bar. It was not unusual for a strange group to come into the pub, and though there was a lot of rivalry between dockers from various wharves, it was nearly always good-humoured banter. Today it was different, however, and the big docker who seemed to be the ringleader was ranting off about conscientious objectors.

Eddie picked up his ears as the argument got more heated and glanced over to where Frank Sutton and his son-in-law Joe were standing. They seemed to be unaware of what was being said, but the discussion was getting louder.

"Well you can say what yer like, Bob," the ganger was saying, "but as fer as I'm concerned, anybody who says 'e's a 'conchie' is a coward. The only people who can say that are vicars an' priests."

"I dunno," replied Bob. "It's a free country. If yer got them principles about not fightin', yer should 'ave the right ter refuse ter put on a uniform."

"Cobblers!" roared the ganger. " 'Ow long's it gonna be a free country if everybody said the same? You'd 'ave

71

the bloody Germans walkin' in. I bet they don't allow conchies in Germany. They'd lock 'em up or shoot 'em."

"Don't talk silly, Ted, this ain't Germany. Yer can't compare us wiv them. You yerself could 'old the same views. 'Ow would you like ter be banged away?"

The big ganger was getting more irate. His bulging neck was red and he began to shout. "Yer can fink what yer like, but in my book, anybody who's a conchie is a bastard coward. An' I tell yer somefing else, I only wish I was a bit younger. I'd be up that recruitin' orfice like a flash, never mind about bein' in a reserved occupation. I'd make 'em take me."

Frank heard the commotion. "Where's that loud-mouthed crowd come from?" he asked Joe.

"They're from The Surrey. I've seen 'em in The Crown a few times. That ganger's name is Ted Molyneaux. 'E was mouthin' off last time I see 'im. Yer wanna take no notice of 'em, 'e ain't werf gettin' yerself inter trouble over."

Frank took a gulp from his glass and wiped his wet moustache on the back of his hand. "You know what, Joe? I've lived in Dawson Street ever since me an' Alice got spliced more than firty years ago 'an' I've bin comin' in this boozer for all o' that time. You could say this was me local, couldn't yer?"

Joe nodded, wondering what Frank was getting at.

"I treat this pub like me own 'ouse," Frank went on. "I don't abuse the place, an' I don't go on upsettin' the people in it, but that don't meant I've gotta stand 'ere an' listen to that big, fat, ugly-lookin' bastard shoutin' 'is mouth orf, Sunday or no Sunday."

Joe picked up their empty glasses. "What yer 'avin', Frank? Same again?" he said, hoping to calm his father-in-law down.

Frank's face had turned white with temper, and Joe knew there would be trouble. He had worked together with Frank for some considerable time, and had seen him in a rage before. "Frank. Ferget 'im," he pleaded. "What yer 'avin'?"

"I dunno as I wanna drink 'ere while 'e's shoutin' 'is face orf," Frank replied, loud enough for the rival group to hear.

Joe was getting worried. He grabbed Frank's arm. "Look, 'e don't know anyfing about Ben. You're takin' it personal. Ferget it. 'Ave anuvver drink fer Gawd's sake."

It was too late. Ted Molyneaux looked over and then back at the crowd of faces around him. "What's 'e goin' orf about? Can't a bloke 'ave a talk wiv 'is mates wivout somebody pokin' 'is nose in? Does 'e fink 'e owns the pub?"

Eddie had seen enough. He leaned over the bar counter and addressed the crowd of dockers: "Now listen, I don't want no trouble 'ere, understood? Any fisticuffs in my pub an' you're barred, an' I'll get the law in quick an' all. Now drink up an' simmer down."

Ted Molyneaux glared over at Frank Sutton, then he quickly finished his pint. "Who's comin' down The Crown? I don't like the company in 'ere."

Frank leaned one elbow on the counter. "Go on, piss orf an' aggravate some uvver poor bleeder. Yer got too much ole bunny fer this pub, matie."

The big ganger pushed away the restraining hands and made for Frank. Eddie vaulted the counter and barred his way. With a heave Ted Molyneaux threw the landlord aside and grabbed a chair with one hand. Joe Copeland held onto one of the legs as the ganger made to swing it at Frank's head, and at the same time Frank hit him full in the face. Molyneaux staggered back, blood streaming from his nose, Frank went after him, and the two fell in a heap on the floor. Joe tried to pull them apart but the ganger kicked upwards into his groin. Frank pinned him to the floor and was raining blows on his face when Eddie shouted for Arnold the potman, and he waddled over and lifted Frank off Ted Molyneaux as though he were a baby. Eddie hoisted the battered docker to his feet and shoved him towards the door as Frank struggled to free himself from Arnold's vice-like grip.

"Put me down yer bloody gorilla! Let me get at 'im! I'll swing fer 'im!"

Joe was sitting on a chair holding his crotch. "Christ! 'E nearly ruined me!" he gasped.

The crowd followed their ganger out into the street, and Eddie gave Frank a blinding look. "You're old enough ter know better. Yer shouldn't go gettin' inter scrapes at your age, it's bloody stupid."

Frank grinned sheepishly and dusted his suit. "Don't go tellin' Alice, she'll go potty."

Eddie laughed aloud. "You ain't got no chance. I bet somebody's already knockin' at your door. You'd better get orf 'ome before Alice comes in 'ere wiv 'er fightin' irons on."

Frank looked over to where Joe was sitting. "You all right, mate?"

Joe got up gingerly and leaned on the counter. "Did yer see the size of 'is plates o' meat? I got one of 'em right in me 'alf a tea service."

Frank laughed, "C'mon, Eddie, fill 'em up. I got a thirst on."

Ben Morrison climbed the wooden stairs and let himself into his flat in Tooley Buildings. For a while he stood in the darkness looking down into the empty street, the wharves and warehouses opposite ghostly in the dusk. Away down to his left were the premises of Messrs James Brown & Sons Ltd. He could read the gold lettering above his place of employment clearly. For six years he had been bookkeeper for that company, and until the war had broken out his employers held him in high esteem. However, things had changed dramatically at the start of hostilities, when Major Brown had asked Ben's intentions. When he heard of his bookkeeper's decision not to don a uniform, Major Brown, MC, DSO, became apoplectic. He made it

plain that unless Ben had a change of heart and decided to
fight for King and Country, then it would be better if he
'damn well cleared off'. Major Brown was aware of the
tribunal hearing and Ben knew that he was on borrowed
time.

As he looked down into the dark street his thoughts
were troubled. He grieved for Lucy, who seemed to be
taking the whole affair very badly, and he was grateful for
the Suttons' friendly attitude. Alice Sutton was kindness
itself, although Frank Sutton appeared to be slightly offhand at times. Connie often chided him in a good-
humoured way, but then it was understandable. She was
worried about Danny, the news of his injuries had upset
her and made her irritable. He knew that he must bear the
burden. The church was important to him, and he hoped
that one day he would have enough money saved to attend
the theological college and become a Methodist minister.
For the present though he had to get through the tribunal.
He was aware that it might mean going to prison. The
thought of being locked away terrified him, and he shivered as he stood deep in thought in his quiet flat.

Down in the street below Ben saw a young girl hurrying
along. Coming towards her was a young man. They met
and embraced, the young man put his arm around the
girl's waist and the two tripped away happily into the
shadows of the deserted wharves. Up above the roofs a
cresent moon came out of the cloud, and in the distance
Ben could hear the clatter of a tram. Footsteps on the
stairs jogged him out of his reverie and he closed the curtains and lit the gas lamp. When he heard Lucy's distinctive knock, he opened the door. The two embraced,
Lucy kissing him lightly on the lips. Lucy wanted Ben to
hold her tight, to smother her with kisses, but Ben moved
out of reach as she took her coat to hang it on the back of
the door.

"I've been thinking, Lucy," he said, pacing the room.
"Supposing I get through the tribunal okay, I'll still be

forced to leave the job. I might get sent to another part of the country to do war work. I believe making weapons and ammunition is tantamount to fighting and I can't do it, it would be a betrayal of all my principles. Refusing work of that nature would mean I'd be sent to prison. I couldn't face it, Lucy, I couldn't.''

Lucy Sutton looked at the tormented figure before her. She saw his pale, worried face, his nervous hands that seemed to be forever fidgeting, and his deep-set blue eyes, and she was torn between strong passions. She wanted to go to him and shake him, and she desired him to come to her. She wanted him to forget everything for just one night, and desire her with the same intensity that made her tremble. She wanted to scream out, but instead she just looked at the pathetic figure who paced the floor in front of her.

She had made her decision when she left home that evening, and knew she would go ahead with what she had planned. She might fail, but Lucy knew it could not go on like this any longer. Slowly she stood up and walked to the window. With a quick movement she pulled back the curtains. Ben gasped, ''Lucy! The black-out!''

''Damn the black-out! Turn off the lamp.''

Ben stood rooted to the spot.

''Did you hear? Turn off the light,'' Lucy said in a low and husky voice.

Ben reached up and turned the tap of the gas lamp. The room was plunged into darkness and Lucy moved towards the pale figure before her. Her hands reached for him and their bodies touched. Ben tensed, looking down at the round face, and in the dimness of the room he saw the desire in Lucy's wide eyes. She had her back to the window and her hair seemed to shine against the night light. Her lips were parted and her breath came quickly. Almost automatically his hands came up and stroked her hair. Ben felt its softness, and he closed his eyes and breathed in its fragrance. Lucy nestled close to him, her rounded figure soft to his touch, as Ben kissed her neck and trembled at the excitement. In the quietness of the darkened room above the wharves he could hear her rapid breathing. Her lips searched for his and her kiss was urgent and demanding. Ben felt out of his depth, and he could only gasp as Lucy pulled him down onto the hard floor.

Heavy, faltering footsteps in the street below carried up to the silent room. The drunken songster halted and clung to a lamppost for support, his broad Scotch accent ringing out as he struggled with a rendering of 'I Belong To Glasgow'. His singing died away in the night, and up in the small flat the lovers nestled close to each other, neither feeling the need to speak. For Ben the act of loving had been brief, over almost as soon as it had started; his body felt relaxed and heavy. For Lucy it had been intense; her passions had not been extinguished, rather they had cooled. For her it was a triumph, and she breathed slowly and contentedly as she lay against his chest. It was the first time for her, and she was content. There had been no expectations and no disappointment, only the knowledge that at last they had been able to step outside of their cloistered existence and express their love together. Lucy savoured the serenity of the moment. There would be other times. She was happy and she silenced his embarrassed concern with two fingers pressed against his lips. She rested her head against Ben's chest and listened to his quiet heartbeat.

Chapter Seven

Monday dawned dry and warm. The heavy, billowing clouds held rain and the air was clammy. The threatened storm finally broke at eight o'clock, with claps of thunder and frightening flashes of lightning. Raindrops beat against the windows in Dawson Street and water ran along the gutters in fast-flowing streams, spilling over the roof-top guttering and pouring out from the cracked and holed down-pipes onto the pavement below. The rain washed away the dust and the hop-scotch chalkings; it penetrated the ill-fitting roof slates and caused new stains to appear on the upstairs ceilings. The storm delighted the young children who watched as the growing puddle spread out rapidly over the cobbles. Wide-eyed and impatient, they waited for the rain to abate, and they made paper boats and loaded them with matchstick cargoes.

At number 26 Dawson Street, Danny sealed the envelope and waited. His letter to Alison explained the problem he had in getting down to Dover and suggested that they might be able to meet in London. He also penned a few lines saying how much he wanted to see her again, and he hoped that she would feel the same. It was with trepidation that Danny sealed the letter, after seriously considering tearing it up and starting afresh. Maybe Alison had forgotten all about him. With lots of patients to tend and all the chatting-up from homesick young soldiers, it would be understandable for her to have put him out of her mind. Three weeks had passed since he had seen her, and already the picture of her in his memory had faded. Could he hope that Alison would be interested in seeing him again? He wanted it to be so. He had to make the decision to forget all about Kathy. She was in his past now. Alison could figure very much in his future . . . In any case, it would only mean the cost of a stamp to find out, and he put the letter in his coat pocket.

Alice Sutton had a serious expression on her face as she cleared away the breakfast things. She had had words with Frank that morning before he set off to work. It was bad enough him getting into a fight, without ruining his only suit as well. Alice would be able to sew up the shoulder, but Frank had also put his knee through the trousers. When the rain stopped she would go around to see if Mrs Simpson could do one of her invisible mending jobs. It would probably mean a patch, but he would just have to put up with it. There were enough worries without Frank adding to them. There was Lucy, who had most likely got herself soaking wet on her way round to Ben. She had insisted on going with him to the tribunal this morning and would not wait for the rain to stop. Then there was Danny. He had only been home for a couple of days and already he had come home drunk on two occasions. Maggie's children looked like they were both coming down with something, and the front bedroom ceiling was dripping water. Alice Sutton sighed to herself and shook the tablecloth into the hearth. She was also concerned about the wagging tongues on the street. There had been the odd remark directed towards her about Ben, but she had shaken her head and walked on by when neighbours asked if her daughter's young man had received his call-up papers yet. There was another occasion when two neighbours who were chatting together at the green-grocer's shop raised their voices, saying that in their opinion all 'conchies' should be sent to prison with hard labour. Alice had ignored the remark, which angered the two paragons even more. As she pottered about waiting for the rain to ease Alice Sutton felt worried. It was Lucy she was most concerned for. There would be much anger directed towards her daughter as time went on, and it would be bound to upset her. For herself she didn't worry. If the neighbours chose to adopt that attitude then they could all go and get stuffed. There were other more important things to worry about.

At nine-thirty the rain stopped and Danny walked up to the tiny post office in Tooley Street to get a stamp. It was not quite so oppressive after the downpour and the street looked clean. As he left the post office he saw a number 70 tram approaching and he ran up to the stop just as the tram shuddered to a halt. Danny climbed aboard and sat down on the lower deck. The short run had made him breathless and he realised with a pang of anger that he was far from being fully fit. He sorted out tuppence from a fistful of coppers and handed it to the bored-looking conductor who flipped off a ticket from a clip-board and slipped it into a ticket punch before handing it to Danny. The tram swayed and rocked its way along towards Dockhead and jerked to a stop once more. Danny could see The Crown public house lying back from the road and it made him think of that Saturday evening with Kathy. The tram moved off and swung around a sharp bend into Jamaica Road. Danny was brought out of his reveries by the conductor shouting "Rovverhive Tunnel" in a sing-song voice.

The young cockney walked along Brunel Road, which ran alongside the approach to the road tunnel. At the end of the turning was the Labour Exchange building and Danny could see a small queue waiting outside. There was an entrance at the side of the building which Danny was directed to, and it opened into a hall where a few people were sitting around on wooden benches. A weary-looking individual sat at a desk at one end of the room and he sighed as Danny presented him with his papers. Once the preliminary questions were over, the young ex-serviceman was told to take a seat and wait.

"Got a snout, mate?"

Danny looked at the elderly character next to him and shook his head. The man turned his attention to the floor, hoping there would be an odd discarded cigarette butt lying around. The green linoleum offered nothing to his watery eyes and he turned back to Danny. "Goin' fer a job, then?" he enquired in a squeaking voice.

Danny was about to say that he wasn't waiting for a tram when he saw something in the elderly man's face. The pale blue eyes were dull, and the lined, unshaven face looked thin and trouble-worn. The stranger's expression was apathetic and seemed in keeping with his general appearance — his shoes were down-at-heel and his clothes were shabby. Yet there was something else, there was a friendliness about his face, and Danny swallowed his hard words. "I'm signin' on fer work. I'm just out o' the Kate."

"I was in the last turn-out," the man replied. "Nineteen I was when they sent us ter France. I got gassed. Still get the wheeziness sometimes. Me doctor said I should pack up the smokin', but I told 'im straight, yer gotta die o' somefink."

Danny smiled and looked up at the metal rafters in the high ceiling and at the poster-covered walls. One poster showed a ship sinking with the words 'Careless Talk Costs Lives' emblazoned over it. Another poster showed an air raid warden wearing a gas mask and there was a list of instructions about what to do in the event of a gas attack. Another poster was headed 'Conscientious Objectors'. The poster was too far away for Danny to be able to read what was said below the heading, but his thoughts turned to Ben Morrison. He would probably be at the tribunal by now.

The elderly character had managed to scrounge a cigarette and came back grinning. He lit up and was immediately racked by a fit of coughing. When he had recovered sufficiently he wiped his eyes on a dirty handkerchief and nudged Danny. " 'Ere, son, if the bleeders offer yer work at the lead mills, turn it down. I was there fer six months. It nearly finished me, I can tell yer. What wiv the stink an' the 'eat, I lost over a stone in weight. Can't afford ter lose that much, can I? My ole woman reckons I'm so skinny, I've gotta be out in the rain fer ages before I get wet. Me doctor told me ter go on oats, porridge I mean. Trouble is, me ole woman ain't much of a cook. She made us some this mornin' an' it looked like bloody cement. When I come ter fink of it, it tasted like bleedin' cement as well!''

"Mr Daniel Sutton!" a voice called out, and Danny looked up to see a bespectacled man beckoning from an open doorway.

"Good luck, son," his new friend spluttered between fits of coughing as Danny got up from the bench.

The small office contained a desk, a filing cabinet and little else. More posters adorned the walls: grinning workers staring out from behind machines, their toothpaste smiles looking maniacal to Danny as he glanced at them. The wording urged everyone to join the struggle for victory. The official told Danny to take a seat and he himself sat down at the desk with a loud sigh. When he had made himself quite comfortable he took off his glasses and proceeded to polish them on a large white handkerchief. Finally satisfied, he put them back on and addressed himself to the papers on the desk.

Danny felt an immediate dislike for the man. He slumped down in his chair and glared. The official began his routine by first resting his elbows on the desk and tapping the tips of his fingers together, next he put his thumbs against his forehead in a display of deep concentration and started a low humming. Danny had an almost irresistible urge to scream some obscenity into the official's ear but he ignored the temptation and looked back at the posters.

"I see you are unfit for heavy work," the man said at last. "That makes it rather awkward for me to fit you in."

"It makes it rather awkward fer me as well," Danny said sharply.

"Quite, but I can't fit you in at the lead mills, and I can't see where I can send you. Most of the jobs I've got to offer are for fit men. Do you see?"

Danny could see quite clearly, and his temper began to rise. "Look, I can't 'elp it if I'm not A 1. I didn't ask ter get shot at, an' I —"

The official stopped Danny by holding both hands up in front of his chest. "You haven't got a trade, have you, Mr Sutton? You see I'm looking for skilled workers for munition factories, or for people to be trained to work lathes and milling machines. You don't fall into that category unfortunately."

Danny's eyes focused on the official's rather bulbous nose and his thick-rimmed spectacles, which made his eyes seem like two large marbles. His long, thin fingers were tapping the paper in front of him in irritation, and Danny noticed the cluster of well-chewed pencils sticking out from a round tin. Suddenly the official grabbed one of the pencils and started to make notes. When he had finished he leaned back in his chair and sucked on the pencil, his eyes staring at his unskilled client.

Herbert Snelling had interviewed a few of these ex-service types recently, and in his opinion they were an insolent lot. After all, they shouldn't expect special treatment and, as he had remarked to his colleagues, most of them were probably making heavy weather of their disabilities. A few weeks in the lead mills would have got them back into shape. Sutton looked fit enough to do manual work. It was a pity the Ministry were so tolerant of those types. Everyone had to make sacrifices these days, as he had explained to his wife when she remarked that it was time she had a new coat. It was all so irritating, he mused as he chewed on the pencil.

Danny was getting more angry. He felt as though the official was expecting him to fall down on his knees and plead for a job with tears in his eyes and with his hands clasped together in anguish, just like in one of those old

84

silent pictures. Danny had other ideas, although he was, too, aware of the consequences. After all, he had come here for a job, not to provoke a magistrate into giving him six months' hard labour for assault. Danny took a deep breath and sat up straight in his chair. "Surely you've got somefink ter give us? There's gotta be plenty o' jobs about, now that everybody's gettin' called up?"

The official looked at Danny through his thick lenses and reluctantly pulled open the drawer of a small cabinet that sat at his elbow. He hummed tunelessly as he fingered through the small white cards until he found the right one. "Here we are, Mr Sutton, here's something you could do. The Acme Glass Company are looking for glass inspectors. It's a sitting down job, no hard work."

The young cockney's heart dropped. Bonky Williams had told him all about glass inspectors. He knew that he would not last more than a day at that job and he shook his head. "Yer mean ter tell me that's the only job yer got fer me? What about all those vacancies frew the call-up? That's a rubbish job, it's soul-destroyin'. Yer must 'ave somefink else in that box."

The official looked at Danny over his glasses. "I don't think you understand. All those jobs you talk about are being filled by women. Yes, women. It releases the men for war-work and the forces, you see. We've got vacancies for manual workers, but you are disabled, aren't you?"

It was the emphasis placed on the end of the sentence that finally brought Danny to the boil. He got up and put his hands on his hips, his pale face flushed angrily and the corner of his mouth twitched. "Now listen you," he exclaimed, his voice trembling, "I've bin sittin' 'ere like a naughty school kid who's waitin' ter get 'is arse caned! Yer bin pissin' me about wiv yer bloody papers an' yer stupid remarks. Anybody listenin' ter you would fink I wanted ter be disabled! D'yer know what it was like out in France? No, course yer don't!"

The official opened his mouth to speak but Danny

shouted a tirade of abuse. "If you fink I'm gonna sit 'ere an' listen ter you prattin' off wiv yer snide remarks, yer got anuvver fink comin'. What wiv yer twiddlin' yer poxy fingers an' eatin' yer bloody pencils, an' lookin' at me like I'm somefink the cat dragged in, an' then 'avin' the gall ter offer me a poxy glass inspector's job! I reckon yer takin' the piss!"

The official's face went white and the small cluster of purple veins on his temple started pulsating. He stood up and waved Danny to the door, "I'm not going to talk to you any more. I shall put in a report about your behaviour. It will be for the manager to decide what's to be done."

Danny leaned forward menacingly and the frightened Herbert Snelling backed away. "I tell yer somefink else, four-eyes, yer can do what yer like, an' yer poxy manager can do the same. If yer fink I'm gonna sit in front of bottles all day wiv a 'ammer in me 'and, yer more stupid than I thought yer was."

Mr Snelling waved his unhelpful client to the door again. "We'll see what the manager has to say."

"Get stuffed, an' tell yer poxy manager ter do the same," Danny sneered as he stormed out of the office and into the coolness of the street.

Back in the office the harassed Mr Snelling sat down heavily in his chair. What was that he said about a hammer? he thought. What would a glass inspector be doing with a hammer? These ex-soldiers are getting worse!

Another member of the Sutton household was on her way to encounter officialdom that Monday morning. Lucy slipped her arm through Ben's as they left Tooley Buildings and walked purposefully along the busy street. Horse carts were lined up outside the wharves and the bored nags were snorting into their nosebags. The narrow lanes that led down to the water-front were crowded as vehicles and carts were being loaded. Bundles of foodstuffs and other commodities were lashed tight and kicked out from loop-holes to hang suspended from crane chains. The loads were then slowly lowered onto waiting transport to the cries of: "Up a bit! Whoa! 'Old it, yer silly bastard!"

The shouts of the dockers rose above the din of clanking cranes and revving vans as the working week began. Along the busy Tooley Street lorries and horse carts continued to arrive, and people were hurrying about their business. Well-dressed office workers carried brief-cases and bundles of papers, and heavy-booted dockers and stevedores moved about on the street. Trams clattered by with their warning bells clanging, and the sounds of the river trade reverberated down along the narrow side lanes. The signs of war were apparent in the busy dockland street. Men were pasting up stark reminders that 'Careless Talk Costs Lives' and about what to do in the case of a gas attack. A military convoy of trucks clattered past towing heavy guns, and a bored-looking policeman ambled along, a gas mask pack and steel helmet slung over his shoulder.

Lucy gripped Ben's arm tightly as they made their way to the magistrate's court for the tribunal hearing at ten o'clock. A few people were hanging around outside the court building as Lucy and Ben approached. Ben was silent, his stomach tightening as they climbed the few steps and entered the high-ceilinged hall. A flight of wide marble steps led up to a narrow balcony which circled the hall and gave access to the first floor courtrooms. Some people were sitting on polished wooden benches with worried looks on their faces, while others studied the court schedule. Ben motioned Lucy to the notice-board and saw that Ben's hearing was to be in court 4. His name was near the top of the list and he gave Lucy a wry smile.

"At least we should get it over with quickly," he said.

They took a seat and watched as more people crowded into the hall and policemen moved among the crowd calling out names from their lists. Ben's name was called and he was directed to the upper floor. The lovers sat down close together, holding hands and gazing into each other's eyes. Lucy saw the fear in his face, and she smiled encouragingly. She felt that they now belonged to each other, come what may, and Lucy was determined to remain strong for both of them.

The courtroom was panelled in oak and the windows were high up so that the sun's rays did not penetrate down into the well of the court. Ben stood facing the five-man panel. The person seated in the centre announced himself as the chairman and each of the others introduced themselves in turn. Ben could sense the hostility as he waited for the chairman to begin. A sheet of paper was passed along from hand to hand, and he could only guess that it was his written statement to the panel. There was a slight mumbling from the back of the court and the chairman looked over his spectacles reprovingly. Ben knew that Lucy was sitting behind him and it gave him comfort.

"You are Benjamin Morrison of 16 Tooley Buildings, Tooley Street, Bermondsey?"

Ben answered in the affirmative.

"You registered on January the 6th as a conscientious objector, and subsequently presented this tribunal with a statement setting out your reasons for doing so?"

Ben nodded and was immediately rebuked by the chairman.

"You must answer. A nod will not do. Is that quite clear?"

"Yes."

"Have you anyone to speak on your behalf?"

"No, but I sent in a letter from —" But the chairman interrupted him in mid-sentence.

"I'm aware of the letter, Mr Morrison, I was coming to that."

Ben gripped the rail in front of him. The hostility was becoming obvious and he began to tremble.

The chairman glanced at the person next to him and the questioning continued. "I have a letter here from the

Reverend John Harris of the Tower Bridge Road Methodist Mission. He states that you are a regular attender at that church, and he goes on to say that you are a part-time youth club leader. Is that correct?"

"Yes."

Another member of the tribunal took up the questioning. "The letter also states that you intend to study for the cloth. Is that so?"

"Yes."

"How long ago did you come to this decision?"

Ben coughed nervously. "I first decided over two years ago."

"Are you sure you did not come to this decision after the outbreak of war?"

"No, sir."

"Can you provide this tribunal with any proof that would substantiate your assertion, Mr Morrison?"

"No, sir. You only have my word, as a Christian."

"Mr Morrison," the interviewer went on, "do you consider it wrong for this country of ours to be at war with Germany?"

Ben's knuckles tightened on the rail. "I consider it wrong for people to kill each other."

"You think it is all right for the Germans to march into this country and kill our people? Because that is exactly what would happen if we did not defend ourselves."

Ben looked hard at the questioner. "No, I think it is wrong for Germans to kill, or for anyone to kill another human being."

"I see, and are you conversant with the Holy Bible?"

"Yes."

"Does the Bible tell you that killing is wrong?"

"Yes."

"And does it not tell of how God led the Israelites into battle?"

"Yes."

The members of the tribunal exchanged glances and the

chairman smirked. "Tell me, Mr Morrison, were you brought up in a Christian family?"

"Yes, both my parents were practising Christians."

"Did your parents ever chastise you as a child?"

"I was punished for doing wrong."

"Were you beaten?"

"No, I was sent to bed early, or had privileges taken away."

"Are you prepared for the results of non-resistance?"

"I know I must take the consequences. I realise that."

"Let me put this to you, Mr Morrison. God forbid the Germans ever get here, but in the event, if you happened to see a wounded German soldier lying in the street, would you render first aid?"

Ben felt himself being slowly forced into a corner from which there was no escape. He took a deep breath before answering. "I feel that every human being has the right to receive medical assistance, regardless."

"Regardless of what?"

"Regardless of the fact that most people see it as being wrong to aid the enemy. I feel sure in my mind that we are all one family under God."

"Are you aware that the Royal Army Medical Corps picks up wounded soldiers from both sides in war, and that the medics are strictly a non-combatant corps?"

Ben sensed that the *coup de grâce* was not far off. "Yes, I would expect that to be so."

"Do you still say that despite what has been said you still object to wearing a military uniform?"

"I feel that a military uniform represents a willingness of the wearer to kill."

The tribunal members conferred for a few seconds, and Ben looked around at the panelled walls. He did not turn completely round to face Lucy, but he felt for her and knew of the anguish she was suffering. He looked back at the tribunal members and saw the nodding of heads.

"Mr Morrison," the chairman began, "I suggest to you

that you have been wasting our time. You have told us in the written statement that you intend to study for Holy Orders, but you cannot substantiate this. Reverend Harris also says in his letter that you intend to study for the Church. That is not a substantiation, it is merely a third party reiterating what you have said of your intentions — an indication of intent. You have provided no evidence of any communication between yourself and the Theological College. Reverend Harris does not tell us in his letter when you first confided in him about your intentions of taking Holy Orders. I put it to you that you first indicated your interest in the college after the outbreak of war. We have made note of the fact that you have stated you would succour the wounded. That is the role of the Royal Army Medical Corps. Therefore, the finding of this tribunal is that you will be called up into a non-combatant corps, subject to you passing the army medical. You will have to apply to be posted at the time of your medical. That is all."

Chapter Eight

Alice Sutton sat in her small parlour talking to Annie Barnes. Annie was an old and trusted friend from the days when the two danced the ragtime and wept unashamedly into lace handkerchiefs each Saturday at the silent picture show. The two went back a long way, to the days of horse buses and wide summer bonnets, the days of hard toil in the local tannery for a few shillings a week. Alice and Annie had lived in the same street since they both married, within a year of each other. Annie Barnes was a confidante, and for her Alice made an exception to her rule of keeping the family business away from gossiping neighbours.

"I tell yer, Annie, I'm fed up wiv the lot of it. I 'ad ter take 'is suit round ter Fran Simpson terday. You 'eard all about it, I s'pose?"

Annie nodded. "Bit old fer fightin', ain't 'e?" she said, her florid face puckering.

"It's that bleedin' bitter, gets 'im real narky when 'e's 'ad a few," Alice said, brushing an imaginary crumb from her dress and folding her thin arms.

Annie Barnes looked out of the window from her easy chair and saw the deepening redness settling over the chimney pots of the houses opposite. The evening was warm, and the lengthening shadows lent a tranquillity to the neat and tidy parlour. Outside in the street a few children played, their happy voices carrying into the house as they made the most of their games before being called in to face a scrubbing brush and Lifebuoy soap which tortured the eyes and stung the skin. In the quietness the metallic ticking of the clock on the mantelshelf sounded unusually loudly. Annie stirred her tea thoughtfully and waited for her friend to begin again. Alice made herself comfortable and sipped her tea.

Unable to bear the suspense any longer, Annie Barnes broached the subject. "Well, an' 'ow did young Ben get on at the tribunal?"

Alice put down the cup and folded her arms. " 'E's gotta go in."

"Yer mean 'e's gettin' called up?" Annie asked, surprise showing on her face.

"From what Lucy told me, they was right gits. They've told Ben 'e's gotta go in the non-compatible corps or somefink," Alice answered.

"Yer mean like the medical blokes who look after the wounded?"

"That's right. Ter be honest wiv yer, I can't see Ben doin' that sort o' job. 'E ain't cut out fer it."

"Don't you fret about that, Alice. It's surprisin' the fings yer do when yer 'ave to. Look at Fran Simpson's eldest boy. Times I've seen 'im come 'ome from school cryin' from bein' bullied. 'E's a sergeant in the Coldstreams now."

"I 'ope yer right, Annie. Poor Lucy's that cut up about it. From what she said, 'er Ben didn't 'ave much choice. If 'e'd 'ave refused they would 'ave locked 'im up and chucked away the key."

Annie put the tea cup back onto the table and reached inside her apron. She took out a tiny silver box and tapped on the lid with two fingers. "Wanna pinch?"

Alice shook her head.

" 'Ow's your Connie? I saw 'er the uvver day with that young sailor, what's 'is name, Jimmy, ain't it?" Annie spluttered as the snuff took effect.

"Jimmy Ellis. 'E's a nice boy, got luvverly manners. 'Is leave's up ternight. I do 'ope nuffink 'appens to 'im, a lot of our ships are gettin' sunk. It's a right worry, what wiv one fing and anuvver."

94

Annie smiled. " 'E'll be all right. 'Fore yer know where you are 'e'll be 'ome on leave again."

"I do 'ope so, Annie. All this trouble and strife, an' the worry of the invasion . . ."

Annie looked up at the window, as though she expected a German soldier to be peering in, then back at Alice. "You don't really fink they'll get 'ere, do yer? I mean ter say, they've gotta come over the water. What's our boys gonna do, stan' by an' let em walk in?"

"I dunno," Alice replied. "I tell yer what though, that bleedin' pamphlet they pushed frew the letterbox scared the daylights outta me."

"What, that one about the invasion? My Bill tore it up, 'e said there was nuffink ter worry about, but I'm not so sure."

Alice got up and picked up the teapot. "Fer Gawd sake let's change the subject. Wanna 'nuvver cup o' tea?"

Annie took the refilled cup and went into her thoughtful stirring routine. " 'Ere, Alice, I see your Danny this mornin'. 'E looked like 'e was in an 'urry. I see 'im runnin' fer a tram up the top."

Alice shook her head. "That boy's worryin' me. 'E 'ad a barney down the Labour Exchange terday. Apparently they offered 'im a job in some glass factory. I couldn't get the rights of it, but 'e went mad. Told the bloke down there ter poke 'is job. Gawd knows what's gonna 'appen now. I s'pose they'll suspend 'im fer six weeks, that's what usually 'appens when yer get lippy, or don't take the job they offer yer."

"It's a bleedin' shame if yer ask me," Annie remarked. "Fellers are comin' back wounded an' what 'appens? They get some bloody jumped up git expectin' 'em ter take the first fing they offer. Bloody disgrace I calls it."

"Yer gotta be fair though, Annie. That Danny's always bin 'ot 'eaded. It seems like 'e's got worse since 'e's come 'ome, 'e can be a cow-son at times."

Annie sipped her tea. "Still, yer gotta give 'im a chance,

luv. After all, 'e's only bin 'ome a few days. It'll take time, an' there's no 'arm in 'im.''

Alice smiled at her friend. "No, there's no 'arm in 'im, but I do wish 'e'd find a nice girl an' settle down.''

" 'E's sweet on young Kathy Thompson, ain't 'e, Alice?''

"I dunno, I fink she's goin' aroun' wiv that Jack Mason.''

Annie puffed, "She wants ter keep away from 'im, 'e's a bad one, is Jack Mason. My Bill's told me a few stories about 'im.''

"It's 'er life, Annie. From what I can gavver, 'er farver leads 'er a dog's life. 'E's always drunk, an' 'e knocks 'is wife about. I see 'er the uvver day wiv a shiner.''

"It's enough ter drive the poor kid away, Alice.''

The street noises had died down and dusk began to settle over Dawson Street. The clock ticked loudly, and the two friends lapsed into comfortable silence, their conversation exhausted. Finally, Annie Barnes yawned and stood up. "Well, luv, I better be orf 'ome. My ole man'll fink I've run away. What time is your lot comin' in?''

Alice looked up at the clock. "Frank shouldn't be long, 'e went to a union meetin'. Connie an' 'er young man's gorn ter the pictures. Gawd knows what time our Danny'll walk in. That Johnny Ross called roun' ter see 'im an' they marched out wivout a leave nor bye. Lucy shouldn't be long, she's roun' Ben's place.''

Annie buttoned up her coat. "You know, I envy you wiv your crowd. I often wish me an' Bill could of 'ad children. Still, it wasn't ter be.''

Alice went to the front door with her friend. "I tell yer one fing, Annie, they're more bleedin' trouble now than when they were babies. At least yer could wash 'em an' put 'em ter bed. Yer knew where they were then.''

Annie Barnes started up the street. " 'Night, luv.''

" 'Night, Annie.''

* * *

Most Monday evenings were quiet in The Globe. A few regulars either leaned on the bar counter or sat around with half-filled glasses at their elbows. In one corner two young men were engaged in earnest conversation, empty beer glasses on the table beside them testifying that the discussion was proving thirsty work.

Johnny Ross put his arms on the table and leaned forward, his dark, sallow features taking on a serious look as he made his point. "Listen, Danny, yer wastin' yer time down the poxy Labour Exchange. Come on now, what's on offer down those places? All the good jobs are snapped up. If yer wanna sweat yer cods off, that's okay, but yer gotta fink of your condition."

Danny Sutton drained his glass and put it down on the table with a bang. "That's the second time I've 'ad that said ter me since I've bin 'ome. I ain't exactly due fer the knacker's yard yet, Johnny boy."

The sallow-faced young man got up and moved to the bar with a pronounced limp; he pulled a thick wad of money from his back pocket and peeled off a one pound note. "Two pints of ale, Eddie, an' one fer Yer Lordship."

Eddie Kirkland gave the youngster an old-fashioned look as he pulled on the pump. "You wanna be careful flashin' that roll in 'ere, Johnny boy. The law was in 'ere last night askin' questions about stolen cases of corned beef. Seems someone broke inter one of the ware'ouses in Tooley Street. They asked me if anybody 'ad offered me any bent cans, bent meanin' crooked. I told 'em, 'What d'yer fink this is, a bloody café or somefink?'."

Johnny grinned slyly. "It's all right, Eddie, I 'ad a win down the dogs."

The landlord placed two frothing glasses of ale in front of his customer and picked up the pound note. "This is a new one. What yer doin', printin' 'em?"

As Johnny carefully carried the drinks back to the table, the door opened and Biff Bowden walked in with Shady

Lady in tow. "Evenin' all," he said breezily. "Gi's a Guinness, Eddie, an' a nice arrowroot fer the next champion."

Two old cronies in one corner were exchanging whispers and the one with the large walrus moustache nearly choked into his beer. "Ere, Biff, what's that all over your dog's coat, flea powder?"

Biff gave the old man a wicked glance as he ordered the dog to sit. "Don't you take the piss outta Shady. She's in trainin' fer the big race at New Cross. Them arrowroots are good fer 'er teef."

"Won't do much fer 'er legs though, Biff," Eddie butted in.

Biff Bowden took a saucer from his coat pocket and poured some of his Guinness into it. "C'mon, Shady, get that down yer."

The dog looked up at Biff with large, doleful eyes before lapping up the beer.

"Yer gonna kill that dog wiv kindness, Biff," Eddie said, shaking his head sadly.

"All right, you can all laugh. One day she'll be a champion, won't yer girl?"

Shady Lady shook herself and a spray of powder dropped onto the floor. One of the old cronies jumped up in mock horror, took off his cap and brought it down sharply onto the table. "Got yer!" he shouted.

"What's goin' on over there?" Eddie called out.

"Did you see that flea jump onto the table? Big as a tanner it was! Came orf as that mutt shook 'erself," the elderly character exclaimed, grinning evilly.

Johnny put the beer down on the table and he raised his eyes towards the ceiling. "It's gettin' like a nut 'ouse in 'ere, what wiv them two, and that silly bastard Biff."

Danny looked at the frothing pint of beer for a few seconds then he said: "So yer reckon Tony Allen can fix us up wiv some work?"

"No sweat," Johnny said with a confident nod of his

head. "I've told 'im all about yer gettin' wounded at Dunkirk, an' I said yer done lots o' different fings since yer left school. I told 'im yer used ter take bets fer ole Tubby Green down Dock'ead. I fink 'e'll fix yer up wiv a bookie's pitch round 'ere. I said yer can be trusted an' that's what counts wiv Tony. Anyway, 'e told me ter 'ave a word wiv yer an' let 'im know if yer was interested in workin' fer 'im.''

"When does 'e want an answer?" Danny asked, picking up his filled glass.

"No sweat. Come down New Cross dogs wiv me on Thursday, yer can 'ave a talk wiv Tony Allen there. What d'yer say?''

"What 'ave I got ter lose? Only me freedom. All right, Johnny, yer on.''

The pub door opened again and Bonky Williams staggered in.

"Look out," Danny said out of the corner of his mouth, "there's Eddie's favourite customer jus' come in.''

Bonky reeled over to the counter and blew hard as he leaned on the wet surface for support. "Gi's a d-drink," he hiccuped.

"Where you bin, spendin' all yer money in some uvver pub?" Eddie mocked.

Bonky's one good eye rolled around in its socket. "I bin 'el-'elpin' Flash 'Arry wiv 'is s-stall.''

"Christ! Bonky, ain't you 'ad a wash? I can smell the fish from 'ere,'' Eddie gasped.

"W-wash? Course I 'ad a wash. Wh-what d'yer fink I am? D'yer fink I-I'd come in 'ere all smelly an' dirty?''

Eddie put down a pint of ale on the counter and leaned back noticeably. "Go an' sit down, Bonky, 'fore yer fall down.''

Bonky staggered over to where his two friends were sitting and almost fell into a chair. " 'Ello, fellers, 'ow-'ow yer doin' then?''

"Bloody 'ell, you smell like Billin'sgate," Johnny remarked, pulling a face.

"Don't you start. I-I've 'ad enough wi-wiv 'im," Bonky spluttered, pointing in the general direction of the counter.

Danny picked up his pint. "I'm finishin' this an' I'm off 'ome, Johnny. We can't talk any more. I might see yer before Thursday."

Bonky had swivelled around in his chair and tried to fix the two old gentlemen with his eye. The man nearest wiped his moustache on the back of his hand and returned Bonky's unsteady look with a glare. Bonky's face creased in a lop-sided grin as he reached in his pocket for a handkerchief. His intention was not lost on the elderly gent.

"If you take that bloody eye out once more in front o' me, Bonky, I swear I'll knock yer uvver one out."

Danny pulled Bonky around. "Look, we're goin' 'ome. You be'ave yerself, or me an' Johnny'll take yer out an' drop yer in the nearest 'orsetroff, understood?"

Bonky's good eye tried to focus on Danny's face but his head drooped and he slowly raised his hand. "It's okay, I'm-I'm goin' 'ome meself."

Danny got up. "C'mon, Johnny, let's walk the piss-artist 'ome. I'm ready fer the sack."

Earlier that evening, Connie left the brewery where she worked as a telephonist and saw Kathy Thompson ahead of her on the pavement. Kathy was employed as a typist in a nearby seed merchant's offices. Connie hurried to catch up with her, and the two exchanged smiles and fell into step. Factory hooters were blaring out their end of day racket and tired workers were plodding homewards or joining the bus and tram queues. The sky was cloudless and the sun had started to dip down over the rooftops as the two girls from the backstreets reached Tower Bridge

Road. They had been chatting away, and while they waited to cross the road Kathy looked at Connie as if to say something, but she stayed silent. Connie sensed her need to talk and she took Kathy's arm as they started to cross. " 'Ow's yer love life, Kath?"

Kathy saw the impish look in her companion's eyes and she grinned. "Don't ask me. Men — I'm fed up wiv 'em! 'Ow you doin'?"

Connie's face became serious. "My feller's in the navy. 'E's goin' back off leave ternight."

"Yeah, I've seen yer tergevver. Nice lookin' boy," Kathy said. "You two goin' steady?"

Connie nodded. "Jimmy wants us ter get engaged when 'e's finished this trip."

"What about yer folks?" Kathy asked. "Will they mind?"

"I don't fink so. Me dad'll puff a bit, an' me mum'll give me a talk, but they won't try ter stop me."

"I wish me dad was like that." Kathy paused. "Yer know I'm goin' out wiv Jack Mason?"

Connie nodded. "Yeah, I do. Yer feller's pretty well known around here ain't he?"

"Yeah, 'e was in wiv all the big villains once. 'E works in partners wiv Tony Allen now. You know Tony Allen the bookie?"

Connie nodded. Just as they got to the corner of Clink Lane she asked, " 'Ave yer bumped inter Danny since 'e's bin back?" She wondered what Kathy felt about Danny now and wanted to see her reaction — she knew that Danny was still keen on the girl.

Two spots showed on Kathy's cheeks and Connie didn't think it was due to the exertion of the short walk.

"I seen 'im on Saturday night. 'E was at Tony's party wiv 'is mate Johnny Ross," Kathy said casually as she stopped at the street corner.

" 'E didn't tell me," Connie pouted. "But then that's

Danny all over. 'E'd be makin' 'is weddin' plans 'fore 'e'd tell any of us.''

Kathy felt that their conversation was getting too painful. She moved into the turning. ''I've gotta go,'' she said. ''I promised ter give me mum a bit of 'elp. See yer, Connie.''

Connie waved. '' 'Night, Kath.''

Chapter Nine

The week wore on slowly for Danny. There was no word from the Labour Exchange, and so he took to getting up late and spending his afternoons taking long strolls. Walking made him feel better, and he found that he was not becoming so breathless. His favourite path was to cross the Thames at Tower Bridge and walk to Tower Hill. The weather remained warm and sunny, and Danny would spend time gazing down from the massive iron bridge at the bustling activity along the waterfront. Somewhere amongst the swinging cranes and laden barges his docker father was working, and the young cockney felt a certain sadness for him. His father had toiled on that waterfront since he was a young lad; he had known the hardships of the strikes, and the scrambling for a day's work. He had become bitter and cynical, and he was quick to anger whenever he spoke about his job. Danny felt that his father understood why his only son had chosen not to follow in his footsteps and become a docker. Times were changing: the unions were slowly extracting better working conditions from the employers, and the safety rules which were being enforced meant less unnecessary accidents for the men. Nevertheless the work was still back-breaking, and it was never certain that there would be a full pay packet at the end of the week. Because of the war there was plenty of heavy work available at the moment, but Danny knew that it could not last for ever.

He remembered talking to Albert Sweetland back at Dunkirk. He had told his pal all about the money to be made if you took the opportunities, but right now Danny realised he was a million miles away from making any kind of fortune. His prospects were limited to becoming a glass inspector, or working for the local bookie, Tony Allen. He had been a bookie's runner before and it had not paid all that well. Johnny Ross was enthusiastic, though, and he had implied that there were a few profitable sidelines to be enjoyed once Tony Allen got to know and trust him. Maybe Johnny was right, he always seemed to have money in his pocket, and it did not come from his poorly paid job at the vinegar factory. Danny had made up his mind. He would see the bookie on Thursday evening and find out exactly what was on offer.

On this Thursday afternoon stroll Danny stopped as usual on the Tower Bridge and looked down at the flowing Thames. The day was hot, and the sun was shining from a cloudless sky. The usual stream of traffic rumbled over the bridge, and the laden barges were being manoeuvred into their berths. He was thinking about Alison, and wondered if she had decided to answer his letter. The possibility of meeting her again excited him. If she was eager to see him then she might even have written a reply already, and it could be on its way. He walked further until he reached Tower Hill, and there he sat down to rest on one of the iron-framed benches. Two soldiers ambled by wearing peculiar hats and displaying the word 'Australia' on their shoulder flashes. A sad-looking young woman pushing a pram passed by, and a few yards away a tired horse flicked the flies away with its tail and rattled the chains that tethered it to the cart. Although the afternoon was peaceful and warm, the signs of war were apparent everywhere. Opposite, a wall of sandbags reinforced a surface shelter, and along the road, a timber frame had been erected to protect the Naval Memorial.

The flint chippings in the paving stones caught the sun's rays and the scent of roses drifted up from the Tower Gardens behind where Danny sat. In the afternoon quiet, everything suddenly seemed unreal and frightening. Only a few weeks ago he had been struggling to stay alive during the fighting in France. He thought of Albert Sweetland, and how his life had been suddenly snuffed out on the beach. He thought of Oggy Murphy, the ugly misfit to whom he owed his life, and he felt a lump rise in his throat. Many of his comrades in the regiment had been local lads, a lot of them he knew very well. He had seen many of them fall, but there must have been others who had somehow struggled back to England. Danny promised himself that he would go round to the drill hall; they would probably have a record there.

A long tug whistle carried up from the river. Then it became quiet again, and as Danny eased his stiff leg he felt a dull pain in his thigh muscle. He decided he ought to start walking again. He stretched and set off down the sloping road, into Lower Thames Street and through the fish market. He strolled along steadily until he reached the Monument. For a short while he leant against an iron post and stared up at the high stone column, a reminder of the Great Fire of London. He recalled the time his father had taken him to the top of the Monument and pointed out London's famous buildings, and then carried him down most of the spiralling stone staircase. He felt sad and a sudden dread of the future possessed him. He thought about the wireless broadcasts he had listened to, and he wondered how long it would be before an invasion took place. What would happen to his family and the people in the little streets then? He'd seen the ravages of the German invasion of France and the thoughts of the same thing happening in London filled him with terror.

Two scruffy-looking characters came past Danny carrying pieces of wood. They walked down the sloping street by the Monument and disappeared into an alley. Another individual in a filthy raincoat and boots tied up with string passed him. He carried a paper bag and a quart bottle of beer under one arm. Danny had often seen the 'up-the-hill' men before. They slept rough in the market alleyways

105

and hired their muscle for a few coppers to the market porters. The vagrants' pennies were hard-earned as they threw their weight against the laden fish barrows and helped the porters negotiate the slippery cobbles. Their pittance bought them their basic necessities and a little beer, but that was all. The tramps dried off the wet fish boxes to use for fires and they slept warm, oblivious to the stench from the burning wood. The 'up-the-hill' men were as much a part of Billingsgate as the Monument and the white-frocked fish porters.

London Bridge swarmed with bowler-hatted City workers carrying rolled-up umbrellas and briefcases, and everyone seemed to be carrying a gas mask. As he walked among the throng Danny recalled his conversation with the old gentleman on the bus. He was right: everyone seemed to be walking with their heads held rigid, eyes directed to the person in front. The river traffic and feverish activity hardly merited a passing glance from the homeward-bound masses as they streamed over London Bridge and into the railway station.

The station clock showed ten minutes past five as Danny walked down into Tooley Street. Tea wouldn't be ready yet, he thought, so he decided to drop in and have a chat with Ben. He should be home from work by now, and from what Lucy had said he probably needed a bit of cheering up. The tribunal result must have been a shock for him, although Lucy hadn't said too much about it.

As Danny climbed the wooden stairs an elderly lady appeared from one of the flats and gave him a suspicious look. Danny smiled at her and she looked even more warily at him as he passed her. Ben's rooms were on the top floor, and when Danny reached the landing he was puffing hard. He waited for a short while and then rapped on the door. Ben looked surprised when he saw his visitor. But he smiled and stood back for Danny to enter.

"Glad to see you, Danny. Anything wrong?"

"No, I was jus' passin' an' I reckoned yer might wanna chat or somefink."

Ben closed the door and motioned Danny to a seat. "I'm just about to have a cup of tea. Would you like one?"

"Great," Danny replied, making himself comfortable in an armchair.

Ben disappeared into the scullery and came back carrying two mugs of tea. He sat opposite Danny and put his mug down on the floor beside him. "How's the job situation? Lucy told me about Monday morning."

Danny grinned. "I'm afraid I blotted me copy book. I 'spect they'll suspend me fer gettin' lippy. Still, I'm seein' somebody ternight, I fink there's a job in the offin'."

Ben picked up the mug and sipped his tea. "Lucy told you about the tribunal?"

Danny nodded. "Bit of a shock, wasn't it?"

Ben shrugged his shoulders. "To be honest, I wasn't surprised. As soon as I went in I could sense the atmosphere. At least I was given a choice. I knew that if I refused to go along with their requirements I would end up in prison."

Danny looked at Ben's pale face and saw the fear in his eyes. "Lucy was tellin' me you was gettin' some aggro from your boss. What's 'is attitude now you're goin' in the Kate Carney?"

"To be honest I'm not sure," Ben said, scratching his head. "He knows that I haven't changed my views and he thinks I've been frightened into putting on a uniform. He's an old soldier and doesn't look on me as being very patriotic."

Danny put his mug down on the floor and crossed his legs. "What 'appens if yer don't get inter the medical corps? The medics are not the only non-combatant lot. You could be in the stores or somefink."

Ben's face became dark and he said quietly: "I tell you, Danny, as much as the thought of prison terrifies me, I'd have to accept it. The only reason I'll agree to wear a uniform is if it's in the medical corps. All right, it's a compromise, but at least I'd be helping to save life, not taking it."

Danny nodded, but he felt uncomfortable. He always did when Ben started to talk so seriously.

The noise of the homeward bound traffic and the grating sound of a tram carried up to the room, and Ben got up and closed the window. He came back and sat down heavily in the chair. He looked hard at Danny and folded his hands in his lap.

"Danny, I want to tell you something," he said with deliberation, and his face was serious. "You've been in action, you might understand. I'm scared of what's in front of me. I went into that hearing on Monday with all the wrong answers. I was prepared to stand up and say just why I felt I couldn't join the services, I thought I had it all worked out, but when they started asking those questions I began to shake. My stomach was in a knot and I wanted to be sick. I knew that Lucy was sitting there behind me, and I think it was only that knowledge that kept me from breaking down. I was scared then, and I'm scared now. I started to question my own reasons for being there. Was it really my beliefs? Or was it that I'm a coward? Do you know, I looked at those faces on the bench and I felt they could see right through me. They seemed to be smirking at my discomfort. They could tell I'd crack, I'm sure they could. I haven't slept properly since Monday, you know. I'm scared of pain and suffering, I can't bear to see anything suffer. Yesterday, Danny, a dog got run over below. It was yelping and whining, and instead of going down to see if I could do anything, I just sat in this chair until the yelping stopped. I finally looked out of the window and I felt ashamed. A young lad had picked up the dog and was struggling down the street with it. I don't think it was badly hurt, but I never even went to find out, I just sat there. How, for the Lord's sake, am I going to cope with the carnage in a battle? Tell me, Danny."

Danny Sutton looked down at the floor. Ben's outburst had taken him by surprise and he felt inadequate. He didn't know what to say. As a medic Ben would be picking up wounded soldiers who were screaming in agony; he would be breathing in the stink of grisly butchery, and mangled bodies waiting to be laid to rest in makeshift graves; he would be shaking with a stark fear that turned his legs to jelly and twisted his stomach into a tight knot. Could Danny explain how it felt when the bullets whistled past and thudded into flesh and bone, when the man beside you fell and you could expect to be the next to get shot? How could he explain the terror to Ben, sitting opposite him, his face white with worry? It was impossible. He could still feel it vividly, but he knew of no words which would help him. Danny looked up at Ben and saw the anxiety in his eyes.

He took a deep breath. "I don't know the answer, Ben. I'm jus' like you, I get scared of silly fings. We're all human, ain't we? I can't stan' spiders. There's no reason ter be scared of bein' scared, that sort of reasoning only gets yer killed. You'll be okay, there'll be uvvers wiv yer. They'll all be scared, but they'll still do what they're s'posed ter do. You'll get the proper trainin', you'll be all right."

Ben brushed his hand through his hair and sank lower in his seat. "I hope you're right, Danny. I expect you think I'm being stupid, talking that way."

Danny got up from his chair and stretched his stiff leg. He looked into Ben's eyes. "I don't fink yer bein' stupid," he said. "I'm scared. We're all scared. You're no different." He paused and looked down. "Anyway, I'd better be orf 'ome. I'll get a rollockin' if I'm late."

Ben saw his guest to the door. "Thanks for dropping in, Danny, I appreciate it."

Danny grinned. "Yer'll 'ave ter come up The Globe wiv us an' 'ave a drink, even if it's only orange juice. We can 'ave anuvver chat, okay?"

Danny walked out onto the landing and Ben smiled at him. "I never knew you were scared of spiders, Danny."

Danny hunched his shoulders. "I'm terrified of 'em. Keep it ter yerself though. If they find out in the pub they'll be puttin' spiders in matchboxes jus' ter see me shout out. Oh well, I'd better get 'ome fer me tea. See yer, Ben."

"Cheerio, Danny."

From the London docks and from other ports around Britian the ships assembled in convoy for the hazardous North Atlantic crossing. Tankers and freighters and the destroyer escorts left their home shores under cover of darkness and steamed out into the dangerous ocean. There was now a war at sea and U-boats were searching out the convoys. The destroyer escorts were increasing in size, and more U-boats were being sunk, but the losses at sea were still mounting as Convoy Q407 steamed into mid-Atlantic on the night of the 6th of July 1940. On board the accompanying destroyer, HMS *Prowler*, everyone was at battle stations. A tell-tale blip on the asdic had indicated that a submarine was in the area.

The look-out let his night glasses hang from the strap as he squeezed his eyes tightly against the strain of watching the water. The moon lit up the waves and a myriad stars shone down from a velvet sky. Although a full alert was in operation, an uncanny calmness seemed to surround the convoy. Other destroyers could be seen moving among the merchantmen and guarding the flanks of the stragglers. The look-out blinked and put his glasses up to his eyes once more.

The steady thump of the powerful engines and the roar of the sea were music to the seaman as he scanned the shimmering water. Ever since he was able to remember, the sea had held a fascination for him. He had seen those big ships come up the Thames, and he had watched as they slipped inch by inch into their berths. He had read the names on the sides and learned to recognise their national flags. At night he had scoured his small atlas and studied it until his eyes drooped; the ports around the world were magical names to the lad. He dreamed of becoming a sailor. When he got older his father took him to the Royal Docks in his van. There he stared open-mouthed at the great cargo ships from the Orient. It fascinated him to see those dark-skinned seamen who were not much taller than he come down the gang-planks carrying their white jugs of steaming water. His father had laughed and said they were going off for their tea. The young lad did not question his father, but it seemed strange to him that the little men should all go to the brick shed marked 'Asiatics' for their tea. What his father did tell him however was that the little men were Lascars, and that they were the only race who could stand the conditions in the boiler-rooms of those huge coal-burning ships. Sometimes in the Indian Ocean the temperature in the boiler-room could soar to one hundred and twenty degrees.

As he scanned the starlit sea the young sailor remembered the time he had been waiting on the quayside with his father at the West India Dock and saw one of those little men brutally kicked by a ship's officer. The Lascar had gone aboard without protest and the young lad had vowed that if he ever got to become a seaman he would treat those dark-skinned little men with kindness. He remembered how his father had laughed at his concern for the seaman, and had said that Lascars were a lazy lot who had to be thumped now and then or they wouldn't work at all. Now the sailor wondered how many of those little men were sweating away now down in the boiler-rooms of the merchantmen as they sailed across the danger area.

Spray soaked the hood of his duffle jacket and dripped from his steel helmet as the look-out searched the ocean from his position up on the bridge. He could see the merchantmen spread out to the horizon, and occasionally he caught sight of one of the escorts cutting in through the lines. His own ship HMS *Prowler* had dropped back to hurry on the stragglers, but now it was racing full-speed to take up the vanguard position.

The officer of the watch called out to him, "You awake, Ellis? We've picked up a signal."

Chapter Ten

Alice Sutton brushed the crumbs from the red and white checked tablecloth as she set a place for her husband Frank. She glanced over at Connie, who had her head buried in the evening paper. Alice banged a knife and fork down hard and then gave her daughter a sharp look, but Connie seemed completely absorbed in the news. Alice came round the table purposefully and tapped Connie on the shoulder. "What's goin' on 'ere ternight, girl?" she asked curtly.

Connie looked up in surprise. "What d'ja mean, Mum?"

"Danny's what I mean. 'E rushes in 'ere like the devil's after 'im, rushes 'is tea down, an' scoots orf out again. All I got from 'im was, 'I might be late, I gotta bit o' business ter see to'. What the bloody 'ell is goin' on 'ere?"

Connie shrugged her slim shoulders. "Search me, Mum. I s'pose 'e's gone off ter New Cross. Danny always used ter go on Thursdays, didn't 'e?"

Alice puffed and folded her arms. "I'm sure I don't know, what wiv one an' the uvver of 'em, they take this place fer a coffee shop."

Connie put down the paper and gave her mother a smile. "You still mad at Dad?"

Alice fought against letting her face relax. "I've warned yer farver. I ses to 'im, 'If yer come in 'ere ternight smellin' o' beer an' yer don't eat yer tea up, I'm gonna let you 'ave it'."

"What, 'is tea, Mum?"

"No, I'm gonna give 'im a piece o' me mind. I'm fed up

wiv keepin' 'is tea 'ot. An' don't you be so lippy, my girl.''

Connie gave her mother a special smile, and as she looked at her Alice felt herself starting to grin.

"Sit down, Mum an' I'll make us a nice strong cuppa,'' Connie said laughing.

Danny walked briskly under the railway arch and crossed the street into Bermondsey Lane. He was taking the back-streets to the Old Kent Road where he could catch the tram to New Cross. He had to pass the Arpinos' shop and so he decided to look in on Tóny. They had often taken a stroll to the dog meetings together before Danny had been mobilised. The clock in the chemist's window showed 6.30 — if he hurried he'd catch the first race. Tony was inside the shop talking to a couple of tall, burly characters as Danny looked in.

"Fancy the dogs, Tony?'' Danny called out from the door.

"Sure fing,'' Tony said quickly. "Walk on, I'll catch yer up.''

Danny strolled slowly on towards Tower Bridge Road and soon Tony caught him up. "We got trouble I fink, Danny,'' he said with a backward glance. "Did yer see those two monkeys I was talkin' to? They've bin doin' the rounds of all the shops round 'ere this last few days. They're talkin' a lot a nonsense about us joinin' a shop-keeper's federation. I've jus' told 'em ter come back when me ole man's there. It's no good them talkin' ter me muvver, she won't know what they're on about anyway.''

Danny frowned at him. "Sounds like the ole protection racket ter me, Tony. Yer wanna be careful, somebody tried ter pull a stroke like that in Tower Bridge Road a few years ago. Me ole man told me about it. This geezer got a right goin' over. Yer wanna make sure all the shopkeepers stick tergevver. It's the only way ter beat 'em.''

The two friends crossed into Tower Bridge Road and

walked up until they reached The Bricklayers Arms. They stood chatting together at the tram stop.

"I've gotta see that Tony Allen while we're at the meetin'," Danny was saying. "Johnny Ross 'as 'ad a word wiv 'im about me doin' a bit o' bookkeepin'."

Tony laughed. "You workin' in an office? Do me a favour, you'll get the right bleedin' 'ump in no time."

"I'm talkin' about takin' bets, yer berk," Danny replied with a grin.

Tony winced. "Yer wanna be careful there, Tony Allen's got 'is fingers in a lot o' pies. Yer might get in over yer 'ead. An' anuvver fing, yer wanna be careful o' that Jack Mason. 'E's in wiv Tony Allen. One nasty bastard that is."

"Don't worry, Tony, I'll be cute. At least it'll be better than what that ponce at the Labour Exchange offered me on Monday."

A young woman joined the queue and Tony gave Danny a nudge. "That's a bit of all right!" he said, his eyes widening.

The woman turned round and gave Tony a cold stare. Tony smiled back at her with a ridiculously innocent look on his face. A number 38 tram pulled up at the stop and the queue boarded. Tony winked at his pal and followed the young woman onto the top deck. As the tram rocked and swayed in the tracks Tony continually glanced over to where she was sitting. At first she ignored him, but as he kept on looking at her she began to wonder whether he was a complete nutcase. But by the time the tram reached New Cross railway arch the two were exchanging smiles.

Danny nudged his friend, "C'mon, Casanova," he said, "this is our stop."

The first race had just started as the two entered the stadium and climbed the steps into the stand. People were milling around and a roar went up as one of the dogs was bundled over. Dog number 6 went out in front and held the lead until the finish of the race.

"Not much of a price that," Tony remarked, looking at the odds on a bookie's stand in front of them.

Danny was searching the crowd with his eyes when Tony gave him a nudge. " 'Ere, look at this."

Danny glanced down at the race card in Tony's hand and saw that Shady Lady was entered in the third race. He grinned. "That'll be a rank outsider, they'll prob'ly give yer two 'undred ter one on that."

Tony looked up at his pal. "Biff Bowden told my ole man ter get a few bob down on it next time it runs."

Danny laughed aloud. "It'll be too pissed ter run. If it gets out o' the trap it'll prob'ly fall asleep 'alf way round, or keel over wiv its legs up in the air."

The dogs were parading for the second race and Danny handed Tony a ten shilling note. "Do us a favour, Tone, stick this on number 4 dog. I wanna look out fer Tony Allen."

Tony Arpino trotted down the steps to the trackside and while he was gone Danny scanned the crowds again. He finally spotted Tony Allen by the track talking to Jack Mason. Then he saw Kathy. She had just walked up to them and he saw her hand Jack Mason something. Danny had forgotten the race completely and his eyes stayed on Kathy as she took her escort's arm when the bell sounded. The mechanical hare was building up speed and as it passed the traps the dogs shot out and went into the first bend in a bunch. Slowly the number 4 dog gained ground. Danny turned back to Kathy and saw her jumping up and down excitedly. When he looked back at the race he saw that his dog was now being overtaken.

Tony came back as the dogs crossed the finishing line and pulled a face. "Oh well. There's still Shady Lady," he said, but without much enthusiasm.

Danny pointed the bookie out to Tony. "I'm goin' down fer a word. Comin'?"

Tony shook his head. "You go on, I'll stop up 'ere. I'll see yer later."

Danny Sutton walked slowly down to the trackside and held out his hand. " 'Ello, Tony, remember me? Me mate Johnny Ross told me ter come an' see yer."

Tony Allen shook Danny's hand. " 'Course I remember yer. This is Kathy an' Jack, they're both good friends o' mine."

Danny shook hands with Jack Mason and was unsettled by his limp, clammy grasp. He smiled at Kathy, who nodded back without a flicker of recognition in her dark eyes. Tony Allen studied the card for a while and then looked at Danny. "Tell yer what," he said, "I'm just away ter put a few bob on number 6 dog. We'll 'ave a drink in the bar after the race, okay?"

Danny nodded. "I'll see yer there then."

Jack Mason looked at Kathy. "I won't be long. I'm goin' wiv Tony," he said shortly.

Danny watched the bookie walk away with his associate, then he turned to Kathy to find her smiling at him. "I didn't expect ter see you down 'ere," she said. " 'Ave yer bin offered a job?"

Danny nodded. "Johnny Ross put the feelers out fer me."

Kathy put her hand on his arm. Danny felt her warm fingers and he looked into her eyes. He could see that she was anxious. "Do yerself a favour, Danny," she said seriously, "don't 'ave anyfing ter do wiv Tony Allen or Jack. Don't ask me why, jus' say no, an' walk away while yer still can. You get in wiv that crowd an' you'll regret it."

Danny reached down and took her hand in his. "You concerned fer me? I . . ."

Kathy stopped him. "Don't start that again, Danny, I meant what I said. Yes, I'm concerned fer yer. Jus' take my advice."

Danny searched her dark eyes. "Yer know I still want yer, Kathy, yer must know that."

"Don't, Danny, don't. Please. It's too late fer us now, fings 'ave changed since then. It's too late."

Danny squeezed her hand until she winced. "Look, Kathy, it's not too late. You're not married to 'im. Come out wiv me termorrer. I'll tell 'im if yer like."

Kathy shook her head and tears came into her eyes. "It is too late, Danny. I 'ad a big row wiv me dad. 'E chucked me out. I'm livin' wiv Jack now."

"Christ! What did 'e do that for?"

Kathy looked down at her feet. "I'm 'avin' a baby. It's Jack's. When I told me dad 'e went mad. Mum tried ter stop 'im goin' fer me an' she got a good 'idin' too."

Her words stunned him. It felt as though icy fingers had suddenly gripped his insides. Feelings of anger and pity rose up in Danny's breast as he stared in despair at the slim girl in front of him.

"Yer mean yer ole man gave yer a pastin', wiv you 'avin' a baby an' all?"

Kathy gave him a weak smile. "Yer know 'ow my farver gets when 'e's 'ad a drink. 'E gave me ten minutes ter pack an' get out. I went roun' ter Jack's place, I 'ad to. Anyway, Jack's bin wantin' me ter move in wiv 'im fer a while now."

Danny shook his head sadly. "Why didn't yer come roun' ter see me? I'd 'ave 'elped yer, you know I would."

Kathy blinked back her tears. She looked into his worried eyes and felt a strong urge to collapse into his arms, but she breathed out deeply and pulled her hand away from his. "Be sensible, Danny," she said. "I'm 'avin' 'is baby, I'm sleepin' wiv 'im. 'Ow could I possibly come runnin' round ter your place an' say, 'take me in, I've bin chucked out 'cos I'm pregnant'? It's not your baby."

"I wish it was, I wish you'd 'ave told me before. I wouldn't 'ave took advantage."

Kathy smiled at him. "Don't be silly, you didn't take advantage. I wanted it as much as you. Yer know that, don't yer?"

Danny's mouth twitched. "Kathy, come with me, the

118

baby don't make no difference. Leave 'im. 'E'll be no good ter yer."

"Don't, Danny. Please."

He gazed round the stadium in dismay. Kathy saw a hollowness in his eyes and she said anxiously, "You'd better go now, luv. Please. They'll be back soon. I'll see yer in the bar later."

The third race was about to begin. Danny walked back morosely to his friend and they stood waiting for the off. Tony sensed that there was something wrong with his pal but he refrained from asking questions. The bell sounded and five dogs bounded from the traps, but one dog had not moved.

"I told yer she'd be pissed, didn't I?" Danny shouted.

Tony grabbed his pal's arm. "It ain't Shady! Look, she's in the lead!"

Shady was dashing round the track, to the roar of the punters. The rest of the field was left far behind as Shady Lady increased her lead. On the final straight she was ten lengths clear, and she romped home to the cheers of the surprised spectators. The bookmakers, who had expected a run on the money if the hot favourite had won, were openly smiling.

"Bloody 'ell! It done it! It bloody well done it! She won!" Tony shouted.

Danny looked at him. "You didn't back it, did yer?"

Tony Arpino was beaming. "Yep, I 'ad a dollar on the nose! Jus' fer luck."

The numbers tumbled about on the totaliser and when they settled the crowd gasped. The forecast was over ten pounds. Tony Arpino rubbed his hands together with glee. He had backed Shady Lady at one hundred to six.

The bar at the rear of the stadium was packed. Danny stood facing Tony Allen in one corner and Jack Mason was with Kathy some way off, talking to Johnny Ross, who had just walked in. Danny was listening to the bookie.

"I've 'ad a word wiv Bernie Marsh," Tony Allen said.

119

" 'E told me yer was ter be trusted. That's good enough fer me. 'E told me yer run a good book fer 'im. Yer see, I've got a few little earners goin'. Play yer cards right an' I might be able ter put a few bob your way. Fer a start yer can take the bets on me Clink Lane pitch.''

Danny nodded. "Is it the usual set up?''

"Yeah, the rozzers won't worry yer. I pay their guv'nor orf each week. When they've gotta make a pinch they let me know an' I get somebody ter do the honours. It works the same as it did wiv Bernie. We put a couple o' bets in the geezer's pocket an' 'e makes sure 'e gets caught. We pay the fine an' everybody's 'appy, includin' the coppers.''

Danny had already made up his mind. He gave Kathy a furtive glance and then looked at Tony Allen. "When do I start?''

"Next Monday. I'll put one o' the lads wiv yer fer a few days, until the punters get ter know yer. You'll be all right, I'll do the business at the Labour Exchange, I know the geezer there. 'E'll give us yer green card fer me ter sign. For all intents an' purposes, yer workin' as a bookkeeper's clerk. That okay?''

Danny nodded. "Fanks, Tony. I know the game, yer can count on me ter do the business.''

Tony Allen smiled and downed his Scotch. "You'll be all right. Be straight wiv me an' I'll look after you.'' He reached into his pocket and drew out a thick wad of money. He handed Danny a five pound note. " 'Ere. Take this on account an' enjoy yerself. Yer can pay me back when yer flush.''

Danny tried to refuse but the bookie pushed the white note into his hand. "You'll find out I look after my boys if they're straight. Go on, take it.''

Early that evening Frank Sutton came home to number 26 Dawson Street and walked through the front door without stumbling over the coconut mat that was spread out along the length of the passage. He went out into the scullery and

120

gave Alice a peck on the cheek before rolling up his sleeves and scrubbing his hands with a stiff brush. "Is Danny out?" he asked, taking a towel from the back of the door.

Alice nodded. " 'E wasn't in five minutes. Gone on some business, so 'e said."

"I thought I caught sight of 'im goin' under the arch as I come in," her husband said. "What's fer tea, Alice?"

"Boiled bacon an' pease puddin'. I know it's yer favourite. Now get in there an' get yer feet under the table. I wanna get cleared up early ternight, I'm goin' round ter see Maggie. The kids 'ave gone down wiv the measles."

Lucy and Connie were both sitting in the small parlour when their father walked in. Lucy was reading and Connie was sitting on an upright chair, one knee drawn up under her chin.

"Bloody 'ell, what's that yer usin'?" Frank exclaimed, pulling a face.

Connie grinned. "It's nail varnish, Dad, I'm makin' meself pretty."

Lucy looked up quickly and put her head down again into her book. Frank sat himself at the table and picked up a knife and fork. Connie gave him a cheeky smile. "You're 'ome early, Dad."

Her father fixed her with a telling look as Alice put his tea in front of him and he began to eat in a deliberately sober manner. Connie winked at her mother who grinned back and walked out of the parlour with her head in the air. Frank ate his tea in silence and when he had scraped the last morsel from his plate he leant back in his chair and sighed contentedly. Lucy had gone to help her mother with the dishes and Connie sat with both feet outstretched and her arms behind her head. Frank hooked his thumbs through his braces and burped loudly.

" 'Ow's yer young man, Con? You 'eard from 'im yet?"

"Give 'im a chance, Dad. 'E only went back on Monday night. 'E's prob'ly gone straight ter sea. 'E won't 'ave much time ter write any letters."

Frank nodded. "Don't s'pose 'e will, girl. What boat is 'e on?"

Connie raised her hands in mock horror. "Yer musn't call 'em boats, Dad, they're ships. Jimmy's on a destroyer. 'E's bin on convoy duties."

" 'E's doin' a good job, Connie. It can't be very nice out there on the water. Mind you, though," Frank went on, "we've always relied on people like your young man. It's in our blood, the sea. We're an island. Wivout ships we're done for, an' wivout a navy we'd be a plum pickin' fer every little dictator that fancied 'avin' a go at us."

Connie looked at her father with a saucy grin. "Look at Sir Francis Drake. 'E sorted 'em out, didn't 'e?"

Frank felt he was wasting his time trying to talk seriously to his daughter this evening. "Don't sit there mockin' yer ole dad, go an' get us a cuppa."

The clock struck ten. Connie had gone up to her room, and Alice had just returned from visiting Maggie's children. She was sitting in the easy chair listening to the wireless. Frank shifted his position yet again and stretched. "What's our lad up to then, Muvver?" he asked suddenly.

Alice folded her arms as she usually did when she had something to say. "I dunno, Frank, but that Johnny Ross was round 'ere on Monday. 'E was eager ter see our Danny. I don't trust 'im, an' 'e's in wiv a bad lot. I 'ope Danny don't get too much involved wiv that crowd."

Frank looked into the empty hearth. "Yer can't wipe 'is nose now, Muvver. After all, 'e's over twenty-one. 'E's gotta make 'is own decisions."

"I know that, Frank, but yer can't 'elp worryin', can yer?"

"No yer can't," Frank said, straightening up in his chair. "An' yer can't 'elp gettin' firsty, neivver. 'Ow's about me an' you poppin' up The Globe fer a quiet drink?"

Alice tried not to look too eager. "Oh, all right then," she said. " 'Ang on, I'll get me coat."

Chapter Eleven

Early on Saturday morning the postman delivered two letters to number 26. Danny was still fast asleep, but Connie was up and about. She took the letters out into the scullery and raised her eyebrows when she spotted a Dover postmark on the letter addressed to Danny. The other letter was for Lucy, but she had already left for work. Connie's sister was employed as a secretary to the manager of a manufacturing tailors who had their offices in Tower Bridge Road. Since the outbreak of war her firm had been working on a government contract to supply uniforms to the armed forces, and now everyone was working regular overtime.

Connie took Danny's letter up to his room with a cup of tea and shook him gently. Danny mumbled something unintelligible and pulled the clothes over his head. Connie shook him again without success and left the letter with his tea on the chair beside his bed. Alice had gone to the market and had left Connie the washing to peg out in the backyard. Outside the sun was shining and children's voices sounded in the street. Presently she heard the cry of the rag-and-bone man as he pushed his squeaking barrow into the turning. She went in and picked up the rag bag lying at the foot of the stairs and went to the front door to await Old Jerry.

For as long as anyone could remember, Old Jerry had trundled his rickety barrow around the backstreets of dockland. Where he came from or where he lived was a mystery. He was bowed and weatherbeaten, with a beer-stained moustache and bushy eyebrows. His faded blue eyes glared out from under a greasy trilby and he wore a tattered grey raincoat without buttons that was tied around his middle with string. It was filthy and he wore it in all weathers, and underneath he carried a money pouch, a spring balance that was rusting and did not work, and a roll of money secured with an elastic band. The most striking feature of Jerry's appearance was his brown boots. They were always clean and polished, which led some people to believe that he was an old soldier.

The barrow that Old Jerry pushed around the back-streets looked as worn out as its owner. The wheels squeaked and the shafts looked ready to fall off. It was piled high with rags, bits of old iron and an assortment of empty glass jars. How he managed to get a living from such rubbish was a puzzle to the local folk, but they were aware that Old Jerry was never short of cash. He struck a hard bargain and the locals learned not to haggle. He swore that his spring balance was correct to the ounce, and if it was ever doubted the bag of rags would most likely be deposited on the pavement and Old Jerry would be off, mumbling under his breath. Connie knew this as she walked up to his barrow and handed Old Jerry the rags her mother had sorted out the previous night. He fished out the spring balance and hooked up the bag, he squinted at the reading then tossed the bundle on his barrow before counting out three pennies and one sixpence.

Later that morning Danny took a leisurely stroll up to The Globe. A small boy cracked a whip against a spinning top and chased it happily, another couple of lads were setting up their firewood pitch, and women carried laden shopping baskets into the turning. Danny contentedly mulled over the letter he had received from Alison. It had really cheered him up after hearing Kathy's news at the races to know that Alison had been granted some leave and she was intending to come up to London next Sunday morning and stay over until Monday, when she would catch the night train to Cardiff to see her folks. And he smiled to himself as he walked into the pub.

The Globe was busy as usual with its regular clientele of dockers, stevedores and shoppers who called in for a 'livener'. Eddie was chatting to Biff and when he saw Danny he came over.

"Jack Mason's in the saloon. 'E was askin' if yer come in 'ere on Sat'day mornin's. I fink 'e wants a word wiv yer."

Danny ordered a pint of ale and Eddie nodded to the connecting door. "If yer wanna go frew I'll 'and yer beer round."

"Fanks, Eddie," Danny said. "I'd better see what 'e wants."

Jack Mason was talking to a couple of burly men and when he saw Danny walk into the bar he came over to the counter. "So yer joined the firm then?" he said with a slight smirk on his bloated face.

Danny nodded. "Me pal Johnny Ross spoke fer me. I used ter be Bernie Marsh's runner."

"Yeah, so Tony Allen tells me," Mason said, beckoning the barmaid over.

Danny sipped his drink while the bookie ordered another Scotch. He noticed how the man's deep-set eyes seemed to dart around nervously. He was a snappy dresser, Danny noticed. His suit looked expensive and was immaculately cut; his crisp white shirt made his swarthy complexion seem even darker, and his black patent shoes looked like they were from a West End shop. Danny watched as Mason took a swig from his glass and his eyes were drawn to the small, crescent-shaped scar in the corner of his mouth.

Mason laid a fist on the counter and leaned towards the young cockney. "You're a mate o' Rossy then, are yer?"

"I've known 'im since we were kids. We went ter school tergevver," Danny replied.

The villain's eyes seemed to bore into him and Danny

felt uneasy. "Trouble wiv yer pal is, 'e can't keep 'is mouth shut. I 'eard 'e was in 'ere the uvver night chuckin' 'is money about. Yer wanna tell 'im ter watch it. It don't do ter let people know yer business. Yer never know, the law might be in 'ere."

Danny felt his dislike for the man growing as he listened. Jack Mason stared into his face. "Jus' ter put yer in the picture," he said, "I'm what yer might call Tony Allen's right 'and . It's my business ter look after 'is interests. There's bin a few geezers in the past that's tried ter come it and I've 'ad ter sit on 'em, if yer get me meanin'. I 'ope you ain't got no fancy ideas?"

"Yer don't 'ave ter try an' put the fear in me. I'm pleased Tony Allen gave me the job, I'm not out ter take liberties," Danny said.

Mason grinned crookedly. "No offence, son, jus' tellin' yer, that's all."

Danny finished his drink and Jack Mason pointed to his glass. "Wanna top up?"

"No fanks, I've gotta meet somebody," Danny lied.

Mason put his elbow on the counter and looked at Danny, a menacing expression on his face. "Kathy tells me yer know 'er."

Danny felt his stomach tighten, he was afraid of what Kathy might have said. "Everybody knows everyone else round 'ere," he said dismissively. "Kathy, Johnny Ross an' me was all in the same class at school. As I was sayin', we all grew up tergevver."

Jack Mason continued to fix Danny with an intimidating stare. "Me an' Kathy are goin' around tergevver. Jus' so's yer'd know."

"Yeah, I know," Danny replied, returning the stare.

Jack Mason suddenly relaxed. He picked up his empty glass and looked in the direction of the barmaid.

Danny felt it was time he got away from him. "Well, I'm orf. I'll see yer around," he said, walking from the saloon bar and out into the warm sunshine.

Danny walked along Tooley Street; as usual on Saturday afternoons the area was almost deserted, the wharves were locked and only a few locals ambled by. In the sudden quiet Danny had time to think. He would have to be careful of Jack Mason, there had been a distinct warning in his tone when he mentioned Kathy. Maybe someone had seen him leave the party about the same time as Kathy and told Mason, but it seemed unlikely. It was more probable that Jack Mason was suspicious of him for another reason. It was obvious the man did not like Johnny Ross, and it was Johnny who put in a good word for Danny to the bookie.

As he turned into Dawson Street he saw Johnny Ross coming along towards him. Johnny was limping noticeably and he wore a large grin. " 'Ello, Danny, goin' 'ome already? I was comin' up The Globe fer a chat wiv yer. What's the matter?"

Danny scowled. "I jus' got lumbered wiv Jack Mason. After five minutes in 'is company I was glad ter get out inter the fresh air."

"I told yer about 'im didn't I?" Johnny said with a confirming nod.

Danny pulled on his pal's arm. "By the way, Mason told me ter give yer a bit of advice."

"Oh yeah, about what?" Johnny asked, looking serious.

" 'E reckons yer should be more careful about flashin' yer money in The Globe."

"Well somebody must 'ave told 'im, 'cos 'e wasn't in the pub," Johnny said indignantly. "An' I bet I know who it was. I bet it was that barmaid of Eddie's. Mason took 'er out a few times. She's still sweet on 'im, I can tell."

Danny shrugged his shoulders. "It don't matter who it was. Johnny boy. Be careful, or they'll stop yer little earners."

Johnny Ross grinned. "Don't worry, Danny. I've got a

nice little touch comin' up. I'll tell yer about it later. Take it easy. I'll see yer soon."

Danny stood beside his front door and watched his pal hobble up the turning. It looks like I've gotta look after both of us, he thought as he pulled on the door string.

The bows of the destroyer rose and dipped into the heavy swell, and up on the bridge Ordinary Seaman James Ellis wiped the salt spray from his face and stamped his numbed feet on the wet steel deck. His eyes were begining to play tricks with him and he blinked hard. "Christ! Where's that dopey git wiv me cocoa," he mumbled aloud as more spray lashed his raw face. Lofty Boulter was struggling for'ard and Jimmy could see him leaning into the wind, his hand protecting the steaming hot cocoa.

"Bloody 'ell, Lofty. It's about time. I was givin' you up."

Lofty Boulter grinned and handed over the beverage. "Fink yerself lucky, Jimmy boy. I nearly went over on me arse a couple o' times."

Jimmy Ellis gulped the drink and felt the warmth penetrate into his stomach.

Lofty pulled his duffle coat up around his ears and leaned on the guard rail beside his pal. "What a poxy night," he groaned, ducking as the spray flew up from the bows. "I knew it was a mistake ter sign on in the Andrew. I could 'ave joined the Brylcream mob an' got meself a nice little WAAF ter keep me warm on nights like this."

Jimmy handed back the empty mug and took another scan of the dark horizon. "D'yer ever get scared on these patrols, Lofty?" he asked after a while.

"You tell me when I'm not," his pal replied. "I don't like these cat an' mouse games wiv the U-boats. I don't like what I can't see. I know very well there's a bloody German down there somewhere jus' waitin' fer the opportunity ter stick a tin fish inter the first ship 'e can. I tell yer, Jimmy, it gives me the creeps."

The *Prowler* continued the 'cat and mouse' manoeuvres and was now sweeping a wide arc ahead of the convoy. Clouds were gathering below the cold stars and spots of rain fell on the steel deck.

"Funny 'ow the weavver changes at sea," Jimmy remarked, wiping his face on the back of his hand.

"Yeah, it's somefink yer can't predict, mate," Lofty answered, bracing himself against the bulkhead and digging his hands deeper into his jacket pockets. "I read somewhere that the sea's like a woman. It's right, I s'pose. Women are unpredictable, at least a few I know are. Yer fink yer got 'em sussed out, an' they kick yer right in the cods. Now you take this girl I used ter know. Rachel 'er name was. She was a good-lookin' sort, an' all the lads round Balham fancied 'er. I was cartin' 'er out fer a spell before I joined up. D'yer know I tried me 'ardest ter get 'er inter bed but she wasn't 'avin' any of it. All I got out of 'er was, 'let's get engaged, Freddy'. Well, I thought ter meself, play yer cards right, Freddy boy, an' you'll crack it, so I ups an' ses, 'Yeah, all right' an' I got 'er a ring. Cost me a few bob as well. I took 'er out fer a good piss-up on the night we got engaged, but it didn't make no difference. 'Wait till we're married', she said. Anyways, this went on an' on until I was gettin' like a dog wiv two dicks an' a double line o' trees. Frustration, Jimmy boy. That's what I was sufferin' from. Well, one night we 'ad a right ole barney. I called 'er a frigid prune, an' she called me a lecherous git. She threw the ring at me an' it dropped down a drain 'ole. Off she stormed an' next day I joined up."

Jimmy grinned as he wiped the eye-piece of his night glasses. "So that's why yer joined the Andrew then. 'Ave yer seen anyfing of 'er since?"

Lofty shifted his position against the rail and leaned closer to his pal. "Yer never gonna believe this, Jimmy, but after our last trip I bumped into 'er in the Balham High Road. She was in the club. Honest. She was out 'ere,'' he said, gesticulating with his hand held out in front of him. "Bloody pregnant, an' there's me couldn't get a look in."

"She wasn't married, then?" Jimmy said.

"Married nuffink. She ended up wiv this geezer who 'ad a shop in the Balham market. Right flashy sort o' bloke 'e was. As I said, women are unpredictable. They're like the weavver."

Lofty left the bridge and Jimmy Ellis put the glasses to his eyes for the umpteenth time. He could see the fitful moon playing down on the rolling sea and the distant stars as they broke from the rain clouds. Away to starboard he saw the billowing smokestack of a small freighter, and the oil tanker that had been running abeam for some time. He was looking forward to the warmth of the mess when his spell of duty was over and his thoughts turned to that last night in London. They were sitting in the back row of the stalls and Connie had snuggled up close. He couldn't remember the film, but he recalled the fragrant smell of her body and how her red lips had searched out his in the darkness as they whispered promises and everlasting love. They had walked slowly and sadly to London Bridge Railway Station where he was to catch his train to Chatham. Connie had given him a small locket as a good-luck charm and he wore it around his neck. He had wanted to take her in his arms and make love to her, but there had been no time. Connie had suggested that they see her father when he returned home, and then they could have all the time in the world.

Bright flashes suddenly blinded the look-out as torpedoes exploded in the dark. The silence was shattered. A freighter lay dead in the water and her crew were scrambling into lifeboats. The tanker was burning as its bow rose up out of the water and it began to sink stern first. The wild sea was full of flotsam and bobbing lifeboats. Oil was burning on the water and the other ships became shrouded as the convoy put down a smokescreen. The

Prowler was speeding forward into the smoke and the surrounding chaos had dissolved into indistinct shapes.

Suddenly Jimmy Ellis saw the ugly wet shape of the U-boat dead ahead and he could read the number 107 clearly on its conning tower. The destroyer ran straight into it and the sound of crunching steel plates was like a scream out of hell. The *Prowler* rose up on the hull of the sub and then settled back in the water. Oil bubbles broke the surface as the 107 went down to the depths and then a fountain of water rose level with the bridge. The destroyer was beginning to swing around when a torpedo exploded amid-ships. Ordinary Seaman James Ellis shut his eyes as he felt the cold sea smash into him and close over his head.

When he struggled to the surface the *Prowler* had gone. Only pieces of wreckage remained. His thoughts were of Connie and he called her name aloud, but he was alone in the angry sea. He hoped that he would spot other survivors, or a lifeboat, but he soon realised that none had been launched, it had all happened too quickly. He tried shouting but he felt too shocked and tired and though his life jacket was keeping him afloat, the coldness was beginning to numb his body. In the loneliness of the vast ocean Jimmy waited for the end to come. He felt a strange sense of calm. His eyes were starting to close and he saw his pal Lofty walking down the street with a dark-looking girl on his arm. Lofty smiled at him and was gone. In his confused mind he saw the large ocean-going ship coming up river. "Look, son! Can yer see it, Jimmy? 'Ang on, I'll lift yer on me shoulders. There you are, see it now?"

Chapter Twelve

The second week of July remained warm and sunny, but now the street drains began to smell and the pavements were hot and dusty. The council water cart plied in and out of the backstreets laying the dust and swilling the drains while children jumped in and out of twirling skipping ropes and chased marbles along the gutters. In Dawson Street, old Charlie Perkins sat watching the daily spectacle. Charlie's leathery features were composed and serene; from time to time his eyes drooped and his head nodded. The children of the street left him alone and Charlie gave them little thought. When little ones chased a bouncing ball or a skidding marble they passed him as they would the lamppost, for Charlie was inscrutable.

In the next street Danny started his job as street bookie. His pitch was in an ever-open doorway at number 18 Clink Lane. The little turning looked very much the same as Dawson Street, with two rows of terraced houses and a railway arch at one end, but unlike Danny's road there were a couple of tiny shops wedged between the tumbledown houses. In Sadie Frost's window flies buzzed around sticky toffee apples and Liquorice Allsorts and crawled over boxes of wine gums and sherbet dips. A little way along on the other side of the turning was a boot mender, where Sammy Hopgood sat for most of the day with a line of brads clenched between his teeth as he concentrated on shaping and nailing new leather onto worn-out footwear. The tap-tap of Sammy's heavy snobbing hammer continued constantly throughout the day. A few doors along from Sammy's was Mrs Coombes's house.

Her brood was large and fatherless — Reg Coombes had met with a fatal accident at the tram depot when his youngest was only a few months old, and his wife Ginny had been left to bring up their seven children. Ginny's door was always open — there were so many comings and goings at number 18 that she found it easier that way. Tony Allen was quick to take advantage of the fact, and it suited him to have a bolthole for his bookie when the police dashed into the turning for a pinch. The arrangements suited Ginny as the payment she received for her co-operation paid her rent and bought a few bits and pieces for her children.

The week had started well for Danny. Most of the street folk knew him, and his helper Tubby Smith was able to clue him up about a few awkward punters. On Wednesday Danny was left on his own, but on Thursday Tony Allen popped into the turning with a worried look on his face. "They've got a new Chief Inspector down at Riverside nick. I've just 'ad Fat Stan come in ter see me, 'e reckons the Chief's wavin' the big stick. They've got some raids set up fer termorrer. The dice players are in fer it an' so are we."

Danny winced. "Bloody 'ell, they ain't given us much time ter get used ter the job, 'ave they?"

Tony Allen nodded. "Don't worry, Johnny Ross is gonna 'ave a word wiv Bonky Williams. 'E might do the honours fer us. You know this Bonky, don't yer? Is 'e reliable?"

Danny thought about it. Bonky was okay, but things always seemed to go strangely haywire when he was involved. He could be a walking disaster. Suppressing his fears Danny nodded. "Bonky's a good lad, 'e'll know what ter do."

That evening a subdued family sat down to their tea at number 26 Dawson Street. Lucy had come in with the news that Ben had been summoned to a medical and Connie was upset too — the news broadcasts reported

134

heavy sea battles in which there had been many losses. She picked at her meal and then left the table hurriedly. Later, Danny listened at her door and heard her crying. He tapped gently and walked in. Connie's face was wet and puffy, and her eyes were red. Danny sat on the edge of her bed and picked at the counterpane.

"Don't yer worry, Con," he said quietly, "Jimmy's all right. 'E'll be 'ome soon, you see if 'e's not."

Connie dabbed at her eyes. "I 'ad an 'orrible dream the uvver night. I dreamt Jimmy was callin' me. I saw 'im plain as day, but I couldn't move. 'E was in the sea an' 'e 'eld out 'is 'and. I tried ter reach 'im, but it was no good. It was really 'orrible, Danny."

Danny put his arm around her shoulders and she buried her head in his chest. He could feel her sobbing gently as he stroked her fair hair.

" 'E'll be all right. In any case, you shouldn't take notice o' dreams. 'Ere, I've got somefink ter make yer laugh. The police are gonna do a pinch termorrer, and who d'yer fink's gonna get nicked?"

There was concern in Connie's eyes as she looked up at him. "Not you?"

Danny laughed aloud. "Not me. They've set Bonky up fer the pinch. 'E'll get six months 'ard labour if 'e takes 'is eye out in front o' the magistrate."

Connie laughed, and for a moment her face relaxed, but then she went quiet again. After a while she looked up. "Danny," she said, "who was that letter from, or is it a closely guarded secret?"

Danny leaned against the bedrail. "It's no secret from you. I met a nurse in the 'ospital at Dover. 'Er name's Alison an' I'm seein' 'er on Sunday. She's comin' on leave. But don't tell the others — I don't want 'em ragging me!"

Connie grinned. "What's she like? Is she pretty?"

Her brother pursed his lips. "She's fat and cuddly, with bright ginger 'air. I've never took a fat girl out, it'll make a nice change."

Connie threw her pillow at him and Danny caught it. "No, she's pretty — like you," he said, tossing the pillow back at her.

Bonky Williams was feeling important. He paced up and down Clink Lane with a smirk on his face and his hands clasped behind his back. He had had a 'Trotsky' haircut and a shave, and he had put on his best coat, even though the morning was warm.

Danny had just finished paying out a punter when Bonky strolled by. He called out sharply, "Don't go wanderin' too far, you're s'posed ter be on 'and."

Bonky grinned and scratched his cropped head. "Don't worry, I know ter what ter do." He had been given two one pound notes to pay the fine, and two more for his trouble, and a few fake betting slips to put in his pocket as evidence.

In Riverside Police Station Detective Constable Stockbridge — Fat Stan — was feeling irritable. On the rare occasions he had to arrest the bookies his income had suffered. He was on the take, but he was proud of his integrity, and it was unthinkable for him to go around nicking the bookies and still hold his hand out. It wasn't right, he rued. Why did that bloody inspector have to go and get caught peeping through the dormitory windows at the hostel for young women? Bloody old pervert. Now there was a new chief at the station, and he had turned out a bright bleeder.

Fat Stan mumbled angrily to himself as he raised his considerable bulk from the canteen chair. "Better get goin'. Musn't ferget me ole Rennies."

At eleven-thirty a police car pulled up at the end of Clink Lane and Fat Stan got out. At the other end of the turning a police constable stood in a concealed position under the railway arch. Danny had spotted the car draw up and he shouted out to Bonky. " 'Old tight! 'Ere they are!"

Bonky Williams was ready. He was determined to make the pinch look genuine. As Danny slipped into Ginny Coombes's passageway and slammed the front door, Bonky did a quick shuffle. Fat Stan came waddling down the street and already he was puffing. Bonky took off in the direction of the arch, with Fat Stan in hot pursuit.

"Stand still yer soppy git," the fat policeman gasped. " 'Ow am I s'posed ter catch yer?"

Bonky looked over his shoulder and grinned evilly as he trotted on.

PC Entwhistle was observing. He had been told to stay put under the arch and just observe. No one had told him that a dangerous-looking character would be fleeing from the strong arm of the law, and in his direction. PC Entwhistle braced himself. It would be a feather in his cap if he was able to apprehend a dangerous criminal. Fat Stan was a few yards behind Bonky and puffing like a concertina. His face was scarlet, and he was concentrating on what he would do once he got the idiot to the station. PC Entwhistle suddenly jumped out in front of Bonky, but he ducked neatly under his outstretched arm and carried on running through the arch. But Fat Stan could not stop in time and he crashed into the startled constable. They fell in a tangle of arms and legs.

"Get yer big feet orf me chest, yer stupid oaf," Fat Stan gasped out. "Yer've let 'im get away. The chief'll 'ave me guts fer garters."

"Sorry, sir," PC Entwhistle blurted out, attempting to get Fat Stan up from the ground.

"Don't worry about me! Get after 'im fer Gawd's sake!" Fat Stan screamed.

The crestfallen constable ran through the arch and looked both ways. Bonky had disappeared. As he stood nibbling at his chinstrap PC Entwhistle felt a tap on his back.

"Excuse me officer."

He turned around and saw a little old lady standing there looking very flustered.

"What is it, madam?"

The old lady took out a lace handkerchief and dabbed at her eyes. "It's me Bertie, I'm afraid 'e's gorn."

"Gorn, madam? You mean 'e's dead?"

"Oh, I do 'ope not," replied the diminutive old lady, dabbing at her eyes again.

Fat Stan had now reached the constable and had just opened his mouth to bark out some choice profanities when he saw the old lady standing there. He slapped his hand to his forehead in frustration. "Christ!" he muttered, tramping off past them along the road.

"I'm afraid it was my fault," the old lady went on. "You see Bertie was naughty. I didn't give 'im any supper last night. 'E smashed me best vase, you see."

PC Entwhistle took out his notepad. Things were going wrong for him today, he decided. Maybe if he could solve the mystery of Bertie it would redeem him in the eyes of his superiors.

"Please 'elp me find 'im, Officer. I'm frightened 'e'll kill 'imself," the old lady sobbed.

"Don't worry, madam, we'll see what we can do," the constable said, sucking on his pencil stub. "I'll need a few particulars. Now then, full name, age, and description."

The old lady sighed. "Bertie Smith. 'E's about two, an' 'e's blue and yeller."

PC Entwhistle bit through his pencil. "Blue an' yeller?" he echoed incredulously.

"Well, sort of. 'E sings luv'ly, 'cept last night when I scolded 'im. What 'appened was, I let 'im out of the cage an' 'e flew inter me best vase, an' it smashed. 'There will be no need fer you ternight', I said and Bertie knew I meant it."

"Just a minute, lady," the constable said, puckering his forehead. "You're talkin' about a bird?"

"Of course. Bertie's my little budgie. I left the scullery

door open an' Bertie jus' flew away. I 'ope those nasty cats 'aven't got 'im."

PC Entwhistle put his notepad back into his breast pocket. "I'll keep me eye open, madam," he said with a frown. "What's your address?"

"A hundred an' eleven Bermon'sey Lane. I'm on the top floor. You'll 'ave ter give two knocks, an' if 'er downstairs answers yer'll 'ave ter shout. She's very deaf yer know."

"All right, madam, leave it ter me."

"You'd better write it down, Officer, you might ferget."

"I won't ferget, madam. One blue an' yeller budgie, answers ter the name of Bertie Smith. Okay?"

Satisfied that she had done everything possible to secure Bertie's return, the old lady toddled off. PC Entwhistle blew out his cheeks. He was only half-way through his shift, he had already allowed a criminal to escape, and now he was saddled with a missing budgie report. A policeman's lot is not always a happy one, he thought grimly.

Fat Stan was fuming. He stood against a wall while he recovered his breath and cursed the stupid idiot he had been chasing, and he cursed the constable who had caused him to lose his pinch. When he felt less exhausted Fat Stan walked slowly back to Clink Lane railway arch. The constable was still waiting there, hands behind his back. Stan gave him a blinding look. Bloody war, he thought to himself, they're taking anyone on the Force these days.

"No luck, sir?" Constable Entwhistle asked.

"Does it look like it?" Stan sneered.

At that moment Bonky decided it was time to give himself up to justice. He had realised there was a slip-up in the proceedings when he trotted out of the arch. His pursuer was not behind him. Puzzled, Bonky had popped into the little tobacconists on the corner of Bermondsey Lane for a packet of Woodbines. He knew the shopkeeper, and they began to chat away. Now, as he stepped from the shop and saw the two policemen standing by the arch, Bonky could see by the expressions on their faces that all was not well. He ambled up to them and took the betting slips from his pocket. " 'Ere, you'd better 'ave these," he said, looking sheepishly at Fat Stan.

PC Entwhistle reached for his truncheon, just in case Bonky should cut up rough.

"All right, all right, I'll deal wiv this," the fat detective growled, taking a handful of Bonky's best coat in his grasp. "C'mon you, jus' wait till I get you down the nick."

As quick as a flash Bonky put his hand up to his face and called out, "Mind me eye."

As Fat Stan steered him along Clink Lane Bonky brought his bunched fist down from his face and slowly unclenched it. A glass eye stared up at Fat Stan.

The detective gagged. "Put that bleedin' eye in yer pocket," he shouted, his face white. "An don't give me any more trouble. You're already on a good 'idin' when I get yer down the station."

Bonky walked on passively beside the puffing detective. The police car had gone and Fat Stan cursed. "That's anuvver one I owe yer, makin' me walk all the way ter Dock'ead."

Bonky was beginning to feel depressed. Two pounds had seemed a good bargain when Johnny Ross put the deal to him. Getting a good hiding wasn't in the deal. "Jus' wait till I see that cripple bastard," Bonky mumbled.

"What's that?" Fat Stan spat out.

"Nuffink, jus' finkin'."

"Well keep yer poxy thoughts ter yerself."

Behind lace curtains at number 18 Danny sat with Ginny Coombes. They stared out into the street for a time before Danny spoke. "I can't understand it. Fat Stan should've got 'old of Bonky an' brought 'im back by now."

"Maybe they've gone round Dawson Street," Ginny suggested.

"They wouldn't do that, unless Bonky's playin' a funny game. Yer never know wiv 'im. I don't know why Johnny lined 'im up. 'E should 'ave known. Jus' wait till the guv'nor finds out, 'e'll skin Johnny alive."

Ginny shook her head. "That Bonky's as nutty as a fruit cake."

Danny looked up to the top of the street just in time to see the police car drive away. "That's done it," he groaned.

"What's that?" Ginny asked.

"The police car's pissed off."

Ginny looked through the curtains. " 'Ere they come. The fat git's got Bonky by the scruff of 'is neck. 'E must 'ave upset 'im."

Danny peered through the curtains. "Blimey! Look at that tec's face. Bonky's in fer a rough time at the nick. 'E can be right evil when 'e's put out. I remember Tony Arpino tellin' me about one of 'is Italian mates. That fat bastard gave 'im a right goin' over down the station."

"There's nuffink we can do," Ginny said.

Danny thought for a few seconds. Suddenly he clicked his fingers. "I've got it!" he shouted. "Quick! Got any pills?"

"Pills? What pills?"

"Any sort," Danny said impatiently as Bonky and his captor drew level with the window.

"I've only got these, they're cascara."

Danny grabbed the three little white pills from Ginny's hand and ran out into the street. Bonky and the detective were almost at the corner shop when he reached them. "Excuse me, mate, I've bin lookin' everywhere fer 'im," Danny said, pointing to his pal.

Fat Stan gave Danny a wicked look. "Yer can't talk to 'im, 'e's nicked."

"I've got 'is pills 'ere, 'is landlady told me ter give 'em

141

to 'im," Danny said. " 'E went out wivout 'em. They're fer 'is 'eart. 'E as ter take these every day, or 'e's likely ter go off jus' like that."

Fat Stan looked at Danny suspiciously. " 'Is 'eart didn't stop 'im runnin' away from me. The bastard nearly gave *me* an 'eart attack tryin' ter catch 'im."

Danny shook his head sadly. " 'E'll never learn, Officer. One o' these days 'e's gonna do it all wrong."

Bonky was listening to the conversation with a pained look on his face. He wondered whether or not to have a heart attack there and then. He decided against it when the fat detective released his coat collar and took his wrist instead.

The rest of the journey to Riverside Police Station was slightly more civilised. Fat Stan did not want any complications at this point. Bonky for his part walked on quietly. After a while he thought he ought to show some distress.

"Can we slow down a bit, sir?" he asked with a grimace. "I'm gettin' a pain in me chest."

Fat Stan slowed down and gritted his teeth in anger. "Yer givin' me a pain," he said.

They had reached the junction with Tower Bridge Road and Bonky spotted the drinking fountain. "All right if I take me pills, sir?" he asked.

"Go on then, I'm not stoppin' yer, am I?" snarled the detective.

"I gotta take 'em wiv water, sir. They stick in me froat uvverwise."

Fat Stan released his grip on Bonky's sleeve. "Go on then, an' be quick about it."

At last they reached the police station. Bonky's captor was in an ugly mood, now that his bit of sport was stymied by his prisoner's condition. He had realised the danger of slapping a heart case around in the cell, and he decided that the sooner he got rid of the idiot the better. Bonky co-operated as the formalities were taken care of, and he

142

was bailed to appear the following day on a charge of street gaming.

As he walked home Bonky felt relieved, but by the time he reached his home in Dawson Street the relief had turned to pain. After frequent excursions to the toilet Binky was cursing Danny viciously.

"Couldn't 'e 'ave given me some Dolly Mixtures instead?" he groaned aloud. "That fat pig wouldn't 'ave known the difference."

Chapter Thirteen

Waterloo Station was a sea of colour as uniformed figures in Air Force and Royal Navy blues mingled with khaki. Every now and then there was a poignant glimpse of innocent bright summer dresses and waving summer bonnets as the military mingled with the civilian population, hurrying to and fro or waiting around on the noisy concourse. Announcements came over the tannoy scratchy-voiced and flat, and only when a train was re-routed to another platform did any passion appear in the tone. Among the milling passengers hurrying from the platforms or rushing to their trains, there were many who were just waiting, lolling around on hard benches, on bulging suitcases and on piles of kitbags and military packs. The big clock that hung from the arching girders clicked away the minutes of Sunday morning above the crowds. Harassed parents watched the clock as though it might suddenly spin, their stern glances defying their children to drop any ice cream down their best clothes. Their eyes darted from their tickets to the clock that hung high above them, and then to the platform number, almost in disbelief that everything was as it should be. Surely the suitcase clasp would snap and scatter clothes everywhere? Or little Mary would be sick, and young Billy would wander off just when the train arrived? But no, young Billy and little Mary were still there, looking perfectly happy. The noise of the protesting steam engines made them laugh and cover their ears, the soldiers and their guns were fascinating and soon they would be sitting in a big train watching the world whiz by.

One young man watched the clock and eyed the soldiers

with interest. There were five minutes to go before Alison's train arrived at the station, and Danny had spent the last fifteen minutes pacing up and down, watching as groups of servicemen mustered by the platforms on their way to strengthen the garrisons along the South Coast. He felt some regret at not being a part of what was going on, and at the same time he was very relieved. He had been shot at, shelled and dumped in the sea, and he considered himself to have been very fortunate. If that shell fragment had been a little to one side he would have perished. He caught sight of a soldier with a Middlesex shoulder flash and he wondered how Oggy Murphy was. It seemed strange that he had only known the man for a very short time and had hardly spoken more than a few words to him, and yet he felt so close to him. They would probably never meet again but Danny knew he would often think of him and he would always wish him well, for he owed his life to that ugly gypsy.

Slowly the minute hand crept around to one-fifteen, and Danny saw the billowing white smoke way down the line. The announcer's voice crackled as he called out: "The one-seventeen from Dover is now approaching platform three." Danny walked slowly towards the ticket barrier and watched as the train came to a stop. Doors flew open and the platform was filled with hustling travellers as they struggled with luggage and kitbags. It was some time before he saw Alison. She was coming from the far end of the train and Danny could see her short dark hair bobbing around her ears as she walked briskly to the barrier. Danny had time to study her before she spotted him. She looked slightly slimmer than he remembered and she held her head high. The cotton half-coat which she was wearing over her summer dress was unbuttoned. Her feet look tiny in those high heels, he thought. She was holding a shoulder bag with one hand and in the other she was carrying a small suitcase. Her complexion was rosy and Danny was instantly captivated by her expression. She looked prettier than he remembered and he felt his heart start to beat faster.

Alison saw him and her face broke into a warm smile. There was a delay at the barrier before she joined him and put down her suitcase. Danny held her arm as he kissed her softly on the cheek and she replied by squeezing his hand.

"How are you, Danny? You look very well."

Danny flushed slightly as he grinned. "I'm fine. No pain, no aches. It's nice ter see yer again. I've bin finkin' about yer."

Alison displayed her even white teeth. "I bet you've not given me a thought, with all your old girlfriends clamouring round their hero."

Danny pulled a face and looked into her large dark eyes. "They've not come knockin'. Still, I might 'ave bin out at the time."

They laughed and Danny picked up her suitcase. "Would yer like a cuppa or a drink? They're open till two."

Alison smiled. "A drink would be nice."

They walked quickly from the station and down the steps that led into Waterloo Road. They passed the Union Jack Club and took a side turning. Danny steered Alison through the door of The Bell and looked for a place to sit. He put her suitcase down and pulled out a chair from under an empty table. "What d'yer like?"

"I'd like a shandy please."

Danny soon returned with the drinks and they sat facing each other. Alison had a sip of her shandy and then took out a powder compact from her handbag. "I must look a proper mess," she said, opening it and peering into the mirror. "You look fine," Danny replied, aware that his voice sounded strange.

For some time they talked. Danny told her of his new job and made her laugh when he told her about Bonky Williams's arrest. Alison told him that the pressure at the hospital had eased since Dunkirk, but that there were still

147

some nasty cases to deal with due to accidents during training. Danny felt relaxed with her and asked her several questions about herself, but Alison quickly switched the conversation around to him. She liked the way he smiled self-consciously and the way his fair hair seemed to curl above his ears. She liked his warm manner and his blue eyes which seemed to bore into her at times. She knew that she would have to be careful. It would be quite easy to fall for someone like Danny, but it was too soon. She wanted breathing space and a friendship, not another romance now.

Danny looked into her eyes and liked what he saw. She was so different from Kathy. Mystery shone in the depths of her eyes. She was alluring yet seemed somehow unobtainable. She both confused and attracted him, drawing him close yet keeping him distant. He felt no such conflict with Kathy. Their years together had built up between them an easy assurance, and implicit knowledge. It was a feeling of familiarity. But with Alison there was something that churned his insides, a challenge to be met. And there was a sense of urgency and it worried him. He would have to be careful, his impatience might be seen as a sign of immaturity, and Danny was anxious not to create a wrong impression. He realised then that he wanted her and he hoped she felt the same. He looked at her sweet face and imagined he was loving her. He could picture those dark eyes mirroring her sensations as he held her to him. He wondered what locked-up passions would be released if he were able to reach her intimately and love her completely. Alison had flushed at his intense look, and turned her face away. Danny suddenly smiled and shook his head. "I'm sorry, I was staring. You look a sight fer sore eyes."

Alison laughed. "I bet you say that to all the girls."

They had been talking over empty glasses for some time without realising. When Danny noticed he reached for them but Alison stopped him. "I must get going, Danny, I

148

promised my mum I'd look in on her old friends in London. They've got a dairy in Southwark Street. They said they'd put me up if I wanted to."

Danny grinned. "That's not far from where I live."

"I know," Alison replied.

Danny reached across the table and put his hand on hers. "Look, can I see yer ternight?" he asked. "We could go fer a stroll, or a ride up West."

"I'd like that, but I really must make a move now or they'll be worried. They know what train I came up on. I wrote and told them."

Outside the day was bright and warm. Alison took Danny's arm as they walked down Waterloo Road. "D'yer wanna get a bus?" he asked.

"Let's walk, it's a lovely day," Alison said, and then added with concern, "that's if you're feeling up to it?"

Danny threw out his chest. "I'm as fit as a fiddle. It's not a long walk anyway. I know the back doubles."

They walked on and turned into the Cut. The wide market street was almost empty today and the shops were shuttered. A jellied eel stall stood outside a pub, and further along a circle of Salvationists were playing 'Onward Christian Soldiers'. A few children and some old men from the lodging house in Blackfriars stood listening to the music as Danny and Alison walked past, and one of the Salvationists held out a copy of the *War Cry*. Danny dropped a sixpence in the collection box and politely refused the magazine. "If I take that 'ome me dad'll start ter worry. We've got one religious member of our family wivout me startin' ter go all 'oly."

Alison was curious, and so Danny explained all about Lucy and Ben. In return Alison told him about her upbringing in Wales. She told him of the huge family bible, and how all the births and deaths were recorded inside the cover. She said that there were pubs which would still not allow women inside and remained closed on the Sabbath.

"Sounds a mis'rable place on Sundays if yer ask me," Danny said, pulling a face. "What d'yer do fer amusement?"

"Oh, we get by. There's a lot of big families in Wales," Alison chuckled. "Then there's the choirs. Welsh people love to sing, but you know that already."

Danny nodded. 'Me mum loves ter listen to 'em on the wireless."

Alison's face took on a look of sadness as she spoke of her dead father. "My dad was in a choir. He went to a local Baptist mission every Sunday evening. I remember when I was little Dad always sang as he cleaned his boots in the backyard on Sunday mornings. He said it was good practice. He had a beautiful voice. It seems such a long time ago now, but I can still remember him clearly."

They had reached Southwark Street and Alison pointed to the shopfront a little way ahead. "There it is, Morgan's Dairies."

They walked across the street and Danny put the case down by the door. "When shall I call round? Will seven be okay?"

"Can you make it eight? I must spend a bit of time with them," she said.

Danny grinned and raised two fingers to his forehead. "Okay, ma'am. See yer then."

The smell of roast lamb and baked potatoes drifted up the passage as Danny let himself in. In the front parlour he saw the prone forms of his father and Joe Copeland sprawled out in the easy chairs with Sunday papers lying opened on their laps. Both had their mouths gaping and Frank was snoring. Danny walked out into the scullery and found his mother and Maggie washing up the dinner plates. Alice gave her son a long hard look. "And where might you 'ave bin? I've 'ad yet dinner in the oven fer ages."

Danny gave his mother a peck on the cheek. "Sorry, Ma. I met somebody."

"I guessed as much. You know I put the dinner up as soon as yer dad gets in from The Globe. 'Im an' Joe 'ave 'ad theirs an' fergot about it."

Danny glanced at Maggie and pulled a face. "I was waitin' fer a train at Waterloo. I was meetin' this nurse an' I walked her . . ."

Alice looked surprised. "A nurse yer say? Was that someone yer met when yer was wounded?"

" 'S'right, Ma. She's a Welsh girl an' she's stayin' in London till termorrer night, then she's off ter Cardiff. I'm gonna show 'er aroun' town ternight."

Maggie picked up a pile of plates and bent down to put them in the cupboard of the dresser. "Are yer gonna bring 'er 'ome, Danny?" she said, winking at her mother.

"I dunno. I might do. Yer'll 'ave ter wait an' see, won't yer?" Danny replied offhandedly.

Maggie grimaced. "Sorry fer breavin'."

Alice handed her daughter the tea tray. " 'Ere, take this in the front room an' wake them two piss artists up. Wiv them two sprawled out there's no room fer anybody else in there. 'Ere you are, son. Take yer dinner in, an' don't spill the gravy. When yer finished yer can tell me all about yer nurse."

Joe and Frank were rousing when Danny walked into the parlour. Maggie gave her husband a cold stare and started to pour the tea. Frank sat up and rubbed his hand over his face. "Ello, son. I reckoned yer might 'ave come up The Globe. We 'ad a good session, didn't we, Joe?"

Maggie handed her father a cup of tea. " 'E 'ad ter meet somebody, didn't yer, Danny?"

The young man buried his head over the plate and sawed away at the meat, but Maggie's remark was lost on the drowsy pair anyway. Frank yawned and stirred his tea with deliberation. "I was talkin' ter Eddie Kirkland. 'E said Biff Bowden's dog's runnin' at Catford next. 'E said ter ask yer if yer got any more o' them pills. 'E said they made Bonky Williams run like nobody's business. What's

151

that all about then? Eddie wouldn't tell me, 'e said ter ask you.''

Danny told them the full story and the two older men burst into laughter. Alice had come into the room just in time to hear Maggie voice her disgust. "I reckon yer done a silly fing. Fancy givin' 'im cascara. Yer could 'ave made poor ole Bonky really ill.''

Danny cut a potato in half and held one piece on the end of his fork, " 'Ow the 'ell was I ter know the stupid idiot would take 'em. 'E could 'ave made out.''

"What, wiv the copper breavin' down 'is neck? Strikes me you men are all the same. You ain't got no savvy.''

Joe Copeland laughed aloud. "C'mon, Maggie, what about the time you an' Lil Franklin put gin in your forelady's orangeade at the party?''

Maggie sniffed. "That was different, we all detested 'er. Bonky is s'posed ter be 'is pal,'' she said, jerking her thumb in Danny's direction.

"Well 'e is, sort of,'' Danny said, chewing on the potato. 'Anyway, what's a dose o' the runs between friends. I mean, it could 'ave bin worse. That fat git of a tec looked like 'e was gonna give poor ole Bonky a right goin' over when 'e got 'im ter the nick. If it wasn't fer me Bonky could well be walkin' around wiv a couple o' cracked ribs — at least.''

Maggie was beginning to see the funny side of it but she kept a straight face and walked back out into the scullery.

Danny looked around. 'Where's the kids?''

Alice was folding the tablecloth. 'Lucy an' Ben 'ave took 'em up Black'eath. Ben's made 'em a kite,'' she said, brushing her hand over the table.

"Connie wiv 'em, Ma?'' Danny asked as he leaned back in his chair and rubbed his stomach contentedly.

Alice Sutton became serious. "No, she's gone round ter see Jimmy Ellis's mum. Somebody told 'er they 'eard ole Lord 'Aw-'Aw on the wireless last night. 'E was goin' on about our ships gettin' sunk, an' 'e give out some ships' names. People should 'ave more sense. I dunno what they mus' be finkin', worryin' the poor little cow like that.''

"Jimmy's ship wasn't mentioned, was it, Ma?" Danny asked.

"No, but she's all worried. She's gone round ter see if 'is mum's 'eard from 'im.''

Frank Sutton was nodding off to sleep again and Joe was trying to fold the paper without much success. Danny got up and stretched. "I'm gonna go up an' 'ave a read of the papers, Ma. When I get married can I still come round fer me Sunday dinner? That meal was 'andsome.''

Alice smiled. " 'Fore yer go upstairs, I wanna 'ave a word wiv yer. In the scullery.''

Danny followed his mother out into the tiny backroom. Alice folded her arms and looked at him. "What's she like?''

"What's who like?" Danny smiled.

"You know who I'm talkin' about. The nurse. What's she like?''

"She's pretty, Ma. She was the nurse who looked after me at Dover 'ospital.''

"Why don't yer bring the girl 'ome ter meet me an' yer dad? We could fank 'er fer lookin' after yer, couldn't we?''

"I dunno about this visit, she ain't got much time, but I'll try an arrange it fer next time she comes, okay?''

Alice Sutton looked into the faded mirror that was hung on the wall by the yard door. She pressed and patted her hair and her eyes caught Danny's in the reflection. "You know you ought ter fink about settlin' down wiv a nice girl, Danny. Me an' yer farver don't like the idea of you workin' fer that bookie. You ought ter see about gettin' yerself a decent job. That Tony Allen's got a bad name, 'e gets in wiv a nasty crowd. I 'eard yer farver an' Joe talkin' last night. The police 'ave got their eye on 'im, they fink 'e's in on the black market game.''

Danny puffed. "Look, Ma, it's only people talkin'. If

the law knew or suspected anyfing they wouldn't broadcast it, would they? Some people are jealous of what 'e's got. 'E ain't a bad bloke. 'E give me a job, didn't 'e?''

"I ain't sayin' 'e's a bad bloke, Danny, but that Jack Mason is a rotter. I've 'eard a lot about 'im. Some of them uvver blokes 'e goes wiv ain't very nice either. Jus' you be careful, that's all I'm sayin'. We don't want ter come visitin' yer in prison. The 'ospital was enough.''

Danny put his arm around his mother's narrow shoulders. "I'll be very careful, Ma, I know what I'm doin,'' he promised.

Up in his bedroom Danny kicked off his shoes and sprawled out on his bed. The room was cool and quiet. He lay with his hands clasped behind his head and stared at a crack in the ceiling, thinking about Alison, going over their meeting in his mind. He let his eyes follow the line in the ceiling and his thoughts drifted. He found himself comparing her with Kathy. They were both pretty and both nice to be with, but they were so different. With Kathy it was easy to read her thoughts, and he thought of that Saturday night. Then he remembered the night at the dog track when she had told him in no uncertain terms that they must not see each other again, yet he was sure she wanted him to. He was sure too that Kathy was desperately unhappy with Jack Mason. She had realised her mistake but she was stubborn and was determined to stay with him, especially now with a baby on its way. Alison on the other hand was mysterious, she had a way of switching the conversation away from herself and he wanted to know more about her.

He followed the line in the ceiling and noticed for the first time that it was starting down the wall. The gaff's falling apart, he thought to himself as he twisted onto his side and bunched up the pillow. Through the bedroom window he could see chimney stacks and cracked chimney pots standing out stark against the sky. The view was too familiar and he rolled over again. Maybe he was being too impatient. No doubt Alison would relax a little more and talk about herself in her own good time. Perhaps he was comparing her too much with the girls he had known before — after the first five minutes most of them had given him a potted life history. Maybe Welsh girls were different. Alison had told him something of her life in the Valleys and about her father, but there seemed to be a curtain which she pulled down when he prompted her to talk about herself, and about her life at the hospital where she was working, and her social life. Maybe he was expecting too much of her, he thought. There would be time enough tonight to talk more.

He would take Alison up West, maybe they would stop off at The Globe on the way back and he could show her off to his pals. The only problem with that idea, he suddenly realised, was Bonky Williams. Bonky was still a little offhand with him over the cascara episode and it would be just like him to get up to one of his tricks. It might be a better idea to pop in at The Horseshoe in Bermondsey Lane. He could show Alison off to Tony Arpino, who was always to be found drinking there.

Danny drifted off to sleep, while down in the tiny parlour below things were rather subdued. Frank and his drinking partner Joe was also sleeping off the effects of their Sunday drinking session. Their snores had driven Alice to her friend Annie Barnes's house while Maggie sat alone in the scullery. The *News of the World* lay open at her elbow as she fretted over her two children. Maggie had just read that Churchill was going on the air that night to deliver an important speech. She was convinced that she would be doing the right thing by the children in getting them out of London, but she and Joe had had words about it the previous evening. He thought she was being hysterical and he didn't seem to realise that it wouldn't be long before the whole war blew up around them. All the papers said that British cities could expect severe air attacks and there would almost certainly be heavy casualties. What if anything happened to her children? Joe had got angry with her and stormed off to the pub saying that if the kids were sent away from London they could get ill treated. What then? Maggie sighed and picked up the paper again. She started to read an article about a bishop and a chorus girl. It all seemed very familiar to her and she turned the page. Joe's snoring carried out to the scullery and Maggie threw down the *News of the World* and walked out into the backyard.

Chapter Fourteen

On the stroke of eight Alison left the dairy and saw the figure of Danny Sutton sauntering along in her direction, looking very smart in a grey suit. Danny saw her walking towards him and he quickened his step. He kissed her on the cheek as they met and he could smell her freshness. Alison's hair shone and her face looked rosy. She was wearing a printed dress that hugged her slim figure and accentuated her small rounded breasts. She carried a cardigan over her arm and a small handbag was slung over her shoulder. Danny smiled at her as they started towards London Bridge Station. "You look very nice," he remarked.

Alison was aware of his strong clasp and she felt strangely excited. "You look rather smart," she said softly as they strolled on, shoulders touching.

The electric train rumbled over the railway bridge that spanned the Thames and slid into Charing Cross Station. Danny and Alison alighted and walked out into the Strand. The evening was warm and pleasant, and a slight breeze was blowing. They skirted pigeon-infested Trafalgar Square and stood for a while hand-in-hand, gazing down on the fountains that spurted up from artesian wells, the couchant lions guarding the high column and the war-scarred admiral, Lord Nelson. And other young couples were sitting around the fountains or strolling among the strutting birds, servicemen and women and nurses still in uniform mingling in a colourful throng. Children chased the pigeons and dipped toffee-smeared hands in the cold water, while souvenir sellers

157

plied their tin badges and tiny Union Jacks. The base of the column was boarded up, and at the north end of the square the imposing National Gallery was ready for war, a wall of sandbags reaching high up the stone pillars. Scurrying clouds seemed to brush the head of the august admiral and a pink evening light softened the fronts of the stone buildings. Starlings chattered noisily in the trees and flew away in wheeling formations as a taxi-cab backfired in the Mall.

For a time the young couple merely stood and took in the scene without saying a word. Danny felt at home here. He remembered his childhood, when for a penny ticket on a number 36 tram he would set off to see the sights of London. He was proud of his knowledge of the capital, and when Alison asked him about their famous surroundings he was able to elaborate on some of the finer points.

"See those lions? They were designed by a bloke called Lan'seer. That column is 145 feet 'igh. See over there? That's St Martin's in the Fields. They 'ave lunchtime concerts there nearly every day."

Alison leaned against his shoulder and watched his face as he talked. She noticed the occasional nervous twitch of his lip, and she liked the way he laughed aloud. Danny was beginning to intrigue her, and she wanted to savour the feeling. Her racing thoughts worried her and a spasm of excitement passed through her. "Let's walk on, Danny," she said, squeezing his hand.

"Okay, let's go this way. We can go ter Piccadilly Circus. I used ter do this walk when I was a kid," he grinned.

In the Charing Cross Road they stopped to have a drink. The pub was full of weekend visitors and all the seats were taken. When Danny finally managed to get served he steered Alison into a corner and they stood very close while they sipped their drinks. The pub was noisy and bustling. An elbow caught Danny in the back and he gave the customer a long hard look. Alison giggled, finally drawing a reluctant grin from her escort.

"Let's get out of here. I want to see this famous Piccadilly Circus you've been telling me about," she said.

"Okay, but there ain't any Eros. The statue's bin took away fer safety."

Alison slipped her arm in his as they strolled leisurely through Leicester Square. They sat on a bench for a while, idly watching passers-by, and then made their way into Piccadilly Circus where they climbed onto the memorial steps.

Danny pointed in the direction of Shaftesbury Avenue. "I know a nice little café over there. Shall we get some-fink to eat?"

Alison nodded and held his arm tightly as they dodged through the traffic and walked to a side street off the Avenue. Luigi's Café was quite full, but they found a table for two beneath the arch of the stairs, and after consulting the crudely worded menu they decided on a meal of egg, bacon and chips. Danny grinned slyly when he ordered two large teas and when they arrived Alison put her hand up to her mouth and giggled at the absurdity.

"They're big enough ter drown in, ain't they," he laughed, grasping the huge mug in both hands.

When they had finished their meal they sat for a while, chatting happily together as customers came and went. Finally they left the side street café and walked out into the late evening air.

Danny slipped his arm around Alison's slim waist as they skirted the Piccadilly Circus and sauntered into Regent Street. Danny could feel her body brushing his and her softness troubled him. He wanted to reach out and hold her, he wanted to wrap his arms around her and kiss her soft neck. He looked down at her and it seemed to him that she was gently mocking him. She had a guarded look that dared him to reach out for her and yet seemed to warn him off. There was a strangeness about her — she appeared to be worldly-wise, confident and discreet, but he wondered if it was panic in her dark eyes. Was there something in her past that made her wary of him, or was it just her mystique? He was determined to respond to the challenge. His thoughts tumbled over and over in his mind as they walked on silently. The curve of Regent Street spread out before them and Alison pulled on his arm suddenly. The strap of her shoe had come undone and as she stooped to fasten it she sighed, "My feet are beginning to ache, Danny. Can we get a bus back?"

Danny pointed to a nearby bus stop. "A 53 stops 'ere. It goes ter the Old Kent Road."

After a ten minute wait Danny and Alison exchanged smiles at the welcome sight of an approaching 53 bus, and soon they were passing over Westminster Bridge. They sat close together on the back seat, looking out at the flowing River Thames. Danny sighed. "That's a nice sight. I've swum in there many a time. We used ter dive in orf the barges near where I live. I tell yer, Alison, there was a time not so long ago when I didn't ever expect ter see Ole Farver Thames again."

Alison was quiet for a while and then she looked at him closely. "Tell me, Danny, does it still worry you, Dunkirk?"

Danny shook his head emphatically. "I used to wake up some nights in a cold sweat, but I'm okay now. I still fink of the lads I left be'ind there though."

Alison squeezed his arm. "I'll never forget that night they brought you in to the hospital. I didn't think you were going to pull through. Do you still get any pain from the wounds?"

Danny grinned. "I've told yer, I'm fit fer anyfing 'cept a cross-country run. I'm still a bit breafless at times, that's all."

"What about your mates, Danny? Do you see any of them?"

"Yer mean the ones who made it back? I ain't bin roun' the drill 'all since Dunkirk."

Something in his tone surprised Alison and she looked

round to see that his face had become dark. Her questioning eyes encouraged him to continue. "The drill 'all is only a few minutes from my 'ouse," he went on, "but I can't seem ter face goin' there. They'll 'ave records of who made it back but I jus' keep wonderin' about the lads. D'yer fink I'm bein' stupid?"

Alison laid her head on his shoulder. "Of course I don't. It's only natural I suppose. Names on a scroll are so final, perhaps that's why you can't face it. Maybe you expect to see your mates in the street. What you have been through must have left some scars. Don't worry about it, one day when you're good and ready you'll go and find out for sure. In the meantime you've got to give your mind the opportunity to adjust to the terrible things you've been through. Give it time."

Danny's face relaxed slightly and he pressed his shoulder against her as the bus headed for the Elephant and Castle.

Danny had attracted the attention of a small passenger on the seat in front. Enquiring eyes stared into his and dirty hands gripped the seat rail tightly. The tot's lank blond hair hung down to her shoulders and a button nose twitched. Danny winked at the child, but she ignored his gesture. He folded his arms and closed his eyes, then slowly he opened one eye then shut it quickly. Still the child did not respond. Alison watched as Danny tried to bring forth a smile. He made faces and rolled his eyes but the child just stared at him, her pale eyelids heavy with tiredness, and as the bus jerked to a halt the child rocked back in the seat and was scooped up by her mother who cuddled her and crooned into her ear. Blond hair cascaded over her face, and presently she fell asleep. Alison watched Danny smiling.

At the Bricklayers Arms the large woman and her daughter got off the bus in front of Danny and Alison. Her child slept on peacefully. Danny took Alison's arm as they crossed over into Tower Bridge Road and walked along the quiet thoroughfare. The night was closing in quickly, birds slumbered in the tall plane trees and stars twinkled down from a velvet expanse. They walked for a while until Alison broke the silence. "I've really enjoyed this evening, Danny," she said.

"It's bin 'an'some," he replied. "I was goin' ter see if yer'd like ter meet me mate Tony Arpino, but the pubs are shut by now. By the way, what time yer s'posed ter be in by?"

Alison shrugged her slim shoulders. "I've got a key. The Morgans run a dairy, don't forget. I expect they'll be snoring by now."

They walked through a maze of drab grey backstreets and alleyways as the moon rose over lop-sided chimney pots and blue-grey slated roofs, and at last they reached Southwark Street. They halted at the diary where there was a dark recess beside the shop front and Danny could see the empty milk carts through the slatted gates. The shadows closed round them as they moved together and held each other closely. Danny could smell the fragrance of Alison's hair as he bent down and kissed her open mouth. Her breathing came faster as she responded to his embrace and her fingers stroked his fair hair while Danny's searching hands ran down her back. Alison rested her head on his shoulder and he kissed her ear, his mouth moving down onto her smooth, soft neck. But suddenly Alison tensed; she stepped back from his embrace and put both hands on his shoulders. "You don't like wasting time, Danny. Let me catch my breath," she said quickly.

"I've wanted to do that ever since I saw yer at the station. You're really somefink, d'yer know that?" Danny said smiling.

"Go on, I bet you say that to all the girls," Alison chided.

Danny's face became serious and she felt his grip tighten. She could not trust herself to relax with him now

162

that the first barrier was down. Her body cried out for him but her mind was troubled. It must not be like the last time, she vowed. Her painful memories had been kindled by his kiss and his searching hands had stirred her stifled feelings. She needed time to find herself again, there could be no hurried love until she was absolutely sure of herself. She knew in her heart that it would be so easy to give herself to him there and then. She tingled at his touch, but she needed to be certain that there would be an understanding, she had to make him see somehow. It was important for them both and she had to tell him everything.

Danny gazed down at her and saw her eyes misting over. He pulled her gently to him and they remained quiet for a while, both content to let their early passions abate. Alison felt his arms relax their hold on her. "I must get in. It's been a lovely time, but I'm feeling very tired, Danny. Do you mind?"

Danny moved back and his hand went up to adjust his shirt collar. "What about termorrer? I mus' see yer again before yer catch your train 'ome."

Alison looked into his pale blue eyes and saw the urgency there. "Yes, I'd like that."

Danny's face relaxed into a huge grin. "Look, I'm takin' bets up until about one o'clock. We could 'ave all afternoon tergevver. What d'yer say?"

"That would be nice."

"Okay, I'll come round fer yer at two o'clock."

Their goodnight kiss was soft, and Alison watched him as he walked off into the darkness.

The figure standing in the dark doorway changed position to ease his aching foot and peered impatiently at his small silver pocket watch. It was half past midnight and the beat policeman had just appeared from Shad Thames. He turned left and walked slowly towards Dockhead with his hands clasped behind his back. Johnny Ross moved out of his hiding place and saw the tall figure of Con Baldwin coming towards him. The approaching figure jumped nervously as Johnny hissed at him. "Over 'ere, Con. It's okay, the rozzer's gone."

Con joined Johnny and they quickly crossed Tooley Street and walked into Shad Thames. The narrow cobbled lane was deathly quiet as they reached an arched doorway. Con took out a crowbar from beneath his coat and inserted it into the heavy brass padlock. Johnny held his breath. Had Ernie Baines done his job properly? If he had, the padlock would spring open under a little pressure. Con grunted with satisfaction as he removed the padlock and slipped the hasp. The heavy oak door creaked as it opened and they stepped inside.

" 'Urry up," Con hissed, "I'll give yer five minutes an' I'll knock on the gate. Fer Gawd's sake don't move till I give yer the signal."

Johnny disappeared into the warehouse and Con stepped back into the lane and gingerly closed the warehouse door. He replaced the hasp and levered the doctored padlock back into place. Satisfied with his efforts he walked along Shad Thames and passed by the gate of the adjoining warehouse. He was ready to adopt a drunken pose should the policeman appear again, but he need not have worried — PC Harriman was hurrying on to the road works in Jamaica Road, where old Bill Jones the council night watchman was busy brewing up some fresh tea over his coke brazier.

Johnny climbed the dark stone staircase to the roof. At the top of the stairs he put his weight against the iron fire door and it clattered open. He was now standing on the flat roof of the warehouse and he swallowed hard as he shut the door behind him. Johnny was only too aware that there was no way back. The door could only be opened from the inside. Ernie Baines had gone over the plan with him until Johnny was convinced he could find his way around blindfolded. Above him was the wide darkness of the night sky, and the fire escape staircase loomed up ahead. Johnny ducked low as he limped down the iron steps that ran down the outside of the building into the yard below. Ernie Baines has come up trumps this time, he thought. The laden lorry was there, standing by the massive iron-plated gate. Johnny hobbled quickly to the yard office, took out a scarf from his coat and wrapped it around his hand. Looking over his shoulder as though he expected to be seen he punched out the small glass panel of glass nearest to the door lock. As he left the office holding the bunch of keys Johnny heard a soft tap on the wicket gate. He threw the keys under the gap below the gate and soon Con Baldwin was in the yard beside him. While Johnny sorted out the keys for the main gate Con jumped up into the lorry cab and checked that the ignition key was there. Johnny beckoned urgently to him and the two of them pulled the heavy gate open. There was one more task left to do before they drove away. Johnny went over to a sand bin opposite the warehouse and lifted the lid. Con started up the lorry, drove it over to the gateway and stopped, then Johnny limped across the lane carrying a coiled length of rope that was knotted every couple of feet. Clambering up onto the cab roof he looped the rope over the spiked tips of the gate then hurried down into the cab as Con drove off.

They drove the stolen lorry steadily along Dockhead. It was not unusual for lorries to use that route at night, traffic from all over the country began to arrive in the early hours ready to load and unload at the wharves and docks. Con and Johnny were confident that their cargo would be stowed safely before the theft was discovered. They could feel the gods of fortune smiling down on them as they reached their destination without being stopped. The warehouse theft went undetected until after Ernie Baines arrived for work and switched padlocks.

Before he went off duty PC Harriman found himself

having to answer some awkward questions. He should have patrolled Shad Thames once more before he finished his rounds, but the place gave him the creeps and he had opted out of his responsibilities in favour of another mug of old Bill's tea. The Station Inspector called in Detective Constable Stanley Stockbridge after he had finished with Harriman. "I'm going to lay it on the line, Stockbridge," he said, "I want you off your fat arse and on your way to Sullivan's Wharf at Shad Thames. The guv'nor there has reported that a lorry's gone missing from his yard. Apparently they got in using a rope, they lassoed the spikes and shinned over the gate. On your way, Stockbridge."

Later, a phone call from Limehouse Police Station informed him that a lorry belonging to George Sullivan and Sons, Wharfingers, had been found abandoned in a lorry rank outside the West India Docks.

"It wasn't exactly abandoned," the desk sergeant explained. "One of our constables found a couple o' Chinese seamen asleep in the cab. They had adopted the vehicle. Their dabs were all over the cab."

"Can't we nick 'em for theft?" Inspector Flint asked.

"No chance," was the reply. "We're charging the two of 'em for an affray in a gambling house in Pennyfields. They sliced another Chink's ear orf during an argument over a game of Mah Jong."

Inspector Flint shook his head sadly and looked out of his office window. Down below he could see the activity in the local timber yard. Two men were leisurely stacking pine planks while another worker lolled against a covered pile, busily engrossed in rolling a cigarette. Inspector Flint returned to his desk and picked up a pile of papers. That stupid fat Detective Constable had better come up with something pretty quick, or it's back on the beat for him, he vowed. Inspector Flint was determined to 'ginger up' the station, as he put it. Already he had made some drastic changes in his efficiency campaign. Had Inspector Flint been gifted with X-ray vision he would have made more progress, for down in the timber yard behind a stack of deal boards, and out of sight of the station window, were three tons of corned beef and eighty cases of canned peaches.

Chapter Fifteen

On the Monday morning of the 15th of July 1940 all the daily newspapers carried a front page report of the Prime Minister's address to the nation. In the backstreets of dockland the speech was being discussed on doorsteps, in the corner shops and behind crisp lace curtains in the small parlours. Winston Churchill had seized the attention of almost everyone when he delivered what the papers were calling his masterful speech. Pubs had stopped serving to listen, and those with no wireless set had crowded round their neighbours'. The dire warning frightened the wits out of Granny Bell, as she confessed to the Brightmans. " 'E fair put the fear o' Gawd inter me last night," she said . "What wiv 'im goin' on about fightin' 'em in the streets. 'E said they're comin' any day now, by all accounts."

The content of the Prime Minister's speech had an effect on Maggie Copeland too. She was now more than ever determined to see that Joe would allow the children to be evacuated from London. "Even 'e said it. London's gonna be laid in ruins before we'd surrender."

Joe licked a dob of marmalade from his finger and shook his head in anger. " 'Ow many times we bin over this? I've gotta get ter work, I ain't got no time ter argue wiv yer."

Maggie threw down the morning paper. "It's in there. Read it, sod yer! Read it!"

Joe pulled a face and picked up his tea cup. Maggie saw that she was getting nowhere with him and she sat down and pulled the paper towards her. "Listen ter what it says.

'Be the ordeal sharp or long, or both, we shall seek no terms, we shall tolerate no parley. We may show mercy, but we shall ask none.' You listenin'?''

Joe tried to hide a smile but Maggie saw his face and she got even more angry. She ran her finger along the type. "There's more: 'London itself, fought street by street, could easily devour an entire hostile army, and we would rather see London laid in ruins and ashes than it should be abjectly enslaved.' What about that then?''

Joe felt the toast sticking in his throat and he realised he was late for work. "Look 'ere, luv, we'll talk about it ternight, okay?''

Maggie was having none of Joe's procrastination. "We'll talk about it now, or I'll leave yer, Joe, I mean it!''

Joe Copeland saw the determination in his wife's eye and he pointed to the teapot. "All right, you win. Pour me anuvver cuppa, an' we'll talk.''

"I thought you was late for work?''

"Sod work. Let's talk.''

When The Globe opened Danny Sutton was the first one through the doors. He was soon joined by Johnny Ross who looked particularly pleased with himself.

"You look like you jus' found a fiver stickin' ter yer shoe,'' Danny remarked.

Johnny winked and called Eddie Kirkland over. " 'Ere, Eddie, give me an' me mate a drink, an' 'ave one yerself.''

The landlord of The Globe pulled a face. "Leave me out, Johnny. We 'ad a late session last night. Biff Bowden was in 'ere wiv some of 'is cronies. Even 'is dog got pissed.''

The joke was lost on Danny, who sipped his drink thoughtfully. Johnny watched as Eddie moved away to serve an old gent who had just walked in, then he leaned over close to his pal. "Done a bit o' business last night, we did. Might be able ter put some easy money your way.''

Danny was used to Johnny's boasting and he ignored

the remark. Johnny looked around to make sure they were not being overheard and he put his hand to one side of his mouth. "We knocked over a ware'ouse. Got a lorry load o' tinned stuff. Most of it's spoken fer, but we've gotta punt the rest. I'm seein' a bloke later terday. Fancy givin' us an 'and? I'll row yer in fer a few bob."

"Sorry, Johnny, I've got a date. I'm seein' 'er soon as I'm finished takin' the bets."

"Oh yeah? An' who's the lucky little bird then?"

Danny leaned back and folded his arms. "Anybody ever told yer you're a nosy git, Rossy?" he said, his pale eyes glinting.

Johnny grinned. "All right, all right, I'm only tryin' ter be sociable."

"She's a nurse I met when I was in 'ospital. I took 'er out last night. She comes from Wales, an' she's on leave," Danny said, hoping to satisfy his pal's curiosity.

"What's she like?" Johnny prompted.

"She's a little darlin'."

"Does she do a turn?"

"Bloody, 'ell, Johnny, you don't stop, do yer?" Danny exclaimed as he picked up the empty glasses and walked over to the bar.

When he returned Johnny was ready with a suggestion. " 'Ere, if yer wanna place ter take 'er, yer can use my drum. I'm goin' up town ternight ter celebrate me good fortune. I won't be 'ome — if yer know what I mean."

Danny sat down and sipped his pint thoughtfully. There would be little time before Alison caught her train to Cardiff but then it might be some time before he could see her again. Trouble was, if he accepted Johnny's offer, everyone in the pub would know within a day or two. But it wouldn't hurt to take the key, just in case. "Okay," he said at last.

"Okay what?" Johnny said absently, fixing Eddie's barmaid with a malevolent stare.

"Okay, I'll borrer yer key," Danny said.

Johnny fished into his coat pocket and pulled out a key on a length of string. "There we are. The only fing is, don't go blamin' me if yer put 'er in the pudden club."

Danny finished his drink then glared at Johnny. "I ain't cut out ter be a daddy. What do I do wiv the key when I'm finished wiv it?"

"Leave it wiv Ginny Coombes. yer can spin 'er a yarn, she don't 'ave ter know what yer borrered it for. I can call in fer it termorrer."

"I won't tell 'er if you don't," Danny mocked as he stood up to leave.

Johnny gripped his pal's arm. "You sure it's a nurse yer takin' out, an' not Kathy Thompson?"

Danny looked down at his friend with a murderous stare. "Yer gonna get yerself in a lot o' trouble wiv that tongue o' your'n. No it's not Kathy Thompson. She's not my concern since she shacked up wiv Jack Mason."

"Sorry, Danny," Johnny said. "Water under the ole bridge, eh? By the way, she was in 'ere fer a spell last night."

"Wiv 'im?"

"Yeah, but they went out early. I was in the piss 'ole an' I 'eard 'em naggin' each uvver as they went by the winder."

Danny walked to the door. "See yer aroun', Johnny, an' fanks fer the you know what."

Joe Copeland was not the only member of the Sutton family who missed work that Monday morning. Connie had opened the paper and seen the heading: 'Destroyer sunk'. Her heart pounded as she read on. "The Destroyer *Prowler* (Lt Cmdr W. Bass) has been sunk by a torpedo in the North Atlantic, it was announced by the Admiralty last night. There are reports of some survivors. The *Prowler* was launched at Greenock in 1935 and carried a complement of 145 officers and men. She had a speed of

36 knots and was armed with . . ." Connie could read no more. Her eyes were swimming and she dropped her head onto the table. Almost immediately there was a knock on the door and sounds of someone in distress.

Alice Sutton came into the parlour looking white and shaken. "Connie, luv, it's Missus Ellis. She's 'ad a telegram. It's Jimmy."

The plump figure of Mrs Ellis followed Alice into the room. Her eyes were red from crying and her face was ashen. In her shaking hand she clenched a plain, buff-coloured envelope. Alice led her to a chair and Mrs Ellis sat down heavily. "It came late last night. I couldn't come roun' before, I was too upset."

Connie bit on her knuckles. "What does it say? Is Jimmy —?"

Mrs Ellis held out the telegram. "You read it, Connie."

The young girl took out the buff slip with shaking hands and read it quickly. "It only says about 'is ship bein' sunk an' they'll keep yer informed when there's more news. I've jus' read that much in the paper," she blurted out.

Mrs Ellis dropped her head and sobbed. Connie got up and went over to her. She knelt down and clasped the distressed woman's hand in hers. "Listen, Missus Ellis, Jimmy's gonna be okay, I know 'e is. We've jus' gotta wait."

"And pray," Alice said as she laid her arm round Mrs Ellis's shoulders.

Ben Morrison had received a letter that angered and shook him. Now, a week old, it rested behind the mantelshelf clock, but still a fury burned inside him whenever he saw it. Lucy had argued with him to destroy it, but he was adamant. "Those sort of letters are evil," he had said. "The writers should be exposed and locked up. I'm determined to find out who wrote it, however long it takes." Lucy had given up the argument. There was no shifting him. More than the letter, she was startled by Ben's

173

attitude to the affair. He had talked to her often of having compassion and understanding, and he had preached to her about the need for forgiveness and mercy, but he had changed since the tribunal hearing. He was becoming bitter and cynical, although in their most intimate moments together he was tender and romantic and Lucy found their lovemaking exciting. When Ben received the anonymous letter, however, he had shown her an anger that was alien to him. Lucy was shocked by his reaction and it worried her. She had come to the conclusion that he must be smarting from the taunts at work and the lack of any support at the mission; he must be feeling isolated and shunned. She sensed it in his growing need to be with her as much as possible, and she was more than willing to spend her time with him. One nagging worry, though, clouded Lucy's mind. Her period was overdue. It had never happened before, and she had always been as regular as clockwork. As she felt no different she put it down to worrying over Ben. She had wanted to tell him but decided to wait another week, and now he was preoccupied with the letter.

When the letter had first arrived Ben would not let Lucy see it, but she persisted until he gave in. The envelope bore a Bermondsey postmark and the message was hand-printed and badly constructed, although Ben was sure that was intentional. The letter vilified him. It condemned his pacifist views and called him a bastard. It went on to express the hope that Ben's family would be the first to get shot should the Germans arrive, and it ended by wishing him a syphilitic death, a plague on his offspring, and agony as they all burned in the fires of Hell. Lucy had been overcome when she read it and urged him to consign the evil thing to flames, but Ben had stubbornly placed it behind the clock.

Down below in Tooley Street the usual traffic was converging outside the wharves. Now and then a number 70 tram rattled along until it reached the foot of Duke

Street Hill, where it waited until the next tram arrived. The points were then switched and the trams changed places. The area was noisy throughout the whole day. Vans and horse carts were called from their ranks into the wharves and onto the quays, more vans and carts arriving to take their places as the laden vehicles struggled past and drove away. The main topic of conversation on that Monday morning was the Prime Minister's speech. The carmen discussed it as they stood beside their vehicles or drank tea from tin mugs in the cafés; the dockers and stevedores chatted about it in the ships' holds and on the quayside. Almost everyone felt that what had been said needed saying. It had been spelt out, and at least everyone knew exactly where they stood.

The tall, stooping figure who walked along Tooley Street that Monday morning had known all along precisely where he stood. In 1914 he had stood on the street corner and watched the men march off to war behind blaring brass bands, and he had seen soldiers in their uniforms drinking and singing in the pubs before they sailed off to France. He had stood on the street corner and watched the parades as the ragged survivors were cheered and clapped upon their return. He had cursed his bad luck and envied the adulation the exhausted heroes received. A curvature of the spine, bad eyesight and flat feet had prevented him from joining up and being part of the parade. Embittered and envious, he had buried himself in his clerical job, and now he saw the whole process being re-enacted. There was a difference now, however, for this time he had found what he considered to be a worthwhile vocation. This time he was able to play a part, and as he walked towards the magistrates' court he smiled to himself. Who was it who said "The pen is mightier than the sword"? Well he was making his own particular contribution to the war effort, and this morning he would begin a new episode. He would remain quiet and unobtrusive in the public gallery, and when the names were called and the addresses were read out, the slouching figure sitting on the polished wooden bench would decide on what action to take. It would not be a difficult decision to make, for he knew exactly where he stood.

Danny Sutton stood in Ginny's doorway. A few lucky punters had walked up to collect their Saturday night dog winnings and there was only one query.

"Look 'ere, son," the old man said, "yer must 'ave made a mistake. I'ad a tanner each way on an 'undred ter seven. If it 'ad bin an 'undred ter six I'd 'ave copped 'undred tanners an' me place money, now wouldn't I?"

"Yeah, but it wasn't 'undred ter six, was it?"

"I'm jus' sayin' s'pose it was?"

Danny puffed loudly. "Look, Pop, 'undred ter six is just over sixteen ter one. That means yer get sixteen tanners, not 'undred tanners. You'd get about eight an' fourpence plus yer place money."

"But it wasn't 'undred ter six, it was 'undred ter seven."

"That's what I'm tryin' ter tell yer."

"Well my ole woman worked it out fer me. She don't make mistakes. She reckons she only ever made one mistake in 'er life."

"Well she's made anuvver one, Pop."

The old gent pocketed his winnings and walked off grumbling about the unfairness of it all. A short while later Danny handed over the day's bets to Ginny and sipped the tea that she had made for him. " 'Ere, Danny," she said, "I see that Thompson girl up the corner shop earlier on. I meant ter tell yer, she's got a nice shiner. D'yer reckon 'er feller give it to 'er?"

Danny gulped the hot tea in anger and felt it burn his gullet. "That's an animal she's wiv, I'd take money on it."

Ginny picked up a pair of torn trousers and searched for the cotton. "I reckon she's a nice kid. Too good fer 'im. I don't know what she got 'iked up wiv that slob for.''

"I dunno, Ginny," Danny said coldly, "there's no accountin' fer taste."

Ginny gave him a playful nudge. "She'd 'ave bin better off wiv somebody like yerself. If I was twenty years younger yer wouldn't 'ave ter ask me twice."

Danny grinned. "You're all woman, Ginny, an' what's more yer make a luvverly cup o' tea."

Ginny nudged him again and took his empty teacup. Danny watched as she rinsed the cup at the sink in the back scullery. She would still be a fine catch for someone, he thought. Her figure was still round and firm, and even with her hair pulled up untidily into a bun on the top of her head, Ginny looked attractive. Her skin was soft, and the few lines around her eyes did not lessen her good looks. Danny had to admit that he wouldn't say no to her in different circumstances.

Ginny put a fresh cup of tea down on the table beside him. While he sipped the tea she picked up the torn trousers and pulled the frayed material together. Occasionally her eyes moved up from her sewing and she watched him. Her husband had been gone almost three years and she felt a stirring in her belly. It was worse at night, when the solitude and the growing desire became an ache. The young man who had taken over the pitch figured in her fantasies. Her face would flush in the darkness as her hand reached over to the pillow beside hers. Her desire was tempered by feelings of guilt; he was a mere boy compared to her, yet in her fantasies he was the one who climbed into her bed and loved her. The ache would then be drowned in a sea of passion, and in its wake a serene feeling would flow over their united bodies like an incoming tide. In the lonely silence the woman could do nothing about the salt tears that soaked her pillow. Her dead husband would come to fill her drowsy thoughts, and she always sought his forgiveness for her infidelity before sleep overtook her.

* * *

177

The sun was high as the carman climbed down from his dickey-seat and wrapped the wheel chain around the wooden spokes. As he strapped the nosebag over his nag's head the animal reared back. The carman spoke quietly to the horse and stroked its neck reassuringly. Normally he parked his cart in Tooley Street while he went for his lunchtime drink, but today the horse seemed nervous. Dawson Street was quiet in comparison to the main road, and before he went off to the pub the carman satisfied himself that all was well. The horse munched away at the oats and occasionally shook its head in an effort to get rid of the pain from its abcessed ear. Along the turning Crazy Bella was kneeling at her front door and putting the finishing touches to her stone step. She mumbled to herself as she gathered up the block of whitening and the house flannel. Across the street the Brightmans' baby slept peacefully in its pram by the front door, and a ginger-haired lad sat day-dreaming, his feet in the gutter. The sun shone down into the street and a pencil of bright light made young Billy Birkitt shield his eyes. He could see a glass marble lying in the middle of the cobbled roadway, and he got up to take a closer look. The marble was trapped between two cobblestones. Billy knelt down and tried to prise it loose with his fingers but it was firmly wedged there and the young lad ran back in his house and out into the backyard. He soon found the pointed stick that he used on the cat when it sauntered through his carefully arranged army of tin soldiers. He ran back to the middle of the street and knelt down to dig away at his prize. Crazy Bella was still wringing out her house flannel in the kerb. Up at the top of the turning, a horsefly flew into the infected ear of the cart horse throwing it into a frenzy of pain and fear. The horse reared up and bolted. The unladen cart with one wheel locked and its iron rim drawing sparks from the cobbles careered down the turning and gathered speed as the nag's hooves thundered onto the stones. Billy Birkitt had loosened the marble but was too absorbed to hear the horse charging down towards him. Someone screamed and Crazy Bella dashed out in front of the wild animal. She only had time to grab the little lad and throw him aside before one of the shafts of the cart hit her between the shoulderblades. Bella was trampled under the horse's hooves and the cart ran over her lifeless body. As if sensing what had happened the horse stopped at the railway arch and stood shivering, its head held down low.

At one o'clock the ambulance pulled into Dawson Street to take the body away. A hush had fallen over the turning. Every door was open and people were crying silently. Billy stood beside his mother, his head buried in her apron. Alice Sutton stood with Annie Barnes and Mrs Brightman, and together they watched the ambulance draw out of the backstreet.

When it had disappeared, Alice turned to her friend. "Gawd rest 'er soul. She's at peace now, Annie. The poor cow couldn't find any while she was livin'."

Mrs Brightman sobbed aloud. "I seen it 'appen," she said, "She didn't 'ave a chance of savin' 'erself."

Alice was staring at the screwed up flannel and the piece of whitening which lay beside the gleaming front doorstep. "We'd better close 'er front door, Annie," she said softly.

Chapter Sixteen

Danny Sutton stepped down from the tram and took Alison's arm as she alighted. Together they walked through the wide gateway into Greenwich Park. Danny had gone directly from Ginny Coombes's house to meet Alison and knew nothing of what had happened. His spirits were high as he took the young girl's hand and guided her towards the steep footpath that led up to the observatory. Only a few people were in the park and they strolled in pleasant solitude past banks of summer flowers in the shade of the leafy chestnut trees. When they reached the top of the hill and walked out onto the paved area they saw the silver band of river far below them. Cranes swung and dipped, tugs slid along with squat barges in tow, and down in the foreground the white stone Maritime Museum shone from the centre of an emerald carpet. Alison sighed and sat down on a wooden bench facing the view. She watched Danny's slim figure as he put one foot up on the low wall and stared down the grassy hill. After a short while he turned and walked over to the bench.

"What d'yer fink of the view? I reckon it's gotta be the best view in London," he said.

Alison nodded. "It's lovely here. It's so quiet and peaceful."

Danny looked around. One old man sat nearby stroking a mongrel that was tethered with a length of string, and away to his left he saw the gun emplacements with their protective walls of sandbags. " 'Cept fer that yer wouldn't fink there was a war on, would yer?"

Alison was staring down at a tiny river craft that seemed

to be bobbing about in mid-stream. A puff of smoke arose from its funnel and seconds later the muted hoot of a tug whistle reached her ears. The peaceful setting and the open sky made her feel ready for the talk she must have with Danny. Alison reached out her hand and as he took it she pulled him down beside her on the bench. "I've got to get that train tonight, Danny," she said. "I'm going to miss you."

The young cockney reached over and gently kissed her ear. "I'm gonna miss yer, too," he said. "The time seems to be flyin'."

"We should talk, Danny."

"What about?"

"About us," she said, her dark eyes opened wide.

Danny averted his gaze for a moment and stared down at his shoes. When he looked up again he said quickly, "I want you, Alison."

"I want you too, Danny, but I'm scared for us. We hardly know each other. In some ways we're like strangers. Well, almost."

Danny gave her a kiss on the side of her mouth but Alison pulled away. "Let's be serious, Danny, we've got to talk. It's important."

"Listen, Alison," he said, taking her hand in his, "there's a bloody war on. Nobody knows what's goin' ter 'appen in the next few months. I fink we've got ter take what little 'appiness we can get, while there's still time."

"That's just it, Danny. We can take, but what will we be able to give to each other?"

"Do I 'ave ter spell it out ter yer, Alison? I want yer because I luv yer. Not fer any uvver reason. Surely that's somefing, ain't it? Ter me that's what luv's all about."

"You say the word easily, Danny. I can't find it that easy to say."

"Yer mean yer don't feel the same way?"

Alison looked up at the thin clouds high in the sky and knew that she could not delay any longer. She must not allow herself to become trapped, there must be no side-tracking. She had to be bluntly honest. "You ask me if I feel the same way. All right, now please listen to me. I want you. I want you to love me, but I don't think I'm ready for the strings to be tied. I don't want to be owned, I don't want to be tied down to a home and children yet, Danny. Marriage is what I'm talking about. There's got to be an understanding between us."

"I'll go along wiv that, Alison," he said, squeezing her hand in his. "I want an understandin' too."

The man with the dog got up and strolled off with his pet trotting along obediently by his side. They watched him in silence. Then Danny turned back to Alison and he could see that she was uneasy. She stared down at the gritted surface and moved the point of her shoe against the stone chippings, and when she looked up he could see the pain in her eyes. She sighed deeply and Danny felt he was about to learn something which he had been secretly dreading. As if to brace him, Alison put her free hand on his tensed arm and began.

"I think I told you that I came into nursing when I was nineteen, just over three years ago. When I finished my training I was sent to the hospital at Dover. At first I was worried that I'd made the wrong decision and it took some time before I realised that nursing was the only thing I really wanted to do. Maybe it came to me as I gained confidence, I don't know, but I was sure that nursing was going to be my whole life. I had been at the hospital for a year when I met a man at one of our hospital dances. He was a pilot whose family lived in the Midlands, and he was stationed on an airfield in Kent. His name was Wilfred Haggerty, though everyone called him Bill. He was good fun to be with, and I must admit he swept me off my feet. Maybe it was because I was naïve and away from home for the first time in my life, I don't know. Anyway, we seemed to get on very well together. We began to see each other regularly, and after a couple of months he asked me to marry him. At first I was taken aback, I don't mind telling you. It was impossible for me to even consider it. We came from different worlds: he was an officer who had gone straight from Cambridge into the Air Force, and I was a twenty-year-old from the Valleys who was just starting out on a career — I had never even had a steady boyfriend before he came along. But Bill wouldn't accept that we were different, I couldn't make him see it. He was a persistent type, I'll give him that. By this time we were spending every weekend together, and most of the nights too when I was off duty and he could get away from the airfield. Bill was sure that after a time I'd change my mind and agree to marry him, and I must admit it was good at first. We were happy and he seemed content the way things were.

"We had been together about six or seven months when the rows started. I think it had a lot to do with the realisation that there was going to be a war. He was beginning to press me again to marry him — I suppose he knew that he would be in action soon and wanted something to hold onto. I know a lot of people wouldn't consider getting married the way things were, but Bill was different. And he began to get irritable. When I couldn't get to see him because of my duty rota he thought I was deliberately avoiding meeting him. We had some blazing rows and we knew we couldn't carry on like that. One weekend Bill asked me again to marry him, and in a weak moment I said I'd think about it, and he took that to mean that I'd changed my mind. He was so happy. Early next morning he gave me a lift on the back of his motorbike as far as the hospital. He left me and set off for his squadron.

"I'll never forget that day. Mid-morning the ward sister called me into her office and broke the news: Bill had been killed in a road accident not far from his airfield. I was devastated. And worst of all, he died believing in a lie. He never knew, Danny, that I hadn't changed my mind. He never knew that it was all a lie."

184

While Alison was talking to him, Danny's eyes were riveted on her. His face was set hard, and when her dark eyes filled with tears he could find nothing to say. Alison remained silent for a short while. When she had composed herself again she went on. "You see, Danny, I've asked myself the same question a thousand times: how can I love a man and yet deny him marriage and children? That's what it comes down to. If I had loved him enough I would have married him and had his children. I would have given up nursing for him."

Danny swallowed hard. "But yer didn't 'ave ter give up yer nursin'. The kids would 'ave come later if yer both wanted 'em that much."

"Bill loved kids," Alison said, looking down at the river below. "He wouldn't have been happy without them. I may be wicked to think it, but I had a feeling he expected something to happen to him if there was a war, and he wanted to be able to leave something behind. He wanted children to carry his name on. I'm sure in my mind he felt that way, although he didn't ever mention it."

"I don't fink you're wicked ter 'ave them thoughts locked away inside yer. I fink yer stupid ter punish yerself. It wasn't ter be. If yer'd 'ave said yer'd marry 'im it still wouldn't 'ave prevented the accident, would it?"

"I know," Alison replied, "but it doesn't stop me asking myself the same question. Could I love a man enough to give up everything for him? Have I got that much love to offer? I feel I'd be trapped inside a marriage."

"Only yer know that," Danny said quietly. "Yer said a little while ago that the word 'love' comes easy ter me. I tell yer this. Maybe I can say it easy, but it's not an easy feelin'. It's a bloody 'ard feelin'. It grips at me inside. It's painful, an' it makes me feel terrible when I'm not wiv yer. It makes me want ter jump up an' shout me bleedin' 'ead orf one minute an' cry me eyes out the next. No, Alison, it ain't an easy feelin'."

Alison had to smile through her sadness at the way Danny expressed himself. His flippant nature had intrigued her in the beginning, yet there was another side of him she was fast discovering. He seemed to have an intensity that he tried to cover up, but now his words revealed his strength of feeling. Her body suddenly ached for his. She wanted to know his love before she left that evening, and at that moment she also wanted his understanding desperately. He must give her the space she needed to adjust to a new relationship. She had tried to make him understand, to warn him not to expect too much, and now it was up to him.

The sun had passed its zenith and the brow of the hill was becoming less private as people arrived and children ran up to the bench next to where the young couple sat.

"Let's walk a while, Danny," Alison said.

His face brightened. "I know," he said, "let's go down ter the pier. There used ter be a nice coffee 'ouse there. We can get a drink."

They left the hill-top view behind them and walked quickly down the grassy slope. In a few minutes they had reached the gate and crossed through into the busy road. They walked on past ancient-looking shops that displayed tattered books and faded paintings of ships in full sail. They saw the high-pillared Church of St Alphege ahead and when they reached the corner they turned down towards the pier. The little coffee house was still there, and soon they were seated comfortably in the shaded interior. An elderly lady came over and Danny ordered tea and cakes. The only other customer was a harassed mother who was trying hard to contain her young daughter. Cream oozed from a cake that the child held in her small hands, dripping onto the checked tablecloth and dribbling from her chin. Her mother smiled lamely at Danny and Alison as she attempted to clean up the mess while the elderly proprietor watched sternly from over her half-rimmed glasses. Soon hot tea in blue china cups and two large cream cakes were placed on the table beside the young couple.

Alison watched as Danny got into difficulty with his cake; he reminded her of a child in some ways. He was uncomplicated and straightforward, and his self-conscious grin pulled at her heart. There in the quiet, old-fashioned coffee house Alison felt she was being unavoidably drawn into a situation she had fought against. Why had she agreed to see him again? It would have been so easy to have said no in her letter to him, but she had been strangely attracted to the young patient and the chance of meeting him again had excited her. It was also an opportunity to test her emotions once more in the safe confines of a meeting that could only be brief. Even if their affair were passionate, it would certainly be short-lived. Time would not permit, nor would she. Now, as she watched Danny blowing on his tea, she felt ashamed. She wanted him badly but she could not fully trust herself, and yet she was using him to test her own emotional strength, and he was going to get hurt in the process. She felt a sudden panic and wanted to rush from the shop. She might experience love again, but in time she would have to walk away. What of him? Her thoughts tumbled around inside her head. Maybe she was being too presumptuous, he might merely be making a play to seduce her. He was young and good-looking, why should she assume he was in love with her? Because he had told her so? She realised it was getting more and more difficult to remain detached, a net seemed to be closing around her. Maybe it would be better to swim with the tide and allow events to bring her closer to a clear understanding of herself. That was the answer, she decided, and she felt an inner calm replacing her feelings of panic.

Out in the street the sun was dipping down behind the rooftops as they walked slowly to the tram stop. Danny had asked if he could escort her to Paddington Station that evening and she had accepted his offer gratefully.

Now it was time to get back to the Morgans, to pack and to say goodbye to her hosts. As they waited for the tram, Alison couldn't help but smile to herself — she had been so preoccupied with her thoughts of an affair, of passionate love and heart-rending decisions, but in reality there had been little time and no opportunity. Soon she would be speeding towards her home town, and later there would be more agonising, more decisions to be made, she would be on her own again. Parted from Danny and back with her family, she would have time to think, to examine her feelings and to question herself again, and perhaps she would be able to discover some peace.

Danny looked along Greenwich Road. He could see the approaching tram away in the distance. His hand was clasped around the key that Johnny Ross had given him but he knew in his mind that he would not take Alison to the flat. It was too contrived. He realised that suggesting it might make Alison feel cheap and degraded. Maybe he was getting soft, maybe he was losing his nerve, and his confidence. Maybe Alison's disclosures had thrown him. In his heart he knew that such vanity was out of place. She had known love and was quite able to make up her own mind; it would not be a question of his taking advantage of a virgin. If she agreed to spend the night with him it would be her choice; she was an experienced woman and knew the consequences. Whichever way he looked at it he knew that the flat was out of the question. He was going to kick himself later, but that was the way it had to be.

The journey back to London Bridge was strained. Danny attempted light-hearted conversation but Alison was preoccupied. He sensed a disappointment and sadness, and his hand tightened on the key. He went over and over in his mind what Alison had told him of her affair with the pilot. His mixed feelings made him angry and regretful. He resented the pilot for having known her love, and he was upset because he could not bring himself to suggest that they use Johnny's flat. Danny felt inadequate and unhappy, and he was glad when the tram arrived at London Bridge. The short walk to Southwark Street was carried out in awkward haste, both struggling to make conversation, and when they reached the Morgans' dairy, Danny half expected Alison to change her mind about him going to the station with her. She kissed him lightly on the cheek. "Thanks for this afternoon, Danny, and thanks for being patient. Can we leave at eight? My train goes at ten past ten."

"I'll be on the dot," he said, as she let herself into the dairy.

Detective Constable Stanley Stockbridge was in a foul mood. He had gone to Sullivan's Wharf and stood scratching his head at the scene of the crime. "The bloody gate's more than twelve feet 'igh. Whoever it was must 'ave bin part monkey."

The uniformed policeman nodded. "Mr Sullivan's up in the office on the first floor, Stan. 'E's waitin' fer yer."

"Well 'e can bloody well wait," Fat Stan growled. "I've gotta 'ave a decko round first."

Accompanied by the policeman he walked into the yard and saw the broken window. "When the fingerprint Johnny gets 'ere I want 'im ter go over that door 'andle."

The police constable had already taken a look round the yard. "Yer won't find anyfink there, Stan. There's grease all over the 'andle. The mechanic's bin in there 'alf a dozen times already."

Fat Stan cursed. "Didn't anybody try an' stop the silly bleeder?"

"Bit awkward really, Stan. The piss 'ole's at the back o' the office, an' the mechanic told me 'e's sufferin' from a weak bladder."

"Christ Almighty! Ain't there anuvver piss 'ole in this place?"

The constable merely pursed his lips and stood with his hands clasped behind his back. Fat Stan looked up at the rope. "That don't tell us anyfing. The sort o' rope yer can buy anywhere round 'ere. No keys bin found?"

The constable shook his head. "Must 'ave took 'em wiv 'em."

Fat Stan took the constable's arm and whispered in his ear. "This is your beat. D'yer know any o' those who work 'ere?"

The constable's eyebrows lifted in surprise. "D'yer suspect it was an inside job then, Stan?"

"I ain't made me mind up yet," Stan growled. "I'm off ter see this Mr Sullivan. You 'ang around, I'll talk ter yer later."

A tall matronly figure in thick spectacles gave the puffing detective a disapproving look as she led him into the inner office. Mr Sullivan did not bother to get up. "I'm Sullivan. And you are . . .?"

"Detective Constable Stockbridge, sir. We'd better 'ave a description of the lorry an' its contents first orf."

The wharf owner looked hard at the fat detective. "They've found my lorry," he said. "It was parked outside the West India Dock. Empty, I might add, except for two orientals. They were asleep in the cab. They weren't involved, so I'm told."

Fat Stan looked embarrassed. "I didn't know they found yer lorry. The report must 'ave come in after I left. What about the load?"

Mr Sullivan pulled a sheet of paper towards him and scanned it while Fat Stan flipped open his notebook. The wharf owner scratched his ginger hair and moved his tortoiseshell spectacles up from the tip of his nose. "Here we are. One hundred and twenty cases of Argentine corned beef. Brand name 'Swan'. Each case contained forty-eight sixteen-ounce tins. Then there were eighty cases of best Californian peaches, brand name 'Sunrise'. Same packing: forty-eight sixteen-ounce."

Fat Stan was struggling to get all the information onto

his small notepad. "What about yer staff? Any ex-cons workin' fer yer?"

John Sullivan flushed indignantly. "I don't employ that sort of person. All my staff have been with me for years. They are all honest, hardworking types."

Fat Stan grunted. He was convinced that that particular species just did not exist. "Who's responsible fer openin' up in the mornin'?"

Mr Sullivan beckoned to his secretary through the open door. In the outer office Monica Adams was straining her ears in an effort to catch the conversation. This would make exciting gossip at her weekly women's sewing circle. She got up quickly and adjusted her dress before tripping into the inner office. She smiled sweetly at her boss and gave the detective a cold look.

"Will you ask Basil to come in, Monica?" Mr Sullivan said peremptorily.

Miss Adams turned on her heel and Mr Sullivan beckoned the detective to a chair. "Basil will be down in the warehouse, Officer. You might as well take a seat. Basil Bromley has worked for me for over thirty years and he's honest as the day is long. It was Basil who discovered the theft when he arrived to open up at seven-thirty."

Fat Stan glanced through his notes. It wouldn't be the first time an esteemed and trusted employee had turned crooked. Basil Bromley sounded like the sort of name they gave to music hall villains. A trusted servant with keys to the wharf. It wouldn't be too difficult to set it up — a rope over the gate to allay suspicion, and Bob's your uncle. Basil would have got himself a buyer for the swag easily. There were plenty of crooked shopkeepers around the neighbourhood willing to put some corned beef and tinned peaches under the counter, what with the food shortages. They'd most likely charge double the price. "Basil Bromley" he mumbled to himself and looked up at Mr Sullivan, but the boss was studying an insurance claim form and ignored him. Fat Stan went back to his notes and pencilled a cross beside the trusted employee's name. It would be a feather in his cap if he made a quick arrest. The new inspector was already reading the riot act out to his officers and Fat Stan did not relish the thought of pounding the beat. His feet wouldn't stand it. Basil Bromley, he thought to himself, I arrest you for the theft of five tons of corned beef and canned peaches. It's no good you struggling. I think we'll have the handcuffs on. That's all right, Mr Sullivan, no need to thank me. All in a day's work. How did I get on to him? Well, it was intuition, Inspector, I've got a nose for a villain. I can smell 'em a mile off. Very few of 'em get by me . . .

The sound of voices brought Detective Constable Stanley Stockbridge back to reality. The outer office door opened and he heard Miss Adams's strident tones. "Go right in, Basil, Mr Sullivan's waiting for you."

A white-haired, stooped old man walked painfully into the inner sanctum and leaned on the desk for support. "I'm sorry, Mr Sullivan. Those stairs seem to take it out of me lately," he said in a cracked voice.

Mr Sullivan smiled sympathetically and motioned Basil to a chair. Fat Stan looked at the pathetic figure whose suit seemed to be two sizes too large for his frail body while Basil peered at him over metal-rimmed spectacles and blinked owlishly. His sunken cheeks puffed in and out as he fought to regain his breath, and his bony hands made motions of washing. Fat Stan began to get the feeling that pounding the beat again was becoming a distinct possibility.

Chapter Seventeen

The tragedy in Dawson Street left a cloud of gloom that hung heavily over the small turning. There were no children playing in the street, and the few people who stood at their doors were talking in little more than whispers. While she lived, Crazy Bella had been ignored by most of Dawson Street's folk, but in death everyone had some anecdote to tell about the unfortunate woman.

"She 'ad a son, yer know," announced Mrs Brightman.

Annie Barnes did not know. "Go on with yer," she said.

" 'S'right. 'E run away ter sea years ago when poor ole Bella lived in Tower Bridge Road. Wasn't much good by all accounts. I 'eard 'e was dead rotten to 'er. Brought 'im up all on 'er own as well."

"Didn't she ever marry?" Annie asked, digging into her pocket for her snuff.

"Not as far as I know," replied Mrs Brightman. "Accordin' ter Granny Bell, she was a smart woman when she was younger. She used ter go up West quite a lot. She was always bringin' fellers back. Still, she wasn't doin' no 'arm. Granny reckons she was on the game, but I don't fink she was."

"Somefing must 'ave turned 'er brain," said Annie, shaking her head sadly. "I've seen 'er up on London Bridge Station. She used ter give the toffs a lot o' verbal. I've seen 'er walkin' be'ind 'em City gents swearin' 'er 'ead orf at 'em."

"I did 'ear that she 'ad 'er son by a well-ter-do feller. 'E wouldn't marry 'er but 'e gave 'er a few bob ev'ry week.

193

That's if yer can believe it," Mrs Brightman said, folding her arms under her apron.

Annie Barnes shivered although the evening was still warm. "Did yer see that poor carman's face? White as a sheet it was. That copper was 'oldin' 'is arm."

"Yer can't blame 'im, Annie. They reckon somefink frightened the 'orse. Yer can't foresee these fings. I say it was an act of the Almighty."

Annie Barnes looked up the turning. "There's young Danny Sutton goin' 'ome fer 'is tea."

"What's 'e doin' now, Annie?"

" 'E's got the bookie's pitch in Clink Lane. I was talkin' ter Alice Sutton earlier on. She's all upset. 'Er Connie got some bad news about 'er chap. 'E's on the boats and 'is muvver come round cryin' 'er eyes out. They got a telegram ter say 'e's missin'."

"Gawd Almighty, Annie! Whatever next?"

As the train jerked to a stop at Paddington Underground Station and the doors slid open, a tide of uniformed figures rushed out towards the exit stairs. Two young people who were holding hands and talking let the hurrying travellers pass them by. They were early, and they emerged onto the railway station almost reluctantly. Danny carried Alison's small suitcase as they came to the station departure board and studied the train times. A large clock over the display showed ten minutes to nine. Alison looked at Danny and at her case he was holding. "I won't be a minute. I'm just going to powder my nose," she said.

Danny eyed her slim figure as she walked swiftly towards the Ladies. Unlike Waterloo Station, he found Paddington depressed him. He watched servicemen pass to and fro, all laden with heavy equipment and rifles and all looking grim and tired. Tearful families and sweethearts waved handkerchiefs as a train grew smaller in the distance. The station tannoy announced yet another delay, and two porters began to argue over who should shift a heap of luggage the few yards to the nearby taxi rank.

Danny felt it was one of those forsaken days when everything went wrong. Back in Dawson Street everyone was mourning poor Bella, and Connie was shut up in her room crying. He had tried to cheer her up before he left to meet Alison, but on this occasion his playful chatter did no good. Now he was waiting to say goodbye to Alison, who seemed quite happy to be on her way home. As he stood beside her case a large lady in a mink stole and feathered hat dragging a tiny dog on a lead beckoned a porter over and addressed him with her high-pitched voice. The hysterical-looking dog sniffed at the case by Danny's feet and began to cock its leg. Danny quickly lifted the case and resisted a strong urge to drop it on the dog's head. He turned angrily and walked away.

Five minutes later he saw Alison emerge from the Ladies and talk briefly to a porter before walking over to him.

"What shall we do, Danny?" she said. "We've got almost an hour before the train leaves."

"This station's givin' me the willies. Let's get a drink."

They walked out into Praed Street and found a little pub a short distance from the station. In the smoky atmosphere they sat in a corner sipping their drinks. Alison put her stout down on the table and ran her index finger around the rim of the glass. "Tell me something, Danny," she said, "are you disappointed?"

Danny looked up into her dark eyes. "About what?"

"About what I told you today in the park. And about us not having much time together."

"No, I'm not disappointed," he lied. "What 'appened wiv you an' this Bill was yer own affair. As fer not 'avin' much time tergevver, I'm not really disappointed, I'm more sorry. It wasn't on the cards, was it?"

Alison fished into her handbag and took out a small mirror. While she was studying her reflection she said, "I'm sorry too. Really sorry."

Danny laughed mirthlessly. "Now if I was an Arab sheik or somefink I'd 'ave carried yer off this afternoon. You'd 'ave bin a prisoner in my tent, an' I'd 'ave dismissed all the uvver wives while we made love."

Alison stroked his hand and Danny felt the softness of her skin. She looked into his pale eyes and smiled. "I don't want to be ravaged by a sheik, Danny. A soldier boy will do — or should I say ex-soldier."

They were silent for a while, then Danny said, "Alison, do yer fink I'm a bit slow?"

The young girl laughed aloud. "Slow, Danny? I think you're as sharp as a pin."

"I don't mean that way," he said quickly, "I mean slow — you know — ter get goin'?"

Alison picked up her drink again and Danny had the feeling she was laughing at him. "Of course I don't. Let's face it, Danny, we've not had any opportunity to . . . Well, you know what I mean." She looked up at him and noticed the tell-tale twitch of his mouth. He put his hand into his coat pocket and laid Johnny's front door key down on the table in front of her.

"Yes we 'ave," he said. "A pal o' mine loaned me that key. 'E said I might wanna take yer to 'is flat."

Alison looked surprised. "Why didn't you?" she asked.

"I'm not sure," he replied. "It seemed wrong. It seemed like it was all arranged. What's more, the bloke that give me the key can't keep 'is mouth shut. If I tell 'im I used the flat, 'e'd be a walkin' *News of the World*."

"Why did you take the key then, Danny?"

"It was the way I was feelin' at the time, I s'pose."

Alison studied her long fingernails. "Do you feel different now?"

"Yeah, I want yer twice as much," Danny said quietly.

"Danny."

"Yeah?"

"There's another train leaving at ten o'clock tomorrow morning. We could go to a hotel."

Their eyes met, and for a moment they clasped hands, the noise and movement around them forgotten. Finally Danny smiled sheepishly and picked up the glasses. "Let's 'ave anuvver drink," he said.

Night was falling as they emerged from the pub. Taxis hooted and swerved in and out of the station and evening revellers sauntered through the busy street.

Danny took Alison's arm. "Let's cross over," he said. "The side turnin's are the best bet."

They found themselves in a narrow backstreet where almost all of the Victorian terraced houses offered rooms for the night. The first two places were full, but at the third attempt they were successful. A bleary-eyed man with his shirt-sleeves rolled back over his forearms span the register and watched as Danny signed them both in as Mr and Mrs Halleron. He handed Danny a key and called out, "Beryl, take Mr an' Mrs Halleron up to number six."

A fat woman with a cheery grin waddled up the carpeted stairs ahead of the young couple, and when she had recovered her breath she opened the door at the end of the landing. "There you are, me dears," she said. "If there's anything else you want, you just tell hubby. Breakfast is from eight o'clock."

The room smelled musty but it was clean. The curtains were drawn back and the bed with its white counterpane seemed to fill the room. Danny looked at Alison in the dimness and she stepped close to him. Their lips met and their bodies came tightly together. The kiss was long, and when they moved apart Danny pulled the curtains shut and switched on the light. A tall wardrobe of dark wood, an old chair, and a washstand were the only furniture in the room. Over the bed was a gilt-framed picture of Victorian Bayswater. The walls were covered with a floral wallpaper, and hanging from the ceiling above the bed was a tasselled shade around the light which gave out a pinkish glow. Danny opened a door which led, amazingly, to a private bathroom and Alison began to undo her suitcase.

197

"Look at this," he called out to her, eyeing the large bath. "This beats our ole bog in the yard. A real tub as well. We take our'n down from a peg be'ind the back door."

When Alison went to the bathroom Danny turned off the light and opened the curtains. He sat on the edge of the bed and gazed at the moon. The room felt strange and he suddenly realised he was trembling. The bathroom door opened and he saw Alison standing on the threshold. He caught his breath as he saw her figure silhouetted in the dim light; her hair seemed to shine, and as she came over to the bed Danny noticed her small, firm breasts standing out beneath the white cotton of her nightdress. "Christ! Yer beautiful," he breathed as she sat down beside him.

"Thank you, kind sir," she said with a coy smile.

Danny reached out and pulled her to him. She did not resist as he kissed her chin and neck, and when he pressed her down on the bed Alison shuddered with pleasure as his fingertips traced a very gentle ring around her taut nipple. After a lingering kiss Danny drew up on his arms and looked down at her flushed face and sighed deeply. "I won't be long," he whispered as he rose and went into the bathroom.

Alison climbed into the comfortable bed and pulled up the bedclothes. She had been aroused, and the desire for full love made her feel impatient. "Come on, Danny, don't keep me waiting," she whispered aloud.

Danny was standing in front of the wash-basin. He had washed down in cold water to ease the growing feeling that threatened to overwhelm him. He eyed his pale skin and looked at the thin white scar that ran from his right side to his sternum. He ran his trembling fingers through his fair hair and reached for the towel which he wrapped around his middle. From somewhere deep in the recesses of his mind a strange alarm was beginning to interrupt his thoughts. He was reaching out for the unobtainable, a mutual attraction was drawing them both like two moths fluttering around a brightly burning candle flame. He shivered as he turned out the light and opened the door.

Alison saw the slim figure come to her and remove the towel from around his stomach as he slipped in the bed beside her. She turned to face him and felt his fingers stroke her hair. She had wanted their love-making to be slow and gentle, but now as his anxious hands caressed her aching body she became impatient. Suddenly Alison sat up, and with one smooth movement she pulled the night-dress over her head and guided his trembling hands up to her naked breasts.

In the dark hotel room, with the moon gently streaming over the bed, they became lovers at last.

A cloud had covered the moon, and now monstrous shapes seemed to loom up in the shadows around the ghostly white counterpane which covered Danny and Alison. The wardrobe creaked and occasionally the distant sound of a train drifted in through the open window. The lovers lay close, their demanding passion spent. Alison rested her head on Danny's chest and gently ran her fingers down his arm. He held her close and watched the eerie light playing tricks around them. Danny could smell the fragrance of her hair and her warm body scent that had drawn him to the summits of pleasure. Now, his body calm and heavy, he whispered into her ear: "I've never experienced anyfing so good. You was fantastic."

Alison sighed and nestled even closer. "I didn't want it to end. Was I greedy?"

"You was great."

"So were you."

Danny stretched out and yawned. "It's funny really. 'Ere we are in a bedroom of a strange 'otel, an' only a couple of hours ago I was gettin' ready ter see yer off. I 'ad the feelin' yer wanted ter get on that train as soon as yer could. I was gettin' the 'ump on that station. I like comin's not goin's. I was jus' gettin' used ter the idea of a lonely trip back ter Bermon'sey when yer told me about the uvver train. Was that what yer was speakin' ter the porter about?''

There was no answer and Danny realised that Alison had fallen asleep. Her breathing was shallow and even, and as he eased her head onto the pillow she sighed and slipped her arm around him.

The early morning was dull and humid. When Danny awoke he found that the place beside him was empty. He sat up with a start and then dropped back onto the pillow when he heard the sound of water running in the bathroom. In a while Alison came into the bedroom fully dressed, her face fresh and pink. She squeezed his big toe. "Come on, sleepy-head, breakfast started ten minutes ago."

Danny got up and washed his face in cold water, grimacing at the puffiness under his eyes and the light stubble around his chin. He dressed quickly and went back into the bedroom. "I'm gonna remember this room," he said, pulling Alison to him. She held him at bay and smiled. "Come on, let's get some breakfast," she said.

Down in the dining-room two other couples sat at breakfast. A dark-skinned man was chatting incessantly to a woman who nodded at him between mouthfuls of egg and bacon. Another couple was utterly silent. Danny became intrigued as he waited with Alison for their breakfast to appear. The man was much older than his partner and he continued to glance at her while he ate. The girl returned his look occasionally with an angry glare. Whatever row had happened between them last night was spilling over into the morning, Danny thought. He saw the man point to the last piece of toast on the plate and in answer the girl with him nodded her head. The man picked up the slice of toast and dipped it into the yolk of his egg with a vengeance, the girl watching disdainfully as he greedily devoured the toast. It's a good job bedrooms can't talk, he mused.

Alison touched his hand briefly. "Don't stare, Danny," she chided him.

"You ought ter be sittin' where I'm sittin'," he whispered. "There's a full-scale war of silence goin' on be'ind yer."

Two portions of egg, bacon and tomatoes were placed in front of them with a plate of thin, crispy toast. The fat cheery lady who had shown them to their room came in carrying a tray with a small china teapot, cups and saucers, milk and sugar. She placed the tray on the table and smiled. "I hope you both slept well?"

"I was off as soon as I 'it the piller," Danny grinned, and Alison flushed slightly.

They ate their breakfast in silence. The other couples had left and the only other person in the room was a weary-looking girl who was busy laying fresh tablecloths on the cleared tables. She yawned as she carried a pile of plates out to the kitchen. Danny watched her exit with some amusement. " 'Appy soul, ain't she?"

"I don't suppose she's got much to laugh about," Alison answered, sipping her tea.

Danny could sense some irritability in her tone but chose to ignore it. He glanced at the wall clock. "It's only jus' nine, we've got plenty o' time."

"I don't want to leave it to the last minute, Danny. I don't relish standing in the corridor all the way to Cardiff."

Danny gave her a quick look, surprised at her brusque tone. Maybe she was always sharp in the mornings, he thought. It was the first time he had been with her at this time of day. His sister Lucy was the same, it was almost impossible to get a civil word from her before midday. Danny felt a little confused. Though she had given him some insight into her feelings during their conversation in the park yesterday, she still remained mysterious. He sensed her sadness was never far from the surface. He had first begun to notice it back at the hospital in Dover when even in her light-hearted moments she had seemed to be under a shadow. He sensed that the loss of her pilot was only a part of it. Danny was sure it went deeper. She had told him of her fear that she was unable to give a total love but he was puzzled. Last night she had given herself with abandon. She had been willing and eager to lead them both to the heights and had succeeded without any hesitation, without any apparent anxiety. Maybe she desired the very thing she rejected, and snuffed out any chances of finding it with casual flings. Danny hated himself for even thinking that he might just be one of her brief affairs. She had told him that there had been no one before her pilot, but she might have taken lovers since. His thoughts tortured him and he felt a strong urge to get away from the hotel, to walk out into the dull morning and leave his twisted, confused feelings behind.

The weary maid appeared carrying clean folded table-cloths. Alison looked at Danny. "We'd better get started," she said. "I think she wants to clean up."

Danny settled the bill and they walked out of the side street and into the morning crowds at Paddington Station. Danny bought a platform ticket and walked along beside the carriages until Alison jerked on his arm. "Here's an empty one."

Danny climbed aboard the train and put Alison's suitcase on the luggage rack. He stepped down again onto the platform and Alison joined him. "I'll always remember last night, Danny," she said. "It was wonderful."

"Don't ferget ter write. I can meet yer when yer come back ter London."

Alison nodded but said nothing.

"I could come down ter Dover if they ease the restrictions, Alison."

She touched his arm. "Don't let's make any plans yet. I'll write to you, I promise."

The railway guard walked along the platform, his green flag held ready. The lovers kissed and Alison pulled away from his grasp. As she climbed aboard the train the guard raised his flag. Danny stood watching as the train drew away, and he waved until Alison's head disappeared into the carriage. He thought about their conversation in the park, and the quiet moonlit room in the backstreet, and then turned on his heel to walk away down the platform.

Chapter Eighteen

Frank Sutton was prowling around the house waiting for Joe Copeland's knock. It was the time of day when Alice made her views known, and she chose this particular time for good reason. Frank could be argumentative and was inclined to 'argue the hind legs off a donkey', as she put it, so when she had something important to say or a telling point to make, Alice caught him when he was getting ready to go to work. Frank had to get to work on time or he would miss the 'call-on', so he didn't have time to argue with her. And then he would have all day to dwell on what she had said, and in the evening after a hard day's work, Frank would be too tired to argue. It was the way Alice made sure that she was listened to.

Today Alice had a point to make and she timed it to perfection. "I don't mind Danny comin' and goin', Frank," she said as her husband looked anxiously at the door, "but 'is bed wasn't slept in last night. Gawd knows where 'e is, but I do know 'e was takin' this nurse out." And she looked at Frank to check that he understood her.

Frank sighed as he looked through the curtains and saw Joe hurrying along the turning. "I've told yer before, Alice," he said. " 'E's over twenty-one. I can't stop 'is sweets or smack 'is arse, now can I?"

"It ain't the point, Frank. 'E could 'ave told us 'e wasn't comin' 'ome. Somefink could 'ave 'appened to 'im. You'll 'ave ter talk to 'im, you're 'is farver."

"I ain't got no time ter argue wiv yer, Alice. Joe's comin' along the street. Anyway, I don't s'pose 'e knew 'e was gonna stop out."

"Well I want yer ter 'ave a word in 'is ear. 'E might take notice o' you."

Frank opened his mouth to utter a choice profanity, but Joe's rat-tat stopped him. "I'll see yer ternight, Alice. We'll talk about it then."

Alice felt pleased with what she had accomplished. She reckoned that there was enough on her plate, what with Connie being all upset over Jimmy, and now Maggie springing it on her about sending the kids away from London, without having to worry about Danny's roamings. Young Tony Arpino had come round to see him and had had to leave a message. It wasn't good enough, Alice told herself, as she took the broom to the passage carpet. Frank will have to say something to him. Stopping out all night is asking for trouble. Danny might have got the poor girl pregnant. Worse still, he might be lying in some hospital. Her thoughts were beginning to make her feel panicky, so she decided the housework could wait. She would go over for a chat with her friend Annie instead. She scribbled a short message on the back of a brown paper bag and after looking it over she propped it up in front of the teapot in the centre of the kitchen table.

In The Globe Eddie Kirkland was having a chat with the subdued owner of Shady Lady, the dog who had broken the track record at Catford last Saturday night. After three consecutive nights of revelry, Biff Bowden was feeling the effects. His winnings had all but disappeared and he was being consoled by the landlord.

"You looked drunk as a sack on Sat'day night, Biff," Eddie said. "Sunday night yer didn't look much better. Don't yer remember offerin' ter buy everybody a drink? Then there was those games o' darts at a fiver a time. No wonder you're skint."

"Tell yer the trufe, Eddie, the weekend's a bleedin' blank. I don't remember much about it at all."

Eddie grinned. "Yer don't remember the ruckus last night then?"

"No."

"Well I'll tell yer what 'appened. It must 'ave bin about 'alf nine when Bonky Williams walked in wiv a strange geezer. I've never clapped eyes on 'im before. Proper scruff 'e was. Anyway, Bonky starts 'is tricks in front of 'is mate — you know what Bonky's like. Last night 'e 'ad a black patch over 'is wonky eye. You was proppin' the counter up an' tryin' ter date our new barmaid, when up walks Bonky. 'E stan's next ter yer an' orders a drink fer 'im an' 'is mate. Now, when Carol puts the glasses down in front of 'im, dear Bonky opens 'is fist an' tells the girl to 'elp 'erself. Right in the middle of the coppers was 'is glass eye. Carol screams out, an' you, yer soppy git, knocks Bonky's 'and up in the air and the money goes everywhere. But Bonky ain't concerned about 'is money, 'e's more worried about 'is glass eye. We 'ad the customers on their 'ands an' knees lookin' fer it. You was tryin' ter organise the seach an' yer offered a fiver reward. Bonky's copped the needle by this time, 'e wants ter crown yer wiv 'is pint mug, an' 'e would 'ave done if it wasn't fer our potman. 'E calms Bonky down an' we got you stuck away in the corner. Proper to-do it was."

"Bloody 'ell, Eddie, I'm sorry about that. Did Bonky find 'is eye?"

"Yeah, Arfur found it. 'Course, that started it off again. The ole chap was doin' 'is nut 'cos yer wouldn't pay up the reward. Honest, Biff, you was as pissed as an 'andcart. If that bloody dog o' yours ever wins the Grey-'ound Derby I'm gonna shut the pub up fer a week. I'm gettin' too old fer all this aggro."

At noon Danny walked into the pub. His message from Tony Arpino had been that he should look in The Globe around twelve and that it was urgent. Danny was due at Ginny's at twelve-thirty, and it was on the half hour that Tony walked in looking agitated. "Sorry I'm late," he said breathing hard. "I gotta see yer, Danny, there's trouble brewin' in our street an' I'm scared fer me ole man."

Danny looked up at the clock. "I'm due on me pitch, Tony," he said. "Walk round wiv me, we can 'ave a chin wag on the way."

They left The Globe and walked towards Clink Lane. Tony seemed reluctant to begin. "Look, Danny, I know yer in wiv Tony Allen's crowd, but . . ."

" 'Ang on a minute, Tone. I take bets fer 'im, that's all. I don't socialise wiv 'em. Least of all Jack Mason."

"It's 'im I wanna talk ter yer about," Tony said as he grabbed his pal's arm and halted.

"Go on, Tony."

"Last time I see yer, Danny, I told yer about those two fellers what come round our street. Well they come back. They called in all the shops an' they give us all the spiel. It's a protection racket."

"What's that gotta do wiv Jack Mason?" Danny asked.

Tony gave his pal a hard look. "I'd bet a pound to a pinch o' shit 'e's be'ind it."

"What makes yer say that, Tone?"

" 'Cos I've seen Mason wiv those two ugly gits, that's why."

"Where?"

"Down New Cross dogs last Sat'day night."

"It might 'ave bin a coincidence, Tony."

"No chance. I was wiv Johnny Ross. 'E told me they're always tergevver. It don't take a Sherlock 'Olmes ter work it out, does it?"

Danny started to walk to Ginny's front door with Tony falling in beside him. "Tell me, Tone, 'ow are they workin' it?"

"It's the usual fing. Accordin' ter them, there's a team from over the water tryin' it on, an' we're bein' offered protection — at a price."

"Ain't none o' the shopkeepers gone ter the police?"

"Leave orf, Danny, yer know the way they work. They've scared the daylights out o' most of 'em. 'Cept me

208

farver, that is. 'E was gonna go roun' the nick, but me muvver wouldn't let 'im.''

Danny stopped at Ginny's house. "I don't know what I can do, Tony," he said.

The young Italian looked down at his feet. "I know you an' Kathy were close once, an' I 'ear she still goes a bundle on yer."

"So?"

"I also 'ear that Jack Mason's givin' 'er an 'ard time an' she'd leave 'im if she wasn't so terrified of the consequences."

"Go on, Tony."

"Look, Danny, I know it's askin' a lot, but can yer 'ave a talk wiv 'er? See if yer can get 'er ter find out when those two monkeys are comin' round again. She might 'ear somefink."

Danny shook his head. "I don't s'pose they'd tell Kathy anyfing, an' she can't very well ask 'em, can she?"

"All right, it's an outside bet, Danny, but she might just over'ear somefink. They might use Mason's place fer a get tergevver. We've gotta know when they're comin' back so we can be ready fer 'em."

"Listen, Tone, even if the law grabs 'em, yer won't get Jack Mason. 'E don't do 'is own dirty work, 'e leaves that to 'is mugs. All right, they might try ter implicate 'im, but it's on the cards Mason's boys'll keep their mouths shut."

Tony gave Danny an entreating look. "I wouldn't ask yer, Danny," he said, "but I'm scared they're gonna do the ole man some 'arm. We want those gits o' Mason's right out o' the way, an' if the law don't pull Mason in I'll take care of 'im meself."

"Don't be stupid, Tony. Jack Mason is an animal. 'E'd eat yer alive."

"You let me worry about 'im," Tony said, gritting his teeth. "Will yer 'ave a chat wiv Kathy?"

Danny puffed out his cheeks. "Okay, Tone, I'll see what I can do."

Tony Arpino's plea only added to Danny's feeling of depression. His problems seemed to be piling up without any answers. When he had returned home that morning his mother had berated him about staying out all night, he was playing with fire in keeping a young girl out all night. Danny had ignored her and stormed out to The Globe but there was no one around. The street was in mourning for Bella and seemed uncannily quiet. Even old Charlie Perkins was foregoing his seat in the sun.

Danny stood in Ginny's doorway thinking about his brief liaison with Alison. He knew that she was not going to rush a letter off to him as soon as she got home, and he was sure that she was trying to tell him in a roundabout way that they were not going to get too serious. The chat they had together on the platform at Paddington Station made him feel that she was preparing him for a rejection. Why did it all have to be so complicated? It seemed as though a dark cloud was settling over everything, even Dawson Street and his own family. His sister Connie was walking around in a perpetual daze since she had heard about Jimmy's ship going down, and Lucy was getting very irritable and unapproachable. Even Maggie seemed to have lost her calm 'big sister' image and was wearing a constant frown.

Just as Danny was ready to finish his morning stint he saw Jack Mason coming down the turning towards him looking like he was about to burst a blood vessel. His face was flushed and he was clenching his fists, and as he got closer Danny could see the vicious look in his eyes. Mason stopped in front of Ginny's house.

"You seen that berk Rossy?" he blurted out without any greeting.

Danny felt dislike welling up inside him. "I bin 'ere fer the last hour an 'alf, an' 'e ain't showed. What's wrong?"

"What's wrong?" Mason sneered. "Rossy's s'posed ter be collectin' some gear from Tony, an' 'e ain't turned up. Tony's copped the needle an' I'm left ter do the

210

errands. If yer see the cow-son tell 'im ter get 'imself roun' Tony's quick as 'e can, or I'll put one in 'is chops.''

Danny gave Jack Mason a sideways glance. "I thought Johnny Ross was workin' at the vinegar factory?" he said.

"So 'e is, but 'e's signed on the panel again. That's why the job was arranged fer this week. I tell yer, son, if it was down ter me an' not Tony I'd give 'im the elbow. It ain't only 'is mouth that annoys me. The bastard's unreliable.''

Danny nodded. "Okay, if I see 'im I'll pass the message on.''

Mason suddenly relaxed a little and he gave Danny an evil grin. "You ain't seen nuffink o' that fat git Stockbridge round 'ere, 'ave yer?" he asked.

"Not since 'e nabbed Bonky Williams. Why?"

"Just askin'. By the way, 'ow's the pitch goin'?"

Danny forced a grin. "Not bad. Biff Bowden's mutt cost Tony a few bob, but it's pickin' up a bit.''

Jack Mason rubbed the sweat from his forehead with the back of his hand. "Well I'll be off. Yer keep yer nose clean an' we won't ferget ter put a little somefing your way later on.''

Danny watched as Mason hurried out of Clink Lane. A couple of weeks ago he would have been eager to work his way into the set-up, but now he felt that no good was going to come out of it. If he got involved any further in Tony Allen's organisation there would be no backing out. He thought over what Tony Arpino had said, and he realised he would have to be very careful in arranging a meeting with Kathy. Mason had a house in Dockhead and it was out of the question to go there to see her. Maybe Ginny Coombes could help him. She had seen Kathy at the shops in Tooley Street, she might know if Kathy ever came round to see her mother since her father threw her out. If she visited her mother at all it would have to be during the day when her father was at work. That would be the best time to catch her, he thought.

* * *

211

The warm, sunny weather continued throughout the rest of the week. Danny was constantly sullen and miserable. There had been no letter from Alison and no news for Connie, and on Saturday morning Maggie was reduced to a flood of tears as she bade farewell to her two children. Alice joined Maggie at the school gates and stood around with the rest of the local parents while their offspring were tagged with their names and given a bag of fruit and a packet of sweets each. The kids seemed excited at the new adventure, although a few tears were shed by the less adventurous ones. Buses arrived and the fond farewells began. There were last minute hugs and kisses, and a general dipping into handbags for handkerchiefs, and finally the parents walked away toward their homes in the backstreets looking sorrowful and apprehensive.

On Sunday morning Lucy joined Ben for the early service at the Methodist mission. When the Reverend John Harris climbed up into the pulpit in his white cassock, his greying hair flattened to his head with brilliantine, Ben whispered to Lucy, "The organist is late."

Lucy glanced up and gazed at the huge instrument with its multitude of gilt and blue pipes that stretched up to the rafters. She wondered how the minister was going to start the service, now that the usually dependable Mr Craddock was not in his place. The Reverend gripped the rail of the pulpit and beamed down benevolently at his flock. "Good morning, brethren. While we are waiting for Mr Craddock let us begin this morning's service with a short prayer."

Heads bowed and a silence reigned in the cold, sterile hall. When Reverend Harris lifted his head at the 'Amen' and saw Mr Craddock enter the back of the hall he was delighted. He had selected some rousing hymns for the service, and good old Mr Craddock had not let him down after all. The organist nodded to the congregation as he hurried to his place. His tall, stooping figure and flat-footed gait drew some sympathy from two elderly ladies who were sitting immediately in front of Lucy and Ben.

"Poor Mr Craddock, he's such a dear soul," one of the ladies whispered.

Her companion touched her Sunday hat with the tips of her fingers and nodded. "He's so pleasant to everyone. It's a shame. He seems hardly able to do the collection lately. I think it's getting too much for him."

Mr Craddock had reached the organ and settled himself at the keyboard. He pushed up his pebble-lensed spectacles onto the bridge of his nose and squinted at the opened music sheet. He rocked back and forth a couple of times, then the opening bars of 'Onward Christian Soldiers' shattered the silence. The old ladies' kindly mutterings about Mr Craddock's health and humility were drowned out as the congregation sang with feeling.

Monday morning the 22nd of July dawned wet and windy. The recent glorious weather changed suddenly on the day Bella Corrigan was to be laid to rest. The horse-drawn hearse and its attendant coach stopped for a few seconds at the top of Dawson Street as a last respect, and in the coach Alice Sutton, Annie Barnes and Billy Birkitt's mother held handkerchiefs to their faces. Bella's neighbours stood silently by as the cortège passed along Tooley Street. Dockers doffed their caps, and a strolling policeman halted and gave a stiff salute. At noon the rain stopped and the sky cleared. The period of mourning was over, and in the early afternoon when Alice was hanging her black coat up in the wardrobe, she heard loud shouts and laughs in the street outside. Mrs Ellis came hurrying into the turning, beaming and waving a telegram. Her son Jimmy had been picked up and landed in Newfoundland. He was quite well and recuperating in hospital from his spell in the cold waters of the North Atlantic.

That lunchtime Danny was anxiously watching along Clink Lane. He had spoken to Ginny about Kathy and was told that she visited her mother every Monday during her

213

lunch-hour. Danny was getting worried. Tony Arpino was pressing him for information, and he said he had heard that there would be a visit sometime during the week for a pay-off. It was ten minutes past one when he saw Kathy walking down the turning and he was shocked by her appearance. She looked tired and jaded, her usual bounce and vitality replaced by a leaden walk. Danny noticed the dark circles around her eyes as she got closer. He waved to her and Kathy smiled. " 'Ow are yer?''

"Not so bad," Danny replied, moving his hands in a rocking gesture. "I need ter talk ter yer, Kath. Soon as possible."

"I've got no time now, Danny, I'm jus' poppin' in ter me mum. I've gotta be back ter work by two."

She looked at him and saw the anxiety in his eyes. " 'E goes out most nights. I might be able ter get out fer a while ternight. I can't promise though."

"Where can I meet yer?"

Kathy thought for a moment. "There's a little pub down by the riverside — The Bell. D'yer know it? It's only five minutes from my place."

Danny nodded. "Yeah I know it. Is it okay there?"

"We'll be all right there," Kathy assured him. "It's a family 'ouse. None o' the villains get in there. I'll try ter get there by 'alf-eight, it should be quiet then. Okay?"

Danny grinned with relief. "That's 'an'some. I'll be there. Try an' make it."

"I'll do me best, Danny," she said as she hurried back to the other side of the street.

She waved to him as she reached her mother's house.

It was a momentous Monday morning for Ben Morrison. He had his army medical and passed A1. He also saw the selection officer and asked to join the Royal Army Medical Corps, but he was not too encouraged by the officer's response. The man shrugged his shoulders. "You'll be told in good time," he said dismissively. Ben hoped desperately that his request would be granted. If not, he could only envisage a confrontation with the military and a spell in an army prison. He was troubled by something else too that had been niggling away at him for the past few days now. When he got back from his medical he went up to his flat and made himself a mug of tea. In the quietness of his room he took the letter down from behind the clock and sat for a while looking at the envelope. Was there something he had missed? he wondered. Was there something in the content that would identify the sender? Ben put his mug down and turned the envelope over. It was an ordinary kind that could be bought anywhere. His name and address had been printed in bold lettering: childlike but legible. Almost reluctantly he took out the folded sheet of paper that had one rough edge.

It was lined paper and had obviously been torn from an exercise book. The wording was upright and neat, and the spelling mistakes seemed to be more deliberate than natural. Ben stared at the letter until his eyes were tired. Maybe Lucy was right, maybe he should burn the evil thing instead of becoming obsessed with trying to identify the writer. After all, there were thousands of these sort of letters received every day by conscientious objectors, according to the newspapers. They were the product of sick minds. Ben sat for some time thinking about whether or not to destroy the letter, then finally he folded the sheet of paper and replaced it in the envelope. He heard Lucy's familiar knock on his door and before answering it he put the envelope back behind the clock.

Chapter Nineteen

Danny strolled along in the cool of the summer evening until he came to Jamaica Road. He walked on for a while then turned off into a backstreet leading down to the river where moored barges rocked on the incoming tide. That particular stretch of the Thames was quiet, almost rural. A patch of green stood out across the river at Wapping where the ancient churchyard held back the threatening wharves and storehouses. At the river wall a lane ran along beside the warehouses until it narrowed into a pathway. It was there that The Bell stood. The pub had none of the trappings associated with riverside inns, apart from a couple of faded pictures of the *Cutty Sark*. The one long bar was sparsely decorated and the proprietors, an elderly couple, seemed content to keep it that way.

When Danny walked in he aroused no more than a casual glance from the few folk who sat around on hard chairs resting their beer on iron-legged tables. He ordered a pint and took a seat. Now and then a customer came in, but there was no sign of Kathy. Danny finished his drink and eyed the bar clock: five to nine. He decided to get a refill, and if Kathy had not shown up by the time he had finished his second pint he would leave. Danny was halfway through his drink when Kathy walked in. She came over and sat down with a sigh. "I didn't fink 'e was goin' out ternight. 'E's only jus' left," she said, breathing heavily.

"D'yer wanna drink? I mean, are you . . ." Danny began.

Kathy laughed. "I'll 'ave a stout, Danny. It's all right, me doctor ses it's good fer me — an' the baby."

Danny returned with the stout and watched while Kathy took a sip. When she put the glass down onto the table he leaned forward and put his hand on hers.

"Listen, Kath, I've got a big faver to ask. It's not fer me really, it's fer Tony Arpino. You know Tony."

Kathy looked at him with a mischievous glint in her eye. "I thought yer got me 'ere so yer could carry me off ter some exotic place," she said smiling.

Danny squeezed her hand and grinned. "Later, Kathy. Right now I want some info. Will yer 'elp me?"

"What is it, Danny?"

"There's a mob goin' roun' puttin' the squeeze on Tony's family, an' the rest of the shopkeepers in Bermon'-sey Lane."

Kathy stared at her glass. "Yer fink it might be Jack's crowd?"

"Tony's pretty certain 'e's be'ind it, Kath. Can yer give us any idea if it is 'im?"

Kathy's eyes flared angrily as she looked at him. "You've got a nerve. Do yer really expect me ter snitch on 'im?"

Danny returned her angry stare with a hard look. "Listen, Kath, I wouldn't even think of it if yer was 'appy wiv 'im. Don't try an' tell me 'e don't knock yer about. Don't tell me yer 'appy wiv 'im."

"There's such a fing as loyalty, Danny. I've made my bed an' I'm lyin' in it."

"Yeah, an' yer 'avin' 'is kid, an' the cow-son's knockin' yer about."

"I ain't said Jack's knockin' me about, Danny. You said it."

"C'mon, Kath, it's yer ole Danny yer talkin' to. Tell me the trufe."

"All right, maybe we do 'ave our ups an' downs. So do lots o' people. Yer can't expect me ter tell yer if

218

'e's involved, even if I did know 'e was — which I don't.''

Danny swallowed the rest of his drink and put the glass down heavily on the table. "I didn't know if yer knew or not. I thought yer might over'ear somefing an' be able ter tell us when they're goin' roun' ter put the boot in.''

"Look, Danny, Jack's always got somebody callin' round ter see 'im. I don't stay in the room when they're talkin'. Even if I did over'ear somefing an I told yer, Jack would know it was me. 'E'd kill me.''

Danny toyed with his empty glass. "Yeah, yer right, I can't expect yer ter take that sort o' chance. Ferget I asked yer.''

Kathy's eyes misted and she stared at her drink. When she looked up at him Danny saw the torment on her pale face. He squeezed her arm gently. " 'Ow yer feelin'? I mean bein' — you know —''

"Pregnant,'' Kathy said, finishing the sentence for him. She got some looks from the people near to them. "You don't 'ave ter be frightened of sayin' it, Danny. But to answer your question, I'm okay.''

Danny looked at her, his pale blue eyes showing concern. "Why don't yer leave 'im? Surely there mus' be somewhere yer can go?''

Kathy sighed. "I can't go back ter Clink Lane, and where else is there? I s'pose I could throw meself on the mercy of some woman's 'ostel, but I ain't gonna bring a kid inter the world at one o' those places. No, Danny, I'm gonna stick it out, fer the baby's sake.''

Danny twisted his glass. "I wish I 'ad me own place,'' he said. "Yer could stay wiv me.''

Kathy smiled. "Yer mean yer'd take me in, an' me 'avin' anuvver man's kid?''

Danny became embarrassed. "Yeah, well I'd be doin' it fer you, not 'im.''

"Danny, you're a luv'ly person. Why don't yer find yerself a nice girl an' get married?''

"Chance would be a fine fing," he grinned. "I don't seem ter be 'avin' much luck lately."

"I wish we could put the clock back, Danny. Me an' you'd make a good team."

"Yeah, we sure would," he smiled.

They left The Bell together and strolled slowly along the riverside. The night was warm, with the pungent smell of mud rising from the foreshore. Heavy, dark clouds were drifting in, and they heard the water lapping and the moored barges creaking and thudding as they lifted on the tide. The two young people stopped on the corner of a small turning.

Kathy squeezed his hand. "I've gotta leave yer 'ere, Danny," she said. "Take care of yerself. I'll be seein' yer around."

Her kiss was soft and her gently rounded body pressed against him briefly. He watched her disappear into the dusk, wishing things could have been different.

On Tuesday there was new cause for gloom and a new topic of discussion around the backstreets and in the docks and wharves. Frank Sutton sat beside Joe Copeland on the quayside during a lull in the unloading. "That's a bit much, Joe. Income tax up ter eight an' six, a penny on a pint, an' this bloody purchase tax they're bringin' in," he said with a scowl.

Joe threw his wet cigarette stub into the water. "I fink it's scandalous. I know there's a war on, but it's always us that gets it."

Frank scratched his head. "Well they've 'it the rich this time. That purchase tax is on lux'ries. What lux'ries do the likes o' you an' me 'ave?"

"Yeah, I s'pose yer right. Fancy puttin' the beer up though, it's bloody outrageous. After all, it's weak as piss as it is."

Frank grinned. "I reckon we ought ter change our boozer, don't you? I'm sure ole Kirkland's waterin' the beer. Why don't we try the brew over at The Castle?"

Joe pulled a face. "I don't like that 'ouse. It's full o' nancy boys."

Frank laughed. "I know a few of 'em get in there, Joe, but they're all right. In fact they're a bit of a laugh. Ole Billy Farnsworth goes in there reg'lar. 'E's a scream. Bent as a nine-bob note 'e is. I see 'im the uvver day pushin' 'is sister's kid in a pram. When 'e see me lookin' 'e shouted out, 'It's not mine!' "

The crane swung around and the dockers went back to work. "We'll try The Castle if yer like, Frank," Joe shouted as he grabbed a swinging rope, "but if one o' them 'iron-'oofs' tries ter kiss me on the lips I'm pissin' orf."

The backstreet folk seethed at the budget news. The price of beer overtook the pending invasion as the main topic of conversation, and it caused long faces among the old gents who used The Globe.

"Now if we was workin', Bill, we'd get anuvver shillin' in the pound stopped. On top o' that, we drink about two dozen pints a week. That's anuvver couple o' bob out o' pocket. This rate, we're gonna suffer both ways."

" 'Ow d'yer make that out, Fred? Me an' you ain't workin'."

"I know we ain't, Bill, but when yer fink about it, if we was, an' we come in 'ere fer a pint, we'd 'ave ter fink twice about buyin' a drink fer anybody now we're gonna be worse orf. See what I mean?"

Bill turned his head and spat a stream of tobacco juice through the open door of the pub. "It looks like we ain't gonna be drinkin' two dozen pints a week now, Fred."

The gloom persisted throughout the week. Danny had still not heard from Alison, and Maggie was missing her kids. She was even more miserable when she listened to the street gossip. Rumours of evacuees being ill-treated were rife, and some of the parents were considering fetching their children home. Lucy too was very touchy. She was unapproachable in the mornings, and when Danny mentioned about Kathy having a baby she suddenly rounded on him. Only Connie brightened Danny's day. She was eagerly looking forward to being reunited with Jimmy, and she suggested that it would be nice if they could have a street party to celebrate his safe return.

"What d'yer fink, Danny boy?" she bubbled, her button nose screwing up and her deep blue eyes widening.

"Anyfing ter liven it up a bit, sis. The way fings are 'ere, I wish I was back in the army."

Connie was alone with Danny in the front parlour. She had been concerned about her brother's depression and decided to try drawing him into conversation. "What about that Alison, Danny? Ain't yer gonna see 'er any more?" she asked.

"I'm waitin' fer a letter, sis."

"She still on leave then?"

Danny shrugged his shoulders. "I don't fink so. She was s'posed ter drop us a line so I could meet 'er in London again."

"Is that why yer fed up? You fink she's given yer the brush-off?"

Normally Danny was reticent about discussing his affairs, but Connie had a special way with him and he found it easy to talk to her. "Yeah, I reckon so," he said.

Connie pulled her legs up under her as she sat in the easy chair and sighed. "I was 'opin' you'd get serious with Kathy. I fink she's nice. She likes you, I can tell."

Danny winced. "Yer know she's livin' wiv Jack Mason now?"

"Yeah, I know," Connie replied. "She's 'avin' a baby, ain't she?"

Danny was keen to change the subject. "What about you? Are you an' Jimmy gonna get married?"

"Soon as we can, bruv. The way fings are, we don't want ter wait. D'yer fink that's right?"

"Them's my sentiments, Connie. Marry yer sailor boy. Grab what 'appiness yer can, while yer can. There's no sense in waitin'. Yer can wait fer ever."

Connie's face suddenly became serious. "Danny, can yer keep a secret?" she asked.

"Try me."

"Promise yer won't let on ter Mum an' Dad?"

"Promise."

"Lucy reckons she might be 'avin' a baby."

"*What*?"

"She's pretty certain. Gawd knows what Mum an' Dad's gonna say when they find out, but they've gotta know before long."

Danny puffed out his cheeks. " 'E's picked a fine time ter get 'er pregnant."

Connie pouted. "It takes two ter tango, Danny. She's jus' one o' the unlucky ones."

"Well at least she'll 'ave a better chance than Kathy. I can't see our ole man chuckin' 'er out like Kathy's ole man did."

Connie got up and took her coat from behind the door. "I've gotta get back ter work. See yer ternight, bruv."

"Don't you get pregnant, Connie, fer Chrissake," Danny said as she opened the door.

"Chance would be a fine fing," Connie called back from the passage, slamming the front door shut behind her.

Danny put his feet up onto the vacant chair and closed his eyes to think. It was Friday, and since he had talked to Kathy he had been unable to contact Tony Arpino. On two occasions he had gone along to the Arpinos' shop in Bermondsey Lane, and each time Tony's father had told him that his son was up town trying to get some information as to the whereabouts of Maria and her family. Danny had bumped into Johnny Ross in Clink Lane that morning and heard that Tony hadn't been to the New Cross dogs the previous evening. Johnny had been edgy, and asked if he could stand in Ginny's doorway while he talked. Danny grinned to himself when he recalled the conversation.

"I'm in the shite, Danny."

"I know yer are. Jack Mason's bin lookin' fer yer."

Johnny winced. " 'E's gonna give me a good goin' over when 'e catches me. It's about somefink I done."

"Bloody 'ell, Johnny, you're a walkin' disaster. What yer done now?"

Johnny peered out from Ginny's doorway to make sure he wasn't in any immediate danger and then he spoke in a low voice: "Yer remember me tellin' yer about that load I 'ad away? Well, Tony Allen stuck it in 'is timber yard."

"Not that one next ter the nick?"

"Same one. Anyways, 'e paid me fer the stuff, but 'e was left wiv a couple o' dozen cases 'e couldn't place. 'E wanted 'em out of 'is yard, just in case the law got sensible all of a sudden. That's what Jack Mason was gettin' all stewed up about. What 'e didn't know was that I was puttin' around tryin' ter get a buyer. There was no way I was gonna get lumbered wiv the gear. I must admit though, Tony Allen was fair about it. 'E'd already paid me fer the lot an' 'e said I could earn a dollar a case fer placin' 'em. Anyway, I got a buyer in Deptford. Fing was, I stuck a couple o' bob on fer me trouble. The bloke seemed 'appy wiv the price, but what I didn't know was that 'is mate a few doors away 'ad already bought some o' the corned beef from Tony. They got talkin' an' my bloke finks 'e's bin took on. 'E gives Tony a ring, an' I'm called inter the office. Tony went on about losin' 'is credibility an' I'm standin' there noddin' an' lookin' all sorry fer meself. The result was, I got a slap on the wrist an' told not ter do it again, when in walks that bastard Mason. 'Im an' Tony get at it, an' I'm told ter wait outside. I can 'ear 'em goin' orf at each uvver an' I'm gettin' scared. Jack Mason's ravin', an' I know I'm in fer a pastin'. So I scarpers quick, 'cos if Mason gets 'old o' me I'm gonna look like a sack o' coal — all lumps an' bumps."

Danny had been horrified by Johnny's tale, and now he eased his position in the chair and wondered how he was going to locate his pal Tony Arpino. He would have to make him see that Kathy couldn't help him without putting herself in danger. Danny thought about his own situation too. Jack Mason appeared to be pulling the strings, if what Johnny had said was anything to go by, and Tony Allen wasn't into protection rackets, he felt sure. That was one of Mason's sidelines, and Jack Mason was a force to be reckoned with. The whole business was putting him in a very precarious position. Being the local bookmaker's runner was jeopardising his loyalty to his pal Tony Arpino. Danny thought about talking to Tony Allen but rejected the idea. It would only bring the bookie's minder down on him, and everything would then get very nasty. He was beginning to regret ever having became an employee of Tony Allen and Co.

Alice Sutton brought the news back with her Saturday morning shopping. There was to be a christening party in the street. Alice was full of it as she unpacked the week's rations and laid them out on the table.

"I'm so pleased for 'em, an' what's more it'll cheer us all up. I was talkin' ter Missus Mitchell, an' she said she was gonna borrer some forms an' some trestle tables from the church 'all. Everybody's invited. If the weavver stays fine the party's gonna be 'eld in the street. That'll be nice, Frank."

Alice's husband was reading the morning paper and uttered an unintelligible reply. Alice stood in front of him with her hands on her hips. "Frank, will you put that bleedin' paper down an' listen ter me?"

"I was listenin', Alice. What d'yer say?" he asked, scratching his moustache.

"I said the Mitchells are 'avin' a street party termorrer. Their baby's bein' christened."

Frank chuckled. "That'll be nice. We'll get Bonky

225

pissed an' doin' 'is Nelson bit. Then we can carry ole Charlie Perkins up ter the top o' the turnin' ter stop any traffic comin' down.''

Alice tried to look stern. "I don't want yer showin' me up, Frank Sutton. I remember the last street party. What wiv you an' Annie Barnes's ole man dancin' up the street in those red flannel drawers, an' the pair of yer grabbin' ole Granny Bell. Showed me up proper, yer did.''

Frank grinned. "Blimey, Alice, that was a few years ago. That was when Charlie Perkins 'ad that set-to wiv 'is ole woman an' blacked 'er eye. On their weddin' anniversary as well.''

Alice shook her head. "That was a different time. You 'ad them drawers on at the Brightmans' party.''

"No, yer got it wrong, girl. I know when I got dressed up, 'cos Charlie Perkins give me the drawers. They was 'is ole woman's, that's what the row was about.''

Alice conceded the point; it wasn't worth arguing when there was so much to do. She had to sort out her best dress, and maybe Maggie could do her hair up for her. Frank was still belabouring the point when Maggie looked in a little later.

"What's all this about red flannel drawers?" she asked as she walked into the parlour.

"Take no notice of yer farver, Maggie, 'e's comin' over all unnecessary in 'is old age,'' Alice grinned as she smoothed down the clean tablecloth. Frank realised he was now outnumbered and decided it was time to retreat to The Globe.

Chapter Twenty

The Mitchells lived at number 17 Dawson Street. John Mitchell was a Scot who first saw the light of day in a croft, and had travelled down to London to seek work, and instead had found himself knee-deep in mud on the battlefields of France. By the end of the war he had risen to the rank of sergeant in the Scots Guards, and had been awarded the Military Medal. His friends reckoned that John Mitchell was a hero, but the dour Scot disagreed. The medal meant very little to him, and the jubilation had soon evaporated in the rush for work and the endless dole queues of the thirties. John Mitchell was lucky, he had got a job with a Bermondsey blacksmith who taught him well. When the next war began he was established in his own business with a young apprentice articled to him. He had also found a wife, a Bermondsey girl whom he doted on. He and his blond-haired Janie desperately wanted a child and, just when they had begun to despair, Janie became pregnant. John Mitchell hoped it would be a boy, who would of course follow him into the business. The birth was a difficult one, and when the tiny bundle was placed into his muscular arms John Mitchell swallowed his disappointment, and promptly fell in love when he looked at his daughter's puckered face. Janie allowed her husband to name the child and he picked the names Heather Louise: Heather, because he said the child smelled of the heather-covered braes; and Louise after his late mother. The Mitchells were a respected and well-liked couple who stayed in the street despite their growing business. Janie could not envisage leaving the turning she was born in and the folk she loved, and John Mitchell was happy to pander to his wife's wishes, and so they stayed. Sunday was going to be a big day in their lives, and everyone in the little back-street was invited to the party.

The idyllic weather continued, and Sunday was bright and warm. The revelries began at lunchtime and The Globe was packed with back-slapping customers who threatened to overwhelm John Mitchell with their offers of drinks. The proud father had to refuse all but the first pint. The chris-tening was at three o'clock, and for him the party would begin after the naming of Heather Louise. The landlord of The Globe was also being cautious. Biff Bowden was in full swing following Shady Lady's narrow victory at Catford and Eddie was watching out for the arrival of Bonky Williams. He was aware of the hostility between Biff and Bonky and realised that he would have to take on the role of peacemaker.

At one o'clock Bonky Williams walked in the pub, and as soon as he saw Biff Bowden standing at the bar his face became dark. Eddie did not miss the omen, and he hurried to serve Bonky. " 'Ow the bloody 'ell are yer, me ole mate?'' he cried.

"I was all right till I see that ugly bastard," Bonky replied.

Eddie poured the stout carefully. "It's a shame yer feel that way about Biff."

"Why's that?" Bonky asked, eyeing the landlord suspiciously.

"Oh, nuffink."

Bonky was hooked. "C'mon, Eddie, why is it a shame?"

Eddie leaned over the counter in an exaggerated gesture of secrecy. "If I tell yer somefink, can yer keep it ter yerself?"

"You know me, Eddie, I'm as tight as a drum."

"I know that, Bonky, but can yer keep a secret?"

Bonky Williams puffed and slapped the counter in frus-tration. "You gonna tell me or not?"

"Right, now listen carefully, 'cos I gotta whisper," Edie said, trying not to laugh.

Bonky gave the landlord a sideways glance. "Look, I might be short on eyes, but me poxy 'earin' ain't affected."

"Okay, Bonky lad. Biff Bowden's dog's goin' inter retirement soon."

"What d'yer want me ter do, go roun' wiv a bleedin' collection fer it?"

"Now don't get all shirty, Bonky, jus' listen. Biff told me in confidence that Shady Lady is goin' fer breedin', an' when she 'as 'er first litter, Biff's gonna name the first pup 'Bonky's Gem'. What d'yer fink about that?"

Bonky Williams looked over to where Biff was standing, then back to Eddie. "Cor! That's decent of 'im, ain't it?"

Eddie turned away and fiddled with the spirit optics until he had regained control of his facial muscles. "I fink it's a nice gesture, Bonky. Ole Biff reckons yer a good sport."

"Did 'e tell yer that, Eddie?"

"Sure did, mate."

"Well I'll be! I fink I'll buy 'im a drink."

"That'd be 'an'some, Bonky."

" 'Bonky's Gem'," ruminated Bonky "Now that'd be somefing ter drink to!"

Eddie winced noticeably. "Don't let on I told yer. Biff'll do 'is nut."

"Don't worry, Eddie. Mum's the word."

Bonky walked over to Biff and tapped him on the shoulder. "Wanna drink, Biff?"

Biff, slightly the worse for drink, looked at the one-eyed character, his face contorted. "Fanks, Bonky, I'll 'ave a pint of ale."

Eddie stood at the counter, his fingers crossed behind his back, and when Biff looked in his direction he saw the landlord winking at him urgently. Old Arthur Smith saw the gesticulations too. " 'Ere, Eddie," he said, "when yer get rid o' yer affliction can yer pour me anuvver pint? I'm dyin' o' thirst."

Before The Globe had shut for the night, the Mitchell's christening party was in full swing. Charlie Perkins sat beside the crates of ale, his bony fingers tapping in time with the wheezing concertina, Granny Bell was doing a soft-shoe shuffle with her skirts held up to her knee, and the street folk clapped in unison. All the children were allowed to stop up late while the guest of honour, Heather Louise Mitchell, slept peacefully in her bassinet. All around her the merriment went on: Frank Sutton took his wife Alice out onto the cobblestones and held her firmly as he whisked her around; Joe Copeland was talking to John Mitchell, a pint glass clutched tightly in his large fist; and Maggie sat with Lucy and Connie. "My two would 'ave loved this," she said sadly.

Connie put her arm around Maggie's shoulders. "I fink yer did the right fing, Mag. I got a feelin' it's gonna get really bad before long."

Lucy nodded her agreement. "It's only a matter of time. The children are much better off being out of London. I feel sorry for the little mites here, they're going to be in the thick of it."

Maggie sighed. "I 'ope I did do the right fing. It caused a right ole barney between me an' Joe."

"Ain't you an' 'im talkin'? Connie asked in her usual forthright manner.

"We're all right now," Maggie replied. " 'E soon got over it. I fink deep down 'e knew I'd done the right fing. 'E didn't like admittin' it though."

Danny Sutton walked back from The Globe to the street party, his thoughts centred on his pal Tony. He felt ineffectual and useless, and it worried him. The two of them had run the streets together as kids and got into the usual scrapes. Now, when Tony asked him for help he was unable to do anything. The pints he had drunk were beginning to take their toll and Danny felt he was well on his way to getting drunk. Maybe he should sink a few more pints and blot out the depression that was gnawing away at his insides and tightening the base of his skull like a vice. Maybe he should tell the bookmaker to poke his job, and tell Jack Mason to get stuffed. Perhaps he could find rooms and move Kathy in with him. At least she would be away from that bullying bastard. He would have to give it some thought, but first he was going to join the party and drink himself into a state of sublime intoxication.

The young cockney heard the sound of the concertina before he turned the corner. Dusk was settling down around the merrymakers, and he could see the outlines of people dancing in the light that shone out from the gas-lit passages of the tumbledown houses. All the front doors were open, the black-out regulations apparently forgotten, and the street warden Archie Madden was waltzing around with the aged Mrs Jackson who owned the little sweetshop on the corner of the turning. Bernie Wright the concertina player was grinning widely as he stamped his foot in time to the melody he was squeezing out from his beloved instrument.

Connie came up to Danny and grabbed his arm. "C'mon, bruv, I've bin waitin' fer yer. Let's 'ave a dance."

John Mitchell and his Janie were passing among the guests, filling their glasses and exchanging pleasantries. Their pride and joy, Heather Louise, slept on as the music got louder and the raucous laughter filled the street. Charlie Perkins was rocking in his chair, with a pint glass in his hand and a toothless smile that infected everyone who looked at him. The war and the troubles that might come were far from the minds of the Dawson Street folk on that balmy Sunday night. They toasted John and Janie and their baby, they drank the health of each other, and they remembered absent friends. The music rang out again, and the strains of 'Roses of Picardy' drifted through the backwater of dockland. John Mitchell felt a wave of nostalgia wash over him, and he remembered the Somme and Ypres. Danny was transported back in his mind to more recent battles. He thought of the young soldier who died at his side on the beaches, and the imperturbable gypsy Oggy Murphy who held him safely in the dark, freezing water off La Panne, and his eyes filled with tears.

The drinking carried on as the midnight hour came and went. Old songs were sung and the strains of 'Alice Blue Gown' and 'She's Only a Bird in a Gilded Cage' carried down the turning and echoed through the railway arch. Sleepy, happy children were hauled off to bed and their parents rejoined the revelry. Two lovers sat close together in the shadows and kissed tenderly. The girl was happy to be sharing the secret, and her beau was a little overcome.

"Tell me, Ben, are you happy for us? Are you really happy?" she asked.

He tried to answer but the lump in his throat prevented him, and he nodded, his glowing eyes answering her fully. She snuggled up to him and felt a slight shiver run down her back. He was fearful for the future, but the night was magical.

She could see the river from her bedroom window. The dark sky held no magic, only a foreboding. She had been happy that morning but the feeling was shortlived; the future held no happiness, only sorrow. She saw the days ahead as too burdensome to bear. Her head ached, and the dark swelling below her eye was tender to the touch. She raised her hand to her forehead and stared out into the night. It seemed that her whole life had been one of constant unhappiness; there were very few occasions when she had felt really happy and wanted. She could count the times on one hand. She thought about the young man who had brought her brief happiness and tears welled up in her

232

eyes. It was too late. She could have gone to him, but the baby inside her would soon come into the world and be a constant reminder of her past. There would always be secret thoughts which would eat into his mind and destroy any true happiness.

It was too late for tears. If only, she rued. If only there had been more time with Danny before he left. Maybe things would have been different. Maybe he would have realised just how much she cared for him and wanted him. Her anger and pride had led her into an impossible relationship with a man whose thin veneer of respectability and decency had peeled away so quickly to reveal the true character beneath. Why had she been so blind? Why had she been attracted to a man like Jack Mason? Why had she succumbed to his surface charm and not seen the real man beneath? Had she gone with Mason to punish Danny? Or to punish herself? It didn't matter now . . .

It was all too late.

The room became dark and Kathy drew the curtains. She turned on the small bedside lamp. The letter was still lying on the dressing table. It would not have been so bad had he tried to excuse his actions or say he was sorry. Instead the confrontation had been violent. She had found the letter quite by accident. It had fallen out of his pocket when he threw his coat over the back of a chair that morning. She had noticed it when she was tidying up, and now she wished that she had never read it. It was from a woman she knew slightly. She was a barmaid in one of the pubs in Deptford which Jack Mason used. It was a passionate letter, referring to the happy times they had spent together, and went on to say how she was missing him while on holiday, and how she looked forward to seeing him once more. Kathy recalled the shock and blind fury she had experienced as she held the letter in her shaking hands. There were many things she had endured with him — the beatings and the rough, inconsiderate way she made love to her — but there was one thing she would not endure. She would not share him with another woman. She was having his baby and she tried to make him see that he owed her his loyalty. His answer was to tell her that he never wanted the kid and that she should have got rid of it like he told her. Her anger spilled over and she tore at his face with her hands, only to be sent sprawling by a cuff. He had stormed out in a vile temper at lunch-time and had not returned. Kathy had spent the rest of the day crying hysterically, but now, as the night drew in, she had composed herself.

With calm deliberation she went to the bathroom and filled a tumbler full of water and then placed it beside the bed. Next she undressed and put on her nightgown. She filled her palm with the contents of a small glass phial and swallowed the lot between gulps from the tumbler. She turned off the light and pulled open the curtains. The bed felt cool as she closed her eyes. The cold, distant stars twinkled through gaps in the cloud bank. After some time the soft moon shone into the room and lit up the prone figure on the bed, then the stars faded and the moon was covered once again by clouds. The pin-points of light went out, and a velvet blackness smothered her heavy eyelids.

Sadie Comfort sat in her comfortable front room listening to the evening service. Boss, her red setter, lay at her feet and looked up with large, doleful eyes. Sadie Comfort felt uneasy, and the hymn-singing on the wireless did little to relieve her. Maybe Albert was right when he said she should mind her own business and not get involved. After all, it was nothing unusual to hear banging and shouting next door. The man who lived there was a pig, in Sadie's estimation, although she thought the girl was very pleas-ant and polite. They seemed an odd match; he was a lot older than her, and was always going out alone. He was prone to raise his hand to the girl and there were often tell-tale marks on her face. Albert said they had to sort things out for themselves, and as long as they didn't interfere with anyone else there was nothing to be done, but Sadie could not get rid of her uncomfortable feeling; something was wrong. Since that morning when she heard the row the girl had not made an appearance, which was unusual. The man had gone out though, and Sadie's horse-brasses had rattled as he slammed the door violently.

Sadie Comfort's eyes dropped, and the sing-song voice of the minister reciting the evening prayer sounded far away. Boss put his head on Sadie's foot and made her start. She looked down at the dog and saw the large eyes staring up at her enquiringly. Sadie yawned and looked up at the clock on the mantelshelf: ten past ten. Albert would be in from the pub soon and then she would feel better. Being left alone didn't normally worry her; Boss was a good house dog, and Albert was rarely gone for more than an hour. Tonight though was different, though Boss seemed restless, too. He had had his walk and his supper, and by now he should have been curled up asleep on the hearth rug. Albert would no doubt think she was being silly, but Boss knew there was something wrong.

At the sound of a key in the door Boss stood up and growled. Albert walked in and took off his coat. " 'Ello, Boss, ain't yer asleep?" he said.

Sadie glanced at the clock. "There's not bin a sound from next door, Alb. I'm sure there's somefink wrong."

"We gonna start all that again, Sadie? I told yer, it's not our concern."

"But there ain't bin a sound since 'e went out. I usually 'ear 'er movin' about, an' she nearly always goes out some time durin' the day. 'E could 'ave killed 'er fer all we know."

"Ain't 'e bin back?"

"Nope. I would 'ave 'eard 'im. I would 'ave 'eard the door go."

Albert scratched his head. "It's a bit late ter go knockin' on 'er door. It'd frighten the life out of 'er this time o' night."

Sadie got up. "Look at Boss, 'e knows there's somefink wrong, don't yer boy?"

The dog gave a short whine and rubbed himself along Albert's leg.

"It's no good, Alb, I'll 'ave ter knock. I wouldn't get any sleep if I didn't."

Albert sighed and followed his wife out into the street. He knocked on Mason's door. "She's not answerin'."

"Knock a bit louder, Albert."

Albert rat-tatted. 'She must 'ave gone ter bed," he said.

"She never goes ter bed early. Yer can normally 'ear 'er movin' about till late."

"Look, Sadie, p'raps she felt tired an' got an early night?"

"No. I'm goin' fer the keys. She could be dead in there."

Albert pulled on her arm. "Yer goin' ter get yerself in trouble if yer not careful. She told yer ter mind the keys fer 'er. She didn't give yer the spare set ter go moochin' around 'er place when yer feel like it."

"Well that's jus' too bad. Somefink's not right. I gotta find out, Alb."

When Sadie returned with the keys Boss was trotting along at her heels. Albert opened the front door gingerly, with Sadie wide-eyed looking over his shoulder anxiously. The downstairs was in darkness and the only light came through the landing window. The moonlight shone on the steep staircase and lit up the gilt-framed picture at the head of the stairs.

"Kathy, yer asleep?" Sadie called out.

"That's a daft question, Sadie. If she is asleep she can't answer, can she?"

"Albert, take a look in the front room. She might be in there."

Albert opened the door and switched on the light. Everything looked tidy. Breathing a sigh of relief, he turned the switch off and closed the door quietly. "C'mon, girl, we'd better get goin'."

"D'yer fink we should take a dekko upstairs first, luv?"

"Now listen, Sadie, yer told me the row was in the front room. That's when yer 'eard 'er scream when 'e thumped 'er. Now if 'e 'ad a done 'er in, 'e wouldn't 'ave carted 'er up the apples, now would 'e? She's asleep. If we go up it's gonna scare the bleedin' life out of 'er. C'mon, let's get back."

"I s'pose yer right, luv," Sadie conceded, and she turned towards the front door.

Suddenly Boss dashed between the two of them and ran up the stairs.

"Christ! Albert, get 'im quick!"

Albert Comfort raced up the stairs expecting to hear Kathy scream out, but when he peered into the dark bedroom he could see the outline of Boss with his front paws on the bed licking the face of the prone figure. Albert put on the light and quickly drew the curtains. The girl's face was pale and still.

"Gawd Almighty! She's dead!" he said aloud. "Sadie! Quick!"

Sadie came hurrying into the room, fearful of what she would see, her mouth hanging open. She crept over to the bed and looked down at the wan face of the still woman. She saw the empty phial and the tumbler beside the bed.

"She's took an overdose!" she cried out. "The poor cow's took an overdose!"

"Is she . . .?" Albert whispered, stepping back a pace.

Sadie picked up the limp, cold hand and could feel no pulse. In desperation she looked around and saw the small oval mirror lying on the dressing table. "Give me that mirror. Quick, Albert!"

Sadie held the mirror close to the girl's open mouth. "She's still breavin'! Quick, run up the top o' the street an' phone fer an ambulance! While yer there yer'd better phone the police as well!"

Chapter Twenty-One

Monday the 29th of July began the same as any other Monday in dockland. The corner-shop owners had to listen to the customers' moans and groans, everything seemed in short supply. The greengrocers took a large share of the complaints. Bananas had disappeared entirely from the shops, stalls and barrows, lemons and oranges were fast disappearing too, and only home-grown produce could still be bought in quantity. Corner-shop customers in the area had read of the recent haul at Sullivan's Wharf and hoped that they would soon be able to purchase a tin of under-the-counter corned beef or peaches but knowing winks and vague gestures did no good. They finally realised that any goods that fell off the back of that lorry had not landed in the Tooley Street area. However, the odd luxury did find its way into a shopping bag, and the satisfied customer realised that all was not lost.

On that particular Monday morning the usual glumness was forgotten when the news of Kathy Thompson spread through the little backstreets. Alice Sutton heard it from Annie Barnes, who had just returned from getting her shopping.

"It's terrible, Alice, 'er poor muvver's goin' mad. A copper knocked on 'er door an' told 'er the news. I bet that bastard Mason's drove 'er to it."

"Where they took 'er to, Annie?"

"Guy's. Missus Thompson's rushed up there. Gawd knows 'ow bad it is, what wiv 'er bein' in that condition."

"Well she's in the right place. They're marvellous at Guy's, Annie."

Annie Barnes nodded her agreement. "She's 'ad an 'ard time of it, one way an' anuvver."

It was Alice's turn to nod. "You're right, 'er ole man's got ter shoulder the blame as well. 'E kicked 'er out when 'e found out she was carryin'. 'E's anuvver no good cowson. 'E knocks Kathy's muvver black an' blue."

"I tell yer, Alice, I wouldn't stan' fer it, if it was me."

"Me neivver, Annie. I'd stab the whore-son when 'e was asleep."

Danny did not hear the news about Kathy. He had left his house early to call in on the Arpinos' shop. As he walked towards Bermondsey Lane he tried to think clearly about what he was going to say to Tony, but he was still feeling the effects of the party. His head was pounding and his legs felt leaden. As he walked along the line of shops he could sense something was wrong. The usual array of goods was absent from the pavement outside the Arpinos' store. When he entered the shop, Danny stared in disbelief. The floor was littered with cans and packages, and one of the shelves had been yanked away from the wall. The grey marble counter had been smashed, and the large brass scales were lying on the floor. Lou Arpino stood amid the litter, his face grey with misery.

"Dey done ma shop, Danny. Dey 'urt ma boy Tony. Look at da mess. It's a no good, I'm tellin' you, Danny. Dey ruined me."

"Where's Tony?" Danny asked, taking hold of the Italian's arm. 'Where is 'e, Lou?"

" 'E's in da back. See if ma boy's okay, Danny. Mamma's wiv 'im."

Danny walked through into the back room and saw Sofia bending over her son. Tony sat slumped in a chair, blood coming from a cut above his eye. Sofia was parting his hair gently with her fingers and Tony winced. "It's all right, Ma, it's only a bump," he said impatiently.

"Bloody 'ell! What 'appened, Tone?"

Tony Arpino looked up as his pal walked in. "They

done us, Danny. They done us proper. They was too quick fer us.''

Sofia held her hands up to the ceiling. "Dey nearly killed our Tony," she cried. "Why dey do dis to us? We don't 'urt anybody. Why, Danny?''

Tony took his mother's hands in his. "Mamma, it's okay. Yer go an' make Danny a cup o' tea. Go on mamma, yer forgettin' Danny's a guest?''

Sofia dabbed at her eyes as she disappeared into the kitchen, and Danny sat down facing his pal. "Tell us exactly what 'appened,'' he said.

Tony winced as he pressed the cut over his eye. "We'd just opened an' they walked in large as life. Two of 'em there was. I ain't seen eivver of 'em before. They didn't say a word. One of 'em pulled the shelf over an' the uvver git took an' 'ammer from under 'is coat 'an smashed the counter. I jump the one wiv the 'ammer but the uvver bastard clobbered me over the crust. It looked like a pick-axe 'andle 'e 'it me wiv. I saw stars. Our pop tried ter grab the geezer that whacked me, but they pinned 'im ter the wall an' they told 'im 'e'd better fink again about not payin' up. They said they'd be back.''

Danny puffed out his cheeks. "I come down 'ere a couple o' times last week lookin' fer yer. Did your farver tell yer?''

"Yeah, he told me. I'm sorry I wasn't 'ere. I was over Clerkenwell.''

"What yer bin doin' over there?''

Tony winced again as he felt the bump on his head. "There's a lot of Italians live over Clerkenwell. They call it 'Little Italy'. Ain't yer never 'eard of it?''

Danny nodded. "Course I 'ave. But what was yer doin' over there?''

Tony looked towards the kitchen, then lowered his voice. "I ain't told Ma what I'm up to, but I've gotta do somefink, Danny. It was lucky she wasn't in the shop at the time. I bin ter see some people I know. Some o' Pop's family live over Clerkenwell. They 'ad the same trouble there a few years ago but they sorted it out fer themselves. This crowd round 'ere won't stick tergevver. Most of the shopkeepers ain't exactly friendly wiv us, I fink they reckon we're spies. They don't see us as bein' the same as them, but we're no different, Danny, you know that. Take me: I was born in Bermon'sey, I speak the same as you do. Me pop took out English nationality papers years ago. It's 'is country as well, but they can't see it. Anyway, all the shopkeepers 'ad a meetin' last week. Pop said we should all stick tergevver an' not pay up. 'Course, a few of 'em agreed wiv 'im, but most of 'em reckoned it was easier ter pay up an' avoid the aggro. What they don't seem ter realise is that this is jus' one foot in the door. Once that mob get us payin' up, they'll be pushin' the dodgy gear on us. All that under the counter stuff. Yer know what they're like, Danny.''

''Yer still ain't told me what yer was doin' over Clerkenwell, Tony.''

Sofia Arpino came into the room carrying a tray with two cups of tea. ''It's nice you come to see us, Danny. You stay wiv Tony. I mus' 'elp Papa clear up da mess.''

She left the room, and when she was out of earshot Tony leaned forward. ''Danny, I've looked up a couple of ole pals. They're gonna 'elp me take care o' Jack Mason. We're gonna give 'im a goin' over, an' if 'e don't get the message an' leave us alone, we're gonna get really nasty. Those two pals o' mine ain't no powder puffs. We can 'andle Jack Mason.''

Danny looked at his friend affectionately. ''Tony, yer me pal, an' I like yer family. I'd 'ate it if any of yer got 'urt. Yer don't know what yer lettin' yerself in for. Yer ain't dealin' wiv some ole plum. Jack Mason's got 'is fingers in everyfink, 'e knows a lot o' people. If yer not careful, yer gonna start anuvver war of yer own. There's bound ter be comebacks, it's a certainty.''

Tony's face was set hard. ''All right, yer tell me what

242

we're expected ter do? If yer fink we're gonna pay up, yer wrong. We ain't gonna do it.''

Danny sighed and leaned back in his chair. ''I don't know the answer, Tone. I tried ter get Kathy ter come up wiv some info, but she was scared. Yer can't very well blame 'er, can yer? She's terrified of Mason. And I ain't gonna ask her again, it's too dangerous.''

An argument was developing in the front of the shop between the Arpinos. Sofia started to raise her voice and Tony looked at his pal and sighed in resignation. Danny put his hand on Tony's shoulder. ''Stay put, Tone. I'll give 'em an 'and ter clear the mess up. When yer feelin' up to it we'll 'ave a drink an' a long chat. Okay?''

It was a week since the warehouse break-in had been reported and Inspector Flint was getting impatient. There were no leads, and no information forthcoming from the usual informers. It was as though the whole load had vanished into thin air. Inspector Flint stood up from his desk and looked thoughtfully out of his office window. Down below people were moving around in the yard; timber was being neatly stacked, and two workers were loading deal boards on to a lorry. For a few moments he watched the activity. At times like this, it would be nice to have a job that ended when the five o'clock whistle went, he thought. That idiot Stockbridge is an incompetent ass. I seem to be surrounded with brainless idiots. Surely someone would have spotted that stolen gear being sold off by now? Apparently Limehouse nick was drawing a blank, too. Still, maybe the impossible has happened, maybe Stockbridge has got a new slant on the business. Anyway, it's about time I shook him up a bit, he decided, opening the door and screaming out for his subordinate.

Detective Constable Stockbridge was dreading the call. He had contacted all his snouts and filled up two notebooks with memoranda, and his feet were sore from all the walking. Stockbridge was convinced that the stolen cases had been unloaded locally and shipped out of the area. The lorry belonging to Sullivan's Wharf had been left in Limehouse to draw the scent away from Bermondsey, he told himself. If none of his snouts had seen anything, then there was nothing to see. They had never let him down before. Problem was getting that dopey git of an inspector to see how sensible his assumptions were. It was a pity that the inspector's predecessor had let his sexual hang-up become his downfall. If he had been a little more discreet, he could have pursued his pastime and still kept his job, there would then have been no threat of going back to the beat.

When he walked into the inspector's office, Stockbridge feared the worst. Flint had a face as long as a month of Sundays, and he was drumming his fingers on the polished surface of his desk.

"Well, Stockbridge, it's been a week now. What have you got for me?"

Fat Stan grimaced. "It's quiet, sir, none o' me contacts 'ave reported anyfink. They've 'eard nuffink, an' there's no whispers about the local villains bein' involved."

"Well someone broke into the warehouse, man, and it wasn't the bloody fairies. The lorry was found in Limehouse, okay? It was full of Orientals and Oriental fingerprints. The results are, the local police make a pinch and we've got sod all!"

Fat Stan winced. "I reckon the stuff was unloaded in Bermon'sey, sir. There's loads o' railway arches an' yards round 'ere."

"What about the lorry?"

"I fink it was a red 'errin', sir."

"That's what the villains want you to think, Stockbridge. While I'm wasting manpower turning over the thousand and one likely sites in Bermondsey, they're knocking the stuff out in another area. Think about it, man. I'd be a bloody fool walking into, say that timber yard opposite, and telling them I'm looking for some corned beef! I'd be a laughing stock. No, Stockbridge, the stuff's being sold in the East End. What we've got to do is apprehend the thieves. Tell me, Stockbridge, you must know the local villains, have you got any suspects?''

Fat Stan thought hard. Tony Allen would be the most likely person among the local criminal fraternity to be involved, but Tony always played ball. His name had to be kept out of the frame. There was no way he was going to cut off his own private source of income by nailing Tony Allen. After all, no one had got hurt, and Sullivan was probably well insured against that very eventuality. Fat Stan realised, too, that he would now be able to put the squeeze on Tony Allen for a little more security against being named as a suspect.

''Well, sir,'' Stockbridge began, ''there's a nasty little team tryin' ter put the clamps on the shopkeepers in Bermon'sey Lane. Me snout tells me they're not from this area. 'E reckons they come from over the water. Maybe they was involved in the robbery?''

Flint banged his desk. ''Cobblers! The other side of the water used to be my manor. The East End villains don't get involved outside their own patch. Take my word for it, Stockbridge, they're local villains who clobbered the warehouse, and they're local villains operating in Bermondsey Lane. Now you get out there and bring back something. I want action! Understand?''

Fat Stan understood only too well. His feet were already reminding him of the rigours of walking the beat.

Ginny Coombes spread margarine over a thick slice of bread and then smeared a thin coating of strawberry jam over the top.

''Now take that an' get out in the street wiv yer bruvvers an' sisters,'' she said to her son. ''And mind the road.''

Joey Coombes grabbed the slice of bread in his grubby hands, a grin breaking out on his dirty face. ''Cor, fanks, Mum. Is Danny comin' roun' terday?''

" 'E comes round every day 'cept Sundays. Now get out from under me feet."

Joey bit into the bread and a blob of jam stuck to his nose. He looked up at his mother with large blue eyes and said, " 'Ere, Mum, 'ow much d'yer like Danny?"

Ginny glanced at her son enquiringly. "What d'yer mean, 'ow much do I like 'im?"

"Well, Billy Brightman's mum said it's on the cards you an' Danny could get really friendly. What cards she talkin' about, Mum?"

Ginny hid her smile. "Look, Joey, yer get out an' keep yer eye out fer yer bruvvers an' sisters. Don't stand there askin' stupid questions. I've got a lot o' work ter do."

Joey took another bite from the slice and jam dripped onto his tattered pullover. "Are we gonna 'ave anuvver dad one day, Mum?"

Ginny felt the question strike into her insides and she wanted to hug the child, but instead she swallowed hard. "Your farver's dead, Joey. Yer can't 'ave two dads," she said.

"I know that, Mum, but we could 'ave a pretend dad if yer got married, couldn't we?"

"Look, Joey, I am not goin' ter get married. I was married ter yer farver, an' I don't wanna get married again."

"I wouldn't mind Danny fer a pretend dad," Joey said as he made for the door.

Ginny felt tears welling up and she dabbed her eyes with the apron. Sleep had come slow last night, and she had been troubled by her guilty thoughts. Her lad had caught her off balance, and she was worried about the rumours. There was obviously gossip going around about her. She would have to be careful not to fuel the fire, but she knew that the backstreets did not allow for much privacy. Everyone lived in each other's pockets, the slightest impropriety was discussed and disseminated at one end of the houses until it became scandal at the other end of the row. News travelled fast in the backstreets. Word of Kathy Thompson's suicide attempt had spread around in minutes. The terrible news added to Ginny's own sadness, and she tried to blot out her dismay by working about the house. She got so involved that she forgot the time, and when Danny knocked on her door the kettle was not yet over the gas. When he walked in Ginny expected him to say something about Kathy, but he was cheerful.

" 'Ello, Ginny, I saw yer brood outside. School 'olidays started?"

Ginny pulled a face. "I've got six weeks o' this. 'Mum I fell over' an' 'Mum gi's a slice o' bread'. It'll be Mum this an' Mum that. It's a wonder I ain't grey."

Danny smiled. "Ginny, yer don't look a day over firty-five."

Ginny suddenly became serious. He can't know she thought, he would have mentioned it. "Danny, 'aven't you 'eard about Kathy?"

Danny's face took on an anxious look. " 'Eard what, Ginny?"

"She took an overdose."

Danny's face went white. "Bloody 'ell! Is she . . .?"

"They took 'er ter Guy's 'Ospital, Danny. 'Er next door neighbour found 'er. That's all we know."

"I wanna go an' see 'er, Gin."

"It's no good, they won't let yer in. 'Er muvver's up there wiv 'er, but they won't let anybody else in yet. Please Gawd she'll pull frew."

"When did it 'appen, Ginny?"

"Last night. The police came round. I 'eard a commotion when I was puttin' the milk bottles out. It must 'ave bin well after twelve. I'm normally a-bed by that time, but last night I fell asleep in the chair. The kids wore me out yesterday."

Danny sat down heavily in the chair. "Did yer know she was carryin'?" he asked.

Ginny nodded. "It was no secret, yer could tell anyway. That was why 'er ole man kicked 'er out, wasn't it?"

Danny nodded. "What'll 'appen ter the baby, Ginny?"

"Gawd knows. If they manage ter pull 'er frew it's quite possible she'll lose the baby. It 'appened ter that girl in Tooley Buildin's only last year. She took an overdose. She was all right, but she lost the baby. Four months gone she was."

Danny ran his fingers through his hair. "Kathy's gonna be all right, ain't she, Gin?"

Ginny smiled. She had noticed how he reacted when she told him the news. She sensed there was something between them, it showed on the lad's face. "She'll pull frew, Danny. If she gets over this okay it might be a blessin' in disguise. She can make a clean break from that 'orrible bloke. I knew all along no good would come out of 'er goin' wiv 'im. Did yer know 'e left 'is wife an' kid?"

"No, I didn't," Danny jumped up, his face dark with anger.

Ginny picked up the teapot from the table. "I'll make a cup o' tea, you look like yer could do wiv it."

Danny suddenly felt drained, and sat down again. "You ain't seen anyfink o' Johnny Ross, 'ave yer, Gin?" he called out, brushing his fingers through his hair.

"Not since yer spoke to 'im last Friday. What's 'e done now?"

"You know Rossy. 'E's upset Mason, an' I told 'im ter stay out the way fer a few days. If Mason or Tony Allen asks yer 'is whereabouts, Gin, yer don't know, all right? Cor, what a bloody mess."

"Don't worry, Danny, I know Rossy's a bit of a cowson, but I wouldn't wish that bastard Mason on me worst enemy. I won't let on."

The morning punters walked up to Ginny's door with their 'tanner each-ways' and their 'shilling win doubles', and the backstreet rang with children's happy voices. Trains rumbled over the railway arch and the din of traffic carried down Clink Lane from the Tooley Street end. Women came in and out of the turning carrying shopping baskets, and the street knife-grinder treadled his whetstone and sent sparks flying. Joey grazed his knee and tears ran down his sticky face. Cigarette cards changed hands at the turn of a playing card, and another egg-crate was carried into the street by two youngsters ready for the weekend 'wood-chop'. Up above the grey slates and the crazily leaning chimneypots the sky was blue. Lazy clouds drifted on the summer breeze, and cooking smells wafted from open doorways. The midday sun warmed the flagstones and children, tired from their exertions, sat in the shade and talked of the coming hop-picking season.

"Bodiam? Where's Bodiam?"

"It's in Kent."

"Is Kent very far?"

"It's 'undreds o' miles from 'ere. Takes hours on a train."

"What's it like, 'op-pickin'?"

"It's smashin'. We go scrumpin' an' the gypsy kids show us where the rabbits are. We go crab-apple pickin' as well."

"What's crab-apples?"

"They're tiny apples, an' if yer eat 'em yer get poisoned."

"What yer pick 'em for then?"

"To aim at the rabbits."

"Cor! Wish we went 'op-pickin'."

"We sleep in 'uts, an' we 'ave straw beds. Fousan's o' spiders though."

"Ugh!"

"Spiders can't 'urt yer — not like bugs."

"We 'ad bugs. My mum got rid of 'em wiv a burnin' stick. They suck yer blood, bugs do."

"There was a stag beedle down 'oppin'. They can sting yer dead."

"Cor!"

They were interrupted by calls to dinner, and the street was quiet once more. Joey Coombes dipped a chunk of dry bread into his lamb stew.

" 'Ere, Mum, why don't we go 'oppin'?"

"We've never bin, that's why."

"All the kids go 'oppin'. We never do nuffink."

"Yes we do. We went ter Soufend once."

"There's no stag beedles in Soufend."

"Eat yer dinner, Joey."

Chapter Twenty-Two

For three days and nights Kathy was in danger. On Thursday, as the first August dawn broke, she drifted from a misty greyness into the starched white of the hospital ward. Her eyes hurt, the pressure around her hand tightened, and the uncertainty was over. The pressure that had prevented her from floating away, that had kept her clinging on at the edge of death, became warm and comforting. Kathy blinked and focused her eyes. Tired, worried eyes stared back into hers, and she began to understand what had happened. She tried to speak but her mouth was parched. Gentle hands lifted her head and bitter liquid was held to her lips. Hearing words whispered and feeling a cool hand on her forehead, she sank back into a peaceful sleep that was free of dreams. The crisis was over at last.

Mrs Violet Thompson left the ward and walked wearily down the wide, stone stairs and felt the cool morning air rush at her face. The chapel door was open, and inside the quiet and solitude seemed to lift her spirits. The early rays of the sun hit the stained glass arched window and played on the tiny altar. For a time Violet prayed, then she raised her head and sat deep in thought. The heartbreak was not yet over. Soon she must go back and tell her daughter about the baby, though for the moment Kathy must sleep and recover her strength. It had been agreed with the doctor that Violet should break the news. She had also impressed on the doctor and nurses that no one else should visit her daughter, at least for the present. She was adamant that Jack Mason should not be allowed in under any circumstances, and when she'd explained her reasons they acquiesced.

For three days Mrs Thompson had walked back and forth from the hospital in a daze, but this morning there was a spring in her step. The usual band of neighbours would be waiting by their front doors. This morning she would be able to smile at them, and the good news would soon spread. Her only worry was Jack Mason's reaction. She had never spoken to him, but someone would no doubt pass on the news. Violet knew that her husband would not take Kathy back, and it was useless to argue any more, but she hoped that when her daughter left the hospital she could go to stay with her aunt in Ilford for a couple of weeks until the fuss died down. Violet decided she must write to her sister that very day.

As she turned the corner and walked into Clink Lane, Violet met her neighbours' solicitous looks with a huge grin. Pinched, morning faces beamed, and their hugs and tears caused the passing dockers to wave as they hurried to the call-on.

"She's gonna be all right, Fred. Tell Bill, won't yer?"

"Fank Gawd fer that, Vi."

"We'll 'ave ter get 'er some flowers."

" 'Ere, there's a tanner. Put me in."

Violet looked anxiously down the street. "I mus' go, luvs," she said, "I've gotta tell my Charlie 'fore 'e goes off ter work."

Beaming faces grew serious and pitying looks followed Mrs Thompson down the turning. "She's 'ad enough on 'er plate, what wiv one fing an' anuvver," someone said.

"You're right. I 'ope this pulls 'im to 'is senses."

"It won't alter the ugly git. 'E's disowned 'is own daughter, the rotter!"

"Well it might quieten 'im down fer a bit."

"Yeah, fer a couple o' weeks, then 'e'll get pissed an' take it out on poor Vi, yer mark my words."

"If that was me I'd open that Charlie Thompson. 'E's a no-good whore-son."

"I said ter my Frankie only the uvver night: 'Yer an' yer

252

mates ought ter send the bastard ter Coventry'. My Frankie only laughed. Yer know what men are like — all pals tergevver.''

Danny heard the good news as he was going down the street that morning, and before he started work he called in on Mrs Thompson.

"Come in, son, I'm jus' makin' meself a nice cuppa,'' she said.

Danny sat in the scullery while Violet filled the kettle and stood it on the iron gas stove. "Kathy's out of the coma, fank Gawd. She'll be all right now. She'll look a lot better when I go in, I'm sure.''

"Can I go in ter see 'er, Vi?''

"I'm sure Kathy would like ter see yer when she's feelin' a bit better, son. I'll tell 'er yer called round.''

Danny picked at the oil-cloth covering on the creaking wooden table. "Any idea what made 'er do it, Vi?''

"Why, it was that whore-son, wasn't it? 'E's led 'er a dog's life since she's bin livin' wiv 'im. She should 'ave known better. Kathy's seen enough of it 'ome 'ere wiv me an' 'er farver.''

"What about the baby?'' Danny asked.

Violet Thompson suddenly reached for her handkerchief and put it to her eyes. "She lost it. She ain't bin told yet. I'm jus' 'opin' it don't upset 'er too much. That git Mason got 'is wish, didn't 'e? 'E wanted Kathy ter get rid of it right from the start.''

The kettle came to the boil and Violet filled a small china teapot. Danny watched while the frail-looking woman busied herself about the scullery.

"What's goin' ter 'appen to 'er now, Vi?'' he asked.

"She can't come 'ome 'ere. 'Er farver's washed 'is 'ands of 'er. I'm goin' ter write ter me sister in Ilford terday. She'll 'ave 'er there fer a couple o' weeks. We'll jus' 'ave ter see what 'appens then.''

Danny put a half-crown down on the table. "Can yer take Kathy somefink in?''

"Fanks, son. I'll get 'er a nice bunch o' flowers. The neighbours 'ave bin real nice. They say in times o' trouble yer find yer real friends. And they've come up trumps round 'ere. Even ole Missus Johnson said 'ello this mornin'. I ain't spoke wiv 'er since me ole man clouted 'er boy when 'e broke me winder."

While Danny sipped his tea Mrs. Thompson studied him. Presently she said, "Yer know, I often wondered about yer an' my Kathy. I fink everybody round 'ere expected the two o' yer ter get married one day. I mean, yer was always tergevver. Even when yer was kids. Why the bloody 'ell she got mixed up wiv that 'orrible bastard, I'll never know."

Danny shrugged his shoulders. "I got a letter from me sister, Con, while I was in France. She told me Kathy was goin' aroun' wiv 'im."

Violet Thompson folded her arms and tucked her hands under her armpits. "Did you an' Kathy 'ave a bust-up, son? 'Fore yer went overseas, I mean?"

Danny nodded. "Yeah, we did, sort of, Vi."

"Yeah, I guessed as much. I remember 'er comin' in cryin' one Saturday night. It was about the time yer got called up. I remember that night well. My Charlie followed 'er in. Pissed 'e was. 'E wanted ter know who it was she was wiv in the doorway. I told 'im ter leave 'er alone 'cos she was upset an' me an' 'im gets at it. I got a right ole shiner that bleedin' night."

Danny finished his tea and put the cup down on the table. "I wished we could 'ave patched it up, Vi. I tell yer, she's too good fer that bastard."

Violet Thompson nodded. "Trouble was, son, even when 'e turned bad, she stuck wiv 'im. And then 'e got 'er pregnant. There was a terrible row 'ere when me ole man found out. 'E went up the pub an' got blind drunk. 'E'd already told Kathy ter be out o' the 'ouse by the time 'e got back, and I made sure she was. 'E give me a good 'idin'. 'E was in a terrible state. So was I by the time 'e'd finished wiv me."

Danny drank his tea and stood up. "Fanks, Vi. I'd better get over ter Ginny's," he said. "Give Kathy me love. Let me know when it's all right ter go in, won't yer?"

On Friday morning the early breeze sent pieces of paper swirling down the street and billowing clouds raced across the sky. Danny came down into the parlour to find a letter with a Maidstone postmark addressed to him. He knew it was from Alison. He opened it and read through it quickly. He had been despairing of ever hearing from her again, and now it seemed she was eager to pick up the threads of their brief liaison. At first he had wanted to take up a pen and write back in anger, but he had read the letter through once more and felt the hot blood coursing through his veins. Their time together had been an exciting one, she had been hot, demanding and moody, which both excited and puzzled him. He realised that he would probably never really understand Alison. He felt she did not fully understand herself. In the letter she said that she would like to see him again and that she had spent a lot of time thinking about her future, but it was clear she had still not decided whether or not she was ready for a steady relationship, and it angered him. She told him that she had been transferred to a hospital in Maidstone and wondered whether he could come down to spend a weekend with her, but she didn't explain why she hadn't arranged to meet him on her return from leave. Danny puzzled over that. Maybe she had needed more time? He remembered that morning on the station when he had been left with so many questions unanswered. The feeling he carried around inside him since then had been a mixture of anger and rejection, a state of depression which was only just beginning to lift. He had resigned himself to believing that Alison would not bother to contact him again, and now here was a letter that threw everything into confusion — and just at the wrong time.

255

Kathy was back in his life, and with serious problems that had taken her to the edge of death. What had happened to her was terrible, and it had allowed a deep loyalty to become reawakened. Danny knew he needed time, but he wanted to see Kathy very soon. The future could now be very different. Did they have a future together? What would Mason do when Kathy came out of hospital? The questions twisted around in Danny's head and he found himself thinking again of Alison. Could he learn to cope with her demanding and unpredictable moods? Could the passion they had felt together ease the tension in their relationship? Why did he feel so uncertain?

Danny put the letter back in his pocket and stepped out into the morning air. He needed to be alone for a while to clear his head of his painful thoughts. The day was bright and he found himself strolling towards Tower Bridge, always his favourite place when he was in a pensive mood. The high white stonework of the bridge and the massive sweep of the supporting girders towered above him as he reached the first span. On either side the wharves were busy as usual, and down below the river swirled around the curved bastions of the bridge and eddied in oily patches in midstream. On the far bank, the narrow strip of muddy sand was partly exposed and two young children were prodding at something by the water's edge. Above and behind them rose the indestructible Tower of London. Danny recalled his halcyon days, when he had bathed in the muddy river and scoured the empty barges for coconut husks and kernels of nuts and fruit. He remembered those walks down dark, scary lanes that led to the water's edge. It had been pure adventure, uncomplicated and exciting. Now those idyllic days were gone. He had been on a slowly rotating carousel which had gone faster and faster and suddenly he had been pitched off into adulthood. It was now a different place; life had become complex and twisted, and the bones of everything were laid bare. Danny grinned to himself when he realised how serious he had become. This walk always seems to have that effect on me, he thought as he turned for home.

The large, shapely woman lying on the bed raised herself on one elbow and chuckled at the antics of her companion. The pale, nude figure hobbled about the bedroom, frantically gathering up his clothes. He tripped over the carpet and cursed loudly. "Look at the bleedin' time, Cora. If 'e finds me 'ere 'e'll spifflicate me!"

Cora lit a cigarette and watched as the young man dressed hurriedly. "Don't get yerself in a panic," she said, " 'E won't be 'ere yet. Jack won't leave the pub till closin' time. Come an' give us a kiss," her painted lips pouted.

"Bloody 'ell, Cora, ain't yer never satisfied? Mason's out fer me blood. I can't take a chance of 'im findin' me wiv yer."

"Are yer gonna come back an' see me soon, Johnny?"

"Course I am, darlin', but I can't 'ang around 'ere now. The pubs'll be turnin' out soon. There's too many of 'is mates know me. If they clock my dial they'll punch 'oles in me. I'll look like an ole clockin'-in card."

Cora chuckled and drew on her cigarette. "Jus' one little teeny kiss?"

Johnny Ross finished tying up his shoe-laces and gave her a quick peck on her lips. "I gotta go, it's ten ter ten now."

Cora watched him make for the door and then called him back. "Don't ferget yer cigarette case."

"Christ, Cora!" he said, putting the case in his pocket. "Well, I'm orf. Keep it warm fer me, won't yer?"

The long daylight hours were fading and dusk was deepening in the backstreets of Dockhead. The sounds of music and laughter came out from behind the heavy curtains at The Ferryman as three figures walked briskly up to the saloon bar door. Inside the air was stale, with cigarette smoke hanging like a cloud. A fat man with shirtsleeves rolled back over his wrists was tinkling on the stained piano keys, while behind the counter a huge man with pugilistic features and a shaven head was sharing a joke with one of his customers. The bar was full, and it took some time before the trio were served. They stood in one corner and studied the customers. Presently Tony Arpino nudged his companions. "Don't look now, but 'e's over there near the pianer talkin' ter that brassy bird. See 'er? The one wiv the bunch o' grapes stuck on 'er 'at. Don't let 'im see yer lookin' over, fer Gawd's sake."

The taller and heavier of Tony's two companions nodded. "I've clocked 'im. 'E don't look all that tough ter me. What d'yer reckon, Mario?"

The other smiled and showed a gold tooth. "Don't yer worry, Tony. 'E'll be no problem."

Tony Arpino grinned nervously. "Don't underestimate 'im. 'E ain't gonna be no pushover."

The big Italian gripped Tony's arm. "When yer ready give us the okay. We'll be waitin' fer 'im."

The Ferryman was a dockside pub with a dubious reputation. The local criminal fraternity drank there, safe in the knowledge that they were on friendly territory. The pub was owned by an ex-fighter who was very careful to handpick his staff; the barman matched him for size, and everyone agreed that the features of the diminutive potman were enough to frighten babies in their prams. He had been a handy flyweight in his time and knew how to get rid of the dallying customers at closing time. If anyone did try it on with him, they could be sure that he was backed up by the ex-heavyweight champion of the Grenadier Guards.

The place was busy from Friday onwards. The local bookies, villains, and other mysterious characters met there regularly. The local police were well aware of the pub's reputation for harbouring and succouring the less law-abiding, but their attempts to infiltrate the premises had come to nothing. On one occasion, a covert attempt to put an 'ear' inside the pub had ended in disaster. The plant spent the last hour before closing time with a funny-tasting pint in his hand, and a notice pinned to his back that said: 'Beware the bluebottle'. The strange-tasting pint gave him a bad attack of diarrhoea and vomiting which necessitated a trip to the doctor. The landlord of the pub calmed the outrage quickly. He listened intently to what the visiting police inspector had to say and then informed him that the person responsible for the atrocious behaviour, so alien to the respectable character of The Ferryman, was a stranger who had been barred for life that same evening. A five pound note donated to the Police Orphans Fund and an afternoon drinking session with the inspector put everything right, and the pub was left in peace.

On this particular Friday night the beer was flowing and the customers stood shoulder to shoulder. Tony had moved away from his two companions as planned. He had visited the pub on a few occasions with Danny Sutton and Johnny Ross, and he did not want to draw any attention to the two Italians who stood in one corner keeping their eyes on Mason. When Tony Arpino eased his way towards the piano, the bigger of the two nudged his pal. "C'mon, time ter go."

Tony had reached Jack Mason, who gave him a strange glance. "What you doin' 'ere? Bit out of your way, ain't it? he said in a malevolent tone.

"I got a message fer yer, Mr Mason. It's from Johnny Ross."

Jack Mason's eyes glinted. "Where is that little rat? I've bin lookin' fer 'im."

Tony gulped and prayed that his ploy would work. " 'E's outside by the oil shop. It's urgent. Can yer meet 'im there right away?"

"Why don't 'e come in 'ere? What's the matter wiv 'im?"

Tony took a breath. " 'E's got some money fer yer. 'E said 'e don't want anybody ter see it change 'ands."

"All right, I'll be out in a minute."

Tony nodded casually but felt his heart pounding. If Mason brought anyone with him it would ruin the plan. He walked out of the pub and blinked as the darkness enveloped him. When he moved along to the oil shop Tony could see his two companions standing in the recess of the doorway. " 'Old tight! 'E'll be out in a minute," he said breathlessly. 'Mario, you stan' wiv me. 'E'll fink you're Rossy. Al, keep back fer Gawd's sake! If 'e sees yer 'e'll know it's a set-up."

The saloon bar door opened and Tony bit on his bottom lip. An old gent emerged and walked unsteadily past the shop without noticing the three who were lying in wait. Tony took out his pocket watch. It showed ten minutes to ten.

Suddenly Mario nudged him. " 'Ere 'e is!"

Mason had emerged from the pub and was walking towards them with his distinctive gait. His eyes opened in surprise as he saw the three men facing him.

Tony's features were set hard. "We've got me ole man's pay-off, Mason!" he said, and he struck Mason full in the face.

Mason staggered back a pace and blood started to drip from his nose. Like an angry animal he charged at Tony, but Mario tripped him and stood back. Mason fell against the shop doorway and reeled back in a daze. Mario brought his foot up hard against the villain's jaw. Mason spat blood through his broken teeth and tried awkwardly to stagger to his feet, but Al stepped forward and grabbed Mason's coat collar. With a huge bellow he threw the man against the shop wall and pummelled him in the face. When Mason put his hands up to protect his head, Al kneed him hard in the stomach. The attack was too fast and too vicious for Mason to respond, and he sagged against the wall. The big Italian finally grabbed at Mason's coat-lapels and head-butted him across the bridge of his nose. The three

260

looked down at the sprawled unlovely heap at their feet.

Tony leaned over the groaning figure. "Keep away from Bermon'sey Lane, Mason. This is just a sample. There's money bin put up. Try it on again an' you'll be goin' fer a swim — wiv yer 'ands tied. Okay?"

As the three started away from the doorway Mason rolled over onto his side and swore at them through his swollen and bloody lips. Al stopped and turned back. Tony winced as he heard a thud. Al walked back casually. "I fink 'e's got the message at last," he grinned, and the three walked briskly out of the backstreet.

Jack Mason's beating had not gone unnoticed. A skulking figure had been standing in the shadows and watched the villain leave the pub. Cora was going to be the death of him, he rued. Five minutes later and he would have been caught with his trousers down. As he watched he noticed that Mason was not going to the buildings but towards some shadowy figures in the shop doorway. Johnny Ross held his breath as the assault took place. In the growing darkness he could recognise only one of the assailants. It was Tony Arpino. In seconds it was all over and he saw Jack Mason turn on his side and curse the three as they walked away. He saw the largest of the attackers turn back and bend over the sprawling figure. He heard the thump and saw Mason go limp. Only when the men had left the scene did he make his move. Slowly he walked over to the prone figure and looked down at him, an evil grin spreading over his pale face.

The last tram rumbled past, and the hands of the church clock were nearing the hour. Amy Wheelwright and her friend Carrie Horscroft had left the sewing circle meeting and were dissecting their fellow members' characters in a particularly brutal fashion.

"I wouldn't mind, Carrie, but she walks in the place like Lady Muck. She really upsets everybody wiv 'er fancy ways," Amy said with an expression of disgust.

"You're right, Amy. I 'eard she's sweet on Billy Whybrow. You know Billy Whybrow, the one what does the books at the institute."

"Oh, 'im. 'E's a dirty ole goat. Fair undresses yer wiv 'is eyes 'e does."

Carrie touched her confidante's arm. "I know you won't let this go any furver, Amy. I 'eard Liz Springett's 'avin' it orf wiv 'im from the greengrocer's in George Street."

"Not 'im wiv the funny eye? What can she see in 'im?"

"Let's face it, Amy, she ain't no oil paintin' 'erself, is she?"

"Did yer see 'er the uvver night, Carrie? Proper madam she is, moanin' about the biscuits. Did you 'ear what she said? 'I only like Peak Freans'.' She should fink 'erself lucky. She ain't backward in comin' forward, 'cept when it's time ter pay 'er subs."

The two women reached the parting of the ways. Carrie stood with Amy on the street corner and was about to come to the juiciest tit-bit, which she had saved till last, when a hurrying figure pushed past them and disappeared into the night. "Well I never!" Carrie gasped. "The manners of some people. Not even a 'sorry', 'oops', or 'by yer leave'. 'Ere, while I fink of it, I mus' tell yer . . .."

Back in The Ferryman the merriment went on. The brassy blonde was feeling very put out. Her prey had somehow extricated himself and it seemed that all her efforts that evening had been in vain. She looked around the bar and realised she was going to have an early night after all. The usual crowd of drunks would no doubt be trying their luck at closing time, and the pawing would start in earnest. She finished her drink and decided it was home to bed and sod the lot of 'em. The cool air made her reel and she leaned against the wall of the pub until she recovered herself. Those drinks he had been plying her with must have been doubles. He needn't have bothered, she told herself, he could coax me into his bed any night of the week. She walked on from the pub and almost tripped against the bundle lying in the shop doorway. A stream of blood had formed a pool in the gutter and had stained the pavement dark red. Lillie Stannard fell against the shop-front and let out a piercing scream. Curtains were pulled back momentarily, and the less drunken customers emerged from the pub. Soon a crowd had gathered. They took the hysterical prostitute to one side while someone threw a coat over the body.

"It's Jack Mason! 'E's bin done in!" someone said.

"They've smashed 'is 'ead in!"

"Quick! Tell the guv'nor ter 'phone the law!"

"Gawd Almighty, what a sight! I was only talkin' to 'im only 'alf hour ago!" said an old man, shaking his head.

"Well 'e ain't talkin' now, Bert."

Chapter Twenty-Three

The news of Jack Mason's murder made the Saturday morning papers. The story was on everyone's lips. There were very few sentiments of sympathy expressed, for most of those who knew him felt that he had had it coming. Mason had many enemies and someone had exacted vengeance. And there was concern for Kathy, who had still not heard the news, for Mrs Thompson was determined not to let her daughter know at least for a day or two. Her own feelings had frightened her when she had been told of the murder. It was as though a heavy burden had been lifted from her shoulders now that Kathy would not have to suffer any more at his hand. Mrs Thompson was a devout Christian who believed in the power of prayer and her pleas for Kathy's recovery had been answered. She had prayed that her daughter would be spared the ill treatment she herself had been forced to endure. But her hopes were fulfilled in a way that she had not foreseen, and Violet Thompson felt very humble.

When Danny walked into The Globe on that Saturday morning, the discussions raged around him. Eddie Kirkland was leaning over the counter talking to Biff Bowden. " 'E didn't come in 'ere much. 'E only used this pub on the odd occasion. It was The Ferryman 'e used. That's where 'e was found, wasn't it?"

"That's right, Eddie. It ses 'ere that a young woman found 'im. 'E was layin' in a shop doorway. Accordin' ter what it ses 'ere, someone went an' smashed the back of 'is 'ead right in. Apparently 'e'd also bin done over, beaten about the face."

Eddie leaned over the copy of the *Daily Mirror* that Biff had in his hands. "What else does it say?"

Biff squinted his eyes up and moved the paper away to focus the wording. "It ses a young man who was limpin' was seen leavin' the street in an' 'urry by two ladies who 'ave given the police a good description."

"Bloody 'ell!" laughed Eddie. "That could fit Johnny Ross!"

"It couldn't be 'im," Biff snorted. "Rossy couldn't punch 'is way out of a paper bag."

Eddie pulled up a pint of ale for an old gent who was moaning about the quality of the beer. "It's the 'ops, Fred, it's bin a bad year fer 'ops."

When the old gent took his pint and moved away from the counter Eddie went back to talk to Biff. "Silly ole sod. 'E's bin moanin' about the beer fer donkey's years. 'E still gets pissed on it though."

Biff grinned. " 'Ere, Eddie, talkin' about Johnny Ross, I ain't seen 'im around 'ere lately. 'Ave you?"

The landlord shook his head. "It's funny, but Bonky come in 'ere last night. 'E told me Rossy's on the run from Mason. Over some money by all accounts."

"Well Rossy ain't got ter run any more, that's fer sure," Biff chuckled.

Danny sat at the bar with a pint of ale at his elbow. He recalled the conversation he had had with Tony Arpino, but he found it impossible to believe that Tony could have been responsible for Mason's murder. A good hiding was one thing but murder was another story. It couldn't be Tony, he decided. Poor Kathy, how would she take the news? Did she still have any feeling left for Mason? Whatever she felt, it was still going to be a terrible shock for her.

"Yer signed the pledge then, Danny?"

The young cockney looked up and saw Bonky Williams standing next to him.

" 'Ello, Bonky, I didn't see yer come in."

Bonky grinned. "I was watchin' yer starin' at that pint,

266

an' I ses ter meself, Bonky, 'e's on the bleedin' wagon."

Danny grinned. "Wanna drink?"

"Ta, I'll 'ave a nice pint o' bitter, me ole mate."

Danny ordered the drink. " 'Eard the news?"

"Yeah. 'E's in the shite, ain't 'e?"

"Who?"

"Why, Rossy."

" 'Ow d'yer mean?" Danny asked impatiently.

"They've got 'is description, ain't they?"

"Don't be stupid, Bonky. That description could fit anybody."

Bonky glanced around the bar furtively and leaned forward until Danny smelt stale breath on his face. "It was 'im."

"What d'yer mean, it was 'im?"

"It was Johnny Ross, the one the paper said was runnin' out the street."

" 'Ow d'yer know it was 'im?"

Bonky looked around the bar again, then his voice lowered to a whisper. "Rossy was knockin' one o' Jack Mason's birds orf, wasn't 'e?"

"I dunno, was 'e?"

"Yeah, 'e told me 'imself. You know Rossy, 'e can't keep anyfink to 'imself. Anyway, this bird's called Cora. She lives in the buildin's opposite the boozer Mason used. I told Johnny ter be careful, 'e's in enough trouble as it is."

Danny looked into Bonky's good eye. "You ain't tryin' ter tell me Rossy done 'im in, are yer?"

" 'Course I ain't. What I am sayin' is, it's a pound to a pinch o' shit that it was Johnny comin' out o' the turnin' last night."

"Christ Almighty!" Danny gasped. "They should lock Rossy up fer 'is own good. 'E's a livin', breavin' disaster!"

"They prob'ly will," Bonky said, picking up his drink.

"Do yer know where Rossy is?" Danny asked.

"I ain't seen 'im around. If 'e's got any sense 'e's scarpered. If 'e stays round 'ere they're bound ter pull 'im in."

Danny finished his drink. "Well, I've gotta be orf. If yer see Rossy about tell 'im ter get in touch. Okay?"

"Right. See yer, Danny."

Danny left the pub and hurried to the Arpinos' shop. When he arrived Sofia and her husband Lou were serving some customers and he could see that they were trying to hide their anxiety. Lou waved Danny through to the back of the shop and followed him into the small room.

"Danny, ma Tony's in a lotta trouble," he said. " 'E's a gone away. 'E say the police they're a gonna come for 'im. What's ma Tony done, Danny?"

"Ain't yer seen the papers, Pop?"

"I donna read so good. What's a dis in da papers?"

Danny took the old man by his shoulders. "Look, Pop," he said, "you've 'eard Tony talk about Jack Mason, ain't yer?"

"Yeah, I know dis Jack Mason. 'E's da gangster what break up a ma shop."

" 'E's bin killed, Lou."

The old Italian bit on his knuckles and his face drained of colour. "Not ma Tony. 'E don't kill nobody. No ma Tony."

"Where is 'e, Lou? Can I talk to 'im?"

" 'E's a jus' gone away. I swear I donna know where 'e's a gone. Maybe ter ma family in Clerkenwell. Ma family dey look after ma boy."

"Whereabouts in Clerkenwell? 'Ave yer got an address?"

Lou Arpino raised his hands to the ceiling. "I gotta no address. Ma family all over da place. Dey gotta shops in Clerkenwell. It's all I know, Danny."

"Don't worry, Pop, Tony's clean. 'E didn't kill Mason."

As he left the shop Danny thought about going straight

to Clerkenwell, but he realised that he might be followed. It was evident that the police had not called on the Arpinos yet, but someone might have spotted Tony and given the police a description. He himself might have been pointed out as a friend of Tony and there might be a tail on him. But the more he thought about it the less likely it seemed. Surely the police would call on the shop first. If they were unsuccessful in finding Tony there then they might tail him, or even pull him in for questioning. Danny was getting nervous and it was becoming difficult for him to think straight. Still, he knew it would be better not to go near Clerkenwell until he could work out a plan. He hurried along to Ginny's and found a few punters standing around waiting for him.

"Where yer bin, Danny boy?" one old gent said. "I've got a fistful o' bets 'ere. 'Alf the street's left 'em wiv me."

When it was a little quieter Ginny poked her head out from the parlour. "Danny, when yer finished can yer pop over ter see Vi Thompson? She wants a word wiv yer."

Detective Constable Stanley Stockbridge walked quickly towards Tony Allen's offices situated off Jamaica Road. He was a worried man. Jack Mason's murder had thrown his plans completely. The boys from the Yard were involved and the Station Inspector had made it plain that they were to get full co-operation. Stockbridge knew the identity of the man seen running from the scene of the crime. He had had his eye on Ross for some time, and his snout had informed him of the strained relations between Ross and Mason. The detective was certain Johnny Ross was his man, but before he named his suspect he thought he should have a word with Allen the bookie. As he walked up towards the offices in Wilson Street Fat Stan saw Tony Allen standing at the door.

"I've bin expectin' you, Stan. Let's go over the road fer a drink," Tony said.

The Jamaica was almost empty at that time of the

morning. There were only one or two regulars sitting around the small bar.

"Give us a Scotch an' soda an' a gin an' tonic, luv," Tony Allen said to the barmaid. "Oh, an' can we use yer snug bar? We've got a bit o' business ter take care of."

Doreen flashed Tony a smile. "I'll unlock it," she said. "You'll be okay in there."

When they had seated themselves and the drinks were in front of them Fat Stan looked hard at Tony. "Look, I can't afford ter mess around, Tony. Murder's way out of my league. The Yard are involved. You gonna put a name my way?"

Tony Allen smiled. "I'd like ter 'elp yer, Stan. Jack Mason had 'is own little fings goin' fer 'im. I 'ad nuffink ter do wiv 'is killin'. I know we 'ad our differences, but 'e was straight wiv me. 'E wasn't turnin' me over, if that's what yer fink."

The detective toyed with his glass. "You've read the papers? Yer know we've got a description of a man seen runnin', or rather, limpin' out of the turnin'?"

The bookie nodded. "'Ave yer got a name?"

Fat Stan looked at the bookie. "Me an' you go back a long way, Tony. Don't let's play games. Yer know who that man was as well as I do."

Tony Allen smiled. "Yer don't honestly fink Johnny Ross is capable of murder, do yer?"

"Maybe not. 'E's gotta be brought in though. If 'e's in the clear 'e ain't got nuffink ter worry about, but it looks suspicious all the same."

The bookie downed his drink and called out to Doreen. "Fill 'em up, luv."

When the barmaid had replaced their drinks Tony leaned back in his seat. "What else yer got ter go on, Stan?"

The fat detective emptied the remainder of the tonic into his gin. "There was a conversation in the pub between Mason an' a stranger. Nobody knew 'is face, or they're not tellin'. Anyway, Mason followed this geezer out an' 'e didn't come back. The prosser who was chattin' Mason up before was the one who found 'is body. She can't tell us much. She was too pissed ter remember what the geezer who was talkin' ter Mason looked like. There's anuvver fing worryin' me, Tony. The squeeze that's goin' on in Bermon'sey Lane, was Mason involved in that?''

Tony Allen nodded. "That was nuffink ter do wiv me, Stan, that was Mason's little perk. Yer know I don't work against the local traders. I employed Mason ter look after me interests at the race tracks. Yer know what it's like. It's a bleedin' 'ard business, an' we need 'ard men ter back us up. I tell yer one fing, when I found out about the Bermon'sey Lane affair I 'ad a set-to wiv Mason. Those mugs 'e brought in were bad news.''

Fat Stan showed a ghost of a smile. "Yer didn't take an iron bar ter back up yer argument, did yer?''

The bookie's eyes narrowed. "If it 'ad bin my intention ter do away wiv 'im, I'd 'ave made a tidier job of it, believe me.''

"I'm only jokin', Tony, but I've got a problem. There's a new gaffer at the station as yer know. 'E's a different kettle o' fish ter the uvver lecherous ole bastard. This one wants results. Take it from me, 'e's no mug, 'e's out ter cripple the likes o' you. So far I've kept yer name out o' the frame, but the gaffer ain't left me alone since the ware'ouse job in Shad Thames. If I can nail Ross, bring 'im in as a murder suspect I mean, it'll take the pressure orf, if yer know what I'm gettin' at?''

"Well yer won't find 'im at 'is own address, Stan.''

"Where's 'e 'oled up?''

Tony Allen studied his glass for a second or two. "Try 'is married sister's place. She runs a pub in Deptford, The Galleon, just off Tanners 'Ill. Yer'll find 'im there I reckon.''

The detective finished his drink. "I'm orf. Keep yer nose clean, Tone.''

271

The bookie reached into his coat pocket and pulled out a sealed envelope. "There's a little appreciation of yer support, Stanley. I only like ter see 'orses' names goin' in the frame, if yer get me drift."

Danny Sutton walked along St Thomas's Street and stopped at the gates of Guy's Hospital. A large, ruddy-faced woman in a man's cap, wearing a blue apron tied around her waist, smiled at him and stood with her hands on her hips while he inspected the colourful array of flowers. "What's yer fancy, luvvy?" she asked. "There's roses, carnations, an' there's some luvverly . . ."

"Jus' do us up a bundle, will yer?" Danny said quickly.

The flower-seller gathered a selection from the vases and wrapped them up in a large sheet of paper. "There we are. 'Old 'em up, they won't bite yer," she said, smiling wickedly.

Danny climbed the stairs and joined the waiting visitors outside the ward. He held the bundle of flowers down at his side and looked around self-consciously. Mrs Thompson had told him that Kathy wanted to see him, and that on no account must he talk about Jack Mason. She had also told him that Kathy was very depressed over the loss of the baby and she hoped his visit might help to cheer her up. Danny felt uncomfortable as he followed the Saturday afternoon visitors into the long ward. He spotted Kathy and walked over to the foot of her bed where she lay propped up against the pillows with her hands folded outside the bedclothes. He was shocked by her appearance; she looked white and drawn, and her dark hair spread out across the pillow made her pallor seem worse.

But Kathy smiled at him, and for an instant he saw a glimmer of welcome in her large dark eyes. He moved around the bed and bent down. His lips brushed her pale cheek and he could smell the scent of Lifebuoy soap. He sat down and leaned forward, covering her hands in his, and grinned. "D'yer like the flowers?" he asked.

She nodded, her eyes fixing him solemnly. "Fanks fer comin' in, Danny. I 'oped yer would."

"Yer couldn't keep me away. 'Ow yer feelin'?"

"I'm okay. Yer know about the baby?"

Danny nodded. "I'm sorry. Yer mum told me."

"Did she tell yer not ter mention about Jack?"

"Yer know then?"

Kathy nodded slowly. "They tried ter keep it from me, but I 'eard two of the patients talkin' an' I've seen the paper."

Danny winced. "It must 'ave bin an 'orrible shock, gettin' it that way," he said.

Kathy turned her head towards him. "There's nuffink inside me, Danny. I feel no pain, no sadness, nuffink. It's scary."

Danny squeezed her hands in his and saw the tear slip down her cheek onto the pillow. "Don't be scared," he said, "there's nuffink ter be scared about."

"I'm scared 'cos I'm empty, Danny. I should feel somefink, shouldn't I?"

Danny took out a handkerchief and dabbed her cheek. "Yer need time, Kath. It's shock. I know what me ole mum would say if she was 'ere. 'You 'ave a good cry dear, an' yer'll feel better.' "

"I want ter cry, Danny. I want ter cry buckets, but I can't, I'm empty."

Danny drew a line along the white counterpane with his finger, then he looked into her dark eyes. "Listen ter me. I'm not very good at this sort o' fing but I tell yer, Kath, when I was in Dunkirk I saw grown men cryin'. They was soldiers who 'ad gone frew 'ell. I see 'em sittin' at the roadside cryin', an' you know what? I wished I could 'ave done the same. We'd all bin frew a bad time an' some of us didn't know 'ow ter cry. I wished I could 'ave cried. Nobody was laughin' at 'em, we all felt the same. Some of us bottled it up, an' uvvers jus' cried. There's no shame in tears. Yer know, I saw me dad cry once."

Kathy's eyes travelled over his face and he looked down at his clenched fists. "We was at The Trocette. It was a real sad film. People was blowin' their noses an' I could 'eard the ole girls sobbin'. Me, I was tryin' 'ard not ter laugh. Anyway, I looked up at me dad, an' 'e was brushin' a tear away from 'is eye. 'E caught me clockin' 'im an' 'e said 'e 'ad a bit o' dirt in 'is eye. I knew 'e was cryin', an' 'e knew I knew, but 'e wouldn't admit it. I wouldn't 'ave minded though. I wouldn't mind if yer cried, Kath. Yer can cry all over me if yer like."

Kathy's eyes filled with tears and she bit on her bottom lip. Danny reached out to her and her arms came up to him. He held her close and felt her sobs as she buried her head in his chest. "Oh, Danny, why did I go to 'im? Why didn't I wait? I never stopped finkin' about yer. Every day I wondered if yer was gettin' wounded. I always wanted yer, but yer was never around. Yer never seemed ter be there when I wanted yer. Why didn't I wait, Danny?"

The young man gulped and patted her back gently. He could feel the tears falling onto his neck. "I'm 'ere, Kathy, I'm 'ere," he said softly.

The ward sister stopped at the foot of Kathy's bed and gave Danny a concerned look. Danny winked and eased Kathy back onto the pillow. "There. Yer'll feel better soon. Dry yer eyes," he said, handing her his handkerchief.

Kathy dabbed at her face and gave him a sheepish smile. "I'm okay. Fanks."

He pocketed his handkerchief. "I've gotta be orf," he said. "Close yer eyes fer a while. Yer mum's comin' in soon."

Kathy gripped his hand. "I'm goin' ter me aunt's fer a couple o' weeks, Danny. I need some time ter meself. Will I see yer around when I get back?"

"I'll be around, Kath. I'm not goin' anywhere."

Danny left the hospital and walked slowly back to Dawson Street. He felt a tightness in his chest and a heaviness weighing down on him. In his coat pocket he still had Alison's letter, and even while he had sat with Kathy the letter had flashed into his mind. He felt that he had betrayed Kathy. He had encouraged her to show her emotions, and then she had asked to see him and he had led her to believe that he would be around when she needed him. Danny realised he had promised too much. She might dwell on what he had told her and expect more of him that he was sure he could give. He might be around, but he could not guarantee his feelings. His need for Alison pulled hard on him; the thought of her sent his pulse racing — and he knew in his heart that he would answer her letter, very soon.

Danny battled with guilt as he walked home. He had not made any actual commitment to Kathy, he had only said that he would be around. She couldn't expect him to be forever ready to drop everything and rush to her when she called. He had his own life to lead. Then he suddenly realised how selfish his thoughts were. Was it love that made him want to dash to Alison, or was it purely lust? Was it love that made him go to Kathy or was it pity? What was that word 'love' Alison had said rolled easily from his tongue? Was it many different things appearing as one? He needed desperately to discover a real answer, but instead a hollowness had opened up inside him. As he turned into Dawson Street he was aware of nothing but pain tightening like a steel band around his head.

Right on closing time that Saturday two men walked into The Galleon in Deptford.

"Sorry, gents, it's after three o'clock," the barman said, stiffening.

A warrant was flashed, and soon after Johnny Ross was led out between two large detectives. A bundle containing his personal belongings was collected and he sat quietly as he was driven to Deptford Police Station. When he arrived he was taken to a room where there was nothing but two chairs and a small table. He was left alone for over an hour, with only his thoughts for company, and he saw the whole picture opening up before him: the trial would be held at the Bailey of course; the many witnesses would naturally testify that Jack Mason was a law-abiding citizen, who had been cruelly murdered for the small amount of money on his person; the number one exhibit, an iron bar, would cause the jury to shake their heads in horror as it was passed among them. There was only one verdict he could expect, and the twelve good men and true would not even retire to consider. The formality over, the judge, who, in his mind's eye, looked remarkably like Bonky Williams, would put on the black cap and pronounce sentence. Johnny heard the words echoing around the court. '. . . and you will hang by the neck until you are dead.' He would try to stay calm and learn how to play chess. The warders would be okay, they would look pityingly at him as the footsteps in the corridor sounded and the mumbling priest read from the good book.

The door opened and Johnny jumped like a scared rabbit. "Come on, Ross, you're goin' ter Dock'ead nick."

Johnny Ross tried to control his shaking knees as he stared into the ugly face of Stanley Stockbridge. A huge hand took his arm in a tight grip and steered him out to the waiting car. "I've seen you 'round the manor, Ross, ain't I?" Fat Stan leered.

Johnny could only nod as he was bundled into the police car.

Chapter Twenty-Four

On Monday the 5th of August Johnny Ross was hauled from the police station cell and the questions began once more. At first he had insisted that he did not go near the body, and he established through Cora a reason for being in the locality on that particular night. But the police were confident that a charge could be brought within a matter of hours. A distinctive footprint in the blood matched up to the suspect's shoes, and traces of blood were found in the tread. Johnny then changed his story and said that he had seen three men attack Jack Mason and he had gone over to find out if there was anything he could do to help the victim. When he had realised the man was past help, he had panicked and run away. The police interrogated Johnny for hours but he stuck to his story. A thorough search of the area around the scene of the crime was in operation and the police felt sure that as soon as the murder weapon was found their suspect would crack.

As he sat alone during a brief lull in the grilling, Johnny Ross could almost feel the hangman's noose tightening around his neck. They had even established a motive for the killing: they knew of the bad blood between him and Mason and they had supporting statements, or so they said. The lack of sleep and the futility of it all overcame him and he lowered his head onto the hard table top. He fell into a troubled doze and when he awoke he felt stiff all over. It seemed to Johnny as though he had been asleep for hours. Then he heard the gruff voices outside the locked door, and the key in the lock. Two stern-faced detectives came into the room and one of them sat down opposite him. A sheet of paper was thrust in front of him and a pen slapped onto the table.

Early on that Monday morning the pale, drawn figure of Violet Thompson walked wearily along Tooley Street. Her shopping bag seemed extra heavy and her legs felt as though they were going to give out on her. Alice Sutton had just left the greengrocer's and almost bumped into her.

" 'Ello, luv," Alice said. "Yer look done in. 'Ow's young Kathy?"

Violet put her bag down at her feet and pressed her hand against the small of her back. "She's doin' well, Alice," she said slowly, wincing visibly. "Yer Danny's visit perked 'er up no end."

Alice looked at Violet with concern and noticed a discolouring around her left eye and a swelling in the corner of her mouth. She put her hand on Violet's forearm. "Yer all right, luv?" she asked gently. "Yer don't look at all well."

Kathy's mother drew in her breath and tears welled up in her eyes. "Alice, I've gotta talk ter somebody," she said in a shaky voice. "I'm worried out o' me life."

Aliced picked up Violet's shopping bag and nodded her head towards Dawson Street. "C'mon, let's 'ave a nice cuppa roun' my place. We'll 'ave a chat."

A horse-cart trundled through the turning and the sound of its iron-rimmed wheels on the cobbles carried into the tidy parlour. The two women sat facing each other and Alice watched as Violet sipped her tea. When she had finished Alice took the cup out of her trembling hands and laid it down on the table. "Are yer feelin' any better, luv?" she asked.

Violet nodded and dabbed at her eyes. "I'm worried, sick, Alice."

"Kathy'll be all right now, Vi. She's over the worst," Alice said quietly.

278

"It's not Kathy, it's me ole man," Violet replied, looking down at her clasped hands. "We 'ad a terrible row last night. Over Mason."

"Go on, Vi," Alice prompted.

Violet took a deep breath. "Charlie come in late last night, pissed as usual, an' 'e started on me."

"I can see that," Alice said quickly. "Did 'e give yer that eye?"

Violet stared down at her hands. Alice began to feel uncomfortable and she decided to change the subject. She leaned forward in her chair. "My Danny told me they've got young Johnny Ross fer the murder," she said. "Allen the bookie told 'im last night."

Violet's hand came up to her mouth and she closed her eyes tightly. "Oh my Gawd! What am I gonna do, Alice?" she groaned.

"What d'yer mean, Vi? There's nuffink yer can do."

"But yer don't understan', Alice. Johnny Ross never killed Mason. Charlie done it," she blurted out, and she began sobbing loudly.

Alice was shocked. "Gawd Almighty Gawd! 'E can't 'ave!"

Violet's eyes opened wide and bored into Alice's. " 'E told me 'imself."

Alice shook her head slowly. "It don't make any sense at all. Yer Charlie won't 'ave 'is own daughter back in the 'ouse."

Violet laughed bitterly through her tears. " 'E didn't do Jack Mason in fer Kathy. It was somefink else."

Alice looked bewildered. "Kathy ain't Charlie's daughter, Alice," Violet said in a tired voice. "I met 'im after I fell fer Kathy. 'E's never let me forget it neivver."

Alice nodded. "So that's why 'e knocks yer about, an' won't 'ave the poor little cow back in the 'ouse. But why did 'e kill Mason?"

"It's a long story, Alice," Mrs Thompson began.

Alice stopped her. "Let's fill yer cup, luv," she said.

279

The two women faced each other in the small parlour and sipped their tea in silence. Violet studied the flower pattern on her cup. "Yer see, Alice," she began, "I've never spoke ter Jack Mason, but my Charlie knows 'im well. Charlie comes from Dock'ead same as Mason. A long time ago there was some fiddlin' goin' on where Charlie used ter work. I fink it was one o' the wharves in Dock'ead. They was gettin' stuff out an' Mason was floggin' it. Charlie got done out o' some money an' 'e went after one o' Mason's mates. My Charlie was an' 'andful then, 'e give this bloke a goin' over, an' the police got involved. Charlie got six months fer assault. Then a few months ago there was an argument in the pub between Charlie an' Mason. Charlie was pissed an' 'e told Jack Mason ter leave Kathy alone. Mason must 'ave 'eard the talk about Kathy not bein' Charlie's an' 'e frew it up in 'is face. The pair of 'em nearly got at it but they was stopped. Charlie told me the same night 'e would end up doin' Mason in, but he didn't kill Mason fer Kathy, it was fer 'is own pride. When 'e come 'ome on Friday night wiv blood on 'is coat-sleeve 'e wouldn't stop goin' on about it. Now you've told me that Johnny Ross is bein' blamed fer it, I feel so guilty. What can I do, Alice?"

Alice pinched her bottom lip. " 'E'll 'ave ter give 'imself up, Vi. Yer'll 'ave ter tell 'im."

Violet laughed mirthlessly. "I can't, Alice. 'E's gorn. 'E pissed orf on Sunday night after 'e'd finished knockin' me all over the 'ouse."

"Where's 'e gorn to, Vi?"

" 'E's got a bruvver in Liverpool. 'E might 'ave gone there. 'E told me 'e was gettin' out o' London."

Alice gripped her friend's arm. "But yer can't leave it, Vi," she said. "That poor lad'll swing fer somefink 'e never done. Go ter the police, tell 'em. Yer don't 'ave ter say anyfink about yer ole man bein' in Liverpool. It's their job ter catch 'im. Yer'll only be gettin' poor Johnny Ross out o' trouble."

Violet Thompson frowned. "Ain't there somefink about a wife not bein' able ter give evidence against 'er 'usband?"

"I've 'eard it said, Vi, but yer gotta go ter the police. Tell 'em everyfing. It's up ter them ter get the evidence tergevver. At least yer'll be able ter sleep at night."

Violet stood up suddenly. "Do me one more favour, Alice," she said with an imploring look. "Come wiv me."

In mid-August the battle of Britain was raging over the English Channel and Southern England. Every day the blue sky was slashed with vapour trails as planes dived and soared in deadly combat. Stricken machines fell into the sea around the coast and dived into the rolling green countryside. Each day the newspapers carried the tally of planes downed as though they were reporting county cricket scores. The battle for survival had begun, and everyone knew that if the battle was lost the invasion would be a certainty. As the news improved a heady feeling of hope prevailed. People were relieved that at last the months of uncertainty and anxiety were over. In dockland as in other parts of the country folk crowded around wireless sets listening to the news broadcasts, and German losses brought forth cheers. Corner shops stuck up posters with the latest scores in large lettering; pubs filled with merry-makers every evening, and patriotic songs rang out. It was a time of great excitement, and everyone's spirits were lifted.

In the middle of August, Danny Sutton boarded a train to Maidstone. He had mixed feelings as he watched the houses and factories give way to green fields from his carriage window, his sense of unease mingling with high excitement at the prospect of being with Alison. She had filled his thoughts constantly since her letter to him, and for all his misgivings Danny knew he had to make the journey. He had not been able to force her from his mind. There were times when he thought of Kathy and looked forward to her return, but the picture of Alison stayed with him and tortured his emotions; the strong physical urge to make love with her again sent his pulse racing.

The train pulled into Maidstone Station and Danny joined the Saturday lunch-time passengers as they walked from the platform. Alison was there at the barrier, and he was thrilled by her radiance. He held her closely and kissed her, tasting her warm lips. Together they walked from the station and out into the sunshine. They found a restaurant and chatted happily over their meal about day to day things, and Alison told him about her new post at the hospital. And the tension between them had gone. They had been lovers, and they had the night to know each other once more.

In the early afternoon they strolled in the park and found shade beneath a leafy tree. The grass felt cool and the whisper of a breeze fanned their hot faces. Alison lay propped on one elbow and looked down at Danny as he lay on his back and chewed on a blade of grass.

"I've missed you," she said suddenly.

"Me too."

"Tell me, Danny, that night we spent together. Has it stayed with you?"

Danny turned onto his side and looked into Alison's dark, brooding eyes. "If yer mean do I still fink about that night, the answer's yes. I fink about it twenty times a day. Night times I lay finkin' about yer an' I wish I could turn over an' feel yer there beside me."

"I feel lonely at night too, Danny. There have been nights when I've wanted you so badly. I imagine you're on your way to me, you're my secret lover and I'm waiting for you. Can we be secret lovers, Danny?"

Danny reached up and pulled her down to him. Their lips met and he felt her teeth close on his bottom lip.

As the sun dipped over the horizon and the evening sky took on a pinkish hue the lovers strolled hand in hand through the town, idling away the time until dusk. They found a pub with a garden and sat sipping their drinks at a log table. Blossoms overhung the stone courtyard and a grotesque vine scaled the ancient walls. The song of a bird split the silence, and up above grey-blue clouds rolled across a dark velvet sky and revealed diamonds of light. Time seemed to have stopped still for Danny and the war was a world away, the promise in Alison's eyes tantalising him. But deep down he felt misgivings stirring his conscience.

"You're shivering, Danny."

Alison's words of concern jolted him back to reality. "I was jus' dreamin'," he replied, taking her hand in his. "This is like anuvver world. Who'd fink there was a war on?"

"This is magical," Alison said, looking up at the night sky. "Just you and me, and nothing else. We're lovers. Lovers who meet on nights like this and who carry the memory with us till we meet again. That's the magic for me, Danny. It doesn't spoil and get ordinary. I don't want it to be just ordinary. I want it to be magic always."

Danny looked at her with sad eyes. "Trouble is, it's an ordinary world, Alison. It's a real world. Yer can't live in fairyland. Fairyland is fer kids."

Alison looked up again at the twinkling stars. "That's fairyland out there," she said.

Danny grinned. "Them stars are a million miles away. It's a long way ter fairyland."

They left the pub and walked slowly through a maze of little streets. Alison had her arm in his and he could feel her soft breast against him. She steered him down a narrow lane and stopped at a low-fronted house.

"Here we are," she said. "I share this place with three other nurses. We've all got our own rooms."

Alison found her key and turned it in the lock. Inside the air smelt of lavender, and in the hall a rosewood chest and a grandfather clock stood against the white walls. Alison opened a door to their left and held Danny's hand as they entered. She closed the door behind them and switched on the light.

The room was cosy, with patchwork rugs covering the wooden floor, a large settee occupying the centre of the room and wicker chairs arranged around the sides. Close to the settee was a small coffee table scattered with magazines, and pictures of country scenes in ebony frames were hung around the walls. At the far end there was a doorway through to another room, and Danny caught a glimpse of a bed. Alison took off her coat and waited while Danny did the same. She hung up their coats behind the door and came to him slowly. "Well, how do you like my little den?"

"It's real nice," Danny said, looking around.

She was standing close to him and he pulled her nearer. Her arms went around his neck and they kissed long and urgently, and when they parted Danny lifted her into his arms and carried her to the bedroom. Alison rested her head on his shoulder and she could feel the muscles moving beneath his shirt. Her breath came quickly as he laid her gently down on the bed and fumbled with the buttons of her dress. He kissed her soft neck and smooth shoulders and caressed her hard nipples and silky thighs. Alison's quick breathing became faster and, moaning with pleasure, she pulled him to her. When the first light of dawn shone into the room Alison awoke and curled her sleepy body closer to Danny's. Her hands awoke him with gentle caresses, and a delicious giving of pleasure united their sleepy bodies and brought them to a dreamy climax. When they stirred once more it was late morning.

The day was warm, and after a leisurely breakfast they strolled through the town and visited the pub where they had spent the last evening. In the afternoon the lovers went into the park again and walked through the scented flower gardens and along shaded pathways. They rested in the sweet-smelling grass of a lush green field, Danny thinking of their imminent parting, while Alison made fun of his serious expression.

"Why so sad?" she asked.

"Goodbyes do that ter me," Danny said, stroking her smooth arm.

"You shouldn't be sad, Danny. We can see each other again soon. If there were no goodbyes there'd be no hellos, would there?"

"We could get married," Danny said suddenly.

Alison's face became serious and she picked at the grass. "Don't let's spoil it all, Danny. We've got happiness, you and I. Marriage is not for me. I need you, I don't need a marriage."

"I do, Alison, I need a marriage. I want ter wake up wiv yer every mornin', and not jus' now an' then, when yer can get time orf. I want yer, an' I want kids, an' a place fer us ter live in."

Alison's eyes clouded and she looked away. "There's no magic in a home and children, Danny. Not for me. I'm sorry if it hurts you when I say that. You may think I'm strange, but it's how I feel. I can't alter, any more than you can. You remember the last time we were together? I told you then that I needed an understanding. We can be lovers, there's nothing wrong in that. We can be happy, I know we can, Danny. We don't need a marriage to seal our love for each other. There's just no magic in a marriage for me. Can't you understand that?"

Danny looked at her, and knew that nothing he could say would make her change her mind. If he wanted her, it must be like this; fleeting and unsure.

The sun was slipping down as they walked slowly to the hospital gates. Alison looked at her watch and gave Danny a brief smile. "We'd better say goodbye here, Danny. I've got to be on duty at seven."

He pulled her to him and they kissed. She clung to him. "Write to me soon, Danny. Maybe we can meet again soon. We can be happy this way, I know we can."

Danny released his clasp and stood back from her, silent.

Alison touched his arm and walked away up the long gravel path to the entrance of the hospital. At the front steps she waved to him and then disappeared from his sight, and he walked wearily back to the station. It was cooler now and dark clouds were beginning to close out the sky. "There'll be no fairyland up there ternight," he said aloud.

Epilogue

August passed by and cool September breezes heralded the autumn. In the little backstreets of dockland life went on. A chastened and wiser Johnny Ross was welcomed back into The Globe. When he left the police station after signing for his belongings, he felt the dark shadow of the noose lifting from around his neck. On that Friday night when he had looked down on the battered face of Jack Mason he had been mistaken in thinking the villain was dead. Al Vincetti had merely rendered him unconscious with his parting blow, and if Johnny had delayed leaving Cora's for another few minutes he would have seen the grotesque murder.

Charlie Thompson had visited a few riverside pubs and was staggering along the turning that led out opposite The Ferryman. Even in his drunken state he decided that he would give that particular pub a miss as he knew that Jack Mason and his cronies used The Ferryman. The long-standing feud between the two had never been resolved, and Charlie Thompson's hatred for the villain was never more intense than when he was drunk. The docker crossed the street unsteadily and staggered up the kerb. He had left the pub behind him and was feeling his way along when he suddenly tripped over something hard and landed on all fours on the pavement. His eyes rolled and he saw the unconscious figure of Jack Mason lying only inches away from him. Looking down into the battered face he blinked in disbelief. Slowly he staggered to his feet and fought to keep his footing, then he snarled and kicked out hard with his heavy boots. Three times his boot thumped into Jack

Mason's skull, then the docker lost his footing and fell into the gutter. He got up and stumbled awkwardly from the turning unseen. The ladies from the sewing circle had left the street corner only minutes before.

Soon after Johnny Ross was released from custody, Tony Arpino left his hideout in Clerkenwell and made his way apprehensively to his parents' shop in Bermondsey Lane. He had heard that the police had started looking for Charlie Thompson in connection with the murder of Mason after Violet Thompson made a statement at Dockhead police station. Tony was worried in case anything should emerge about how he and his pals had been involved in the Mason affair. The few words in the daily papers seemed to suggest that whoever killed Mason had done so in a very brutal fashion, but there was nothing he read that led him to believe he and his friends were likely to be implicated. The Bermondsey Lane shopkeepers were visibly relieved by the disappearance of the protection mob, relations between the Arpinos and the rest of the shopowners began to improve, and Lou and Sofia were welcoming a few of their old customers back to their store.

Tony was cheered by the letter that was waiting for him when he got home. It was from Melissa. She wrote that her family had been interned on the Isle of Man, conditions there were not too bad, and everyone seemed to be settling down in the camp. Melissa said in her letter that she loved him and missed him terribly, and Tony smiled. For the first time in what seemed to be ages, his future looked rosy.

The Globe carried on with business as usual. Customers moaned over the quality of the beer but continued to drink there. Biff Bowden was drunk for a whole week when his dog won the coveted Blue Cross Stakes, and Shady Lady was then retired on her favourite diet of Guinness and arrowroot. At least once every week Bonky Williams sidled over to Biff and bought him a drink. Then he would look closely at Biff with an earnest glint in his one good eye and ask him, " 'Ow's yer dog, Biff? She puppin' yet?''

Bonky's obsession with Shady Lady's sex life puzzled Biff. "I reckon it's those bleedin' magazines 'e's readin'," he remarked to Eddie, rolling his eyes in an exaggerated gesture of shock.

The landlord of The Globe was reticent. 'I fink our friend Bonky's turnin' over a new leaf. D'yer know, 'e ain't took 'is eye out fer ages.'' Eddie ran a 'sweet' pub as he called it, and he was hoping it was going to stay that way.

Down along the Tower Bridge Road the sounds of the mission organ rang out every Sunday morning. 'Dear old Mister Craddock', the elderly ladies would say to each other at every meeting, gazing at the frail figure bent over the organ keys with fervour. Mr Craddock the organist had given up his part-time job of letter writing — things were getting hot at the tribunal hearings, and his continued presence there seemed to be drawing suspicious glances from the court usher. But he had found another channel for his patriotic endeavours: when the weather was nice he wandered over to Speaker's Corner and heckled the pacifists. "We had enough of you lot in the last war," he would shout out to the orator.

"Go on, Pop, tell the bloody traitor about the trenches and the mustard gas," others would call out.

Mr Craddock ignored the remarks of the audience and walked away. He could still see those soldiers in 1914, marching like heroes away to war.

Ben Morrison had received his call-up papers and he was soon to be drafted into the Royal Army Medical Corps. Lucy's pregnancy was confirmed, and she and Ben were married rather hurriedly at a registry office. Lucy told her family that she had not wanted to wait, and being married would give Ben some extra responsibility and would help him to cope with army life that much better. Alice and her children exchanged knowing winks as she mentioned to her Frank that she had a feeling they would soon become grandparents. Frank, in his usual argumentative way, rejected the idea as nonsense. "Lucy won't start a family yet, Muvver," he said, "she's got more sense."

"All right, Mister Know-All, we'll jus' 'ave ter wait an' see, won't we?" Alice said with a ghost of a grin on her lined face.

Danny's eldest sister Maggie and her husband Joe were very much relieved when letter arrived from a farmer and his wife saying that their two children were enjoying their stay in the Cotswolds. The kids had taken to life on the farm and were both enrolled at the village school. There was a short letter enclosed from the children, saying how much they liked their new home, and Maggie and Joe were also given an invitation to go and meet the farmer and his wife and to stay for a long weekend when they could manage it. Maggie was enthusiastic about the trip, but Joe had reservations.

"It'll be nice ter see the kids, but the farm might be miles from anywhere," Joe said. "I bet there ain't a pub in the village."

"Course there will be," Maggie countered. "I bet the locals won't be as bad as that scatty crowd you get wiv in The Globe every Saturday night."

Joe was doubtful, although he had to admit to himself that the beer could not be any worse than the rubbish Eddie had been serving lately.

Connie Sutton was looking forward to the end of September with excitement. Jimmy was now back home in England and would be given leave soon. Connie had been to see the parish priest and their wedding was planned for the first week in October. Jimmy had been transferred to the Home Fleet and Connie was hoping to find a flat in Portsmouth as soon as the wedding was over.

"That'll be the girls all married off," Alice remarked to Frank. "That only leaves that wayward son of ours. I wish 'e'd get 'imself a nice girl."

Frank Sutton grinned. "Danny's got more sense. 'E ain't in too much of an' 'urry. I mean, there's all that naggin' and moanin'. A man's better off lovin' 'em an' leavin' 'em.''

Alice gave her husband an icy stare. "Yer ain't done so bad. You know where yer arse 'angs.''

"On the bleedin' floor, what wiv all these weddin's in the family,'' Frank quipped.

The Thompsons had moved away from Clink Lane. Violet and Kathy had gone to live in Rotherhithe. The little backwater off Tooley Street held too many bad memories, and being in Rotherhithe suited them. They were not too far away from their friends, and from their front door they could still smell the river and hear familiar sounds carrying into the quiet street. Kathy returned to her old job. On her first day back she had by chance bumped into Connie Sutton, who told her that Danny had stopped working for Tony Allen and was now going into the greengrocery business with his pal Johnny Ross. The mention of Danny's name had sent a familiar dull ache running around inside her, and Kathy knew that there would always be a special place for him in her heart. She had remembered him saying that he would be around, and that he wasn't going anywhere, but she realised he had only said that in an effort to cheer her up. A lot of water had gone under the bridge and she figured it wasn't realistic to imagine that she and Danny could get together once more. It was time now to pick up the pieces and start again. Maybe one day she would be able to meet Danny in the street without feeling ashamed and confused.

The young cockney felt a heaviness weighing down on him from which he could not escape. His surroundings, and the people he had known for years, could do nothing to lift his spirits. He tried to fill up the days by throwing himself into the new venture with Johnny Ross. Sometimes it worked. They were a good team. Their greengrocery shop was attracting customers and the trade was improving. Most of the time however, the nagging emptiness was still there, beneath all the activity and hard work. Danny felt his life was leading him nowhere. His love for the two women had left him feeling lost and inadequate. As much as he thought of those brief sojourns with Alison he realised that it could not go on in that way. The excitement of their meetings would dull in time and there would be nothing left. And yet she insisted on there being no more. It could have been different with Kathy. She was desperately unhappy and he could have said the right words when he held her close in the hospital; she was in love with him and wanted him to say he loved her, but the letter in his pocket had prevented him from grabbing happiness for both of them. In the beginning, the war had parted them just when he was becoming aware of how much she could mean to him, and so much had happened in the few months since his return. Now there was a ghastly shadow in Kathy's past, and he wondered whether she would ever be able to rid herself of the dark ghost of Jack Mason.

Danny realised with a sinking feeling that he had played such a small part in the events around him, and he felt suddenly sad and older. Deep down he had made a decision, and he knew there was only one thing he could do, and there would be no going back.

His pulse beat faster as he reached the little back lane and knocked on the front door. He heard light footsteps and the door opened. The pale, dark-eyed girl stood there looking at him for a few seconds without saying anything. Her eyes widened and two blotches of colour came to her face. Danny grinned, his thumbs hooked into his trouser pockets and his shoulders hunched. " 'Ello, Kath," he said.

Kathy Thompson stepped back a pace. " 'Ello, Danny, it's nice ter see yer. Won't yer come in?"

Danny followed her into the small parlour. It was cool and shadowy, and he could smell the flowers that were arranged in a blue glass vase on the table.

It was a bright day outside. The Saturday afternoon sky was cloudless and sunlight danced on the Thames, making the water sparkle like a river of grey glass. The docks and wharves were quiet and deserted, ships and barges lay at anchor, rocking gently on the turning tide. Seagulls cried out as they glided through the air, diving suddenly down low around the deserted quays, and mooring hawsers strained against the wash from a slowly patrolling police launch. The cobbled riverside lanes were quiet. The street hawkers had come and gone, and inside the open windows the fresh lace curtains hung limp in the still air.

In the tiny parlour the two young people sat facing each other beside the black-leaded grate and gleaming brass fender. The girl looked down at her tightly clasped hands as the young man talked softly.

"What's past is past, Kathy. All the wishin' in the world won't make it any different. I'm talkin' about now. I should 'ave made it clear when I came ter see yer in the 'ospital. I couldn't say it then, Kath, but I can now. I luv yer, an' I want yer. Are yer listenin'?"

Kathy looked up with tears in her eyes. The lump in her throat prevented her from answering. She nodded and his hands reached out and took hers in a firm grip.

"Don't torture yerself, Kath," he said, his voice sounding loud in the quietness of the room. "I told yer once we were good fer each uvver. I meant it, an' I'm sayin' it again. I used ter dream about you an' me gettin' married an' 'avin' kids. They don't 'ave ter be dreams any more, Kathy. We can bury the ghosts an' be 'appy tergevver. We can, can't we?"

Kathy's eyes blinked against the tears and she swallowed hard. "I've never stopped lovin' yer, Danny, but I was never sure about you. You always seemed ter put a wall between us. I dunno what it was, but I was always aware of it. It seemed as though you was frightened ter say the fings I wanted to 'ear. When yer came back 'ome an' I first saw yer that night in the pub I wanted ter die. After we made love I knew that my feelin's fer yer were stronger than ever. That's what made it so bad. It 'appened too late, it should 'ave 'appened before yer left, Danny.''

The drone was far too distant for them to hear as Danny held her hands in his and looked deep into her eyes. "Listen, Kath," he said. "I don't pretend ter understand the reasons fer what's 'appened. I dunno about this fate business, but I've asked meself, 'ow comes I got back 'ome an' the feller next ter me ended up dead on the beach? 'Ow comes Jack Mason gets killed an' you lose 'is baby? I don't know the answers. What I do know, is that yer an' me are sittin' 'ere tergevver. Will yer walk out wiv me?"

The drone was still some way off as Kathy smiled through her tears. "If yer really want me to, Danny."

He reached out and took her in his arms. His lips touched hers and he could taste her tears as they kissed softly and gently and her arms held him tightly. Their lips parted and Kathy buried her head into his shoulder.

"Yer know, I was glad ter leave Clink Lane," she said. "The only fing I regretted was that I wouldn't see yer around."

Along the river estuary the formations of aircraft were darkening the summer sky. As the planes followed the bank of silver water the drone became nearer. Danny smiled. "Anybody would fink yer moved ter the uvver side o' London."

They could both hear the drone now, as he said, "After all, it's only tuppence ter Tooley Street . . ."

When the Pedlar Called

Harry Bowling

When Nell Bailey is wounded in a Flying Bomb attack, it is up to her daughter, Josie, to hold the family together. The traumas of wartime London have left her father a weak and angry man and he no longer lives in the Bailey home in Quay Street. But Josie's new responsibilities don't stop her imagining a brighter future – a future she hopes to share with Johnny Francis, whom she has loved for as long as she can remember.

Her younger brother Tommy, however, does not adjust so easily to the changes in family life. He longs for his father, Frank Bailey, to come home and when the mounting tension between himself and Josie reaches its peak he storms out of the house, vowing to live with his dad. But when, in the search for Frank, he finds himself caught up in the notorious Pedlar's plan to assassinate an eminent political figure, he begins to wish that he'd left well enough alone, for nothing will ever be the same again . . .

'The king of Cockney sagas packs close-knit community good-heartedness into East End epics' *Daily Mail*

0 7472 5883 X

headline